# THE ROSE & THE VINE

# THE ROSE & THE VINE

Lydia Harman

DIADEM BOOKS

Published by Diadem Books

For information, please contact:

Diadem Books
Ocean Surf
CLASHNESSIE
IV27 4JF
Scotland  UK

www.diadembooks.com

ISBN: 978-0-9559852-1-8

Dedicated to my daughter Sonja:
who never lost faith in my ability to bring this story to fruition.

And

In memory of her brother André.

# ACKNOWLEDGEMENTS

Research of facts and figures of historical events, though fascinating and exciting for history addicts, can also be frustrating in that the accuracy of those events are sometimes hazy: many references often not in agreement on a date or point of fact. My research therefore covered a wide variety of books, documents, libraries and archives. If five out of seven of these sources agreed upon a point or fact required for this story then that element was used. Further to points of accuracy, I searched out and was lucky enough to discover, papers and books printed as long ago as 1913, 1885 and 1850. These, though no guarantee of greater accuracy by being closer to the actual event, proved interesting in containing many snippets and facets not found in more recent print. To the authors of all books, papers and documents thus researched, I offer my gratitude and thanks, in particular Thompson's *The French Revolution, Epochs of Modern History*, and Gardiner's *The French Revolution 1789 – 1795,* from whom I gained much inspiration.

An acknowledgement, equally important, also goes to the many people who have encouraged and supported me through the emotional see-saw of research, writing and publishing of this novel that 'had to be written'. In particular, I wish to thank:

Brian Croasdell, author of historical novels of the Roman Times, without whom I would never have identified Diadem Books. My editor Dr Charles Muller, without whom the period of self-editing would have gone on forever! Dylan Parker for the giving of his valuable time in building for me a new, fast computer and talking me through the perplexities of a new programme! Marie Chauveau, for enlightening me in regards to the mysteries and nuances of the French language: *Merci beaucoup*, Madame Chauveau! Shirley Taylor, for reading the manuscript and offering feedback; and for steering me away from over emphasizing the 'proper' way of doing things! Leonie King: for identifying the meaning of the softer horse sounds and other finer details of the equine variety; and Mary Böck, for her unfailing faith in me and emotional support throughout and timely reminders to keep my feet on the ground.

# TABLE OF CONTENTS

# THE DE QUATREAUX FAMILY

Jean-Pierre Mathieu Vermont: Comte de Quatreaux: widower.

Married:

Roxanna Marie Ralston: daughter of Frederick Albert Ralston, Earl of Kelsey, (England).

Children:

Clarisse Estelle Henrietta Vermont.

Married:

Stanilaus-Olivierre Jordain: Viscomte de Lacoste.

Twins:

Emile-Marcellus Renaud Vermont: Vicomte de Quatreaux.

Angelique-Heloise Roxanna Vermont.

Youngest son:

Francois Berthoud Laurent Vermont.

**Close Friends: of the Comte de Quatreaux and his family.**

Odette-Jolie, Comtesse Bayette: widow & friend of de Quatreaux senior.

Rochelle-Marie du Bois, of English birth: close friend of Angelique.

Raoul-Phillip Michel Trifane, Marquis de Savieur: of neighbouring estates and friend of Emile and the de Quatreaux family.

Henri-Marie Pontisqieu: lawyer: No title but of aristocratic (maternal) background, becomes friend of family as dangerous times increase.

Jacques-Lucien Devereaux, 5th Baron Lacy: friend of younger son, Francois.

Jean-Paul Olivierre, Baron de Cotteau                                  "

Berthoud-Roberte Montague, Viscomte de Arriette                 "

Mathieu Hugues d'Arcy son of Marquis de la Molyneaux          "


**Old friends of Jean-Pierre Vermont, Comte de Quatreaux.**

Yves Beaumont, Comte d'Arteaux

Dominique Montmaire, Comte de Brieze.

Marc-Jean de Vries, Viscomte de la Fontesqueu.

Geraud-Juste Tour de Fonté, Baron de Marmoin.

Phillip-Henri Du Toit, Marquis de Saint-Dumas.

# CHRONOLOGY OF FRENCH REVOLUTION

## Beginning for this novel at point of States-General recall.

### 1789

May.

| | | |
|---|---|---|
| Saturday | 3$^{rd}$ | States-General: reception of deputies at Versailles. |
| Sunday | 4$^{th}$ | Procession and mass in Paris at Nôtre Dame and Saint-Louis. |
| Monday | 5$^{th}$ | Opening session followed by six week deadlock. |

June.

| | | |
|---|---|---|
| Thursday | 4$^{th}$ | Death of the Dauphin: Louis-Joseph. |
| Wednesday | 17$^{th}$ | 'National Assembly' |
| Friday | 19$^{th}$ | Council at Marley. |
| Saturday | 20$^{th}$ | Tennis Court Oath at Versailles. |
| Sunday | 21$^{st}$ | Council At Versailles. |
| Tuesday | 23$^{rd}$ | Séance Royale followed by king's surrender. |
| Saturday | 27$^{th}$ | Reunion of Orders. |

July.

| | | |
|---|---|---|
| Saturday | 11$^{th}$ | King's dismissal of Necker: Paris arms. |
| Tuesday | 14$^{th}$ | Fall of the Bastille: death of de Launay. |
| Wednesday | 15$^{th}$ | First emigration fleeing the revolution. |
| Friday | 17$^{th}$ | King's visit to Paris. |
| Wednesday | 22$^{nd}$ | Murder & mutilation of Foullon and Berthier. |

August.

| | | |
|---|---|---|
| Tuesday | 2$^{nd}$ | 'Abolition of feudalism' |
| Thursday | 4$^{th}$ | Abolition of tithes but church retained property. |
| Thursday | 20$^{th}$ | Declaration of Rights began. |

September.

| | | |
|---|---|---|
| Friday | 11$^{th}$ | Suspensive Veto granted to king. |

October.

| | | |
|---|---|---|
| Thursday | 1st | Versailles ritual welcoming banquet for the Flanders Regiment. |
| Monday | 5th | March to Versailles: 'bread riots' & attack on Palace. |
| Tuesday | 6th | King's return to Paris on demand of people; followed by Assembly |
| Monday | 19th | First session of Assembly in Archevêché: Archbishops palace. |
| Wednesday | 21st | Martial Law. |

November.

| | | |
|---|---|---|
| Monday | 2nd | Nationalization of Church property. |
| Saturday | 7th | Decree excluding deputies from ministry. |
| Monday | 9th | First session of National Assembly in Mènage: riding school built for Louis xv; north side of Tuileries Palace, Paris. |

December.

| | | |
|---|---|---|
| Saturday | 19th | First issue of assignats: paper currency. |

# 1790

February.

| | | |
|---|---|---|
| Thursday | 4th | King's speech to the Assembly. |
| | 13th | Religious vows prohibited. |

May.

| | | |
|---|---|---|
| Friday | 21th | Paris municipal law. |
| Saturday | 22nd | Decree on right of declaring war. |

June.

| | | |
|---|---|---|
| Saturday | 19th | Abolition of Nobility. |

July.

| | | |
|---|---|---|
| Monday | 12th | Civil Constitution of Clergy. |
| Wednesday | 14th | First fête of Federation. |

November.

| | | |
|---|---|---|
| Saturday | 27th | Clerical oath decreed: to country (excluding Pope and King) |

# 1791

# 1792

May.
Wednesday        30th       Dismissal of king's bodyguard.

June.
Monday           4th        Paris camp.
Sunday           10th       Petition of 8000 v Paris camp.
Wednesday        13th       Dismissal of Brissotin ministry by king.
Tuesday          19th       King vetoes Paris camp.
Wednesday        20th       Crowd invades Tuileries.
Thursday         28th       Lafayette visits Paris.

July.
Sunday           1st        Petition of 20,000 v June 20th
Friday           6th        Suspension of Pétion .
Tuesday          10th       Resignation of ministers.
Wednesday        11th       'The Country in Danger'
Saturday         14th       Third Fête of Federation.
Monday           30th       Arrival of Marseilles.

August.
Wednesday        1st        Brunswick's Manifesto.
Wednesday        8th        Lafayette exculpated.
Thursday         9th        Insurrectional Commune.
Friday           10th       Attack on Tuileries; royal family shelter in Manège
Saturday         11th       Convention summoned.
Monday           13th       Royal family imprisoned in Temple.
Friday           17th       Tribunal of August 10th.
Monday           20th       Desertion of Lafayette.
Thursday         23rd       Fall of Longwy.

September.
Sunday           2nd        Fall of Verdun and Paris Prison massacres.
Thursday         20th       Battle of Valmy.  First meeting of Convention:
                              replacing the Legislative Assembly.
                              First year of republic.
Friday           20th       Abolition of Royalty.

October.
Thursday         11th       Constitutional Committees.
Monday           29th       Louvet denounces Robespierre.

November.
Tuesday          6th        Battle of Jannappes.
Tuesday          20th       Discovery of 'iron chest'

December.
Monday           3rd        Decision to try King.
Tuesday          11th       King's interrogation.
Wednesday        26th       King's trial.

# 1793

January.
Friday      18$^{th}$      King condemned to death.
Monday      21$^{st}$      King's execution.

February.
Friday      1$^{st}$      Declaration of war v. England and Holland.
Sunday      24$^{th}$      Levy of 3,000 men decreed.

March.
Thursday      7$^{th}$      Declaration of war v. Spain.
Frid.-Sun      8-10$^{th}$      The March days.
Sunday      10$^{th}$      Revolt in Vendée.
Monday      11$^{th}$      Tribunal extraordinaire.

April.
Thursday      4$^{th}$      Desertion of Dumouriez.

May.
Saturday      4$^{th}$      First Maximum.
Friday      10$^{th}$      Convention moves to Tuileries.
Tuesday      21$^{st}$      Commission of twelve.

June.
Sunday      2$^{nd}$      Expulsion of Girondin deputies.
Tuesday      4$^{th}$      Armée Révolutionaire.
Monday      24$^{th}$      Constitution of 1793.

July.
Saturday      13$^{th}$      Murder of Marat.
Sunday      28$^{th}$      Girondin leaders outlawed.

August
Saturday      10$^{th}$      Fête in honour of Constitution.

September:      **New Revolutionary Calender (built on a 10-day week)**
Sunday      22$^{nd}$      (Vendemaire 1): new year starting.
Sunday      29$^{th}$      ( " 8)      Second Maximum.

October.
Thursday      3$^{rd}$      ( " 12)      Impeachment of Girondin deputies.
Thursday      10$^{th}$      ( " 19)      Decree of Emergency Government.
Tuesday      15$^{th}$      ( " 24)      Trial of Girondins.
Wednesday      16$^{th}$      ( " 25)      Queen's execution.

| | | | | |
|---|---|---|---|---|
| Thursday | 31<sup>st</sup> | (Brumaire 10) | | Execution of Girondins. |

**November.**

| | | | | |
|---|---|---|---|---|
| Friday | 8<sup>th</sup> | ( " | 18) | Execution of Mme Roland. |
| Sunday | 10<sup>th</sup> | ( " | 20) | Fête of Reason in Nôtre Dame. |
| Friday | 22<sup>nd</sup> | (Frimaire | 2) | Closing of Paris Churches. |

**December.**

| | | | | |
|---|---|---|---|---|
| Wednesday | 4<sup>th</sup> | ( " | 14) | Revolutionary Government. |

# PROLOGUE

## Paris, 1760

Jean-Pierre Vermont, the Vicomte de Quatreaux, sat very still, staring straight ahead, his eyes cold and flat. Lareaux had to die: nothing less would suffice and even then the scales of justice weighed on the light side. Perhaps in hell the man may really pay but that was small comfort to the living: to the family of the beautiful, gentle, Lady Favièrre.

The hooves of the matching pair rang loudly upon the cobbled streets of Paris against the dawn hush. Next to de Quatreaux sat Yves Beaumont, his oldest childhood friend. Opposite them both sat Marc de Vries. The mandatory appeal against violence, serious duty of all chosen seconds to any duelling party, had been repeated and calmly rejected again: as late as last night.

Arrived at the designated neutral grounds, a small and secluded public garden, they witnessed the surgeon's carriage pulled to the side. De Quatreaux, tall, trim and dark, stepped indolently down from his carriage. No more emotion other than a slight boredom showed on his regular features. Beaumont, of the lighter Nordic features, also stepped down, followed by the darker, solid, de Vries. They gazed about; the bushes and garden beds still enshrouded in dark shadows; a ghostly wraith of wispy mist drifting slowly against dark humps of exotic plants and shrubs.

"Mayhap he'll not show," murmured Beaumont hopefully to de Quatreaux.

"You know better than that Yves, *mon ami*, his arrogance will not allow him to default. Besides, he knows that I shall hunt him down to the ends of the earth."

Pure, cold intent hung in the air.

Beaumont backed a little: never had he witnessed de Quatreaux thus. "No other way? No, I perceive that there is not."

De Vries now spoke, quietly and persuasively. "She is not a blood relative to you, Vermont. I still say it be best to await Marcel's return... as brother to Mademoiselle Favièrre, 'tis surely his to avenge... to challenge the duel."

The icy eyes turned to him and the very stillness of the body told de Vries more than he wanted to know: "The *late* Mademoiselle Favièrre, Marc!"

Seeing the futility of further argument, they moved off to greet the surgeon and inform him that they had extended their best persuasive abilities to avert this duel. The surgeon, thus reassured, turned his back on them. He re-entered his carriage to await the absent party: his position, according to the laws applied to duelling, one of impartiality.

The gloom began rapidly to lighten and the misty tendrils disperse when the sound of a rumbling carriage grew louder; then softened as it hit the grass. It pulled up behind that of the surgeon and Lareaux stepped down, followed by his seconds. The early autumn air was crisp but still, the light good. He glanced at de Quatreaux, a thin smile stretching his mouth. The seconds gathered together, discussed any new laws applied to modern French duelling, then returned to stand beside their respective carriages.

De Quatreaux calmly divested himself of his greatcoat, coat and waistcoat and tucked up the ruffles of his shirtsleeves. He released his small-sword with his thumb, withdrew it and handing this to Beaumont, unbuckled his scabbard and placed it in the carriage. His black, wavy locks were secured by a black riband, tied at the back of his neck. He then accepted his sword and stood perfectly still, waiting. He betrayed no sign of emotion as he watched Lareaux perform the same ritual, then flex his sword and swipe the air a couple of times. A known master of the sword, Lareaux could not help performing to an audience, no matter how small. De Quatreaux' eyes glinted in satisfaction: this, he knew, would prove to be a disadvantage to that man; but he did not underestimate him.

The paces were measured. Each man took his place and moved into that surreal moment of elevated tension and heightened alertness of the primed combatant: awaiting the dropped white kerchief that would commence the duel.

## TWENTY-EIGHT YEARS ON: PARIS, JULY 1788

Jean Pierre Vermont, the Comte de Quatreaux, stared down at the rioting crowds in the street below, a deep furrow between his brows. The storm clouds had gathered: the whole of France was becoming involved. He watched a crested carriage bowl along at unsafe speed, forcing other traffic to direct two wheels onto the narrow, crowded pavement. His frown deepened: impeccable in manners and attitude of respect to all fellow man, he found the crass rudeness of the individual directing his coachman, intolerable. This, to draw attention to superiority of class, could only worsen the building discontent.

Few, however, in the summer of 1788, saw France teetering upon the edge of a wide, deep chasm: as did de Quatreaux. That the ever-present discontent was being cleverly harnessed was no new feat of engineering; but to use it as reason to call the archaic emergency council: the *States-general*, to deal with it; was.

His frown grew deeper: gentle, retiring, Louis XVl, inheriting a disaster from his wasteful, decadent forebears, now battled bankruptcy and famine-driven fears. In attempt to raise finances, he had tried to extend taxes, through the *law courts/'parlements'*, to the exempt upper classes. Though rule at this time was by Absolute Monarchy, these *law-courts/'parlements'*, in place for matters of law, also owned the right to register or revoke edicts sent out by the king's council. Controlled by the privileged clergy and nobility, these had refused outright the extended taxes; and demanded the dismissal of Turgot, the Controller General of Finance. Striking while these turbulent waters still swirled about, they then began to push for the convocation of the *States-general* to sort the matter. Soon they had the gathering weight of popular opinion behind them. De Quatreaux saw the reaching tentacles.

His fears now deepened: could the *States-general*, if the agitators succeeded in calling this *ancien* emergency council, become the nemesis to a very long reign by Absolute Monarchy?  He felt the possibility to be fairly strong: this, though rarely called, being the only 'real parliament' of France.  In this unstable political climate, hijacked by clever, unscrupulous men, it could shake the dust of 175 years in abeyance and take on a life of its own. The risk then of a swift power shift, from the king to a 'States-general-based-parliament', would be very real.

He sighed: Louis could not see it.  For time immemorial, France had been governed by a system of *Absolute Monarchy*: the king ruling by absolute and divine right, answerable to God alone.  A crisis of succession in 1328, on the demise of the last, (childless), Caput king, had brought about the birth of the emergency council: then called the *Estates-general*, saving the throne from Edward the III of England and preserving it for the first of the 'Valois'.  Such was its function: last called in the year 1614.

The *Estates-general*, operating as the only proper parliament, when called, represented the three estates (lawful social divisions) of France: the first the Clergy, the second the Nobility and the third the People (the Bourgeoisie): the latter often referred to simply as 'The Third'.  (A fourth, unrecognised, estate of French men and women: the urban workers and country peasants—the vast bulk of the population—owned no place, lawfully or socially, within this tiered structure.) Normally, crises over, the country reverted to monarchical control: his orders directed through the King's Council to the *law-courts/'parlements'* of France.

The *'parlements'/law courts* were run by local authorities and controlled by the local Seigneurs (Lords), owning also the added burden of tax collection for the crown, via the *collecteurs*.  These Seigneurs were the *Noblesse de l'épée*—Nobility of the Sword, (hereditary nobility of many generations with the right to carry a sword), hence the expression 'tax collection by the sword', bearing no resemblance to collection of taxes at the point of a sword.

Towards the end of the 1780's, the rising tax demands of the crown, added to the feudal fiefs, *champarts* (giving the Lord his portion of the harvest), *banalitiés* (small charges for the use of the noble's mill, wine press, ovens, etc.) and other innumerable taxes; to use the markets but one, contributed to the falling popularity of the monarchy and the rumblings of revolt.  By 1788, the volatility of the country had reached crisis point and Louis needed to deal with the catalyst: bankruptcy and famine effects.

Jean-Pierre Vermont, the Comte de Qautreaux, absently swirled the deep red burgundy and took a sip. There had to be a way through Louis' stubbornness. Times were changing swiftly: many countries were discarding the old and installing governance by the people. And the rioting here in France had already turned to full-scale rebellion in some provinces.  But Louis' policy of 'do nothing and it will go away' had thus far worked for him.

He focused upon the people again. The people were the bridge. It was not too late to turn the tide and at least avert a full-scale rebellion: if Louis could bring himself to communicate with them; before the agitators did so on a large scale. He tossed off the last of the burgundy and glanced at the mantle clock. It grew late and he had an appointment with Beaumont this night. Perhaps tomorrow, he would be able to make some headway.  He smiled ironically: he was asking the king to convert from an ancient, patriarchal stance to one hinting of democracy, a new and alien concept.

♣

Thus July 1788 finds Louis XV1 wrestling, with his finance minister and advisors, for a solution to these problems. The Comte de Quatreaux, as friend, secret emissary and skilful advisor to Louis, agrees with the suppression of a calling of the *States-general* but this to be achieved with kid gloves. However, his idea of the royal family moving to the Tuileries Palace in Paris, for the summer season and holding open fetes and festivals, falls on startled face. De Quatreaux tries harder, pressing for a warm and personal communication between the crown and populace: to appear to lead rather than to direct. His Majesty, however, with no template to follow, finds great difficulty in a vision beyond that of patriarchal rule, or of governing from anywhere other than the Palace of Versailles.

The Comte de Quatreaux exits Versailles and de Brienne, the finance minister, pushes for a slow investigation into the *running* of the so demanded *States-general*, as a pacifier, buying time in which to somehow raise foreign finance. He feels cautiously confident: his position that of the last speaker within a court trial.

Louis now listens to de Brienne's soft words, his face a mask against his rising irritation within; his thoughts on De Quatreaux: that man is possibly right, but his radical plans, to draw attention away from the *States-general*, by engaging the people in such manner, unthinkable. Marie Antoinette would never reside in the ancient, dark and rambling palace, *Tuileries*, of Catherine de Medicis, not to mention the filth of Paris. No: the desire to call the *States-general* rested upon the famine and financial crisis; therefore these must be remedied before all else. De Quatreaux *must* succeed in raising foreign funds. The only alternative: raising the taxes. If this occurred, again, those of the Third Estate, the bourgeoisie, those wily lawmen, businessmen and entrepreneurs, would rocket France into the strongest rebellion ever experienced by France. This he *did* know.

# CHAPTER ONE

## Versailles. July 4ᵗʰ 1788

The black carriage, accented in gold and silver, the coachman, footmen and postboys liveried likewise, swept along with speed: the four gleaming, black thoroughbreds straining against their collars. The gold and silver crest, visible upon the door by the light of passing vehicles' lanterns, gave identity for those curious to see just whom it was that travelled so recklessly—a judgement swiftly redressed as they identified the owner. De Quatreaux could never be accused of recklessness, and he certainly demanded the same behaviour from his coachman. Though none could touch him in driving skill and horsemanship, even higher stood his standards of manners and respect for fellow man.

Angelique Vermont sat alongside her silent *père*: Jean-Pierre Vermont, the Comte de Quatreaux. She stared ahead in deep thought; then caught hold of the dangling leather strap and swayed with practiced ease as the carriage slowed. They had hit the rougher Paris section of road. Behind them lay the eternally smooth surface to the Palace of Versailles. The Comte also gazed into space, a faint frown between his brows.

Angelique glanced at him. "*Mon Père*? You have not shared with me the reason for our departure from Versailles. I do know that Estelle Pontac and indeed Marie Antoinette expect me this night at the soirée."

De Quatreaux appeared, for a minute, not to have heard and then in his deep, even voice said, "*Mon enfant*, I must return to Paris and will not leave you back there to face alone the hidden dangers of court life. Louis knows this and so it follows that the queen also will."

She frowned, not accepting this but only said, "Your meeting with our monarch was successful then?"

"How does one measure success in this case? I attempt to reason with His Majesty; regarding the looming disaster that he does not admit. That is all."

"He is not stupid; but I think does not really believe it could happen." Angelique gazed at his sombre features and frowned slightly. "But be it so bad: the States-general recalled...to deal with this crisis? After all, this is only the third time in 500 years; not so? When all is settled again; it returns to the archives."

"Not necessarily so: this time." He turned his head, light grey eyes gazing steadily into hers. "The actual structure and intended usage of an emergency council

1

is a very fine idea. The danger however, this time, lies in the possibility of designing persons using it to launch a political coup d' é-tat within the present climate."

She nodded thoughtfully. "Of instability...famine fears and revolts of the people; and bourgeoisie demands. Not to mention a large portion of discontent nobility! Poor Louis, I do feel for him: he is such a gentle man, a kind man."

De Quatreaux smiled grimly. "A monarch has no business owning such gentleness."

A slight chill entered her soul at his tone. "You think that he will bow to the finance minister's persuasions: to actually call the States-general?"

"If he does not perceive the degree of danger within such a move: yes. And it will give strong evidence of loss of faith in the king: something of use to designing persons!"

"Do they not have faith then, in his ability to deal with the financial troubles?"

"Not when his only remedy be yet more increases in the taxes."

"But those opposing this, the discontent of the nobility, are exempt."

"On those Louis tried to inflict a share of the taxes: on *all* nobility. And many of them see that a complete axing of those exemptions and concessions could be the final solution, especially when *le peuple* cannot pay another *sou*."

She stared. "And much nobility live with pockets to let! Panic would be extreme! So...to call and then *control* the States-general is their aim. *Mon Dieu*...but it is diabolique!"

Her *père* reverted to expressionless mien and remained silent. Angelique's heart grew colder. She felt a shiver run the length of her spine: sure that the day for deep concern would come. She fought to annihilate it. Where this sensitivity to flashes of deep and graphic insights came from, she did not know but hated it: they were always accurate and always spelt disaster. Her *père* could have told her: her *mère* had also been burdened with 'the sight'. The days of burning people as witches, however, were not far removed; and so the silent burden remained silent; even to her *père*. In an effort to escape the heaviness within, she turned her thoughts to the court now behind them and smiled suddenly.

"And what devious thought amuses you now, *mon enfant*?"

She chuckled; a deep contagious sound that was her signature. "Marie Antoinette is at this moment, I believe, persuading Louis to a ball. The first in a yearlong drought of such entertainments; he will be hard pushed to refuse her!"

"He had better!" The stern mouth and set features startled her. "The pamphlets and magazines are just waiting to pin the deep troubles of France upon her avarice."

"Oh? But of course; already the templates were drawn...in her enthusiastic youth. But she was only fifteen years old when she entered France as Dauphine...how unfair!"

She leaned back against the satin squabs; wrist comfortably caught in the looped strap, swaying with practised ease, wide golden-brown eyes shadowed now with deep concern. The sway of the carriage lulled her. The long, filmy, silk scarf slipped from her thick tawny hair, fell to her shoulder, slid to her lap. There, in the half-world, between drowsing and sleep: the alpha state, she drifted. The heat and dust, even, did not penetrate her mind. The sudden picture of spreading blood did however; followed by a slowly evolving toothless crone, crowing at the sight of a dripping head, held high by its hair. Angelique started violently; and aware suddenly of her *père*, converted a gasp to a cough.

The Comte grimaced, waving a hand at the swirling dust; entering even the closed carriage. "We will soon be home, *mon enfant*. And then I must depart with speed, across the frontier. You will of course obey your brother in my absence."

Buying time to recover, she threw the old family joke: "But *Mon Père*! He is senior to me by three minutes only…and then I am never sure about that." Feeling slightly better, she gave a small chuckle. "Ah, but I forget; it matters not: he is *male* of course!"

A small, indulgent smile crossed the Comte's features. "Precisely. Therefore please do control that independent streak in you! And I warn you, *mon enfant*, should you ever follow the dreadful Madame Roland in her insistent political writings, but worse, her tasteless, unfeminine, participation in political discussions within company, I shall disown you totally! And I do know that you scribble, you know."

The deep chuckle increased, and, ignoring the accusation against her 'journal', she exclaimed, "Never! You *could* not disown me. Besides, times are changing: one day the female of the species shall be equal to the male. Indeed it has always been so within some tribes of the South Americas. You had best prepare, *Mon Père*."

Steely eyes turned upon her. "Shall I buy thee a grass skirt then?"

She subsided but clung to the sudden foray into a rare warm moment with her *père*.

♣

Back at Versailles, July 4<sup>th</sup> brought to a worried king no such warmth. Instead, a sudden wraith of chill premonition, regarding changing times, entered his troubled soul. On a more prosaic level, it brought to his mind his minister of finance, de Brienne.

Louis XVI<sup>th</sup>, at last ridding himself of the Gentlemen of the Wardrobe and bringing the morning *coucher* to a close, nodded to one of the pages. On soft padded feet, the page left the *chambre*. The hour was eleven, of the morning. Louis glanced longingly out over the rolling green landscape: the day was perfect for hunting.

He moved to that window and stood, hands clasped behind his back, bracing himself to grapple once more with de Brienne's ponderous efforts to convince him that the pressure to call the States-general be insurmountable. The face of de Quatreaux swam before him: a strong, dark, decisive face, the face of a man who definitely did not lose one within an avalanche of words. And, he was convinced; here was the exception to the rule that a king could trust no one. And de Quatreaux would, *must*, elicit support from their neighbours: in the very least from 'Toinette's brother. A sudden boost of foreign finance from Austria could stop the clamouring for the convocation of the States-general.

He gazed intently at the beauty of the scene beyond the window and frowned. Versailles had been a monstrous burden on the national revenue from the moment of its conception: the latest statement announcing one quarter of civil expenditure going to its support. Now his enemies used the opulence and extravagant lifestyle of the palace, the more so of his wife, as propaganda launching-ground for missiles of discontent. The small army of royal gardeners suddenly caught his attention: surely that Versailles gave many people employment was a good thing. He sighed: his heart belonged with his people, always, and their unrest was, he was certain, not directed at the king but at the monarchy; the *system* that he had inherited.

Etienne-Charles Lomènie de Brienne, Archbishop of Toulouse, Controller-General of Finance, entered the *chambre* on the heels of the page and coughed softly, "Good morning: Your Majesty."

"It is?" Then, ever polite, Louis turned. "Good morning, Brienne."

De Brienne bowed, his movements deep and precise. "Sire, I know that the current situation is food for concern, but we shall prevail."

"Ha! How? The '*parlements*'' standoff is becoming perilously close to an army dug in for the duration. Can *we* break their siege? That is the question."

"Majesty, '*Parlements*' is simply trying its strength against the power of the monarchy; by these refusals to register any edicts which lesson its own privileges, of course, but..."

"And I wish that I knew the answer to such insubordination."

"It is buying time, Sire, by taking this oath of non-compliance, while it gathers popular opinion for the demand of the States-general by which, some say, may be spawned an *English* style parliament."

"*English style*: it could never work here!   But that does not enter into the equation. *I* am Absolute Monarch and *I* decide what is best to do." He paused. "They challenge me, Brienne: challenge *my right*; to impose new taxes...to make these decisions and govern France.  I will not have it, Brienne!"

"Indeed it is so, Your Majesty, but it is most unwise to lock horns with the angry bull, I feel.  But to appear to *lead* it, Sire, by a *slow investigation* into the *running* of the States-general, may turn the enemy's cannon back upon himself."

Louis gazed at de Brienne, brows raised. "How slow?"

"Very slow, Sire; if worked upon.  This would buy time for us: to turn their minds away from such a measure; by proving its impossibility."

"Nothing but magical appearance of new funds will reduce the desire to call the States-general, Brienne." Louis paused, then, "By popular opinion, I think you said. But the populace understands only what is fed to them by men of no scruples: men who would use them as a bridge to a platform of power."

"Indeed, Sire."

"There was a time when such treasonable action would beget exile, or incarceration, if not beheading. In fact, the axe remains the most effective manner of silencing such Machiavellian individuals!"

Watching his Monarch's jaw set and eyes gleam, Brienne panicked. "To resort to such counter measures, now, would convert the riots into rebellion—in the fastest possible time."

"This situation, Brienne, is insupportable." The king resumed his pacing, ending before the large mahogany desk.  He picked up a finely carved, ivory letter-opener and balanced it on his upturned palm, lace ruffles falling and moving delicately over his wrist, and continued: "Balance, my unfortunate Controller-General of Finance. It is about balance: of the taxes! Some semblance of which would have prevailed had the reforms been registered when I recalled the *parlements* last month. The judicial system, that first obstacle, would have been totally overhauled: the court judges' stranglehold of power, over my edicts, broken."

"But *parlements* were quick to block them. We have a terrified tiger by the tail, Sire."

"A tiger rounding up the tidal-wave of civil unrest: an effective power tool, hmm?" Louis halted his pacing again, replaced the letter opener upon the desk and turned to face Brienne. "We must find a way of flinging that tiger so far that it will not return."

"Tigers are night animals, Sire. It is difficult to see their stealthy manoeuvres." Brienne stared at the floor: how to tell Louis that the building of the present situation called for nothing less than at least a show of interest in their demand. "Sire, we shall come about."

Louis smiled sourly. "How... hmm? The *Assembly of Notables* defied me. Then the *Parlements of Paris*! Even my exiling the whole to Troyes had no effect, other than to create great riots across Paris and cries of liberty. Liberty!" He paused, then began to pace again. "But the strength of the discontent of the nobles... is our first worry."

"Indeed Sire. But you do have the backing of some of our neighbours, should it be necessary."

"But of course... the insightful work of De Quatreaux!"

Startled, de Brienne paused a moment, then continued: "For the present, however, I feel that to issue a decree," he paused for emphasis, "*investigatory* into the *running* of a convocation of the States-general, shall buy us time, Sire, and settle these aristocratic revolts. They are the ones to lead; the opportunistic bourgeoisie simply follow."

His Majesty stared at him. "I comprehend, Brienne, that you see no alternative; but these are not de Quatreaux' feelings!"

De Brienne controlled his features: de Quatreaux was growing far too close to the king. The man had interests all over Europe; and something dark lurked in his past. His daughter also now sat close to the queen. Tonight he must bring in his informant.

He marshalled his thoughts along lines of fragile diplomacy. "Well Your Majesty, such a move should call for a very long research; the last convocation, 1614, was a long time ago! No Royal Intendant knows his way through the dusty maze of ancient writs, and records involved. That is to say, those that can be found: almost all have been destroyed; even maps of the old constituencies, were lost in the great fire of the archives. And as no *parlement house* has ever existed before, a debate... a no doubt long debate... must be held as to where the States-general must sit: Paris or Versailles? As to the choosing of the deputies to represent each of the three Estates: what rank, education and social level must they be? Even what costume they must wear. And identifying signage: an armband or cockade, or hat even? And does the Nobility of the Sword wear his ceremonial sword, or is this provocative to a new breed? And: whom to make the decisions on all these issues? Every detail of procedure must be defined, Majesty, by an army of men, over whom much time and care must be exercised in *their* selection." He paused, a deep smile lurking in his eyes at the king's bemused expression, then continued, "The antiquarians must review the records that *can* be found; then correlate these lengthy reports. My decree would invite the co-operation of all bodies across France in this investigation: for it would of course be impolitic to leave any institution out, Majesty. Archivists and officials, from the most distant border to the remotest mountain corner, may collect relevant documents and traditions, bearing any information on the history of the National *Parlements*: the States-general. Committees, representing local authorities and provincial assemblies, shall then study this mountain of material. Learned men, guided by the Academy of Inscriptions, for all of this will be 175 years old at least, should then be brought in to weigh up the results of these mass findings; following of course investigation into *their* right to the position. By then the Lord Privy Seal may just be in a position to offer a final report upon the outcome of all this... er, learning, Sire. Once he has digested it all."

A staring Louis, visibly rousing himself, offered in faint tones, "My dear Brienne, I had no idea of your incredible ability to amuse!"

Brienne bowed with exquisite grace. "Majesty, I do my best, but to amuse you was not my aim. I could go on Sire, there is much more, to slow the whole operation."

"No, no, no! Thank you, but I, er... fully understand the, er... difficulties that may be arranged." He paused, frowning. "But in the interim, we are still *broke,* Brienne!"

"Well Sire, the days of selling Noble ranks are over but... there *is* the Clergy, Sire."

"*Mon Dieu* Brienne, you do not go there for finance? They shall never acquiesce." Louis' gaze was severe. "Do not be upsetting Rome, Brienne. Whatever else you may do."

"Pius is very aware of Your Majesty's faith and loyalty, but no, I shall not upset Rome."

A rustle of silk and a movement at the door caused him to pause. The queen had entered the room and he knew that his interview with the king must come to a close. He turned to face her as she came forward: entrancingly lovely; her diminutive and willowy figure dressed in flowing white, drenched with gold lace.

"Ah, so this is where I must seek my husband. But always of these days I find him here." The sweet low voice was a caress and he knew that the interruption was designed.

He tensed in anticipation of a request for more money to finance some new project. That she was the owner of an astute brain he knew but a cloistered life, both in Austria and here in France, following her early marriage, seriously hindered any grasp of reality. No such request eventuated, however, and he relaxed a little: the rumours of her avarice were of course exaggerated. Behind her now drifted her Lady-in-Waiting, Estelle Pontac, dressed in blue satin and white lace, her dark attractiveness a perfect foil for the pale beauty of the queen.

Bowing low, Brienne took the delicate hand of the queen, just brushing it with his lips. "Your Majesty. As beautiful as ever I see. You are well I hope?"

"Why Archbishop, but yes, thank you indeed... I trust that you too are well this day?"

"Quite well, Madame." He bowed again and turned back to the king. "Sire, I beg your leave now… but first: may I send out the investigatory decree of which we spoke?"

The king frowned in thought: if de Quatreaux returned with foreign finance; mayhap from 'Toinette's brother, then this debacle would surely dissolve. He turned to Brienne. "After all that… it seems that I must: there being no realistic alternative."

Brienne's bow to the king and queen was deep, a degree less so for the Lady-in-Waiting. Turning, he left the chamber, wondering how long before Louis was forced by the wretched *parlements* to dismiss him, for inability to pull the financial rabbit from the hat. He smiled grimly: Calonne, Necker and Turgot had also trodden this road and Turgot the best statesman since Richelieu.

The queen floated to her husband's side. "You look so tired, *Mon Louis*! 'Tis all so grim, these troublesome tidings of the *parlements*; but all is not gloom for we are here to beg your indulgence regarding a ball, Louis." She turned to her companion. "Not so?"

"If it would please Your Majesty," responded Estelle quietly, moving forward with a low curtsy to her Monarch.

"But we, er, abandoned such activities in the drive for economy, 'Toinette."

"Ah, was a time Louis, when you held a ball every Wednesday in my honour."

"Yes *ma chérie*, but not last year; that was when we decided…"

"*You* decided, Louis. And it is a whole calendar year since the last and so it cannot be regarded untoward now. We have been very economic."

"And how would it look with Louis-Josephe in such poor health?" Louis responded.

A look of concern for her sickly elder son crossed her fine features; then she brightened. "But he is much improved. You *know* that that is his habit during the summer months. Come, my Louis, you become blue-devilled. This is the very thing to cheer your downcast soul."

"*Ma chérie* I cannot be easy on such a head. The extravagances of Versailles are being denounced the more every day and Brienne tells me that bread grows scarce following this year's poor harvest."

"Ah, but that old complaint rears its head every harvest: it is but a fear tactic, used by clever men to increase their demands; *they* do not care about the people! Do banish matters of state from your mind and listen a moment. A masked ball shall cheer the court out of the doldrums: the brooding goes on here too, you know. But you do not notice; hunting and books your only care. And this is all very comfortable, I know, but is not good in one who must indulge the court that supports him. Now, a ball would dispel any courtly anxiety and show *le peuple* that all rests well between monarch and state. That the discontent of some Nobility be mere rumour, that you are indeed united." She paused; then knew, as Louis gave a faint smile, that she had won.

She turned now to her Lady-in-Waiting. "It shall be a masked ball, Estelle. We shall announce it at the soirée this night. Which Louis shall not attend, I am convinced. But all is forgiven… though I do wish that you would come!"

Her smile of pleasure softened as she watched him. Louis' simple tastes and gentle disposition rendered him poorly suited to the savagery of court life. Others, less acquainted with him, saw only his stiffly held head and penetrating gaze. Few knew this last to be due to severe myopia and that the appearance of pride covered extreme shyness. Court life was hard work for him. His expression now returned to one of deep concern, as he stared into space.

She took his hand suddenly. "*Mon Louis*...the practice, adopted by middle-ages kings...of consulting the three Estates from time to time, was never a threat. The king took into account their opinions but always retained his power and made the decisions."

"*Ma chérie*; that was so, but little by little it became customary for the three orders to elect deputies, for the meeting of the Estates-general. In those early times, it represented no threat, for Absolute Monarchy was the only known manner of governance. Meeting over, the clergy, nobility and bourgeoisie returned home and it was disbanded until required, very rarely, again."

"And now: Louis? What has changed, think you?"

His frown deepened. "Now... I do not know, but have the feeling that once called it will not be easy to dissolve... that is all." He met her concerned gaze and smiled suddenly. "But we shall contrive, *ma chérie*... go now and prepare for your soirée!"

She returned the smile and turned to Estelle. "Come, we must not dally!"

Walking back to the queen's ground-floor apartments, Estelle wondered whether the charming Count Axel Fersen should await them there: his consideration a balm to the soul, in this Versailles filled with conniving, court sycophants and political engineers. Also she would feel Angelique's absence: the message had read that she returned to Paris for matters of family. She smiled suddenly: if the Comte de Arras attended tonight then she would have some amusement after all. His increasing years were no deterrent to his pursuit of Angelique: his countenance this night would be that of a sad spaniel at her absence.

"Where be your romantic mind travelling now, ma belle?" laughed the queen.

"Angelique and Comte Arras," she chuckled.

"*Grand Dieu*... never! Besides, he has so many dis... er... *ailments*, that one!"

# CHAPTER TWO

## Château Quatreaux: Christmas 1788

"'Tis enough I think... what say you?" shouted Raoul, wheeling his mount. "We shall cause delay to the luncheon!"

Emile grinned. "And be cast out for our tardiness. *Mon père* owns low tolerance over such ill manners!" He turned in his saddle. "Marcellus! 'Tis finished... the hunt; the carcases to the château, if you please." He turned back to Raoul and grinned. "Race you!"

"Ah-ha! Think you can, *mon ami*? To within a hundred yards of the party I think."

Emile squinted against the white glare. "To the large oak there," pointing.

The great bay roan, impeccable pedigree evident in his every line, thundered along the track, virgin snow flying from his hooves as he challenged his equal: a dappled grey. The two competing riders, leaning forward and lifting to enhance lightness for their mounts, focussed entirely upon the race. Neck to neck they flew, two dark figures against the pristine landscape, those about to follow pausing their mounts to watch.

"Lay you a gold louis it be Raoul!" chuckled Berthoud.

"With those two: one can never tell," replied Francois, "but I am left to back my brother I see!"

"I say a draw!" said d'Arcy, joining them. "The whole of Paris concedes their superiority of horsemanship be above all others... but equal to each other... makes the gamble irresistible, of course!"

The two arrived beneath the oak, arguing the point of accuracy of judgement minus a witness.

"A half-nose I tell you!" laughed Emile. "I swear!"

Raoul patted his mount's neck. "But of a certainty, in my favour of course!"

"No, no, no... ask my mount... *he* will tell you!"

"*Prejudiced, mon ami...* prejudiced!"

They trotted sedately now, behind the remaining hunters thundering past them and continuing down the slushy track towards the knot of gathered people, hounds baying at heel, jovial voices echoing in bursts of infectious laughter. The valleys and wooded hills lay cloaked in glistening white and crisp air sharpened the far horizon against a clear blue sky. The incredible beauty of the scene surely denied any approaching ugliness.

"'Tis no wonder half the court like coming to Quatreaux estates Ange," said Rochelle, pulling her hand from the mink muff and waving at the scene before them. "It would surprise me not, should the queen follow!"

"The queen never follows. She leads," smiled Angelique.

Snow crunched underfoot as footmen tended the family and guests, gathered about the long, white-linen draped trestle and the breath of animal and man misted in little puffy clouds. The sharp tang of conifer needles, crushed underfoot, drifted on the air; melding with the aroma of the hot roasted deer, fowl and wild duck, still sizzling upon the braziers to the side.

The last of the younger set now appeared, racing each other on steaming thoroughbreds. Wheeling to a halt by the small stand of trees at the edge of the forest, amid teasing hilarity and festive good cheer, they dismounted. Handing the reins and hunting weapons to their grooms, they approached the gathered company already sipping champagne or claret from cellars that knew no economy. A pair of brilliant eyes, watching this, hid their emotion as they contemplated the ease of a small *coup d'état;* slaughter even, after all, the pamphlets said: why keep the hated nobility alive? The head dropped in servile manner as the elderly butler approached: loyalty swam in the very bone marrow of this man. The owner of the brilliant eyes turned to his tasks.

Serfs dragged in the closer kills of wild boar and deer, loading them onto the carts to be carried back to the château. The hounds, panting with tongues lolling, flopped onto the snow but soon fought for position behind the carts, as these pulled away from the scene, dripping small splotches of blood as they departed.

A red splash lay brilliant against the virgin snow, centred by gleaming, darker, congealed patches. Angelique withdrew her eyes: set beneath perfectly arched brows above a perfectly straight nose. But those eyes were drawn again, against their will, to that darkening stain: spreading, running in little rivulets, to pool in a shallow hollow of snow. She felt a sudden premonition steal down her spine. Unable to break the hypnotic power of that bloodstained snow, a dark agony of feeling shadowed her soul. It dragged her on to the far distance, running until it covered all before it, turning at last to a dark purple shadow, spreading all around until day was as dark as night. She stood transfixed and then a gentle hand, barely touching, a sensation rather than a feeling, fell upon her shoulder and her father's deep voice sounded in her ear: 'Be not afraid, this too shall pass... there be but one.' Choking back a rising sob of relief, for she had gone very deep this time, she half turned, fighting through the blackness and muted sounds of wild cheering. Forcing herself to move and reaching for something tangible, she put up her hand to cover his but found her shoulder bare. Searching for it completed her return and she turned her head, then witnessed him at the other end of the company, laughing with his oldest friend Yves Beaumont, the Comte de Arteaux.

She took a shaking breath and struggled to return to the present, hating this thing that had been hers from early childhood, wanting now to share it with her *père*. But Fanchon had warned her: such gifts were dangerous in the extreme and her stories of burnings at stake of the 'seers,' had been graphic. Once again she held her tongue and pondered the ambiguous words 'there be but one': one in their family, one in a hundred, fifty... ten, two; and one for what?

"But Ange... whatever be the matter?" queried Rochelle, gazing at her in puzzlement, then following her gaze to the blood on the snow, "Ugh!"

"*Ma chérie*," the voice of the Comtesse Bayette was full of concern, "do not look! 'Tis one of mans' more base pleasures, the hunt, I do concede... but one must eat. So too do the very animals themselves. It is the order of things."

Angelique attempted a lightness of voice. "Then I do not like the order! The animals' kill however is swift and knows no pleasure, only hunger."

A tall figure on her left, laughing at some jest, ceased his laughter and leaned forward.

"But Mademoiselle, 'pon my honour, every beast that *I* take dies as swift, I promise you!"

She turned to look up into twinkling, slate-grey eyes. The black brows rode high with good humour and the generous mouth lifted slightly at the corners. She stared silently.

He caught her agony, caused obviously by something very deep and attempted to relieve her pain; by the means that almost always worked: light-hearted satire. "What, no argument from the female of the species? But this *is* cause for celebration," he lifted his glass in gentle mockery, "or is that a pleasure yet in store for me?"

She couldn't decide just how to read him. She was aware that Raoul Trifane, the Marquis de Savieur, boundary neighbour to the far-side Quatreaux estates, had recently returned from long absence whilst at law school, upon the death of his *père*. Prior to that, though he was good friend to her twin, Emile, she had met him infrequently: she often in England, he at the Sorbonne. She gazed steadily at him now but her ability of swift and accurate assessment of fellow man deserted her. Though a genuine gentleness and compassion surrounded him freely, something puzzled her. That he knew of her puzzlement and was laughing at her, suddenly took precedence. This she could not allow.

"Seigneur Trifane, I am sure that I cannot argue on your personal hunting skills, but in general, I hold man's bloodlust in abhorrence. As for law by nature, certainly 'tis so, but the animals take only that which they need, no more, no less. They do not hunt for the pure pleasure of it, leaving excess carcasses to rot."

"Mademoiselle, not all of us kill for pure lust and though I do enjoy the hunt, when enough is bagged I turn away. And indeed our estates do not waste: following just supply to our tenants any excess goes to the orphanages and the destitute, as should happen on all estates. But come," he added teasingly, "more wine, to drive out the cold and toast the day's success, for this after all, is the Comte's ritual festive-season hunt."

She attempted an expression of severity but failed, smiled faintly then turned at the approach of a slim young man.

"Ange...I took a huge buck...a magnificent creature!"

His face glowed from the exertion and his eyes sparkled in exhilaration. His golden-brown curls, so carefully tended that morning by his valet, stood up in a dishevelled mop.

A soft chuckle sounded by Angelique's side again. "Ah, but 'tis in the family blood after all; is it not... this lust for the hunt? There is no dampening your brother, Mademoiselle."

"Francois!  Pray do preserve your killing-fields anecdotes for those who care," responded his sister acidly.

"All Christendom is aware of your strange abhorrence for the hunt, I own, but Ange, think of the practice gained. In these dangerous times more so than any, a man must acquire skill, hone his marksmanship," he continued; undeterred by Angelique's rising brows. "For the coming of the civil war. The village talk is of naught else!"

"Taproom gossip, Francois?" asked Raoul Trifane softly, eyes brimful of laughter.

Angelique's brows reached a frigid peak and she opened her mouth for a scathing retort, both for her brother and for Seigneur Trifane. Before she could speak, however, the Comtesse' voice sounded across the table.

"But 'tis enough! I shall *not* have the politics at table, *though* it is so informal."

"But Madame, I only refer to the coming rebellion. Every man knows 'tis so." His stubborn chin set hard: a familial trait.

An elderly man of lean proportions and still erect figure, Marc de Vries, Vicomte de la Fontesqieu, spoke softly from across the table. "Let the lad alone, Madame. He is assuredly astute and if we continue to turn a blind eye to that which is staring us in our faces... it well may happen."

"But what can *we* do, when Louis buries his head, along with the rest of Versailles?" asked his friend, Geraud, leaning in to inspect the dish of baked fowl pieces.

"Ah, but Geraud, my friend, he knows naught of the outside world and listens to those fools that surround him," interposed Seigneur Montmaire as de Quatreaux hid a smile. "He hopes to bluff his way through by conceding to the *Parlements of Paris* and calling the States-general... all the while, I might add, turning a blind eye to the Queen's spending frenzies. Between them all they will bring nothing but destruction and disaster."

"Nothing unusual for court behaviour: the fifteenth Louis' spending upon Madame Pompadour could have supported three countries, they say, for a hundred years," chuckled Berthoud as he approached the trestle table, then paused in thought. "Mayhap that be a trifle exaggerated!"

"Ah, but she was a mistress well worth it: a creature of unsurpassed beauty," said d'Arcy, accepting a glass of champagne from a liveried footman.

"Had she lived today, however, Madame Pompadour would have competition from our own Marie Antoinette," said Trifane lightly, "but anyway, 'Toinette has moderated her avarice as she has grown older.  And Louis' concern, I read, for his unpaid staff from his predecessor, was such that he paid them out of his own allowance."

"Yes, yes, yes... and he has reduced court spending by 25% but 'tis a drop in the ocean." Seigneur Du Toit turned to Montmaire. "So much for so few. And the rabble grows the more discontent with the increase of orators.  And what a mob it is: well over 22 million of them; just ripe for the use of clever men!  If the day comes when

Absolute Monarchy is replaced by a rabble of Absolute Government, then Louis must be held to blame."

"Have a care, my friend; men have lost their heads for less treasonable remarks. And ears are everywhere," murmured Yves Beaumont.

"What? *Here*?" Du Toit's brows reached for his hairline.

Beaumont did not reply, leaning in to inspect the roasted quail with his elegant quizzing-glass. "These morsels appear beyond resistance; roasted to perfection, Jean-Pierre."

De Quatreaux, his host and oldest friend, smiled. "Fortunate in my chef, I can assume nothing less. Garvois turns his staff inside out in the hunt for perfection."

Montmaire turned to Beaumont. "But come! What is the real news from the court, my friend?"

Beaumont frowned. "The court whispers have it that the King is gathering about him those in whom he feels that he may repose his trust."

Expecting court gossip in response to his light query, Montmaire was startled. "To do what?" he asked, eyebrows raised. "Raise a secret army?"

"None know, but you can be sure that beneath that apparent weak hesitancy of his resides a wily brain," replied Beaumont.

The outer environs of the company had drawn closer to the trestle table as he spoke and the Comtesse intervened suddenly, "Wily? I do not agree with that, Seigneur Beaumont. What say you, Angelique?"

"But yes Angelique…from the moment of your presentation he took a shine to you, *ma belle*," smiled her friend Rochelle, from across the table.

"But of course, Mademoiselle. He would take a shine to *all* the beauties at their presentations. No doubt it offers relief from the fubsy-faced ones," chuckled Beaumont softly, drawing a glance of icy disdain from Angelique and a grin from Raoul.

Jean-Pierre glanced in appreciation at his slender, tawny-haired daughter but offered no opinion on Louis' personality.

Rochelle persisted: "Well, *wiliness* of character does not, to me, marry very well with extreme reservation. The word is that he can never find words for the debutantes."

"Oh no: he had much to say, I assure you," exclaimed Angelique.

"Ah, ha…! Then Beaumont is in the right of it," laughed d'Arcy. "His warming to you no surprise: you are after all a reasonable female to observe!"

Raoul's brows shot up and his eyes sparkled. "*Reasonable, mon ami*?" he murmured.

Angelique heard only the slight on Louis' character. "No, no, no: I protest! There is nothing of the profligate about him. He is quiet, gentle and interesting. Reads prolifically! And he dotes upon Marie Antoinette; all do admit to this. It is a known fact that he has never taken a mistress."

Berthoud shook his head. "Bad mistake, you know! Unnatural! All monarchs have a mistress…"

"Or two," grinned Mathieu.

"His people *expect* him to," continued Berthoud, then shaking his head again, very sadly, "Sign of weakness…not good for control of the people!"

"Well, I find him to be a genuine man. *More* important, wouldn't you say?" said a determined Angelique.

"Then the genuine man had better look to his kingdom and his people before this rumbling rebellion takes a strong hold," murmured Seigneur Du Toit. "Not so, Jean-Pierre?"

His host and very old friend smiled placidly and stepped forward, waving the outer groups of people forward around the table. "The subject grows weighty and stirs the appetite and so, *Messieurs-Dames, bon appétit!*  We do not stand upon ceremony this day.  Louis' calling of the States-general to assembly is not until May 5$^{th}$ and time is everything in these things." He turned to the Comtesse. "This hunt has been the most successful to date, do you not agree? Our Christmas table shall rival that of Versailles."

The Comtesse Bayette laughed and threw up her hands in protest. "Not a word more of the Royal Court shall I hear this day, nor the foolishness of the *parlements* and their puppets or any other political nonsense. This is *our* day.  *A votre santé*, everyone," and lifting her glass high, "May the future continue as bright as this day!"

"*A votre santé*!" echoed the company.

Angelique sipped the champagne, a small frown creasing her fine brow now as she gazed out across the valley, absently twirling her champagne glass.  She did not hear the quiet voice beside her and started as the glass was taken from her grasp. Looking up she found Emile beside her, smiling gently.

"*Ma soeur*... your restless fingers betray you. Be not troubled so, there have been many rebellions. Our family is well protected."

She stared at her twin, her gaze direct and serious, "By our allegiance to His Majesty, Emile?  He can barely protect himself these days...his army spread so thin."

"Ange, an additional army is at this moment quietly building for the protection of King Louis. It follows that our *père* will have already laid his plans." He gazed in the direction of Francois, and chuckled softly. "He shall not risk *that* one to a rebellion. His resemblance to our *mère* is too great."

She stared at him, her voice acid. "Do not treat me as cockle-brained because I am female and to be protected!  *Brewing* trouble? It was brewed long ago and is fermented to perfection. Emile... you *must* have noticed the change in our staff.  Feel the avoidance, the scurry of persons when one approaches, the sometimes almost sly smiles and the worst of it: the feeling that always a person is listening at the door."

His thick black brows above the aquiline nose shot toward his hairline and his dark eyes were bright with controlled laughter. "My humble apologies! Never for a moment could anyone think such a thing of you as er, cockle-brained. Your recent stay in England seems to have exacerbated your independence of spirit and speech, my volatile sister. Does your English friend," glancing with unconcealed admiration in the direction of Rochelle, dressed in rich burgundy, "share this outspokenness?"

Rudely ignoring this, she stared, "You must agree Emile; this is not going to go away."

He sighed impatiently. "Rid your mind of a bloody rebellion here, Ange. Our people are amenable. They are fond of the Comte...generosity begets loyalty. And that is as good as it can be. 'Tis the Paris bourgeoisie that carefully breed then stir unrest and it is wealth and property that they want. They will not destroy that which they covet."

"And to get it... they shall just *ask*? Oh Emile!" She almost stomped her foot.

"Ah, let it be, Ange. 'Tis Christmastide, do not spoil our *père's* pleasure. This is his day, *ma soeur*. It is *our* duty to smile."

"Ah yes, duty reigns supreme!"

He lifted a humorous brow. "When did it ever not?"

He turned, retrieved her glass and handed it to her, smiling; but she saw that his eyes, too, were deeply shadowed as he turned away to answer d'Arcy, speaking at his elbow.

Angelique sipped her champagne and nibbled on small wings of game birds, relaxing into the ebb and flow of the laughter and chatter that surrounded her. But it did not work entirely: feelings of urgency racing through her central being. Her frown cleared suddenly to a delighted smile, as she remembered that Fanchon was to return to the château at week's end. There, was the very being with whom to discuss this madness of the mind. That was when it had all begun: on her maternal parent's death, when the château herbalist had allowed her to trail around behind her.

"Well, wet goose, you have come out of your doldrums, yes?"

Angelique glanced around on the soft voice at her side and smiled at her elder sister. "Thinking of Fanchon, Clarisse. I cannot imagine her siding with the rabble... should sides become an issue!"

"Pray do not let this Paris nonsense cut up your serenity, Ange. As for village gossip: 'tis hot air, it will always be so, it is the system. You *know* that."

Angelique gazed at her elder, gentle sister and smiled fondly. "You really are happy, Clarisse! I wish that I could be as serene. No, it is more than that. Accepting: that is it."

"But of course I be happy my love. I do not believe the rumour-mongers and trust my husband to protect us." She smiled. "You should try the married state, Ange my love; it be a marvellous experience. And one has far more to think of rather than the politics: so very unfeminine, my dear."

Angelique gazed at her sister. "Clarisse, do you never wonder what...?"

"What would have happened had I a choice of husbands?" laughed Clarisse. "My dear, this new, *English* I believe, habit of falling in love and marrying the man of your choice, is fraught with trouble and confusion. Believe me, I have witnessed it."

"But where... did you so?"

"Oh, we have many such, deep within France. They buy the destitute estates from ruined French nobles. Or occasionally win them in those wretched gaming salons and retire quietly, in disgrace with their own back in England, or Belgium or wherever."

"You mean those of *mésalliance*?"

"Those too, and they do not prosper any more than do ours. The rigours of opposition *beget* the love *because* it is forbidden, but once beyond that point the interest seems to wan. I do believe that a deeper love grows out of arranged marriages when one falls in love with one's husband, slowly, permanently and... delightfully."

"Oh!" Angelique had nothing to offer on this issue. She could not imagine accepting an arranged marriage, but then the convent was the other option. She could not decide which was the worse fate and dismissed the gloomy subject. She shrugged, then, suddenly, teetering on the very edge of her mind, lurked the dark shadow of a tall, lean figure, with laughing, slate-grey eyes deep-set below thick, black brows. Emile spoke beside her again and she turned to laugh at his jest; but the image remained, startling her in its intensity.

# CHAPTER THREE

## Château Quatreaux

The carriages rumbled over the cobbled surface beneath the avenue of stately trees, barren branches intertwining overhead. Muted horses' hooves thudded softly on the snow-covered verges beside them as the hunters rode alongside. The château ahead, set upon a high rise and etched sharply against the clear late sky, gave off a distinct sense of peace and security. Topping the last undulation the guests caught the full majesty of the scene. From this aspect, the western approach, the sun sank rapidly over the snow-sharpened horizon behind them. In doing so it glinted off the long windows and lent a lotus-flower pink hue to the château's ancient limestone walls.

Gazing in adoration at the sheer beauty, the Comtesse murmured softly, "None in their right minds could *possibly* imagine unrest or rebellion against that!"

All eyes within the carriage dwelt on the fairytale scene. All were held in silence by the pristine aura of holiness: white-blanketed undulations, topped by the soft pink, cathedral-like lines of the château.

Exhibiting a greater reality, the rear courtyard of the château now reverberated with noise and activity. Scullions and yard-boys raced to and fro, emptying the returning carts, hindering the bucket-laden dairymaids battling to keep their feet on the slush-slippery cobbled surface: against the leaping, slobbering, baying hounds. Delivery wagons from the village added to the crush.

In the enormous kitchen the chef berated his assistants with rapid-fire speech and up-flung hands as he organized a suitably impressive dinner for Monsieur le Comte and his guests. Here also yard-boys fuelled the ovens and scullery maids battled valiantly with the mountain of returning dishes from the hunt picnic.

Footmen went about quietly lighting the candelabra and wall-brackets within the now darkening rooms, on the east side of the château. Their circuitous route led them back again to the front; where the wide entrance, great dining hall, salons and the ballroom, waited their turn before the guests descended that evening to dine. Urns of hot water and laden coalscuttles were delivered to the upper floors and below stairs piles of logs sat beside the great, now blazing, fireplaces.

The front entrance, lit by flares and lined by waiting staff, showed a more dignified activity than the rear. Certainly grooms ran to the carriage horses' heads, as the returning vehicles drew to a halt at the front entrance, but the waiting footmen moved forward with practiced grace to open the doors and let down the steps.

Personal grooms of the gentlemen took their masters' mounts, leading them away to be rubbed down, baited and stabled, for the long cold night ahead, as the hunting party climbed the wide, shallow steps to enter the cavernous entrance-hall.

Siffred, having returned long ago and organized his long line of footmen to assist the now cold and tired guests, moved forward silently as the Comte entered chatting lightly with Seigneur Montmaire. A footman took the cloak, hat and riding gloves from Jean-Pierre, as the butler arrived at his side.

The Comte raised his brows in enquiry. "Well, Siffred? You have a problem?"

"Not precisely, Monsieur le Comte, but I arrived to find that a royal courier had called, carrying a message bearing the royal seal."

The Comte regarded him with raised brow. "'Twas he that caused your long face?"

"Well, Monsieur, I believe *le courrier* was not impressed by the lack of senior members of staff within this household. Perhaps I should have stayed."

"Waste not another thought on the matter. I place far more importance upon the success of the luncheon, Siffred!"

"A trusted footman stands guard, Sire."

The Comte gazed at him coolly. "As are they all. Otherwise they no longer work for me."

"Yes Monseigneur, but Jacques comes of good family."

"Many a traitor has come of good family, Siffred. We should know!"

Siffred permitted himself a small smile, sliding down the long road of their union to the Comte's younger days: of that fateful duel and his own efforts to prevent it. He frowned; the evil family enemy was dead as a result, but his young cub was about these days, he had heard, and seeking revenge. His own surveillance over his staff revealed nothing; but that the cub would have spies within the Comte's establishments, had to be.

The Comte strolled towards the library door and entered as a footman hurried to open it and then close it again behind the emerging 'guard'. A slight frown creased Siffred's normally bland features: he had witnessed other occasions of royal summons necessitating the abrupt departure of M. le Comte. He waited a few minutes in the lofty entrance hall, eyeing that closed door, but no orders were issued for immediate departure and so he returned to his many duties of the evening. Jacques slid back into his duties again, indistinguishable from the retinue of other footmen: the time to move may be many months ahead; perhaps years. He simply followed orders and those at this moment were only to watch, listen and relay: but the royal seal had been impossible to break.

The winter dark crept across the slopes outside as the guests ascended the broad staircase to the deep, wide landing; housing upon its facing wall two old paintings of previous de Quatreaux,' gazing imperiously out over the new arrivals below. Here also resided two chintz sofas, though nobody could say why one would wish to sit half-way up the stairs, whereat those stairs divided, curving away to the left and the right.

Angelique and Rochelle reached the gallery that ran along the top; housing many more haughty ancestors within gold frames, defended every few metres by heavy suits of armour of medieval magnificence. They turned to the left, continued on and then turned right, down the long, wide corridor to eventually reach Angelique's apartments.

"*Mon Dieu!* But you must remain in a perpetual state of exhaustion, *ma chérie,* living here," exclaimed Rochelle, giving her light, irresistible chuckle. "It challenges Versailles... I do declare!"

"Versailles," smiled her friend, "be one third of a mile long and that is going in one direction only.  But a place of great beauty and light also: designed to glory in the summer sunshine and thus capitalize upon what light can be caught in the winter."

"Did you not become lost?" asked Rochelle, intrigued.

"Many times...terrifying experience, let me tell you. I never did see so many predators, as roamed those corridors, in all my life." Angelique paused at her door as her *femme de chambre* held it open. "But do dress for dinner quickly and return here so that we may go down together."

Having completed her ablutions, Angelique seated herself at the mahogany dressing table and, looking at the array of pots, decided upon only a little face dusting and the slightest touch of *rouge*. She paused—perhaps a very light touch of kohl. The pomegranate-tinted cream for her lips took only the first bite of food to delete it. She shrugged; one day there would be an improvement. The fire glowed red in the grate and the air was warm, but she knew this would not be so in the great hall in which they were to dine.  It contained two great fireplaces but the expanse of that room, coupled with the lofty arched ceiling, caused the impossibility of heating to any real comfort.

"Do not allow me to forget my shawl, 'Belle," she said, pausing indecisively over the placement of the tiny silk patch, staring critically and then leaning forward to place it, then leaning back to view it and, changing her mind, leaning forward again. Isabelle stood behind her; hands out, about to dress her hair in the latest fashion. They had agreed to pile it high this night. She spoke now, in English, a sure sign of frustration.

"*Will* you be still please—My Lady!"

Angelique grinned into the mirror. "Oh! Are you ready to start? So sorry, my love, but you see, I cannot settle my mind to the patch or not the patch. What do you think?"

A knock at the door caused further interruption as Isabelle left her position to admit Rochelle.

"But *mon amie*, you look stunning in that colour!" exclaimed Angelique into the mirror. Rochelle advanced into the room, dressed in pale pink silk, with rustling, dusky pink, satin underskirt.  A silver riband threaded her dark curls and another accentuated the waist of her gown, falling from there, at the front, in two long curled, silver tails.  This, complemented by silver slippers and a simple silver locket, created a picture of willowy simplicity.

"Ah! Merci, *ma chérie,* but I do not own the eyes to match it."

Startled, Angelique looked a question in the mirror, glancing at the dusky pink. "You wish for the eyes of a diseased *rabbit*?"

Rochelle laughed, then, "As do yours match your honey-gold gown: that changes colour from gold, through variations of this, to a deep brown, as you move... exactly as your eyes do with your changing moods, though you cannot know this of course."

"Oh. A trick of the light and if indeed that is so then I cannot claim the effect; for it was indeed the Comtesse who decided that the elles of material were just the right shade for me. I do not much mind what I wear, unless of course the choice causes me to become an antidote."

"You could never be an antidote, my friend. So enviably slender: you could wear the veriest rags to advantage!"

Angelique chuckled. "You mean skinny, of course! But, *mon amie*, look in your own mirror."

"No, no, no... another five livre; at *least*; must go. *Then* the stays need not hold one permanently on the edge of the vapours!"

Angelique chuckled. "Another torture for the demolition! If I could but change the fashion: for 'tis the *gowns* that demand their use! But the Comtesse does not agree!"

The Comtesse," Rochelle paused. "You er... do not find her... um, intrusive, *mon amie*? Choosing your very materials even? I mean, your *mère*; and now *her*?" Rochelle's voice was soft and compassionate but she glanced at Isabelle as she spoke.

Angelique laughed. "You must not mind 'Belle, must she, my dear?"—looking into the mirror, at her *femme de chambre* who gave a tight smile but maintained a mute attitude. "Isabelle has been with me so long that I cannot imagine her not being here."

"But of course, I forgot; you came with Ange from England."

Isabelle nodded briefly and spoke again in English. "That I did My Lady, and long gone is the day since I was able to show her the birch of schoolroom days: I would that I could use it now too."

Angelique chuckled. "But my 'Belle! I am *very* well behaved these days."

"Ah, the pleasure of hearing the English," sighed Rochelle.

"But surely you do not wish to return so soon?"

"No, no," Rochelle looked serious suddenly and reverted to French tongue. "This trouble in Paris, Ange, what think you about it? Already it is driving out the foreigners."

"You be no foreigner *mon amie*! But at the luncheon you would have none of it."

Rochelle picked up a haresfoot brush and played with it. "Mere social etiquette. Does the Comtesse Bayette truly not listen to the very real evidence of her changing world?"

"She does not see what she does not wish to see."

"As with many of the nobility; but if they do not soon open their eyes, there will be trouble too great to handle. They cannot leave it all to Louis... and the few *perceptive* nobles."

Angelique chuckled. "To do that they must bestir themselves from their mentally recumbent position. But do you really think so?"

Rochelle stared. "You of all people should see it! And M. le Comte be at the hub of affairs, I be sure. He is always at Louis' court. When he is not abroad, *for* Louis I suspect."

"Yes, but surely you do not believe he shares even a hint of information with us? And I do not see, when it comes to it, that Louis will allow the heinous stirrers to create a large problem. It is for him, as monarch, and Necker, to deal with surely... now that the ponderous de Brienne has gone. And surely, now that we are to have a meeting of the States-general, the people shall be content; for *there* they may air their grievances."

Rochelle looked serious suddenly. "Ah! France's only real *parlement*, stuck in a cupboard for centuries. Our Louis must have a care there."

"Yes, the play for power will be strong: within the unstable period of its convocation. He will have his plans in place, though. However, let us return to festive mood! And do not be having an opinion upon the politics, at dinner, whatever you do my friend. An intelligent female is *not* all the crack within our society."

Rochelle grinned. "But *mon amie*...how does one *resist*? But do you think it shall *ever* be accepted that a female's brain is no less than a males?"

"In the year two thousand and something, *if* even then," laughed her friend: the chuckle grew deeper. "Someone actually ran around measuring heads, would you believe; and declared, on average, the female brain smaller than the male. No... truly... I read it!"

Rochelle stared, then collapsed back against her chair in laughter. "Oh Ange! Only you could be relied upon to find that snippet. All your reading not in vain: Monsieur le Comte *must* not complain!" She replaced the hares-foot brush on the dressing table and stood, wandering around the room. "Do you stay here for the entire winter?"

"No. We go to Paris again soon: but when? *Mon père*, he will tell us eventually. You know his way, mysteriously silent to the last. He can make a plate of porridge appear exciting, that one. But that is, he tells us, how he survived all those years away from France and travelling from royal court to royal court. By holding his own council that is: not with porridge."

"Heavy stuff, porridge; but speaking of royal courts... someone should enlighten our queen of the current nation wide gossip trends, regarding her 'continued spending on the *Petit Trianon*, while the nation starves'." Rochelle paused, then grinned. "Mayhap you can have some influence. She listens to you, they say."

Angelique gazed at her in astonishment. "I? But I am a mere guest. I may never go again. One must after all be invited, unless requested by Louis to reside at Versailles."

"Do you not mean 'ordered'?" Rochelle asked dryly. "A gentle hint, then. It is said that she took a liking to you and you are now great friends. *Do* you not know her so well then?"

Angelique hesitated: de Quatreaux had asked her to kill such assumptions. "Rumours. *Mon Dieu*, what rumours can do! She merely took a fancy to me because I offered her a cure for her megrim and it happened to work. That is what began the rumour and yes, we connected. I found rapport in her sense of humour and ready wit and due to a certain affinity of ideas we rubbed along very well indeed and for a while she requested my company. The *Petit Trianon* did not use the large amount of *livre* that it is rumoured to have done, by the by. But question her spending? And likely lose my head?" She ended lightly, "But I do feel…"

"But no. They do not, for such petty offences as insubordination, *execute* over here do they?" Rochelle chuckled, resuming her seat again.

"Ah! Why do I worry then? It is a simple matter of imprisonment!"

"But not the dreaded Bastille; that is only for male prisoners… political prisoners, mainly, I think."

"Ah-ha, it grows better and better. Only, then, the *Conciergerie*… or perhaps *La Force*! But to continue from where you so rudely had my head severed at the neck…"

"But no *mon amie. You* did that," laughed Rochelle, settling herself the more comfortably in her chair, gazing at her friend in the mirror still as Isabelle put the finishing touches to Angelique's hair. "Besides, it eventuated to mere imprisonment after all."

"To continue," responded Angelique severely, "More of a worry is the welter of printed material: revolting writings about her by unscrupulous and disgusting men of *lettres*, of a certain *style* of *lettres* you understand."

"You mean the '*Love Life of Charlie and 'Toinette*' and the '*Essay on the Life of Marie Antoinette*'? Certainly they portray her as barbaric and adulterous and, what was the other thing—oh yes, debauched. I always thought that they were the same thing."

"Well, whatever you do, do not be airing that very bad language in public," laughed Angelique. "We are after all not supposed to know that such even exists."

"Oh, never fear, blind, deaf and mute am I, a picture of maidenly innocence. But surely she could *demonstrate* that it is not so."

Angelique shrugged. "The king is aware of her virtuosity and so she disdains to even acknowledge such revolting trash. No, I do not blame her for her haughty silence."

"But then she looks guilty."

"Useless to deny: mud sticks. And in her case, heinous stirrers of the masses have realized the power of the quill, especially in cartoon; to the delight of the uneducated."

"Ah yes. My cousin d'Argmont says, upon return from his forays into the seedier side of Paris… not that he actually admits such… that disgusting cartoons and pamphlets pour out an endless barrage of filth and criticism, which of course are read as common truths."

"Oh yes. *And* her supposed affairs: with the Duc de Coigny and the Duc de Biron… and now poor old Axel, whose adoration be of the purest form! But her greatest crime is that she is a Habsburg and that she presented a female first-born."

"Must admit I was drawn to her when I met her; and her gentleness surprised me."

"And she *does* feel for her people, but is powerless. She escapes into her family now." Angelique paused reflectively. "You know 'Chelle, we sat often, simply playing with her children, nothing more; all the while during which time, I learned later, she was supposed to have been entertaining her many lovers, male *and* female.

Did they think all together, I wonder? I be not sure whether *I* was supposedly one of the other females or not."

"*Vraiment*! De Quatreaux had better not get hold of *that*. But she did deny the immorality, surely?"

"No, *ma chérie*, the more the rumours the stronger her pride... and I cannot bring myself to criticize that, for I'd sooner have my head severed than bow to these awful people."

"I thought we decided upon imprisonment for you!"

Isobelle intervened, as she pinned the last curl in place. "Imprisonment may be closer than you think; should you both be late for dinner; and then of course it shall be my fault."

Angelique laughed. "Saved by my 'Belle again. Come, Isabelle is in the right of it. We must not be late, if we wish to avoid *mon père's* acid tongue regarding tardiness."

"Then we run! I have past experience of such as he."

"Do not stay up, Isabelle dear," said Angelique as they departed. "Who knows how late this night may go; there be whist and charades, following dinner."

They hurried along the corridor and turned into the upper gallery, there to meet others also making their way to the great hall below, among them Berthoud Montague and Mathieu d'Arcy.

"Well met, Mesdemoiselles; may we escort you against the dangers that lie in wait upon your long and perilous journey to the great hall?" grinned Berthoud, waving an elegant hand towards the descending staircase and bowing.

Seigneur de Vries peered down the wide sweeping stairway at his feet, quizzing-glass to one eye. "No, no *mon ami*," he chuckled. "I see no lurking enemy but your gallantry is commendable—one never knows these days."

"Better then check out that suit of armour there, Berthoud," responded Mathieu gaily.

"Ah yes, what better place to hide!"

Mathieu's brow's shot up at the sudden serious note in his friend's voice. "Eh?"

Berthoud grinned again. "The spies: they lurk everywhere. 'Tis just a feeling, *mon ami*; we may soon own reason to check out even the suits of armour."

"Perish the feeling then, much more pleasant things to do. Case in point: dinner!"

"Which, you certainly will not see if you dally here much longer!" Berthoud turned to Angelique and offered his arm, "Mademoiselle Vermont?"

The dinner, of an excellence that gratified even the exactitude of the chef Garvois, was well into its second hour when the conversation showed signs of turning towards a more serious nature. But Francois, Berthoud, and Mathieu determined to keep a jovial face, the bounden duty of any good guest.

Mathieu smiled across the table at the Comtesse Beaumont. "But no Madame, time enough for such reflections. Our national debt has always been of the highest within Europe anyway: in which case it must therefore read that we can afford it."

"But no, no, no... I only asked *why* Calonne used such to push Louis to raise taxes."

"And why do we discuss him? There have been two controllers of finance since he was dismissed, have there not?" asked Rochelle suddenly. "And still the mire grows deeper."

Angelique raised her brows at her friend's deliberate foray into the man's world of finance. Emile smiled quietly into his wine glass. Raoul Trifane also grinned but at Angelique's mobile expressions.

"Because, Madame, he started it all," responded de Vries. "But because Louis sniffed danger in the air, and did not wish for outright confrontation with the *Parlements of Paris,* he first took the reforms to the *Assembly of Notables.* But they sniffed a threat to their exemption of the *taille* and were suspicious of hidden agendas. And when they were dissolved, he finally approached the *Parlements of Paris* with the same result. They too had to be dissolved."

"And those following have not done any better," muttered Montmaire. "De Brienne lost all credibility; as finance minister—and now we have a return of Necker."

"Mayhap 'twill be better, a banker seems always able to raise funds," replied Seigneur Beaumont. "But it be a greater issue than finance."

"You are saying?" asked Berthoud, now suddenly interested.

As Beaumont paused in thought, De Vries responded, "Until now, the serfs put up with anything at all as their 'lot'… even unto death… for king and country. But this generation growing up in the period of plenty, ending only, roughly, a decade ago, know nothing of famines, diseases and disasters that toughened their forebears."

Angelique regarded de Vries with poorly camouflaged distaste and Raoul Trifane watched her with sudden interest.

She could not let it go, and reverting to schoolroom impetuosity, turned to de Vries. "So you feel that they should continue to *put up* with their lot, Seigneur de Vries?" her voice, soft and polite, accentuated the criticism. "These are not Madame Roland's sentiments. And she digs and ferrets deep, in her attempts to search out the truth of the serf's existence… not that one must dig at all to see their dreadful plight."

A sudden silence dropped over the immediate company. Raoul worked hard to hide a grin but Emile glanced in mock terror toward the Comte at the head of the table. De Quatreaux was, however, involved in concentrated dialogue with his left-hand neighbour. Rochelle's eyebrows wanted to reach for her hairline but she controlled this and lowered her sparkling eyes: de Vries was, after all, a very long-standing friend of de Quatreaux.

The urbane tones of the eternal diplomat now covered the ice. "You are saying, de Vries," murmured Phillippe Du Toit, "that today's generation, unaccustomed to these er… bracing discomforts of hardship, are unwilling to tolerate famines, economic strictures and the like?"

"And neither should they," said their host, now returning his attention. "But, the wily bourgeoisie hope to *use* this new wave of unrest supported by radical thinking."

Beaumont grunted. "Radical thinking spawned of Voltaire, Rousseau and their ilk! But they are dead now and though I suspect their theories, Rousseau's in particular, strongly influence our newer rebels' thinking, today's snakes in the under-grass be the real danger."

"But one can never find out who they *are*," complained a bemused Comtesse.

"And never will, until too late; they do not stand on the soap box, they pay the orators to do that: to fuel the growing discontent."

"Nothing new there surely: the people are trained from the cradle to be dissatisfied!" said a desperate Berthoud.

Raoul Trifane grinned at him. "Deny and it shall surely go away?" Then suddenly, looking at Angelique: "There were similar rebellions and riots in England, of late, not so? Were you not there at the time?"

Before she could answer de Vries replied, "Ah yes; but *they* used the military. The nonsense ceased immediately, or as good as."

"Only thing to do," agreed Francois, reaching for another sweetmeat.

"But we do not have full rebellion here…yet," said Angelique at last. "And I do believe that it could be much averted if only the rumour mill would cease its endless stirrings."

"Ah, that clever, indefinable weapon," smiled Raoul. "But a revolt based on rumours?"

"Why not? There is nothing more powerful. Rumours supply indecision, quandary and fear.   Cleverly designed common gossip has brought down governments before now."

"It takes little, I agree," said Yves Beaumont. "How long before open revolt?"

"They'll never dare." Berthoud found the very idea impossible to absorb.

"Not while we have the army to keep them in check," asserted Francois firmly.

"What of you, Seigneur Trifane, would you fight?" asked Angelique suddenly.

"But most assuredly, Mademoiselle, to the bitter end, under *any* threat, to defend that which is mine." His eyes held hers as he added softly, "The lot of the workers *must* be improved but it is not they who would benefit from a rebellion: in fact the very reverse: cannon fodder be their destiny under such. And to preserve our heritage; for my heirs; and for those very people that its canopy protects, I would do whatever was required."

"I would that all were as loyal as you, *mon ami*," murmured Seigneur Montmaire.

"But surely if it came to it everyone would be so?" said a startled Comtesse Bayette.

"No, Madame," replied the Comte de Quatreaux gently. "There are those who would sell their souls to survive. Mere history tells us so."

"Show them to me," said Francois. "Cowards! *I* should run them through!"

"Good thinking," Mathieu chuckled. "Now. Before they can do damage."

"Enough! The politics I can, at a push, tolerate at table… and these days just try for anything *else*.  But the bloodletting… I tell you *no!*" cried the Comtesse Bayette, laughing and throwing down her serviette. She glanced down the length of the table, saw that one and all were replete, then rose, glancing at the Comtesse d'Arteaux on her right; and began the procession of the ladies from the room to the long salon.

# CHAPTER FOUR

## Versailles

Comtesse Bayette hurried along the long gallery. "Are they coming or are they not?"

Siffred, approaching sedately from the opposite direction, diverted to one of the long windows and peered through. "Extra heavy snowfall Madame."

"Well, the ball shall just be late, that is all!"

Rochelle smiled gaily. "Starts late... ends late!  But 'tis Xmas Eve—does it really matter, Madame?"

The Comtesse rolled her eyes. "Not when your years do not exceed much beyond the nursery!"

Rochelle chuckled and also diverted to a window.  Many flares at that moment appeared: bobbing across the black expanse, accompanied by muted voices lifted in song. "There!  Do you not hear them? And where, for the goodness sakes, is Angelique?"

"She will appear in her own good time, that one." The Comtesse now slowed and moved, in dignified manner, down the broad stairs, stepping before a politely waiting Rochelle.

She moved across the hall to the grand-ballroom, causing a pause in the lively chatter of the guests, as she entered through the door opened by the waiting page.

De Quatreaux moved forward to meet her. "Comtesse."

She took his arm and, turning, he escorted her to a chair beside the cavernous fireplace.

At this moment Siffred entered the room. "The carol singers, Seigneur."

The voices, many meriting credit should circumstances allow, lifted and echoed to the high arched ceiling of the ballroom.  Following the last note of the last carol, they swept into more riotous songs as Emile, Francois and friends led the retinue from the ballroom, one behind the other, snake-like, beneath the decorations, dancing and singing, all the way to the very large kitchens and staff dining hall. Here traditional mulled wine to keep out the cold and Christmas fare was offered to the carol-singers before they set off again, taking with them fancy foods and jars of wine. A thoroughly festive air predominated; convincing the Comtesse Bayette that last night's more serious discussions were naught but hot air. These people were full of goodwill. She smilingly saw off the last villager and turned to M. le Comte de Quatreaux.

"There now: do you *now* see why I will not tolerate the bad tidings that people *will* visit upon us? It is just too much, Monseigneur; all this distressing talk of rebellion. I shall *not* allow it to be true."

He smiled. "Your wish shall be my command. Until the end of the festive season, all political discussions shall be under ban: if not by royal decree, then that of de Quatreaux."

"Which amounts to the same thing," muttered Emile mischievously in Angelique's ear.

She laughed softly. "Does he realize the difference?"

"Such filial disrespect: you both deserve horsewhipping at the very least," chuckled a deep but muted voice behind Angelique, but it was Emile who swung around, grinning, to answer Raoul.

"*Mon ami, you* have not the benefit of our experience at his hands."

"Ah! So, I shall enquire no further. May I take you in, to the ball, Mademoiselle Vermont?" responded Raoul, with an elegant bow and offered arm to Angelique.

"Well, it shall be better than *me* taking her," chuckled Emile, then glancing up to see Rochelle descending the stairs, "And if you shall both excuse me, I must not cast my chance to others!"

The elegant decorations of the ballroom heightened the grandeur of the ancient château. The light from the chandeliers lent sheen to the swirling silks and satins, and reflected as tiny fairy lights within the occasional wall mirrors. Doors and windows were opened at intervals by a waiting page, to allow a swirl of refreshing breeze to the heated faces. The musicians remained tireless and the dancers invigorated. Footmen stood at each arched entrance along the walls and seamstresses waited within a fire-warmed room above stairs, for any repairs to torn dresses or collapsing hemlines.

Angelique and Rochelle, their program booklets filled, stood up for every dance, but it wasn't until close to midnight that Angelique danced with Raoul; but any smooth flow of conversation became impossible as they continuously pulled apart and came together again, within the moves of the quadrille. This being so, she simply gave herself up to the rhythm of the music and the light amusement of his dry wit, offered in fragments.

Supper, served from the dining hall, occurred at the end of the Quadrille. The musicians ceased their play, the announcement was made and Raoul Trifane bowed elegantly, offering his arm. "You must be thirsty by now, Mademoiselle—come."

He escorted her to a vacant chair against the wall, then disappeared to the adjacent salon and, returning, produced two glasses of champagne.

"Thank you, Monsieur, this is a welcome sight indeed," she confessed, taking the long stemmed glass from him and sipping its cool and sparkling contents.

"The pleasure was all mine; you own a dancing skill and grace unequalled this night," he replied, offering the usual accolades, then laughed suddenly at her slight smile and faintly raised brows. He settled in for an enjoyable few minutes of her company; knowing that here was not your usual shy country lady of gentle birth or, even worse, the practiced court socialite full of grace and wit and complete insincerity. Of the latter, he was practiced in politely and charmingly evading. The Comte's younger daughter, however, he found intriguing: she owned more than mere beauty and it was that indefinable 'something' that now drew him.   Twin to his staunch friend Emile, she had remained illusive: seen only occasionally, as sisters were, since the family's return to France and then only for polite exchange; or from a distance or across the floor.  Of adult life, their paths had rarely crossed: she was often in England, he at university. He regarded her now with hooded eyes over the rim of his glass; she had grown graceful, in a natural sense: as was a reed in the breeze or a hawk gliding the air currents high in the sky.  Was that it, the difference he felt about her, one of *naturellement* and freedom?  Certainly she owned a freedom from routine accepted thought, causing a delightful lack of compliance of speech to popular opinion. He paused at this thought, suddenly afraid that this attitude, though captivating, could lead her into trouble if not danger, in the uncertain future.

"Monseigneur Trifane?" observing his faint frown, she raised her brows high, "You have a problem with some aspect of my person?"

His chuckle was appreciative. "Was I staring? I do apologize: forgive me please. I did not mean to put you out of countenance.  You are very obviously unaware of how beautiful you are."

"Ah but no, Monsieur, 'twould be irritatingly naïve of me to pretend other's have not tried to tell me so... though some flowery speeches *have* left me in a definite state of suspended belief. Therefore I know that I be not an antidote at least; and that be all that matters on that front... a false and doubtful accolade anyway... transient, in the very least!"

He smiled suddenly, sardonically. "But whole estates may be snared on nothing more... indeed, have been... routinely *are* so!"

"Then these designing individuals must thereafter work exhaustively, to maintain their status quo. However *that* may be... 'twas not my degree of beauty, or otherwise, that was under appraisal, wherever it may reside on the scale... set by goodness knows whom, not so, Seigneur Trifane?"

He was delighted by her perception and opened his mouth to reply, but as happens in such moments, Berthoud suddenly appeared before them, bowing to Angelique and begging her hand for the next dance, a minuet; approaching at the same moment as a laughing Emile and Rochelle. He rose, bowed and offered Rochelle his chair.

"What a crush," breathed Rochelle to Angelique. "I did not realize so many people would come from Paris!"

"But what a night, eh Angelique, this be the best Christmas Eve ever," said Emile. "Trifane; do you not agree?"

"It was," a slow accent on the last word, "until you appeared *mon ami*," replied Raoul under cover of Rochelle's bubbling accents, as she laughed with Angelique.

"*Ah-ha*, what is this? That is my sister, *mon ami*! What is more, she is my *twin sister*, Savieur. We are close! Remember that. Do I call you out, I wonder?"

Raoul-Phillippe Michel Trifane, Marquis de Savieur, raised mock haughty brows, "Do you think you *could*, de Quatreaux?"

Emile laughed, "Depends, Savieur: pistols or sword?"

"Pistols or swords?" asked Mathieu, joining them at that moment. "Which is the better? I say pistols. They be exceedingly improved these days, especially in the field, do not throw so much to the left, they say, and much less blood; mind you, nothing like the sword for silent stealth and one does lose time by having to reload a pistol."

"I do agree," replied a grinning Emile; then bowing to Raoul, "Best leave it there, *Monseigneur*; I do not wish to carve you up er… stealthily!"

Raoul Trifane responded with a bow of mock exquisite grace and a grin. "Or me shoot you, *mon ami*...with a, um, left-throwing pistol!"

The very early hours of the morning saw the first of the older company drifting up to their rooms and by four o'clock the musicians ceased their tireless activity. Such gentlemen as were not enthusiastic about dancing had withdrawn long ago, following the mandatory two or three appearances on the floor.  These could be found in an above stairs salon and continued their card games until well after five. All agreed that the Christmas of '88 had been well and truly ushered in and with such cheer and good will as had not been seen for a long time. Perhaps it was the particular mix of good company or perhaps a determination to cling to the old order; that refused admittance this night to the chill of sombre change in the air, stealing as a silent wraith across the land.

Angelique sat, in demure fashion, within the window embrasure, leaning towards the late afternoon light as she set the next intricate stitch in her embroidery.  She glanced up in time to see the shallow arc of a round, red, orb slide behind the western snow-clad horizon. Bands of deep pink shafted upwards into the sky; and crested the snow-drenched undulations. She sighed and put aside her work of an indifferent quality. She had brought it down only to avoid boredom, having read all the current journals and magazines. She glanced again at the clock on the mantle and then at Emile slouched in a chair by the fire, deeply absorbed in the latest agricultural journal.  A log fell, causing the fire to splutter, and rolled, smouldering, to the very edge of the fireplace lip. He neither saw it nor was disturbed by the wafting tendrils of smoke.  Francois tended to the fire, lifting the offending log with the toe of his highly polished knee boot and pitching it forward to land upon its compatriots again, with a burst of sparks and smoke.

"I wish he would hurry," he said, "I cancelled a card party with Armand and Jean-Paul for this night. I believe that even Devereaux, too, was coming."

Emile continued to read but Angelique smiled fondly and replied, "*You* know our *père*."

"Well, shall be Garvois to whom he shall have need of apologizing. It shall be dinner time soon and you know what our very dear chef be like if his work spoils."

"Our esteemed *père* is up to *something*; nothing is surer and these times it has to be tied to the king," said Emile, emerging from the articles that had absorbed him so intently: the new English method of soil drainage to the benefit of crop production; and even newer ideas on dry seed preservation.

Angelique, about to speak, paused at the sound of a quick footstep towards the door.

Emile and Francois rose. Angelique sat very still, a faint smile upon her face as their father entered the book-room as would a breath of fresh air, dropping his fashionable, indolent attitude reserved for social occasions: in particular those at Versailles.

"Ah *mes enfants*, we are all here. Good. It grows late, did any one call for drinks?"

"Well no, we thought rather to wait for you *Mon Père*," responded Emile with a straight face.

The Comte smiled slightly and reached for the bell pull just as Siffred entered with a tray carrying a bottle of burgundy and four glasses.

"Ah Siffred: timing perfect as always."

"Monseigneur," the butler bowed his thanks then poured and handed out the goblets. He then stood to one side and waited: avoiding irritating unnecessary speech.

"*Merci*, Siffred, I shall call if I need you."

"Very good: Monseigneur."

Jean-Pierre took his drink to a chair, sat and took a tentative sip of the burgundy. Then, placing his glass on the small, ivory-inlaid table by his elbow, he withdrew his snuffbox, flipped open the lid and offered it to Emile and then Francois. Startled, Francois responded, as his turn came, thanked his father and then sat back and waited.

"I see someone has had the instruction of you Francois. You handled that very well; Emile's influence, hmm?"

"Well, I er, thought that someone should, as he was making a mull of it."

"I'll be having you know..." Francois didn't chance to finish as his father broke in.

"All sibling rivalry relegated to the nursery, *mes enfants*. Now to matters of the moment: you will not be aware but on return from our hunt luncheon I received a message from the royal court." He paused, but the response was conspicuously absent; this was not after all an unheard of event. "And so I called you all to tell you that I set out for Versailles on the morrow and am taking some of you with me."

"Not I?" asked Emile, watching his father over the rim of his glass.

"Just so: you shall be required here."

"And I, *Mon Père*?" asked Angelique. "To Paris... or Versailles?"

"'Toinette has been asking for you and therefore court etiquette denies our refusal. But on the night of my appointment with the king, simultaneous to some *levée*, I shall attend alone... not knowing how long the meeting shall go."

"Be there an offer for Angelique in the wind?" Emile grinned, remembering the aging Comte de Arras, then chuckled at her expression of horror.

"I do not expose my daughter to such hunting grounds again. The mandatory presentation is enough," replied the Comte and Angelique's relief was palpable; but this became short-lived as he continued, "When I decide it time for her to wed, then I shall choose outside that den of...savage hunters."

Emile's grin broadened at the rapid changes to his twin's expression.

"We go tomorrow, *Mon Père*?" asked Francois unwisely.

"Hearing impairment, Francois?" Jean-Pierre's brow lifted just faintly.

"Then I must go immediately to Isabelle," said Angelique. "She shall require time for the packing." Then, turning to de Quatreaux, "How long do we stay?"

"Until I see His Majesty I really do not know, this time. But," with a smile bordering on fondness now, "a Flanders Regiment, for you Francois, is in the wind. So; we shall travel by the family coach and leave Emile the chaise and all else."

"*Monseigneur*... you mean it?" Francois leapt up, excitement shinning in his eyes, "'tis of all things what I have wanted most!"

"We know," chorused his long-suffering siblings.

"But yes... but you do not know *how* much I have longed," retorted Francois, striding about and punching the air with his fist.

Perfect in unison, the chorus came again, "Oh yes we do!"

"*Mon fils*, you shall go nowhere if you do not sit down and behave as a gentleman."

Francois subsided reluctantly, but nothing could keep the glow from his eyes.

Emile gazed at his *père*. "Is it related; your call to Versailles, to the calling of the States-general next year?"

"Such would not surprise me. The country is alive with a ferment of speculation and those inciting honest men to revolt against the monarch, the *parlements* and law and order, have many months in which to work their evil. We must have a counter plan." He shook his head. "The streets of Paris, the villages even, now evidence a bubbling pot of disaster. Not from the peasants; but the orators there, pushing their own causes and not so quietly or secretly now. Every town and every village parish is at this moment meeting to draw up great lists of grievances: to send to the first meeting of the States-general. The complaints shall be many but these honest complaints of the people, which would be accepted... at least by me... will be twisted so far from the truth as to be unrecognisable. While the scribe pays attention to the claims of the peasants, he is busy with fancy turns of phrase that will in no way bear resemblance to their complaint; but lead into a more beneficial avenue for his own agenda. While he is thus employed, his assistant be imparting to the assembled crowd, all the gossip and subversive ideas brought from Paris."

"You have obviously witnessed this, *Mon Père*; and view the coming States-general with trepidation," said Angelique; then slowly, "But surely, when the crisis is over, operations of the country *will* revert to governmental control... directed by the King's Council? For what excuse can they use to retain it?"

"The difference this time is just that: one of time. Changing times: changing of attitude, throughout the world...toward Absolute Monarchy...encouraged by America's hard won Independence: an exhibition of what could be done. This has not been an overnight event. One hundred and seventy five years have passed since its last recall and a lot has happened in that time. The new philosophies of Voltaire and Rousseau, Diderot even, have enlightened many but now their words are twisted to suit the anarchists among us. I like the idea of a *true* democratic *parlement*; based on a Monarchical Constitution, with equal rights for the *Commons*... but I will not exist in a fantasyland... for it cannot happen with these Machiavellians in the driving seat! But of greater concern is the demand by the bourgeoisie: the Third, for an increase of votes: from 300 to 600... for themselves."

"But this is unreasonable: if the First and Second are left with *300* each! Is it because they outvote the Third by always voting together?" asked Angelique slowly.

"That is the bone of contention. If the States-general be constituted in the same manner as 1614: with only 300 votes each estate, the rights that they... the Third... hope to wrest from the king could be snatched from them; by the still powerful nobility and clergy again voting together.  The church and the châteaux shall then supplant the prerogatives of the crown.  And the interests of the *Commons*, the vast majority of the people, will be ignored... again."

Francois looked shocked. "*Grand Dieu*: no wonder the King is threatened!  From the discontent of the aristocracy *and* The Third." He shook his head. "Definitely not fair."

"Francois meets reality," Emile grinned. "Welcome to life, *Mon Frère!*"

"*Mon Père*, who sanctioned these meetings that are happening now? Or are they happening *because* of the States-general recall?" asked Angelique.

"Electoral edicts of January, this month, were sent out by Necker, inviting primary assemblies to draw up *cahiers* and to appoint electors. The peasants are to have a voice this time apparently: not just the bourgeoisie of the towns and wealthy country farmers, who were to represent them... supposedly."

"Shall the peasants actually *know* what this is all about? I do not believe so. Their lot has been grossly unfair certainly but they know nothing of liberty of press, separation of powers, assemblies and the like. They would stare with open mouth to hear such talk."

"Of course they would, *mon enfant,* but an idea suggested to them at the right moment by clever orators they shall accept.  However, none of the oratory be of the building up but of the pulling down! First and foremost upon the list of demolition is the public image of the crown, the futility of Versailles, collection of taxes by the Sword and the like. Unfortunately they know nothing of the blueprints in place to rectify these matters: eventually; any change must happen slowly." He frowned in thought and they waited. "Their numbers have increased slowly but surely; until the balance of the scales be dipped almost to ground level on their side. This, the deliberately blind and self-absorbed, of the upper classes, cannot—will not, see... they sit in the elevated upper dish of the scales and swing their legs blithely. The heavier, the more desperate and destitute the lower classes become, the more they see this as a power to use: to drive themselves even higher. And now the famine increases; exacerbating the problem of rising numbers of persons to feed. Their problems *must* be amended first: sustenance foremost, then employment and then education."

Angelique gazed at him. "And then, *Mon Père*? Once educated, the cycle begins: education begets employment, which begets higher income, which begets better standard of living, begets enthusiasm, begets a happy and forward driven France...etcetera?"

"Seems obvious to me but I, personally, cannot persuade anyone that this is so. Without some change, immediately, all is in place for an upheaval that has never been witnessed within France. There are, however, some upper-class individuals who do see the threat from this angle: the turncoats of *our* society and they will pander to them, in a non-beneficial way, in their desperate attempts for self-survival! *They* will be our downfall... not the demands of The Third or the unrest of the workers."

"And these turncoats of the aristocracy: the deserting rats, *Mon Père?*" asked Emile with interest.

"Ah yes: the 'Rodent Brigade.' They percolate through all strata of society of course, but the Robe and Bourgeoisie have the means to plot and plan and run if it does not succeed. However, rest assured there be many rodents also among the Sword."

Francois stared. "Does our code of honour, loyalty, valour, brotherhood, honesty... and ancient traditions of generosity, even of performing great deeds without self-interest—because it *does* still occur—mean *nothing* to them?"

The Comte smiled gently. "Trust no man, these days, until he has proved his loyalty, no matter how deep his roots; or character even, be he ever so likable; appear ever so trustworthy"—his voice dropped to a low sombre note—"even known to one for a long time."

Emile laughed suddenly. "I like it: 'The Rodent Brigade'."

"Be not so amused, my brother. Rats breed like rabbits. In fact, the rats must have an edge for everyone avoids them; they are difficult to trap and indeed no one knows what to do with them, once caught. One cannot after all eat a rat," said Angelique thoughtfully.

"Just kill 'em," said Francois. "There be no use whatsoever for a rat, that I can see."

Emile was staring at the Comte. "Well Monseigneur? We know that look."

"I had thought to never have to do this but I feel the time has come to warn you all. About a man with whom I never thought you to meet but he has been seen about Paris of late and even somehow managed to acquire an invitation to Versailles. Should you meet him, honour him with politeness and give him nothing. Do not discuss our affairs."

"As if we would... with anyone!" said Francois hotly.

"Ah yes, my young fire eater. But he is clever, though not as clever as myself I think."

They smiled at this, for they knew it to be born not of arrogance but self-belief, of his own intelligence, nothing else, to be above most others but only 'most': always, he had said, beware that there can ever be someone sharper than yourself: and without ethical restraints, these had a decided edge.

"And this man is?" asked Angelique now.

"Phillippe-Jean Bernierre, Comte de Lareaux: charming of manner, rather the fop of dress, and the flat, black, unblinking eyes of a snake."

She gazed at him curiously. "Shall we listen for the hiss, *Mon Père?*"

"Most definitely; stay well clear until you hear more from me, my children. I tell you this only as I may be absenting myself from town for a while."

"If you come across a snake, do not touch its tail, for its fangs are never far away," murmured Emile.

The Comte lifted a brow. "Just so."

Knowing it useless to pump him further, Angelique shrugged and, rising, curtsied and moved toward the door. "I really must run up to Isabelle and arrange the packing if I am not to be late for dinner."

"We are already that—I told Siffred to hold dinner until I called him," he replied. "However, much longer and I shall not own a chef."

"I make haste then. Garvois' temper does not bear thinking about."

"More to the point is the food that he throws on table *when* he is distempered," grimaced Emile.

The gleaming Quatreaux carriage slowed to enter the gates of Versailles, rumbled past the pedestrian guests, then entered the *Cour Royale*. The three-sided courtyard blazed with light: from the long windows but also from great *flambeaux*. Coaches streamed in a long line to the entrance, pausing to release their passengers, then passing on to allow others' access. Finally the de Quatreaux coach drew up at the door, the steps were lowered and the Comte stepped indolently down, yawning affectedly: this night was some birthday or saint's day celebration. His lack of accuracy mattered not, however, for the king would not be in attendance: and it was the king that he attended this evening. He glanced around at the inching coaches: then strolled forward, allowing a page, greeting him by name, to divest him of his cloak and take this and his cane.

Looking every inch the courtier in white-powdered wig and sky-blue, silver embroidered jacket with matching waistcoat, he proceeded through various antechambers to the Marble Court where he was soon absorbed into the crowd, greeting some, nodding to others. With knee breeches and silk stockings fitting as an outer skin, and lace ruffles falling delicately from his throat and wrists, he outshone all fashion statements at court this evening. Making his way slowly through the crush, he arrived at the great marble staircase heavily encrusted with gold. Up this streams of people were now moving and falling in with a much-painted gentleman, known only slightly to him; he chatted lightly as they mounted the stairs and crossed the hall at the top. Still speaking with his acquaintance, he traversed several chambers until they reached the *Œil de Boeuf*.

From the *Œil de Boeuf* the mass of glittering guests moved on to that vastly renowned room: the *Galerie des Glaces*. Here he slowly made his way to one end of the gallery where sat the regal party, on gilded chairs, before the fire. He made his bow to the Queen, spent some few minutes with her and then removed quietly as more came to pay their respects. His absence would be unnoticed: surety of this the more so within the vast crowd.

His sky-blue, high-heeled shoes, matching the silk coat, now tapped purposefully as he walked the long corridors; passing red and gold liveried footmen; standing at intervals as wax effigies, against the walls. Arriving at the king's apartments he was met by an old friend, the king's head valet, Hanet Clery; old friend in that he had been enough times to the royal apartments to warrant recognition and the faintest hint of a smile.

"Seigneur de Quatreaux, I do hope that you be well, Monsieur."

"Thank you, Clery, that I am; and yourself, I hope. Certainly your composure remains intact I see! That must count for something."

Clery gave almost a full smile; a privilege not afforded many. "But yes, Monseigneur. Do please enter, His Majesty awaits you."

The Comte's eyebrows rose. "He does? You mean to say that he is *alone*?"

Clery responded to the laughter in the Comte's eyes. "But no, Monseigneur, not quite."

"Ah... who then, have we within?"

"Messeigneurs Montmorin, Luzerne and Necker; they await your arrival." So saying he moved to the double doors, as a footman sprang forward, and ushered M. le Comte de Quatreaux in to the king's apartments, then announced his arrival.

The king, standing within the window embrasure, his favourite position, turned and greeted him warmly as he crossed the expanse of the room.

"Ah... de Quatreaux... come." He paused only slightly as the Comte made his deep bow and waved a hand towards the company. "You know of course my ministers."

Jean-Pierre bowed politely to Messeigneurs Montmorin of Foreign Affairs and childhood companion of Louis, Necker the Finance Minister and long-standing friend of Montmorin and Luzerne of Navy and Colonies. All made like responses. Burgundy was offered to the Comte, the others already holding glasses of varying levels of the deep red liquid.

In the slight pause of polite pleasantries Seigneur Montmorin glanced at Jean-Pierre and smiled a little. "You came via the levée, tonight, d' Quatreaux? A frightful squeeze, I think." He frowned faintly. "A threat to security, I cannot but feel," he bowed to the king. "My pardon, Sire."

The king smiled and shrugged.

De Quatreaux, replied to Montmorin, "But no worse than the 'Openness of Court' tradition, I dare swear."

The king bowed to them in heavy satire. "Any danger, I feel, gentlemen, shall not come from the public! But of course the Queen, born to more reserved and austere national traditions, would agree with you both. For such a reason, did she conceive the building of the *Petit Trianon*."

De Quatreaux nodded. "It was perhaps a very necessary refuge for her, Your Majesty."

"Oh yes, de Quatreaux, but its erection has been attributed to today's state of affairs. Upon its head lies our financial difficulties apparently and 'twould not surprise me should the famine origin be laid at its door also."

"Sire, these threats shall die down. By the calling of the States-general: for although it must have disturbed you to do so, it can be now used to allay their fears. What direction does it take, Your Majesty?"

"The nobles hope to establish a constitutional monarchy, based, of course, on aristocratic institutions, ensuring a dominance of their own Order. The middle classes: absolutely to destroy every distinction given to the nobles and clergy: which set them apart from the State."

"And the church, Sire; where stand they?"

"Firmly... they propose to maintain authority in their own hands and answer to none but Rome. Pius is aware of events but not worried apparently. Perhaps he should listen to Abbe Seiyes, asking just who and what the *Third Estate* is."

"Pardon, Sire?"

The Monarch smiled. "Precisely my reaction, d' Quatreaux: such ridiculous notions."

De Quatreaux looked at Necker.

"Ah, Sieyes says I think, de Quatreaux, within his recent article: *'Qu'est-ce que le Tiers Etat'* that the people of France, with the exclusion of nobles of course... form an identity of their own. Certainly their numbers are prolific... when including the lower classes. And now that their numbers can swell those of the Third, they *are* included!"

"On what grounds does he make such a claim, Necker?"

"That the commoners are the workers, therefore deserving of much more than their current lot! He continues that the privileged classes be the, er... pampered drones, and that the Third Estate has always worked for nothing, counted for nothing, received nothing, except heavy taxes that left them nothing. He claims that the general will of the people must draw up a constitution limiting, of course, the powers of the government."

"The Bastille," recommended de Quatreaux in bored tones.

The king smiled at the affectation. "I would that I could, Vermont."

De Quatreaux relaxed a fraction at the king's use of his family name. "And the position of the crown, Sire?"

"That of an isolated castle, it seems."

"Then we must increase the guard, fill the moat and pull up the draw-bridge."

"I am pleased to see that you are awake, Vermont, but it is not so of all castles. There be those that still slumber and believe that the wave of discontent shall bypass them, not even reach the village, let alone the drawbridge."

Looking at Necker, the Comte said, "You are in contact with Turgot, I believe. Does he read the people as volatile as rumour has it?"

"No," thoughtfully, "except for that very thing: the rumour mill. Alarm can spread faster than the fastest royal *courrier*: like fire, always among the illiterate and superstitious. Not in print or within the cahiers but by word of mouth. They live in darkness and darkness always begets fear. So, cleverly controlled, they could be a formidable force. Mayhap education *is* the answer after all but slowly and *I* should not like to have that responsibility; in its infancy mayhem would rule."

De Quatreaux looked suddenly at the King. "Our defences, Sire? Should this States-general issue turn from mole-hill to mountain?"

The King smiled rather grimly, glancing at his minister of Navy and Colonies. "Correct me if I err in judgement, Luzerne, but at last reckoning I believe it stood something like this. Army: 79 infantry; that is regiments of the line, recruited by drink, bribery, press-ganged; be there loyalty *there*? 23 regiments of foreign mercenaries; all very well with high pay packets. Territorial militia: conscripted by lot from amongst the peasant population again... but the cavalry, artillery and engineers attached to the regimental forces are the best in Europe, apparently.

Altogether with mounted police and coast guards these standby forces amount to 270,000 men."

"From what Puységur tells me, Sire, these forces have been recently reorganized and freshly trained in methods learned from the Seven Years War and so are a very formidable army," added Luzerne.

"Ah, but this army, be it so excellent, is stationed on frontiers and at provincial garrisons, Luzerne," replied the King dryly.

"Need they be, Sire?" asked de Quatreaux.

"Yes, to suppress riots and apparently ensure safe transport of food wagons. If the serfs looted these to eat, one could but understand but they destroy and burn."

"I see. So you could count on how many troops in Paris Sire?"

"Ten thousand," stated the King in flat tone, as he once again stood gazing out the window and across the undulating beauty there, hands clasped behind his back. The Comte stared.

Turning, Louis saw and gave a wry smile, "And we are losing many commissioned officers, de Quatreaux. D'Boullé says that of all his power, there are only a probable five or six battalions of foreign troops on which he may rely."

"Well Sire, if I may ask, what *is* his power?"

The king indicated to Luzerne to answer.

"One hundred and twenty battalions of infantry and eighty squadrons of cavalry: even the Household Troops, so Necker's spies tell him, cannot be relied upon. He can only rely upon mercenaries."

"Then, Sire, it appears we find more mercenaries... and substantial foreign aid."

Montmorin and Luzerne exchanged glances.

"And quickly, de Quatreaux; the edicts are out and we may expect an avalanche. Rioting across the country," replied the king, "not may, but *will*, occur."

The Comte frowned suddenly. "Sire, where do stand the industrialists in all of this? Deitrich of Strasbourg Iron, Teraux, the cloth manufacturer and de Fontenay of the Rouen cotton mills? People like that hold sway and there must be many of them?"

"Where else but on the fence: one wishes, uncharitably, that they may slip; the pain may swing them one side or t'other. In reality they dine with Lafayette and company and though he raised his own finance and army to take to America, I somehow distrust him," replied Louis and paused, lost in reflection. "And, should Lafayette's plans not produce easy profits, then they are just as ready to turn against him... as against me! But who can blame them? It is but survival."

"We rather thought, de Quatreaux; that perhaps your contacts may be of assistance in this instance," said Necker, coming forward at last.

"Oh?" The Comte's face became a mask of politeness.

"When I was in Geneva, de Quatreaux," said Montmorin now, "I well remember the company that you kept, the homes to which you were welcome at any hour. And so, with Necker's banking connections and your, er, high ranking connections, we may be able to come to some sort of foreign arrangement."

"Of military support, Sire?" replied the Comte bluntly, turning to the king.

The king smiled. "Not quite so simple, de Quatreaux. Something similar but in a way reversed and so I do have a mission in mind for which, should you accept it, I shall owe you."

"But no, Your Majesty, 'twould be an honour," bowing.

"The information required of... and to be conveyed to... the crown of Austria, requires the greatest discretion. You see, what began as a protest by clergy and nobles to the monarchical powers this last year of '88, indeed afore that, has set in motion a chain of events in which many sections of France now see opportunity to exert greater political power. The Queen's brother, amongst many others, even unto England, Prussia and Poland, observe us with interest, since the rumour of a States-general has spread."

De Quatreaux wondered just how much reliance could be placed upon these foreign powers.  Joseph and Catherine were engaged in hostilities with Turkey. England, Holland and Prussia were close to lending support in the conflict on behalf of the Porte.  This war in the east would be diverting their attention from France's affairs, whilst Hungary and Belgium were still in a disturbed state.  And Austrian eyes were gazing defensively toward Prussia, in anticipation of an attack from that direction.  Who would have time or concern for France?  The carrot would have to be very large.

The king returned to the large mahogany desk standing in the middle of the room, waving them all forward.  The Comte moved with them, his swift mind analysing the character of those about him and in general finding that he trusted them as much as he trusted any man. Of Montmorin he was not so sure but then mayhap it was only his manner of hesitancy that gave off an unreliable air.  An honest man, he had been a boyhood friend of the king for as long as could be remembered and therefore must be in that man's confidence.  Certainly he worked ceaselessly for his monarch's good and he *was* the least unpopular of Louis's ministers. Aside of Saint-Priest, whom all knew to be very attached to Louis and whose thoughts were of little else than his monarch's safety, there were none so close to the king. With him stood Luzerne, a complete royalist and veteran of the seven-year-war against England and Prussia. The Comte gazed at them, then decided on a lone run: his mind reaching ahead to those countries in which he had resided for long periods.

The lone sound within the *chambre* was now the occasional sputtering of a candle, as faint draughty gusts of air circled the room, finally drawing to the fireplace and curling up the chimney, causing a sudden flare in the grate. The two remaining of the company were still and silent, each lost in their own thoughts.

Louis, one elbow leaning on the mantle, stirred the fire with one boot, pushing a red crumbling log to the centre and watching the sudden acceleration of the flames. He then straightened and turned to look at Jean-Pierre.

"Vermont, my hopes lie with you," and gazing in deep admiration at the Comte's dandified attire, "Certainly you will dazzle the foreign courts!"

The Comte laughed. "You like my camouflage, Sire?"

"The frivolous, insincere, court dandy: perfect! There is nothing to hold you from immediate departure?" and at Jean-Pierre's shake of head, "The papers for your son shall be prepared and ready for retrieval within three days. The Lord knows I have need of such as he; there be few loyal subjects within my armies these days. 'Tis no favour I be doing you."

"Nevertheless, for that I thank you, Sire. The boy needs structured activity at this time of his development. And now I must take my leave of Your Majesty. There is much to organize.

"May God go with you!" The king paused and gazed at Jean-Pierre. "Remember; if 'Toinette's brother be very reluctant, then we offer him the land concessions."

"And if it falls apart? He is to be trusted?"

"What think you? You have most likely seen more of Josephe than I."

"My few associations with him tell me that he is. But to trust *us* may be *his* problem... It is not a common plan... to offer to lose a war to your enemy. He may think he smells a rat."

"But he'll not find one. The only condition: to reinstate Absolute Monarchy, *Mine*, within France," Louis frowned. "The only tricky part will be to decide at just which moment it is prudent to set the plan in motion. Too soon could be disastrous."

"Yes Sire: it cannot be too soon or too late; a very fine line to walk. But who knows... a threat of war with Austria may unite the people, in perceived times of national crisis, behind their leader: their king."

The king smiled faintly. "That, also, is my hope, de Quatreaux."

"I must take my leave now, Your Majesty."

The king turned, waving his hand toward to door. "Please, May God go with you!"

"Au revoir, Your Majesty." The Comte bowed low, then moved toward to the page, who opened the door and ushered him through.

The king watched him go; some hope within his heart.  He trusted de Quatreaux as none other. His thoughts turned to the other chore for that man: that of finding a solid and safe base for the funds to buy the émigrés already settled across the frontier; this only to be activated should they be so desperate as to need their support.

The Comte, retracing his steps to the *Galerie des Glaces*, dwelt upon the king's obscure plan: who to trust? They had little time, for the States-general assembly was set now for May eight. He did not, for a moment, repose any real reliance upon the heads of state of their neighbours, as did the king, holding his Majesty's hopes of Marie Antoinette's Austrian connections in little faith. Her brother's acerbic comments regarding the conduct of the French court, he had heard only too often. But with an annex large enough, who knew what Josephe's reaction would be?

His thoughts turned to the Princes of the Blood: that the Prince de Conti was and would remain rigidly loyal to the old school and his brother, nobody could deny, but his aggressive antipathy towards change could, probably would, prove a burden. Of the king's more liberal brother, the Comte de Provence, he was uncertain: assuredly the more diplomatic of the two and therefore mayhap the more believable, should his assistance be gained. But Louis had chosen lesser men for his plans. That General Dumouriez was also reliable he knew and of Calonne he wondered. Louis had not mentioned him. To Vermont he seemed a likely ally. His total loyalty to the Crown, indeed his acquiescence to Marie Antoinette's financial demands, had earned him dismissal from his position of Controller-General of Finance; and therefore his hatred of the *Parlements of Paris*. Already he had founded the *Compagnie de Indes* and its foreign contacts took a convoluted route impossible to follow. He mentally moved Calonne into the group of 'possible contacts'. His own estate, the nobility, were next on the list but here he paused his thoughts, having reached almost the gallery and switched into light social mode as he entered the crush of be-silked and bejewelled, majorly sycophantic, humanity.

"De Quatreaux! You come from the gamming salon? Your luck: *mon ami?*"

De Quatreaux turned to greet the Comte Saint-Menou, his voice an urbane and affected drawl. "But no, dear Comte; tonight the ladies' company be simply too irresistible... Have you spoken with the Lady Vergemont? *Ravissement!*"

"Ah, the toast of the new debutantes," Saint-Menou grinned, looking the Comte up and down. "So you come from one of the more private anti-rooms! But certainly none could possibly know your real age, *mon ami!*"

The impassive features of de Quatreaux showed none of his rising disgust: the Lady Vergemont had just passed her sixteenth birthday. "Ah, no, no... these days I but look upon a pretty sight, Comte. But come," taking his elbow and turning them both about, "Somehow... can't think why... I *do* now feel the draw to gamble! Be my guest, *Monseigneur*. Perhaps I may even fleece you!"

The unsuspecting Comte shrugged. "If the king be in attendance... stakes shall be low! But yes... let us hazard a throw; it need not be serious; and a drink I certainly need!"

De Quatreaux smiled amiably. "But my dear Comte," he complained, "gambling is *always* of a serious matter." The soft drawl showed none of the cold hard intent within his eyes. "Mayhap one of your estates..."

# CHAPTER FIVE

## Paris: Late winter 1789

4 00,000 candles flickered within their crystal chandeliers, reflecting to great effect from the seventeen long mirrors of the famed *Galerie des Glaces*. Standing against one of these, candlelight casting a golden sheen to her gown and dressed hair was Angelique. Fanning her flushed face, she turned to her friend. "Rochelle, I only know that *mon père* acquired a commission for Francois, in the Flanders Regiment. That he is gone beyond the borders of France is a fact but for what business, I have not the slightest notion. I must suppose it to be of no more import than to gain a fitting at Westons, London, for the new English cut of a coat. It is almost *de rigueur* at the moment in Paris!"

"Your *père* and an *English* style coat... the Comte de Quatreaux? Humbug, my friend! But more to the pity is Francois."

"A *pity, mon amie*? But he has pined for nothing *less* than a regimental commission—a twelve month or more, *ma chérie*."

"A pity about his being so much younger than us. I mean, his friends, you know—they most likely to be of similar age. And a man in uniform! So romantic," chuckled Rochelle.

"*What* is this I hear? Must I challenge mine own brother? *I*, after all, saw you first," exclaimed Emile, emerging from the crush of people, clutching three glasses of champagne from the liveried footman. "Or would I advance my cause by obtaining a set of regimentals?"

Rochelle spun around, blushing deeply. "My pardon, Monsieur. An idle and wretched tongue: I would that I could control it! 'Twas but a jest." Blushing further beneath his laughing eyes, she ceased speaking to avoid further stammering.

Gazing in amusement at her twin, Angelique suddenly saw him with fresh eyes. He surely did not require regimentals to enhance his dark attractiveness.

"Ah so, your *père* would do well to teach his daughter to hold her tongue in a man's presence I see," he responded severely, "but I do indeed find your total honesty diverting and of course you may look, *ma chérie*, yet awhile."

"But?" Angelique gazed at them both as sudden understanding flashed through her brain. She opened her mouth to delve further when a voice sounded on her right as the throng parted to allow passage of Princess Lamballe. Beside her stood a man of indefinable age; possibly thirty to thirty-five years.

"*There* you are, *mon amie*. I have looked all over, for there be someone to whom I would introduce you, though I believe that it is *he* who fervently presses the issue," laughed Princess Lamballe.

Angelique curtsied to Her Highness.

"But Your Highness," intervened the gentleman, now with a glittering smile, "it is that I have been away for so long; and to return to find someone to whom it is said that I am related, even should it be rather distant... and so very beautiful," here he bowed with exquisite grace to Angelique, "I could not wait to see if it were true."

Emile, standing behind him, glanced at Rochelle, eyebrows reaching for his hairline and the corners of his mouth for his jaw-line; causing her to fight for control.

Princess Lamballe turned to Angelique. "May I present Seigneur Lareaux? Monsieur, be pleased to meet Mademoiselle Vermont and her brother the Vicomte and Mademoiselle du Bois... er... English! There now, I have done my duty!"

Lareaux bowed again. "*Enchanté de faire votre connaissance, Mademoiselle Vermont!*"

Angelique responded, then drew a breath of relief as the princess commanded her attention again.

"But you do not visit us of these last months *mon amie*, you have been out of town, yes?"

"Yes,Your Highness. We spent Christmastide and much of the winter at Quatreaux," replied Angelique, relieved to focus upon inanities while she recovered from the shock of meeting the Comte Lareaux. Certainly he owned the eyes of a snake.

"Ah, a château of *ancien* history and extreme beauty if I remember," said the Princess. "Then you must return soon to court. Her Majesty charged me with the direct order, should I find thee. But, you have paid your respects?"

"I have. When we arrived... but the crush was such," she shrugged.

"Oh yes, 'tis impossible, but there: 'tis Versailles! They say the *Gallerie* holds six thousand people but I do declare tonight there are far more!"

At that moment Princess Adelaide, the deeply religious and formidable aunt of King Louis, descended upon them: to bear Princess Lamballe off to the other end of the ballroom and the regal clique there, casting a patronizing smile upon the immediate company surrounding Angelique. Her eyes warmed faintly, however, as they passed over Emile. He in turn bowed elegantly and offered his escort, which was accepted with charm and grace. He departed with a meaningful glance at his twin and repressed a grin at the whimsical glint in her eye.

"Well my good Vicomte, 'tis so long that I hardly recognized thee," exclaimed Princess Adelaide. "Have you abandoned us, *Monsieur*?" She rapped his lace-drenched wrist with her fan.

"Matters of the estates have kept me from Versailles, Your Highness," murmured Emile. "These are times of..."

"Oh do not! For I know, Vicomte. Though it be rumoured that princesses care for little but their raiment and extravagant hairstyles; I do know of the distressing drift towards rebellions and such. My poor Louis, he inherits his ancestors' financial indiscretions. I fear deeply for him. He needs the unfailing support of those few in whom we may trust. And how many *are* trustworthy, *Monsieur*?"

Emile smiled gently, gazing at this severe but worried, dominant figure of the court. "Do not be concerned, Your Highness, for while there exists *mon père* and his ilk, then you and the Crown do remain safe from this rabble unrest."

"Ah yes, from the rabble, but it is from the court that the danger does threaten, does it not? And they hide well. But if *I* had control, I should *ferret* them out and be rid of them!"

"The execution of which would perhaps not be so simple a matter, Madame... but come; there can be no gain from such speculations. We shall prevail henceforth. But for now, may we finish this distressing discussion upon a lighter note? Your Highness, may I have the privilege?" He smiled and bowed elegantly.

Princess Adelaide gazed at him thoughtfully for a moment, then laughed gaily. "Why not? I have not danced the Quadrille for many a year. Come, let us show our mettle." And with that they literally romped into the quadrille with gusto unheard of in the elderly aunt of Louis. The ballroom paused for a moment at this sight and Angelique, staring along with the rest, laughed suddenly.

"Well Rochelle, you must look to your laurels, there be *competition* for thee," she chuckled deeply and then turned as their new acquaintance bowed low, begging the honour of the next dance: the graceful minuet.

Annoyed now by the fact that this was the one dance in her programme deliberately not occupied, to create a welcome break, she could but accept.

"But your dancing grace is unrivalled, Mademoiselle. And your beauty, I had not an idea of such in our family," he offered as they came together then moved apart again.

"*Our* family: Monsieur? In what way do we be related, for I cannot recall the Comte's mention of you or indeed the name Lareaux on our tree," she responded at the next union.

"But we be cousins, Mademoiselle, a little apart certainly, second cousins I believe. Has not de Quatreaux mentioned us? He and *mon père* were cousins."

She executed the turn, wishing it would take her a thousand miles from him and answered, "But we do not delve along the tree's branches to that extent, Seigneur Lareaux. Who knows what the dense leaves may hide!"

She immediately worried about her indiscretion, then dismissed it: if she knew nothing about him and his family, then she *would* make such light-hearted remarks. Her smile was angelic and she hoped that it was not over done, for de Quatreaux was correct in his estimation of this man. His eyes were those of a cobra, coal black, mesmeric and unblinking, with a gentle smile that managed to send lumps of ice down one's spine. He was certainly very handsome. His address was faultless, his dancing prowess matched the best and his formal attire exquisite: a very beautiful cobra.

As the dance ended, he returned her almost to her original place, then veered away to an arched opening into an adjacent salon. "'Twill be cooler here for a moment, without the crush."

She could not object for she had no just cause. He was all propriety and concern, chatting of inconsequential issues about court and the light from the ballroom flowed through the arched exit and over them. Others too, were seeking a little cool from the overheated room and while this was so she managed to keep up a casual, relaxed flow of dialogue. After some minutes of light but sincere conversation with him, however, she began to wonder if perhaps her *père* had exaggerated the facts. The smooth, hypnotic charm lulled her; until he mentioned the absence of the Comte and then she could have blessed the sudden voice from behind, gay and bantering, fitting to the frivolity of the ballroom.

"Ah, there you are, Mademoiselle! I have claim to this dance, I believe. Forgive me if I am wrong; my lamentable memory you know, but it *should* be there within your dance card, I think. Your pardon, Lareaux, but your loss," drawled Raoul, bowing in his direction, then offering his arm to Angelique. She took it with a polite smile of regret to Philippe-Jean, who bowed low to her in return, then performed another, stiffly, for Raoul.

"Your servant, Savieur." He watched them leave, calculation filming his expression.

Raoul gazed down at Angelique, "You did not enjoy that company I think?" His eyes laughed then his manner changed to one of concern at her serious expression. "He was not... did not cause any discomfort to you, I hope?"

"No, Seigneur Savieur," she replied slowly, "There was... nothing."

"But...?"

She glanced up at him, a question in her eyes and then they parted yet again. Her instincts told her she could do no better in matters of trust, but then her father's statement returned; trust no man until you know where his loyalty lies. And this man, after all, dined often with Lafayette: and Lafayette's leanings towards democracy were well known, as was his support of the American Revolution and warm friendship with Washington. She smiled with an apparent lift of spirits as they came together again and he did not press the issue but was in no way convinced.

"You know, Mademoiselle, that you may call upon me at any time, do you not?" and at her faintly raised brows, "No, no, no, I am serious now!"

"I thank you, Seigneur, and shall avail myself of your kindly offered services, should I feel the necessity."

"And with that I suppose I must be content. But be careful of that one, *mon enfant.*"

"You know him, Monsieur?"

"Enough but also not enough; in the clubs he is guardedly accepted: but because of his introductory body, namely La Fayette and of course Mirabeau, who all regard as," he stopped short, "Ah but never mind all of that. Lareaux is new on the scene but there is something about him. I have yet to find what it is."

Gazing at him, Angelique was suddenly very sure that he would do so. The swirl of people and the descending partner for the next dance parted them. It wasn't until later that she realized he must have been watching over her to witness the detour into the salon and note her discomfort. This illumination stilled her thoughts, for if Raoul Trifane had seen her discomfort then so too mayhap had Lareaux. She must do better than this. Who on earth *was* he? Their *père* must surely furnish them with more information if the Vermont siblings were to avoid the pitfalls that apparently surrounded them.

♣

The last months of winter '89 hung beneath a thick cloak of snow, leaning determinedly into early spring, but by early April the snowdrops and daffodils forced their way through the hardened ground, just as determinedly announcing that spring had right of way at last. This however brought the usual showers not appreciated by the gentleman stepping around and over the many puddles on his way to his club in Rue St Honoré. Reaching his destination at last, he stepped into the wide entrance hall, handing his gloves and hat to a page. He turned his back to another who removed the long, many-caped cloak, revealing lace ruffles at throat and wrists, falling as snow against his plum-coloured coat and waistcoat. Climbing the few shallow steps and reaching the salon he paused to glance around and was hailed by Dominique Montmaire, sitting at a card table a few feet from the entrance.

"D'Arteaux! Come. A hand; I insist: my luck is out, rest assured."

"Badly dipped," nodded de Vries sagely. "But no need of old man's scythe yet."

Seigneur Yves Beaumont, Comte d'Arteaux, arriving at the table smiled derisively, bowing to Seigneur Montmaire. "You think that my luck rests upon your bad luck? *Mon ami*, I have won, over you, more times than I can remember. Your servant, DuToit, Geraud, de Vries," nodding to each at the table, then, "No, no, do not rise, *mes amis*."

They responded variously and then Montmaire chuckled. "Be that a challenge?"

Yves Beaumont smiled gently. "If you wish it to be. A little later... the numbers..."

"But no, Beaumont," said Geraud now. "I must be gone, an appointment, you know. No, do not disturb yourselves," he added as he rose, took his leave of each and left the table, pausing at the door to greet a friend just arriving, then moved indolently down the stairs.

Beaumont took his chair and Seigneur Montmaire held up one fine-boned, dead white, hand to a page and asked for a new pack and more wine. The play commenced in serious silence.

"Seen de Quatreaux, anyone?" asked Beaumont after some ten minutes of play.

"No, but has returned, I do believe, some time ago and left Paris immediately for the château," replied Du Toit. "At least that is the story."

"Went to Vienna, not so?" asked Beaumont lightly.

"No, no, to England: some family member, English side of course, sailing close to the wind, or slipped his wind... not sure which." Seigneur Montmaire paused. "Pity about that wife of his, taking little thing, pretty too, but English, you know. Surely an abundance of French blood for him to have picked from and tougher; a French woman wouldn't have gone to roost so soon. But that was a time ago, of course. Now the daughter: *there* be a diamond of the first water and taken the eye of Trifane, me thinks."

"You think so? No, no, no but Lareaux... now there walks another matter," responded De Vries.

"Lareaux... who the devil *is* he anyway?" asked Montmaire suddenly. "Saw him at Mdm Corot's salon t'other day. In fact, seems to be all over Paris! Fellow gives me the creeps!"

De Vries cocked an eyebrow at Beaumont. "*You* remember; *mon ami*."

"What's this? Come now, you cannot leave it there," complained Montmaire, looking from one to the other.

"Ah 'tis history, naught but a duel: De Quatreaux you know… and Lareaux," said Beaumont.

Montmaire shook his head decisively. "Cannot be so. He is too young by far."

"Not the present Lareaux… the *old* Comte: now deceased… of course," supplied de Vries.

"Oh? By de Quatreaux' hands? Why then do I not remember it?"

"Er… ahem… out of the country yourself then, Montmaire," chuckled du Toit.

"I *was*? Well, of course, often out of the country those days. Well, so too were we all from time to time." Montmaire tilted his head, dredging up some memory from the mists.

"Ahem, yes, mayhap you remember not. The little opera singer, lovely little barque of frailty she was too but got a little too demanding, remember, *mon ami?*" said Beaumont now, laughing softly and shaking his head. "Nasty things, rumours."

Suddenly remembering the issue as closer to blackmail, Montmaire nodded, "Ah yes, something does, unfortunately, drop into the mind. So! De Quatreaux won the duel."

"Yes."

"The old wolf's cub, eh… returns from the Gods know where to avenge his *père*? But surely not legal within the duelling etiquette: too much water beneath the bridge. If when *I* left the country, then that will be at least; *Grand Dieu*, thirty years ago," said Montmaire. He shook his head thoughtfully. "No, won't wash: too long… besides: the age difference."

"For duelling certainly," responded Beaumont smoothly.

Montmaire shot a penetrating look at him suddenly, an unusual trick that he owned. "You would have been one of de Quatreaux' seconds, eh? You were always close."

"That I was; and clean as a whistle it was. De Quatreaux the deadlier of the two, that was all, eh de Vries? And the evil creature deserved it if anyone did. Not a soul wept."

Du Toit gazed at his hand of cards. "Hmmm, the young coxcomb shall bear watching, that I see… he be as evil as his *père*, if not the more so. Could pick a fight with the son I suppose. Loss of his first born would flatten de Quatreaux." He glanced up suddenly, in horror. "Oh *Grand Dieu*; the daughter!"

"Ah yes, but she is no bird-witted green girl, that one, and neither is she pudding hearted, come to that. Not that it has to say to anything… yet! No, no, he be not first oars with her—I witnessed them at 'Toinette's ball," smiled De Vries. "Must keep an eye on these things in de Quatreaux' absence, you know! Besides, there's her twin the Vicomte *and* the younger one. She will inherit little of what Lareaux wants, though a generous dowry of course. No, he could not despatch both sons… look bad. And she is a de Quatreaux after all. Bit of a problem for him: breaking *her* into bridle."

"Taking his place at the Assembly, is he then?" asked Beaumont casually.

"De Quatreaux? Ah! Well he *was* present at the Assembly of Notables last year. What goes forward in that direction, Beaumont?" said de Vries now, his hands busy shuffling the cards and fanning them out on the table with a flourish, sweeping them all together again and repeating the process, lace wrist ruffle moving with grace; snowy white against the plum coat-sleeve.

"*Politics*... I will *not* allow it to spoil my game," grimaced Montmaire good-humouredly. "And that it shall, for there is no hope these days of a sensible political discussion. Why, no one *knows* what is happening, it is all such a mish-mash."

"I agree," sighed Beaumont. "All *I* can see is a massive clash on the day: the numbers game is still raging. The first writs were issued on February seven and still the last of the Paris Bourgeoisie, are not ready. They are missing twenty deputies."

De Vries frowned. "But they have achieved their increased allowance of six hundred deputies, haven't they?" he brightened. "But we still have our combined six hundred, as before; therefore we shall prevail!"

"Unless," murmured Du Toit, who had remained silent, "some cross the floor."

Montmaire and de Vries stared at him, the thought diabolical and Beaumont smiled, "Ah just so; de Quatreaux's 'rodents'!"

Montmaire grunted. "But Louis is going to have to lean in a little more if he wishes for the support of The Third: and he could use them. And the bourgeoisie, surprisingly, are quite the royalists, most of them."

De Vries continued shuffling the cards. "Unfortunately our Louis expects them to aid him in the subjugation of the nobles to taxation... and in carrying out unavoidable administrative reforms... but cannot see that they expect him to show an interest; lip service would be sufficient at this moment, in their attempts to establish a democracy... at least the shadow of!"

Du Toit lifted a brow. "Do you blame him? God forbid: a democracy... real or shadow of... led by uneducated rabble leaders! And shadows deepen, as light disappears! But the king shall always go as far as suits his purpose and no further anyway."

"The rabble is naught to do with it! 'Tis the scurvy Bourgeoisie—The Third—shall need watching," replied de Vries.

"*Using* the rabble: take little to stir *their* grievances to blood-lust!" responded du Toit. "Been to the new clubs and cafes, Beaumont?"

Beaumont grinned, "*Have* I? The grounds and arcades of d'Orleans' *Palais-Royal* now contain more gambling houses, taverns, and the good and beautiful ladies, than all the rest of Paris! And one can pick up any information one wants in the arcade outside the *café du Berceau-Lyrigue* and the *café du Conti*. Forged notes, should you have a use for such, abound at the *café de la Rotonde*. The place is a seat of all manner of subterfuge, intrigues, spies, and runners... what you will. One may find a man to do anything that you wish, on count of gold louis of course."

"And secret gaming-tables are known to exist at the *café Mècanique*, the *café* du *Roi* and *des Variètiès* I heard," chuckled Du Toit. "But the fearful thing is the political discussions going on in these places! Horror of horrors: the people are being educated!"

Montmaire gazed dolefully. "New age madness," he paused. "But they cannot hold sway over the Assembly when it sits, surely."

"But you must roll with the punches, Montmaire! Times are a changing! The clubs will be a monitor—of the political climate—and will of course influence the deputies' stand," replied Beaumont, leaning back indolently in his chair. He frowned in thought. "Club political argument will ensure the deputies' ultimate course of action at the Assembly, I be thinking. The shift of power hath begun and who would have guessed via the Clubs?"

Montmaire glanced but a split second at Beaumont and read more than that cautious man would suppose; however, he only said, "Ah, give me the old salons where a man can have a decent conversation: literature, religion and the natural sciences... *and* good female company!"

♣

The calendar moved relentlessly towards May second 1789, causing some angst to the finance minister as he battled to cement the involved plans for the grand opening of the States-general: today the king his stumbling block.

"But Your Majesty, we cannot scorn the political correctness of holding the States-general convocation in Paris. I know that Tuleries is neither comfortable nor..."

"I have made up my mind Necker. They shall make their bow to their Monarch, *if nothing else*, here at Versailles," stated Louis stubbornly and Necker, the new Finance Minister, knew that it was useless to proceed further with the argument and sighed.

"Very well then, Sire."

Thus it was that at Versailles, on May the second 1789 that King Louis XVI formally welcomed the 1200 deputies of the three Estates, the long ceremony occupying ten hours. Received in the *Galerie des Glaces* for this ritual, deputies of the Third Estate gazed in stunned silence at the wasteful magnificence of Versailles. Dark mutterings could be heard throughout as they gazed into the seventeen great mirrors of the famed '*Galerie des Glaces.*' These would have reflected many historical and momentous gatherings, thought a suddenly astute deputy: but never before had it held members of The Third, of this he was sure. That this momentous event would be documented in the annals of history he had no doubt; but could not guess that this could be the last event, ever, within the *Galerie*.

Two days later, Monday, May four 1789, Paris, that capricious city renowned as none other for its fickleness, reverberated with the sounds of excited babble and gaiety. All that were able flocked into the city centre. The pressing crush of people further swelled the normal overcrowding of the narrow streets. Brilliant tapestries, flags, silks and satins draped the walls. Sightseers vied for position; citizens leaned from windows, waving colourful ribbons, silk sashes, scarves, shawls, flags and kerchiefs. Gone were the angry riots, declaring famine and national bankruptcy the devise of the *Famille Roi* and nobility. The people of France would issue in the States-general, after one hundred and seventy five years of absence, in fine pomp and ceremony.

They awaited now the parade through the streets to the Notre Dame to mark the opening of the States-general. Here the deputies were to meet to sing the Veni Creator and to escort the Host in solemn procession to the church of Saint-Louis. At this church, the opening of the States-general was to be consecrated by a mass, a sermon and a Te Deum.   For this colourful event, the masses of street audiences waited.

The music of the combined drums, fifes and trumpets now heralded the royal entry into the Notre Dame; the interior a vision of colour and splendour: the choir hung with cloth of gold and bright embroideries. The King moved to the throne upon the right of the choir screen. The Princes of the Blood, ministers and grand officers, moved in to sit below him on seats of velvet adorned with fleurs-de-lys.

The Queen, Princesses and the ladies of the Court, in their glittering, jewel encrusted robes sat on the other side. All eyes now turned toward the colourful spectacle of the procession of the deputies. These marched two by two, candles in extended hands, the nobles in black and gold; plumes in their hats, the clergy in their cassocks and birettas. Following them, the bishops in the exotic vestments of the Gallican hierarchy, now contrasted with the stark black of the *Commons*.

The ceremony over, the colourful company exited into the bright sunshine of that perfect spring day, moving through the glittering ranks of the Swiss and French Guards to the great cheering and hand clapping of half a million people.

The contrast between Paris yesterday and Paris today defied all reason, except that this was France: the France that one and all knew to be superior to all other nations; in that it could put aside troubled times to celebrate in fine form.   And here surely was France in all her glory, exhibiting the colour, the emotion, the warmth, the love of King and country.   What French man or woman could possibly do otherwise?   Surely this could not all be swept away: all for a little understanding and giving on both sides?   The crowd felt it, moved to cheering the deputies as they emerged two by two: the States-general convocation *was* the answer to all their problems.   No longer would they bow to Absolute Monarchy but thrash out their problems within the establishment of the States-General: king and Assembly together. The balance of power must surely now maintain an even keel.

The cheering died slightly to a natural lull but then Orlèans, that infamous contender to the throne, who appeared as a deputy, not a Prince, stepped out into the sunshine. The sound then took on an almost hysterical note, rising in an almighty crescendo, receding only to swell again at the appearance of the Comte Mirabeau: for though a noble, he walked, dressed in stark and sober black, with the *Commons*. Then followed a rise in decibels: for the traditionally drab ranks of the Third Estate, echoing through the narrow street for many minutes.

Louis received the *Vive le Roi* with more enthusiasm than he expected.  A sudden silence however greeted the Queen and her entourage: a still, sullen, malevolent silence, as they emerged from the gloom of the Notre Dame. The rumour mill had done its work well and Angelique, walking alongside Princess Lamballe to the rear of their company, felt a sliver of ice run up her spine.  The ice instantly melted however, on the sudden heat of anger, of pounding fury: at the power of the spoken word, of the quill in scurrilous hands.  She kept her eyes strongly ahead; chin lifted and heard the Princess' soft voice beside her.

"Bravo *mon enfant*! Smile!" breathed that remarkable lady, with a soft cynical laugh.

They reached the church of Saint-Louis at last, for the sung mass by the choir of the Chapel Royal. The two-hour sermon by the Bishop of Nancy allowed them a brief respite, the king not the only one to be seen dozing on and off throughout that man's dull monotone. To many who actually listened, the bishop rambled wide of the mark in his welcome of the States-general. His main thesis, however, that of religion as a basis of national life, could not be argued. Touching upon the barbaric tax collection, he caused a loud applause, brought to an abrupt halt by the people themselves as they realized, of one accord, where they were. The reaction, however, would be well remembered.

The candles in their silver branches were at half-mast and flaring slightly in the gentle breeze from the open windows, when the ladies removed from table to the salon at the end of the gallery, leaving the gentlemen to their politics and cognac. The dinner had been enlivened with talk of the day's events and the morrow's assembly of the States-general, but now the ladies of the company, near as possible, flaked and lounged against chairs and chaise-longues grouped around the low, central, Persian table.

La Comtesse Bayette yawned and, lifting her feet from the Aubusson carpet, stretched her long legs out before her on the chaise. "Allow me a minute 'afore the gentlemen appear," she sighed. "I am positively undone, my dears! Are not you?" looking around and then to Angelique, "But you *mon enfant*, must be exhausted, for not only was it a long day but the strain of it all for you."

Angelique smiled a little. "But we *sat* for the better part of the day, Comtesse."

"Ah yes, but those so uncomfortable pews. But I did not like what I observed toward the Party Royal in the streets. Ah me... I fear we enter dark times *mes amies,"* offered Beaumont's wife gloomily, declining the Ceylonese tea and Brazilian coffee: accepting more wine as though it would be her last goblet of the Comte's best vintage.

"No, do not say so; shall all come about now that the Assembly commences, you shall see," responded Madame du Bois, Rochelle's aunt.

"Ah *but* 'tis the *form* to be taken by the States-general, Madame," sighed Rochelle. "That shall decide whether political supremacy shall rest with the first two orders or the Third Estate." She beamed around at the blankly staring faces, proud of her hard earned knowledge. This gathered from Emile and a relentless Angelique, delving and diving inexhaustibly into all things political: for knowledge was armour these days of looming uncertainty. She continued, "Should each order sit separately and each *chambre* vote apart, then some control shall prevail; however, should *The Third* get their way and the three sit together as one, forming a single *chambre*... then intimidation during voting; just one issue, be a very real threat." She shrugged, then brightened. "But the Robe must now work hand in glove with the Sword, for they *must* co-operate, to oppose the reduction of their privileges. No more can they indulge their petty jealousies and suspicions, rivalries and envies, for they shall surely fall without the backing of the Sword."

"Ah but," laughed Angelique, taking up the challenge, "the Robe outnumber us enormously these days and I do believe that here we shall find many of *mon père's* 'Rodent Brigade', for to fall back into manner born is easier, under pressure, than to stand firm on the foreign, and harsh, soil of the Sword... and all that that demands! Therefore, it stands that they could join the Bourgeoisie." Her eyes gleamed as she watched her friend marshal her thoughts into battle lines.

The Comtesse Bayette, however, laughingly brought the discussion to a halt. "My dear girls," she interrupted indolently, "you both exhibit a shocking lack of femininity. In my day we would not have any idea of the politics... much more exciting to discuss the very newest fashions of the ladies in the procession... *and* of course the gentlemen!"

But Angelique was not bowing to that lady within her own home. "Madame, with all due respect, for I do indeed admit that the femininity of your day far outweighs ours, which is sadly declining... I do believe that one should at least understand how it all *works*, even though we females shall never have our say.  Why, we only need see the danger of people like the Comte de Mirabeau. You saw his position amongst the Third today! As to the Duc d'Orleans..."

"But *Mirabeau*: what can one expect? He has been barred by the Society of Parisian drawing rooms long since. *And* every man in the *Parlements* of Versailles distrusts him. I suppose I must now say the 'old *parlements*' of Versailles!  But he is after all one of the poor provincials of the aristocracy anyway, so boring," drawled the Comtesse de Vries, speaking now for the first time with a smothered yawn. "But his line be *quite* impeccable, Madame; even his uncle is a distinguished sailor, a colonial governor, almost a minister of the crown and the old Marquis is the renowned author of '*L'Ami des Hommes*' so there must be *some* brains in the family," responded Angelique laughing. "But there... his two passions be his downfall, women and the quill.  He apparently cannot encounter a subject of controversy without writing about it."

Rochelle chuckled. "And a female without..." She ceased abruptly beneath her aunt's steely gaze.

"Then he must be having a field day now.  And his quill has indeed a poisonous tip; along with that dreadful man Hebèrt and his appalling '*Père Duchesne*': and his pamphlets are deteriorating into sordid gossip. But Mirabeau, why even his own father acquired the *Lettres* for his imprisonment: several times. The man is poison, I tell you," supplied Madame du Bois.

Rochelle turned to Angelique. "But you, Ange... I have yet to hear *your* explanation."

Angelique smiled. "How I happened to be in the entourage today? I cannot satisfy you *ma chérie*; except that Estelle Pontac could not attend and I imagine that I filled her place, as she supported the First Rocker, and the vast army of Royal Attendants there, including Gabriele de Polignac: for Louis-Joseph does slip away rapidly now. 'Toinette had no choice but to abandon him for this day but she agonizes over him daily, be sure of that."

"Ah then Louis-Charles *shall* be Dauphin after all. I always said so, did I not? 'Tis the bone disease, not so? And his sister, Sophia, had the same I hear. Died back in '87… poor little darlings. But one wonders if it be not contagious," said Madame Beaumont gloomily.

"Do you go to live at Versailles then, Angelique?" asked Madame du Bois, ignoring bone disease in the hope of its deflection.

"I am there now, Madame, but I manage at times to return to Paris for matters family."

"Or so you tell them," chuckled the Comtesse. "Impossible place to live! *I* found the vapours the most effective deterrent to roaming profligates! And forgetting one's salts causes a great search to be set up by an ever-increasing crowd, for one cannot rebuff them; then one *would* suffer, may as well be banished forever, or even dead."

The gentlemen's footsteps sounded along the gallery and the ladies henceforth straightened both their physical form and their mentality. Pleasantries exchanged, the M. le Comte de Vries made his bow to his host and held out his hand to his wife.

"We must be gone: the morrow brings a long day. We commence very early!"

"No, no, no. Louis shall not arrive afore one. This I know. We congregate in the little salon, afore the sitting in the *Salle des Menus Plaisirs du Roi*. It shall be needed; for the twelve hundred deputies and as many spectators, so they say," responded de Quatreaux.

De Vries laughed. "Oh to be privy to court moves. Be thee advanced to Gentleman of the Wardrobe yet, I wonder?"

"But no, *mon ami*," de Quatreaux threw up his hands in mock horror, "I beg of you."

The company departed and the family de Quatreaux relaxed but the twins glanced at each other as de Quatreaux took snuff, offered the same to Emile and that done, reached for his goblet. Something was afoot.

# CHAPTER SIX

## Paris: Summer 1789

Noting a slight frown on de Quatreaux' face, Emile turned his attention to the now empty fireplace before him. Angelique stared tiredly and vacantly ahead, her shoes kicked off and lying beside the chaise-longue. Following a soft knock, Siffred entered the room with a tray carrying a bottle and three glasses. Angelique raised her very expressive brows at Emile who, under the light of the candelabra and in full view of his father, remained stone-faced.

"You wish for perhaps the *English tea*?" asked the Comte in chilly voice that caused Siffred to wince, noting his master catching the glance between the twins. Now in competition in the eyebrow department, the Comte gazed at his daughter.

She laughed suddenly, a deep laugh from the heart, a sound that, unknown to herself, had first captured the Marquis de Savieur. "No *Mon Père*, how could I? I am a Vermont. But oh, I did absorb so much this evening, could not leave the Comtesse to carry her reputation alone, now could I?"

"What? Was *she* the only stalwart?"

"I be afraid so, *Mon Père*."

The Comte smiled gently, then dismissing that woman's amazing alcoholic capacity, said, "So, *mon enfant*, etiquette satisfied; are you of the world at the present?"

"But of course *Mon Père*: always am I so."

"Have a care my child; when we are so sure, then often it is not so." He paused, faintly frowning. "And there be those who may try to be your undoing, with the assistance of a little liquid fire. Case in point: Lareaux."

"I shall be extra wide awake then, Monseigneur! Besides, you taught us a trick or two."

"In that event, I rest my case, but beware of all who would have the entertaining of you."

The twins looked at each other. Angelique groped for her shoes with her bare feet.

"No, no, be comfortable."

"*Really* comfortable?" laughed his daughter, suddenly swinging her feet onto the chaise-longue and curling them, child-like, up beneath her skirts.

He smiled indulgently. "Should you fall asleep, then, 'tis nothing for it but a bucket of cold water."

Emile grinned. "Allow me: there be many unavenged moments in my life."

"I believe that you have both had the dubious pleasure of the Lareaux," said the Comte.

"Well yes, Monseigneur, and the eyes have it. As you did warn us; those of a cobra," replied Angelique.

"So here then is the trick.  School yourself to hold those cobra eyes; for as he locks onto your gaze, he is busy thinking that he has you in his power and does not feel your manoeuvres.  Do not forget this, burn it into thy brains, *mes enfants!*" Jean-Pierre leaned back, stretched his long legs and settled more deeply into his chair, taking his glass in one hand before he continued, "You know that you entered France at the age of, what was it, twelve years of age?"

"Er, thirteen, it be twelve years ago, *Mon Père.*"

"Well, no matter... the thing is that on arrival here, at the château that is, you had no idea of the hardships courted by your parents; though your *mère* did not utter one word of complaint. She did not mind a thing as long as we were together and it was not until her death that I saw her wisdom." He paused and took a sip. "My return here followed nigh on thirty years exile—England, Austria, Netherlands, Italy: you shall yourselves no doubt account some of them good and exciting years *but* 'twas not the home of your birthright." He paused again, taking not a sip this time but deep swallow of the red liquid. "And to reclaim that birth right I had much trouble. In point of fact, I had to win it back."

They stared at him but remained still and silent and he continued, "For you to understand, I need to regress. In those days the aristocratic youth were wild."

But surely not... er, yourself, Monseigneur?" said Emile with bland face.

"Out of order, *mon fils*," the Comte's tone was severe but the faint curve to the corners of his mouth caused the twins to ignore it. "However, in my youth I led the life of all young aristocrats, of our time, those things were accepted then." He paused, frowning slightly, then continued, "The point of the fact is, that I killed someone in a duel. My history with *mon père* otherwise was also not good. Women, wine, gambling, overreaching the boundaries..."

"You need not go on, Monseigneur. We appreciate it was the lifestyle, for that generation."

The Comte cast his son a penetrating glance. "Oh yes, but had *you* leanings of that nature I should have had the disciplining of you, but thankfully you showed more of your *mère* in you. For that reason I had Francois into the Flanders Regiment... best place for any slight instability of character; not that he showed instability but his type of extreme energy requires channelling.  However, to continue, *mon père*, justifiably, had reached the end of his tether and threw me out of the château and the country: a necessary action of course, due to the duel, even though it was fair and above board.  You see, the man I killed was the son of *mon père's* archenemy.  This being so, it did not look good for him: and so my exit laboured beneath a very black cloud."

"Was this duel over our *mère*?  But you did not meet her in France!"

"That is so, Emile... we met in Italy. This was long before. The cause was the abduction... and worse... of a good friend's sister.  She instantly took her own life.

And yes, I had feelings for her at the time.  He, the brother, being in Italy at that moment and his father in England, I took on the duty of defending her honour."

"And our *mère's* family, did they know about this duel?" asked Emile.

"Oh, they were all sympathy; the family name of de Quatreaux stood well but the name of my opponent was known to them as an evil enemy of society; they were half French themselves and so I was hailed as a hero and the matter kept at home. But that is not the present day issue. *Mon père* had no other sons and unknown to me my sister, Charlotte, died from a minor resurgence of the plague a little after I left and so that left him alone. About twelve years into my exile, by now I had proudly established myself and could turn my arrogant back on the family estates, *mon père* also died, leaving the estates empty and by rote of ancestral hierarchy it fell to the care of the nearest next of kin that could be found, no matter how remote, until I could be traced."

"Now why does the name of our contemptible cousin, *second* cousin, *Lareaux*, come to mind?" breathed Emile softly.

"Ah yes, and in the execution of this duty he found that should I be untraceable within seven years of disappearance, I be presumed dead and the estates may then be transferred to the next in line."

"*Him!*" said Emile with a snort of disgust.

"Yes. But more than that is the aspect of just who he is."

The twins remained silent.

"He is the son of…"

"The dead man of the duel," broke in Emile suddenly. "My pardon, Monseigneur, but I begin to see."

"Ah. But do you see also that when I arrived back in France, several decades later, any solid proof of my identity and possession of the estates were missing: a certificate claiming my own death existed and the deeds had been transferred to him. This included the Château Quatreaux and all other estates belonging to our family…"

"But could you not prove who you were? Certainly you were absent a long time but…"

"*Mon fils*, you would be in the right of it should there be no dispute, but no matter how many people can verify one's identity, when papers declare otherwise there exists much legal doubt. I had not even my birth certificate on me when I left."

"You left with all speed; birth certificates far from your mind," said Angelique.

"So *that* is why we stayed in the château of the friend in South America. I remember it well; you were fixing Château Quatreaux for us," Emile murmured, "Thought that you meant structurally."

"I thought of forgery of the essential papers, deeds and such, but did not like it; so clumsy." A rare, whimsical, smile crossed his features as he murmured, almost to himself, "I had not then, a good forger within my acquaintance."

"*Anton!*" nodded Emile, then grinning, "So you then set out to win the château. What game did you play?"

"Be it of consequence?"

"But yes."

"It was, I believe, Lansquenet: a very old game of chance; actually suggested by Anton."

"And he was not...er, so familiar with it?"

"He was not. It was sheer luck, but I won and all was fair and above board with many solid witnesses. Many estates changed hands in such a way... still do occasionally. He has of course never forgiven me for the death of his *père* in that duel: considered his take-over of my estates recompense, I imagine. 'Tis always such with the likes of he... never accept the consequences of their own deeds... in his case those of his *père*. He is almost as bad but not quite: he has not abducted a lady of tender age... yet! At least: that we know of!"

"And the problem is now exacerbated, *Mon Père*?" asked Angelique.

"He is becoming very vocal. Taunting that I be not just who I say that I am, or more to the point that I do not own what I am believed to own: Château Quatreaux and the estates: hinting that legally they are his. Our family's history of feuding was recalled. I could see that some were impressed and of course curious."

"But can he, regardless of legal documents... so many remember you?"

"Ah yes, but who really knew the ramifications of the property ownership? A Frenchman loves an intrigue and who can say, where there be smoke: there *was* a card game, the duel, his *père* lay dead by my hand; *and* the enmity between both families was widely known." He shrugged. "I have seen many unbelievable things in my time occur through rumour and chance. A story only needs catch the interest of bored club patrons and it leaps to life. No *mes enfants*, I *must* find my original birth certificate and the deeds must be transferred back into to my name. We face turbulent times ahead."

"Why were they not returned to you when you won the estates back?" asked Emile.

"Under normal gambling law of course, etiquette even, an honourable person would have done so. He claimed them stolen from the Chateau Lareaux. There was a theft... a rather large and clever one in which much family jewellery was stolen I believe... but the documents? I do not believe it true... but how to force the issue? It falls beneath the grey area of the law. And we all know that one can get stuck in there forever!"

Silence reigned a moment as Jean-Pierre rose, stretched and poured more wine then, shoulders against the mantle, stood gazing at them. "So, there you have it. I wanted you to be aware of the degree of this man's hatred." He paused thoughtfully for a moment. "But I shall contrive, oh yes, I shall contrive. He fears me. And as are all bullies, he is a weak man and so that is why I warn you, for he will strike in the dark. And he *will* strike: he cannot assuage the revenge that still burns within, without doing so."

Emile stared at him. "Can we not be of assistance... in locating the documents?"

"And just how do you mean to do that?" smiled the Comte.

"Break and enter?" chuckled Angelique. "Where is he now? In Paris, that is where. Where is all the fuss going forward at the moment? In Paris—therefore his château would be empty. Does he have family, this repulsive cousin of ours? *Second* cousin! Ugh!"

"No, no, no. You must not interfere. I would not have enlightened you had I thought that you would both be irresponsible. I have an idea that could work."

"*Lettres de Cachet*?" asked Angelique suddenly with a wide smile. "Louis would not hesitate! Before the Assembly abolishes them! *Then* we could raid the Château Lareaux."

His father gazed at her for a moment. "I hope I have not misplaced my confidence, hmm? *You* will not do anything! Now, no more, I have a heavy day ahead: to bed, one and all."

"And all for one," murmured Emile.

They headed up the staircase, M. le Compte stopping off at the book-room for a moment, the twins moving along the gallery.

"Emile, how *would* one get hold of one of the *Lettres*?"

"Local magistrates; or the Abbe even: under the fifteenth Louis, they say, there was something like one hundred and fifty thousand or so *Lettres de Cachet*: that it is said he signed for families of errant sons."

"Ah! So, my deep admiration of your filial respect for our *père* has been misplaced I see. All the time you were mindful of the dreaded *Lettres*," laughed Angelique and dodged a lightly flying fist, then turned at her door.

Versailles resounded with noise. The noise of voices: the voices of well over a thousand deputies and as many spectators. The babble rose to the heavens, as they waited the first meeting of the saviour of the nation: the *States-general*. This national parliament of France would never again be relegated to the dusty archives: for there were now those among them that would make sure of that.  Summoned for eight o'clock in the morning, the representatives of the Commons, The Third, gathered within the dim lobbies for their names to be called. Their places were eventually assigned them, according to correct procedure, as drawn up in 1614, thanks to de Brienne's lengthy harvest of matters of antiquity. The king arrived at one o'clock, and a series of official speeches opened the drama of the first such meeting in one hundred and seventy five years.  Listening to this were twelve hundred deputies and twice as many spectators.

Louis, the first speaker, gave a successful, carefully prepared oration.

"There are dangers ahead, my people," he ended, "if we do not deal immediately with this grossly exaggerated desire for change, and the general unrest, that now exists and be growing daily. Well informed men of great wisdom, moderation and long experience, are here for you, here to deal at once with these new issues at stake. But also, my people; over and above this: *I* am always here for you; my love, regard and duty to the people of France ever focused towards that which is good for all. My ministers also, are ready to offer wise and prudent advice, during these times of difficult change. I cannot emphasise enough, that this gathering of national representatives should pay close attention to these men.  They have long experience and much knowledge.  We must all pull together; work together, fight together, to free France of our current problems! *Together*... with my Council and, whilst it be in existence, the Assembly of States-general, we shall reverse these problems and set a path to build a mighty France."

Moderate applause followed this but all were left deep in thought at the real meaning of these words and surely the King's Council would cease to exist?

The Lord Privy Seal expounded his Majesty's remarks. "His Majesty has acquiesced to the double representation of the *Commons* and sanction of voting *par tête* should you so desire.  The privileged orders are ready to bear their part in the burden of the taxes: of which they have thus far been exempt. The deputies are at liberty to debate a number of subjects: freedom of the press, reform of criminal law, education, maintenance of public order just a few.  Under such co-operation, France can only go forward."

Of constitutional reform, however, there was no mention and a restless shuffling began amongst the deputies: success or failure, it was felt, rested on a new constitution.

Necker, the Controller-General of Finance, rose next and faces brightened for here stood a man who had always managed to find finance no matter what. Necker however was a Genevan and his manner abrupt. He disdained to perform to the emotional atmosphere of his audience and his lengthy speech soon exhausted himself as well as those listening; for he now spoke not to the *Ancien Regime* but the New Regime: in which the speaker must be a great actor of oratory and wit, to captivate and hold the audience.  For this reason, he had pre-arranged for Dr Broussonnet, a celebrated speaker of the Royal Agriculture Society, to finish for him.

Dr Broussonnet carried on: on a monetary level, Necker's statement admitted a deficit of 5.5mll livre. The remedy for this bankruptcy lay, apparently, within the ministers' operations on the money market, bearing no relationship at all to the issue of taxation or expenditure. In point of fact the ministers could do all that was needed, without this assembly of deputies of the States-general. A low rumble began within the audience. The attitude, within Necker's speech, of the government towards the people, however, caused the most stir.

"The king," continued Dr Broussonnet, "is a gifted Monarch; gifted with wisdom beyond his years, due to his elaborate education and intelligent birth lines. Over and above this, however, he is now an experienced and astute man: due again to his intelligence but also to many experiences of deep and recent crises.  As such, as soon as this assemblage does reveal the common opinion upon the greater of our problems, he will be able to decide his response to these deliberations. Should these be for the betterment of the nation and the will of *all* the people, then he will sanction their wishes. From this shall spring great human benefits beyond compare and unchallengeable national power. With such leadership, France can only progress to greatness beyond our imagination!"

Wild cheering rose from the deputies and then slowly quietened, as they tried to digest what had really been said. Just as slowly it became clear that the king, as always, remained in power.  What was more, it appeared that they were to accept reforms, immaterial issues and old orders; modified according to his wise and manifold judgement.  Was this to be the end of all their debates?  After so many hours producing pamphlets, so much lobbying, so many speakers growing hoarse on street corners, so much expense simply to be there and so much angst?  Following so many revolts, so many lives lost and all in vain: all to gain an Assembly that carried no weight at all? Where was the open discussion and honest decisions of the States-general deputies, following deep and thoughtful contemplation regarding the millions of cahiers sent in to the capital?

They looked at each other and sitting at the back of the Commons, dressed in neat but severe black clothing, was a young, thirty-year-old lawyer. The habitual cynical smile sat on his face, as the flat cold eyes took in the scene before him, his hatred and distrust of all above him clearly evident to those who cared to look. Maximilien de Robespierre hailed from the town of Arras, in the district of Artois to the north of Paris. As one of the eight deputies from that area, he represented the Third Estate. He had been greatly influenced by Rousseau's teachings: equality, democracy and fraternity for fellow man, taking firm root in his mind. As he watched and listened, however, this idealism dissipated as he realized the powers offered by a possible absolute government of the future. His dry and acrid tones sounded now, amid the uproar following Necker's speech, lawyer-like drawing attention to every discrepancy he had heard so far. He appealed to the lower classes, inflaming the distrust felt by them towards persons of rank, wealth and talent.

Maximilien Robespierre, cold and unemotional, unable, from the cradle, to love within any capacity, began to focus upon pure self-advancement. Gazing now at the noisy public gallery, he saw suddenly a possible power tool, wrapped within the unmentioned: those, for whom France had no name, the 'great unwashed:' the serfs, the peasants. Here surely, could be harvested then moulded, a strong force to stand against the First and the Second Estates. Great in number: 95% of France's population, suffering the worst lot in life and owning no rights at all, they could surely, as their eyes slowly opened to a possible better future, soon be very easily manipulated. He eyed them speculatively; under the current disturbances, they were as pliable as soft dough, their uses manifold.

As the days passed into weeks, battles personal and battles of a large body, evidenced by the demand for single *chambre* meetings for the entire States-general, were enacted daily now. The *Commons* dug itself into a bunker, the king equally as stubborn. Many of his supporters saw that if the king wished to retain direction of affairs, then it was imperative for him to at once declare a single *chambre*, for behind the deputies of the Third Estate stood the strength of a nation: the as yet unharnessed masses. Blind to the subtle threat of this invisible power, he was however unprepared to do so, for the formation of a single chamber implied the abolition of all class distinction and the swamping of the Nobles by the Third Estate: disastrous for the monarchy. A separate sitting for each of the three estates, enabling them to vote separately, must be maintained to protect the crown and the King's Council.

Two tired men, Necker and Montmorin, sat in consult within the king's *chambres*. Nothing, it appeared, could breach the stubbornness of His Majesty.

Necker, the finance minister, tried again: "Your Majesty, to establish a constitution with *two chambres*; comprising the upper; of the combined Nobles and

Clergy and the lower; the Bourgeois... the Third: each then with 600 votes, and get on with the restoration of our finances seems to me to be the...er, most desirable of the moment."

The king stared at him, tired, his mind distractedly tearing at the problem and did not answer. The *one-chambre* issue was a nightmare threat: to lose his support, the First and Second Estates, unthinkable. His childhood friend softened to compassion at Louis' turmoil, but knew he must be brought to see the changes raging around him as substantial.

"*Mon ami*," he smiled gently now at Necker, "a *two-chambre* sitting will never be accepted. The deputies of The Third have set their heart on civil and political equality. Until this occurs: under a one *chambre* sitting, they shall pay no heed to mere administrative or financial reforms. I know that it is your intention that the three orders sit together only when financial, and administrative, matters are under discussion. All other subjects to be discussed sitting apart, but..."

"Yes Montmorin: and should there be disagreement, the king to make the final decision," replied Necker, gazing at him in perplexity. "What could make more sense?"

Montmorin sighed. "Ah yes, Necker, to *you,* but The Third shall never accept this. A combined upper *chambre*, and a second for the Third Estate, can only thwart them in doing what the whole nation is now expecting them to do, and quickly. Your only hope is to declare a single *chambre*... they must meet; the three estates, as one body."

Louis, rising from his chair and beginning to pace from desk to window embrasure, spoke with a stubbornness they knew only too well. "To overcome those of the privileged orders in *opposition* to the crown, has long been my wish—but one cannot, under any circumstances, *separate* them from the crown. And to make one *chambre* for the three estates together, does tear them away from the crown... I will not have it!"

"Sire, I feel deeply and sadly that should you refuse to lead the attack, ahem... my pardon, the, er... changes, on the privileged orders, it may be made with great violence. And so Sire, I feel that your only hope in retaining leadership of the Assembly is by declaring unreservedly for a single chamber." Montomorin paused but his Monarch did not reply. "I know this causes the demarcation line to shift to exactly below yourself, Sire: placing 'all on one footing' with *one chambre*, appearing to tear away your support... but we are on the brink of civil war."

"They surely cannot claim such an issue as grounds for violence, Montmorin!" said Necker.

"The people are pumped up," replied Montmorin. "They have been for months on end... waiting the magical change! Already disorder and riots rage in many parts of the country, and now parts of Paris, and we have 700,000 of them here. The winter past was the longest and coldest on record, the death rate the highest since the plague. Bread price is rising again and their misery, which they expected to vanish on the first meeting of the States-general, is on the increase."

The king grunted in disgust. "And this, The Third are using!"

"As tools to stir the masses, yes Sire; and I know full well that it has always been difficult to prevent rioting in Paris in times of scarcity or political excitement... but now we have the both together: to create disorder *and* the added insult of weeks of debating with no sign of any progress." He paused and looked at the king tentatively.

The king stared back at his old childhood companion. "There is *more*? Do not hold back, *mon ami:* give it to me with the bark off if you please... the raw inner works of it!"

"Well, Your Majesty, to the faubourg St Antoine and other poor quarters of Paris where already breeds the ruffians, beggars and destitute workers, have been added many migrants to the city. Brought here from the country on the promise of things better; labour and bread at the very minimum, but they are, after all, starving and idle. These are ripe to be worked upon to dangerous effect; by pamphleteers and street orators. Indeed, tenant land holders are already refusing to pay taxes and feudal dues. Educated men..."

"*Partly* so: herein lies the problem," muttered Necker bitterly, "the great avalanche of today's self-educated 'academics'! Lawyers from the Petit Bourgeoisie etcetera! Curse this new-wave of 'enlightenment'... it shall bring only violence and disaster!"

"Men who can read, then," conceded Montmorin, "are spreading suspicion upon the intentions of the government. Officials are powerless to act with the old rigour. In every town and hamlet the people apparently wait with eagerness for the speedy accomplishment of their desires expressed in the millions of *cahiers* laid before the States-general, Sire. And while they wait the redress of their grievances, there is no lack of evil and poisonous stirrings going on around the clock."

The king, leaning back against the great mahogany desk, arms folded as tightly as his lips, continued to stare, his myopic eyes, disconcerting to most, boring into his friend. "But is that the lot, Monty? Surely you can rake up more?"

Montmorin kept a sober countenance but could not suppress the twinkle in his eyes as he gazed back. "Well..."

"No, no, I was jesting! Do not, I beg of you," laughed Louis now, not in any great humour but in relief, for to be able to laugh these days was a luxury mostly denied him.

The atmosphere relaxed a little then, until Montmorin mentioned the state of the still daily sittings of The Third in the Great Hall. Necker, much to his chagrin and bitter regret, had omitted to provide a separate meeting place for the *Commons*: believing displacement to be a great deterrent and so there, beneath the chin of the dragon; indeed within the very dragon's lair, they, the Third Estate, silently staked out their claim to a new '*parlement*', refusing to proceed to business until the other two orders joined them.

The fourth week, following that momentous event of the convocation of the States-general, now flowed into the fifth. In that time, no letters had been opened, no business transacted, no money voted, no reforms discussed let alone passed, for as such the delegates may be seen; in the absence of the other two Estates, to be acting as a class. And it was not three separate orders of three separate assemblies that had been convoked but one national body: sitting together. Until the three sat together as *one chambre*, they reiterated, the Assembly could not begin its work. This then became their refrain.

Within his apartments, the king paced. His mind searched in vain, answers to the *'chambre'* battle; a way to keep the three Orders separate within a sitting. A combined sitting of the three orders together could only bring disaster: an opportunity for a swift power shift. Even were he amenable to such a move, The Third was too green and too emotional to prevent even further disaster: though most were partially educated, they were still ignorant regarding the running of a country. He paused a moment, gazing unseeingly out over the great beauty of the distant blue-tinted low hills, then turned and spoke to the two waiting his decision.

"This deliberate inaction of The Third is some miserable member's master stroke, Necker. It places the Privileged Orders in the wrong and is reducing the government to impotence! I wonder if, whoever he is, he realizes how powerful a manoeuvrer it is: for the purse be coming up to mighty low tide now. How much can you scrape up, Necker?"

"Another six months, no more, Sire."

"I am prepared for anything, my ministers, even unto ceding constitutional rights to the country, which shall of course set limits to *my* authority. *But ...I shall not* suffer abolition of the classes. Any fool can see that this is how it must be! There shall be complete mayhem should all power slide to the uneducated Third. There can be *no other direct result* should the real governing power pass from myself to them. Has any one the imagination to see just what is ahead of us, should the upper lose control?" finished the king.

"Sire, I do agree, but in order to improve the lot of the government, you may be obliged to at least reduce the power of the Privileged. But primary to our concerns be the one *chambre* demand. As things stand, while the Third Estate are performing their glorious inaction, the Nobles and Clergy are also refusing to sit with the *Commons*: are proclaiming themselves a separate order and are operating out of the committee rooms close by. I shall not exhaust thee with the tedious comings and goings. They are knee deep in crackling parchment and it becomes clear that the Nobles wish to dictate and the Clergy to negotiate."

"And...?"

"The Third..."

"Don't tell me: won't bend in any way. Did they learn that from Lafayette by any chance?" asked the king bitterly.

"Pardon, Sire?" Necker's tired eyebrows had just enough energy left to lift a little.

"Oh, something about the strength of arrows, of course: all things *American* are of the greatest moment in his book. One arrow is able to be broken but a bundle tied together is unbreakable. The principle seems to be working." He paused suddenly. "*Unless*...we can untie and separate them! So, what goes forth now?"

"Well Sire, as of this midday, The Third are leaning towards verifying their own credentials, not as representatives of The Third but as one of the nation as a whole. They are at this moment deciding another name for themselves. I believe the running favourite is *Assemblèe Nationale*."

"*Grand Dieu*! What next shall they waste their time with?" said the king.

"And," added Necker bitterly, "Bailly's arrival in the chair seems to have strengthened them; policies abound to win over the waverers of the upper and outmanoeuvre the reactionaries. To do this, they must transform the conference of three orders into the, er... abovementioned National Parliament; ready to co-operate with, er... yourself, Sire."

"Co-operate...bah! 'Tis blackmail. I say again... I shall *not* lay my crown at their feet." He paced again, hands gripped behind his back, then spinning round to a stop, "But they are not legal, my ministers... there has to be a way of proving that."

Necker and Montmorin glanced at each other. "Sire, I be afraid that their every move has been carefully studied and researched and worded, so that it is indeed all legal and, what is more, their final weapon involves potential non-payment of taxes. The taxes shall only continue to be paid so long as the Assembly continues in session but should it be in any way dissolved, they will cease to be payable: no longer carrying the free and formal consent of the nation."

"Enough!" The soft voiced king had not been heard to actually roar before. He now looked old suddenly, the lines of care and grief deepening. He glanced at the ornate Louis X1Vth clock on the mantle. "Well, be what it shall, I am still going to Marly for a few days. 'Toinette can take little more of this Versailles at the moment. She has had no chance of rest since Louis-Josephe..." His jaw stiffened; then he continued, "'Tis but a few miles—let me know of their resolutions poste haste."

Bowing deeply in silent respect and compassion for the king's grief, the two ministers left the chamber of King Louis XV1. The king slumped suddenly and slid into a chair.

Several days passed for the king and queen within the simpler comforts of Marly-le-Roi and away from the din and distraction of Versailles. These drew them together even more staunchly than ever, for without the hurly-burly of court life, ministerial demands and bullying, they could relax and be themselves: a thing that even the closest courtier never witnessed. Had these known of the depth of love and devotion of each toward the other, they would indeed have been surprised.

Louis turned now, seated on the rustic seat beneath the fragrant old roses climbing the arch before them and gazed at Marie Antoinette; at her exquisite willowy grace; her increasing slenderness: the death of the Dauphin causing great loss of weight. "Did I ever tell you that I loved you?"

Startled, she turned, lifting her head from the buried position within a long branch heavy with flowers, inhaling the delicate perfumery and gazed at him: a slow smile spreading across her face. "My love, many times, but never I think, in such isolation as here at this moment. We did need this so very much! No court, no *courtiers*, no heavy responsibilities, no functions. None would believe me of course... but every day now, I wish to do nothing more than love my children and husband. I have come to crave simplicity, Louis." She came and sat beside him, taking his hand in hers and gripping it tightly. "The death of a child does change one so... the mind, the heart, they are in a different place now. I wanted only to be with Louis-Josephe every moment, but it was impossible. The States-general opening and oh, many, now more important than ever, functions I was compelled to attend. Oh how many hours did I miss? And I am not the person that they say, Louis. *I am not.* I suppose next I shall be accused of neglecting my son in his dying days! They shall rake and twist every possible thing, Louis." She choked on the words then forced back the tears, for they could only be described as self pity, she knew; and Royal life offered no place for such. "Why oh why, Louis?"

"My dear, when you came here you were so very young and so full of life that you left me gasping. You grabbed life and ran with it, you were beautiful and gay and kind and generous. You dished out favours left right and centre but this caused many jealousies, vicious and lethal; but more than that, you became a figure that shone and a shining light can be seen for miles. It draws the more deadly moths as well as the gentler and there were those very black moths that saw how to use you, my dear, for their ambitions. But you know all of this *ma chérie*... a queen, worldwide, is only ever seen for her uses. Do not feel guilty for you have done nothing that you have not been trained to do for your position. My dear, we sit at the edge of an abyss, the rumblings of change sounding from before I mounted the throne. I saw it then, dully, but now," he shrugged, "the vision clears and without support from the Nobles... ah, but we came here to rest *ma chérie* and *I your Monarch*, ban the subject from this stay."

She smiled, took his hand and kissed it in mock supplication, then rested her head upon his shoulder. They sat thus for several more minutes, but even this brief respite was to be doomed, for approaching them across the green lawns was a liveried messenger. Louis broke the seal of the proffered parchment, read and then called a page standing close by.

"Call Clery if you please—to organize our immediate departure for Versailles."

The queen looked at him; saw his deadpan face and her eyebrows lifted, "Sire?"

He handed her the parchment and she read. She read that at a pivotal meeting on June 17$^{th}$ 1789, the deputies had passed a motion that since they represented 95% of the people, the Third Estate should be renamed as a new body and called the National Assembly with the right to control taxes. As the king was absent they planned to proceed without the Monarch.

She threw it upon the grass and turned to him. "*But Louis...* this is... this is... treason! Treason of the people! Grand *Dieu* Louis, you cannot stand for it! It is a rebellion!"

"Of the people: the masses will be harnessed now to add pressure to their cause!"

She stared at him in horror. "The causes of *The Third*... and much of the discontent nobility; *Mon Dieu:* 'tis *diabolique!*"

# CHAPTER SEVEN

## Mid-Summer Madness

The *Gallerie des Glaces* buzzed with loyal subjects, messengers, courtiers, and spies, though of the last two, one could not know one from another. Nobility, that had not graced the court for years, flocked to Versailles. All of this swirling activity should cause, thought Necker, the king to feel that loyalty abounded for the Crown. As he watched, however, along with Montmorin and now Luzerne, he witnessed Louis' face, normally in gentle repose, grow more and more cynical.

De Quatreaux moved to stand beside Luzerne now; his face a mask of courtly politeness. The king's feelings for his country ran deep. The torture he must be suffering, beneath the turmoil and persuasion of his surrounding critics and supporters, would be great. He frowned: Louis was still in shock; nothing like this had ever occurred in France before. That a people could so easily suddenly *announce*, that they had now formed a National Assembly, *with the right to control taxes without the consent of the king,* was a thing difficult to grasp. Surely it could be proved not legal. He smiled grimly: no legal structure had ever had to cope with such. Deep in these thoughts, de Quatreaux shook his head faintly: he had expected bloody revolt but nothing like this. This was somebody's very clever and substantial move: providing a strong basis for a power shift.

The *Galerie des Glaces*, none other would accommodate the swelling numbers, now reverberated with the buzz of excited demands from some and fearful anticipation from others. To the excited courtiers, it seemed as easy a matter for the king to impose his will upon these newly spawned representatives of the nation, as it had been for his predecessors to impose theirs upon the old *law courts/parlements* of Paris. Few could grasp that this new parliament however, was no shuttle service, or assembly line for the conveyance of orders from the King's Council, as had been the old.

A tight knot of people surrounded the royal couple at one end of the gallery. Here the queen found great difficulty in preventing herself from pacing. "Mon Louis... you must stop them! This surely cannot be allowed!" she cried now.

"Close the *parlements*, Louis!" d'Artois, his strongly counter-revolutionary brother, flung out his arms in agitation. "It be the only remedy for a disobedient Assembly!"

"Not so easy, d'Artois," murmured his more liberal brother, the Comte de Provence.

65

"What's difficult about it?" shouted d'Artois. "Stop it all *mechanically* at least: lock the room in which they meet! They cannot meet in the rain! Use the troops! At least do *something* that shows *strength*, Louis!"

Provence looked at him thoughtfully. "Certainly it will hold them up for a short period... give time to plan."

"While the King's Council find the... *illegalities* of this monstrous... event!" added the Queen.

Urged on by his two brothers and the queen, and unable to find an alternative, Louis complied. Orders were sent out to close the 'parlement-house' against the deputies and to prepare it for a *Séance Royale.* Versailles was placarded with notices of a Royal Session for June 22$^{nd}$ and the Mayor, now Bailly, received an official letter saying that the new Assembly's meetings must be suspended while the hall was renovated by a team of carpenters.

June 20 dawned chilly and wet. The deputies, scornfully disregarding these notices, assembled outside the building as usual and found the doors closed. They listened but no sounds of carpentry could be heard: instead, soldiers were now in possession, a precautionary measure of the king's brother. The foremost deputies glanced at each other, reading these signs as the forerunner to dissolution.

"*Quickly*... another venue... there must be *some*where we can hold the meeting!" said one urgently. "The very sight of those soldiers will inflame the mob!"

The deputy on his left gazed swiftly around. "You two... take the left. We the right; find *something*!"

"The *jeu de paum*," gasped one on return, "enough room."

Soon the large bare spaces echoed with many voices: not those of tennis spectators but angry protests from the deputies of the displaced Assembly.

On his arrival, Bailly gazed about him. "Mounier! This could turn into a bloodbath. We must move quickly to prevent more provocative action!"

Mounier raised his brows. "Provocation being?"

"Seiyes' proposal to remove to Paris: that the Assembly must set itself up in Paris!"

"Imbecile! The king would never agree to move it all from Versailles and *then* what would happen be beyond me! We cannot allow bloodshed!"

Mounier thought a moment, then, "An oath! Drum up an oath... all persons hold an oath sacrosanct... and would keep them busy for a little time at least."

The suggestion of an oath, which was to make them famous and to become a charter of French liberty, caught hold of their imagination. The more gifted scribes among them set to work and soon, deleting the picturesque offers from the more poetic individuals within this small circle in conference, an oath was transferred to parchment. Mounier read it aloud, ending with:

"And the Assembly declares," he said, "that: 'nothing can prevent us from continuing our deliberations, in whatever place the Assembly may be obliged to meet; and considering that whatever and whomsoever of its members may meet, here then *be* the National Assembly. All members of said Assembly should here and now, take a solemn oath, never to abandon it and to go on meeting wherever circumstances may dictate, until the constitution of the realm be set up and consolidated on firm foundations.   And, when said oath has been taken, all the members, severally and in common, shall confirm, by their signatures, this unshakable resolution'."

All signed this oath, to the last delegate but one: the Tennis Court Oath was born. And Mounier had been correct: the word of a man; the age-old honour of an oath he took was held in reverence and seriousness, the breaking of which considered the most heinous crime. That one man, however, placed after his name the word *opposant*, for he could not, he said, conscientiously support measures not sanctioned by his king. Try as they would they could not change his mind and allowed his signature to stand. This to the credit, it was said, of the majority as proof of liberty of opinion: albeit following a lifesaving tussle by his friends, against the militant-inclined of their company.

♣

"One man?" the king gazed at de Quatreaux. "One man amongst the entire *Commons*? One man in 600—does that not tell you something, my friend?"

"It tells me that the commons have at one stroke converted themselves into the Long Parliament of Charles 1st of England," de Quatreaux paused. "But it is the few of course... wrapped in the cloak of freedom and all the rest of their newfound, so-called *liberality*. The rest, as usual, are sheep!"

"Oh yes," Louis responded dully; then he suddenly looked at de Quatreaux. "Necker did er...'show me the way', de Quatreaux: to become a sheep, I imagine! Had drafted, ready for my signature, a declaration in which I was to accept a proper English style of government."

"But you did not...er...become a sheep, Sire."

"Not even the stud ram, de Quatreaux," sardonically. "The queen's circle was appalled and I could not distress her further. She has always disliked him and now his reforms do nothing to bridge that gap. The Queen's court hates him but no, on my own account I *could* not, de Quatreaux. Could you?"

"Personally: absolutely not, Sire; besides, the ground be a quagmire."

"The council meet again tomorrow, Vermont, and so let us see what can be salvaged. No legal precedence exists to guide us but this could work for us too. You have everything under control, Puységur, I believe? I have not had time to leave the council chambers but I have been told that the troops are ready?"

"Yes Sire, they are on their way as we speak," replied the Minister for War.

"Good! But I do not expect to have need of them, of course. It is precaution only."

De Quatreaux looked at the king. "Our external plans still stand, Sire, there is sufficient funds in place and the émigrés are impatient."

"Good. But we must not move too soon."

De Quatreaux looked at him in deep anxiety but did not voice his thoughts: that the king could also leave it too late.

The palace was indeed surrounded by troops the next day, 21st June 1789. The Comte d'Artois, the king's strongly counterrevolutionary brother, engaged the tennis court to prevent another meeting of the *Commons* before the Sèance Royale, which had been postponed to the 23$^{rd.}$

Both of the king's brothers: the Comte d'Artois and the Comte de Provence attended the meeting of the King's Council, along with two selected State Councillors, Dr Gallisière and Videau de la Tour, hoping that these votes would achieve a clear majority against Necker and his supporters: in the battle over Necker's conciliatory program, toward the Assembly.

The Royal Séance declared Necker's program a sell-out and turned it down. The National Assembly resolution was quashed. A motion was passed that the tax exemption could only be abolished by the Nobles themselves and their monopolies were to be retained. The king retained the right to impose taxes as he saw fit and without the consent of the Assembly. Further reforms could only be sanctioned if recommended by all three orders separately—establishing the impossibility of, and defeating the battle for, *one-chambre* sittings. Now the deputies must be told.

The 23$^{rd}$ dawned yet again a wet and miserable day. The king arrived in state at the hall where the whole body of 1200 deputies was, by his injunction, assembled. He gazed at them a moment as the shuffling and murmured anticipations died down. The relief at their apparent submission was overwhelming but his face remained impassive. He drew a deep breath then cleared his throat and spoke quietly but clearly, informing of the motions passed and the sitting by three separate orders.

"Therefore," he continued, "I require you all to listen well... for this I shall say once only. You *shall continue* to meet as three separate orders: that must be made clear: three *separate* orders. You have my consent to form one Assembly for matters of common interest, from which however all questions of social, constitutional and ecclesiastical nature shall be banned," he paused and complete silence reigned. "You shall now all disperse and assemble on the morrow in your *separate chambres*. Do not be tempted... for in the case of disobedience I shall not hesitate to secure the safety of my subjects. I am prepared, without qualification, to do this! My subjects I hold dear: their safety of the highest importance. *Nothing* can be higher."

The resultant sombre silence gave evidence that all who had passed through the lines of alert troops, were left in no doubt as to his meaning. They had however also witnessed those soldiers' discomforts and guessed at the fragile loyalty to crown.

The Nobles, with the exception of those few, as did the Clergy, obeyed their king and left the hall but the entirety of the *Commons* sat on. Necker, always respected by the people, had absented himself from the meeting, thereby preserving his popularity, a manoeuvre noted by the king, he knew. It was a thin straight line that he now walked: possibly the finest walked by any finance minister in the history of France.

Still nobody spoke; until finally the Master of Ceremonies, De Brèzè rose and gazed over them all. "Did you not hear the king's orders, Monsieur President, Monsieur Bailly?" he asked.

But it was Mirabeau who responded. "Oh yes! *We heard...* the words that were put into the king's mouth and we know by whom! *That* is our beef, for 'tis not the king that one and all resist but those that manipulate him. And let me inform you, that if you intend to turn us out, then you had better apply for orders to employ force, for we shall only quit our seats at the point of a sword or bayonet!"

The spell of perceived bondage was broken and loud cheering reverberated to the high vaulted ceiling and back; they could not be moved—until the new constitution be born. Feelings of freedom, liberty and above all, victory, carried them on a wave of euphoria.

A speaker shouted: "We shall not move until we are one meeting... one Assembly!"

"We are one!"

"One National Assembly... we be one only!"

"Here! Here!"

"We shall not be moved!"

"One *chambre*! We are one chambre!"

The cry, taken up now by the entire 600 deputies, echoed for long minutes and pandemonium broke across the assemblage in a frightening wave.

"Dissolution of the States... *Grand Dieu...* 'tis the only way to go, Louis!" raged the Queen, striding up and down. "Can you not see that? The entire court agrees... the States-general *must* be dissolved! 'Tis madness! The King's Council *must* regain control!"

Necker glanced at the king, who was deep in thought and not hearing the queen, "But Madame," he said, "there are difficulties. Grave financial ones and matters of military: for if His Majesty was to actually *actively* employ the troops, then he would have to do so across the nation."

The king continued to gaze into space. It was the early hours of the morning and the last sleepless hours, days even, were taking their toll, for no one but the royal family seemed to remember that Louis-Josephe had only been dead a little over two weeks.

"Then do so! Right across the nation if you must!"

"Madame, the class distinction that prevails throughout the army, as it does through all of our institutions, is an obstacle under these circumstances. The Officers are all nobles..."

"But of course, what else: who otherwise to run the military machine?"

"But Your Majesty, resistance within the army *toward* these nobles, would occur, for they would not be fighting a foreign invader but their very own people. Paris would erupt and the troops would very likely refuse to fire on their own classes, Madame."

She stared at him for a long moment. "Then we shall have anarchy in the streets! No moral restraint is possible in a people unaccustomed to self-government."

"There is talk already, Your Majesty, of a march upon Versailles. The *Gardes Francaises* have already gone over to the people and there be rumours that the regiment *Salis-Samade* shall join them. We must move with extreme caution."

"Your Majesty," said Madame Lamballe, very quietly, "there exist rumours that noble deputies have returned to their homes in Paris to find their doors marked."

"They are not rumours, Your Highness," offered Estelle Pontac from her corner. "One... er, loyal noble, whose door was so marked, was dragged from his horse last night, as he neared his home and, er..." She left unsaid the fate of the noble but all knew the story.

The Queen stared, then slumped into a chair, gazing ahead and then driven to movement by racing adrenalin, born of anxiety and fury, rose again and recommenced pacing. "*Vraiment*... the ghost of Herod!"

And so it was, on the 27th, that the First Estate: the Clergy, and the 2nd Estate: the Nobility, received orders to unite with the Third Estate, the *Commons*. They yielded, albeit with bad grace, to a command to *one-chambre* sittings, based in court fear of a successful revolt against the throne.

♣

"Let us hope that they now be happy," said Montmorin, looking at de Quatreaux, "and that our friends in foreign courts, and those on the border, are ready!"

"Oh yes, as much as can be expected, but it is not, my friend, their problem."

Montmorin looked at him thoughtfully. "This was your impression? Including Spain, I imagine."

De Quatreaux merely smiled. "Louis' Spanish cousin is, er..."

"Not in the least interested? Nothing new there! On a brighter note, I have reason to believe Calonne has been very busy raising finance and an army. I can but imagine that his contacts, from his time as Finance Minister, have helped... *your* work, Vermont?"

De Quatreaux did not humour him. "Our Monarch is in a bad way. His power is collapsing, Montmorin. His *Assembly of Notables* defied him, his *Parlements* defied him and now the *Third Estate* defies him. The *Commons* now hold the majority and with the defection of d'Orlèans and Mirabeau, none know how many shall follow: 'tis a complete victory."

"Not quite."

"Tell that to the jubilant rioter in the streets; my guess be that extra regiments be required afore the day is out."

"If that be so, then order all close lying regiments to Paris of this instant!" They both looked up at the familiar voice, as the king entered the *chambre*. They straightened to bow low.

"Sire...with all due haste!" said Montmorin, moving to the door.

The king's stubborn jaw was set. "This rebellion must be put down. The borders, according to you, de Quatreaux, be safe for the moment. And the foreign troops ready, should they be required?"

"They are, Your Majesty. All awaits your word."

"Good, but we do not move just yet."

"Sire," Montmorin, half turning in the open doorway, glanced at de Quatreaux, "this is rather more than a rebellion. Perhaps we should allow de Quatreaux to, er...travel post-haste to Austria: as he, er, trusts no courier and goes himself."

Louis, gazing down at a parchment, merely shook his head. "Not yet."

♣

Angelique descended the stairs of Hôtel Quatreaux, pulling on her gloves and glancing inquiringly at Siffred as he crossed the wide entrance hall toward her.

"Madame, there be here a gentleman but I informed him…" He paused lamely as that same man advanced through the entrance and crossed to the foot of the stairs.

"Ah, Mademoiselle Vermont, I beg forgiveness for the slightly early hour but other attempts of mine to pay my very anxious respects have been thwarted by your leaving the house very early in the mornings. Where do you go I wonder?" he ended teasingly.

"But I am not a lay-about, Monsieur. I have many things to attend to. Please do come through." She turned to Siffred. "Some of that new South American coffee, if you please, Siffred. That is, unless of course you desire claret, or something a little lighter; perhaps a glass of *canary*?" looking at the visitor.

He laughed. "But what an opinion you have of me, Mademoiselle. The stronger liquids have not yet become my friend, I do assure you."

"In that case please do come into the salon," replied Angelique and led Monsieur le Comte Lareaux into that pleasantly appointed room. Her heart beat a little uneasily against her chest wall but she kept up a flow of light inconsequential topics.

"You did enjoy the Queen's soirée the other night I saw, but with a baritone of such remarkable quality I would be surprised should not all the women admire him."

Her face showed no irritation at the patronization. "He was indeed excellent."

The conversation continued in such empty fashion and Angelique managed to direct the flow as she waited his reason for the visit. Nothing of note eventuated however and, reduced to frantic mental search of Parisian gossip to offer, she was relieved by Siffred's reappearance, announcing the person of Jacques Devereaux, the fifth Baron de Lacy.

He entered a little hesitantly, bowed low to Angelique then offered a polite bow to Lareaux. "Your servant, Lareaux," he said; and then, turning to Angelique, "Mademoiselle, I beg your pardon but I am anxious to know when Francois is to be home next. I have need of his direction otherwise and knew that I may obtain such from you, if you please."

"Ah yes. The Flanders Regiment, was it not?" breathed Lareaux. "But they are busy on border business are they not, cousin?"

Angelique gazed at him, a seraphic smile upon her face hiding her grinding teeth at the claim to familiarity. "Yes, and yet I do not know of his regiment's move, Jacques, I am sorry."

Lareaux, ever mindful of proper social etiquette, rose, following a few pleasantries with the new visitor and smoothly bowed himself out. "Mademoiselle, I must now depart, but may I escort you to Versailles—if you be in attendance for the Queen's gathering of the Sun King's favourite roses? Though I am at a loss, in these troubled times, to know why she should persist with an old ritual that can only bring more criticism upon her," he smiled gently.

She returned the smile, relaxed and gay, gazing clearly into those unblinking eyes of a cobra, "But what of it Monsieur? Come now, surely troubled times demand even more gaiety than usual, has it not always been so? Besides, the ceremony is so pretty."

He laughed, "Then I shall call here again to arrange a time," and left the room, leaving Angelique to gather her wit and strength as she turned immediately to Jacques. How to wriggle out of the proposal she did not know but something would offer itself: it must.

"Mademoiselle, I do not know what that fellow is up to, but... oh, I do apologise! 'Tis none of my business to be sure." He bowed apologetically, flustered by his own impolite outburst.

"Jacques, what know you of him?" asked Angelique, waving aside his apology.

"No, no, Mademoiselle... such affront... I was forgetting; he is your relative!"

"A recently discovered relative, Monsieur, and I could wish it otherwise... and so require much knowledge, so please... what know you of him?"

"I know naught but what any man can see. He is not quite the thing you know! Something definitely down river about him. Not quite a captain sharp, or a loose screw, but I do not trust him; but there, mayhap just not my type of fellow." He paused, frowning slightly; then his brow cleared. "Now I know what it was, probably naught but..." He stopped again. "No, mayhap I am all abroad."

"Please Jacques! Do not leave it there," responded Angelique laughing. "You *know* that you cannot leave it there. I am *female*!"

"Ah yes," he grinned. "My sisters say the same. But 'tis his smooth easy-going manner... it be not genuine... and proof of that be in the episode of the cane, now that I remember."

"The cane: Monsieur?"

"Yes, his cane became confused by the new footman at his club one day. Obviously a little green, a little nervous no doubt, but he gave Lareaux as he left the club, the wrong cane. Easy thing to do; why they all look alike, I myself could never hold such a position: memory like a grain-flour-sieve! And I have; now I come to think of it, myself received the wrong one on occasions, but a cane is a cane, what for to make a din?"

"So you are saying that he erupted over a simple mistake?"

"Yes, that was it, an eruption: where anybody else would have shrugged. But mayhap it owned sentimental value; who knows." He frowned again. "No... dash it... it *was* unusual... a hint of panic perhaps. Ah 'twas naught... do not attend me!"

"Yes, perhaps so. However, thank you for the warning. I shall take care not to upset him in any way; but you came on request of Francois—I cannot tell what goes forward with him but his unit is at this address; now, one moment if you please—ah yes, here it is."

She sat at the small secretaire and picking up a quill, dipped into the ink. She wrote for a moment, the only sound in the room the scratching of the quill as it travelled across the parchment. Having used the brevette and folded the paper, she then rose and moved forward to Jacques. "Here we be, 'tis all that I can furnish you with."

"*Merci*, Mademoiselle. Soon, I hope, *mon père* arranges the same regiment for me."

He beamed proudly and Angelique rose, delighted for him, moving forward with her hand held out. "But Monsieur, I am so very pleased for you."

"Well thankyou; but for the moment, you shall keep my confidence, I know."

"But of course. Rest assured; wild horses would not drag it from me." He laughed, "Or the rack?"

"Never the rack; or even the wheel, although I have sometimes wondered which is worse: to be stretched, or broken! And thinking about it: wild horses also do not sound so pleasant!"

"Mademoiselle, you shall never find out."

She frowned but a moment. "I surely hope not but if so, I do be praying for the fortitude required for such experiences."

He bowed himself out and Angelique pulled on her gloves for the second time and nodded to the butler as he turned back to her from closing the door. "Yes Siffred, the carriage, if you please: to Mademoiselle du Bois' hôtel."

Unaware of Lareaux' manoeuvres, Emile spent the day finalizing the payment for forged documents, necessary in the execution of transferring monies to England. Deed complete and requiring a drink, not admitting this to be the end result of tension, he rode the streets to Hôtel Saviuer. Now ensconced in the card room with his friend, he gazed across the small table, lifted his goblet to his mouth, sipped and replaced it; then, gazing at his hand of cards, swept them all together. "Pass! Your deal, Trifane..."

Taking up the cards Raoul commenced shuffling, passing no comment on the slight tension within his friend. "All well with Anton, *mon ami*?"

"Exceedingly well... I am glad *mon père* trusts him... otherwise..."

"But that is the nature of the beast these days, *mon ami*." Raoul's tone was gentle. "And risk must increase as time goes on... especially if Louis does not retain leadership of the Assembly! What think you?"

"Who knows? The *one chambre* victory of the *Commons* is a bad business: intimidation during voting shall swing many to cross the floor."

"But *mon ami*, 'tis political liberty, not so?" drawled Raoul.

Emile snorted. "Liberty! The agitation in Paris is strengthening. The Gendarmes could not get even *near* the *Palais-Royal* the other day. The government, now powerless to maintain order, can no longer affect their duties!"

"The turmoil does however give us a little time; heard from Calonne?" murmured Raoul.

Emile rose, moved to the door, opened it swiftly and peered out. Closing it again, he returned to his chair with a grim smile. "Never thought to see the day! As to Calonne, his man called yesterday; *Compagne des Indes* be structured in such a way that ensures as much safety as can be expected *mon ami*. You are going to run with it?"

"In the name of a deceased employee: you will have taken equal care of course." Raoul placed a card gently on the table.

"Now, how did you do that?" Emile's face assumed a mock stunned expression at the trump card; then he grinned, the relaxing effects of the liquor now taking effect. "Let us hope these plans triumph as easily!"

"Nothing is easy; or completely safe, *mon ami*!"

"*Mon père* would agree with you! Now *he* moves quietly among the bourgeoisie, of late. Melting pot for information and contacts, but I worry—where lie their loyalties?"

"On the fence: hoping for a leg up but ready to fall; especially now that the *Palais-Royale* demagogues are demanding complete abolition of nobility."

"That's so, is it?"

Raoul grinned. "Cannot be allowed of course."

"Never." Emile glanced at the crossed swords on the wall above the cavernous fireplace. "What *would* the ancestors say?"

"So that's the chilly wind I feel down my spine these days."

Emile chuckled, then frowned thoughtfully. "They must not succeed, of course, but counter measure requires serious planning."

Raoul picked up his new hand of cards and glanced at it. "The success of this rebellion rests upon as much certainty as does this hand of mine," he replied thoughtfully. "And so does a counter-rebellion, but one must take a gamble. Louis' Swiss and German troops, however, quartered in and around Paris and Versailles, are also about as reliable as this pack of cards. The city is edgy, *mon ami*."

"Edgy? The city has been rigid, with starting eyes, for months now."

"Does de Quatreaux say what Necker is up to?"

Emile frowned. "Opposed to any intimidation of the Assembly, but has no influence with the king. Oh, Louis listens but it is the Queen that he tends. 'Toinette, and of course Artois and Provence, detest Necker, always have, don't blame 'em... and keep him much in the dark. *They* want the Assembly to be dissolved, to bring them to heel. But Necker argues against."

"It never does work. But Necker is a good finance minister and is correct: Louis cannot do it now; he agreed to the one chamber: creating their National Assembly for them..."

"By armed force," Emile smiled gently.

"Oh! Then gird the loins for insurrection."

"Louis has it covered, he thinks: relies on the troops' presence to overawe the capital but will not resolve to force unless it be in self-defence. You know how his mind works; cannot see civilians attacked: cannot yet see the new National Guard as military."

"He can no longer afford his nice ethics and sensitivity," said Raoul, "and his Royal Troops are increasing the fear and excitement instead."

"Remains only for armed occupation of the town: and a proclamation of martial law."

"Angelique is still at Versailles?" It was pronounced casually but Emile was not fooled.

"Oh yes, but coming home on the morrow."

"Get her to Quatreaux, *mon ami*."

Emile frowned, "You think so? Be it any safer than here? I think it doubtful."

Raoul frowned. "Would she go?"

"Not while Lareaux is in town."

Raoul glanced sharply at him and Emile wanted to tease but he added instead, "Not for the reasons that spring to mind; believe me... thinks she is onto something!"

"I would not believe such bad taste in her," he replied lazily. "But she may be capable of underestimating him: pull the head of the family hierarchy and send her."

Emile laughed. "You think she would acquiesce? You do not know my sister!"

Raoul frowned. "I am serious. Use your authority, while de Quatreaux is out of town, and send her away; at least warn her off Lareaux."

"Ah but 'tis obvious you have not ever had words with her," chuckled Emile. "*I* have witnessed her backed up like an unbroken filly, *without* the trembling of flanks and *that* against our *père*. Besides, he is returned, you know, last eve. And as to Lareaux...," Emile trailed off and Raoul glanced at him with penetrating eyes but said no more.

Emile lifted his head suddenly at the sound of footsteps along the gallery, cocked an eyebrow at Raoul but had time only to murmur, "Speak of the devil!" and rise, as did Raoul, on the entrance of de Quatreaux.

"Ah, there you are, Emile, Trifane," nodded de Quatreaux, accepting their bows; then, glancing at the table, he advanced to the bell-pull and gave it a tug.

"Streets still erupting, Seigneur?" asked Raoul.

"Yes, growing worse by the hour. Are they happy now that they have what they want? But of course not, for they shall now worry over the loss of what they have newly gained."

"And they have certainly gained, have they not?"

"Oh assuredly; by default, of course, but matters not—they have gained their six hundred deputies, who claimed to monopolize the authority of the State, without waiting for the co-operation of the other orders, or the consent of the king. They have turned their decrees into the law of the land, without proper debate or vote. They have abolished taxes and then re-imposed them, widely. They have assumed for themselves the privilege of the Orders and the prerogatives of the crown. They have placed themselves above the law and the constitution; that they now claim. This rabble: couched in Bourgeoisie terms, now represents twenty-five million people. Ah Siffred," he finished as that man entered the room.

Siffred bowed and waited politely.

"A small collation, Siffred, if you please: I must go out again almost immediately but missed my breakfast *and* my lunch. Oh, and some more wine," glancing at the carafe.

"Very good, Monseigneur," replied Siffred.

"So, Monsieur... thrashing it out today in our new National Assembly?" asked Raoul.

"Oh, make no mistake: we do have some brain power there. Our hero, Mirabeau, has a brain that would stand out against a thousand better-educated men. 'Tis unfortunate that that brain be warped, but fortunate that his policies be moderate: now that he walks with the *Commons*. We had Sieyès, with his passion for an ideal state, but with no interest in history to guide him. That of course be no obstacle for from the past there be few good examples, but he could take on the copious warnings there." He frowned. "The bubbling volcano reaches the brim! The abolition of hereditary nobility is their next target."

"Never!" exclaimed Emile. "You cannot simply wipe out whole strata of people."

"A new legislation; one of liquidation of the aristocracy, Monsieur?" asked Raoul.

"I hear so. We must be reduced to dust. They do not understand, apparently, that they cannot stamp out the indefinable with their decrees and laws. We shall of course live and die as gentlemen, no matter what they do, how they pauperise us."

"And they won't be doing that, if I can help it!" murmured Raoul.

"I perceive something serious happened today, *Mon père*," said Emile suddenly.

"Agitation for the king to withdraw his troops: they fear violence against them."

"But he refused, of course?" asked Raoul.

"That he did and went one step further—he fired Necker." De Quatreaux's face was bland and Emile whistled softly; he had seen that look but once or twice.

"And ordered him to leave the country, immediately." This time he poured himself more wine. "The reaction was violent. It was felt that only the presence of Necker in the council gave them security: from force being employed by the king against them and the capital." He paused a moment, frowning. "Without a strong centre of gravity: ministers with enough strength to support the crown as well as the people... this is going to dissolve into chaos."

Raoul stared out the window at the flaring street lamp, listening to the sounds of the still milling crowds though it grew late. "Monseigneur; is your daughter to stay in Paris?"

"No, I am sending her, first to the château and then, mayhap, to England."

Emile sat up suddenly. "She has agreed to *go*?"

De Quatreaux's brows lifted a fraction in a way that his offspring knew well and Emile grinned and sank back into his chair. "Pardon, Monseigneur," he murmured softly.

Raoul glanced at the Comte. "Have you, er, informed her, Monsieur?"

"No, I shall do so when she arrives on the morrow."

But the morrow saw the Comte travelling post-haste to Versailles following an urgent message from that court.

Upon entering the king's chamber, de Quatreaux saw before him Montmorin and Saint Priest, which did not surprise him; but the presence of Mirabeau did. Danton, a young, as yet unknown lawyer, was also present. His mind worked swiftly: if Louis drew these two wily and mildly unsavoury characters into his survival plans the dangers would increase tenfold. Mirabeau played a double game: championing the people, as his secret funds were administered in the king's interests. He also acted as spy for England. He was, however, the most able statesman and his policies of moderation invaluable: in the face of threatening democracy. Danton, on the other hand, owned no distaste of bribes, but this rested not upon loyalty to the crown but upon pure avarice. He hated all of the first two Estates but had no problem taking their money. Jean-Pierre presented his polite court face to this assemblage: these two before him were useful only in that very thing: usage; usage in the interests of the king. He gazed again: willing to be corrected in his assumptions but saw no proof to revise his opinion.

# CHAPTER EIGHT

## The Chaos Begins

The Quatreaux carriage rumbled over the relatively smooth road from Versailles, holding to an admiral speed. A little rocking occurred but not enough to cause the passenger to wake and grasp the broad loop of leather strap swinging above her left shoulder. She remained leaning back against the satin squabs of pale blue, eyes closed, dozing lightly; sliding gently some inch or so, to the left then right then back again. This motion continued for some time. It was however not a peaceful doze, for the image of Lareaux entered her mind and drifted there. She tried, in weak fashion, to chase him away, but the edge of the deep-sleep abyss was too close; so he remained there drifting, smiling, before her. Two things caused her to suddenly start and sit bolt upright. One: the sudden passage from the smooth, Versailles road to the rough Parisian section. The other: Lareaux' voice, 'but what must one *do*; on meeting the man who killed one's *père!*' She shivered: how easy was revenge these days; it required only a lantern, a rope.

The crowds upon the roads thickened as they approached inner Paris, until the carriage slowed to walking pace and then ceased to move altogether. Angelique leaned out of the window, to view the bottleneck of traffic ahead as her coachman shouted down to her.

"Mademoiselle, I do not know what goes forward but up ahead, they pull up the paving stones. We cannot move. I believe that it be prudent for us to go round, to our left. We shall end close to *Palais-Royal*... not good... but 'twill then be but a minute to home!"

"Very well then, do so, Joubeau. We can but do what appears prudent. Go!"

But Joubeau had not reckoned with the rumour-mill causing, it seemed, the entire population of Paris to erupt into the streets; for the news of Necker's dismissal had reached the people that morning. It called for another two hours to move a quarter of a mile through the noisy, milling mass of excited, semi-rioting people, swelling the normal human and equine congestion. Donkey carts, laden for the markets, added to the packed confusion, jostling private and public carriages. Beggars and newsvendors, flower vendors, lamp cleaners, pedlars and water-sellers, added to the crush. An early morning coffee-seller squeezed past the carriage, the aroma from his urn tantalizing Angelique.

The closer to the *Palais-Royal* the de Quatreaux vehicle moved, the noisier and more tumultuous the scene. The dwellers of the narrow tiny attics and lodgings, forced by lack of space within these to eat within the cafes here, vied for tables. Here too were added the clerks, shopkeepers, traders and small-profession men, the artists, students, journalists and lawyers. Every type of man was represented, except for the nobility.

Uneasy troops, of the Swiss and German Guards, patrolled in and around the milling crowds. Nervous equine traffic began to sidle and rear up, infecting the immediate carriage horses. Plunging within their traces, these then caused the de Quatreaux carriage behind them, to come to another standstill. Angelique leaned out again, in time to see a small child dashing in and out of the traffic, casting terrified glances over his shoulder. Saw him trip on a suddenly outthrust foot to stop him, fall, catapult forward and roll beneath those plunging hooves.

Flinging the door open and leaping to the ground, furious with the owner of the foot, she flew to the horses' heads, grabbing and holding strongly. The postboy on the other side, having brought his leader to a stand now, dived among the hooves and pulled the boy free.

"Oh *Mon Dieu*... is he hurt?" asked Angelique as she knelt now on the ground beside him, feeling for a pulse and lifting back an eyelid. The boy lay limp, very white and very odorous, owning matchstick limbs, dressed in the least rags as a human could and remain decent: almost. She glanced at the post-boy who stood, cap in hand gnawing upon his lower lip, gazing nervously around at the gathering crowd.

"You should leave him now, Madame, 'tis but a beggar child!" And with this he swung away to sprint after his vehicle, now turning down a crowded side street. The crowd swelled as a strong tide around the Comte's vehicle, shouting and berating Joubeau for holding up the traffic, forced him on.

"Mademoiselle: come! Leave him!" shouted Joubeau frantically, as the density of people thickened, inching by sheer human wave of force, his vehicle on down the street.

"Leave him?" She gazed at the boy in her arms now. "But of course we cannot leave him..."

Her speech was cut short by the high pitched wailing of a woman pushing her way through the crowd. "This is what we must expect from the likes of them, do you not see, people! You!" A dirt-stained finger pointed: "You have killed him!"

"But no, Madame, 'twas not my vehicle, nor even *any* vehicle's fault, but never mind that, the boy needs a doctor. Please send for one!"

"Then who to blame... tell me that! I see no other," shouted the woman. "*Un docteur?* The boy be *dead*, what need *le docteur*? Huh? Tell me that? To bribe him to say the boy be alive, till your escape? Oh, I know the likes of thee, *Madame*! Your kind wants us all dead but we shall see... we shall see just who ends up dead: *that* we will!"

"Oh, do be *quiet* woman!"

The voice came from behind her as Angelique, chaffing the boy's hands and brushing back his filthy hair, witnessed his recovery, eyelids fluttering then lifting fully to gaze at her in vague suspicion.

"Come woman," said the man now to Angelique's accuser, "the boy is not dead." Dropping then to his knee beside Angelique, his face was grim as he glanced at her.

He took the boy's pulse, felt for breakage of limbs and spoke to him kindly, "Do you hurt anywhere?"

"No."

"Very well, sit up now and we shall see how the head feels, eh... that's it... now..." But before he could speak further another woman, staring suspiciously at Angelique, moved in; inciting the crowd, waving them forward.

"You have brought him back to life!" cried the woman.

"No, no," Angelique replied laughing, "I have not that power. He was but faint."

The woman stared, hands on hips, "But no, he did not breathe! I saw, did not you... and you? And you?"

By now the crowd had closed in, presenting a thick wall of solid humanity and the stranger glanced across the boy to Angelique. "We best get out of here—you have just signed your death warrant."

"But what nonsense, Monsieur," she replied, startled and trying not to hear the muttering growl of the crowd.

He glanced pointedly at the child leaning back in her arms. "That you killed a child be enough, but to bring him back to life? A miracle: one step from witchcraft." A faint smile lifted the corners of his severe mouth. "Do not for the love of God offer recipes for the enhancement of the child's recovery!"

"'Eye of newt and toe of frog, adder's fork and blind... er, something's sting'... I forget the rest, but how ridiculous, Monsieur. We are not dwelling in the middle ages."

"Sometimes I wonder," he muttered. "But for now, Mademoiselle..."

He lifted the boy to his feet and the urchin swayed for a moment and then, remembering his angry pursuer, suddenly took to his heels, and disappeared into the crowd, ducking and weaving out of sight. But for Angelique, escape was not to be so easy.

"How came you here, Mademoiselle? Why have you no escort?"

"Oh but I have. My..." She paused in astonishment as she took in the disappearing carriage; forced around a corner some hundred yards from them, the only visible portion, the upper half, appearing to float upon a sea of humanity. She laughed, uncertainly, "Monsieur, it seems that I must hurry to catch my vehicle!"

"Not so fast," shouted a bystander. "For 'tis a witch that we have here I do believe!"

"A witch: a witch!"

"A rope: a rope!"

"Hang the witch! Hang the witch!"

The crowd thickened to a solid wall and she realized with horror that this was how it happened, how the illiterate and deeply superstitious lived their lives. She glanced uneasily at her mentor and then turned to face them. "Nonsense, the boy was but stunned by his fall." Her voice strong, her eyes holding theirs, she shoved her trembling hands within the folds of her skirt.

"Is this the way you repay a kindness?" asked her mentor now, standing, hands on hips, turning slowly and eyeing the solid mass of people. But they were suddenly sullen.

"Clear the way," he continued sternly. "Have you no manners at all? Do you wish to appear undeserving of your new status? And we are *all one* now, remember, this be what you wanted! Now you have it! Let us pass, the lady is a friend of mine; equal to you and I. Come Mademoiselle." With this her new benefactor guided her, sometimes pushing and sometimes pulling her through the reluctantly parting crowd, the darkling glances and muttered threats following them as they made tortuously to the corner. They found no sign of the carriage. The man; youngish, of moderate height and neat dress, paused and looked down at her.

"Well Mademoiselle, seems that I must find you alternative transport."

"Surely a carriage with a crest would be treated with respect?"

"Where have you been living? Versailles?"

She opened her mouth to confirm this, then realized the satire. "Why so, Monsieur?"

"Only one living such a false and utterly protected life could say such a thing; the crests shall soon be painted over on all carriages of the nobility!  But for now... come down here," leading her down a narrow, mired alleyway, a little thinner of people, winding and twisting until it finally projected onto the side-walks of *Palais-Royal*.

"My name by the way is Henri-Marie Pontisqieu."

"*Enchantée Monsieur*; I am Angelique Vermont. I am exceedingly grateful for your swift assistance; did never require a doctor as urgently as I did back there."

"It is nothing.  And I am not a doctor but a lawyer. However, right now you need to await somewhere safe while I find a *pots-de-chambre*."

"Oh! There *be* such a place, here?" She glanced up the street at the again milling crowd but this time they seemed intent upon surging in the direction of the *Palais-Royal*.

"I know the owner of a café just here and you shall be safe for, believe me, no one of the nobility or indeed the police even, can enter this section of the town, and your attire is rather distinctive." He propelled her into a shop entrance and presented her to the curious proprietor.

"Jean-Rouberte, please look after this young lady, until I return. It is all bedlam out there and I need to track down a *pots-de-chambre*. Keep her safe."

"But assuredly," replied Jean-Rouberte, bowing low to Angelique. "This way if you please Mademoiselle. You are in need of the very strong coffee I not doubt; Marie shall bring it." So saying, he led her through a winding passageway, up a short flight of narrow stairs and into a pleasantly furnished room overlooking the courtyard.

"Thank you Monsieur, you are very kind."

He smiled. "You're welcome." He bowed and hurried away; business promised to be the best ever today, with the *Palais-Royal* gardens and meeting rooms filling already, normally for the speeches and debates of The Third, but today civil war sat upon the edge of everyone's lips.

Angelique poured from the steaming jug and sipped the strong coffee, moving to the window as she heard bouts of cheering rising on that warm summer morning. The cafes and meeting places were open to the air, spilling onto the sidewalk and courtyards and as she watched, a young man leapt onto a table and waved his arms.

"*Citizens*! Are we going to tolerate this?" he shouted. "No! No! No! *Listen* to me; the troops are advancing at this very moment, they say. Our glorious triumph, this Glorious Revolution shall be suppressed in blood! As always! Do we allow it? No, I say again, no! We must fight. We must obtain arms, good people!"

A voice lifted above the mayhem: "But where are they stored?"

"At the Bastille: that is where!" cried another.

"They have driven Necker from office, citizens! Our only insurance against '*them*'! They are preparing for martial law! We shall be back where we were, citizens! Do we bow to them yet again? Do we allow them to feed off tables of plenty while we starve? Do we continue to doff our caps, tug our forelocks, while only three day's supply of baker's flour remains in this city? Do we allow it?" shouted another from a chair atop a table. Angelique stared in horror, realizing that her newfound friend had been correct about Versailles; they had no idea.

At that moment another leapt to a tabletop shouting, "To arms! To arms! We must fight them to the end! We must be rid of them forever! To the gunsmiths, to the armoury! Kill them all; kill them all till not a one be left... to the Carthusian!"

"No, no, no my friends, there is none left there, or the Arsenal. It has all been transferred to the Hôtel de Ville!"

"To the Hôtel de Ville!"

It was however not these bloodthirsty men that shook Angelique but the sight of another, sitting at a table, long legs stretched out before him and crossed at the ankles, casually sipping coffee as he watched and listened, dressed in sober black, neat as a pin, it was true, but nothing to advertise that he be nobility. In fact his cloak, hanging over his chair-back, was quite shabby. As she gazed he glanced upwards suddenly. There was no warning, his glance so lightning swift that it removed any chance of withdrawal from that window and Angelique's eyes met those of Raoul Trifane. His widened a fraction; then, looking around casually after some few seconds, he rose indolently, spoke a casual word to those nearest, a jest to others, and sauntered away and across the street. He moved beyond her sight but she had no doubt that within minutes she would be confronted by him. She finished her coffee in a gulp, working hard to control her shaking hands. Suffering now the full impact of what had almost happened, heightened by the fact that she did not know of Jouberte's fate in that milling crowd, her entire insides shook. She turned to face the door as she heard the firm, decisive steps there.

The door opened and Raoul stood a moment, hand on the doorknob, gazing at her with those penetrating grey eyes that could sparkle suddenly with laughter, black brows faintly lifted. "So, it *is* you after all. Wondered for but a moment whether it was a vision given me." His mouth lifted slightly at the corners. "Or a little too much of your *père's* excellent burgundy last night. Emile you know... played deep, but we both survived." He moved into the room and closed the door, then wandered casually over to the window. There was, however, nothing casual about his demeanour as he gazed down for a minute into the scene below: then turned to look at her, his expression devoid of the preceding grimness.

"You wait an explanation, Monsieur?"

"But no. 'Tis no business of mine." The eyes sparkled: then he took a step closer. "But if we are to get you home safely," motioning to the streets below, "we must make haste. You have not your carriage hidden away somewhere, I suppose?"

"Monseigneur, you may full well laugh but I am not such a ninny-hammer that I wander the streets alone. Wander them at *all*. My carriage was hijacked. But do not concern yourself at all," she concluded acidly, "I have help: Monsieur Pontisqieu is at this moment acquiring for me a *pots de chambre.* "

"Ah! Monsieur Pontisqieu...*and a pots-de-chambre*! Then of course all is well." His eyes laughed still, but she detected an undeniable gleam of understanding. "Madem..."

The door opened suddenly to admit that very being. "Mademoiselle... ah, bonjour Monsieur," he said, then bowing to Raoul, "My name is Pontisqieu."

"Ah yes, Pontisqieu... Saviveur. How do you do?" bowing politely to Henri-Marie, then in sudden recognition, "but we have met, I think: at the Sorbonne? Yes, yes, those dreadfully convoluted lectures on merchant law origins! However of prime importance," glancing toward the window, as the noisy rioters below almost drowned their conversation, "is that of conveying Mademoiselle to her home. Did you manage to acquire the *pots de chambre* by any chance?"

"That I did, but it waits at the end of the street; there is no possibility of getting it any closer. The crowds are so dense one could walk across them with no danger of falling through: as I have witnessed flock-dogs do on tightly herded sheep, in the country..."

"Is there a difference?" murmured Raoul.

"And so I believe that this also be of a necessity, Mademoiselle," Pontisqieu ended, lips twitching; and holding out the summer-weight cloak of inferior quality, to Angelique. Understanding, she took it and draped it around her shoulders, suppressing an expression of distaste at the stale odour rising from its voluminous folds. Raoul moved behind her and adjusted it to her comfort, then looked at Henri-Marie.

"My thanks, Monsieur: I shall see my friend's daughter home now."

Angelique turned to her rescuer, "But Monsieur, I cannot leave it there; I owe you my life; that is certain!"

"Not at all, Mademoiselle," he replied quickly, "But we must move."

"I have not your direction Pontisqieu," said Raoul, "but shall make a point of finding you before the week is out, somewhere down there." He waved to the street below.

"Absolutely; but now best be gone," Pontisqieu paused, "and I do believe that we shall require the both of us."

At this Raoul glanced down into the street at the assembled crowds there, to hear more rousing speeches: now against the tyranny of the monarchy and nobility and denouncing the precautionary troops as impending destruction of the new National Assembly.

"Citizens! They will stop at nothing; they are plotting a massacre of patriots! This city is ringed with Royal Troops! See, they come."

"They come! They come! The Royal Troops come!"

Witnessing the failing attempt at crowd control by the German guards, Raoul's face grew grim but he said lightly, "Ah yes... we shall indeed require the two of us: to get Mademoiselle through the 'sheep'!"

Following Monsieur Pontisqieu, they moved swiftly down the narrow stairs, along the passageway and out another exit into a short back alleyway and paused a moment.

Raoul, glancing at Henri-Marie, nodded in the direction of the soldiers and the furiously milling crowd. "I do hope my friend; that the *pots de chambre* is not through there?"

"Well...er...as I did mention, to get it any closer..."

"Ah. Well, looking at that lot, you have performed miracles. Come Mademoiselle," and with this he held out his hand, glancing down at her by his side as he spoke and then, laughing at her upturned face of pure scorn, "No, no... I do not for a moment imagine you to succumb to the vapours! But if we do not maintain strong contact in that lot out there we shall very soon be separated, make no mistake. And keep your head down as much as possible... that face of yours belongs not to the peasant cape you be wearing."

He pulled the hood over her head and tucked her glossy hair beneath its folds.

"Oh... thankyou." She grabbed the loose material at her throat, to hold it tightly in place, with one hand. She took his with the other and thus they emerged into the maelstrom.

The hand to which she clung during the next fifteen minutes turned out to be a very necessary adjunct to survival. It wasn't until much later that she recalled the comfort provided by its very strength and warmth, for a more terrifying fifteen minutes she had not experienced. And somewhere in the future she would also recall that those hands; long, slender and elegant, had been the very first thing she had noticed about him, across the luncheon table at the Christmas Hunt. The crowds now presented with a mass strength unknown to her; as she was pulled and pushed by her escorts through the maelstrom.

The seething masses fell about as two young men dragged a German Cavalry man from his horse and began beating him. The Cavalry, fruitlessly attempting to rescue him, charged through a procession carrying a bust of Necker before them. Speakers fell from their tabletops, mid-speech rallying and were trampled underfoot as the crowd stampeded. The violence increased. A young man, wild and euphoric, sprang at a soldier, wrestled him to the ground and killed him with a pike. As Angelique stared, his head was sliced off and stuck on the end of another pike. She gasped, her grip tightening on Trifane's hand. He glanced down and then followed her gaze. With a savage oath under-breath, he hauled her fiercely around, pulling her face against his chest.

"Mademoiselle... come... think of nothing but survival! Hear me! Come, this way!"

The scene quickly converted to a wall of moving humanity, wild, cruel and insane. Only the need to continue through the seething bodies kept her focused beyond the rising bile in her throat. Cheers rose above the turmoil and another was attacked, and another. Guns were wrested from others, shots fired and bodies fell: of both soldiers and civilians. Angelique gazed in horror as it happened around her and knew that the troops would be blamed on the morrow for the deaths. However, it was not this that caused her horror but the fact that she was actually *glad* of the orators' misfortunes. The mistruths, the dishonesty, the twisted meaning of the works of the new philosophers, the total usage of class differences as portrayed in those rallying speeches she had heard, turned the people into what they were not. This riled her: converted her shocked mind to anger, to the degree of wanting to kill. Equally she wanted to kill those of the Nobility founding this unrest: to their own advantage. This was not a class war, or a rebellion of starving people, but an age-old situation that leant itself to the grasp of power; and the power-mongers were using promoted famine fears and class division as a very successful weapon. It had done so for the last year or more, slowly building their foundations for a rebellion until now 1789 had become the year of fearful anticipation from all sides. The nobility were now afraid for their rights, the king even, afraid of the building power of the Assembly, and the Third Estate were afraid of royal counter-attacks *and* loss of control of the mob. And that mob feared extermination: believing the pamphleteers. Paris was crowded with the unemployed, starving refugees and victims of agricultural and industrial crisis and these were told, and believed, that the nobility be plotting their extinction. Fear-based riots were erupting all across the country; with brigands looting and burning villages and châteaux. She had been correct in her statement at the château dinner party: 'if only the rumour mongers would cease; much disaster could be avoided.'

All of this flashed through her mind in but a second but she was suddenly ensured of her own feelings in a way that could not have evolved without this immediate experience: knew suddenly that there was no luxury of half-measures. A gasp of self-realization left her as she stumbled along. Something of this transferred itself to Raoul as he held her hand in an iron grip: the sudden convulsive tightening of her own, on this revelation sufficient for him to glance down at her. At that moment she looked up. He smiled grimly but the understanding in his eyes was sufficiently strong for her to recall much later.

She waited: the condemned but perhaps able to come about again. She glanced at her *père*, standing with back to the fireplace. His aura of perfect stillness of body and gaze, gave notice of the degree of his anger. This she recognized, but had not witnessed for a long time. She did not glance at Raoul; sure that his eyes would hold a glitter of amusement but here she misjudged him.

"Monsieur, I believe that your daughter has suffered much already. Mayhap…"

The Comte's voice was low and calm. "Seigneur Savieur, when I require your assistance to know what my daughter has or has not suffered, I shall approach you on the matter. That she has suffered an extreme indiscretion is evident."

Raoul rose from his chair. "Monsieur, then I feel that I must…"

"No. You be part of this now Trifane; nothing that I shall say to my daughter be of the least private." He turned to Angelique, who remained seated before him, her eyes downcast that he not see: for in them was expressed not shame or fear, but a fury that she had rarely felt so strongly, even in her tempestuous schoolroom days.

"*Monseigneur*, I could have done none other than that which I did. You yourself would not have watched a small child die beneath pounding hooves. If you could, then I know you not." Her voice was moderate, so too her demeanour, but her eyes flashed.

"What a man does and a woman *should* do originates from two different worlds! But to detour through the *Palais-Royal* café's... the most dangerous area of all Paris? The utter collapse of authority is universal and Joubeau knew that. All provinces have collapsed and townsfolk everywhere are arming themselves and seizing power. But here in Paris it is worst of all." He turned to Raoul suddenly. "I am in your debt, Saviour."

Raoul shook his head. "Monsieur, it was naught."

Angelique stared, suddenly recalling the moment of her first sight of him at the *Palais-Royal* debating grounds. There was a sound at the door and Siffred ushered in Joubeau. Angelique arose and advanced towards him. "Joubeau! You are *safe*: and the grooms?"

"Ah yes Madame, but 'tis yonself that I be grateful to see."

He ceased speaking as de Quatreaux advanced. "Joubeau, my library."

The Comte's controlled anger silenced all as he led the way and Angelique was left standing staring at the closed door, at the mercy of Raoul's penetrating gaze.

"Do not distress thyself, *mon enfant*."

The gentle voice was almost the undoing of her. She turned away and moved toward the window to gaze out there for a moment. "I do have you to thank also. What, Seigneur Trifane... what has it all come to?"

"To a time of instability, but we shall come about."

She turned. "Do not treat me as a bird-witted female!" Her voice then faltered. "It is that we do not know the whole and it seems that *mon père* does; but for me: 'tis all darkness!"

"He protects you... because..." He paused, searching for words.

"If I know nothing and am arrested then I be safe? But I *could* not be arrested! What possible reason could they find?"

"It requires no reason: they behave as children at this time. The more to the point, you shall appear innocent, the one thing that may save you."

"Innocent of what crime, save me from what? Whom? What is he up to?"

He smiled. "You can be sure that it will be for king and country... and family."

"But what is he..." she gave him a penetrating look, "all three of you...planning?"

"Ah, do not be asking me now. One day," he shrugged and moved to the window, standing alongside her now as they both stood gazing down into the riotous street scene seething below. She felt his strength there beside her and experienced an unruly desire to lean against him. Startled, she reined in her ill-disciplined emotions, colour flooding her cheeks suddenly.

♣

Siffred stood in the wide gallery glancing about him for spying staff but remained the only occupant. He strained to hear the snippets of dialogue through the closed door:

"Hijacked?"

"Yes Sire, I could but try to hold the horses but they were too strong: the crowd Sire... we were forced down the street. I called to the Mademoiselle to come but she be occupied with the scrap Sire, none of us could do a thing and there was the horses and the carriage to consider."

"Your concern for our property is commendable Joubeau but be not the *lives* of this family the more important? I begin to see that you also feared for *your* life?"

Joubeau stared woodenly at the floor. "Well Monsieur, that too, a little I do confess: for though I be a-knowing that to you, concern for one's own life be of the utmost contemptible, in *my* family Sire, I needs to provide... whereas in your's there be provision should you er... well never mind. But I had no time to consider very much. I feared for Madame and I be of no use to her a-decorating the lanterne, Monseigneur... and as to the carriage... I *had* to defend it, Sire... without it I could never get her home again." He waited his dismissal.

The Comte gazed at him a moment, then nodded. "I stand corrected... you are right of course... and the grooms?"

"Well, I tried to send one back to her, Monsieur, but they be not the brightest candles in the branch. And their livery plastering them as turncoats, they were soon within a strong arm-lock of the biggest, meanest men that I have ever witnessed Monsieur!"

The Comte paused, glanced to the window and the sounds coming from there. "Who be behind this particular plot to riot, Joubeau? Who really leads them out there?"

"I know not but I can tell you that the next days afore us be right dangerous. They were a pullin' up the paving stones and building barricades... and looking right ugly toward *us* Monsieur. That is why I did what I did an' went the long way round, though it is through the *Palais-Royal* Sire. An' there was a lot more pikes than *I* ever saw in the city. An' I heard tell that the gunsmiths are a bein' ransacked."

"Did you now," responded Vermont grimly, then, "Your family Joubeau, they be safe in all this?" He smiled grimly at the look of amazement. "Oh yes, I do think of more than my immediate family sometimes."

"But yes Sire, they are well out of it at the moment, thank you."

"But you know there will come a time of choice; what then?"

"I do not know Monsieur."

"I thank you for your frankness. Your own come first of course, that be true of all of us. However, cut the throats of *my* family in the middle of the night and I shall hunt you down to the very edges of the world."

"Sire, how could you think such a thing?"

Shock and genuine horror showed upon Joubeau's face and the Comte was satisfied.

"I overheard two servants talking. Oh not of the house of de Quatreaux, be sure of that but 'twas said that the difficulty of killing members of a family known to one for many years, could be overcome by the servants of each house going to another *unknown* house, to perform this duty. That way no one being guilty of treachery to said household. I must say that I found it ingenious: diabolical, simple, but ingenious."

"Yes Sire," replied Joubeau faintly and again the Comte was satisfied: as far as he may.

♣

Lafayette barely heard his visitor's agitated voice as he gazed intently into the street below: seething with a roused rabble, giving proof to a roused nation. He frowned thoughtfully: they required harnessing, now, before all mayhem erupted.

His visitor's voice finally penetrated. "But why does the king not move to suppress this insurrection? I cannot believe it!"

The Marquis de La Fayette gazed at his visitor and smiled grimly. "He knows not how. It is as simple as that. To suppress that lot," he waved a hand toward the streets below the window, "he must give the order for attack; and Our Monarch cannot sanction bloodshed against his own people. He does not inherit his ancestors' ability to spill blood! In war, no problem, but that of Frenchmen and civilians he cannot face."

"He cannot recognize *traitors*? This is treachery, *mon ami*!"

"After yesterday's debacle, he knows that his troops are not loyal. And his dismissal of Necker is the catalyst to this new upheaval; that and the royal regiments surrounding Paris."

"Ah yes. He who controls Paris controls France!"

"But *Paris* is still to be won. Versailles, the seat of the king, has been won with the successful battle for the new Assembly. But no stroke for the Assembly can be decisive until *Paris* is disarmed of royal troops. To rid it of the king's troops be their aim. But in the main: they are screaming for the return of Necker."

"Louis should never have dismissed him! You are not making yourself available?"

Lafayette glanced at him and then down into the street once more, "To the Throne? I have offered but I am not trusted in that household *mon ami*! The queen is the more against me I know but Louis will never go against her. Even in those matters of state in which she can have no proper understanding at all."

His visitor smiled. "Being female? Or being Austrian?"

"Both!" Lafayette's smile was derisive.

His visitor stared into the street. "So they are planning a complete Revolution."

"To complete the *coup d'é-tat* that they began: with the calling of the National Assembly in the king's absence. Now they want military control; as well as that of the Assembly. The Revolution began long ago; but none believed it possible and so it arrived quietly. No Revolution *begins* with the fanfare of fifes and drums. *That* is the grand finale."

"How final are they going to *make* it? The streets have been in uproar for two days now."

Lafayette frowned. "Unfortunately the precautionary 25,000 troops of Louis' give an impression of preparation for civil war."

"But isn't that what it *is*?"

Lafayette sighed. "Whatever it is, the presence of the troops are not working as a deterrent. And I am told that officers are afraid to act without authorization and cannot trust their men; desertion is rife. The majority of the aristocratic officers, even, have already thrown in their commission and gone over to the exiles in Triers and Coblenz. And the French Guard has gone over in a body to the people. They are building barricades with paving stones. Pike makers are making a killing, as are the gunsmiths. Those not willing to sell have their shops raided, along with military storehouses: enough muskets and powder in the streets now to blow away much of Paris."

"'Tis madness that we face: shall be wholesale slaughter!"

"Which is why I am going to harness a national guard of some sort," replied Lafayette. "They need a leader to avoid the bloodshed that you so ably predict. The recruitment begins as we speak, at the Hôtel de Ville."

"Ah! I thought as much. The Bastille does not worry thee *mon ami*?"

"But I am actually endeavouring to *save* the Monarchy! Not destroy it."

"By harnessing a ready made, fired up army of the people; and thee a staunch supporter of the American War of *Independence*? Even financed your own army to assist?"

Lafayette laughed suddenly. "None would believe I suppose that, for *France*, I firmly believe in a two-chamber Assembly and a monarchical constitution!"

"They would have difficulty...'tis true!"

"Come; to the Hôtel de Ville: let us see what can be salvaged." He led the way out of his house and into the turbulence below.

His friend, striding beside him, wondered; Lafayette had grown bored, following his return from America, but this drive within him evolved from deeper depths than that. He craved attention, admiration, and adoration; was at his best glorying in leadership within battle. To harness a wild mob and tame it into order would bring satisfaction: but gratitude from the king? No: Lafayette was a lot of things but not naïve.

# CHAPTER NINE

## Mayhem

"To the armouries!  To the gunsmiths!!"

"To arms! To Arms! Join the peoples' army!"

"To the French Guard! Join the French Guard!"

"What? Are ye mad… *slaughter* the French Guard! That's what!"

"No, no, no, my friends… they are gone over to the people of this last half hour!"

The voices of the rabble rose on the evening air, the crush of seething humanity frightening to perceive; and dotted above the heads bobbed placards, nailed to poles.

"Hôtel de Ville! *There* goes on the recruitment. Hôtel de Ville!"

"Come. We need every man and every woman… the king plans to crush us!"

"The troops surround us!"

Watching from a window, Emile smiled grimly, "Paris be frozen in fear now, *mon ami*!"

Raoul crossed the floor to stand beside him. "From two opposite perspectives, I think! Of the people: that of an armed occupation of the town and the declaration of martial law. Of the crown: a rising of the populace, ending in dissolution of all authority! I wonder who is the more nervous of the two."

"The crown must have the edge, I think: for the peoples' army will not hesitate! Louis, on the other hand, will not fire on the people; but the *canaille*; they do not know that!"

Raoul, brows raised, looked at Emile. "Someone should convince them!"

"Not possible!"

"Louis must be warned."

Emile grinned. "I'm up for it! Toss?" He paused. "But first we need more information."

"And we need each other in that maelstrom out there: to the de Ville."

The two were soon melting into the crowds, their plain-black cloaks crumpled and muddied along the hems, blending with the sans-culottes as they moved with the flow.

Recruited by the hour, the deserters and the roused rabble youth of the city joined the 3600 French Guard, now gone over to the people.  From these milling, leaderless masses, during the following night and day, Lafayette, now elected as Colonel,

89

supervised the enrolment. Thus was born the military force of the people: the new National Guard.

During this time, a wild orgy of indiscriminate violence and pillage assaulted the city. Fires flared: excise barriers, at each entry into the city, burned. The prisons were stormed and opened. Soon a scene of total carnage leant new horror to those narrow, mired, twisting streets deeply shadowed by their overhanging tenement houses. No authority existed and none obeyed simple human decency.

The deputies assembled at the Hôtel de Ville tried what authority they could, within the raging mob, on imminent peril to their own lives. Lafayette paused a moment, within his own military construction, to appeal to the deputies of The Third: to organize a militia force within each of their own sixty districts of Paris. Hopefully this would throw some control over the violent insurrection. Time, however, was against them, for any orderly action to come of this. As waves of panic swept the Paris streets, people rushed to arms: with anything that could be grabbed. Soon a melting cauldron of fear, fury, excitement and elation bubbled over as the driving force that raged through the night. Noise, flames and smoke dominated the city and above it all rang the incessant tocsins.

Emile and Raoul returned, with difficulty, to Rue St Honoré, with no real backing to their fears, except for an apparent building of a fear-driven peoples' army. This knowledge they sent to the court via a fast and trusted courier.

Emile watched him ride off and turned to Raoul. "*Mon ami*, 'tis still not enough to convince our monarch! Mayhap one of us should have been the messenger."

"No...we need to follow their moves. They go to the *Invalides*, for arms no doubt, but their plan? We need that."

"*Can* they plan?" muttered Emile as he moved behind Raoul into the street again and they melted into the tumultuous river of seething humanity.

Thus, in such violent manner, did Parisians pass the night, until the dawn of July 14 shuffled in, pushing before it the orange hue of still raging fires. 80,000 people now gathered at the *Invalides*, overwhelming the troops remaining there. Here they obtained a further 30,000 muskets and a number of cannons. Emile and Raoul consulted softly with each other, deciding knowledge of these weapons' destination was paramount, before they retreated.

The moment was right to fan the flames of insurrection. Faster than the fury of the fires, now spread the groundless rumours of Royal Troops on the move. The citizens' army, it was said, needed even more gunpowder and this, it was rumoured again, was kept at the Bastille. It was enough: the crowd swept forward as stampeding buffalo upon an African plain, driving with blind, unstoppable force, all before them.

"To the Bastille!"

"Take the Bastille!"

"Of course!" muttered Raoul to Emile, "The badge of tyranny."

A man nearby spun quickly, "What's that you say?"

Immediately he knew that it had not been the words, but the accent that had betrayed him. With the smooth teamwork of long association the two spun away and leapt for the alleyway on the left, vaulted a mule, aimed a swift, accurate kick at his underbelly and left their followers fighting over the braying, rearing animal and jerking cart.

"Stop them! Stop them! They are nobles!"

"A lynching! A lynching!"

A tide of humanity now surged down the alleyway. Leaping boxes, collapsing their stacks to hinder their assailants, they moved with a speed motivated by dire straits. Raoul, glancing behind, slowed a fraction to bend and pull the dagger from the sheath inside his knee boot. Entering a second and then third alley they were now totally lost, fearing the inevitable blind alley. The crowd were gaining, to the point of almost grasping them, until Raoul slashed at a clothesline stretched from one side to the other. The large, wet sheets collapsed over the followers. Emile and Raoul disappeared through an exit and melded once more into the massed people. Pushing and shoving in peasant manner, they moved with the tide towards the end of the street. To turn and make their way back was impossible on two counts: the strength of the tide could not be breached and the fact of their reverse direction would attract unwanted attention. After a further half hour of travelling in this manner, they managed to exit the dense crowd into a narrow side street.

"Me thinks that we will not be returned in time to warn Louis," Raoul said softly.

Emile grimaced. "Be a miracle if we return at all!"

The commander of the Bastille, the Marquis Bernard-Réne de Launay, had long since pulled up his drawbridges and made ready his defence. From here he watched the insurrection grow. His small garrison consisted of only thirty-two Swiss Guards and eighty-two old French soldiers, but he relied upon the fortress itself as defence enough.

The high, grey stonewalls and menacing towers of the Bastille fortress rose, as a great dark edifice, on Rue Saint-Antoine in the east end of Paris. Here it guarded the approach from the slums and wharves of the faubourg Saint-Antoine, over-looking the poorer, muddier area of the town, of rough paving, noisome *égout* and over-crowded tenements. For centuries now, enemies of the crown could be detained; by the simple issue of the *Lettres de Cachet*, here within this mighty, almost windowless representative of royal tyranny and oppression. De Launay knew that the anticipated attack upon them rested on this symbolism, rather than to free the few prisoners within. And the hatred of a nation could be quite a force to combat. But they were rabble; and his men those of military discipline: he felt no anxiety.

"What to do... *Mon Commandant*?" The nervous young man admired the toughness of character and spirit of the old school, but as far as he could see, they did not seem to comprehend the twists and turns of modern strategy and events.

"Worry not my boy, these walls be built five-foot thick; they and the double moat shall guard us against the assault of that ill-disciplined mob! They shall never get through."

"But moats have been crossed before, *Mon Commandant*."

"Ah: but the second moat and the unscaleable walls, now *there* lay their difficulties."

"But if they have strong weaponry?"

"This is an unruly mob, *Sergent*. They have no discipline, no leaders and no weaponry required to blow through these walls!"

The Marquis, however, had reckoned without the organized deserters of the old French Guard. First entered the deputies from the Hôtel de Ville, summoning him to surrender.

"I shall rather set fire to the powder magazines and blow the place to the skies! Over my dead body shall ye enter," replied de Launay and watched again the effect of his reply, as thousands streamed to the main entrance. Soon they surrounded the fortress. The population milled about, impeding the old French soldier as he cut the chain that held the drawbridge of the outer moat.

"Move away, will ye!"

"Well hurry old man! Hurry!"

They moved, a few feet, waiting with impatient urgency the fall of the chain. The chain finally clattered to the ground. A shout of triumph rent the air as the assailants rushed over the fallen drawbridge, only to be confronted by the second moat and incredibly high walls of the fortress. De Launay smiled grimly; then stiffened. The French guards pushed cannons before them. Operating behind a very effective smoke screen of carts of burning dung, they aimed at the second drawbridge. All their best efforts to force the passage of the moat were however frustrated by de Launay's troops.

Five hours of incessant musketry fire passed. Cannons sounded across the city.

"Load!"

"Fire!"

"Load!"

"Fire!"

And so it went, until a hundred of the assailants lay dead. The people, however, by sheer numbers, were the stronger and finally the last garrison standing compelled de Launay to surrender.

"*Mon Commandant*: we cannot resist longer! It is madness!"

He stared in astonishment. "You *mutiny*? Fire! Fire I say, fire!"

But his soldiers refused to longer resist. He swung around, pointing his firearm at them, fury and impotence battling supremacy. At this moment Hulin, an officer leading the French Guard newly gone over to the people, approached de Launay.

"*Mon Commandant*...surrender, please! To stop wholesale slaughter! A pardon and immunity for all," Hulin's voice was calm and reasoning.

Suppressed fury reddening his face, de Launay gazed at his remaining soldiers, then at the sea of humanity gone mad before him. He had however no choice. Accepting his nod as surrender, Hulin turned to the crowd, raised his arms and tried to shout above the din.

"My people! The Bastille is ours! The battle is over! The Commander has my promise of immunity!"

He could not enforce their observance of these terms however, and the mass of people behind him forged forward, those following knowing not the terms, only that here stood the fortress: those held within, imprisoned without trial. More to the point, here lay the munitions that they badly required. The mob now breached the fortress, those behind pushing aside those in front and striking blows at random, killing six of the garrison.

"Ye be animals, ye dolts and idiots!" bellowed de Launay, swinging around in defence, ignoring the fact that he had been disarmed. Though old, his close combat skills were second to none but the sheer numbers surrounding him were also second to none. He was soon grabbed and dragged with the escort of the French guard, toward the Hôtel de Ville for trial by the people of France. Trial of a few minutes only, he knew.

He looked about as he stumbled and fought his escort: here then were the new French and what he saw made his blood boil. He struggled against the holding hands, stared into the leering faces. "I'd rather die…than…allow you imbeciles…to rule France!"

"*That* is no problem, old man!"

A long-sword flashed and a great insane cheer rent the air, as his head parted from his body and fell with a thud to the ground. De Launay finished the march to the Hôtel de Ville with his head impaled upon a pike, carried in triumph through the streets. His fate was shared by three of his officers, three of his men and Jacques de Flesselles, a man recently turned Revolutionary and working hard for them but somehow reckoned by the people to be a traitor.

The city streets now echoed, day and night, with the incessant ringing of tocsins, musket fire, running excited crowds, and endless marching of the inner city Militia. These sounds drowned out any impression of the siege of the Bastille, on the outer environs of the city; the only change that of drifting smoke and dull orange skyline. This Angelique noted suddenly as she glanced through the window but shrugging, returned to her writings. An extraordinary cheering, accompanied by a sudden swell of the crowds running along the Rue Saint-Honoré towards the *Palais-Royal*, however, lifted what had become a normal bedlam, to a higher level.

Angelique stayed her quill and lifted her head at the sound elevation, then moved swiftly to the window. She looked down in time to witness Rochelle stepping from her elegant, low-slung chaise. The wave of jubilant humanity surged just a few dozen yards behind her. Angelique gasped and ignoring the bell-pull for Siffred, raced down the stairs to the front entrance. She flung one of the heavy, nail-studded doors open and dragged her in. She then bolted it and turning, leaned against it, gazing at her friend.

"That was mighty close, my friend!"

"But nonsense, what would they want of me?"

Angelique stared and then laughed suddenly, "There is no one, I tell you, like the *English*! What do they want *anyone* for, *ma chérie*? Some one to lynch; anyone… mob mentality! Come, to the salon and I shall show you. You live not on Rue Saint Honoré."

"A doubtful privilege, it seems!"

Ensconced within the window embrasure of the long salon, they watched the mob surging beneath them for some time. Soon a pole appeared, carrying a set of keys, a flag and a paper. Following this, were two pikes bearing the dripping heads of de Launay and Flesselles.

"What on earth is *this* all about?" said Angelique, twisting her head and trying, unsuccessfully, to read the paper.

"Ugh! How can they enjoy it so? Look at them! How can they *do* it?" said Rochelle in disgust, then turning away from the gruesome sight and moving to the middle of the room. "Well *mon amie*, appears we be imprisoned here for a little. None shall leave Paris in one piece in a hurry. Or shall you still try for the château?"

Angelique, a little pale from the stark reality before her, stared at her. "Are *all* the English this cool? Do remind me to include you on any errands of a dangerous nature!"

Rochelle thought a moment, head on one side, then shook it decisively. "No, I do *feel* of course: a lot of anger, fury in fact; and impotence... but no crumbling emotion ever accomplished *anything*. Now we must plan!"

Still staring at her friend, Angelique chuckled suddenly and said, "And I thought *I* was mad...but am only half English of course! Now, you shall stay here the night." She paused as the town cryer went by, his handbell in competition with incessant tocsins.

"Keep indoors. Stay awake. Keep your lights burning... the Royal Troops are coming! Ready your ammunition and missiles. Aim to kill. Watch your backs... your masters are your enemies!"

He moved on, the muskets continued, the Town Guard ceaselessly patrolled, the rioting and looting could be heard in streets to the left and right, and the red and orange skyline flared and died, flared and died.

"The Royal Troops... I wish they would," said Angelique, "If there be any left! The attack *we* prepare for be that of the 'new army'! Now... hunting weapons... and swords and, ah yes, the duelling pistols. And ammunition: goodness...do you know, I have no idea where *mon père* keeps it these days. Now if this were the *château*, then the armoury would be the place."

"Er, Ange, be there anyone else here: your brother... the Comtesse Bayette even?"

"Oh no, gone on business of their own; *mon père* to Versailles and Emile to join Trifane and Berthoud, the goodness knows what be *their* business. Mayhap a simple card game! The Comtesse has not been for three days."

"A card game!"

"The sans-culottes do not have the monopoly on rebelliousness, *ma chérie!*"

Rochelle frowned suddenly. "That is their story of course. My heart leaps at the danger of their... work."

"Hush my friend. They live entirely innocent lives. A card game it is."

Chin stubbornly set, Rochelle stared but only said, "So we are alone."

"Yes."

"Ah ha," looking around searchingly, "Priest-holes or er... tunnels?"

"What? Where now is that English courage?" Angelique chuckled.

"Only *you* said I had courage."

"Modesty serves no purpose, my friend."

"Of course, not a fearful bone do I own. *Gammon*; more prudent a priest hole!"

"Well we do actually have *one*; more than one at the château."

"Thank the Lord for the Templars! It *was* them... that required such? But one will do."

"Mayhap 'twas not them... I do not know if this house is that old, Rochelle."

"Sadly for the priests... I really do not care *which* of them required such but do lead the way, just in case I am found to have mislaid this courage you insist on talking about!"

"Sire, this is the only information that I be in possession of at the moment: that the Bastille was attacked and has fallen; with the, er... death of de Launay, Sire!"

The king strode up and down, causing the procedure of his morning *levée* much interference. "Tell me again what happened and then tell me *why* it happened; why it was not anticipated. The Lieutenant of Police *must* be aware, at all costs, of all that goes on in the streets. How did this slip past him? And was it not enough that they won their infernal one chamber Assembly? It is nothing short of a revolt!"

"Sire," responded his informant, the Duc de Liancourt, "it is no longer a revolt. It is a full scale revolution!"

The king ceased his striding suddenly, turned and stared. "What mean you?"

"The fall of the Bastille Sire, is the, er..."

"The fall of the Monarchy? We shall see about that, we have survived many rebellions!"

"But unfortunately Sire, you said... forgive me Sire... but you did say to the Assembly, as you brought in more troops, that unless you were obeyed you would *secure* the safety of your subjects and the peoples' response is this very thing before us: the rising in support of the Assembly against er... yourself, Sire!"

"How can words so clear be so twisted? I meant it when I said that I cared for their security! It meant just that... not what it was apparently blown out of all proportion to mean: forced obedience by means of slaughter!"

"Sire, you know what people will do with words these days; was not long since that Réveillon was almost murdered outside his wall-paper factory by mob violence: for saying that his workmen now lived less well on forty sous, than they had on the fifteen sous; previously found to be sufficient. This was twisted away from an indictment on rising costs to mean that a man's worth be only fifteen sous."

"So...and d'Artois...whilst pretending to be an enemy of the rebels, calling himself a patron of the die-hards, plans to be gone before daybreak. And my other brother follows him; *and* those other extravagant courtiers, just you watch, the de Polignac and de Noailles and a thousand other helpers of the Queen to spend her money. Seems that I have two elderly aunts, my wife... and scant courageous nobility only: to trust. I cannot sanction such cowardice; it is shameful! They shall never return to France as free citizens. They *have* gone, it is so?"

"Ahem, well Sire, as to that I am not sure, for of such an uproar is the court at this moment. But the Comte d'Artois and the Duchesse de Polignac did continue their efforts to win over the wavering mercenaries, even until this morning Sire."

"And then there is the pretender to the throne... d'Orlèans. *He* shall make as much hay as he possibly can now; seems my case is serious, not so, Duc?"

"Well Sire, his evil reputation may keep his popularity among the people at bay and without them he dare not move but of immediate import is the question of the return of Necker," replied the Duc de Liancourt.

"*That* is their demand?" asked the king now, returning to the subject of the Bastille.

"And the withdrawal of troops from Paris," replied the Duc de Liancourt. "Your only safety lays in immediate co-operation with the National Assembly, Sire!"

A discreet knock at the door and Clery entered. "De Quatreaux, Sire."

"Send him in!" The king turned, smiling grimly. "Not a pretty sight, eh Quatreaux?"

"No Sire," de Quatreaux bowed to the king, then to the Duc.

The Duc acknowledged this, then turned again to the king. "If I may, I shall get on with the business of Necker's return and the troop removal, Sire?"

The king looked at him long, wrestling with the impotence of the situation, then nodded slowly. The door closed quietly after him and Louis turned back to gaze across the room at de Quatreaux' bland face. "What a debacle!"

"Ah yes, Sire and, forgive my abruptness, but I am here to see whether you yet agree that the time may have come for the plans to become operational."

Louis frowned, "Not, I think, with Paris armed to the teeth with thousands of *canaille: Lafayette's army*," he snorted. "The queen was right to distrust him!"

"By the time a message is relayed to Austria, Sire... considering travel time."

Louis was silent a moment. "I cannot risk harm to the civilians, Vermont."

"Well, if I may venture, Your Majesty, the civilians now be Lafayette's 'new army', the National Guard, and no less dangerous for the lack of a uniform, Sire... a *revolutionary* National Guard; attacking the crown."

"But one sniff of a rumour of war and Paris be bathed in blood... of this I am sure. Paris be armed and the foreign troops far off as yet. No, we will yet come about!"

De Quatreaux bowed, quashing a deep sigh: the moment to strike was now. All was in place: all the months of difficult and dangerous manipulations within and without the frontiers had paid off—if Louis moved now. He paused: suddenly very sure that it would all be in vain; the king merely required the security of the *knowledge* that military backing was there. His heart plummeted: the king would not fight.

The Assembly sent, from Versailles, eighty-two of its deputies to Paris with the good news of Necker's return. These were escorted, by the thousands, to the Hôtel de Ville. Here the electors affected the function of a provincial municipality and two deputies were singled out for special honours: Lafayette; position of Commander-in-Chief of the new militia the National Guard, and Bailly, position of the Mayor of Paris.

Whilst street celebrations were being enacted for victory over the king, Versailles emptied of almost all its inhabitants, fleeing north to Belgium and to the coastal ports. Though the nobility, of the highest rank, invited (drafted) into the Palace of Versailles, had long wished for escape from the gilded cage, they had not envisaged this extreme anarchy. Though they had bowed and exhibited the virtues of '*l'honnête homme*', this method of control had long been a thorn in their sides: a method cleverly devised by Louis X1V to strip them, especially the provincial nobility, of power; for Versailles had not been built merely for reasons of glory and prestige.  Disguised now as laundry persons, street sweepers, *femmes de chambre* and valets, tutors and domestic staff, many nobles ran for the frontier. The Duchesse de Polignac, dressed as a *femme de chambre*, stepped up to ride as a servant, with the coachman. Controlling with great difficulty her grief and anxiety, she reflected that soon the people would wake up to these poor disguises. Her soul sank to a depth before unknown to her, at the state of France, and the knowledge that this surely was but the beginning. Despair, guilt and shame at her cowardly escape were now her companions forever.

The Royal family remained at Versailles. The king stood now before the window; seeing, as was usual these days, nothing of the view. The queen paced up and down.

She glanced at him. "Louis! What to do?"

"I shall not run."

She stopped still a moment to gaze at him. "I understand that your devotion to your ancestry and country be indestructible, but we cannot simply sit here... as if nothing had happened; not any more, Louis!"

"Any escape efforts will be seen as abdication, my dear. I cannot go. But you, and Elizabeth and the children, must."

She stared. "I will not go without you! We stay together, Louis!"

"Then we work together."

"Then let us begin! We must make a stand... a noisy stand! *Mon Dieu*... they must know that we will not tolerate this mayhem!"

Louis turned slowly to face her. "*Ma chérie*... I will go to Paris as they demand. You will not like this I know... but I must bless the Revolution that I can no longer control."

"*What*! Louis... for the Gods' sakes! You walk into their net!"

"The madness must be stopped... before a complete bloodbath wipes out most of the Paris population—the bulk of whom did not ask for this. I shall go tomorrow: after hearing mass. I will also empower Provence to rule in my stead, should I not return alive."

"I suppose it be better than d'Artois!" muttered the queen beneath her breath.

The queen, left weeping for his safety, soon found her tears turning to a fury inexperienced even by her, as she frantically burned papers and packed jewellery.

Louis travelled to Paris, as requested by the National Assembly, with only a few officers and members of his bodyguard and a handful of the Town Guard of Versailles. At the barrier of Passy, Mayor Bailly presented the king with the keys to the city: the same as those presented to Henri 1V, when Paris had surrendered to him.

"He," said Bailly, "had made a conquest of the people of Paris. *Now* the people of Paris have made a conquest of their King!"

The fall of the Bastille did indeed represent the fall of the old Monarchy in which the king alone represented the nation.

♣

The insurrection of July the 14th, 1789, soon to be celebrated as Bastille Day, ended in the utter disorganization of the old order of government. Royal officers, where they remained, could not now maintain authority; the army was in mutiny and the people armed. New ineffectual authorities were evolving countrywide and the National Assembly, though also yet ineffectual, became the new government.

Watching the noisy mayhem that was the new Assembly at sitting, Montmaire smiled cynically. "The absence of the overlap of one government to another, to assist in a smooth transition, is causing chaos, *mon ami*!" he said softly to de Quatreaux.

De Quatreaux nodded. "And the countryside, if possible, fares worse than Paris. In many areas châteaux are burning, I hear; and the taxes and feudal dues remain unpaid nationwide. Our economic framework of society is collapsing." He smiled sardonically. "Every man is free now and his crippling tax gone, but as yet the machinery to collect public money has not begun. And Paris, already in semi-starvation, starved over the days of the taking of the Bastille. But worse is to come, *mon ami*... no evading it!"

He sat back and watched the high proportion of the 'Rat Brigade' grow higher. The Assembly, now responsible for the founding of the new order amid this ruin, owned no political experience or recognized principles of action. He watched reports of *le Grande Peur* drive many Nobles and Clergy to cross the floor: the National Assembly was about to sweep away feudal privileges, serfdom and tax exemptions.

Some two weeks later, the evening sitting of August 4th 1789 saw the commencement of the axe to the very roots of the old order. Decrees were passed offhand: declaring the feudal order destroyed, along with the abolition of serfdom and servile dues. All privileges of Seigneurs: exemption from the *taille*, church tithes, exclusive rights to some civic, ecclesiastic and military positions, hunting rights and many more special privileges to the nobility of the provinces, were abolished also.

Geraud arrived quietly and slid into his seat next to de Quatreaux. After a moment he leaned closer. "You were here yesterday, de Quatreaux: God knows how you do it! I cannot stomach this mess more than a day at a time! But tell me... the taxes, *mon ami*?"

"Changes for us... talk about it later; but the same old taxes for the people remain in place until the new system, based on principles of equality, is introduced," responded de Quatreaux in low voice.

Geraud raised his brows, speaking very softly. "But the people will not understand, or acquiesce, to this!"

De Quatreaux lifted a sardonic eyebrow. "And so the public purse remains light in weight and the tax collectors light in authority!"

"This Revolution of Paris, and that of the towns, would not have won their way without the supporting Revolution of the countryside; occurring separately but simultaneously and yet there be no provision for them, that I can see," muttered Montmaire. "The people of the villages remain largely ignored."

De Quatreaux grunted. "And of the total population of twenty six million, only five and a half million live in towns. The country people: now peasant-proprietors, and freehold owners, are finding that the axed feudal fiefs and attached charges have now been replaced by new, inexplicable, charges... multiplied to greater than before!"

The two friends, gaining knowledge by regular Assembly attendance, had assessed the situation accurately. Slowly the peasant turned landlord, if only of a few acres, did indeed begin to see that things were little changed. The village in the de Quatreaux hamlet had been fortunate in their Seigneur, but this made little difference to the newly brainwashed. Fear, fostered by the media, now overshadowed positive experiences at the hands of men like de Quatreaux. Resurrected tales of past cruelties bathed the countryside. Fireside stories abounded: of the wheel, and the rack in châteaux dungeons, of tar and feathering on the village green, amputation of the arms and putting out of eyes of the rebellious and the indebted, and many more heinous punishments. Blinded to the fact that the changes, now claimed as 'no change at all', grew directly out of the Revolution, they saw but one thing. The nobility had always been to blame; they had to be to blame now: *somehow*, for this unaccounted delay to their demands. The Revolution had not even begun: time now for revenge against a long history of cruelties.

De Quatreaux stood in the small salon, back to the fireplace and looked at the twins. "All roads to all ports are blocked, as are the main exit barriers... so to exit this city requires heavy bribes. Now I must make my way, in a few days, across the frontier but you, my daughter, shall go to Quatreaux. I have engaged some mercenaries to escort you. You shall exit by the Barriére de Belleville. Bribery is easier there, Emile."

Emile nodded, "Yes, *Mon Père.*"

"And another thing," turning to Rochelle, seated by the window, applying intricate stitches to her embroidery, which she abandoned now to pay heed to de Quatreaux. "Your *père* has, I am aware, informed you of his impending journey back to England and will not subject you to the dangers of the travel involved. We have agreed therefore, as you cannot be alone within this madness in Paris, that Château Quatreaux be your destination also... all remains relatively quiet there as yet."

"Yes, *Monsieur le Comte.*"

Within two days, Angelique and Rochelle, along with their *femmes de chambre,* set out in the de Quatreaux closed carriage. The hour was early, as they travelled down the Rue Saint Honoré, to the east-by-northeast gate of the city. Here, suffering silently the insults of the drunken barrier guardsmen, they managed, with the swift tongue of Emile and threatening muscle of the four mercenaries, to pass through without incident. Following this, they rattled on at a decent pace towards the east for the better part of the day.

Emile, riding alongside the carriage, moved close to the lowered window. "Ange, it be prudent, I believe, that we ride on through the night to Quatreaux. Will be tiring I am aware, but I do not feel it wise to stay in foreign villages."

"Emile," smiled Angelique, her head and shoulders through the window, "none could disagree. We still have cattle at our remaining posting stages?"

"So far as I know and there we shall refresh ourselves while they are changed but to arrive I am impatient."

"Then *dépêchons nous!*" She smiled and withdrew her head.

"Ange, does he always confer with you on decision-making matters?" asked Rochelle.

"Do not raise your hopes my friend. He grows the more each day into his *père's* shoes. The system between us is of long-standing. I *always* denied his three minutes ahead of me at our birth, convinced that the times were switched to ensure a male first-born," she laughed. "The birthing papers stated otherwise, I discovered much later, and of course the first-born male child always carries the position of authority anyway. But our *mère* was plagued many times with the necessity of breaking up our fights in those early days."

Rochelle regarded her speculatively and, feeling this, Angelique turned suddenly, smiling at her friend. "You know, if what I feel between you and Emile is imminent, then I could not be happier. Please know that."

"Ange, for goodness sake," Rochelle looked at her in some anxiety, glancing but a second at the wooden faces of the two *femmes de chambre*, "There is nothing. I tell you, nothing!"

"Ah-ha! So... that English courage hast limits so it does; and now I have found them." Angelique chuckled with great glee, then relented as Rochelle coloured: sobering suddenly, she continued, "It is just a pity that things are as they are at this moment."

They fell quiet and rocked and swayed their way to the next posting-house where they took what refreshment that hostelry offered while the horses were changed. So far so good, the services offered were no less than usual and mine host his affable self.

"Mayhap it be that the de Quatreaux' are generous of purse, Ange; but I feel nothing but friendliness here."

They resumed their journey and before long she was to see that for the most part, after all, the people retained their sullenness and aggression. As they travelled the further eastward the countryside could now be seen to contain scavengers, hunting late mushrooms and wild root vegetables, in the wooded slopes either side of the rough dirt road, casting the crested carriage malevolent looks as they passed.

Angelique gazed in compassion but unsure whether or not they were paid locals, to spread the rumour of starvation, murmured, "Abbe Seiyes would make much of this sight! Add it, somehow, to his Declaration of Man."

"What, *now*, is he declaring... more new age illuminations?"

"Man born free and equal and every citizen owning right to liberty, property and security; to resist tyranny, decide taxes, freedom from unlawful imprisonment, of speech, of the press... assistance during famine... he be correct of course... but *slowly, mon amie*! Slowly! Nursery children cannot be let loose to run the household!"

"But this is new! Condensed into an actual statement, I mean."

Angelique continued: "Religious liberty also and well anyway, basically the declaration announces the abolition of all orders and corporations. But liberty of press appears to be a big one... because of course that is part of their arsenal. As to worship," she paused thoughtfully, "now that one comes to think of it, Mother

Church has not entered into the affair. Now I wonder why? But the general theme of the so-called Declaration of Man seems to be that of middle-class elevation. By equality they mean the lowering of the old privileged aristocracy, to the level of the newly privileged bourgeoisie, rather than the lifting of those poor souls from the very depths of peasantry to a new and fairer working system. But the peasants will always remain at the bottom of the pile! No one cares! And in the middle sit the clever ones, scooping benefits from both directions. That is what infuriates me: the declaration makes noises about the poorer population but aims its 'equality rights' at the bourgeoisie only! They could be elevated to better position so very easily, the serfs. I would give all that I have... if it really went to them!" She sighed. "Mayhap they shall be elevated from their dreadful situation in a few decades' time."

"Don't you mean centuries? If they do not destroy France first! But right now, from our perspective, the big question is whether the king will be given the right to veto."

"Hopefully a compromise will be adopted... that he be able to veto the same decree during two consecutive sittings, to attain validity... but we shall see."

They rounded a relatively sharp and blind bend to be confronted by a convoy of flour and other lumpy bags of unidentifiable produce, under military escort to Paris. The de Quatreaux carriage pulled to a halt, and then moved to the side, the offside wheels sinking alarmingly into the shallow ditch. The occupants clutched at the arm straps, the two *femmes de chambre* uttering gasps of fear, but Emile rode up to the window and instructed them, through the now closed curtains, to remain in the vehicle no matter what.

"No matter what?" shrieked Rochelle's *femme de chambre*. "We are about to be turned onto our heads... that's what."

"Come now, Lucinda. Joubeau is an old and accomplished coachman! Control thyself," said Rochelle sternly and Angelique hid a smile. Rochelle would do well at the château as Emile's wife.

The arrogant soldiers and sullen ox drivers pushed their way past, some casting dark glances at the now closed curtains of the carriage. Soon they were rounding the bend and the de Quatreaux party continued on its way. The next town saw long queues at bakers' doors, many turning away empty-handed. Rochelle gazed intently at this, a small frown creasing her brow.

Angelique glanced at her, "What bothers thee, *mon amie*? Again, the bread shortage is orchestrated... if you searched out the cellars and attics there, you would find it! To spread anger and fear of starving, the fact must be genuine!"

"Yes but, Ange, I was thinking of the queen... be it true; what she said of the peasants... about them eating cake... when told of the bread shortages? I find it hard to imagine that of her!"

Angelique frowned. "You *see*? What the foul men of *Lettres* can do! Yes, she said it, but her words were, as usual, twisted away from her meaning! Remember: for these people, cake is a solid, plain, filling food, heavier actually than bread... not the fairy-light, fancy *millefeuille* that we understand cake to be. She was saying that we must use what we have... must restrain ourselves where necessary... if we cannot do a thing, have a thing... then so be it. The people cannot appreciate that these words were based in her own severely disciplined upbringing... her every move and word controlled by the discipline of what a Royal can and cannot say and do! She sees them as unruly children, needing discipline. They see *her* as free as a bird… to do as she likes. It did not help of course, that she voiced this sentiment impatiently; and that she then went on to demonstrate by remarking her own restraint regarding 'That Necklace' that she declined, knowing it to be beyond her means."

"Ah yes. We all know about *that* debacle!"

The countryside was baron, dry, dusty and hot, with no relief in sight of the now five-day-old heatwave. Château Quatreaux presented cool and welcoming, as they stepped from the carriage and up the wide steps of the southern terrace to the deep cool of the entrance hall.

♣

De Quatreaux; having given of his wisdom regarding a sticking-point, now sat in his seat and watched, casting a cynical eye round the Assembly's theatre-like organization of semi-circle of seats, facing the Presidents chair. Beneath it stood a tribune. Now it seemed the country's future was to be directed by the most popular and persuasive young players to a fickle audience: replacing the older, more disciplined men. His smile grew grim; the future of France was tenuous enough, without irresponsible, power-seekers holding dangerous sway over a vast, uneducated population. Worse: over semi-educated lower bourgeoisie. Sway held by perfected theatrical technique.

To the *extreme right* sat the majority of the Nobles and Upper Clergy, regarding the Assembly's work as resting on no justifiable foundation and working hard to reverse it on the first opportunity. That the old order was gone forever they could not absorb.

The second section, the *centre-right*, comprised deputies from all three orders, somehow managing to agree on the defence of individual liberty and parlementary control. In favour of two houses, in which the landed wealthy predominated: these were bitterly opposed to the establishment of a democratic institution. Restoration was, from their viewpoint, of prime importance.

The Third, the largest section, forming the *centre left* of the Assembly, consisted, he could see, of curés and deputies of The Third and a sprinkling of Nobles and Upper Clergy. Though differences existed in this body of seven to eight hundred men, two main sentiments prevailed: equality and self-government. These were not pure democrats *or* republicans: their real aim being government by the middle classes.

The fourth section, sitting *extreme left* consisted of a few deputies, some twenty or thirty in all, who, as pure, fanatical democrats, included in their program male suffrage and eligibility of all citizens to office, without property, educational or other qualifications. They pushed hard for a republic. Here, amongst these, sat a young lawyer by the yet unknown name of Robespierre.

So far, noted de Quatreaux, it was obvious that the extreme left wished to exterminate the aristocracy, the extreme right to reciprocate with equal fervour the authors' of the Revolution and the two middle sections wanted to build a better France. No one section, however, pushed to delete the throne but just at that moment, a voice floated toward him.

"The sooner we destroy the throne the better!"

"And... while the pot still boils!"

De Quatreaux turned his head slightly. The voices were those of Robespierre and Pétion. He gazed rather intently at them for a moment, noting the fanaticism of both and suddenly hoped fervently that those of the extreme left would not eventually control the Assembly; for if so then France was doomed, not only as it was known but completely and utterly. He stared, suddenly knowing, and wishing that he did not, that the outsider could creep in along the barrier to take the race. Suddenly he felt ice slide down his spine: and de Quatreaux was not known to admit ice to his inner mentality, unless he was delivering it.

A raucous noise rose from the public gallery and he smiled wryly: they would not wait very long for their demands to be met. Their excited, noisy interruptions of the debate, was a real menace to the speaker of the moment. Their immediate worry was now registered on the face of every republican: that the king would use the powers given him, that of the veto, to bring about a restoration of the old order. He watched and listened for a little longer then, having made his mandatory appearance, rose quietly and moved unobtrusively to the exit; his next port of call was to a certain wine merchant at the lower end of town and then a silent and invisible exit from the country.

Arrived at the wineshop, de Quatreaux bowed to Anton. "You are well, my friend?"

Anton gave a fat chuckle that matched his rotund belly. "In health or purse?"

"Hopefully both, *mon ami*; now tell me all that goes forth."

"In my line of work, I hear a lot, Monseigneur," he grinned, "but first; the drift at the new *Parlements* and the Palace: *that* is far the more useful I am thinking, for all that *I* know of the comings and goings of Paris... *you* already know."

"As regards the new taxes on your good drop," nodded de Quatreaux, glancing around the cellar at the stacked barrels, "and the export outlets, and excise dues... certainly... and that you shall have my friend: but first, I have a matter of delicacy to discuss with you."

Anton waited until the yard boys finished stacking, sent them off on errands that would take an hour each and then closed the door to the staircase leading up to the centre of the shop. He drew back an old threadbare tapestry and, unlocking a door, waved Jean-Pierre in. Letting the rug drop, he moved to a lamp, lit it, then locking the door again, he moved to a large, overflowing central desk and offered his guest a chair. He opened a jar of his finest, filled two goblets, then sat across the table, in a plush, high-backed chair.

"Well Monsieur, what be it this time? Or should I ask for whom? Many have passed through my hands already and methinks that it be soon the turn of the *Famille Roi*."

"Not yet Anton: although I do try to persuade His Majesty to at least ready himself."

"Ah, but to run is cowardly, an' that be not his way... whatever else he be... besides, there's a plenty to jump into his shoes if he does... in particular a nasty blood relative!"

"Ah yes. D'Orleans *is* of concern. However, what I have come for is of a personal nature and may be difficult."

A wide smile greeted this. "Not stopped old Anton afore, Monsieur... but first the going rate."

De Quatreaux smiled and waited.

"Now don't mistake me, my risk is great and my nest over the border not yet complete."

"Then in that case, better the gold in hand than the promise of more."

"Ah yes, but what I ask in return be a commercial barrier pass for it becomes more and more difficult and more and more expensive."

"Ah: the bribes."

"Just so, but you and I, we have a business deal—no bribe shall besmirch *these* premises. A paper for a paper... I am right?"

"A small matter of a birth-certificate, Monsieur: in fact, five of them."

"Not difficult."

"In the name of an authentic family."

Anton raised his brows. "*Which* authentic family, Monseigneur?"

"A dead authentic family... but unknown of course."

Anton remained calm. "Ah. Well... shall be difficult but a quick eyeball to a register could offer such. Famine victims lie all across the country of course, but a whole family? More like to find one from the recent small plague resurgence in the south."

"As I thought, Anton; you are, of course, the best."

"But assuredly. So... we need birth certificates... five of them... in the name of a deceased family. Leave it to old Anton! And, I take it; passports, *barrierre* passes... in fact, the whole gamut of travel paraphernalia: regard it done." Anton beamed. "And of course the necessary peasant clothing and transport: an old carriage or farmer's cart."

"Mayhap the farmer's cart a little extreme, Monsieur... it be not the discomfort, you understand... but the odour! But as I said... you are the best. None can touch you."

Anton smiled, poured more wine and watched the faint frown on his guest's brow.

"I may *not* need them, of course."

Anton shrugged. "Of course! The greater portion of preparation, of anything, is rarely used! That is its own success."

"One more thing: title deeds; but this is the more difficult. I have no access, now, to the register for folio numbers and the like."

"No! Is that scoundrel still pushing his case agin' ye, Monseigneur? Now that's *too* bad—I told you it be best for thee to take him out!"

Monsieur le Comte de Quatreaux leaned back in his chair and laughed suddenly; he really liked this man. "Anton, you know full well that that was what caused all of this in the first instance!"

"Ah me, I did *tells* you so, Monsieur... that the young cub would grow!"

"Into a half-decent being? But it did not eventuate, *mon ami*," complained the Comte.

"I did not say *how* he would grow! But with *that* blood running through his veins?"

"Hmm... but this is not for the present, but for my return."

"I have my contacts. If not, then you will know someone with register access?"

The Comte frowned. "I do, but wish not to implicate him. He already been of invaluable assistance to my family. I actually owe *him*."

"Can I have a name?"

"Pontisqieu."

Anton stared. "Ideal... his popularity as a lawyer of the people unbeatable!"

"Only if necessary, Anton... the dangers for him would be extreme," de Quatreaux stood, "But now I must depart... *au revoir, mon ami!*"

Anton also rose; and bowed. "I shall be in touch, Monsieur!"

The Comte strode through the streets; something of his bearing defying any would-be assailant to attempt assault upon him. He approached his club and passing in found Beaumont, Du Toit, de Vries and Montmaire enjoying a quiet game while the talk raged around them of Mirabeau and Necker, going head to head over the king's veto issue.

"Ah Vermont! Long time since I have had the pleasure, take a seat, do. Play?" cried Du Toit while Beamont sent for more wine and a new pack.

"Thankyou *mon ami*, I shall not disturb the numbers... but a bottle I *will* share."

"No, no. I have had enough!" said Montmaire, rising. "Take my place, please."

De Quatreaux settled himself, took up the hand dealt him and studied it. The evening passed for another hour or more very peaceably. He did not glance up or show in any way that he had witnessed the entry of Lareaux some two hours later. His mind however lifted into alert mode; the alcoholic fumes lifting and dispersing by sheer will.

"Well, well. Back from Austria, de Quatreaux? They did not keep thy head I see?"

Staring in deep and frowning concentration at his hand, de Quatreaux did not appear to hear him. The company paused, a second only, at the slight and then continued play.

Lareaux rocked back on his heels, a stiff smile upon his face and then de Quatreaux spoke in drawling, bored accents: "Austria? Monsieur, you are quite mistaken, haven't been there for an age." He lifted his cool, flat gaze at last to Lareaux and that man suddenly felt a deep fear slide over his entire body.

"No, Monsieur? But you were seen there, by all accounts," he stated with a curl to his lip and those at the nearest tables paused their play, for here could be an entertainment worth the watching, though few could remember the ramifications of the de Quatreaux-Lareaux scandal.

Jean-Pierre raised his brows just faintly and then spoke. "Then, by all accounts, they were wrong." He paused and leaned back in his chair. "But come, seems you have taken an aversion to something, Lareaux; could it just possibly be me?"

"One cannot like a man whom one cannot trust... a man who has no proof of his identity, or one who also duels *and* plays, to unfair advantage, Monsieur."

There was, of a sudden, perfect silence and then a stir. People began to gather; at some little distance, in a circle around the table.  Soft offerings to be seconds followed.

"But let me see this clearly! You are saying that I am somehow *not* de Quatreaux? Who then am I? I shall, by the way, deal with the insult at a later date."

"*Monsieur*, if you are indeed de Quatreaux, then you should not have had to gamble for the estates Quatreaux. I challenge you to produce the deeds... that be all that I say!"

"Lareaux! Enough of the insults!" thundered Beaumont. "*I* have known de Quatreaux from childhood."

"But he was out of the country for a very long period. Can you be sure?"

De Quatreaux turned a bored face toward Lareaux. "I should call you to book for that, Lareaux, but you shall sight the deeds. It is not necessary, of course, except for the expediency of closing your mouth, forever."

"We shall see!"

"Indeed we shall. And after that... I am afraid that you have bought yourself a duel, Lareaux. No man could swallow your accusations of... er... foul play, was it not?"

Frank offers as seconds were now clearly heard: for de Quatreaux.

Lareaux bowed politely to the company and then turned away but no offers were forthcoming from any of the tables and heads turned away, absorbed suddenly in their play. He was forced to leave, within the deadly silence that ensued, without the faintest offer of a single game. De Quatreaux turned back to his hand and studied it in cool concentrated manner for some seconds, then placed his choice of card upon the table.

"Well Vermont, you win," laughed de Vries, pushing a promissory note towards him.

He glanced at his friend of long standing but knew there would be no telltale signs of that man's thoughts or emotions. He was correct: Vermont's face remained simply bland. He also knew that de Quatreaux would place Lareaux on ice, until he was ready: but a duel there certainly would be. It could not be otherwise. He wondered how Lareaux would handle the stress of waiting. Though a master of the sword, he was not well balanced emotionally. And mentally: De Vries reviewed his assessment. Yes: instability roamed there in the attic also, of this he was certain. He shivered suddenly: evil did exist. One could have no doubts, once having gazed into those black eyes of a very cool, emotionless cobra. He puzzled a moment, the physical beauty overlying this evil; then gave it up and returned his focus to the game, resolving to watch his friend's back.

# CHAPTER TEN

## 18c Witchcraft

"I *will use* the veto regarding any decrees despoiling the rights of nobility and clergy! It is my only wedge, Monty! How many times must I repeat myself?"

"Er, I do not know that they are listening, Your Majesty. The stormy debates have raged several weeks now," replied Montmorin. "The strongest voices those of Mirabeau, Mounier, Necker, Lafayette and of course Abbe Séiyè, selling his Declaration of Man."

Louis snorted. "Rights of Man! The place will go mad: handing power to men with no knowledge! Were you there, day gone but one? The uproar within this new Assembly was disgraceful!"

"Indeed Sire, but I worry more about the daily meetings held in the alleys of the *Palais-Royal*. Petitions from there, regarding your power of veto, arrived this morning, Your Majesty, and rioters threaten to nominate new deputies... if your power to veto be not renounced immediately."

Louis stared. "Is our Assembly in the hands of the club demigods? Are our deputies so weak that they be *dictated* to?"

"We do not know... yet," replied Louis' old friend in deep sympathy. "One hopes not!"

Louis gazed in disbelief. "Do they expect to vote in new deputies every time something does not suit them? *Mon Dieu*, Monty... we are the laughing stock of Europe!"

A march on the Assembly at Versailles, of fifteen hundred men was organized, offering violence if the power of veto to the king was not renounced immediately. The Assembly deputies, however, stood their ground and would not be dictated to by their constituents. They refused them audience and the seat of anarchy, the *Café de Foi* at the *Palais-Royal,* was raided and closed.

The fifteen hundred trudged the fifteen dusty miles back to Paris but the entire episode was not wasted: ending in the granting of a suspensive veto not unlike that exercised by the President of the United States. This began many losses of the *Commons* on unanimity and the breaking of the parlement into a decisive left and right for the first time. This then was the beginning of a true parliamentary 'left, right' conflict: the first of its precise kind in the history of the world.

The Assembly now waited for the procrastinating king to honour his promise to publish, by royal press, the resolutions of August 4th; whereby the Assembly had laid its axe to the roots of the old order. During this wait, bread riots and marches routinely dominated the city.

Life at Château Quatreaux, however, continued on in country fashion but now beneath an atmosphere of stifling heat and reluctant staff, some even deserting but then returning. The prospect of no wage at all in times of famine daunted even the most revolutionary of them.

"Ange…is it simply my imagination, or do your staff appear even more surly to you too?"

"Yes…and they actually have better conditions than before: Emile pays a higher than usual wage, has taken on more staff, to alleviate the unemployment in the village and supplements their poor harvest with grain for grinding. But they are infected."

"With the disease of fear: orchestrated by the professional rabble rousers! Emile's goodwill shall not make a whit of difference of course; but I do wish that he – or your père - were here, they would not dare to offer *them* this veiled insolence."

"No, but we must continue on as though nothing were afoot. Many a mutinied ship has been controlled simply by the mind-power of the captain."

"Aye, aye Captain," laughed Rochelle and continued her sketching of the magnificent landscape falling away before her, gently undulating down to a stream reflecting the azure sky and then climbing again to the far horizon, steeped in summer haze.

"But you know," she added suddenly, as she moved her easel again, now into a new patch of dappled shade, then gazed restlessly about, "I do not feel right, sketching, whilst all France falls apart. It is obscene, Ange!"

"Oh certainly it is," Angelique, wrestling with her latest verse, glanced up, "But what else would you have us do then? We cannot entertain and draw attention to ourselves. One can no longer enter the village, unless appealed to, even to aid the ill and destitute: as *ma mère* was used to do! So many she saved from dying, you know… she, and Fanchon together, with their herbs and medicinal potions."

"There *must* be something that we can do! To demonstrate we are not all as blackened as the insurrectionary orators would have us." Rochelle paused, settling the legs of the easel into a more stable position and watching Angelique's thoughtful frown as she sharpened a quill.

"The orators, shaking centuries of conditioning at the very foundations, hold sway at the moment. All the Emiles in the world will make no difference." Angelique shivered suddenly. "It shall come, I believe, sooner than we think."

Rochelle gazed at her friend's suddenly pale countenance. "Why, what ails thee Ange?"

"Ah: 'tis nothing."

"But no...of *course* 'tis something!"

Angelique looked at her friend and almost broke a code of silence lasting her lifetime, but then said, "Nothing, just that, I feel that bloodshed is imminent... a large amount of it!"

"*Bloodshed*... better then have ready your spiked posset!"

Angelique smiled. "The potion in the ring? But 'tis only a man's ring that be large enough to cope with the amount required, for to half do the job does not bear thinking about."

"Your locket then or stitched into the edge of your chemise. Anything, rather than go beneath the mob! Shall not just be murder; at least for the female population it won't, especially if the sackings and pillaging be conducted by the army rabble."

"Ah yes: our salubrious National Guard!" Angelique paused as the head of a groom, of the First Stable of Château Quatreaux, appeared above the gentle rise behind them. She squinted against the bright sun as he approached and Rochelle raised her brows in query.

"Worry not, he be old and trusted. Besides," responded Angelique, opening her reticule; and smiling at Rochelle's widening eyes as she exposed a small silver pistol, "it is Marcel. He be third generation château groom and taught me to ride French style."

She rose and moved forward to greet him. "Why Marcel, what brings you here? You should have saved your legs—we were soon to return."

"Madame, it be my son. I would not bother ye but I knows that ye be a great healer. It is known in our village; you healed the son of Jean-Christian the chandler that time and…"

"Yes, yes, well no, actually, *I* did not heal him, 'twas the herbal recipe left to me by *ma mère,* but what is the matter with your son, Marcel?"

"'Tis the black cough, Madame, he be real bad, an' we depend upon him, these times an' you was known to…"

"Yes, yes, I shall see Fanchon and come immediately with the medication. Worry not: I am sure he shall be well soon."

"Thankyou Madame, I tolds 'em that you would, an' I be right an all!"

"We come now, Marcel," replied Angelique gently; then to Rochelle, as he turned away, "So here be your chance, *mon amie*... to demonstrate that we are not all the same!"

Angelique stood in the drying room and gazed at Fanchon, noting age creeping upon her work-hardened features. "Why Fanchon… what mean you?"

She had the posset of herbs, and other cures for the groom's son, stowed in her basket and turned now to look at her oldest friend. Fanchon, herbalist, overseer of the kitchen gardens, keeper of the keys to the drying room, had been the figure, with more compassion than any other, to whom Angelique had turned in those early days in France. Days when the loss of her *mère* was intolerable, days when she had sought comfort and had found none; and later when the teenage growing pains of body, mind and soul had left her confused and lonesome. None but Fanchon, that daunting lady of the severe countenance, strong resolution and strict discipline, saw or cared. None other would have sought compassion and guidance from this hard-faced lone woman: even amongst her own. But Angelique, through long hours spent under her direction, amongst the herbs and flowers whilst grieving, closing her mind to all but the backbreaking work required to make things grow, had slowly built a strong connection with her. But Fanchon shook her head, as she worked and would not answer now the question of Angelique's vision, at the luncheon of the Hunt.

"But my dearest Fanchon, you have never failed me. 'Tis you have given me wisdom from my visions! None other could, even were I daft enough to ask. But this time, the blood, *Mon Dieu*! There was so much of it."

"Hush child," glancing around the drying room as she sealed the stone jars and earthenware pots again, "what ye did see was naught but the 'coming'... and it shall come... best thee leave this country, Madame."

"Oh Fanchon, you have been a mother to me. 'Tis *I* should be addressing you as 'Madame'. Indeed it is!"

"Ah no, you be mistress of the château... *born* to the big house Madame; and now 'tis the big house that shall extract deep price."

"Do you not mean 'high price'?"

"No. It weighs heavily and drags deep, upon all who live and work here. We shall all go beneath the tide. Run, my dear, run, you who are able."

"Never: my good and wonderful Fanchon, *never*."

Fanchon's face was grim: "Then say your Hail Mary's and Our Fathers without respite."

Angelique stared at her. "Then, if events turn so diabolical that we must, you must get a passport and come with us: I would not go without you!"

"No. I have too many dependent on me: and few wish to care for the crippled."

Angelique gazed at her in deep compassion and affection but only said, "Come, we shall be late if we do not move speedily."

"*We*: Madame? I shall go alone and 'tis to walk that I shall."

"You shall certainly not: it will be dark on arrival if you do. No, we take the small estate-carriage. Emile has the travel coach."

"But you must not come! 'Tis not like the olden days."

"But of course I am coming, Fanchon. I do not trust the atmosphere any more than you do but do not believe our people to be hostile, as are those of the towns and cities. Besides, a show of faith is very necessary to counter the evil crowd-inciters."

Angelique and Rochelle stepped, with Fanchon, from the carriage into the village square. From this point a narrow, winding, cobbled lane led to Marcels' dwelling. The people stared but maintained a distance as Marcel came forward, bowed and then motioned them to follow him.

"You know, Ange, I did note that 'twas awfully late to do this. And I do think that Emile would readily beat us if he knew," said Rochelle uneasily.

Fanchon, hearing this, nodded with grim satisfaction.

"Twaddle, my dear, best to show from the very beginning that you do not fear him. As for me," she gave a rich chuckle, "he would have a hard time beating *me*. I learnt to fight *and* fence with my brothers. My dear sister tried, you see, to teach me the occupations becoming to a lady, but all too soon she married and moved away... and *la compagne* gave up; then left! Then I spent much time in England... as you know. Then came *la Comtesse*... but she also threw up her hands and abandoned all attempts to draw from me the fine embroidery and light fingers of the pianoforte! And much energy I did own; and so you may add fishing, though I was far too impatient for such sport. But archery and shooting: now *that* I *was* good at."

"But you abhor the hunt."

"Target shooting...*you know the one*: the round white board... marked with red circles."

"Jest all you like, I would still be more comfortable that we went on the morrow."

"Afraid of the dark?" laughed Angelique. "Besides, another night for Marcel's son without the medication is another night in the clutches of the disease."

"But which disease... he did say the *black* cough!"

"Would you be thinking the plague?" asked her friend softly, glancing at Marcel some few feet to the fore: it would take little to stir panic by the word plague.

"Well? Would it be so outrageous? We know that it lurks about; never far away."

"Nonsense! And I am sure Fanchon agrees with me!"

But Fanchon remained mute, her eyes on the rutted dusty road as that particular silence, often accompanying dusk, now surrounded them. They followed Marcel to his abode, twisting and turning through the narrow dusty streets. At the last bend a man on crutches, bent and malformed of all limbs, struggled, one foot throwing out to the right, across their path. Angelique stopped and waited, her compassion stirred as she motioned him forward on his attempt to stop and bow; his body a wreck but not his dignity.

"What happened to him, Marcel?"

"Ah, it is nothing," muttered Marcel.

"But no, one is not usually born like that. Not often at least."

His voice dropped even lower. "'Twas the wheel, Mademoiselle."

Angelique stopped and stared aghast, "But 'twas not *mon père*. I would swear to it!"

"No Mademoiselle, he comes from the next village but one: the land of Lareaux."

"*Lareaux; he* did that?"

"But he did own great debts: could not pay his Seigneurial dues, Madame; 'twas deserved, he himself do admit that."

"*None* do deserve that, Marcel!" she replied grimly. One day Lareaux must pay, she thought. "How does he live?"

"He is lucky to have family and is strict, regards eating little. An' he is lucky to own family that persisted in teaching him to walk again. Now here we are, please do forgive my humble home, Madame," he said to Fanchon, then turning to Angelique and Rochelle, "You must go back to the carriage now. You should not have come at all but I could not leave you alone within the carriage; and to the escort of Fanchon I had to attend. But you must make haste home now. My brother, Jean-Paul, shall see to your safety. I shall see Fanchon back to the château."

They stood outside the simple dwelling and then Fanchon, hearing the wracking cough from within, turned and shunted them away from the doorway. " 'Tis no sense or indeed room for us all to be in here Madame," she said. "Go now with Jean-Paul."

Bowing to the sense of this and also now worried regarding the exposure of Rochelle to contagion, Angelique handed over her basket of special broths and turned to obey that woman's stern orders. Rochelle gave up hers, carrying the stone jars and folded extra blankets. Fanchon had the herbs and potions, including several restoratives, a generous clyster and several poultices ready made for the heating.

They followed Jean-Paul through the people gathered to watch their progress, now with darkling and sullen glances, though Angelique smiled and greeted some known to her as servants of the château. These made their bows and curtsies as they paused to speak but of the old warmth and friendliness there was none.

They arrived back at Château Quatreaux late, taking dinner on the terrace, chasing the faint summer evening breeze and watching the round, red, haze-covered disc sink rapidly behind the skyline. The sky turned salmon-pink, then pale white as they ate: a small collation of chilled soup and cold meats, washed down with burgundy. They then retired to the book-room, or, as Angelique called it, the work room, for here she had spent many hours reading and writing, always the embroidery in evidence for the sudden appearance of her *père*. This usually avoided for her, censure of her rather political scribbling.

"Ange, did you see that well-dressed man at the market? Perhaps a businessman of some sort?" asked Rochelle now, glancing up from her book suddenly.

"Ah yes, I did," responded her friend, pausing her quill for a moment; the concentrated frown vanishing from her brow.

"He seemed familiar somehow, can't think why and I felt Marcel's uneasiness at his appearance."

"Probably some city stirrer: that he was embarrassed for us to see! 'Chelle, I am going up for a moment, I need that other book to cross reference and it is beside my bed *and* I need to stretch my legs."

"I shall not die of boredom; we have not spoken a word for at least two hours!"

"But how rude... please, my apologies!"

Rochelle grinned. "But how comfortable; none required."

"It is, isn't it?" agreed Angelique as she left the room, moving along the gallery and turning down the great lengthy corridor to her apartment. Here she found the girl turning down her bed for the night and renewing her water jug. She nodded a polite goodnight to her and moved to her ornately carved bedside table and located the book, buried beneath others. Exiting through the boudoir, she moved back along the corridor and had reached the long gallery when Siffred appeared at the head of the stairs.

"Pardon Mademoiselle. But a moment, if you please: there is a person from the village to see you. I did inform him that Monsieur le Comte was not available; or the Vicomte for that matter but he said it did not matter. He insisted upon seeing you Mademoiselle. I can get rid of him..."

"No Siffred, do not; show him to the little salon."

He hesitated. He did not like it but Angelique held his gaze firmly. "Yes Madame."

She watched him reach the foot of the stairs and then turned to walk along the gallery to the book-room, but changing her mind suddenly, a feeling of urgency enveloping her, followed him down to the cavernous entrance hall and across to the salon. Here she saw a man not before encountered, but his obvious agitation and fear brought her quickly forward.

"Madame," said Siffred in haughtiest tone, face devoid of expression, "Monsieur Jardine."

She placed the book on a side table. "Monsieur. You have need of the Comte? He does return on the morrow but one."

"Madame," bowing low and casting furtive and fearful glances at Siffred, "Even the morrow shall be too late; 'tis Fanchon."

"Fanchon...! Then tell me immediately. Thankyou Siffred, you are busy I know so I shan't keep you."

Siffred bowed and reluctantly vacated the room, knowing that the door to this one be too dense to allow sound through.

"They hear tell that she be a-curing the son of Marcel. They are sure that she be a witch, Madame. There be much talk of such of late, an' he being of such low level that naught but witchcraft be the work to cure him," said the man now that Siffred was gone.

"But surely his cure, no matter how, is a good thing, Monsieur Jardine."

"But no, Madame, not if it be God's will that he die." He ran trembling hands through his hair. "An' she be watched... and you an' she be overheard today; speaking of things of magic and visions. Therefore the cure be the work of the devil... they says Madame. They be a building a, er... bonfire right now, Madame!"

She suddenly stood very still; then, thinking rapidly, moved back and forth in front of the empty fireplace. How to do it? The crested carriage would take time to be harnessed but would show authority. Then she remembered that very crest had inflamed her situation in the Paris street riots. Better to use stealth. Suddenly ceasing her movement, she turned to him.

"Monsieur, where be she at this moment?"

"Locked in the inn, Madame: while they prepare the stake and faggots."

Angelique gasped. "Oh *Mon Dieu*, then you are in the right of it: we have no time to spare. Go to the stables, quietly. Can you ride? No? No matter: my mare Tiffany shall carry the two of us. It is not a matter of more than three miles and I do believe that I witnessed a full moon last night. Go to the stables and find Phillippe and tell him to saddle her: as for the Vicomte... come, the less the butler knows the better, go now." She stood by an open French window leading onto the terrace and motioned him through: "Along the edge of the château and through the shrubbery, none shall see you. I have done it a thousand times as a child!"

She turned and ran back up the sweeping staircase, along the gallery and to her dressing room. Here she dragged off her light house-shoes and pulled on, not riding boots, but solid walking boots: who knew what was ahead of her? Catching up her very dark, but lightweight cloak, with hood, she left the room. Changing her mind, she re-entered it; and moving to the writing-bureau released the spring to the hidden recess and took out the small silver pistol. This she slid into the concealed, long inner pocket of her cloak and headed out again, her satin petticoats rustling as she hurried. She frowned suddenly, glancing down at her skirt and then, upon inspiration, ran to her brother's room. Following some minutes in there she then ran lightly and now silently down the service stairs, casting Rochelle, in the book-room, but one thought as she ran. She was remorseful at her deception but dare not involve her friend; or waste time arguing. Leaving by the heavy wooden door, she listened and then made her escape, running across the stretch of grass to the path leading to the stables.

Here she found a slack-jawed Phillippe, staring at her as she approached. She took the reins from his hand, placed a foot in the stirrup and flung herself onto the mare, gathering her cloak around her again, thus hiding the gentleman's attire.

"Where is the Monsieur from the village, Phillippe?"

"Ah, he set out on foot Mademoiselle, said not to bother about him, he can run almost as fast and has a head start. He shall meet you by the millwheel among deep shadows of the Poplars, dead reeds an' tall canes. Do not do anything until he comes!"

"As fast as *Tiffany*? But never mind; I shall likely overtake him on the road. Now Phillippe, should any word of this reach the château, your secret poaching habits shall be revealed. Believe me; and to the *Comte* himself when he returns."

Phillippe gasped and stared in disbelief. "No Madame, you cannot know such... I mean I haf never..."

"Save your breath Phillippe. I have known since my young days; my brothers followed you as the best bet on places of fair game!"

"But they never *told*?"

"It is obviously so my friend," she smiled. "Some of us are actually decent people, Phillippe! As for these hungry times, perish the thought; I only hope that you snare enough. But should you..."

"No, no Madame, I shall not, but if you be gone long and becomes a concern?"

"Then...then tell only Siffred, he shall know what to do."

"Yes Madame," he responded doubtfully and Angelique gave a brief chuckle, as she dug her heels and set off for the village, for she did not blame him. Siffred could not know what to do any more than anyone else in these times.

The sounds of uproar carried across the village, to the old mill on the very outskirts of this large village, as Angelique tethered Tiffany in deep shadow and amongst the tall canes. Suddenly she did not feel quite so courageous now that she had nothing to do; each burst of applause causing her heart to jump and each moving shadow her mind bending to a lurking enemy. A dog barked in the distance and some hedge animal rustled in the long reeds. Smoke now wafted on the air and panic enveloped her. Where was Monsieur Jardine then? Making up her mind to creep along to the inn, she paused suddenly as a movement stirred in the silent shadows.

"Come," breathed Monsieur Jardine softly, "We have little time, I have the keys. I would rather you wait here but we needs two. One to bring up a cart full of empty sacks and to cause a disturbance if need be and one to unlock and get Fanchon out of there. That be you; bring her down to the end of the lane behind the inn with all haste. Beneath the sacks you shall both reach the mill and the mare." He paused to gaze at Tiffany's strong, sleek frame as he spoke. "She shall manage the two of you alright. Now hush!"

"Monsieur...surely the uproar is unusual?"

"Orators: smart city persons; the people are impressed! *They* are responsible for the proposed burning! Though it is an archaic ritual... the people are infected and pumped up."

"And Monsieur, the smoke?" she whispered.

"No," grimly, "That is from cooking fires; they do not light the faggots until after she is tied up to the pole. Now, follow me: I shall take you to the inn and then double back for the cart, Mademoiselle... by the by... yon animal's name? I may need to move her."

"Tiffany."

She shivered and followed him, twisting and turning so that she began to doubt how she would find her way back, then settled to the idea of skirting the village to the Old Mill Road if need be. They made it to the Inn unmolested, all either at home for the evening or involved in the commotion that grew louder and louder.

Crossing the yard as two silent black shadows, Monsieur Jardine, silencing the lounging yard dogs with a soft practiced whistle that they knew, they slipped into the back of the inn. Here they found themselves in a wide lobby, at the beginning of two staircases, one leading down to the cellar, the other up to the *chambres*. He nodded up and then slid behind a stack of empty barrels as he exited the inn. Angelique, keys tight in her hand, stepped silently upon each stair, holding her breath against their creaks, though she guessed that little would be heard against the roaring and cheering from the taproom and the tables outside.

Creeping up towards the landing she heard a masculine laugh sounding from a room exactly opposite that landing and another step gave her a view of that room with its door partly open. The laugh had sent shivers down her spine and it did not take the gentleman to turn around for her to recognize that tall, lithe figure with, she knew: the eyes of a very beautiful cobra. Just what he was doing here was more to the point; and he would have heard what went forward and was apparently in accord with it. She shuddered at such cold-blooded evil but just then a girl, young and beautiful and of city smartness but apparently lacking maturity and wisdom, appeared from the room beyond. Angelique dropped and crouched against the balustrade, clinging to the shadows between the flickering candles within their widely spaced wall brackets; clinging also to hopes that no one would come out of the taproom below and head up the stairs, or the two leave the room above her to descend them. Neither of her fears eventuated and she heard their voices recede and a door close. She rose and ran lightly up to the landing, but it had been an inner door that had closed and she could, but rather not, guess to what purpose. She glanced into the outer room for a moment, dreading a third person, but it was empty of all but a chair and small table holding a glass and a half empty bottle of wine. On a hook on the wall, there hung a gentleman's coat, hat and cane.

She turned back onto the landing, then swiftly ducked back in, returning with the cane clutched firmly in her hand. Devereaux had thought there was something of note about it. That Lareaux may eventually guess just who took it was a problem that she would think about later. At this moment Fanchon remained the only important person.

The third door: one, two, this one. With shaking hands she fumbled with the key and almost dropped it at the sudden explosion of noise from the taproom below. The pseudo mine-host had opened the door and now moved in the direction of the kitchens for more food for the hungry crowd. Unknown to Angelique and Fanchon, the real mine-host was also imprisoned, for his apparent reluctance to the imprisonment of Fanchon.

Fanchon sat on a chair, smiling grimly at the sound of the key and then stood suddenly, pale and shaking. "Mademoiselle! You should not... oh *Mon Dieu*... the Comte shall never forgive me!"

"And I could never forgive *myself* my dear, or live with myself otherwise. Now come."

They made it to the bottom of the stairs but an eruption of drunken humanity from the taproom into the small parlour round the bend to their left, caused them to leap back, pressing against the wall.  The hard handle of a door pressed into Angelique's back and fumbling with it she turned it and they both slid in.  She looked around—the room was empty but for two sets of gentlemen's coats and hats on one wall.  The city gentlemen: the orators.  Suddenly she ran across and grabbed all the belongings on one hook. Motioning Fanchon to remain quiet and put out the candles, she left the room and ran lightly upstairs.  She placed the cane with the coat and hat belonging to Lareaux. Bundling the extra hat and coat into a tight wad, she shoved it up the fireplace chimney, promoting the belief of theft of the entire outfit, deflecting attention from a single missing cane. The difference between them was inestimable, as far as she could ascertain. This done, she sped back to Fanchon and they both left the inn via the back door, sliding out into the moonlight, keeping to the shadowed walls, searching for the promised horse and cart.

It was nowhere in sight. They stopped at the sound of a door opening and someone leaving the building ahead of them. This personage turned down an ally-way however and was swallowed by darkness. Inching further along the wall, as two silent shadows, they made it to the bottom of the lane but here traffic still moved back and forth. Of a sudden Angelique heard Monsieur Jardine's voice and felt relief flood through her but it was to be short lived.

"Out of the way man, can ye not see that I need to move this mule and cart?"

"Ho! And where are you going, *Monsieur*?"

"That is my business."

"But now I make it mine, there can be no reason for such at night. Something smells about this!" The man's voice was slurred.  Staggering, he leaned over to look into the cart. Seeing the rumpled and empty sacks he snorted, "You have no produce here for the morn! What need you of the village centre? Is this a pretence... a reason to visit the city lass that I see'd in your company t'other night?"

Glancing over the man's unsteady shoulder, Monsieur Jardine saw the two shadows tight against the wall. Raising his voice a little he challenged the drunken man: "Monsieur; your mind resides in the egout, 'twas to answer a query that I did speak with Tiffany... but anyway that be no business of yours!"

"Ah, Tiffany was it... hey? Share an' share alike my friend: that is village law!"

"Not of our womenfolk!  There be no *Tiffany* for you... believe me!"

"Ha! And what mean you by that?"

Angelique and Fanchon left Monsieur Jardine stirring a heated argument, shot through a dark side lane and bolted but it wasn't long before Angelique knew the reason for the cart; Fanchon, approaching sixty years of age, was soon blown and they had to slow.  She said nothing, however, slowing and pausing from time to time, her mind racing faster than her legs. Who had taken Tiffany? But there was no time for speculation. Somewhere on the way in she had witnessed some horses and then she remembered: outside the tannery, saddled still and tied to the post-rail.  Hope built as she saw it in the distance, the wall brackets and street flares still glowing. If they could but reach it before midnight, closing time, just some few minutes away.

Keeping to the shadows as much as possible and leaping behind crates, bushes and barrels and beneath wagons as people appeared along the way, they made it unobserved to the row of beech trees standing along the edge of the long, low building.

"Stay here Fan, I'm going to hijack one of those animals," whispered Angelique.

"But I cannot ride!" hissed Fanchon.

"You are going to be the fastest learner in France, Fanchon... and worry not: they are in too poor a condition to hold much of a speed. Hold this please, while I grab one," holding out the cane.

All quiet reigned; the only sound the flapping nostrils of blowing equines; and whining hounds at her approach.  Quietening the hounds with soft speech, Angelique worked swiftly and returned with an animal of uncertain parentage and even less condition and stamina.

"This is the best that I could find," she said softly. "Now, your foot in the stirrup and then the other in my cupped hands...quickly!"

Fanchon obeyed and following three failed attempts, after which Angelique grabbed an old box from the stack against the building, she at last managed to sit upright on the depressed but stoic animal, clutching the pommel and pulling at her skirts.

"Do not bother how you look my dear," chuckled Angelique. "No person shall pass judgement this night I am sure.  Now this is what you do: to steer, this... gently... and to make him go faster, this, and to pull up: this.  And all else fails, you just hang on for dear life and let him have his head; for it won't be very fast but do urge him in the right direction!"

"But Madame, are you not coming?"

"I shall but that poor animal cannot carry two. You are on your own but I shall not be far behind you.  Please say you rode as a child!"

"Well, I did an all but that be a *very* long time ago... fifty years!"

"Ah! Then be quick to recall. Now go!" So saying she gave a thump to the animal's hindquarters and stepped back. Fanchon, clinging to the animal and crouching low over the pommel, disappeared around the corner and into the shadows just a second before the doors of the tannery opened and men emerged into the street, calling goodnight to each other.

Angelique looked frantically about; no chance now of a horse for herself and no Monsieur Pontisqieu here to help her and Monsieur Jardine had played his part and indeed did not need further involvement to brand him a traitor, likewise Marcel. She shrank behind a beech tree, hugging her black cloak tight about her, flattening herself against the trunk; wishing that it would open and swallow her. Glancing up she shoved the cane into the long inner cloak pocket, then suddenly leapt to grasp the lowest branch. As she had as a child, feet against trunk, she then hauled her body up, cloak trailing behind. Trapped she certainly was if anybody thought to look up, well hidden if they did not and surely any horse-thief would not hang around to be caught. She hauled her cloak tight around her and found the cane an impediment, sticking out now at odd angle, like an extra shoulder, beneath the cloak. She drew it out, clutching it in front of her, running her hand absently up and down its shaft as she held her breath against discovery.

The uproar over the theft of the horse was a sight to behold, as the men spilled out of the tannery and valuable time was gained for Fanchon with every passing minute. The search was futile and Angelique was beginning to feel just a little secure when flares were brought in to search out the very dark areas, causing her to pull up her feet and tuck them under, hugging the fat trunk deep within the dense leafiness, trying indeed to become the trunk. A jutting and rotting stump from a fallen branch, supporting her left foot, snapped suddenly beneath the pressure and she froze. A man carrying a flare turned toward the sound, moved right around the tree and then held the flare aloft. Hood of dark cloak already covering her entire head, she flattened herself further, rigidly immobile, breath held: causing a black bulge in the trunk. She knew the bright flare held in his hand would blind him. Within the dark shadows of the leafy branches she would be safe; but if others came to examine them, she would be discovered.

"A mare up a tree?" chortled a voice. "It's daft ye be man!"

"It be one of them travellers at the inn I bet!" said another, "That took the 'orse...all their new-found knowledge ain't no guarantee of honest character... me thinks!"

"If 'tis so then he an' horse be far gone by now," replied another, "*not* up a tree!"

The search moved away towards the village centre and listening intently, she heard the last of the tannery workers leave, extinguishing the lamps and flares as they went, bathing the place once again in comforting darkness. Shaking violently now, she leapt to the ground. Her knees gave way beneath her. Forcing them to support her again she headed, shakily: legs still behaving erratically, for the old mill wheel, for from there she could find her way home. It would take but a couple of hours, at most, on foot.

Reaching the ancient wheel, she gazed around without much hope for her mare and thought the exchange not really fair, considering the opposing qualities of the involved horseflesh. However, perhaps Tiffany would break free and make her way home as lost horses do. About to leave the shadows she was arrested by new sounds: almost inaudible sounds of stealth. She backed into the reeds then slid under the low bridge. Mayhap she had imagined it: then she saw them. Saw lightly running men, calling softly to each other, fired with fanatical zeal strengthened by alcohol, their silent fervour unmatched by any previous, overtly rioting crowds Angelique had witnessed. She shivered and prayed that Fanchon would reach the safety of the château. Listening for the last of them she hugged the black shadowed buttress of the bridge and discovered that she still clutched the cane. Waiting for total silence, she ran her fingers again idly up and down the cane, was at the point of disciplining herself to cease fidgeting when she became conscious of a fine seam, or join, mid-shaft, camouflaged in a knot. With feel alone, the darkness here almost total, she discovered the cane unscrewed at this point. She grinned: much easier to carry! She gave a few more minutes and then crawled out. Pushing through the reeds she began to run lightly in the direction away from the village, along the road east, towards Château Quatreaux.

Running, half crouched, she moved from tree shadow to tree shadow even here, for in the country nothing escaped the natives. Every sound, every odour, every humped shadow of bush or animal was familiar. The ear, eye, nose and inner senses, were tuned so that the faintest unfamiliarity acted as a tocsin to the mind. She carried on for several minutes more and then, her senses drawn, she glanced across to the wooded hill rising gently on her left.

There, before her, was the most terrifying sight that she had ever witnessed. It was something to do with the darkness and quietness of the night she supposed but the dark, silent, hunched, running figures there, spreading up the hill in military manner, long pikes protruding before them, sent a chill sliding down her spine. Like black hunchbacks, they continued at a steady, silent wolf-trot, the ends of their pikes ever preceding them. On and on they trotted, up the lightly wooded hill, in the direction of the château. Panic seized her for the first time, for she would not reach home in time to warn them. Desperate now, she stared into the darkness for a horse, but could see nothing. Just at that moment a faint sound of rumbling carriage wheels caught her ear. Trembling with relief she ran into the middle of the road and waited, for only aristocracy en-route to the city travelled at night: and not many of them. Hopefully the coachman would stop and the owner turn and take her back to the château, for it was travelling toward the village, now behind her.

The coachman rounded the corner at a fair pace and stared in amazement at the figure right in the middle of the road: for to stand to the side would not halt a carriage in these dangerous times. She gritted her teeth and stood until the coachman brought his team to a sudden halt and then dealt with their stress at such treatment. Finally calming them and trying to answer the irascible voice from the interior of the carriage, demanding to know what went forth, he turned to Angelique in the light of the carriage lamp.

"What! But 'tis a woman, Monsieur," he called down, staring incredulously at Angelique, smiling sweetly up at him, simply waiting. As she knew it would, the window was let down and the curtain pulled aside to reveal an older man and his wife. Two female servants sat with them. The valet rode up front with the coachman and two footmen rode up behind. She knew now the prospect of persuading them to turn around, if only for a mile or two, was bleak.

"What do you want woman?" His voice was severe, the tone of that to a servant.

"I should like the chance to explain why I very seriously need you, if you please, to turn and convey me quickly to the Château Quatreaux."

Realizing now that this was no country maid, he threw up further fear-based reserves: what was a lady of gentle birth doing in such position? She explained, he listened and then about to speak, his wife, the Comtesse spoke sharply from the interior and Angelique knew that she was doomed. They would not take her, and when the rioting of the village was known and that they were headed to Quatreaux, her last chance followed the rest.

About to tell the coachman to drive on but uneasy to leave a lady in the road in the middle of the night, the Comte was vastly relieved to see a second vehicle appear, travelling east from the village.

"Ah, now you *see*, all shall be well I am sure. The vehicle goes in your direction Mademoiselle. Henri! Get thee down and stop that carriage."

But this was not necessary; the carriage in question was drawing to a halt. From the front could not be seen the crest but they could be in no doubt that it belonged to a nobleman. Angelique, courtesy demanding that she thank her reluctant helpers at least for stopping, did not see the gentleman descend. She then turned at the sound of his approach—to gaze straight into the eyes of a cobra.

She was never more thankful for the night and blessed the dense and timely cloud drifting across the moon, as she gathered her shaking body into stern order. Forsooth, here was a pretty pickle; what would Emile do? What would any of her family do? Possibly run him through? The age of duelling was not yet over; and the rabble mob seemed to be at liberty to run people through *and* chop off their heads at a whim. She felt a surge of hysterical laughter well up inside and struggled to control it. 'Never let the snake *see* that he has you; hold his gaze, call his bluff,' de Quatreaux had said.

She realized that he was speaking to her and the family carriage beginning to roll forward. Then it was gone and she was left standing in the centre of a rough country road, in the middle of the night, with the family's most evil enemy beside her. There was nothing for it but to get in, as he was at this moment suggesting: refusal would indicate fear; and this he must not be allowed to think. What to do she would think about as they travelled. Stepping upon the carriage step, her foot slipped and she bent down in the struggle to regain her balance. His arm shot out to assist. She swiftly waved it away: there was the cane to consider and he must not touch her before she had mastered the shaking aspen that her body had become. Hopefully not touch her at all.

"I am alright Monsieur…thank you!" she said calmly and finishing the entrance into the closed carriage, under cover of the deep darkness there, she slid the cool metal object into the wide sleeve of her brother's shirt. Settling herself against the lush squabs, she draped her cloak in such manner as to allow the two halves of the cane to sit unobtrusively within the deep, inner cloak-pocket, against her off side to Lareaux.

"You are comfortable my dear cousin?" he purred, leaning across to adjust the light silk cover for her, then leaning closer still to pull back the curtain, for visibility was void. Now the fitful moon, entering the window on her right, gave some light to her face.

"Why thank you Monsieur, I am most comfortable but oh so tired, such a long walk." She smiled sweetly and he would never know how much steel it took to not flinch at his touch and proximity. "I am most grateful to you for your detour of a mile or two, 'deed I am."

He smiled gently, his hand playing with his quizzing-glass, long, very white, fingers running up and down the narrow velvet riband holding it. She repressed a shiver, wondering suddenly what cruelties the girl at the inn had had to suffer. She then began to wonder how this long night would end; the girl was possibly accustomed to rough treatment but then again, Angelique was supposedly born to courage. And though her emotional response to him was majorly one of revulsion and scorn, she was neither the less obliged to suppress a rising panic at her predicament. Her thoughts turned to escape.

His voice was velvet soft as he answered her: "My dear cousin, from what I saw, I do believe that it would be prudent for you to avoid the château until this dust-up is over. 'Twill not be long: without direction they soon lose vision and organization." He knocked on the roof with his cane and the carriage moved forward, travelling eastward still.

"Oh but I cannot," she replied softly. So the cobra knew what went on then; but right now to escape claimed her attention. She needed a brilliant plan to force his hand; persuasion would be useless. No brilliance of mind occurred. In fact, that particular portion of her physiology seemed to be filled with a dense white fog. Or was it ice? Certainly her entire being seemed to be frozen.

"Cannot?" the dulcet voice held an unmistakable threat.

"I cannot leave my guest, Monsieur; the château shall be taken by surprise!"

"Never worry, I shall send a carriage for her convenience, after we arrive at my château."

"Your château: Seigneur?"

Somehow she managed to sound bored and he laughed: her courage was unmatched. He settled in to enjoy her imprisonment, for he could not pass up such good luck as this: he was as talented in mental torture as he was in swordplay. And of swordplay his skill was renowned. The entertainment provided by the city orators in the form of a Parisian wench, back at the village, paled in significance, measured alongside this piece of good luck. There were some few miles yet, in which to torment her, build her fear of him: in fact, if they went slowly, fine tune it to a high degree. Once arrived at his estates, there would be no coachman to hear the screams, no limits to inhibit him. He smiled gently: her display of courage did not fool him; they all broke, eventually. Glancing at her, however, he suddenly caught an essence of scorn and derision. His deadly intent rose.

# CHAPTER ELEVEN

## Pillage and Burn

Raoul Trifane rode into the village with his mind still on affairs of Versailles and the business of the Comte de Quatreaux that had come to his ear, which should not have. Here he found the flares still burning and the horn gently sounding the arrival of a visitor at late hour. His eyebrows lifted faintly as he glanced at the mess of table and street, the sounds of activity and, in particular, at the inn still not closed and shuttered. His mind deserted suddenly the problem of getting in touch with de Quatreaux. A carriage of nobility stood in the yard and he recognized the crest. He noted their piled luggage and wondered whether Paris be their destination or whether they be more of de Quatreaux' 'Rodent Brigade' heading for the frontier.

He gave the reins to the ostler appearing around the corner of the inn and ambled into the taproom. The room was empty now, except for Monsieur Jardine and an agitated mine-host, both known to him. His indolence hiding his extreme wariness, he gazed at them, an eyebrow raised in query; suddenly alert. The ride through the cooling night air of a few miles from the other side of the village could certainly claim its cleansing work: the drinking had been hard and the game deep but political information carelessly dropped had been worth the play and the struggle to keep his wits.

They turned to him as to the returning Saviour and, offering a jar of porter on the house, poured forth a jumble of drama, self-flagellation and outright anger. It took him but a few moments to sift fact from emotion and grasp the events of the evening just gone. With a grim mouth and pale face he left the taproom and the porter, mounted and galloped off in the direction of Château Quatreaux. Passing with savage anger the pole and pyramidal faggots, now bathed in moonlight on the square, he urged his mount as never before. The girl in the road, reported by the travelling family, was of course, Angelique. He cursed the despicable nobleman, snorting at the word 'noble,' that had left her there for it could only have been Lareaux approaching from the village: the timing was right and his the only other carriage to depart and travel east. He had longed to thrash the nobleman but the urgency of Angelique's situation disallowed this. He rode on; pushing his horse beyond what was kind but that animal only revelled in the race.

"Well done old man!" urged Raoul, lifting and leaning forward and the animal surged beneath him. "Keep going, *mon ami*! Just a little further and I do believe we shall catch them. He shall not reckon on being pursued."

Sensing the urgency, the horse shuddered beneath him in attempts to reach greater speeds than he had ever performed before.  Raoul pushed on, passing the turn-off to Château Quatreaux, sure that she would not have been able to persuade him to turn there. The de Quatreaux/Lareaux duel ran through his brain as a hot flame: that girl too had been abducted; then raped, tortured and left for dead by a Lareaux.  This man was his son and, many said, much worse. Fear flooded through his very being: he could taste it rising up to his throat and mouth. Sweat poured from his pores that had nothing to do with exertion.

At this time, inside the Lareaux carriage, a silent battle for supremacy continued. Angelique, staring into those unblinking eyes, developed a fascinated horror at their soft gentleness as their owner proceeded to kidnap her without a worry or interference. In fact, could it be called kidnapping: for had she not simply stepped into his hands?  She sank deeper into the corner and, feigning tiredness, closed her eyes; but they flew open at his hand on hers, closing gently as he spoke.  The fingers were warm and silky smooth, conversely sending a chill through her veins and she struggled to control a shiver.

"My dear, we shall deal profitably together me thinks, if you play your part well and I shall not object to you; you are a diamond of the first water and of a family of the first consequence." He laughed softly and his hand tightened. "But should you deny me…" He shrugged indifferently.

"But Monsieur," her hand remained very still in his grip, "I do not know just what it is that you want."

He smiled in bored fashion. "Poor effort, Cousin! Your *père* would not leave you without warning. I want the Quatreaux estates and shall have them… eventually: de Quatreaux is without proof of ownership… and now perhaps I have you also, for you are not a bargaining tool but an unexpected bonus.  One night under my roof shall be enough to undo you forever.  So you shall be obliged of course to marry me."

She gazed at him, no doubt now that insanity lingered in his family. What did one do with the insane?  If an animal, one shot them of course: a mad dog did not get a second chance. Her irrepressible humour had been her downfall and her saviour; but just now she did not know which, only that it threatened to bubble over into wild hysteria. The turn-off to the château they had passed long since and travelling at this rate; but no, she could not work it out, only that to stop him she must, before many more minutes and miles passed.

To get her hand free became the object of the moment: to obtain the pistol from the sleeve covering that same arm. The cane was also a problem; she could not make many moves without revealing it. But worse: his hand holding hers needed only a slight shift to discover the pistol held only by the fabric of that sleeve. And did he guess that she carried a weapon, or was he simply exercising his power, or caution even? But make her move she must.  She plied her shell-shocked brain; cudgelled it into activity and arrived at the only solution, weak though it was.

Of a sudden she bent forward in a noisy sneeze, face turned away, her hand jerking within his at the spasm. She began sniffing rapidly, causing him to release her hand at the obvious demand of a kerchief.  He glanced away politely then back again, to stare into the end of a small, silver-mounted pistol. He leaned back in his corner and simply gazed at her, the black eyes unblinking; a lingering half-smile upon his thin lips.

"Well? Do not hesitate *now*! Shoot me."

"I shall if you do not tell your driver to turn around or at the very least put me down."

He made a mistake, rare for him. He laughed. She fired. His eyes widened and he found himself clutching his left shoulder, a red stain appearing between his fingers but otherwise he showed no emotion.

"Tell him to stop or this time I shall take great pleasure in sending you to join your despicable *père*. I am sure he is waiting, for not a soul on *this* earth could want you... come to think of it, I have grave doubts about him even."

At this moment a shot sounded from behind the carriage, then thundering hooves. The startled coachman pulled to a halt; the vehicle rocked by the plunging horses. The door flew open and in its frame stood a swaying Raoul, but the pistol in his hand was rock steady. Silence reigned, other than the driver's voice endeavouring to calm his animals. Raoul suddenly laughed, eyeing the red seeping stain to Lareaux' shoulder, "Well done Mademoiselle, although you *have* robbed me of the chance to run this fellow through... but," he shrugged, "no hurry, heal well Lareaux; to be sure, there can be no claim of foul play! Come Mademoiselle." He stepped down backwards to the dirt road, pistol still trained on Lareaux, then held out his hand to assist Angelique's jump into the road without the use of steps. He slammed the door shut again.

Lareaux, having not uttered a word, knocked twice on the roof with his impostor cane and the carriage rumbled forward. Angelique was left standing beside her rescuer, the moon flitting unconcernedly in and out of cloud cover. She was silent, and shaking, her abstract thoughts wondering vaguely whether her loathsome cousin felt any differences about the cane yet. The fact that her legs could barely hold her upright took precedence.

"Come." Raoul took the pistol from her shaking hand, checked its safety and dropped it into his pocket; then taking her shoulders, pulled her onto his chest, holding her until the shuddering ceased, then putting her away, still holding her shoulders and looking down into her strained face. "*Never* do that to me again! When I heard, at the inn, that you had been taken up by Lareaux... and then that shot... but we'll discuss all of this once you are home. And I shall not leave there until Emile returns; he could not object to my presence under the same roof as two ladies, under these abominable conditions that we suffer."

She laughed shakily. "And if he did?"

"Then I suppose that he may rightfully call me out." He smiled gently. "Better?"

She nodded but her legs still felt like jelly.

He mounted and then reaching down held out his right hand and understanding, she took it in her left and placing one foot on top of his rigidly out-stretched one, vaulted up and managed to get her leg up and through as she settled in front of him, dragging through and adjusting the folds of her cloak.

"Ahem...tell me Mademoiselle, do I ignore the no skirts situation? Or do you, er, explain?"

She settled her breeches clad legs more comfortably and said, "You ignore it!"

"Ah! Now why did I guess as much? A difficult discipline but I shall contrive."

She laughed—a sound that had always captivated him but he did not miss the shaky quality lacing it now.

"Steady *mon enfant*, steady."

The mild everyday tone served to settle her more than any expressions of sympathy or concern could do and she leaned back against him, naturally and unthinkingly. They rode in silence back toward the pike-road turnoff and headed into the two-mile journey, almost all uphill, toward the château.

Deprived of their quarry, the mob moved as one, now bonded in unspoken revenge, for the nobility had always won and now here again they had won; and the victor two wretched females: it was intolerable. They ran at a wolf-trot: gently, unerringly, indomitably, determination their driving force. The whole château should burn; Monsieur le Comte and his family; and his staff. No thought of their very own kith and kin within that staff emerged, only that of genocide of a hated class, inflamed by the Comte's daughter's daring attempt to rescue the 'witch': for this woman had healed many a hopeless case. Was that not proof enough, for only the Lord Jesus owned that right. Her use of herbs and fungi, foreign leaf and root matter was surely a blasphemous thing: a thing of the devil.

Fanchon's ride proved one of debatable comfort but she did get a head start. She held to her animal for a good part of the first, wooded uphill climb and for this she was grateful. Topping the rise she could see the château upon the next. But it was then that her luck and rusty riding skill deserted her. Riding beneath low leafy branches, Fanchon could not see the owl, directly overhead. The close, cannon-like hoot caused her to suppress a scream and the horse to shy. It was sufficient. She tumbled to the ground, and the panicked animal galloped off snorting and whinnying, sounds heard by the more acute ears of the wolf-trotting men.

"There…over there!"

Soon her presence was detected and Fanchon, wrists tied with rough jute rope, struggled along in the hands of her captors until they at last reached the château, the mob splitting and running to the front and back, covering all sides.

Seeing the candles still burning in Siffred's butlers' quarters, Fanchon gave it her best shot and opened her mouth, screaming at a pitch that even she could only dimly remember from long ago childhood; a strange sound from the throat of an old woman. A fist came out of nowhere, cutting the sound off and darkness descended around her. She fell limp to the terrace and was left there for the moment.

The château was not altogether unprepared, for Siffred had had the entirety searched at Rochelle's concern and of his own accord. The search continued, outhouses, barns and stables and it was here that he heard the story from Phillippe. Returning to the château, he pondered the wisdom of informing Mademoiselle du Bois, as he mentally chose those of his staff to take with him to the village. But just then Fanchon's scream sounded. He flew to Rochelle, seated in the book-room, restlessly turning the pages of an old London fashion journal and pushed her towards the largest of the priest-holes.

"Do not…Mademoiselle, come out no matter what you hear! Do you hear me?"

She stared at him now, horror in her eyes at the sounds of the breaking glass and stampeding humanity within the château, aghast at the turn of events.

"But Siffred…I must help her!"

Unceremoniously he shoved her into the gaping hole. "Do not come out!" he hissed again. "They do not have her with them. *I* shall go look for Mademoiselle Vermont!"

"How do I get out again?"

"Place pressure on the centre of the panel to your left but do not use it until you experience silence for at least some hours. They lie in wait sometimes. Now go!"

He watched until the panel closed firmly, then ran to the Comte's library. That the documents entrusted to him were safe he knew but let them get hold of the book of promissory notes and such like, he would not.

Ransacking the château, they carried out jewellery and anything that gleamed of gold, heirlooms centuries old; and wine and cognac. But clothes, of materials and elegant cut were the greatest draw.

The housekeeper, Madame Vinue, white of face but cool and calm, stood in the Great Dining Hall, back to fireplace. Believing that she could reason with the intruders, she had gathered her immediate staff around her; all girls and young men from the village but now termed traitors. They screamed and fought against the attackers. Soon overpowered and slaughtered with crude weapons, their heads were cut off and stuck onto pikes to be carried back in triumph to the village, leaving the black and white tiled floor splattered with irregular patterns of blood. The headless body of Isobelle draped one window seat. Rochelle's *femme de chambre*, Lucinda, lay, also headless, at her feet.

The master's valet, not required upon this excursion of the Comte, and a person from Paris, tried to defend his master's personal belongings upon the dressing table and suffered like experience. Siffred: that known loyal man to his employer, was held down while his head was severed with an axe. The desk he protected was turned on its side and searched for secret draws and hiding places.

Outside on the front terrace, upon the second level, a bonfire was built and Fanchon knew her fate to be inescapable, no matter how her mistress had tried to rescue her: when the good Lord called, then he called. She asked for her hands to be freed to say her last prayers. After a debate on her rights of such, her hands were freed, though her legs remained tied to the pole stuck into the ground beneath an uprooted flagstone. Lifting her hands to the sky, she muttered softly and the mob pulled back superstitiously. She then lowered them to her chest and prayed again, unseen fingers curling into the seam of her gown. She raised them above her head again, palms together, head thrown back and muttered more strange words, driving the audience even further away. At last bringing her hands down again, she crossed herself and none saw the slight pause over her mouth on the downward movement. She smiled faintly, grimly: her gaze lifted to the heavens and the now fading stars. Or was her vision fading? She smiled again: please good Lord, make it quick, before the flames licked her feet, and God have mercy on such a cowardly soul. The stars blacked out completely but she forced her eyes to stay open and she could still hear, just faintly, then the kindly shadows of darkness cloaked her mind forever.

Her hands were retied behind the pole and the crowd grew silent in awe, for she neither pleaded nor showed distress in any way. Her head drooped now in servile manner and none could make her lift it again though her eyes gazed in gentle reproach. Here then was proof. It was unnatural to contemplate death by fire and not flinch. The mob drew back in silence as the faggots were lit and then flared in the night breeze, soon licking the feet of its victim but still she did not cry out. Fear fed upon fear and they withdrew further and further from the scene, muttering protective curses against such a person. Here surely was a witch. They did not feel the triumph or savage glee prompted by the victim's screams and, denied this, they turned and rampaged toward the steps leading to the great double doors. But the vision of those calm eyes on them, as the body burned, would never be reduced in effect; no matter how long they lived.

The barns were ablaze, sending plumes of smoke and flaring shafts of orange skyward, by the time the bonfire burned its most fierce. It then began to collapse, flaring from time to time in the gentle summer night-breeze and it was this that welcomed Angelique and Raoul as they topped the last low rise.

A choked cry escaped Angelique and the arm tightened round her waist.

"Steady *mon enfant*, steady. 'Tis only the barns." His voice was soothing and gentle, belying the grim fury writ across his face. "And you know that Emile has had a contingency plan for just this, no? You did not? But he did not tell you? He has the grain in the cellars and the dungeons beneath the old section of the château, along with a store of food and water. But of course it will not come to that. Soon this great upheaval shall be but a bad dream."

He continued talking in everyday accents until he felt the rigidity leave her body.

"Rochelle," she whispered in accents of horror.

"Come now, the château stands." His voice changed: stern and imperative, producing the desired effect.

She straightened and said no more until they grew closer and saw the bonfire on the terrace. She was silent as he dismounted and as silently allowed him to lift her to the ground. She stood a moment, gazing in stupefied manner, walking forward in trance, hand over mouth until she stood staring down at the still hot ashes and blackened lump of remains of Fanchon. She choked on a cry of anguish, flinging herself to the ground, reaching out but not quite touching the charred body: wherever she touched must surely hurt. But no, dead people did not hurt anymore. She reached closer and gingerly touching the burned eyelids, fearing them to disintegrate, pulled them down over the staring pale blue eyes that had somehow escaped the licking flames. She closed her own eyes and swayed a fraction.

"They won," she whispered. "*Grand Dieu*! Beneath all that is evil... nothing overshadows this! They got her." Suddenly vicious in her desire for revenge, she turned and looked blindly up at Raoul as he stood now, watchfully beside her. He bent, took her by the elbows, lifted her to her feet and turned her away.

Flinging the hands off, she turned back. "No! I want to stay! I *shall* stay!"

He did not touch her again but his imperative tone of voice far outweighed any physical restraint. "You must come away... nothing can be gained here."

"No! I shall stay! Fanchon! Oh *why* did I force you onto that animal! Why! *Why*?"

"*Angelique!*" It was his first use of her name but she did not note it.

"A moment—but a moment longer...she was *une mère*, for so long, to me!"

"Come," he repeated, his accents icily stern now. "There will *never* be moment that you shall be willing to leave her. Come. We must estimate the damage."

She allowed herself to be led away but refused, as he knew that she would, to be installed in a quiet salon while he toured the château and together they made the gruesome discoveries. That he hovered beside her, cradled her as she discovered Isobelle, watchfully guided her, she was not aware but later, years later within the flashbacks and eternal 'replay' that accompanies such trauma, she wondered how it would have been without him. She supposed little would have been different, for at such times one is aware of nothing; within the hollowness of mind and soul. That he had guided her decisions; softened the anguish and shielded both she and Rochelle from even more heinous acts within stables and outhouses, she later learned from Henri.

They found Rochelle, sitting in the Comte's library, holding Siffred's hand, his severed head lined up against his shoulders, propped up by heavy books; the only one to escape the pike journey back to the village: his particular assailants turning their attention then to ransacking the château. She looked up as they entered the room then down again.

"Look Ange. Humpty Dumpty. And they were right: we cannot put him together again!" She began to giggle and Angelique, now operating within a vacuum of false calm, walked swiftly toward her and before Raoul could move, dealt her a hard slap across both sides of her face.

She gasped in shock, then rising from her knees turned to her old friend. "Thank you," she said, "Undisciplined of me!"

Raoul's eyebrows shot toward his hairline. "Harsh, but effective," he murmured.

Rochelle, now partially restored to her former unflappable English self, led them into the untouched little salon, a place that had been reckoned not worth searching.

"Well Ange?  What to do?" She looked at the bell-pull and then at her friend. "Tea? Isn't that what people do—drink tea?"

"Tea forsooth: this is France! *I* need a cognac!"

A hovering footman, pale and shaking still, came forward. "Monseigneur," he bowed to Raoul, "I do not know much but I do know where there be a store they did not find."

"Thankyou: good man. Do get it please."

The footman returned with a dented silver tray carrying the bottle and three glasses and Raoul gazed at him, a wry smile across his features. "Already had yours, hmm?"

"But no Monsieur," the footman was horrified.

Angelique spoke gently. "Then go get some Henri... you possibly need it more than us... you were here! Then round up all remaining staff to the staff dining-hall and give them some also. We shall then take stock and see what is to be done."

It was now growing close to dawn, the smoke from the smouldering barns hanging in the hollows and caressing the smooth, flat surface of the stream. The sky, clear and windless, promised another hot day. Angelique moved, talked and thought without emotion: that would come later.

They joined the servants in their dining-hall and Angelique set some order to the tasks for the day, of cleaning up the château, as Raoul marshalled the remaining stable and field staff to remove and bury the bodies: it was summer. Daylight arrived; bringing shock and exhaustion; but action to a job of work he knew to be the only answer to the immediate post-disaster aimlessness of its victims.

The family carriage rumbled up to the front entrance. The destroyed barns and stables were hidden from view on this approach. Casting a puzzled frown around at the absence of butler and footmen, Joubeau ordered one of the two riding up behind to lower the steps for the Vicomte. Not waiting for this service however, coatless in the heat, he leapt down and ran lightly up the wide shallow steps to the front entrance. Here also emptiness of persons met his frowning gaze. He moved purposefully towards his father's library: also silent and empty. He turned back into the hall, noticing the missing artefacts now. He frowned: taken off for cleaning and polishing? But they did not enter the festive season, or a wedding or any function that he could remember. He grew cold suddenly as he turned to witness the now promoted Henri enter from the service door.

"Ah...Henri, where is everybody? Do not tell me that they have been recalled to Paris by the Comte?"

"Ah...er...no... Monsieur le Vicomte! I shall send for Mademoiselle, she be within the drying-room Monsieur... but a moment." He bowed politely and turned but the Vicomte's voice froze his movement.

"Henri! What is Mademoiselle Angelique actually *doing* in the drying-room?"

"Er...she is occupied there with the herbs and spices, Monsieur. I believe that the bottling of some such be due just now. Brigette has just taken more stone jars across, Sire."

Emile frowned at the 'Sire'. Much was amiss and this man did not want to tell him about it. "Henri. Do empty your budget! What is afoot?"

"Monsieur, I shall send for Madame poste-haste. Please let me do that for there is too much for me to explain."

Tension born of alarm tightened his chest. "Thank you Henri... I shall go myself."

He strode from the hall.

Angelique, engrossed in the task before her, did not hear her twin until he stood beside her. Startled, she stared up at him silently. She took his proffered hands, staring up into his face; then, unable to stop the sweeping tide of violent emotion, leaned against him and wept.

Emile felt the chill of before deepen and, waiting for the storm to abate, held her, the quip regarding the spoiling of his very favourite waistcoat dying on his tongue. This was the first of such emotion he had witnessed since her pony had died. Afore that: the long nights following their *mère's* death. After a few minutes, perhaps only seconds even, the storm abated and the shuddering of her body slowed.    She marshalled her wanton emotions and stepped back, making efforts at apology.

Holding her shoulders, gazing down into eyes dark with grief, he cut her short, "Tell me."

It grew late as they sat in the small salon, the one room unaffected by the attack but also uncluttered of heirlooms and heavy furniture and owning the widest and longest windows, to allow the summer breeze entry.  Raoul sat on one side of the empty fireplace, Emile the other, Rochelle a little to one side of him and Angelique over by the windows open onto the terrace. The silence was deep, fraught with shock and grief and Raoul watched Angelique beneath hooded lids.

"Château Coste is alright?" she asked now in a flat voice.

"Oh yes, nothing that cannot be rebuilt."

The silence returned.

"And Clarisse and Stannilaus: and the children? They actually stay in Italy?" asked Rochelle suddenly.

"Yes, until things settle and they may return." Emile did not know what more to say and then, gazing at his twin, "I shall take you one day, you perhaps need to go. It is a very beautiful part of Italy. The peace there is what you need perhaps."

"No. What I *need*, Emile, is to cut the throat of every murderous Machiavellian in this country." It was a flat, cool statement.

Emile glanced at Raoul but before either could move Rochelle was at her side, taking her hand and gazing in deep concern, then spoke in gentle tones.

"My dear, it was but their property: not that I belittle such, but after this week there is… there must be… worse to come, collect yourself do, to deal with it."

Angelique turned her face to her friend. "I am ready. But *Fanchon*," she paused, swallowed, "was a mother to me… and Isobelle… my beloved Isobelle… those days in England… then here… so much more than a *femme de chambre*, a *compagne even*… so, so long were we together! But *why* the village staff! Why them: *their very own!*"

Henri knocked and upon call entered. "Dinner is served, Monsieur… Madame," he said looking from Angelique to the Vicomte, not sure to whom he should address this.

Angelique turned her head. "Well, I suppose we must eat… somehow."

"At least the chef kept his head!" muttered Emile

The carriage rolled to a stop. The château was uncannily quiet and the ever-present and incomparable Siffred nowhere to be seen. The Comte frowned: senses heightened by the preceding weeks fraught with danger and suspicion.  Working alongside Danton and Mirabeau had not been easy, as he had watched his back *and* the interests of the king.  He wished the king would accept brief exile: until things settled a little.  Smelling disarray, he moved cautiously into the hall noting the missing artefacts, crossed it, and climbed the sweeping staircase. Noting suddenly the absence of a portrait on the landing he stood still a moment and finally entered the library: cautiously. Looking around briefly at the changes he moved to the bell-pull.

"You rang Monsieur...oh! Ah," bowing low Henri then straightened and looked at the Monsieur le Comte. "I shall send for the Vicomte, Sire!"

"One moment," the Comte's voice was soft and calm, "Where is Siffred?"

"Sire...I cannot say...I, er, mean..."

"Will not."

"Er...well Sire, will not, that is, I mean...cannot...that is, I think it be better..."

"That you send for the Vicomte, Henri: and as you appear to have lost the faculty of speech, I quite agree."

"Yes Sire!"

The family sat together again in the small salon. The Comte stared at the floor for some time and then, the twirling of his claret glass the only evidence of his emotions, looked up at Emile. "We take the closed coach and travel to Paris, following the breaking of the fast on the morrow. Angelique and Rochelle shall stay at Hôtel Quatreaux until we go to Versailles for the welcoming of the Flanders Regiment."

"Oh, the whole regiment?"

"Yes, Emile. Francois will be there."

"Shall Paris be safer than here, Sire?" asked Angelique. "The attack be over and to escape that place we came here."

"It shall probably be safer in Paris now that Louis is bringing in that Regiment but also there is no guarantee that a second attack here shall not occur. After all, they did not manage to kill any of *us*," the Comte smiled grimly. "And as I *must* go, so we all go."

"What battles are being fought at the Assembly then, beside Louis' troop reinforcement? We have been somewhat busy of late," said Angelique apologetically, glancing at him warily for he had not as yet reacted to her actions over the village affair. Grief took precedence; Siffred had been more than a butler to him: they had spanned, together, more than thirty years, shared many adventures and dangers. This, none fully appreciated.

The Comte gazed coolly at her now. "*Ma fille*: that much is evident. And I am wondering just what maggot got into your head, hmm?"

Raoul began to rise from his chair but the Comte waved him back again. "You be part of this family now," he smiled wryly. "Be that fortunate or unfortunate for you...I suspect the latter! Indeed, since the affair of the Parisian street riots and now this added involvement, I owe you more than I can say."

Raoul subsided, and shrugging this off, sat very still, watching Angelique, aware that he could do nothing to spare her. His eyes, filled with deep understanding, caught hers. For a moment she basked there before again meeting her *père's*, hard, icy stare.

"Well?" asked the Comte, the dulcet tones causing Emile to sink a fraction lower in his chair, with a surreptitious grimace at Raoul.

"No maggot Monseigneur, except to retrieve Fanchon. I could not leave her there." She gazed at him defiantly. "I cannot see that there was any other option, for had I stayed at the château and left her to burn, then I could rest, apparently, within *mon père's* good grace. But never could I live with myself again."

Emile gave a mental groan and inched deeper into his chair. "You appear to miss the point, Angelique. Your riding off *ventre a terre* to the rescue pre-empted the attack upon the château."

"But I gave it my best efforts, Monseigneur. I can think of no other decision that could have been executed at that time."

He stared at her and then, with the extreme gentleness and politeness that had sent a chill down the spine of his offspring and staff over the years, enlightened her upon *other decisions*. These, thus explained, may have resulted in rather less than the violence experienced by the occupants of Château Quatreaux.

As she listened politely, Angelique remembered past chastisements but she was a child no longer and life had changed dramatically. Now, sometimes in but a few brief moments, decision of action must be made and then hope for the best. That he chose not to chastise her in the privacy of his library but before others, showed, she knew, his deep concern for her. His exposure of her to embarrassment was meant to burn the lesson into her brain: in effect he was fearful of repeat event should circumstances further deteriorate in this country. And there was, he knew, nothing surer. She stood her ground, informing him that she failed to see that he himself would have acted any differently. Raoul hid a smile as he listened and could but applaud her courage. Of that attribute, though, he had already more evidence than any man needed.

"Besides, I have in my possession that which you seek, Monseigneur," she ended quietly.

The Comte's slender, elegant hands, about to fob his snuffbox, stilled of a sudden and he shot her a keen glance. He said nothing but waited.

Emile sat up suddenly. "*What?*"

"If you will bear with me for but a moment," she responded and moved to the door. Some few minutes later she reappeared with a gentleman's cane and two very tightly rolled parchments in her hand, moved across the room to the Comte and handed them to him.

The Comte carefully unrolled the first, glanced at it and then the second one. Allowing them to spring back into their tightly rolled state again, he looked up at her.

"Your arbitration skills are unequalled, *ma fille*, for I shall not insult you with the term bribery. I know you too well. You know that there was no excuse for your behaviour in going to the village. The fact that I, as you say, would have done so makes no difference to the fact that *you* as a female should not have. However, for these," glancing down at the documents, "I must obviously thank you, but did it occur to you that I may have had plans of my own? That I may have had the means to extract them from him no matter where he had them hidden?"

"Well, I suppose that now you are relieved of that office. I am sorry Monseigneur, but you cannot blame me for taking advantage of his situation there."

"Oh but I can: and I do! You did not think the matter through; think of all the probabilities. At every moment during your foolish venture you could have been caught. You had completed your rescue at that point and should have got out of that inn poste-haste. How is it that offspring of mine suffer such appalling lack intelligence?"

"So Lareaux had them on him all the time... carried them everywhere with him in fact," grinned Emile now. "What made you hit upon the cane as the hiding place?"

She told him about Devereaux' perplexity over the issue of the cane incident: that it had dwelt always on the edge of her mind for some reason.

He smiled suddenly. "Good old Dev. He shall go far in the army with such instincts!"

Raoul picked up the cane, only very faintly fatter than any gentleman's cane, balanced it on his palm and then experimentally unscrewed it. He looked at her suddenly, his eyes dancing for the first time since the tragedy. "Concealed it under your cloak I suppose?"

"Yes, in a deep inside pocket."

"Ah yes," he grinned but said no more about what else she had concealed beneath her cloak and she suddenly smiled faintly at his restraint. The general chaos and overt thievery would, she hoped, have covered any discrepancies within Emile's wardrobe, for she had disposed of the stained and ruined breeches and shirt.

"The pistol?" enquired Emile suddenly, grinning. "Throws to the left?"

"Yes. When the blood showed through from his shoulder I was for an instant worried that I had killed him. I aimed for his upper arm only."

"Why the worry, one more skunk despatched."

"No," said Raoul now, cold intent lacing his voice, "that privilege be *mine!*"

The Comte gazed at him beneath hooded lids and saw and was satisfied but all he said was, "Come now, we cannot fight over the issue. He is mine from way past."

"But Sire," laughed Emile, "be fair... you have already despatched one Lareaux!"

The journey to Paris was fast to the point of danger, the passengers swaying in practised manner, the groom beside the coachman clinging on and casting darkling glances at Joubeau.

"'Tis a killed that we be," he said between his teeth now and Joubeau laughed.

"When the Comte says to go speedily that better be what we do. And 'tis naught agin the Vicomte when *he* decides the issue!"

The Vicomte and Raoul, now also travelling to Paris, rode escort. Two chosen and trusted, as much as one may trust any man now, grooms rode on the other side; Phillippe being one of them. The carriage also carried Henri; now butler in training; from memory of Siffred's behaviour and stringent reminders from the Comte, and the chef, a person of Paris, begging not to be left behind.

Blackened and charred remains of other châteaux stood grim reminder of the unrest within the countryside, as they rattled toward the city; all the effects of riot and crime still deep at work. The rise in bread shortages and prices, caused by interference by the Assembly with the corn trade, resulted in an increased pillage of corn on transit.

Upon the municipality and the National Guard, now fell the chore of maintaining order; the current chaos exacerbated by new fears of starvation: the National Guard forming as an organized police force. Most who served were volunteers but 6,000, incorporating the French Guards, were paid and lodged in barracks. The soldiers now elected their officers: following the abolition of the four-aristocratic-grandparent regime of the old order for commissions. Lafayette, the commander-in chief, was popular with these men but his influence over them was confined within very narrow limits. The Guard retained its character of citizen force, possessing strong political bias, capable at any time of taking its own course. Of this Lafayette was aware, but having controlled worse in America, remained confident in his own ability.

During September the idea began to take root and grow in strength, of marching to Versailles and bringing the *Famille Roi* to Paris, amid rumours of their intended flight across the frontier. The people believed their sufferings, supposedly due entirely to royal and noble intrigues, would abate with the king securely established in their midst.

Within Versailles, since the July 'Bastille Day' Revolution, plans of retreat to Metz and Rambouillet had been urged upon the king but it was impossible to adopt this course without resource to arms. De Quatreaux' carefully laid original plans were dissolved. The Queen was now more than willing to leave but Louis had concerns regarding the similarity of such action with that of Charles the 1st of England that had aroused civil war. He decided finally to bring a thousand troops, the Flanders Regiment from Arras, to Versailles, as a precaution and preparation commenced for the traditional banquet of honour, for the newcomers. All aggression was banned but aggression was far from the minds of the Household Guards anticipating the age-old, welcome-banquet tradition.

# CHAPTER TWELVE

## Banquets and Violence

The king looked stonily at Necker. "And still they are not happy: though the Assembly reigns supreme. They have abolished feudalism, created the Declaration of Rights and asked me to accept a suspensive veto, but the government of the city, in less than two months, has changed three times! Each of these accompanied by manifestos, demonstrations and intrigues, each successive body immediately stood upon its head by the very people who put them in place. Paris remains in uproar." He smiled cynically. "Semi-independent districts dispute the control of municipal affairs, the most troublesome being the *Palais-Royal* and its cafés and clubs and everywhere the *Grande Peur* reigns. Bread is still in short supply, the Seine is so low that the Paris water-mills are out of action and the corn that you purchased at the beginning of the month, from Morocco and Burgundy, is now reduced to only ten days baking. Supplies from Flanders, Italy and England have run dry and so now you place orders with Hamburg. Am I correct thus far?"

"Yes Sire…but…"

"Oh, do not spare me whatever you do! To continue; the starvation is exacerbated by the émigrés…200,000 passports issued to date…the recipients taking their wealth with them and causing a flotilla of domestic servants and other workers of the luxury trades to be thrown onto the street. And the countryside remains in uproar; revolts rage against the constitutional protection army and the people refuse to pay the taxes that now replace those they had got rid of. The burning, slaughter and pillaging of châteaux is increasing by the day, so that soon the face of France shall resemble that of the moon... and I dare say that be a slight on the moon."

"I believe the moon to be a beautiful planet, by comparison, these days, Sire."

The king stared: Necker the sombre, the sober, was jesting. He continued, "And now to the issue of my Flanders Regiment: is it really going to be the cause of yet another insurrection? Even though you informed the deputies that they are here at the *request* of the municipalities: to *support* the Town Guard?"

"Our informants, Sire, tell that defence strategies are being placed within Paris to repel a royal attack. Nothing will convince them otherwise. They have ordered the transfer of powder from the magazines at Essonnes, and the purchase of bullets and cannonballs."

"All the more need for the Regiment then… and the dinner tonight, Necker. 'Tis an ancient traditional welcome by the Royal Guards to the Flanders Regiment, and I shall not abandon a tradition that this court has always offered to their incoming officers!"

"Sire, if you could pardon me from the dinner? I have business in Paris that cannot wait. I had planned on leaving from here this night, if I may, Sire?"

The king looked at him for a long moment and Necker knew that royal trust in him was growing to low tide. He was approaching the precipice and knew not whether he would be able to leap the abyss but the opinion of the people he feared more.

♣

October 1st, 1789, and the welcoming dinner given by the king's bodyguard to the Flemish Regiment officers, gave evidence of considerable enjoyment: the humour of the hosts and guests increasing as the hours advanced and the barrels emptied. The scene was exceptionally colourful: the officers smart and handsome in dress uniform and sword; the tables, glittering with crystal and crowded with fine china, competed with the surrounding opulence of the Royal Theatre. The toast was the royal family and loyalties centuries old echoed through the palace theatre beneath the gold and blue canopies. The sumptuous banquet, offered by the royal chef, was served against a background of a royal orchestra. Inevitably, deeply royalist songs were played and shouts of 'Vive le Roi' cannoned through the surrounds for several minutes.

The king and queen appeared with the Dauphin, suddenly, and it began all over again. The crowded room erupted, with many tears and many officers saluting the king with their swords. The royal family walked among the guests with the Dauphin in the queen's arms, the tears in Her Majesty's eyes causing undying loyalty to King and Throne.

Jean-Roberte Gregoiré, an officer close to retirement, was saddened and infuriated by the coming death of these traditional loyalties, inextricably linked to the tottering throne, for with it went the loyalty of man to man. The brotherhood, that was on everyone's lips now as a new revolutionary innovation but had its roots in thousands of years of history, was about to die: as that very Revolution, he was sure, would rent all asunder. He watched, as the night wore on, with deepening anxiety. The national cockade, fallen and trampled underfoot in the highly charged atmosphere; was replaced by the black badge of Austria. He wondered of a sudden, who had been idiot enough to procure them for this night. He leaned back in his chair and turned to a fellow officer and long companion, as Francois, splendid in his regimentals and seated half way down one of the tables, leapt to his feet to propose yet another toast: *"Vive le Reine!"*

Another sprang up in his wake: *"Vive le Dauphin!"*

He vented a deep sigh. "My days are numbered within this establishment, *mon ami*, but I hope *that* young man has received an excellent training."

His friend turned to stare. "That's young de Quatreaux, is it not?"

Gregoiré grunted. "Yes, and he shall need all the skill that can be mustered in the coming months."

"But surely 'tis so: *you* have been a large part of it."

"It's the remaining part that I am worried about! But have done my best for the Comte."

"Ah! Promised to look after him, eh?" The grey head moved slowly from side to side. "Bad mistake that. Never promise."

A grim smile crossed Gregoirés face. "Promised to polish him as a piece of ebony... if causing him to be bullet proof proved impossible."

The king's departure, with his wife and child, brought his speech to a halt as shouts of 'down with the Assembly' resounded and Gregoiré groaned, "This is going to spread as did the Great Fire of London," he muttered.

"Rumour in avalanche, propelled by its own weight...'twill reach Paris afore we do."

Gregoiré nodded. "I can see it now: 'Banquet held for Counterrevolutionaries!' 'An orgy: where the national cockade is trampled underfoot.'"

"Someone should cut Hébert's throat!"

"You are offering? You think *mon ami*, that that would extinguish the voice of the '*Pére Duchesne*'? We have freedom of the press now."

"*Something* needs to...*and* that of those disgusting pamphleteers."

Meantime: Angelique and Rochelle, ensconced in the queen's apartments with the ladies-in-waiting, sat talking with Estelle Pontac and Princess Lamballe. They rose as Her Majesty reappeared, kissed her son goodnight and handed him over to the first rocker, smiling happily for the first time in many weeks.

Estelle Pontac looked at her. "Madame? I take it that all went well?"

"Ah but you should have seen them! If only the country contained more of their calibre." She sank to a chair and the company sat again. "But unfortunately it does not." Her smile disappeared, leaving a sadly wistful expression.

"But Madame, you do not know that: out of twenty-six million people there must be! They are all afraid, that is all."

The queen gazed at her sadly. "Estelle *mon amie*, therein lies the essence."

Paris: 3rd October 1789. Gossip regarding the Flanders dinner party grew in dimensions and intensity but had no direction. The leader of the Jacobin party frowned in thought, then looked across the desk at his visitor. Though fastidious regarding manners, he did not offer a seat. His visitor did not expect one: here only to receive orders. He waited.

Robespierre rose and moved to the window. "The streets are reasonably quiet today...even after the Flanders Regiments' dinner party! The mob has gone off the boil."

His visitor waited.

"So...though the fall of the Bastille, collapse of authority and the *Grande Peur*, have caused resistance by the privileged classes within the Assembly to weaken... they have not caused their demise!"

His visitor now spoke, hesitantly. "I know little of the politics Citizen but seems to me that they are indeed rallying from all this. In fact a 'royalist body' of some strength, wishing to restore the king's executive powers, have begun to appear in the Assembly... so I hear. But of this you will be aware Citizen."

Robespierre, for once not irritated by rhetoric, turned to gaze at him. "Indeed! And so we must maintain the upper hand: which is almost ours... against this royalist body. Fear: that is the key. This is where you come in. A protest march on Versailles, by the hungry, especially women and children, shall bring the pot back to the boil. See to it."

Robespierre returned to his seat and took up his quill.

His visitor, effectively dismissed, looked at the bent head a moment; then, "Er...regarding violence, Citizen?"

Robespierre completed a word with a flourish, rested the quill and looked up. "If it takes violence then, regrettably, it does so. But once alight, the fire shall need no fanning... a picture drawn of a starving people, while Versailles feasts, shall be the only faggot required."

His visitor nodded, and turned to leave the room, thankfully: he had not ever gazed into such cold flat eyes as those of Robespierre. Rumour had it that the man was incapable of emotion and he believed it. He reached for the doorhandle but the even, polite tones of his superior halted his step.

"And bring the royal family back to Paris. And before you weary me by asking, I do not care how."

♣

Sunday, October 4<sup>th</sup> and the *Palais-Royal* cafes and clubs filled with patriotic revolutionaries. Gossip, stretched and growing by the minute, of the Versailles dinner for the Flanders Regiment, resounded up and down the streets.

"When there be a serious suffering by want of bread, Versailles feasts and dances!"

"The very soldiers are preparing, it be a pre-battle feast... that what it be!"

"Ah be quiet woman! Were you there? No, of course not, that was no pre-battle dancing but a welcome dinner of *very* ancient ritual. Be fair woman, you know it to be so... cease your witch-hunting and let well alone. We have enough to attend!"

The woman clung, limpet-like, to her mantra. "Agin the good Lord: that what it be, opera-dinners and the like, while the nation starves!"

"*Cease* I said, woman, nobody starves! Flour be a little scarce, that be all."

"Oh Yes? Then *they* hide it... to bring us to our knees... to starve us into submission!"

"Submission to *what*... they already has everything!"

"Well, I hear tell that the green uniforms were adorned with black, Monsieur! The black cockades of the Austrian hoar! Enough reason! March I say! March on Versailles!"

"March!"

"March!"

"March!"

"Paris starves soon... I hear tell... *really* starves!"

"March for bread!"

"Must we starve, while they feast? March I say!"

"*And*: to avenge the trampled French cockade!"

The rioting grew, the mob heard of a baker hoarding flour in expectation of higher prices as the shortage increased. He was dragged before the Hôtel de Ville and lynched; his store then found to be empty. Others had their shops burned and the city police their hands full in efforts to contain the fury, terrified that Paris would burn wholesale.

Monday October 5th, 1789, early morning found the Town Hall surrounded by hungry mobs of women, calling for the Mayor, shouting their desire for a march to Versailles. They waited his arrival, far past the hour of opening and then broke into the building, seizing all the money and arms to be found there.

Abbe Lefebvre tried to reason with the mob of angry women; wishing that he too had recognized them as uncontrollable and also turned his carriage rapidly round, as had the unseen Mayor. He stood his ground, refusing to hand out more arms and ammunition. They grew angry at his change of front, demanding that he assist them as he had during the events of July 13th with arms for the taking of the Bastille. Fighting for his life, he appealed to the womanly heart of the mob. To his dismay he quickly discovered such did not exist; only hatred, hunger and fear; and hostility toward the men of Paris for their faint-heartedness over the issue. They were indeed the more deadly of the species.

"You issued arms for the Bastille! Give us now!"

"But Mesdames, they were men. I cannot give arms to women."

"Huh! That be so? Then move aside... we will not be stopped!"

He gazed around in terror as cries of a lynching rent the air and those on the outer environs found a rope; not knowing the facts of the matter but it mattered not: they believed their sisters. It was only the arrival of the National Guard that caused a pause in the events long enough for him to survive. The Guard at last restored order and the women, searching a male leader, found it in the 26-year-old Stanilas Maillard, a Châtelet employee and one of the prominent heroes of the Bastille-day revolt.

This tall, lean young man now headed the procession of women, armed with the few stolen weapons but mostly with the usual pikes and pitchforks. Achieving the orderliness demanded, he led the way as they moved noisily along the Paris streets and out onto the road to Versailles, recruiting all on the way; all given the tricolour cockade to wear. Robespierre's men worried at the sudden availability of so many cockades in so short a time, defying that this be the spontaneous march that it appeared. It was fifteen miles to Versailles, a wet day and the road increasingly muddy, the deliberately fasting women scantily and poorly clad: by design. Bands of men soon followed. The crowd grew.

The tocsins rang out yet again across Paris, though they had barely ceased, as Lafayette bore the efforts to coerce him into following the marching women, while the municipal council still debated the issue.

He looked at the Guard spokesman in a puzzled way. "Why do you want to go? They are a bunch of women. They cannot harm the king."

"Not, Mon Commandant, to defend the king but to support the demands of the women and to avenge ourselves against the Flemish Regiment's insult to the tricolour cockade."

"And to bring the royal family back to Paris Sir... and the Parliament," said another.

Lafayette looked at him and suddenly knew that he had to go: slaughter could ensue.

"Please, please remember the fate of Foulon," said another, suppressing a shudder, at the memory of that man's terrible death, wondering if it be really necessary to carry torture and mutilation to such debased levels. And Lafayette did remember; not so much the event as Chateaubriand's comments later:

'—"I saw the lot from my window, Lafayette. They were brigands. Worse: worse than the uncivilized tribes of the wildest corners of the earth. Heads on pikes indeed! If I'd had a gun I'd have shot the lot down like the vermin that they are."

"Ah yes," Lafayette had responded, "But what else can one expect from a populace accustomed to a long history of torture and subjugation... blinded now by the bright sun of propaganda; as they emerge from their dark places of ignorance?"

"An eye for an eye... this is the effect that they want of their Revolution?"

Lafayette had shrugged: 'Well, I only know that the *pure* revolutionaries do believe this: that these executions be more than revenge. They be the necessary foundations to a more enlightened life."

"Bah! You know better than that; or is it your plan to use it? Let go the glory Lafayette, you have succeeded, you have arrived *mon ami*. Your place in America is up among the highest, the most esteemed of heroes... *and* here. You cannot ask for more. One day thou shalt reach too far. Leadership of this country be not in your stars, believe me."

Lafayette had smiled gently, "But you mistake me. I have no thought but for a constitutional monarchy"—'

Obtaining an order from the Town Hall, he now set out, reluctantly, hating the ramshackle turn of events. He left with 15,000 Guards and many more irregular and ill-disciplined volunteers, knowing that he would not reach Versailles before midnight. Volunteers were the bane of his life: a law unto their own selves, they were practically uncontrollable. He sent for a messenger and soon the *avante-coureur*, leaving Lafayette and the troops far behind, headed for the Palace with a message for the king, warning him but also urging the Monarch not to fire on the mob.

The National Assembly at Versailles was in uproar: again. This time the cause that of the king's refusal to promulgate certain issues of the constitution, kindly acceding to those articles which had already been voted. His condition: that no attempt be made to lessen his executive powers. He also informed them that he would consider the Declaration of Rights, still hanging in abeyance, after the constitution had been passed.

The anger of the deputies of the centre left and extreme left, had bubbled and boiled for weeks now, hating the unpalatable discovery that the roots of monarchical power had been driven very deep over the centuries. It was going to take more than the creation of an Assembly to eradicate them.

The people wanted total change, immediately, and were discovering the difficulty in even finding the legal origins of acts and decrees necessary for their abolition. The right and centre right still clung to this fact in fragile hope that events would eventually settle to compromise: with constitutional monarchy resulting. But the general populace could not understand why it could not all be swept aside, with the sweep of a hand. That it could not bore evidence to the fact that the Assembly was balanced by the right: preventing unanimous vote. This much was very clear and certain members of the extreme left laid their foundation plans; silently and invisibly, led by one fanatical, puritanical Robespierre; visualizing a future far beyond most men's imagination.

It was 3 p.m. The uproar within the Assembly this day grew intolerable and nothing could be heard of the speaker at all. Mounier sat in the chair ringing his *sonnette*. On the point of donning his hat and suspending the sitting, he was halted by the arrival of the women who demanded to be heard, as they broke into the Assembly Hall, their voices shouting above those of the deputies.

The voices rose as one: "Bread! Bread! Bread!"

The faint-hearted of the deputies attempted to leave. Horror registered on these faces as the women prevented them, their flat, gleaming eyes resembling those of a frenzied, dervish dancer as he danced himself into exhaustion.

It became a chant. Another started up: "Less talk... more bread... you talk, talk, talk... while our families starve, starve, starve... you are the new Assembly, yes? Here to stamp out the old and bring in the new? Yes? *Then do it*!"

"Bread! Bread! Bread!"

The left and extreme left of the Assembly took up the cry: "Bread! Bread! Bread!"

"But there *be* bread," cried a weak voice in defence, "This be fear tactics!"

Nobody heard him above the chant of the combined women and Assembly voices.

"Bread! Bread! Bread!"

Mounier stood, climbed onto his chair, and rang his *sonnette* continuously. His *hussiers* marched up and down, forcing a passage through the seething mass of female humanity, waving their swords and crying out for order until the uproar subsided to a steady rumble.

"I shall *not* have this, in this assembly, while I am *President*!"

"Then listen to us!"

"Then choose a man to speak for you and we *shall* listen!"

They chose Maillard and he conveyed their grievances of bread and cockade and requests of punishment of the Flanders Regiment. The deputies of the left, listening, suddenly saw new tools to use against the king and offered Mounier, as President, to support them at the palace. Hiding his chagrin, he accompanied them, with instructions to acquire the king's three signatures: to three decrees—providing food for Paris, to the Declaration of Rights and to the suspensive veto.

They waited five hours, Mounier and the deputies kicking their heels in the palace, growing more and more furious, whilst the king was sort and requested to return from his hunting within the forest. The queen was found at the Petit Trianon, the last visit that she would ever pay to this place of sanctuary. But this was not the cause of delay: the debate that ensued was; and still the king prevaricated. Food for Paris he deemed reasonable but the other two caused intense anxiety.

"De Quatreaux! What would you do? Hmm? Should I slip away? It sticks in my gullet so it does. They shall *not* command the king. I shall *not* be driven from my palace by a bunch of women. Besides... a fugitive king? No, I say."

Marie Antoinette entered at that moment and de Quatreaux made his bow but she brushed it aside. "Mon husband! We must go! We must flee Versailles now... please!"

The king looked at her and spoke gently. "*Ma chérie*? You would have me abdicate? For it will be read as nothing less."

"The carriages are at the door Sire, Madame," said de Quatreaux. He paused thoughtfully, knowing that they would not escape without notice and that the mobs would overturn the carriage and tear them to pieces. "But my opinion, for what it is worth, is that I should not use them, just yet awhile. I should wait for the dust to settle on this issue. Send the women back with the promise of bread, Sire, for we know just where it is stockpiled. I believe that I have the tools to force the hands of those renegades that starve a people for political reasons. And then go. But not in the royal carriages Sire, but plain, black, crestless ones."

"To Metz?"

"No Your Majesty, to Rambouillet: everything be prepared there for Your Majesties."

"Listen to him, do, Louis." The queen was pacing and then pausing suddenly before him, took his hand in hers. "Louis, I must return to the children now but please do listen to Vermont." She turned then to de Quatreaux, holding out her hand to him in farewell.

De Quatreaux took her proffered hand, bowed and kissed the pale fingers. "Do not worry too much Your Majesty, though I know it be hard; but Lafayette does have them in hand."

"Lafayette!" On a note of savage disgust she turned to leave the room, then pausing, she stared at him. "Vermont, I *cannot* believe that you do not see that... that... Americanised man, for what he is!"

De Quatreaux moved forward again, bowed low and smiled grimly. "Never, Your Majesty, doubt that for a minute. But he has his uses... and this be one of them."

"Even though he hates... loathes me: *without* knowing me?"

De Quatreaux gazed at her. "Even though!" He could not be less than honest with her: would not offer denials and empty platitudes.

She stared at him, a faint smile in her eyes. "De Quatreaux... I hope you are correct."

She left them.

The king, turning from his contemplative state during this interchange, spoke: "But has the moment come to appeal, Vermont, to the country: against Paris and the Assembly?"

"Your Majesty, I cannot but feel that that time is past: from the other side we can fight. The armies are ready and impatient, I do not know how long they can be contained, primed for action, before they wander off, the émigrés very bitter and revengeful and the mercenaries keen to scoop what they see as a windfall but if not immediately forthcoming…"

"I see," replied the king with heavy cynicism, "we are good only for what they can get out of us! Well, every man knows that I suppose... and Austria?"

"Sire, I am sorry to inform you that though I tried hard, the fact is that the queen's brother is in no way now positioned to…"

"Does not intend to support us!"

De Quatreaux hid a smile. "Well Sire, he be very involved with Turkey at the moment and has Prussia breathing down his neck."

"Ah yes, of course. Each to his own set of problems." Louis turned to gaze at de Quatreaux for a long moment; then, "You are a good and loyal friend, de Quatreaux, your work outside our borders for our protection, deserving of reward. I would that I could."

"I require none, Sire," he smiled sardonically. "I am already finding that the title of Comte is buying me enough trouble these days. I am too busy to deal with more."

Louis came close to grinning, a rare luxury now. "No, no Vermont, *mine* be the *first* title that they try to abolish; to topple the crown their deepest desire. You will take your daughter out of Versailles now I think—yes, that be best."

"It matters little where she be, Sire, point of fact where any of us be. Versailles be no more dangerous than Paris."

"Ah, and the attack on your château cancels any retreat to *that* neck of the woods. I am sorry, de Quatreaux, that I cannot send out troops to avenge thee. 'Twas a time…"

"Shall come again; Your Majesty."

The procrastination was over. Louis could hold out no longer, for he had no further excuse and the women were rioting outside his palace; indeed had broken into sections. His heart softened as he gazed at them, not able to resist the picture of starvation, for the most emaciated were deliberately before him now. He embraced the more presentable of them now and sent them away with promises of bread. His advisers gazed at him aghast.

"Sire, it be designed that way! It be a plot!"

"Ah yes, but though I can annihilate whole enemy armies, I cannot tolerate that women and children suffer… and there be no doubt that they do indeed suffer. They are my people: the mothers, aunts, daughters and sisters of my people."

"And as such, are at this moment Sire, the she-wolves of the savage dregs of society. They be cunning and know nothing but to kill or be killed!"

"In defence of their people."

"Shoot them down. You need only do it once! That will bring them to heel!"

The king gazed long at this advisor still residing within the *Ancien Regime* and spoke softly, "No."

The king's advisers groaned, for though the king's signature to the documents might be expected to end the crisis; for the deputies of France and the people of Paris had now what they wanted, they knew that matters would not end there.

Clery entered softly and approached Louis, sprawled tiredly in a chair, gaze unfocused as his mind travelled far away. Disturbed by the movement, he looked up.

"Men of the *Commune* have arrived, Sire."

"What be the time?" But as he spoke the clock began to strike the hour two. Louis listened a moment, then, "And what be their demands now?"

"The people of the *Paris Commune* request that you, Sire; and your family, make your residence in Paris. And er... the Assembly, they say, should also cause its venue to be established in the city."

"Immediately? *Tonight? Now?*"

"Well yes, Your Majesty, that is their desire."

"No, no, none can travel to Paris this night, it be much too late," responded the king.

The deputies were advised to go home to their lodgings for the night and the women to use what accommodation the town of Versailles offered or to camp in the palace court. This they did, lighting bonfires and killing and roasting a horse and three commandeered goats. The feasting commenced.

"Sire, Lafayette does assure your safety here this night."

The king looked at his advisor cynically but sent his assurances to the Assembly that he would not desert them and retired to bed. It was three o'clock in the morning and upon retracing his steps to his apartments he found his wife there, awaiting him.

"My husband, come, rest, the morrow shall be another day and I feel that it shall be monumental in our lives. I have always hated the Tuileries Palace. But if it means we be together, then I shall go... to Paris and to Tuileries." She moved towards him as she spoke, kissed him and then turned to the door.

"You shall not stay...this one night?"

"Louis, I would that I could... but I fear for the children. Always I fear for them."

He looked at her sadly and knew that the fear should be for his queen, though she scornfully denied such, containing her worry that she be the butt of the peoples' hostility.

Day broke across Versailles on the 6th of October with a clear sky, pushing before it the pale and silent clarity of the very early morning that presaged a still, warm, day. All quiet prevailed, for even amid hostilities humans must sleep, but contrary to this order of nature, some women did not slumber well and whispered between themselves, plotting and planning. It took but one step further for the women to search out the pre-arranged unguarded door into the palace and pre-empt the day's plan, creeping through, silent and armed. Soon they found alert sentries and exchanged shots before surging up the main staircase to the royal apartments.

"Madame! Madame!"

Marie Antoinette, woken from her exhausted sleep by her women attendants frantically shaking her, sat bolt upright. Shots and the smashing of doors resounded through the shrieks of the women warriors. Screams of obscenities could be heard, as the bloodlust of the women grew ever stronger.

"Cut off her head!"

"Tear out her heart!"

"Pour hot oil into her gut!"

"Fricassee her liver."

"Fry her kidneys and her guts to ribbons... and even then it shall not be over and do it fast so that she lives while it happens!"

None cringed: these things were common practice against evil and the Queen was the original she-devil, born of Satan's loins: Austria. A bodyguard tried to defend the staircase, fighting to the last but ended stabbed with knives and pitchforks, his body dragged into the courtyard where his head was severed by an axe and impaled on a pike. Passing this, another Guard tried to reach Marie Antoinette's apartments.

Wounded and faint, he reached her door, calling loudly, "Madame! Fly... lock and bar the doors behind you... do what you must but get out!"

The infuriated crowd cornered him there, valiantly holding the door with his musket, unable to shoot because of the king's orders. The attack upon this incredibly brave man was short and brutal; then he also lay dead in a pool of blood.

Running, half-clad, the queen arrived, with her women attendants, at her husband's apartments, but the doors there were also locked: they were caught as rats in a trap.  For the first time panic seized her and held her in a suspension of frozen fear but she was later to learn that here be a safer place; for minutes after her exit, her own bed had been cut to ribbons by sabres and knives wielded by the mad rioters.

Those inside the king's apartments all stood waiting, sure that the clamouring without the door be the insane and rioting mob.

"Mon Dieu...but we have no weapons in here!" cried a distraught voice, searching the room for anything solid: fire irons, letter openers; anything that could be used as a weapon.

Clery turned to answer him, then paused, listening intently. "But no! That be Louise... one of the queen's attendants... quickly!"

He rushed to the door, shaking hands fumbling with the lock then dragging it open; thus saving the queen's life.

"Where is Louis for the Gods' sakes?" she asked now, gazing around in horror at his absence and listening, to ascertain the direction of the next attack.

"Madame, he be gone to you!"

"Oh *Grand Dieu*!" She gazed fruitlessly around, then in further horror, "The Dauphin! But Madame de Tourzel must have him surely!"

She tried hard to control her continuous shaking.  But nobody knew.  In fact nobody knew anything and nobody could find the princess, Marie Therese.

Eventually they were all reunited in the *Salon dé l'Œil de Bœuf*. Here, sheltering behind a solid oak table, they gazed at each other as axes and iron bars thumped against the doors and guards tried to drive the assailants away with bayonets only. These valiant men, obeying still the king's orders not to fire, managed the miraculous task and eventually drove the rioters out into the courtyard. Here the Body Guards were saved at that moment by the late arrival of Lafayette and the National Guard. This ever-slow National Guard surged at last up the staircase and restored peace within the palace, driving the remaining rioting mob out but the noisy courts were filled with more of the same, clamouring to see the king.

He stood now on the balcony, gazing down at them, holding up his arms and at last quiet prevailed, but he did not appease the crowd as they began to shout for the queen.

When, however, the queen, ignoring his shake of the head, appeared upon the balcony with her son and daughter, the voices rose even higher as the crowd shouted.

"No children, no children, send back the children!"

She stared at the musket levelled at her and knew with certainty that they wanted just her: to kill her, to screw her head upon a pike. Sending Marie Therese and the Dauphin, Louis-Charles, back into the palace she stood her ground, chin lifted, staring and daring. It was this very courage, pushing the limits of mob mentality that worried Lafayette. There remained only one thing to do: he entered the balcony and stood next to her, lifting her hand to his lips for the kiss of respect: of subject to throne.

The crowd fell silent and still, in awe of her extreme courage. Nobody fired and after a while she curtsied to her people, turned and went calmly back inside, waving aside the offered arms of assistance. All in that company expected her to be shaken to the point of an inability to stand. That they were very nearly correct only she knew, for even here, amongst their supposed friends, lurked the enemy spies. She turned and looked at Louis and he smiled gently at her as he in his turn moved back to the balcony again to the demanding cries for the king.

Several thousand voices rose on the air: "The King! We want the king. To live in Paris! *Le Roi à Paris!*"

"Yes my friends, I shall come to Paris, but not without my family."

"*A Paris! A Paris!*"

"*Le Roi à Paris*...ever to live there!"

"*A Paris! A Paris!*"

"My people, I shall come."

By 1 p.m. everything was ready for the departure and the royal family escorted to the carriage, via the small staircase, to avoid the areas covered in blood. Soon the King, Queen, Marie-Therese and Louis-Charles, along with their aunt Elizabeth, Monsieur and Madame de Tourzel, were seated and ready to go.

The National Assembly however, declared itself inseparable from the throne and elected to travel with the *Famille Roi* to Paris. Selecting only a hundred of its members to enact this symbolic statement, they arranged to follow on the next morning.

The day was perfect, barely a breeze stirred and the clear early afternoon sunshine lit up the beauty of the landscape. Marie Antoinette glanced at her husband, wondering if he too was remembering a day almost fifteen years ago—the day they had ridden together into Paris in the glittering gilt coach, escorted by the colourful Swuisses and Gardes du Corps in their splendid uniforms. Dressed in white satin and so many jewels that the weight proved a problem, they had been accompanied by the officers of the Royal Hunt and the Gentlemen of the Household. The ladies and gentlemen of the court had followed. She sighed in deep sadness and bemused disbelief.

Within the coach the occupants now stared straight ahead, following the disorderly mob rejoicing in the capture of the royal family. Heads on pikes jogged up and down just outside the windows, on either side of the royal coach. Their carriers ran, jubilant, triumphant, dancing round and round the carriage, their bloodlust ever thirsty for more. Marie Antoinette glanced from time to time at her husband as he dabbed at his eyes with his kerchief, her own expression now one of violent grief. She tried to ignore those climbing onto the carriage yelling ever more crude insults.

Lafayette and the National Guard travelled always in sight of the carriage, an intended reassurance but the following disarmed Household Troops and Flanders Regiment, including an infuriated Francois, did little to reassure Louis. Following these were soldiers and a crowd of civilians. Some rode in cabs, others on carts and gunpowder carriages; and carried the trophies of war: helmets, swords, bandoliers, regimental jackets and the ever-present, dripping heads on pikes, from the defeated troops.

The journey of fifteen miles took six hours, as thirty thousand milled around the royal party. National Guardsmen rode often up to the windows showing, on the points of their bayonets, loaves of bread deliberately turned green and mouldy, others blackened by acid application. Alongside them rode the French Guards, some of the Flemish Regiment and members of the King's bodyguard, now fraternizing with the 'conquerors.' These Francois badly desired to slaughter with his own bare hands.

Count Axel Fersen, in one of the following carriages, travelling a little behind the royal family, leaned back and closed his eyes. His feelings for the queen were widely known, often misinterpreted and the purity of such disbelieved. None of which bothered him. One would not last long at court if wounded by each titbit of low court gossip. He did however worry on behalf of Marie Antoinette. That he adored her was known, that he was often seen in her attendance also was known, but the depth of his instinct to protect the one you loved most was not; and this shameful journey to the city smote him to a depth before unknown by him.

They were at a standstill yet again: the milling thousands of the mob, carts and carriages, causing yet another halt to the journey. Fersen sighed deeply as he estimated that they should reach Paris probably on the morrow at this rate.

"It be not over yet, *mon ami*," said his friend. "We shall come about again. The king must be got out... that is all. And from Paris it most likely be as easy as anywhere."

Axel, opening his eyes and looking at him, ignored this cold comfort and said, "You may delete the platitudes: they enter even deeper into captivity. And I never want to see the like again! May the Gods prevent me from ever witnessing again such a diabolical and heartbreaking spectacle as that of the last few days, *mon ami*! I have seen horrendous sights. Royal persons have been murdered down the annals of history by their own blood relatives even. Wars wreak untold misery upon nations. But this! This... is more than diabolical. The French language has no words for it! And I feel that though it be a first it be not finished yet; not by a long shot."

He closed his eyes again, ignoring the proffered snuffbox. Thereafter silence reigned and his friend did not nudge him to witness the receding glimpses, through a forest of pikes and sharp-ended poles certainly, of Versailles. Home to the Bourbons for a century, it slowly retreated from view. He tried to shut his mind to it all. The endless musketry fire however, by exultant brigands, the chanting of *Vive la Nation* and the continuous shouting of insults, echoed through his head, ever reminding him that Marie Antoinette would be suffering to a degree never before experienced.

The queen, dwelling again in their past journeys to Paris, suddenly shook off these brilliant memories as they approached the barrier and Bailly, for the second time in three months, welcomed the king to Paris. At the Town hall more speeches were made.  Later, the king, Bailly, Moteau and Saint-Méry could be seen standing together in the light of flaring candles within a window overlooking the Place de Gréve. This brought about cheering of several minutes: the king had been conquered and now brought home to Paris.

♣

Versailles stood: eerily silent, naught to be heard but the occasional scurrying and whispered urgings to hurry. Angelique wandered aimlessly, clutching her portmanteau in one hand and reticule in the other.  She stood in the *Gallerie des Glaces* and gazed around, a tear trickling down her cheek. Tears for a lost era certainly but more for a lost people, a lost future and the loss of all that was good and beautiful; for the claimed evil within the royalty and nobility had been but a small proportion of the whole.  Just as now the evil and powerful within the new regime were but the few. Nothing, of course, would alter. The poverty, cruelty, greed and all that was base in man would prevail as always; as the new successors proceeded to climb ever higher.  Certainly power corrupted.  She wondered whether they should join the fence sitters after all; for these were ever prepared to fall whichever side meant survival. But then, she decided, she could not live with herself. She was brought out of her fruitless reverie by a sound to her left and froze suddenly. The rabble, she knew, had left: following the mob back to Paris.  Of the three thousand residents of the palace, however, she was not sure how many were left; also wandering, it felt, forever the halls and corridors of Versailles and unlike herself, perhaps on the prowl for goodness knew what.  It sounded again and then she heard her name called and laughed.  Running now, she moved towards the familiar voice.

"Well, for the great Gods' sakes! There you are! What are you doing here unattended? De Quatreaux is looking all over for you... the closest I have ever witnessed him to outright panic! Don't tell him so! And I've had the very devil of a time finding you!"

"Ah, Emile," she gazed about, "How can something so very beautiful come tumbling down so swiftly?"

He took her bag. "Shall be thee that tumbles down if you do not hasten to the carriage! Come... le Comte waits."

"But wait, Estelle and the Princess Lamballe comes with us; I shall be but a moment."

"They have surely gone to Tuileries? Not so?"

"There was no room in any of the carriages. All efforts were directed toward the safety of the royal family. I er...we er...shamefully I know but we hid... until all was quiet and then I er... well, I knew that our *père*, when released from his duty to the king, would come sooner or later." Tears of relief stood on her lashes.

Emile glanced away, busily scanning the corridor. "*What*? My independent, outrageous, self-willed Angelique *hid*?"

It was enough: emotion controlled now, she chuckled. "Emile, you shall never know what a traitor I felt."

He grinned but only said, "I shall inform the Comte... no, perhaps not. But do make haste. None are sure of the safety of the road now."

"Why? Have they not executed all the damage that they can?"

Tuileries; the abandoned 16<sup>th</sup> century palace in the heart of Paris beside the Seine, had been taken over slowly by servants and artisans, settling in to the rabbit warren of dark chambers and endless, dimly lit stairways and galleries.

The original building: the old palace of Catherine de Medici, had: like that of the Louvre at an earlier date, been outside the city walls. Its front therefore faced west, toward the beautiful and open countryside, so delightful that it had quickly acquired the name of Elysian Fields. At the back, after the city walls there had been demolished, was a courtyard surrounded by stables and outbuildings, the open area named the Place du Carrousel, according to an equestrian fete held there by Louis X1V in 1662. Behind this, there existed a medley of old lanes and houses. High walls surrounded the whole, obscuring much of the palace. To the west were walls and a moat, over which a bridge led to the *Place Louis Quinze*: soon to be known as *Place de la Revolution* and to contain the guillotine. Northwards ran the lane, enclosed between high walls of the Tuileries gardens and the back walls of the residences facing Rue Saint-Honoré. This space had been used as exercise ground for the horses of Louis XV's *menége*.

Disused by the court since Louis X1V, the Tuileries and surrounding buildings had been gradually filled with lodgers, adding to the artisans and servants, those pensioned-off royal servants, bankrupt aristocrats, retired military officers and many others. Many of these had now to be turned out to make room for the royal family and their retainers. There remained, however, still at least two thousand residents within these walls.

"But surely it is so ugly in here...is it not?" asked Louis-Charles, gazing about with wrinkled nose.

"It has been home to many of our ancestors, child! Before Versailles was built it was hearth and home to our ancient family. You should not ask more. And you shall not say such again in the hearing of others! Remember this please!"

Suitably chastised, he fell silent for a bit but then, listening to the uproar still going on outside the palace walls, he looked at his father again. "Why do they not like us? Why are they all so angry? We wish them nothing but well. Have we done something unpleasing to them, Sire? I know that it be the duty of a king to do so sometimes but cannot think of anything so bad that they hate us so. Everything that is done be for their good: even if it hurts; like the drawing of a tooth! Without the tooth drawn... they become poisoned and die! But they sound as though they would kill us all but then where would they be?"

"It be regarding money *mon enfant*; always trouble surrounds that subject. Certain men wanted it and I needed it: mostly to pay for the war expenses; for wars that protected the people of France. These men then roused the people against me."

"But they are stupid then! It be assuredly for their own benefit!"

Louis gazed at his son, his heart growing cold with fear. He marshalled his thoughts along lines that a child may understand and failed miserably. "Never, *mon fils*, ever, let me hear you speak so again. Such words may execute one these days." The king frowned worriedly at his heir, then continued in effort to make him understand. "I tried to do this; gain more money, through the parlements and then through the States-general, but many requested financial concessions, which I could not grant, if the plan to reduce taxes to the poor was to succeed. But do not blame the people *mon enfant* for it be very evil men that used this as an excuse to make the people rise up and have caused the bad experiences of the last few days. Do not blame the people for they are as unlettered children, believing the orators; and wanting what they were told they would have and lashing out when it did not eventuate. But even then they would not, without the wicked men to lead them, push them, to such bad behaviour."

The *Famille Roi* was detained in Paris, within the Tuileries Palace indefinitely. Lafayette was now their keeper, his troops, the National Guard, comprising the palace guard, monitoring their every move.

The Assembly, following the king a few days later, established itself in a large room in the archbishop's palace, the *archevéché*, near Notre Dame. But it arrived minus many of its deputies. The emigration of Count d'Artois, following the fall of the Bastille, had set precedence and now many followed; with full expectations of returning soon to find the old order restored.

Two leaders of the *right-centre*, Mounier and Lally-Tollendal moved quietly out of the capital, pleading danger to their lives and stating that the Assembly was not free. Soon more followed, depleting the right side of the Assembly, leaving those remaining stalwarts infuriated as they watched, day after day, the *left* acquire new sources of strength.

Mounier, the current President of the National Assembly, sent in his resignation October 8th, the first of the Federalists to do so and set off to his native Dauphiné, determined to rouse that aristocratic stronghold to revolt in defence of the liberty of king and a moderate Assembly. Many others, nursing the same hopes, followed his example; however, their scattered geography caused some doubt regarding a unified front.

The new President now faced two to three hundred applications for passports almost daily, following the Versailles exodus. He sent out reprimands to the deputies and placed many difficulties in their way, hoping to slow the mass emigration. Their constituents denounced these cowardly deputies and the *Commune* went bail for the good behaviour of the citizens, a move that did slow the stampede, just a little.

Lally-Tollendal deemed the Assembly a gang of cannibals, others proclaiming it the black pot of boiling political soup, into which all antagonists would be thrown eventually. All slept with swords and pistols beside their beds and their children close by in the anti-rooms. Life in France had inextricably changed: forever.

# CHAPTER THIRTEEN

## Of Property, Gold & Plots

Raoul Trifane, Marquis de la Savieur, dressed very simply, in plain dark attire, stood within the movement and noise of the milling crowds that occupied the *Palais-Royal* arcades now. His eyes ran down the newest placard, containing ninety names: of those who had voted against the National Assembly on June 17. Turning to the next list, he wondered what vengeance was in store for those venturing even further and voting for two *chambres*, or for an absolute veto. Here he found the name de Quatreaux. He smiled grimly: not many owned de Quatreaux' courage and this type of intimidation could eradicate many more of the *right*, leaving the *left* with a growing majority.

His thoughts were proved correct: on Monday October 19th at the first sitting of the Assembly in the *Archevêvé*. Here, it became clear that the Assembly was reduced by almost three hundred members: all from the 'right'. This reduced their 600 votes to nearly 300. The left retained their full 600 and pursued a jubilant and volatile, Revolutionary Patriotic Front.

Paris had changed with a rapidity that had left one and all breathless. Its citizens were jubilant at their October victory over king and Assembly and reminded both, noisily, that they existed for the benefit of the people. The people, it was clear, would rise again and again if results were slow or obstructive. Of the slaughter, however, within those risings, they were quick to deny.

An inquiry, conducted into the assault upon Versailles, the Assembly and the Monarch, on October 5th and 6th 1789, focussed on Mirabeau and the Duc d'Orléans. Four hundred witnesses were eventually heard, by the *Comité des rapports* of the Assembly, and the two cleared of the accusation but suspicion clung to them.

Following advice from Lafayette, the Duc d'Orléans left the country, establishing himself in London; his credit within France dissolved and his hopes of a regency demolished. His only hope, if he returned, lay within the Robespierre led Jacobin society but even here he was mistrusted. Mirabeau; mouthing astringent denials, remained arrogant as ever, his acid tongue and quicksilver brain, dancing as a champion political fencer, holding him safe from all attacks thus far.

Military control was wrested from the army by the rabble National Guard and political control from the intellectuals by the demagogues. Paris, under these two, now owned the power and control to dictate, both legislatively and executively, a policy to the whole country. It did not take a visionary to see that these changes, some visible, most invisible, were going to alter the whole course of life for French men and women forever. Only the blinkered refused to admit this. The see-saw had tipped: weighted still by absolute rule but now by those leading the Assembly.

Raoul Trifane, definitely not blinkered, sat at the café de Foi sipping his coffee and reading the *Courrier Français,* smiling sardonically at the journalistic anarchy. Nothing could now stop the noisy political clubs of the *Palais-Royal* arcades influencing, directing even, the intentions of the Assembly.  He wondered at their next move against the monarch; wondered also if the imprisoned family royal had ventured outside yet and guessed not: the gardens of the Tuileries afforded little privacy. The view from the front windows of the palace was little better, showing a terrace full of the crowding public. That they had been prisoners also at Versailles was no secret but at least the privacy from the mobs and the beauty of the place had acted as some small balm.  Here the gloomy buildings, street odours and noisy environs had to be of the most depressing.

He frowned in concern, for this was not their only problem: even the remaining moderates of the right were being forced out of the Assembly, the radical left gaining the upper hand and some now advocating total abolition of royalty. Also, the Clergy was now at last coming under attack. The leftist Assembly, viewing the Clergy as a pillar of the now discredited *Ancien Regime*, searched out ways to reduce its power: fearing a threat from the Church, to the survival of the Glorious Revolution.

He detected a presence and glancing up from the paper, saw Henri-Marie Pontisqieu.

"We meet again!" Henri glanced at the open page, the headlines praising the new Assembly, and grinned, "Have you attended yet *mon ami*, since it has moved to the manège? But how rude of me: you be well, Monsieur? "

Raoul stood, laughing as he bowed, briefly, and indicated a chair. "But Henri... is it *possible* to have any other dialogue these days?  But I am still free, therefore I am well thank you.... and you also, I can see, unless you own some skulking disease. But no, I have not that privilege as yet: regards the Assembly... empty your budget, do!"

"Crowded certainly; but cosy…easy to accost someone across the narrow floor!"

Trifane nodded to the hovering proprietor and soon a jug of coffee and earthenware mug was placed in front of Monsieur Pontisqieu and poured for him. Taking up the mug of dark liquid, he thanked the proprietor and continued.

"Poor light, no heating other than a tiny, inefficient stove, of abominably inconvenient shape and offering great difficulties to the speakers.  But worse: the *air* is so bad, that the good Dr Guillotin suggests a sprinkling of vinegar and herbs, rose and lavender water, twice a day.  A decree ordering a good monthly personal tubbing of the gallery-mob *I* would have thought more effective, but ah, who am I?  And after all I suppose the Seine *is* at low ebb... if only this cursed drought would abate! The public gallery is extremely cramped but it does seat about 300, great for the likes of Mirabeau."

"Ah yes, easily monopolized by the *claqueurs*. He *would* be the first to see that. I wonder what he pays his *mouchards*."

"Two livre; rumour has it."

Raoul laughed. "I hope they are worth it!"

Henri grinned. "Indeed. But you really should come tomorrow. It promises to be thoroughly entertaining! Two to three speakers battle it out at the same time; as the President, wishing no doubt that his fortnight of chairing be over, fights to keep order. All the while the gallery is shying old fruit and vegetables at the whole, the *claqueurs* are clapping and the antagonists screaming and bellowing at them *and* the speakers."

Raoul smiled derisively. "And this: the new Assembly, born at Versailles! But the president has his *sonnette* and his *huissiers*; and if all else fails, he can throw on his hat and suspend the sitting, yet again I imagine!"

Pontisqieu snorted. "It's a mockery! A parlement that spends its days chasing its tail in such a tangle of resolutions, counter-resolutions, amendments and counter-amendments, that in the end it finds itself debating what it was that it was to decide upon! As for the delivery of set speeches: mostly all lies and fantasies spoken as truths! Besides, that is not the origin of the real power."

Raoul nodded wisely. "Ah! The worm in the apple: the *Commune .*"

"The asps *among* the apples more like: the clubs... in particular the rising Jacobins. Dangerous times ahead, Savieur, for it is within the clubs that battles are won, even before they reach the Assembly. The moderate constitutionalists: the Girondins, only just hold sway at the moment, hanging on by their teeth."

"Certainly they dare not, in their Assembly speeches, go against the power of the clubs."

"But it is the Jacobins in *particular*, that grow sinister."

"I imagine that would be the source of very interesting information but I can hardly comment; I am not a member, Pontisqieu."

Henri looked at him, brows faintly lifted. "That can be arranged."

"Oh?" Trifane smiled gently. "Not at risk to you. I will not have it."

"There shall be no risk. I introduce you to Robespierre and he shall assess you, in the blink of an eye! You shall be in... or out! If in: either to convert you or keep an eye on you! He owns a mind comprising a cocktail of mercury and acid, that one."

"How very charming it is!"

"Could give future protection: to have one's name on their list of membership. But...do not use it as a reliable source of information... treachery slides amongst them as does an eel beneath the cover of seaweed! So I shall see you at the Dominican Refectory tonight then? You know the address, of course?"

"Rue Saint Honoré...but I already owe you for your assistance to the Mademoiselle Vermont; during that horrific street riot."

"Ah, she is safe, Trifane?"

"For the moment: yes."

"Then that is all that we can expect these days. She is of excellent courage."

"Good luck with your case today."

"Ah yes, it be a small matter but of great import to the life of the individual concerned, therefore requires my utmost concentration."

"Oh: and Pontisqieu!"

"Yes?"

"What happens in the mixing of mercury and acid?"

"The Lord knows, but it cannot be pleasant, that is assured." Pontesqieu laughed and left with a brief bow and strode towards the Châtelet, flagging down a *pots de chambre* and climbing on.  It was 10:00 hrs and other legal practitioners began to appear and head in the same direction, wigged and gowned, some managing to also find a *pots de chambre*, their clients running alongside.

Trifane, left deep in thought, glanced at his pocket watch: time to call upon Lafayette, that monument of the National Guard. Also, however, known to few, he was a tireless engineer of the construction of a business government: that would secure property, creating profits and foreign bankers' speculation.  That he also funded foreign emissaries financing the agents of public disorder would have astounded many.  Raoul shook his head: a double-edged sword was dangerous enough, let alone walking its edge.

Raoul stood, dropped a liard on the table and left the *Palais-Royal*, walking in the direction of Lafayette's *club de '89* founded by that man himself, exclusive entry fee 125livre.  This at about the time Malouet and his circle founded the *Impartiaux*, and Lally-Tollendal the *Club Monarchique*.

Stepping around beggars and navigating a convoluted course through the crush of pedestrians, his thoughts dwelt now on the infamous Jacobin club: place of deputies of the extreme left and the even more radical journalists of Paris.  Questions debated in the Assembly were at the same time debated here and with far less reserve.  Here, even Barnave and Mirabeau, though popular speakers, were far behind the rising Robespierre, who gained an audience that listened in silence and awe, followed by applause minutes long.  This man, thought Trifane suddenly, could bring to a halt the invading Mongol hoards just by his silent, deeply controlled manner; emanating a sense of enormous power within the very stillness of his bearing.  His ability to draw and hold an audience, to leave them feeling fulfilled: was above most great orators. He could, thought Trifane, talk absolute nonsense and make it sound brilliant; appear the highest order of enlightenment and the only way to think or go. However, his very lack of emotion could also be his downfall, or that of France: hopefully the former.

Under these influences from the clubs, the Assembly, attempting to complete the Constitution, carried reform into every province. Its principles were those of uniformity, decentralization and the sovereignty of the people, sweeping away every clashing, previous or still existing, institution to these moves.

Provinces were swept away and replaced by eighty-three *Departments*.  These in turn were divided into 374 *Districts*, who then devised an administrative body: the *Directory*. These small units, their boundaries now changed, would hopefully break down the old feudal traditions and ancient local rivalries *and* loyalties: creating new ground for new growth. The *Communes* alone were left intact, all forty-four thousand: placed under the direct control of Municipalities; their members elected by 'active' citizens only.

Arrived at the club of Lafayette, Trifane settled in his chair, gazing across the rim of his glass at Lafayette. "So... you are well, Lafayette?"

His host burst into laughter. *"Mon ami...*cease with the polite, if you please! You *know* that I did not invite you here to assess each other's state of health!"

Raoul grinned. "But *Monseigneur*... I know no such thing... not being er, in touch with higher levels of, um, financial or political wizards! I can but assume that you wish to ruminate over the new voting laws!"

Lafayette stared. "Now you hoax me! Voting laws?" He shook his head, gazing now in serious suspicion. "The stress of recent events has caused your loss of mind?"

Raoul grinned. "But the issue *is* serious! The new voting laws now create a new aristocracy of wealth, Lafayette: no less objectionable, surely, to that of the previously abhorred aristocracy of birth? To be elected... no, even an elector... one must have a stake in the land or own property, or business qualification; no less."

Lafayette took up the cudgel. "Ah *but, mon ami*, as a bright individual at yesterday's sitting put it: 'twill encourage the poor to become rich. They gain, the country gains, what could be better?"

"Become rich... to qualify for *active* citizenship?" Raoul snorted. "How do they do that precisely: metamorphose from *passive* to *active*... in a servile position, in abject poverty, *within* a bankrupt country?"

"You are a man of awkward questions, *mon ami*. I should depress that tendency if I were you," laughed Lafayette. "But whatever you think of it, 'twas passed unanimously. The vote was also extended to a National Guard serving at his own expense..."

"Generous I'm sure! He cannot eat but he *can* vote! Oh: and fight!"

"*And*: to those of 15 years continuous service," continued Lafayette, "and all pauperised clergy."

"Ah, so our spiritual caretakers now have a voice in earthly matters."

Lafayette waved an impatient hand and continued, "Sooner or later Savieur, you will realize the seriousness of all this!"

"None do realize so deeply, mon ami," murmured Raoul beneath his breath.

Lafayette continued, "The first principle of the constitutional revolution was to replace arbitrary rule with a code of law; that be correct? The National Assembly was to be its guarantee, allowing the nation to speak as one man... *but*... freely appointed and empowered to represent the people. Correct?"

Raoul merely nodded, placing a brake on added acid comments.

"But then the voice of the people culminated in the violence that now be history..."

"Of a very recent activity: *and* fruition!"

"And the deputies be afraid of those voices, Trifane: especially those heard on the new 'café strip'. They see the people, accurately, as a set of wild children let loose within a chocolate factory. They will not cease their clamouring to have it all at once."

"And so they set up the qualifying 'monetary' structure to vote, which eliminates a vast number of the population... the children wanting the chocolate!" said Raoul. "They underestimate them! And insult them: by graciously allowing the sans-culottes to listen to speeches and carry pikes; but still the direction of their future is in the hands of those who can write a petition and read a paper! But illiteracy does not necessarily equate with density, Lafayette! The developing fourth estate: the *sans-culottes*, will be a force to be reckoned with: and soon."

Lafayette shrugged. "But the lawyers and journalists shall always maintain control... especially within the *Insurrectional Commune*.  But to the matter of finance, Trifane: hoard or export your *louis d'or* and *écus*; the *assignats* flooding the country since December 19 are depreciating at a high rate of knots. Fraudulent notes abound also, so have a care."

"*Assignats* have been used before and failed, Lafayette; the Mississippi Co. for one; and the debacle of our very own *Caisse d'escompte* discredited notes. Not sure what happened when Catherine used them in '68."

Lafayette shrugged. "Russia! But this *Assignat*, Trifane, was issued by the emergency bank, into which the sale proceeds shall go: of the confiscated property."

"Church Property, yes: and the massive hoarding and export of gold and silver rapidly follows."

"I suspect that you know because... you have found a way to do that!"

Trifane, wanting more information but unwilling to give, leaned back in his chair, his face bland; apparently at ease though he did not trust the private salon to be secure. "The restoration of finances mid-revolution shall not be a piece of work easily accomplished. After all, the Assembly has still not firmly established the new tax system, leaving a hole through which the people slip in their continued refusal to pay the old: the revenue proportionately decreasing; national debt *in*creasing."

Lafayette nodded. "Double that at which it stood at the beginning of the Revolution. *But*, I called you here to tell you that they are looking toward the property, *all* property, of nobility." He smiled gently at the suddenly arrested look in his companion's eyes, then said, "Thought that would draw your attention... at last!"

"One *hears*, Lafayette, everything; and one *expects* such a move but is never in possession of concrete fact. How... do they propose to do this?"

"Well, as you are aware, their piece de resistance; the *ci-devant privileges*; failed; impossible to assess and collect, of course. After all, how far, retrospectively, can one go with that? And so now, a plan is being constructed to confiscate the Privileged Orders' property, and it follows these lines."

Trifane listened, his face bland and untroubled. "But this was expected from the moment of the States-general recall."

"But few could really believe it. Now everything is in place to *do* it. As to your property Savieur, bring the folio numbers to me."

Raoul gazed but did not reply.

"Ah, but you must trust *someone, mon ami*: it may as well be me. I *am* the 'Guard'. And as such... well, let us just say that I hear ideas to destroy the nobility once and for all."

"And ownership of these ideas? Robespierre!"

"A very, very clever man; dangerously so... but few realize it!  So come to Saint-Germaine tonight. De Quatreaux shall also be there, along with my guest Calonne. And Ferriers: has a good head for finances, that one."

Raoul lifted his brows faintly and then smiled, "But assuredly."

"And of course a couple of the cloth manufacturers and iron-masters; also keen financial brains."

"And they all expect to play a political role."

"Lord yes!  After all, they point us in the direction of prudent investment."

"And the deputies?"

Lafayette chuckled. "But we cannot leave them out! Many frequent my table *ad-nauseam*: for 'tis the age of financial speculation. And for us: inner sanctum knowledge."

"Camouflaged speculation... but wrapped in what?"

"But think of it *mon ami*. Commerce requires credit, credit security and security of course, depends upon a business government."

"*Your* driving force," softly. "I *had* heard, Lafayette!"

"Ah but no, *I* am the National Guard. Military life is my *only* passion."

Raoul bowed his head with extreme politeness and Lafayette laughed again. "I shall really look forward to your company, Savieur!"

"Trifane."

"Ah yes. Often wondered why you prefer your family name to your title. Everyone knows of it."

"Lafayette...they can strip me; of my lands, my investments and my titles, but God forbid they take from me my birth name."

Lafayette looked at him, eyebrows raised. "Indeed. God forbid! Funny things, names... your foreign investments and new English, Belgian and Italian estates in yet another of 'em I not doubt!"

Raoul lifted perfectly innocent brows, "What investments and estates?"

"Those God-forsaken, incessant, patriotic drums," said de Quatreaux, walking from his club back to the Rue Saint Honoré.

Du Toit glanced at him, as they moved through the mass of noisy citizens and colporteurs crying their pamphlets and papers; loudly: to rise above drums, the church bells and tramp of patrol feet. "Yes, last sound on sleeping."

De Quatreaux snorted, "If one *can* sleep."

"And a greeting on rousing; overlaid by the wondrous parody of martial music."

"Every morning I own a particularly sweet dream; of firing a cannonball directly down their bugles. Paris, *mon ami*, is a city besieged."

"More to the point...a city *mon cher*, policed by Sieur Goisset and his thugs."

"The spies of the *Comité des Recherches* cause me no disturbance."

"You are right: red-herrings of course."

"But where, in your opinion, do we seek the more dangerous of the deep?"

"You may seek them Vermont. I shall not... but they lurk amongst our own: in our clubs, salons, balls, not that there be a proliferation of those of late. Trust no one!"

De Quatreaux slowed his step a second and turned his head. "Even thee, *mon ami*?"

Du Toit gazed back a moment in compassion. "I suppose that I must be included there if you must not trust a soul. But I am aware of some of your activities, the information not extended by yourself and therefore it stands that somewhere there be a leak. But look closer, *mon ami*."

"Beaumont?"

Du Toit turned shocked eyes on his friend. "Ah no... could not be! Good Lord, if *'tis* he then all be lost, no? For he is one of the your oldest and closest of friends."

"Indeed all would be lost; for he has a copy."

"*Grand Dieu...* but you would never keep... records; surely? I do not believe it!"

"When I feel the beginnings of woolly-headedness I shall inform you. But when an activity grows in size it follows that quill to paper be required to keep track of events and details."

"But why the need? Preventing...*dishonesty*?"

"More importantly for when we return, not monarchic rule, that be gone forever but at least a Girondin way of doing things, then a record of finances and property be required. And these have Beaumont's signature, as does much of the more inflammable material," de Quatreaux spoke softly even though the traffic was light.

Du Toit walked silently by his side; then, turning to look at him, "Then I must suppose that it cannot be he."

"Oh, I shall find him. Doubt you not that I shall."

"How long goes this cursed Revolution, Vermont?"

"Long enough, hopefully, to reverse it," the voice was low and calm.

"*Grand Dieu*! Thee casts high, *mon ami*... have a care."

"I have those among the Jacobins that would warn me."

Du Toit's smile was satirical. "How you keep your head, and your tongue, perhaps that should be the other way around, within that pack of wolves I cannot imagine."

De Quatreaux smiled. "Who can tell what the future shall bring these times? One can but ply what skills he has and add a liberal dash of hope."

They turned at that moment into the entrance of his residence and were greeted by Henri; and Du Toit was left wondering at the Comte's fearlessness; born of arrogance? He glanced at him as they divested their outer clothing and suddenly remembered their childhood and wondered: whether Vermont's severely authoritarian parent, with his demands of perfection in all things had not caused his son a favour after all, leading to a very strong self-assurance and confidence.

Angelique looked at her father as he sat one side of the fireplace, burgundy in his hand, eyes on the gently flickering fire. "But what are your objections, Monseigneur?"

"Those of any father and of any person owning common sense: to go to Versailles now would be fatal; the political ferment is not yet over, *mon enfant*."

"But all those heirlooms; they need to be catalogued and stored, hidden if you will, before the rabble destroy them totally. One day they shall be required again."

Emile, reaching the end of the Assembly proceedings, dropped his *Mercure* to the floor. "If you think that, *ma soeur*, then you are a bigger gapeseed than I thought."

"I will not give up, even if the rest of this family, indeed the rest of the country, does so!"

Her father gazed at her for a moment. "Not writing again, are you, *mon enfant*?"

She turned away and then back to him again, chin lifted a little. "But Seigneur, we live now in a democracy: do we not?"

Emile heaved an impatient sigh and then rose to his feet. "I am not part of this! I go to much more rational, and radically less irritating, company!"

"Ah, would that be the gentle and demure Lady Rochelle?" she teased.

"Anyone; rather than listen to you in one of your belligerent moods! And if you think this a free and democratic country now, then I suggest our *père* sends you to the nearest *Couvent*; housing a particularly severe Reverend Mother. That is the only way to contain your insanity. *And* keep the family name intact."

"Oh no...please...not the couvent!"

"The Couvent!"

"Oh? Not the dungeons at Château Quatreaux?"

"No, you would escape afore we got outside Paris," grinned Emile. "After all, *I* taught you to fence...*and* to hide."

"The attic then, next best thing: I could sit in the window embrasure with pale and sad countenance and watch the world go by; anything rather than the *Couvent*!"

"The *Couvent*!"

She sighed dismally. "The *Couvent* it is then. I shall take Olympe de Gouges' '*Rights of Women*' with me then. I dare say the nuns could use a little liberation."

"That *woman*...if one could call her..."

"Emile!"

He grinned at his father. "Well Seigneur, oh, alright, I'm going... and pray that I never have a daughter in the image of my sister!"

His father gave a faint smile. "Your dressing-chambre mirror broken then?"

Shaking his head and laughing, lifting his hand in a fencer's attitude of defeat, he bowed to the Comte and left the room.

Angelique watched him go and then turned to her father. She waited but her father did the same, not even looking at her and she knew that the diversion was but a temporary respite.

"Yes Monseigneur... I write," she said now, better to face it sooner than later.

"But just what do you write, *mon enfant*?" he asked very gently.

"Oh prose, poetry, random thoughts on this and that." Her voice was casual but to no avail; this was the parent that the twins had called the devil. He suddenly lifted his gaze directly into hers and the severity of those brilliant and penetrating grey eyes brought her as always to the point of total honesty. "*Mon Père*, I write events as they progress; one day they may prove interesting."

"To whom may they be of interest?"

"Well, of that I am not sure; mayhap a hundred years or so ahead they will be read with some interest. None can object, because what I write is nothing but the truth. The Paris papers even do the same though the truthfulness is doubtful."

"Just so: and one day they are legal, the next they are prohibited and their editors thrown into gaol."

"But 'tis simply a record of Assembly proceedings, *Monseigneur*, the six secretaries within the *ménage* do exactly the same."

"Then why bother?"

"Archivists wring their hands *now,* regarding missing information and documents, of the histories. Through today's twists and turns, much of these revolutionary events, I do be thinking, shall be lost."

"Destroyed...for reasons concerning the word treason, according to the power of the day; bring them to me."

She looked at him a moment, then left the room.

De Quatreaux sat long into the evening, reading an illuminating fantasy of France's journey into the last decade of the 18th century, except that it was no fantasy. His brows lifted occasionally at the accurate assessment of the apparent causes, thus far, of this Revolution: this document commencing with the calling of the States-general.

Through close study of the *cahiers*, drawn up in each parish to list the grievances of the people for the first sitting of the States-general, she had given a clear vision of the grievances and desires of The Third: the Bourgeoisie. These showed, throughout the country, that they simply desired a better quality of living: attacking tax burdens, feudalism, social inequality and influence and wealth of the Clergy and Nobility. Speaking then, separately for the illiterate, the serfs: they attacked the appalling lot of the peasant but in no way was the tone of these combined lower classes republican or anti-monarchist. This came later, inflamed by the paid, and unpaid, orators. It was indeed many of the privileged classes, who resented the concept of Divine Right and ministerial despotism.

Founding factors precipitating the current situation included the industrial crisis, following the Anglo-French Commercial treaty of 1786, the agricultural crisis resulting from the famine of '87, '89 and now scarcity and price rise of food. This had created fear and rumoured starvation of the people. The disorder: over and above, in degree, that of the earlier *jacqueries*; had begun even as the delegates had travelled to Versailles for that first monumental meeting of the States-general. Now, increasing insurrection, pillage and street massacres were daily events. Potential British revenge: for the French support of the American War of Independence, contributed to the deepening fears of the country. Added to this was the rumour that English gold was now aiding France's enemies; granting substance to the paranoia of English spies walking the streets of Paris.

He read on then, eventually, sat back and gazed at his daughter a moment. "An excellent piece of work! And Louis... you must have thoughts on our monarch?"

She smiled, "That must be a separate document," then grew serious, her tone sad. "*Mon Père*, poor Louis could only see that he was bankrupt and, try as he would, powerless to enforce his tax reforms on the privileged orders: his only answer. Though courageous, he could not *see*, I think: that he could have taken the lead, within the evolving mood for reform. This, I see now, is what you were trying to promote in your early meetings with him. As we returned from Versailles that night, following your first meeting of any import with him, I did not fully understand but now I do."

"Ah! The intense clarity of hindsight: a wondrous thing."

"But foresight is the better. As had Mirabeau and Lafayette: all the early 'honourable' defectors to The Third... but did they realize, I wonder, how far it would all go?"

"And it is by no means ended yet!" He hefted the sheaf in his hand. "'Tis an excellent piece of work *mon enfant*; if the Assembly owned the clarity herein, we would indeed be a fortunate nation! But you know of course what must be done now."

She smiled suddenly and waited: the Comte's approval of supreme importance, as always. The smile froze within the next instant as he leaned forward, without further discussion, and tossed the whole onto the fire, watching until the last blackened folds lay smouldering and then stirred it with his elegantly booted foot to ensure totality of destruction.

Angelique stood and he at last lifted his head. "That hurt, did it not?"

She nodded, throat too tight for speech.

"Myself also, but believe me, it was of a necessity. Please do nothing to draw attention to yourself in such a way ever again. Every inch of those writings can be twisted to treason! The prisons are filling at alarming rate with ordinary persons accused of treason on a word, a look, let alone quill and ink!" He gazed at her and waited and the expression of deep understanding, mixed with hard reality, within his eyes at that moment she would never, ever, forget.

"Yes, Monseigneur... if you will excuse me." She left the room before her feelings overran her determination but heard her father's soft words as she closed the door.

"*Mon enfant...* in writing ability even Voltaire, or indeed Rousseau, could not compete!"

"But my love, what did you expect? Of *course* the Comte would know! He is not known throughout Paris as 'Lucifer' for nothing, he knows everything!"

"*No* man is omnipotent...even *de Quatreaux!*"

"Ma chérie, I fully believe that he *is*."

"Very well then, there is nothing for it but..."

Rochelle gazed at her friend apprehensively. "But?"

"Quatrains!"

"But of course. Only way to go," knowledgably, then, "What are they?"

Angelique explained.

"Oh *Mon Dieu*! Tell me Ange: is your death wish *so* strong?"

Angelique laughed suddenly. "But no! That is the way to go. After all, if Nostradamus achieved total secrecy, then so shall I."

Rochelle simply stared and Angelique explained.

"But is there any being that actually understands his... er ... quatrains?"

"No, of course there is not."

"Well, it does seem a safer way than your prose and poems, I suppose!"

"Assuredly." Her face took on a stubborn mien, well known to Rochelle. "And this time I shall have two copies, tedious as it shall be to write."

Rochelle groaned. "I still cannot like it... the wrack... the wheel... life in the galley! Shall *nothing* contain thee?"

"*No*. But I do not think that they had *female* galley slaves, Rochelle." She paused thoughtfully, then smiled. "But you *mon amie*, shall the Vicomte contain thee? Is it *his* voice that I hear these days? For it be not the Rochelle of old; that much I do know."

Rochelle smiled wistfully. "Ah, do not ask."

"But surely...I do not understand, I must confess, why so slow?"

"Emile waits *mon père*, still in England, to gain his permission... the convention, you know. Especially now and with France in such turmoil and he says *mon père* may even refuse."

"*Mon Dieu*, I would never have thought my twin to be such a slow-top!"

"He does everything these days to prevent any discomfort to me, or inconvenience to our family and the family name of both our Houses."

"And the revolutionaries had thought to have swept it all away!"

"But they are the *cause, mon amie*. An alliance between us could cause suspicion of Emile's defection to England: resulting in confiscation of de Quatreaux property." Rochelle was quiet for a moment; then, chuckling, "Tell me more of Olympe de Gouges."

Angelique groaned. "He carried that much to you, I see."

"Oh yes, but there: what knows he of woman's rights, even his own. I very much doubt that he has even read that bill."

"Oh he has! Covers all with a facade of bored nonchalance but he is ahead of all that the Assembly can throw at us."

"And the good Olympe... is she ahead? Or do we risk even greater censures because of one woman's writings?"

"Do not excite thyself, *mon amie*, for through it all, all seventeen articles of the Rights of Women thus far, the limits exercised over and above the natural rights of women still stand; those of perpetual male tyranny!  But it is early days yet. Work still to do!"

Rochelle groaned. "I just want to mind my own business, get on with my life and somewhere in there, do the world a good turn if I find a way to do so!"

"You don't stand a chance, too simple!"

Rochelle chuckled, then suddenly reverted to serious mien. "Tell me Ange, where on earth did you come by the results of the cahiers and such for those, now destroyed, insightful writings?"

"You do not really want to know *ma chérie*!"

"Oh but I do."

"Madame Roland."

"Oh *Mon Dieu*... no, you are in the right of it; I wish to know no more... if the Comte *knew*!"

♣

"Francois!" Angelique threw herself into his arms and danced him about the room. "You did not send warning! How long have you been in the city?"

He laughed, putting her off and readjusting his uniform. "I have not returned from the dead, Ange, only the frontier. Do control thyself."

Henri stood grinning at the scene, for he had not yet mastered the bland expressionless features of all good butlers, none of whom could hold a candle to the late Siffred and so he did not bother; he liked whom he liked and that was that.

Angelique turned to him. "Some liquid celebration, Henri, please."

"Yes Madame! Champagne?"

"The best that the Comte's cellar can offer!"

"*Yes Madame!*"

Some time later, all ensconced within the long salon, Emile turned to Francois and grinned. "So how goes the city under arms from a soldier's standpoint?"

Francois chuckled. "The patchwork security? Without it the Glorious Revolution cannot survive."

Angelique looked thoughtful. "The function of the modern army seems a far cry from that for which it was intended."

"'Tis at once an army *and* the police force; a mounted guard for the king, that is, to contain him; not protect him, for the protection of the Assembly, the *Commune*, the Chasseurs on the Barriers, the Town Hall, the banks, cash or corn convoys from the provinces, prisons, bridges, quays and waterways and such like. Even public functions; did you attend the recent patriotic fete? I did not see you but the massed crowd was such that..." He shrugged.

"The July 14th federation celebrations? *Bastille Day:* they are beginning to call it! No."

"Ah: on principle."

"Absolutely: especially when an official arrived on the doorstep to inform us that we would be wise to attend."

The Comte turned his head sharply. "You did not inform me of this."

Angelique met the penetrating eyes a moment, then looked vague suddenly. "Well, Monseigneur..."—too late she realized the title indicated guilt—"you were absent at the time; and I will not be, er...'*instructed*' by those...bullies!"

"Ah, I see, but of course, not to be tolerated." His voice was velvet soft and the siblings converted suddenly to defence mode. "And did you yourself inform him of this? Or was it conveyed by Henri, whom *should* have been attending the doorbell."

Francois and Emile exchanged resigned looks and waited.  Rochelle smiled at this.

"Oh, Henri was there but I was on my way out and er... regretted that I had other appointments to attend," replied Angelique.

The Comte was silent a moment. Nobody spoke.

"This house has long been on the list." The Comte stared into space a moment,

"Therefore you brought about an extra notation...against it."

"The list...Sire?" asked Emile. "They *could* not, surely, run around making lists of families who did *not* attend their wretched celebrations: commemorating slaughter and mayhem!"

"No, but the reply, to the door-knocking vigil, *would* be recorded. That was the purpose of it. There is no no-man's-land now. One is either for the Revolution or against."

There reigned a sober silence for a few minutes as each absorbed the implications of this.

"So Sire, we really are under revolutionary martial law," said Emile.

"I am glad that at last you all realize it," replied the Comte. "Why do you think I led you all to the long salon, for this reunion?"

Emile's eyebrows rose, glancing along the long corridor of a room with a central fireplace and open ends. "No servant, or any person, can linger within hearing distance."

The Comte nodded. "I expect you to take equal care. Of your speech, of your movements, of everything about your daily living now, your facial expressions even, particularly the latter."

"So do beware expressing the agony of a giant toothache," grinned Emile.

"I am serious, *mes enfants*." The Comte's tone was mild, gentle: and frozen.

There was a pause and then, "So how *did* the Federation fête go?" asked Rochelle.

Francois grinned at her attempt to defuse the air. "Well, was a sight to be seen. Poor Lafayette was dragged in to swear the oath again, even though he tried his best to convince them that oath could not be sworn twice."

"But that I thought was from the King," said Emile.

"Conveyed by Lafayette."

"Tell me: why did the bridge collapse?" asked Angelique.

Francois laughed. "Overcrowding was said to be blamed but I say it was the fat lady. I jest not, at least three axe-handles across the, er…"

The Comte's frigid brows stopped him.

Emile hastily filled the gap. "And the two killed during the salute of artillery?"

"Careless discharge."

"I would run a bet that you have no idea why the two drowned in the Seine," challenged Angelique.

"None at all: leaky boat? Foxed? I may be employed to keep Paris safe but disclaim all responsibility of fools and liquor. Of greater interest to me is the fact that Talleyrand spent the evening gambling and broke the bank at his favourite gaming house. I want to know *how* he did it."

"Twice! In one night," grinned Emile; then, "So what do we have by way of armed forces in Paris now, Francois?"

"68,000."

Emile looked thoughtful at this and Francois, glancing at him, raised his brows. "Think not along those lines. The King could not use them."

Emile looked puzzled a moment. "Ah, of course, I was forgetting, since the Decree: 'A standing army that cannot be used by the king against the people', disarming him completely. Oh well, we shall have to think of something else. Not all the best forces of the military are *inside* France's borders." He paused thoughtfully. "He should have gone, on Mirabeau's advice following the October 5th uprising; but even 'Toinette could not persuade him to anything that would result in civil war."

Francois shrugged. "How could he *pay* for it anyway? The king is broke."

Emile thought of the Comte's tireless manoeuvres but only said, "Others have tried too. Augeard, the queen's private secretary, spent most of his fortune on escape plans at Metz for them; and the Comte de Maillebois planned a royal retirement to Lyon. Stupid idea if you ask me: more isolated than ever."

"But financed by the kings of Spain, Naples and Sardinia," said de Quatreaux. "The troops *are* there; 25,000 Savoyard: and could still raise the Midi to march on Paris."

"I be thinking that Fersen be the only one with a sound head for such planning," said Angelique, and then glancing at her *père*, "That is, other than the Comte de Quatreaux!"

"Never! I mind my own business and my estates. And you shall all remember that."

"Yes Monseigneur!" chorused the siblings.

"The *Commune* grows very powerful now, I think," said Rochelle.

Francois grimaced. "Yes. Full of, and fuelled by, Jacobins, they say."

"Robespierrists," murmured de Quatreaux softly.

Emile nodded. "But beside the Jacobin Club, other machinery is being born at a rate of knots in Paris, by which the ultra-democrats are paving the way for power. Danton of the Cordeliers is one such; and acquiring notoriety."

Francois turned to the Comte. "Be it true that Mirabeau tried to gain entry into the ministry... and direct the councils of the king?"

"That is so but Necker moved more swiftly than one would think possible; to force through a decree that no deputy could be a minister."

Francois was silent a moment, then, "But then, I hear, he entered into a secret weekly meeting with the king and queen."

His father stared at him a moment. "Nothing is sacred! But of course while man has the power of speech that will always be so. Hence the tedious double acts, misinformation and worse; that one must plod through to find the truth: a career in itself!"

"But Louis and 'Toinette do not trust him," intercepted Rochelle.

"They do not. But beggars may not be the choosers," replied the Comte, "and Mirabeau is the best provider of accurate information since the axing of the king's *Cabinet Noir.*"

Francois looked at his *père* in some compassion, guessing that to get the king out of France was now the Comte's ambition. He felt a cloud pass overhead suddenly, and controlled a shiver.

"So...the troops of line...still the division of the classes?" asked Angelique now.

"Oh Lord yes, turn against one at the drop of a hat...or a boot: a fact that forces one to sleep in 'em... both... mutiny all over the countryside."

"*Mon Dieu*, this country is sinking but faster and deeper than I thought possible." Emile leaned back and gazed at his younger brother: no longer the snub-nosed sibling but beneath the good-humoured exterior, a man of military and now life experience. He gazed around, noting suddenly that thus far, they were still all alive: and soon, that may be the only thing that mattered.

# CHAPTER FOURTEEN

## The oath. The Pope. Louis

Raoul spoke softly: "You up for it?"

Emile stared into space a moment, then, "I do not necessarily subscribe to the adage that 'more is better'. I have sufficient for a solid foundation in England, *mon ami;* or Italy. However, to listen cannot harm. Perhaps this particular stack of cards of Lafayette's has less likelihood of collapsing." He shifted his gaze now to Raoul. "Very well, let's listen! But it must be isolated from all else."

"Absolutely; these are investments *here*," Raoul grinned. "Yes, yes... a seemingly senseless and worthless plan but a very convoluted path deems it untraceable."

Emile simply waited; amusement in his eyes as he watched Raoul, then, "Buy low—sell high; *if* France ever stabilizes again! I never thought to see you so. Is enough, never enough? When will you call a halt?"

"Yes, yes, a gamble but think... if we return..."

"If...? *When* we return, *mon ami!*"

Raoul shrugged. "Enormous price will be attached to our estates! The bribes, or simply the going rate, will be three times their value... to get them back."

A slow smile began to spread across Emile's features. "Well, well! *Not* greed but foresight. Decidedly relieved about that! But yes, within the see-saw buyer seller act, our desire will be the stronger and they will know that."

Raoul nodded grimly but remained silent.

"You do know of course, that if the Robespierrists' of the Assembly remain in control the price on our heads will remain in place for our lifetime."

Raoul shrugged. "Life itself is a gamble."

They left the rough, wooden, street-table of the café and wound their way through the dense traffic of the *Palais-Royal*. Dressed in ancient, ragged capes, hood casually thrown back, they forced their way, peasant style, through the noisy populace.

Rounding a corner Raoul sniffed the air and turned to glance at Emile. "Smoke?"

"Yes, *mon ami*," the soft voice came from his right shoulder.

Startled, Raoul spun to see Pontisqieu, his face grim. "Glad I bumped into you! I could do little on my own; except plead the illegality of it all: the conscience weighed heavily!"

Raoul merely raised his brows and Pontisqieu continued, "They burn an effigy of the Pope. I am sure it is in no way harming Pius... personally. But they have, to drive home their point, a *curé*, held and ready."

Emile stared. "But we cannot allow this." he turned his head to Raoul, brows raised.

"A non-juror, of course," said Raoul.

The crowded sidewalk now thickened into a tight wad of humanity.

"We must not fail," muttered Emile, "but in this swarm?"

"No, no," said Raoul softly, "It is provident: the crowd!"

Both his companions turned to look at him as he pulled a parchment-wrapped package from his inner cloak-pocket. "Gunpowder; packed in a special way: from Anton, today, his invention; was going to test it at the estate."

Emile raised his brows to their highest point. "And you sat with *me*... drinking coffee?"

They continued their laboured progress so that Raoul had to convey his plan softly, to first one, then the other, separately. "Gunpowder thrown onto the fire would cause sufficient diversion."

"Make a habit of carrying such things around on your person, do you?" hissed Pontisqieu.

"You suggest that I use a courier?"

"But the searches, *mon ami!*"

"Not been used before you say?" Emile grinned: his daredevil grin of more frivolous days.

"Not designed quite like this."

"Range?" asked Pontisqieu.

"Of blast? No idea...'twas not meant for throwing into flames, I think."

"So you could kill him."

Raoul shrugged. "Hopefully not. You got a better idea?"

"Better than the flames anyway," said Pontisqieu, "And nothing surer; without a diversion we three can do little against the sheer numbers here."

They arrived to witness the dying flames of the effigy. Someone doused the supporting pole. Others readied more faggots for the dying base fire. They turned to the *curé*, held by three large, strong men.

"On the count of three," whispered Raoul.

He tossed the package lightly above the heads, into the smouldering coals and they watched. They waited. Nothing happened. The noise of the milling excited crowd rose, as the *curé* was dragged toward the fire.

The explosion was deafening, rocketing flames and debris high into the air, stunning those nearest the fire. The 'strong men' were thrown to the ground, along with the *curé* and many of the closer spectators, creating a domino effect of falling, stumbling, dazed and desperately escaping, humanity. Raoul, Emile and Pontisqieu raced to release the *curé* and dragged him away, beating out the flames of his *casaque*, swiftly ripping it off and draping him in Raoul's cloak.

Semi-conscious, the *curé* proved a heavy burden, dragged by Emile and Raoul, an arm draped over a shoulder each.

"Where now?" hissed Emile.

"Make way! Make way!" cried Raoul, and seeing the injured man they did, without casting him a glance, ever pushing forward to see what had happened.

"Which way?" hissed Emile again.

"Keep going…left…down that alley. To the Mouton *Auberge!*" said Pontisqieu. "It has access to the tunnels."

The post shock phase of the explosion dazed the immediate crowd. They pushed through this, then the milling excited crowd, then the merely curious further afield. Soon they were entering through the back entrance of the *Auberge*. Pontisqieu simply gave the proprietor a nod and was led through the taproom to the passageway beyond. Emile and Raoul staggered their way through the patrons; dragging the apparently inebriated_cure. "Make way! Make way…fellow citizen is ill!"

Thus, following Pontisqieu, they arrived at the cellars and the proprietor turned and left without a word. Gazing about searchingly, Pontisqieu detoured suddenly to a high shelf there and returned with a bunch of candles, lit one from a wall lamp and handed it to Raoul. Pulling away old crates from the wall, he opened a small half-door then led them into the endless tunnels below. They lowered the *curé* to the floor and propped him against the stack of barrels there. They straightened and eyed the tax-evaded contraband.

Pontisqieu set about pulling the crates back as best he could with a long hook kept by the door for that purpose. "Just in case someone enters before Jules: he will do the rest."

"I um…do not wish to insult, Pontisqieu, but know you just where these end?" asked Emile.

Pontisqieu tugged the last crate into place and closed the door. "Well no, only that it is a safe place to hide."

"Inside the Notre Dame," muttered the *curé*, head lifting now.

As one, they turned to look at him. "Ah, the prodigal mind returns," chuckled Emile. "Welcome back *Mon Père*."

He stared at them. "I can but thank you… whoever you are… but you must know that I was prepared to die."

"Nonsense *Mon Père*," said Raoul. "Much better things to do."

"Why, by the way, did they burn the effigy?" asked Emile suddenly. "You of course must be a non-juror."

"I am. But the Effigy of His Holiness was burned by the Constitutionalists; in retaliation against those demonstrating *against* the Revolutionary State Church."

"Eh?" Emile shook his head, "*Mon Dieu*, it is all too much for me! *Who* demonstrated?"

He shook his head, then winced, drew a breath and said, "It is not complicated. The 'conformist' nuns: (equivalent of the priestly jurors)… and 'non conformists': (non-jurors), were forcing their beliefs onto each other. The beautification of Sister Marie of the Incarnation, was turned into the demonstration against the *Civil Constitution*, by the 'non-conformists' of course, and the last word was had by the *Constitutionalists*; they burned the effigy of the Pope."

Emile stared, not even trying to follow this, though he doubted not that it made sense if dwelt upon. "I knew we were coming to a pretty stand but France grows madder by the minute." he shook his head. "Augmented by a bunch of women."

"A bunch of *Holy* women," rebuked Raoul. "And you will end far from anything Holy, *mon ami*, if we do not get our friend out of here."

Emile turned to the *cure*. "Do you know the way... through these catacombs?"

"I do."

"Ah: descendant of the Templars of course!"

The *curé* gave a weak grin. "Your powers of deduction to be commended."

Following, at junctions, always the damper walls indicating that they crossed beneath the Riviere Seine to the Ile de la Cité, the *curé* led them through the maze. The Notre Dame, after wrong turns and blind ends, appeared abruptly, as they stumbled into a crypt. Raoul moved up stone steps and listened at a solid oak door. He tried the handle; depressing it very slowly, halting instantly each time it began to grate. Finally the door swung open enough to slip through and they ascended steep narrow steps to exit behind a small alter holding a statue of the Holy Virgin. Crouching here, they laid further plans. Pontisqieu left first, via a statue, then casually moving past the sporadic, praying individuals, to exit the Notre Dame and seek a *pots-de-chambre*.

Raoul, Emile and the *curé* emerged as it appeared and Emile and the *curé* squeezed on. They moved off to cross the Seine and headed to Hôtel Quatreaux, on Rue St Honoré.

Emile cursed the Revolution. Without this, requiring front doors be barred for added security, he could have used his key as of old, thus circumventing Henri. Standing there, thinking a moment, the door was opened suddenly by Angelique.

"*Ma Soeur*. What providence. But you do not go out surely."

"No Emile," she laughed, ushering them in and closing the door again. "I witnessed your arrival from above... awaiting Rochelle. Something was afoot, that much was evident!" She gazed a fleeting moment at the *curé* with faintly raised brows.

"Ange, please meet er...?" He turned to his companion.

"*Père Guilbert*. I thank you both but you cannot hide me here."

Angelique's brows rose and Emile grinned. "You do not know the de Quatreaux twins. *Not* feeding you to the lions *Mon Père*! Certainly you must stay here. Come."

"Quickly," Angelique moved swiftly up the stairs, glanced along the gallery and beckoned them.

Without hesitation she led them on, along the gallery, always ahead, pausing frequently to listen for movement of staff, to a small bedchamber. Emile moved to the panelled wall surrounding the fireplace, applied pressure to a scrolled carving and that panel slid silently aside. Stepping in, he reached for a taper, lit it and nodded to the *curé*.

"Until no evidence that we be followed and a decision is made, please remain here, *Père Guilbert*," he said softly. "There be extra candles, fresh water and a bed, as you see."

The *curé* nodded, then suddenly, "But all is prepared?"

Emile grinned. "Assuredly, the water changed daily; the periodicals, monthly."

*Père Guilbert* stared. "You feel things are that bad?"

Emile merely smiled and gave him a gentle shove. The panel slid back soundlessly.

Dinner complete, they gathered in the small salon. De Quatreaux and Emile sat reading journals and sipping burgundy. Angelique pulled the candelabra closer for greater light and fed new embroidery on to its circular frame, pulling it taut.

The absent Rochelle entered the room, launching into speech as she arrived. "Père Guilbert is now replete and settled with the journals! He is safe! But... regarding the Church... what *is* this fuss going forward about Tallyrand, Seigneur? I wanted to ask at dinner but," she shrugged, "the footmen were present. The gossipmongers of the salons are full of it; so cousin d'Argmont tells me! What *has* he done?"

De Quatreaux' eyes twinkled as he looked at her, then in severe voice, "Do take a breath *ma chérie*," causing Angelique to smile: Rochelle had certainly captured the Comte's heart, not an easy feat.

He continued, "But it is what the Vatican has done to *him:* Striking at the *Constitutional Church*, the Pope excommunicated the Bishop of Autun."

"Tallyrand," Rochelle raised her brows expressively, "But why?"

"Pius' Secret Allocution of March 10$^{th}$ rendered the new French State Church illegal." The Comte paused and took a sip of his burgundy. "And Tallyrand, having resigned his Bishopric in order to become a member of the *Paris Department* then, under the *State Constitutional Clergy*, consecrated the first two State elected bishops."

Rochelle's face lightened. "Ah yes, I see, illegal now... in the eyes of Rome."

Angelique frowned slightly. "Why did the reluctant Pope make a move at last?"

"Fear of losing his influence and property of Avignon motivated him in the end. That and pressure from the émigrés," then cynically, "which abounds with princes and nobility now. More to the point, of course, be the *Abolition of Annates* by the Assembly; loses the Vatican three to four hundred thousand *livres* per year."

"And his stand on the oath?"

"All bishops and *les curés* who have taken the oath of allegiance to the Revolution, shall be suspended by the Pope: unless they retract their oath within 40 days of taking it."

"The escape route," murmured Emile. "Speaking of which, can we not er... release *Père* Guilbert, *Mon Père*? Seems we are not to be ruthlessly searched. None can be aware."

All eyes turned to the Comte.

He frowned. "No. We did not prepare the staff for a visitor: a suspicious circumstance. But it is not a problem now: he leaves us later this night. I would that I had been here at his arrival. There are other places that he could have gone: hiding a person; against the Revolutionaries draws a severe punishment." His gaze rebuked Emile.

Rochelle, deep in thought, suddenly looked up. "Not that it counts. Any other action could not be contemplated!"

De Quatreaux swirled his drink and took a sip; then, "It counts more than you imagine; imprisonment without trial, then execution." His tone was so subtly cool that she missed it.

She shrugged. "Oh."

Emile laughed. "Are *all* English alike to you?"

"I warned you there was a large portion of insanity within her," chuckled Angelique.

Rochelle raised her fine brows. "Well, whatever be the use in fretting over *possible* consequences?"

De Quatreaux turned a severe face toward her, chips of ice forming in his eyes and Rochelle felt the first of his ire; realizing now what the siblings must have grown up with and that, by joining the family, she sat now in range of that discipline. Lacking practise within the family dynamics, she could not hold his gaze. So, the honeymoon was over: she now must realize her place in the de Quatreaux family and accept that discipline.

The tone matched the gaze. "*Mon enfant*; not 'possible' but of a certainty; should the authorities be aware. Remember that."

Emile snorted, "Robespierre's spies!"

The Comte nodded silently, then rose, walked to the door and searched beyond for any listening servants. Returning, he stood with back to fireplace. "Any criticism of Robespierre is now treasonable, with one outcome. Sometime soon you must all learn to contain yourselves." His voice remained smooth, and frigid. "If you do not, sooner or later you shall find yourselves imprisoned and once there you shall never see the light of day again. If indeed you keep your head upon your shoulders long enough to see anything at all." He stared at the floor a moment; then, placing his glass on the mantel, glanced at the clock there. "I must depart now *mes enfants*... an appointment... you will remember my words, I trust. Otherwise *I* shall have the hanging of you."

Emile stood. "Sire," bowing as the Comte turned and left the room.

Rochelle glanced at Angelique and anxious now to hide her chagrin, launched into the first thing that entered her head. "What are the new laws regarding the oath, Ange? You were reading it I think."

"Ah, forget it," said Emile, "they shall change again afore my sister finishes speaking."

Angelique's face took on a stubborn air. "Knowledge is armour!"

"And in practicality, worse than useless: it is a maze no man shall conquer. Besides: to keep up with the daily changes, is exhausting."

"But even *Louis* found to ignore them be a bad mistake. His support of the Vatican: taking communion from non-juror priests only, brought an accusation of treason," said Rochelle.

"Poor Louis is close to breaking down I believe," said Angelique, "since he has been forced to sanction the *Civil Constitution of the Clergy*... something unthinkable to him."

"But he has his revenge: receiving constitutional bishops as though they are mere state officials *and* turning his back on the juror priests."

"And the Deputies' attitude toward this issue, Emile, the oath: you were there."

"No sympathy: if the rest of the nation's civil servants must swear allegiance to the New State, then so too must the priests, who are now paid out of the tax payers' money."

Angelique chuckled. "So now we have two priests in the one Parish; juror and non-juror. Both worried regarding treason: the one to the Church, the other to the state; neither agreeing."

"Divide and rule. That *had* to be Robespierre's idea," said Rochelle.

♣

A vast crowd formed the funeral procession. Moving slowly with the mourners, de Quatreaux gazed at the casket containing Mirabeau: deceased on April 2$^{nd}$ 1791 at the age of forty-two; following the sudden breakdown of his normally robust health. Coinciding, he noted, with a change of temper drawing over the Assembly. This had to be expected: if anyone could hold the runaway team together, it was Mirabeau and without him, mayhem would rule.

The procession halted at the recently built church, the *Panthéon*, on the south of the Seine, reserved for the special burial of those granted honour by the Assembly. This being so, de Quatreaux had to suppose that Mirabeau's secret work for the king: for which he had been paid a monthly salary, remained a secret. But he knew this to be not necessarily so: those possibly holding this secret could be awaiting opportunity.

He glanced around as the body was interred. The relief of Mirabeau's bitter enemy, Necker, was almost palpable. Equally obvious, was the sorrow and regret of those who saw his policy as one of moderation and thus of durability. Now a very strong push of the ultra-democratic party to dominate the political arena would surge ahead: Robespierre, the power behind this radical, political throne, now battled no competition.

De Quatreaux frowned. He hoped Mirabeau's devotion of the last few months of his life to the king's survival, *did* remain a secret. The planning and devising, of viable schemes to withdraw the king under armed escort to Compiègne or Fontaineblau, with the co-operation of the faithful de Bouille and Lamarck, had been extensive.

In spite of the unproven accusation of double-dealing hanging over Mirabeau's head for some little time, none could deny that his popular policy agreed with the abolition of privilege and destruction of the order of nobles and clergy. Adding to his popularity had been his relentless campaigning to free land and labour, the press, worship and individual rights of property and person.

Few, however, knew that he had detested the new arbitrary government and had had little faith in the wisdom of a collective, elected, body of men. De Quatreaux smiled suddenly, remembering his acid comments on the political intelligence of the middle and lower classes: 'Bah! There is no loyalty either side: the one would sell out for political victory and the other for bread! A king, de Quatreaux,' he had added, 'even if only a puppet, as leader of the nation still be needed, to give strength to the base line of a juvenile government. Stability in this country be founded in a long, long line of Monarchy; and it will take as long again to organize these scattered ants without their leader! Even if only symbolically!'

That loss of stability was now further imperilled by the continued disorder of the people. Taxes still remained unpaid. Peasants continued to pillage corn from wherever it could be found. Attacks on Châteaux; and cash and corn trains from the provinces, increased across the country. Street mobs persecuted non-juror priests and lynched careless nobles at will. Soldiers refused orders of their officers. Clubs usurped authority and papers and journals discredited the Constitution. Insurrection was alive and well still. Now, however, light dawned at last regarding the mayhem. It began to turn and swing in the opposite direction. The Royalist hopes were raised, just a fraction.

Lafayette, Barnave and the Lameths, stalwart nobles still within the Assembly-left, began to fear overshooting their mark by having crossed the floor at the beginning; but to change course now was impossible. They worked hard for popular support and clung to their original principles: as ordained within the early Constitution. Too late, they began to realize the very great steadying influence that Mirabeau had had over the Assembly. This man had had an acute vision of the political battlefield as it really was. Even sharper had been his ability to see what should be done about it.

The death of Mirabeau quickly caused the death of what fragile stability still existed, creating a pendulum swing towards the opposite direction. The fickle and reactionary press now condemned the Assembly and threatened the axe to all who had given it support from the very first States-General meeting. The build up of arms, military and émigrés collected in bands. Invasion threatened and Louis' brother the Comte d'Artois called on foreign powers to restore, by force of arms, the king and the authority of the throne.

The position of the king and queen had long been intolerable, regarding the Constitution as monstrous, Louis bending eventually, with extreme reluctance to consent to the many demands: the Civil Constitution of the Clergy and the imposed oath, the greatest nightmares of all. That he was unable to obtain sanction for this from the Pope destroyed his peace of mind. His depression: once alleviated by involvement in his kennels and hunting at Versailles, now deepened. His gentle nature was dying a slow death at Tuileries, leaving him flaccid and disinterested and it became known that to deal with Louis, one had to have the queen by his side.

The queen's unpopularity continued. Hostilities based in past history, was resurrected with monotonous regularity. Light again shone on the disfavoured pledge of alliance between France and Austria, formerly a long-standing enemy, on her marriage to Louis. Rumoured Court intrigues clung to her. Already branded untrue wife, false queen and betrayer of France, she now apparently sought to put down the Revolution in blood, by aid of Austrian troops. And true it was that she now devoted all her amazing energy and drive, to the restoration of her husband's throne. She found great pleasure, as always, in her duties to her family and by her bearing, calm and dignified, impressed all that came in contact with her. She was Austrian and Austrians did not lie down and die.

To escape this prison became her one driving force. It was of course, more than a political prison, or the bricks and mortar of the hated Tuileries. Her life had been one long imprisonment: of restrictions experienced by all royalty, of an arranged marriage whilst still a child in Austria, to a man that she eventually and truly loved but had found difficult to respect from time to time, in view of his manifest weakness; and imprisonment within a city containing a people that loathed her. Now, both she and the Monarch regarded this new disorder with hope: that the Constitution should fail.

Maria Antonia of Austria had always been a rebel. Born partly of genetic nature, partly of national pride, she had battled the French court and its etiquette at early age, fifteen, on her marriage. She had fought court slanders and intrigues. More recently she had rejected the patronization of Mirabeau and other courtier-politicians and turned constantly back to the plan of Montmedy and an Austrian army. To this end the winter and spring of '90-'91 had passed in total devotion, with the confidence and trust of the Marquis de Bouillé at Metz, the Swedish Comte de Fersen in Paris, Mercy d'Argenteau and de Breteuil at Brussels. Secrecy remained amazingly tight; the only other persons in possession of the plans the Duc de Choiseul, the Bishop of Parmiers and the king's messenger: the Comte de Lamarck.

The queen gazed now at the Count de Fernan Nuñez, the Spanish ambassador. Louis, she knew, had no secrets from his Catholic cousin, the King of Spain and, as early as October '89, had sent him two vital, and eventually damning, documents. These contained bitter protests against the acts of the Assembly, contrary to royal authority.

"But schemes of Bourbon Princes, disjointed and isolated as they are, now can do nothing. We *must* have the simultaneous support of Spain, Switzerland and Sardinia!"

Nuñez bowed politely. "Madame: shall be, in that case, impossible to avoid a border skirmish and perhaps civil war."

"It need not come to that, I am sure. A *threat* of arms should be enough; but to make it work Louis *must* be established on the Rhine frontier."

"Madame, I believe you to be sincere and very intelligent on this issue and certainly desperate straights call for desperate measures; but be there reliable and trustworthy support within Tuileries?"

The queen looked at him. "The escape of Madame Adelaide and Madame Victoire does encourage me. Yes, they were stopped at Arnay-le-Duc, but eventually the deputies allowed them to proceed."

"To Rome, Your majesty, not Austria; and they were not the king and queen but the king's aunts: *elderly* aunts, hardly a threat, if you will pardon me, Madame."

"Carefully planned, Nuñez, 'twill not be impossible."

"Finance, Madame?"

"One million livre plus jewels and notes of exchange and that be added to the 160,000 from the banker Duruey and Crauford's 15,000 and Stegglemann's 12,000. There be almost sufficient... and Trifane has arranged further funds for us. All is in place; Trifane sends his assurances. Why, even Lamarck, on his return from a mission to de Bouillé at Metz, reports that all omens are propitious. There is apparently much political discontent on behalf of myself within that countryside. And also Lady Cowper of England *and* Lady Atkins I hear, raise funds for a Royalist army for us."

Nuñez gazed at her, knowing that her will was stronger than his and not only from the position of Queen. Unable to convince her of the folly of such a plan, he made his excuses and bowed his way out of her presence: just as the king entered.

"Ah, Your Majesty! I leave now... but please, you know my sentiments regarding this issue of, er... removing to beyond the border. I believe that Spain cannot, er... openly support such a move."

The king grinned sardonically. "Or covertly! Oh, I do know my cousin, Nunez."

Nunez bowed again with a smile and made his exit.

The Queen gazed at Louis in exasperation. "He is stupid... that one!"

"Astutely so, *ma chérie*... his objections hold much water."

"But Louis, we only need money and troops enough to *get* us there! Once over the border my brother shall place whatever troops are in Luxembourg at our disposal. He *promises* so."

"Leopold may or may not, *ma chérie,* but to get there first is the thing. Remember the St Cloud affair. We achieved naught but the gates of this courtyard; and that was only to go to that place for a brief rest. And I do not believe that the National Guard shall protect us any more now than they did then: they mutinied and then shut the gates. There are no troops to support the king anymore."

She gazed at him. "I remember it only too well *and* Talleyrand's letter condemning us; for taking communion from non-juror priests... warning us that the whole nation was against us; as if we required a memory prompt on *that* issue! Louis, do you too, feel that this is all a fantastic dream? We are as much prisoners as any wretch that lies within any dungeon."

He smiled tiredly. "I try hard not to think of anything that has happened from the time of the calling of the States-General. How long ago it seems now."

She frowned thoughtfully. "How many National Guardsmen at Tuileries now?"

"Six hundred, according to Lafayette; and an abundance of spies..."

"That many, to guard one family. I do wish that we had the political and military strength to legitimise their fears! But, we have behaved in manner of late that says we are giving way on every count, thus allaying the fears of the Assembly. But before we act, we must be sure that 15,000 men are moved to Arlon and Virton and as many again at Mons. De Bouillé is very anxious that this should be done. He needs reason to mobilize troops and munitions at Montmédy *and* our assurance that a body of 10,000 men shall be at Luxembourg ready to march on Paris. De Quatreaux is rallying the émigrés also. And as to Leopold: he says that until we are in safety he shall make no move and shall prevent the Princes from doing so. But if our plan succeeds, then he will send orders to Mercy, to aid in every way that he can: money and troops, whatever we need. The place is now not Montmédy, as every one in our confidence believes but the *Château de Thonelle*: de Quatreaux' idea, a half-day's journey from the frontier. It be protected by an armed camp and the Austrian troops be but a few miles away. Once arrived, Louis; your first mission will be to dismiss the Assembly and to restore the property of the Church... at one blow destroying the Revolution. If this be not successful then we must march on Paris; with the Austrian army in support. We *must,* Louis!"

"And finance? Leopold is not forthcoming." Louis smiled tiredly at his wife.

"Well, certainly my brother refused the advance of ¾ of a million sterling but I supplied Fersen with 75,000 (sterling) and he added 30,000 of his own! Louis, we must move *now*; secret escape the only plan now, we have not time for anything else... no Guardsman to be trusted."

"Oh yes, there be de Quatreaux' son and a few of his original regiment. But we would be best to wait for my next quarterly; a million and a quarter shall not go astray, plus approximately another 30,000."

"How do you know you can trust de Quatreaux's son? He is young."

"But mature and his loyalty is without question. And if one cannot trust a de Quatreaux then it is indeed the end of the world. Here also be Fersen. And mayhap Lafayette." He spoke tentatively, aware of her mistrust of the Marquis.

"*Not* the Marquis de La Fayette! Yes, he will help us but only within the confines of his own popularity. He would betray us to save his own neck, that one. That is not enough. But first things first: we must use the tunnels to even get out of Tuileries. We must investigate, again, the tunnel from Tuileries to the outside of the donjon of Vincennes. *Then* where to, Louis?"

"By stages to Varennes and then to the Château de Thonelle: General Louis de Bouillé is there and, as you say, together we can challenge the Assembly."

"We can trust every one in our confidence?"

"As far as possible, but who knows these days. Bouillé's loyalty is total. But regarding travel: Fersen wants us to go separately."

"No Louis! I shall not have us scattered all over to be plucked off as pigeons in the clear blue sky."

"In fast light carriages, instead of the cumbersome berline," replied Louis.

"No! We shall never find enough trustworthy men to escort us, for more than one carriage: besides the berline is not cumbersome; large and of obvious noble ownership certainly but no more than would be expected of Fersen's Russian friend, the Baronne de Korff, who has ordered its construction...*and* is paying 6000 livre for it. And its size allows us to store our few things within, escaping the piled up bandboxes that should surely cause notice."

The king looked sadly at his wife. "I am wondering of late how Louis thirteenth managed to surround himself with so many valiant musketeers: all swearing loyalty to their beloved king on pain of death."

"That is *long* ago. I imagine they all roll continuously in their graves at this debacle. But we must remain in the 18th century, Louis. Not slide nostalgically into the beauty of the past and what might have been for us had it continued. All be not lost, the divisions within the Assembly are increasing with a strength and speed that even a month ago one would not have believed. The country is drifting into real anarchy; not a shadow of a doubt about that and we must use it, Louis. Now! What news of Turin and Coblentz?"

"Trifane sends coded messages only but seems that most of the nobility that have left the country are noisily threatening invasion and calling on foreign powers to restore me by force of arms. Those nobility still remaining here, are openly and scornfully defiant and by protests and intrigues are stirring hatred against the Assembly... to bring it into contempt be their aim. And, Trifane tells me, the nobility in support of the *revolutionary* laws are under a social ban by their own order. Of Spain, he holds out no further hope."

"But this is well for us," she replied, ignoring Spanish fickleness: Louis' wavering cousin: escaping always the concrete backing of his verbal loyalty.

"Ah yes, but the word *treason* grows stronger as the Assembly grows the more desperate: placing the remaining royalists in a more dangerous position than ever. The central government is impotent to restore order... its top-heavy structure so unwieldy that its highest authority rests within its lowest administrative bodies now."

"What did they expect... but those areas of our strongest support?"

"Limousin, La Marche, Bretagne, Lyonaise, Alsace and Champagne."

"And our route to Montmédy?"

"Bouillé has stationed detachments in every town and village after Chalons for our protection."

"But shall not that raise suspicion? The Dragoons and Hussars are disliked all over."

"I rest my confidence in him."

"Shall require many staging posts."

"Nineteen in all, I am told, and to install fresh cattle without raising suspicion, will be something of a problem."

"But de Quatreaux is seeing to the fresh horses, is he not?"

"No, he is stretched too far already!  Fersen's contacts are seeing to it. Fersen will ride with us by the way."

♣

"But Rochelle...you look magnificent!" Angelique moved forward and gave her friend a hug, then holding her shoulders leaned back and surveyed her. "*Ma chérie*, I could not be happier for you. When you are married I suppose that Emile shall command your attention. My heart is broken!"

Rochelle laughed. "You goose: of course our friendship shall not suffer and Emile insists that in these times you shall make your home with us.  The Château Quatreaux is large enough to house half of France and not see any of them for a sennight I be sure."

Angelique laughed again, then stepping back, "No *mon amie*, I shall refuse, outright!"

"What be thee refusing outright *this* time *mon enfant*?" the Comte de Quatreaux entered the room silently as he spoke. He turned to gaze on his recalcitrant daughter; waiting in mock frigidity for her response.

"Sire," she curtsied elegantly, smiling up at him demurely, "I merely stand upon my...er...decision not to make my home at Château Quatreaux but..."

"Well? Do go on *mon enfant*, where then shall you live?"

"Um, well, I suppose wherever they are not? Hôtel Quatreaux while they are at the château."

"And when they come to town you shall then run off to the chateau... with no one at your side but your *femme de chambre* and a couple of servants? No, *mon enfant*: time for you to marry also, shall be arranged."

Angelique turned cold suddenly as she gazed at his unconcerned features; then the guests began to arrive, ushered in by a footman: the first three, Madame Bayette the widow Comtesse and the Comtesse and Comte d'Arteaux. Just behind these was Raoul Trifane, Marquis de Savieur, casting his glance towards Emile and saluting, as his friend entered and took Rochelle's elbow. The pair then moved to stand with de Quatreaux and the Madame Bayette to greet their guests as these congratulated the couple on their betrothal and exclaimed over the ring, an ancient family heirloom sapphire surrounded by diamonds. The new guests then moved into the long salon, where they were to take drinks before the celebratory dinner in the long dining-room. Raoul turned to Angelique, aware from the moment of entry, of her disquiet.

"Something has upset your equilibrium, *mon enfant*?" His tone and manner was of gentle concern and understanding.

She gazed at him, stunned by the swift changes his mere tone of voice could now wrought within her. The wild, rebellious desire; to tear away from all humanity; to ride break neck across the fields of Quatreaux, that had held her steady in the face of new threats, now melted away. But it was the deep and intent expression of his eyes that almost had the undoing of her: almost caused her to lean on his strength and unburden herself. Struggling to overcome the weakness, she managed a steady voice.

"But no, Seigneur Trifane, this is after all an occasion for festivity."

He continued to gaze at her, a very faint smile tilting the corners of his strong mouth. "Mademoiselle, if you prefer to do battle with these new demons, whatever they be, without my assistance, then I can but bow to that."

She laughed. "Seigneur Trifane, I shall manage... but thank you indeed. I already owe you. Twice I believe. I must cease to be so careless!"

He laughed. "But the pleasure has been mine; the rescue of a fair damsel is always an amazing boost to the male sense of chivalry. However 'tis your *père* that upsets thee, no? That I did witness! Come, a drink be in order: *that* much I can offer you."

"Thankyou Monsieur."

He took her arm, paying no more attention to her distress, the very antidote that she needed and together they entered the long salon and the noise and gaiety there absorbed them and separated them, as the night of celebrations began.

A voice hailed Emile, above the babble and, glass in hand, he turned to see Beaumont approach. "Good evening, Vicomte. You return I see! It must have been quite wonderful to walk the streets so freely! But England is mayhap preparing for another war against us?"

"Seems so Monsieur; however, I was there such a short time that I really cannot say for sure: being there on other business."

"The business," laughed Du Toit, "of obtaining the hand of this beautiful young lady here. Raise your glasses again I say, to the Mademoiselle Rochelle du Bois!"

"To Mademoiselle Rochelle!"

Francois grinned and lifted his glass high. "To them both... to Emile and Rochelle!"

"To Emile and Rochelle!"

The cry rang out across the room and echoed across the halls and up the stairs.

Angelique gazed about and wondered.  How long could they go on in this manner, ignoring that which was spelt out before them; but then, as her gaze rested upon the Comte, she realized that here was one man that did not ignore anything at all.  But he was, however, determined that his son and heir would enjoy this ritual to the upmost; that the family name would go on, no matter what, that the estates would go on, no matter how hard to retain them; and that France would go on.  She caught the eye of Francois at the other end of the table and raised her glass.  If anyone should be saluted it must also be her younger, military brother, giving his all, fighting his strongest, within a bizarre war of no logical sense.

At Tuileries, plans continued for the escape of the royal family: the queen nervously re-examining every detail. "Louis! We shall soon be out of here! If we can trust everyone; but you know, always there is a leak, no matter what precautions are taken. We must have provision for them. Check again, please Louis, the travel documents?"

"The Russian ambassador arranges the duplicate passports for Frankfort, for the whole travelling party, under the name of Korff, through the Foreign Office."

"How so?" The queen worried eternally of exposure, accidental or otherwise.

"She declared the originals accidentally lost, or was it destroyed?"

"The whole of them? Oh Louis, I cannot like it... it could spark a search and to travel the road frequently used by émigrés: we shall be stopped and questioned repeatedly!"

"But rich and foreign travellers shall be excused much eccentricity.  Better that: glaringly obvious, than sneaking and hiding; eyes are everywhere for that."

"I suppose, but, well anyway," she paused as Clery entered silently and announced Count de Fersen.

"Ah Fersen, come in and relieve my wife do, of her anxiety if you can."

The count bowed low to the king and then the queen and smiled. "Do not allow your serenity to be cut up, Madame: all is in order thus far and all goes smoothly. The plans are all but complete; the waiting all but over, the Austrian troops—that cause of our delay recently—are now in place on the frontier. And the unreliable servant has gone..."

"The most recent in a long line of them: I do not trust *any*!"

Fersen smiled gently and calmly, perceiving that the anxiety of the wait, as any soldier could testify, was taking its toll.  Even on this Austrian stalwart of courage and strength.

"We cannot trust any court servants, Madame, certainly; but our 'leaked' information is misleading for them.  And the placement of de Quatreaux' daughter and others within the court shall lead to the assumption that you widen your court for the summer entertainment. You must allow your natural talent for joy, and love of fun, full reign over the next short period. And then it shall be all but over, Madame."

"Oh *Mon Dieu, 'twas* a natural talent, was it not? No more so, Fersen, I struggle every day. What of our escort? They must be trustworthy, Fersen."

"The Comte de Moustier, known for the journey as 'Melcher', shall ride up front on the box with me, and the Comte de Malden, 'Jean', shall jump up behind. My own coachman, Balthasar Sapel, shall ride as postilion on one of the leaders. M. de Valory, 'Francois', shall ride ahead to ensure the relays are in place and ready. Scattered along the way, travelling at a little distance and separate from one another, shall be the Vicomte de Quatreaux, the Marquis Savieur, Vicomte Montague and Marquis d'Arcy. They too shall have their *aliases* and reasons for travel arranged. They shall ignore our party completely. Also, de Bouillé has stationed bodies of cavalry at various points along the route from Chalons onwards."

"Be that not a little dangerous? Create suspicion?" asked the king now.

"Sire, I agree with you; did not, still do not, like it but de Bouillé knows his work and the movement of these detachments have been carefully co-ordinated. The first is to meet the coach, the *berline*, at Pont-de-Somme-Vesle, eleven miles beyond Chalons, with instructions to safeguard a convoy of 'treasure' on its way to the frontier, Sire."

"And this is under whose command?"

"The Duc de Choisseul, a royal officer of a wealth and pedigree not to be denied."

Louis caught an element of the unspoken. "But?"

"Too young and indiscreet, Sire, but mayhap I be wrong. He is to travel ahead of you to take over his command."

There was a pause as they digested this. The queen then decided, against her greatest wishes otherwise, that no plan could be completely and utterly foolproof. Relying upon the young officer's bloodlines, the queen left the subject, unable to do more about it.

"And Madame Brigney and Madame Fourville?" she said now.

"The *femmes de chambre* shall travel ahead to as far as at least Claye, the second posting house on the road to Chalons; by a *cabriolet*, Madame."

"And leaving this place: the Tuileries/Vincenne tunnel?"

"No: for though its existence is so doubted as to be almost a myth, I had information that it be watched... at least the supposed exit of such."

Marie Antoinette suppressed a shudder. "We are *so* watched!"

Fersen smiled reassuringly, though he knew she was not fooled by this. "Madame: the myth of your escape has been bandied about since your arrival at Tuileries... none, I feel, do expect it in reality."

"You *feel*!"

He bowed at this and continued, "You shall be picked up in a hired carriage from the *Cour des Princes* at the back of the south wing. You shall use the door that I have used," he smiled faintly at the memory of the very odd hours that he had had need of visiting them, "since your arrival at Tuileries, the one leading through the Duc de Villequiers' private quarters via the *corridor noir*. Through there, Madame Royale, 'Amelie' and the Dauphin dressed as the girl, 'Aglae', shall slip to the waiting carriage, with Madame Tourzel dressed as the Baronne de Korff; the children's 'mother'. If there be need of diversion I shall drive around the quays or some such before returning to the Petit Carousel to pick up Madame Elizabeth; now the nursery maid, 'Rosalie'. Then I shall pick up you, Sire, as the valet 'Durand', in your sombre grey coat and wig! Lastly, Madame: yourself, as the governess 'Madame Rocher'."

"I *was* beginning to wonder if I was to be left behind."

The queen's weak attempt at humour caused his heart to contract. If only he could do more for her. Gazing now at her, he knew that his love for this woman would never ever die, no matter what took place, through this life and the next. Suddenly he was amazed at the durability of a real love and cursed the age in which they lived. He glanced at the king suddenly and felt the warmth of a strong friendship for that unfortunate man, wondering if any other would have done better in his unenviable position. A more callous, bloodthirsty man of no conscience may have, in the early days of the States-general demands, ground underfoot those leading the unrest. This however would only have served to delay events and was a moot point now.

"Now," he turned to the king, "Sire, it mayhap take some time to exit Paris with many twists and turns and perhaps delays, depending upon the traffic and unaccounted events, but on no account, forgive me Your Majesty, give up and turn back to the royal apartments. The time to contact you again could imperil all."

"Oh the valet 'Durand' shall be ready and waiting, as are all good valets."

"Good...please inform me, should even the smallest thing alert either of you!"

# CHAPTER FIFTEEN

## Royal Flight to Varennes – 20-21<sup>st</sup> June 1791

Angelique stood, Saturday 18<sup>th</sup> June, in the large entrance hall, draped in her cloak and pulling on her gloves. "Henri, in the unlikely event that the Comte or the Vicomte return while I am away, be pleased to tell them that the Comtesse Bayette and I travel to court in the de Quatreaux carriage. I shall pick her up on the way through…"

A loud clanging of the heavy doorbell caused a pause in her speech, as they both turned to look at it and Henri glanced at her a moment.

"Yes Henri, answer it, though I cannot think just whom it may be, for all know of my departure to the Tuileries for the small function there."

Henri opened one of the heavy double doors and stood aside. "Monsieur?"

Henri-Marie Pontisqieu stood on the threshold.

Angelique moved forward, hands held out. "But Monsieur! Do come in, please!"

Henri ushered them into the small salon on the ground floor. "You require liquid refreshment, Madame?"

"Please, if Monsieur Pontisqieu does have the time?"

"Thankyou, Mademoiselle, indeed; but you, I perceive, are about to leave the house and I do not, unfortunately, have the time. I just needed to see you for a brief moment, though I regret the intrusion at this hour but do need to be at the Châtelet again this evening."

The butler left the room, closing the door quietly and Angelique gazed in inquiry. "You have my full attention, M. Pontisqieu please; sit down."

"Mademoiselle, I do not know how to say this so shall simply do what Seigneur Trifane asks of me."

"Trifane?" she glanced away, then back again. "Goodness, what can he want?"

"Only that you convey this note to the Count de Fersen as soon as may be possible; in fact, immediately—he seems to be under the impression that you attend a court function this evening. Also, he insists, that I escort you as far as Tuileries."

"Monsieur Pontisqieu, that be not necessary but please, do tell me what goes forward."

"Mademoiselle, I am in no way to let you go alone. If by chance your carriage be stopped for the purpose of searching the occupants, then please pass me the note immediately. In which case, you had better know that there has been a leak."

"I am to tell the Count de Fersen just that... a leak?"

"Of what plan or information I do not know, but Fersen shall. And there is to be a lockdown at Tuileries."

"Monsieur…"

"Henri, Please!"

"Very well then, Henri, do you know much about the lockdown?"

"No, only that Trifane came direct from the house of Lafayette, to give me the message for you: be that pertinent to the case, or coincidence, I am uncertain. There is to be a special guard set: the Mayor Bailly and Gouvion the Commandant of the Palace Guard are to spend the next night or two in the building. And the officers doubled in number throughout; and I suppose other innumerable measures of tightening security."

Travelling the short distance to the Tuileries, with the Comtesse and the added protection of Pontisqieu, Angelique pondered the mystery; the sealed note prickling against her skin beneath the low-cut bodice. Arriving at the palace, they entered, the sounds of the ball growing louder. A page escorted them into the ballroom. The dull and drab Tuileries was now transformed and the candlelight from the many chandeliers caught the colourful silks and satins of the ladies and gentlemen of the court, as they twirled, twisted and turned within the moves of a minuet.

The Comtesse, perceived immediately by one of her oldest friends, was carried off and Angelique found herself alone for a moment. She gazed about abstractly, her eyes seeking the Count de Fersen, then turned at a touch upon her elbow to find Beaumont, de Quatreaux' oldest and closest friend, gazing down at her with a faint frown of concern.

"And why is the daughter of de Quatreaux travelling without a gentleman's escort this night, Mademoiselle?"

"Ah…yes, well you see, Emile found reason to return to the château unexpectedly but 'twas no problem; we, the Comtesse and I, had the protection of another for the short journey here, although of course at such short notice he was not dressed for court and therefore could not attend. As to the safety of travel in the Comte's carriage, he has it so secure that I find trouble in exiting the thing! So it stands that none could enter; and the postilions are of extreme toughness."

He gazed at her with an indulgent smile on his lips but his voice was censorious. "Hmm, Seems a shabby set-up to me… and smells of intrigue!  Who is this gentleman?  And I *know* that the Comte would expect you to remain at home under such circumstances: especially these days.  As to females making lone entrance into the ballroom: not unheard of in these abhorrently changing times of course… but… shall I inform the Comte?"

Startled, worried by his perception, and to throw him off, Angelique focused upon the reprimand. "But Monsieur, what a fuss: have you not heard? The English are throwing off such heavy mantle of fustian etiquette! And so it follows that Paris shall do the same. Come to think of it, Paris likes to be *first* at everything. However, please feel free, Monsieur!"

He laughed again and then taking her elbow, "But England is not in the middle of a Revolution. The daughter of my oldest friend shall escape; this time.  Come: pay your respect to your queen before the court censors your tardiness."

Rather to approach Marie Antoinette alone but unable to find a reason for doing so, she allowed him to escort her across the room to the queen's side.  She wished he would leave her then but he remained by her side as they awaited notice and Angelique had time to ponder his chance remark, wondering if he did indeed suspect intrigue.

The queen turned away from the Belgian ambassador and smiled at her. "Angelique, so lovely that you could come."

With Beaumont by her side she curtsied elegantly but some of her anxiety showed within her eyes.

The queen turned to the Comte with great charm. "Beaumont, your company again a great pleasure but I perceive Madame Du Toit gazing in our direction."

He could do no other than bow, smile; and comply with the hint. "Ah, then I go, Your Majesty, but I leave you with the greatest reluctance!"

The queen turned back to Angelique. "*Mon amie*, what be it?" Then, as more sycophants descended, "Come to my apartments at the end of the night; there we shall be secluded from all of this."

"Thank you, Your Majesty, but please do tell me, is the Count de Fersen to be here this night? I see him not."

The queen's brows contracted a little, then. "Yes, of course, I believe he finishes his game soon and shall descend to the ballroom."

Angelique thanked her and made way for the new arrivals intent upon making their curtseys and bows. She moved to join the ladies-in-waiting. Eventually, just prior to the hour of supper, she witnessed Fersen entering the room and with much delicate manoeuvring arrived, within a few minutes, at his side.

"But Mademoiselle Vermont, I am enchanted to see you. Does the Comte delight us with his presence and wit this night?"

"Thank you, Monsieur. No, he be absent at this time, as does the Vicomte, Monsieur; but I must have words with you. I have something for you." Her tone was low.

Reading the anxiety behind the brilliant smile, he glanced casually about, then took her arm. "Mademoiselle; pat your face with your kerchief. You are faint."

"I am?"

His eyes danced. "But yes. Definitely you are. And pull out your smelling salts."

"*Monseigneur*: I have never in my life required such and therefore do not carry..."

"But now you are definitely about to swoon. The kerchief, if you please."

She obeyed, reaching into her gem-beaded reticule for the scrap of dainty lace.

"Good. Now I must find somewhere...ah...there is a place." He led her off into a small alcove, seating her there on a *chaise-longue* and stood with his back to the room, a small potted-palm by his side screening her. He was smiling gently at her and suddenly she understood the queen's feelings for him; he had to be the most handsome man in the room and though he played the indolent courtier, she knew that few exhibited such care and compassion as did Fersen.

"Monsieur, please do not move!"

He stood very still; brows raised, then a slow smile formed on his face, glancing away, as she reached beneath the lining of her bodice.

"Madame? Be this a hold-up?"

"I wish it be as simple; and I am not that bad with a pistol."

"So I heard," he laughed.

"You *did*?"

He smiled as he took the proffered hand and felt the screw of parchment there. "And he deserved it and now rests upon the scorn, and worse; merriment, of Paris."

"As bad as that; but this be not good for me, Monsieur—he be a man of great revenge."

"Fear not: he stands not one chance. Be easy on that head, Mademoiselle. By a ring of security, your friends you understand, you be protected beyond your imagination from the likes of he. And unshakable it is; nothing shall tear it apart."

"Ah, but I seem to be able to tear up any ring of security all by myself!"

"Ah yes, that also be known amongst us."

"*Mon Père...!*"

He laughed. "But you must rest easy, for only the love of a person can create that sense of protectiveness amongst us males. And it is especially strong when the lady be of courage and daring, fidelity, honesty and integrity, gentleness and compassion, to a high degree. These are no exacting qualifications you understand but a natural eminence of such... by the lady concerned, rousing the protective instinct within us gentlemen!"

She stared. "You must be hoaxing me, Monsieur! I *cannot*, sadly, aspire to such lofty virtues!" she chuckled. "Do gentlemen actually *believe* in such paragons? But I perceive that the virtue of obedience be not there. How is this? In a patriarchal world; for such has not yet been defeated by the Revolution I think?"

He laughed. "One cannot, in your case Mademoiselle, insist upon the impossible!" He quietened suddenly. "And before the intrusion of another body, nothing more certain as I see the Comte de Arras descending at this moment; anything to add?"

"Only this, Monsieur: in the inconceivable event that you lose the note," she offered the brief message from Henri.

He thanked her and turned in time to greet the aging Comte. "Greetings Sire," bowing deeply. "I hope you are well this night? And now, I feel sure that I may leave the beautiful Mademoiselle Vermont safely within your hands, as my very doubtful social graces are required elsewhere at this moment. But you should know that she has felt rather faint and still recovers." He bowed to her, "Madame," and then to the Comte, "Sire," and was gone, leaving Angelique to the tender mercies of the tottering and mildly intoxicated Comte.

It needed fifteen minutes to six o'clock, Monday 20<sup>th</sup> June, and the queen was in tears.

The final arrangements had been set in place and Fersen was leaving the palace for the last time.

The king, face rigid with emotion, looked at the Count. "Fersen! Whatever may happen, I shall remain forever indebted to thee. And I shall never forget. Some day... *some* day we shall all laugh at this."

An hour later found Fersen at the house of his old friend Craufurd. Craufurd, going far in financing this plan, had offered his stables to the king's cause; and all known facts collected by him, from the street upwards, to aid the Count in this project. Here Fersen checked that all was in order with the berline for the journey to the frontier. Eight o'clock found him back home again at his desk scratching at parchment with quill, a last note to Marie Antoinette, changing the previous arrangements for the *femmes-de-chambre*, adding coded words of love and devotion. He walked to the palace and left the note there himself, without disturbing the queen again and found all quiet on that front; patrolling the darkest shadows and silent alleys until satisfied.

Next, he checked that all was understood by the three *gardes-du-corps* who were also to accompany the party. He gave them his final instructions and warnings against persuasive spies, naming some, describing others.

At ten o'clock, dressed as the driver, he brought a hired carriage around to the *Cour des Princes* at the back of the south wing of the Tuileries. He had left early to account for unexpected delays but all reigned quiet this night. Expecting tight security following Angelique's warning, he double and treble checked the obvious and the obscure. Officers were on duty at every turn certainly but the one door had been left unguarded. So some, it seemed, could still be trusted but he continued his extreme vigilance.

The door opened and two children and their governess, Madame de Tourzel, passing as the Baronne de Korff, slipped to the carriage.

Fersen, perceiving the approach of Lafayette at this moment, driving to the *king's coucher*, urged them into the carriage. "Quickly! Be quick."

But Lafayette appeared to notice nothing; and Fersen, though he trusted him not, was as satisfied as he could be. He drove around for a further forty-five minutes, trawling the quays and surrounding streets, never the same route twice and then returned to the palace, arriving at the Petit Carrousel at the north end of the Tuileries. A shadow, that had to be the king's sister Madame Elizabeth, emerged.

"Come Madame!" whispered Fersen, leaning down to the 'nursery maid: Rosalie', "We pick up His Majesty next."

She nodded, entered the carriage and he drove on, hoping that the king would be able to quickly eject Lafayette: that always last attendant, from his evening ritual *coucher*.

The king, however, as 'Durand' the valet, was a little late, owing to Lafayette's talkativeness and offers of ingenious plans regarding military control of Paris. He took his time to absorb the information, in normal, cautious, Louis manner and then, Lafayette at last exiting, waited some minutes before changing his attire and silently also exiting the Tuileries. And so he too entered the carriage with no fuss and sat in immobile silence; the day had finally come: to exit Paris in manner of stealth. His very soul revolted at the cowardly aspect of this.

Fersen drove on and soon arrived at the appointed place of exit for the queen. He pulled the carriage to a halt, controlling his terror as they awaited her appearance. They waited an hour, the minutes, the seconds, ticking by loudly in his heart and mind. Within the carriage the tension increased to fine proportions. Restless with anxiety, the king stuck his head out of the window and, seeing the street empty, called softly to Fersen.

"What do you suppose has gone on?"

Fersen turned quickly and whispered, "Please Sire… do remain in the carriage! I am sure she will appear soon!"

At that moment the queen; now the governess 'Madame Rocher,' emerged. Mentioning none of the horrors undergone within the tightened security, she entered the carriage and showed nothing of her deep stress other than a slightly more rapid breathing. The king took her cold, shaking hand and without glancing at her even, squeezed it in empathy.

It was now after midnight.  Fersen used a further hour, driving sedately in random manner, in order to make a final call on his stables in Rue Saint Honoré. Finally they moved along the cobbled streets towards the Barrière Saint-Martin, holding their breath at the ringing hooves in that misty, echoing silence.  Here the travelling coach awaited them.  Now, at one thirty on the morning of June 21$^{st}$ they set out on the hundred-mile journey to Chalons, leaving behind the 'prison' palace, guards, barrières and city guard. The tension, though reduced a little, held them all silent and the queen in deep prayer: of thanks; and for the deliverance yet to come.

At Bondy, a few miles outside Paris, they slowed to a halt. It was still dark but dawn waits no man and Fersen rode up to the window of the carriage.

"Sire, Madame, here, according to plan, I must depart. I will see you beyond the frontier. All will be in readiness, I promise. God speed! And preserve you all!"

The queen, her heart a painful lump in her breast, could not even look at him and stared remotely ahead, tight lump in her chest and stomach, rigidly controlling impending tears. The king simply nodded his thanks.  Fersen, with the upmost reluctance, every bone and fibre screaming out for him to see to this escape personally, left them.  He walked his horse a few yards distant and turned to gaze at the dark hulk of the carriage. He was to make his own escape on horseback to Mons to meet Craufurd and then to Arlon, where he was to meet up with the king again, on the German side of the frontier. This was the plan and so far so good.

He gazed back at the coach for but a minute. The queen, tears streaming down her cheeks now, peered through the chink in the curtains at his silhouette: his Swedish-born figure proud and erect against the lightening skyline. He then turned his horse and rode off sedately, wanting to spur the animal to a reckless gallop: do *something* to ease the sharp thrusts of savage pain within his chest.  He forced his mind to the 'plan', to the future: he *must* believe in a royal future; in a restoration, in a safe and secure Marie Antoinette.  He swore and suddenly thrust his horse recklessly forward.

Not looking but understanding his wife's pain, the king took her hand under cover of the darkness and squeezed it tight, knowing that in every mans' mind this would be seen as a weakness but his wife's returned pressure told him all that he needed to know.  It *was* possible to love within the universal image of the word: a love that transcended the barriers of human emotions and cheap jealousies. That she loved Fersen he knew. That she also loved him, he also knew.  It was that simple; for after all he had been chosen for her and Fersen, had it been possible, had been chosen by her.  He smiled gently into the darkness. His wife, that strong-willed, valiant, fun-loving woman was also one of extreme warmth and incredible generosity, owning an enormous capacity for love of the highest order and deepest feeling.  His smile converted to a frown; the public knew nothing of this woman they so easily denigrated.

It was the longest day of the year and the king swore that it was the hottest in history as they jolted and rattled along, the heat and dust penetrating the interior of the carriage. They stopped only a moment or two at posting stages to change horses and took what meals they could stomach within the inconvenience of the crowded carriage. Occasionally the children, when isolation offered protection, left the berline to walk up a hill as the animals made slow and heavy weather of the issue against the cumbersome berline; Madame de Tourzel accompanying them at times.

"Come Madame! The air is cooler out here and the exercise beneficial."

But the queen remained flaccid and depressed: her treacherous mind periodically replaying without warning, the dreadful horrors of her last hour within the corridors of Tuileries. As the family sat waiting her appearance, she had experienced total, disabling disorientation. Detouring from the designated route, in order to escape notice of the sudden excess of guards, she had had the worst time of them all: ending in touring the long, rabbit warren of unfamiliar corridors. Fighting her way through these labyrinths, she had battled a mounting panic: struggling to control shallow breath and mounting hysteria, as she passed closed doors, muting sounds of noisy soldiers within. Finally, arriving at the designated rendezvous in a state of total confusion, she had fallen, in complete relief, into the *berline*. The flashbacks continued, her body shuddering from time to time.

At Claye they paused and the king, gazing out the window, saw the cabriolet. "Well, seems so far so good *ma chérie*. We have caught up with the two *femmes de chambre*." The queen turned her head in flaccid manner. "They are to follow our carriage, Fersen said; at a small distance behind, for the rest of the journey. Not that they can be of assistance should we require it!"

Golden shafts of light streamed down the centre of the road ahead as the sun rose, throwing the buildings of Meaux into dark relief, as they approached. An artist, thought Marie Antoinette abstractedly, would have made much of it. June 21st had dawned. Montmarail appeared next, without incident, and then Etoges. Here a broken trace brought the first of their troubles. Setting out again they arrived at the town of Chalons: a posting stage. The family descended from the carriage to stretch their legs and take a little refreshment during the changing of the horses.

The town mayor, frowning distractedly at the dangerous ebb and flow of last night's meeting, moved mechanically along the cobbled sidewalk. Reaching the post-house and navigating the berline, he politely sidestepped a knot of strangers stretching their legs. He glanced indifferently at the scene before him then stopped, staring a moment: here, surely, stood the royal family? So the rumours of the royal escape were true. His soul shrank at the idea of exposure. He watched as the mission was completed at that moment and the party re-entered the berline and moved out. His gaze followed them, determining to say nothing. Turning, he found the baker's boy staring at him; then following his line of gaze. He shrugged and gave a half-smile, indicating that non-locals were strange people: the boy had not even travelled to the next village, in his short life. The day progressed and busy with municipal affairs, the mayor staved off the gnawing worry. Finally the thought of punishment reigned supreme: it needed only a chance remark from the baker's boy; and he was inordinately fond of his head. He walked to the bell-pull and then sat at his desk, pulled forward parchment and dipped the quill into the ink.

"You rang Monsieur?" asked his butler.

"Yes Belsar," without looking up. "Go fetch my messenger, if you please."

Belsar left the room and he continued writing, quill scratching across the parchment. The messenger entered the room some minutes later and bowed, but the mayor did not look up a for moment; then shaking the contents of the brevette over the wet ink, waited a moment, then folded the missive and closed it with his seal,

"Take this to the Assembly, if you please. Do not let it out of your sight. Hand it only to the President, even if you must go to his Hôtel."

"Now...Citizen?"

"Are not fresh horses always held in readiness?"

"Yes Citizen!"

In Paris, at ten o'clock in the morning on this same day, the 21$^{st}$, three successive alarm guns boomed across the city and the people knew now that the rumour of the king's escape was true. They were missing and none could trace their path. The streets filled with excited crowds, hurrying to stare at the now closed Tuileries and at the *Menagé*: to demand action of their deputies.

The tocsins sounded from all the clock towers continuously, once again, and the town cryer walked the streets calling his warning: 'Invasion! Invasion! Keep the lights burning upon the night, stay calm, be prepared!' At the Town Hall, the now tattered red flag of martial law once again replaced the white one of peace.

The National Assembly sent couriers out into every *Department* to close the frontiers. Regulations were passed immediately, regarding passports and extending police powers to a degree before unknown. Authority was given for the recruitment of a further 100,000 volunteer emergency force. This chore was handed to the National Assembly ministers. These now ordered the justice minister to stamp, with the seal of state, all decrees blocked by Louis thus far: with his declining powers of veto.

That morning began the first of five long days of continuous sitting for the Assembly. Responsible persons, for the royal escape, must be found. A seal was placed on the Royal Apartments of Tuileries and Luxembourg and investigations made into the catacombs beneath them. A veritable army of officials carrying flares before them became lost so many times, that a method of accurate trail had to be devised. The National Guard was ordered out to search every road out of Paris, in every direction, for the king's route of escape. Having eventually found this; and with nothing further to investigate, Lafayette at last sent two of his officers to trace this and secure the fugitives' arrests.

While this fermenting cauldron bubbled on in Paris the royal party continued their journey, their thoughts far from that place of imprisonment. A detachment of de Bouillé's cavalry arrived at Pont-de-Somme-Vesle, a small post-house some few miles beyond Chalon. These were under instructions to protect a convoy of 'treasure' to the border.

The young, inexperienced Duc de Choiseul, commanding this detachment, sat his mount, gazing anxiously down the road before him. He calculated again: rate of travel, distance and adverse events. Of the latter he could think of none: the weather was fine, the roads fair and dismissing misadventure of any sort, calculated again the speed of travel. Not familiar with the cumbersome berline he now miscalculated its speed. He had had all in order by two-thirty but the king had not arrived and now, several hours later, his troops fidgeted: something must be done; the new breed of soldier was not of the disciplined variety.

His aide, glancing at his commander's irresolute face, ventured a remark: "I believe it to be the hour of four. The troops are restless, their mood fragile."

The Duc glanced about, cursing his lack of experience: he had to do something. "Move ahead!"

Not expecting such radical decision on his simple warning, the aide stared, "But the outrider: Valory, from the king's escort, may still arrive!"

The Duc looked down the empty road. "It grows too late. Send me Léonard, the *Royale Perruquier*. He must inform the next station of troops that the coach will not arrive before the morrow. Restless troops I do not need! He must release them."

A domino effect, at this point accidentally, of collapsing support network for the king, had begun.

Arriving at Pont-de-Somme-Vesle, tired and hungry, the king, finding no one to meet them, gazed about. "We must push on I suppose: to Sainte-Ménehould."

"But Louis, something be wrong I am sure!" responded Marie Antoinette.

"Perhaps: perhaps not; but there we meet with de Bouillé's detachment of Dragoons, under D'Andoins."

They pushed on. D'Andoins, however, having received de Choiseul's message, via Léonard, had ordered his men to unsaddle and disperse, just a half hour prior to the arrival of the royal party.

The late royal party trundled onward: to the town of Saint-Ménehould, eleven miles beyond Chalons, and found it in uproar as the berline entered the heart of town. The queen felt her heart plummet, for the place crawled with far more than necessary military. The royal party was however innocent of the cause for this upheaval. That same day, just prior to the entry of de Bouillé's dragoons, Goguelat, with another body of cavalry, had arrived at Saint-Ménehould. He had, however, entered the town carelessly, neglecting to first notify the Mayor of their passage; and without sounding the traditional fanfare: the neglect of such traditional courtesies stirring deep suspicion and fear. Panic set in and fearing hostilities, the newly formed Town-Guard of three hundred men, armed, smartly attired in new uniforms and filled with patriotic fervour, were ordered out on parade. Suspicion of all new arrivals now increased; but still all would have been well for the travellers but for a moment of sheer accident.

The moment of harnessing the fresh horses, at Saint-Ménehould, occurred with the royal family remaining within the carriage. To the nervously impatient Louis this appeared to be inordinately slow. He leant out of the window to see what was going forth.

Jean-Baptiste Drouet, the *maître de poste,* an ex-dragoon of Condé's regiment and ardent Jacobin, descended into the street at that point and glanced at the foreign travellers. He stopped abruptly and stared: surely not. The king could not be here. He pulled an *assignat* from his pocket and gazed at it. The head and face on the note appeared a replica of the man leaning out of the window. He spun on his heel and disappeared. Soon the alarm spread.

The queen gazed in horror at the swathe of excited people pouring down the street toward them and could barely contain herself: "*Mon Dieu*, Louis... we must go... never mind fresh water and victuals... go, go!"

They went, anxious to reach the next detachment of cavalry at Clermont. As the berline moved out, the support cavalry, escorting the 'treasure', followed. At least, they tried to follow but were now prevented by the milling suspicious crowd.

Lagache, one of the fervently Royalist cavalry officers, stared about him at the seething mob and suddenly made a dash: cutting through the mobs to follow the berline. They must be warned; and the cavalry waiting at the next post, Clermont, brought forward for protection. But his action turned the uncertain rumour now into a truth. Compounding this mistake, his horse was fresh but the night growing dark: he lost his way and did not arrive at Clermont until eleven at night.

Back at Saint-Ménehould, local authorities sent M. Drouet and M. Guilaume to ride after the fugitives at once. These men were locals and did not lose their way.

Ahead at Clermont the detachment of cavalry, beneath the officer Dumas, had also been allowed to unsaddle and disperse: before the late arrival of the royal party. They rallied but again the cavalry were prevented from following the berline as it moved quickly on. But here, also, were others of royalist fervour, in particular Rémy and his companions, who broke free from the milling mob and chased the coach. These too, missed the turn and rode on to Verdun.

The Jacobins, Drouet and Guillaume from Saint-Ménehould, rode on: pushing their mounts until they met the returning postilions with the old relay of horses.

"Wherefore are ye taking these cattle, at this hour?" asked Drouet, bringing them to a halt by manner of authority.

"Back to their owners: Citizen."

"And where headed are the new horses?"

"Well, Citizen, I do not rightly know but heard the order 'a Varennes'."

"A *Varennes*!"

The postilions gaped as Drouet jumped his horse across the ditch and rode off across the open countryside, following a route unknown to most and certainly impossible for a coach to use. Leaving them to draw what conclusions they could, Guillaume followed at breakneck pace, catching Druoet after some minutes.

"Citizen! What the devil?" he shouted, the wind in his ears as he rode.

"Short cut."

"To Varennes?"

Druoet also lifted his voice against the wind. "The advantage of being a local: Varennes is a town split in two by the river Aire. It lies ten miles north of the main road to Verdun at a point where a side road to Montmedy dips into the valley of Aire."

"It has a posting-house?"

"No. I can only imagine that they have arranged their own fresh horses there."

"Oh." Guillaume followed his companion until they dropped into that sleeping town at eleven fifteen at night, just a little ahead of the royal coach.

The shutters of the Bras d'Or remained open and light poured into the street. It was, however, the only inn within Varennes to do so. Drouet slid from his mount, dropped the reins into the ostler's hands and strode in. It took little to persuade the Jacobin landlord and three or four of his late departing guests to assist in the blocking of the bridge at the foot of the hill: with a hastily commandeered removal-cart full of furniture and another of lumpy packages. They armed themselves and prepared to stop the coach at the point of the arch between the church of Saint-Genoult and its bell-tower.

Drouet had been correct; horses had been organized for the royal party and paid for by Choiseul, but of these there was no sign when the coach arrived.

"Louis, what goes forward?"

"I do not know but shall find out."

Descending into the dark and dusty road, he confronted the escort.

"Sire, Varennes be off the road and has no post-house, but fresh horses are at the top of the hill, at the near end of town."

The king, too distracted at this new complication, failed to note the discomfort of this spokesperson and his anxiety to be gone again. He returned to his wife.

"My love we shall find them, no doubt."

At said top of hill, at the queen's insistence, the entire party climbed down from the Berline and spent a good half hour searching, but to no avail. "But they be paid for by de Choiseul! They *must* be here," she stormed.

But in this town, Goguelet had moved the horses to the Hôtel Grand Monarque, *beyond* the bridge, at the further and lower end of the town. Here the fresh animals waited, in the charge of Raigecourt and Charles de Bouillé, son of the Marquis, General de Bouillé. Close by was a reinforcement of Hussars under Rohig.

A Goguelet messenger was now sent off to search for the royal party. Some few yards into the darkness he was halted. On quiet instructions, effective of disciplinary action should he not follow them, he rode to the top of the hill but rode past the royal party and told them nothing.

Dismissing the lone rider hunched against the darkness, as a local, the king now spoke to the gardes-du-corps, "Go down the hill and look for the horses, man!"

The man did so but did not cross the bridge.

Two officers, within the king's confidence, at the Hôtel Grand Monarque heard sounds of disturbance. They looked at each but shrugging their shoulders, lifted their jars of porter and did not investigate. The postilions, who had brought the coach from Clermont, were instructed not to take the horses beyond the entrance to Varennes: their owner, the post-mistress, wanted them to carry hay for the next morning.

"I care not for the postmistress or any other mistress!" said Louis now. "Go on down there, man: there is nothing here! The horses *must* be at the bottom of the hill."

Approaching the archway now, the coach was halted by a small group of armed men.

"What goes forward here? Where is the Mayor?" asked the king, leaning out the window.

"Away in Paris but as *procureur* of the *Commune,* I have a right to stop travellers and demand their passports," replied Monsieur Sausse.

"Very well then: they are here," said the king.

"*Out*! All out! Come, come!" Sausse cried softly, anxious to avoid any mishap, "To the comfort of my rooms."

The fugitives were forced out of their berline, within a few hundred yards of de Bouillé's horses and Rohig's Hussars: within a few hundred yards of liberty. Within the darkness of the night, however; and with little cartographical knowledge, uncertainty held them in its grasp. Now exhausted by the long, gruelling journey and worried at the failure of their plans, the party allowed themselves to be lulled into a belief of Sausse's loyalty. They were ushered into a room over Sausse's grocery shop. It was here, so much against the queen's instincts, that Louis admitted to Destez, unknown to them a local judge aroused from sleep, to identify him, that he was indeed Louis XVI.

The queen smelled treachery. 'No Louis! No! We are the Korff's!' screamed her brain. 'It is a trap: I care not what they assert; these are not men of our support.' Soon she was proved correct.

"Even now, Louis, we may escape," she whispered. "Do not bow to them! Choiseul, Dumas and Goguelat are in this town… the postilion has just whispered to me. With more than fifty men, we are but some hundred metres, apparently, from them. If 'twere not so dark: if we had but known!"

Louis shook his head. "Rohig has ridden off."

"So what if he has done so? His detachment shall not find it difficult to force a way through the local guard. *Go* Louis! *Give* the *order*!"

But Louis, seemingly to pass into his habitual mood of apathy, dread and hatred of violence against Frenchmen, would give no such orders until de Bouillé arrived.

"*Ma chérie…*you do not understand. I am not chicken-hearted but concerned. For my people certainly, for I cannot tolerate that the blood of civilians be let in my name… and in these circumstances I shall be hung for murderous treason if I give the order that will spill that blood. But that be not my concern, 'tis for you … and the family, but especially the Dauphin that I worry. I cannot risk the Dauphin's head!"

"But Louis! This debacle is far beyond these considerations!"

Frantic now, she tried to coerce the postilions into action but they would not move without the express orders of their Monarch. In total frustration she turned away, hiding her streaming tears as her eyes scanned the dark streets for horses to ride even, to no avail. The tocsins rang out, the town entrances were blocked, the citizens roused and within an hour ten thousand inhabitants milled around the party's temporary shelter.

The hour was two in the morning as the municipal authorities sent off Mangin the town doctor. "You are to ride to Paris; inform the authorities that we have the *Famille Roi* secured here."

The royal family remained captive until two emissaries of the National Assembly arrived, carrying orders for their return to the capital.

On the same evening, that of the 20th June, the Comte de Provence and his wife, after quietly dining as usual at Tuileries, set off by another road, passports describing them as the Steglemann family. At the time the king and his party were just setting out for the return trip to Paris, the Comte and his family reached the Belgium frontier.

General De Bouillé waited by the roadside *beyond* Varennes most of the night then returned to Stenay. At four o'clock in the morning, a messenger conveyed the disastrous news. But all was not yet lost, for D'Eslon, Rohig's superior in command, now arrived with a fresh body of Hussars.

"The last chance of rescue comes from here, Boudet," he said now. "We must ignore Louis' orders and attack the town. We shall have no problem, gentlemen!"

But his message went astray: and Boudet's men were already drinking and fraternizing with the locals when, at eight o'clock, Charles de Bouillé arrived with more men, just half an hour behind the departing berline.  When the Marquis de Bouillé himself arrived with the main body of cavalry, the coach was more than two hours on its return journey.  De Quatreaux, hearing the details later, believed this period of time to be easily outrun by a fast riding posse of Royalists.  He wondered long and hard about the identity of the spies within their ranks but it was, he supposed, now a moot point.

♣

"Ange...have you heard? The royal family are on their way back and spending the night at Chalons.  Poor 'Toinette, it was there that she also spent her first night on her entry into France," said Rochelle, tugging off her tight gloves as she entered the reading room, ushered in by the faithful Henri.

"But the *brochures, ma chérie...* tell the king has gone, by Compiègne and the Ardennes, into the Emperor's territory to join the army of the ex-Prince of Conde! Also are we under threat of war against the rest of the entire world."

Rochelle laughed. "Feed it fear and rumours and Paris thrives! The pamphlets are worse: the king of Sweden has ordered his subjects out of France, Catherine refuses an audience with the French *chargé d'affaires*, and all French are to be expelled from Spain."

"And Spanish troops are moving to the frontier. Austrian troops, along with vengeful French émigrés, are crossing the frontier and shall march on the capital.  Within the hour, mind...I *wish*." She stopped suddenly, a strong thought entering her head.  Had not de Quatreaux something to do with the émigrés?  She shook it off.  "But the latest, *ma chérie...* be that the Cordeliers club declares itself ready to exterminate all tyrants: the aristocracy, and their descendants and ties... us; 'tis madness!"

"Ange, when do Emile and Raoul and the others return?"

"*Mon amie*, how can they? When the dust settles, heads shall roll now that Louis is back."

"*Whose* heads? That is the point."

"Worry not. Emile and company split off at about half way I do believe, or so Emile told me as he departed, there to continue on across the frontier, then to split again to go their appointed ways.  Much had to be organized, for the military-backed return of the king."

Rochelle stared at her. "So in that the pamphlets are not so wrong after all? How did you get so much out of him?"

"I am his twin. And if one plays it cleverly, the other of you thinks that you know anyway and opens their budget: learnt *that* much in early childhood.  Must admit though, it *was* a little more difficult this time and he swore me to secrecy but to you he would not mind, I surmise," she ended with a chuckle.

"What then? Where are they now then?"

"I do not know anything more. Except that we cannot expect them back until the dust settles."

"But they shall be arrested; no matter when they return... oh *Mon Dieu!*"

"Not if the Assembly be persuaded that the royal flight was a kidnapping…."

"You really believe that?"

"I must. They would have a contingency plan for the unthinkable: failure of the flight."

"The Cordeliers threat: that does not worry you?"

"Ah 'Chelle…how: would be such a big job of work!"

"They shall begin with the king and then work their way through the treasonably guilty. You watch! At least that is how I would do it. And just being *born* of nobility is treasonable now.    But Emile and Trifane… if any leak suggests their involvement…"

Angelique stared strangely at her and was transported suddenly back to the Christmas Hunt, seeing again in graphic detail the spreading blood of her vision but spoke calmly. "*Mon amie*, we shall no doubt see Emile and company come smiling through that door soon. Or…"

"Or: what?"

"Or we shall be called for.   So, you stay here this night; there be safety in numbers."

"As bad as that you think?"

"We cannot know; that is just it."

"I wish Emile was here!"

Angelique looked at her. "Myself also, *mon amie*, myself also."

Rochelle stood gazing miserably into the street. "They are distributing gun-powder."

"Ah, then we prepare. The Comtesse Bayette is also coming here tonight."

"She is?"

"To lend support: to my emotional sensitivity during this time of trial."

Rochelle stared and Angelique burst into a gurgle of laughter.

"Never mind the emotions, Ange: let's preserve the body first, shall we? Did you not tell of tunnels here: under this building?"

"Ah yes, they lead to the Tuileries."

"That is no good then."

"Oh but it is... before arrival, there, they branch off to an exit, by the Notre Dame."

"Under the *Seine*?"

"Yes.  But as you say, we would want north, not south, of Paris."

"*Any* way out of Paris shall be good!"

"Well, we shan't require such 'Chelle. You shall see."

"And the frontiers are closed anyway."

"But not every inch of those, only the exit barriers and we can both ride, rather well."

"Cross country. Difficult that: water, feed for the animals, without being seen, that is."

"If our ancestors could do it so then can we.  *Carry* the feed.  *Find* the streams, at dead of night."

"But the weight... there be our bundles as well."

"No 'Chelle: we go in our cloaks only, the papers in a shoulder satchel, our jewellery sewn into the clothing lining. The way the king should have gone in the first place. Louis is a bruising hunter and the queen not far behind! He could be across the border by now. No *femmes-de-chambre*, no governess; just the king and queen and the children up in front of them... or even carried up front of an escort each; but no more than that."

Rochelle stared at her. "You have given this some considerable thought I see."

"But of course, have not you? Following the château incident? I shall never be unprepared again."

The dawn of June 25th witnessed the royal party returned to town, surrounded by six thousand National Guard and several thousand peasants. They re-entered Tuileries, this time as true prisoners. The king's supporters claimed the whole affair to be a kidnapping but Danton and the Cordeliers demanded that a Republic be proclaimed and the king put on trial.

The king, prior to leaving, had secretly left a document addressed to the people and a copy to Fersen to be despatched to the Austrian Emperor. In this he criticized the Constitution, complained of his imprisonment and gave his legitimate reasons for flight: that of seeking a place of safety for his family, in particular the Dauphin.

The king and queen sat now before the commissioners appointed by the Assembly.

"We must know and *shall find...* who and what lies behind this plot. Who planned it?"

"There was no plot," replied the king calmly. "I had no intention of leaving France; or intent of insurrection, along with relations, émigrés, foreign powers or anybody else."

"Then where *were* you going?"

"Be a person not free to move about France anymore, Monsieur? In point of fact I was going to Montmedy: it is as safe a place as any to leave my family and a good point from which I may oppose any attempt by our neighbours to invade France. Such an event, I heard, be close to a launching. With the military so excessively busy and stretched, I felt it my duty to see to the security of France, in whatever way that I could. If I had intended to leave France would I have published my declaration *before* I had crossed the frontier? You have such in your possession now I believe."

"And your brother: he fled to Brussels, it is believed! In fact it is known."

"Only did he do so to avoid the same route as mine; which would have cast unjust and untruthful rumour on my movements. He intended to join me at Montmedy."

"I see. And we are expected to believe this. Likewise, that the Count de Fersen had crossed the frontier at Arlon, only to recross it at Montmedy, to join you? Your journey appears to have attracted much convolution of route and purpose, defying I might add, all reason!"

"My journey has been interesting and convinced me that public opinion be in favour of the Constitution after all; and though I disagreed with much within this constitution, I accepted that and returned to Paris of my own free will. Here to work with that constitution."

"Madame"—turning to the queen—"What have you to add to this?"

"Why, nothing, for it all be true and it was of course only affection that caused me to follow the king. As a family we stay together always. Would not any person faithful to his country and family, do as my husband did?"

"Commendable I am sure! And if he had tried to leave the country?"

"I should have done everything to persuade against such a foolish move; another reason for my accompanying him. And, by the by, the *courriers, femmes-de-chambre* and governess had nothing whatsoever to do with the plan to establish ourselves at Montmedy. They simply followed orders."

"I see. We shall follow up on all your claims."

Soon, however, a letter from de Bouillé arrived; in which he claimed all responsibly for the king's flight. 'The Monarch,' he wrote, 'on safe arrival in Montmedy, would have had to create a fresh assembly of wise men and establish rule by reason and the principles of freedom: the very principles of the National Assembly. As such he would be no threat but a wise and thoughtful addition to that Assembly.' De Bouillé then unfortunately ended with the threat: 'Howsoever all of this may be, should anything at all untoward happen to the king then I shall personally lead an army into France and an assault on Paris, leaving nothing still standing within that capital.' This wiped out Louis' diplomatic assertions in one sweep, and the Assembly realized the very real threat of the war of foreign intervention that had been a rumour for so long. Rumour now threatened reality.

At this moment the Emperor, at Padua and the Pope at Rome, unaware of events in Paris, were composing letters of congratulations to the king on his escape and were laying plans and calculating the next step against the Revolution. All was in order for a retake of France.

The flood of Republicanism now rose rapidly in the clubs, the sections and the slums. That provider of abundant fodder to the furnace of fear and discontent, the press, now agreed in denouncing Louis' conduct, and on the introduction of some new form of executive. The *Mecure, Bouche de Fer, Babilliard, Crueset* and Brissot's *Patriotic*, influenced by Madame Roland, the *Revolution de France et de Brabaut* and even the *Orateur du Peuple*; all agreed upon this issue, some openly favouring a full Republic. But, reiterated the more stable deputies, to denounce Louis would be to invite foreign attack. The Assembly was humming as a disturbed hive of angry bees. The king, it was decided, must be kept not only a prisoner but also a prisoner upon the throne of France.  His dethronement, on the only grounds allowable within the Constitution, that of insanity, would afford the only excuse required for a war of foreign intervention.

Back in 1789 nearly all the sensible politicians, writers and respectable authorities admitted that they wished to retain the Monarchy as stock on which to graft the new Republic. The new French Republicanism, they asserted, was not of imported ideology but had grown within France: out of the political *needs* of France. It had arrived slowly, through many fragmented origins. It was, however, the popular press that had spawned the early ideas of such.  The press, the clubs of Paris and the Fraternal Societies, agreed on the education of the people of Paris; education steeped in Rousseau theory and republic idealism. All, however, had long held that the throne was the stability within this idea. But Louis, they now said, by his flight to Varennes, had in effect abdicated and a new stability must be found.

One individual seized upon this hour of opportunity. Using the turmoil, the Duc d'Orleans had driven up and down the Carousel in his cabriolet on the evening of June 23$^{rd}$, reminding the people of Paris that he was available for the restoration, or a republic, whichever they pleased. He was cheered at the Jacobin club on this day and changed his name, there and then, to Egalité, disassociating himself entirely from the royal family. The people, however, showed no faith in him after all, as regent or king: a man capable of such an action not to be trusted. Also, to dethrone Louis was to invite open foreign attack.

Thus the Assembly noisily debated this problematical subject. While Robespierre declared the king's inviolability a myth, the last word on the issue lay with Grégoire the 'old friend of the people' or Barnave, the 'new friend of the queen'. After much debate, it was decided by the Assembly that the king, only, should be suspended and his accomplices brought to trial.

Rochelle heard this with horror, a sliver of ice gliding down her spine. "You see! I told you: they shall be after the Comte, Emile, Raoul, Montague and D'Arcy!"

"But they be nowhere *near* the operation. We must hold faith in their intelligence; and not ourselves be captured: as bait."

Rochelle stared. "*Mon Dieu*! And they would too! Ah, that Fanchon were here!"

Angelique raised her brows.

"For the posset: none other can know the recipe."

"Mayhap it be as well... one could swallow it too soon... only to discover... well, I suppose one would not, being then dead," Angelique chuckled, "that it was not necessary after all!"

"Your infinite calm!" Rochelle stared at her. "Our attitudes reversed! Am I less so now because I be in love, thus heightening the fear? Perhaps it *is* a little different for you... not being so."

Angelique turned away, her eyes also dark with fear but, her voice light, only repeated Rochelle's own mantra: on the subject of fear: "But *ma chérie*... nothing is ever gained by a demonstration of extreme emotion!"

# CHAPTER SIXTEEN

## The New Legislative Assembly – Oct. 1st 1791

Angelique gazed at the Comtesse Bayette and realized suddenly that this woman had grown on her. More importantly, she appeared to make her *père* happy, the only important element regarding this lady. Her attention diverted to the new import: the companion/chaperon; a distant cousin of whom she had never heard, Marie-Therese: brought into the family now that it became obvious de Quatreaux and his sons were now often absent, simultaneously.

The Royal escape fiasco, driving home the point of his daughter's vulnerability had he not been able to return, had pushed de Quatreaux to invite Marie-Therese into the household. To the added matter of social mores and laws, he should perhaps have given observance much earlier: the protective barrier of social correctness, ensured by a chaperon, standard requirement. Previously, of course, the ever-present Madame Bayette had, for many years, negated the necessity of such and before that Clarisse. Now, however, the dangers of street travel kept Madame Bayette more frequently in her own home. To Angelique's vehement protests he had offered in place of the companion in residence, an arranged marriage, smiling gently as her eyes had widened in complete horror.

She smiled now in memory of that conversation and dismissing the companion, her eyes turned instinctively toward the eighth person in the room and looked hastily away again, her thoughts in turmoil. Raoul Trifane had glimpsed, she knew, her relief at his reappearance from across the frontier. The depth of expression in his eyes that day had held her immobile and silent; and the urge to fly into his arms had been strong. But he could not: indeed *would* not, she knew, declare himself whilst the word treason hung over his head: would hold himself remote in protection of herself. She had struggled severely for control that day: cursing the mores and laws but more the Revolution; that kept them apart. Now, to drag her mind away from such fruitless ramifications she focused on Francois, tall and handsome in his uniform, as he spoke lightly of his involvement in the Champ de Mars affair, in July.

"What *really* happened?" she asked.

"In short; king returns and the Assembly reluctantly reinstates him, holding now both the king and the throne prisoner. But he is *there*... lending stability. The July 14th taking of the Bastille celebrations, at the Champ de Mars, causes emotions to run high. The people run petitions demanding Louis' removal: and the Constitution to replace him with some new authority, or executive. Petitions are refused by the

Assembly... for to accede to their demands meant no king... no king meant war of foreign and émigré intervention. People push: republicanism and sedition against a weak government runs high in the streets and the *Palais-Royal* is full of vengeful orators."

"Nothing new there!" muttered Emile.

"No... but the Assembly clamps down on the now very republican press... place in uproar again... Assembly afraid... out with the National Guard again... and when false rumours of Lafayette's assassination run wild; out with the good old red flag of martial law again. People see red, excuse me," he grinned, "resulting in a clash and many lay dead; many more wounded of course. That's it in a nutshell." He ceased grinning. "But the dead were mainly sans-culottes: those gaining nothing out of the whole wretched Revolution!"

"But of course... the more sans-culottes dead, the greater their anger: the stronger the driving power for those directing this insane revolution!" said the Comtesse, then thoughtfully, "So the king's capture brought relief to the Assembly from the fear of civil war; organized by the émigrés with foreign backing and on the point of breaking out. But the king's document made clear his unfavourable view of the Constitution since 1789 and so the people now had no confidence in his re-establishment to the throne." She turned to de Quatreaux. "What do you make of the upshot?"

"The ultra-democrats pronounced his flight an abdication and an end to the throne, but some, Robespierre in point, hinted at d'Orleans as a regency figure... others, Danton, Brissot and Desmoulins called for outright republic."

"*Robespierre* did that?" asked Rochelle now, in shock.

"Yes. He has the ability to temporise his hatred of all above him and see things as clearly as Mirabeau did, and do what it takes, no matter how unpalatable of the moment. Mirabeau was a highly intelligent freethinker: debauched, irreverent, recalcitrant, a daredevil and risk-taker who scorned all criticism. *But...* he was *not* dangerously insane."

"As is Robespierre: cold, remote, puritanical and machine-like in his every word and action! Assumed he could control d'Orleans I imagine. And so what now?" asked Angelique.

Raoul answered her. "The Cordeliers, under Danton, have plastered the walls with placards calling for an outright republic, but the Jacobins, under Robespierre, ask only for the deposition of Louis. The deputies of the centre and left *now* support the tottering throne; Lafayette and Barnave pledging in honour of that throne."

"*Mon Dieu*, one needs be a...a...genius to follow them, they change sides so fast."

"Some tend to do that, as they chase their own survival!" murmured Raoul.

Angelique glancing at him, stilled at the grim line of mouth and sombre voice.

"Lafayette, along with Barnave, has always been in favour of the king in *some* executive position, but Robespierre and his entourage, be another kettle of fish," added de Quatreaux.

"And the schism within the Jacobins that I hear about?" asked Francois.

"The constitutionalists of that club have veered off from the republicans and are calling themselves Feuillants."

"*Another* club named after monks! What do they all suppose? That it somehow gives them divine powers?" exclaimed Rochelle.

"Or perhaps divining powers," grinned Emile. "But that then leaves the ultra-democrats in full possession of the Jacobins."

"And you foresee…what?" asked the Comtesse now of de Quatreaux.

"The dissolution of the existing Assembly and when it happens Robespierre is ready and waiting," he replied, and then turned to the new, shy companion, Marie-Therese, gently drawing her into the family. "What do *you* believe, cousin?"

She shook her head and prevaricated. "I am not of the modern school of females, Monseigneur: brought up as I was beneath 17$^{th}$ century laws and mores: my family were *very* old fashioned, their disciplines established, in my case, for the betterment of females." The twins raised eyebrows at each other and Raoul grinned at the thought of the diversity between the new companion and Angelique. "And I, er… do not have any real opinion to be sure, but following what I can, it seems to me that events swing back and forth so fast that none, no matter how they *think* they can, is able to follow the fast incoming tide of total confusion; compounding the previous confusion. At the beginning of the season, republicanism—previously the catchword of the century—was hardly heard on anybodies' lips. But now, within three months, it is so strong that a campaign of suppression—by the very people who instigated its birth—be in full swing—and that suppression of strength equal to that of the earlier Monarchy, of the 1740's. These speedy reverses make the head spin, so they do." She blushed and apologized for her outspoken thoughts, for after all she was, she said, but a woman.

"No, no, no, my cousin," exclaimed Angelique now, entranced. "Do not be spoiling it. You have hit the nail upon the head. They have, in their maze-like, contorted trail, chasing power, returned to absolutism: of Assembly."

Raoul glanced at her, a half smile on his face but said nothing, aware that she had caught the glance and basked in her confusion, covered by an intense dialogue with her cousin on the political strengths and weaknesses of the Assembly as it stood. He watched her and knew that she knew this and then suppressed a deep sigh, for the time was not conducive to romance of any sort. He was called away so often that it be impossible to conduct a courtship of any duration. He frowned, more to the point, the 'times', before long, would either claim his life or send him into exile; especially if, behind the Assembly's acceptance of Louis' kidnapping, the search for treasonable nobles intensified. His face grew darker: the word treason swung as a weathercock, wildly, in the winds of continuously changing regimes. One minute one was a loyal patriot: the next a treasonable criminal, according to swiftly changing authority. He glanced up suddenly and found Angelique's deeply worried and questioning eyes upon him. He shrugged—a whimsical smile on his face now.

He stood, and making his excuses about the late hour, left the Quatreaux Hôtel, walking the Rue Saint Honoré to his own, his thoughts and spirits diving to a very low level at the impossibility of his situation regarding Angelique. He had desired her from the day of the Quatreaux hunt and had soon realized that he wanted her in his life, by his side, forever. The impossibility of the situation drove those feelings now to a deeper level still, for he knew that he could not put her life at risk; and any connection with Raoul Trifane, Marquis de Savieur, increased that risk. Should he be a suspect, executed even; so too then would she. Worse: she could be interrogated; he stood perfectly still a moment—and tortured, for information on his own movements. No greater draw for the Tribunal than a woman in love. His very soul froze in sudden fear. He must distance himself from her in every possible way. He shook off, with difficulty, this ascent into that dark abyss difficult to climb out of: hopelessness. He *would* come about; it meant only the hastening of his plans for property across the frontier but then again, to hasten those plans involved risk, risk of the loss of the lot, leaving him with nothing to offer a lady of gentle birth, or indeed any lady at all.

Angelique gazed at Her Majesty in great fondness. She could, along with only a handful of people, see the real Marie Antoinette, warts and all. Her strengths and her weakness, however, were all overshadowed by her love of family. The security of that family and the re-establishment of Louis upon the throne now obsessed her mind. Of the people, she did not think, now. They would not, on any terms, give her the consideration that she had given them: had they but known it. They would hang her on the flimsiest excuse, for pure vengeance of *perceived* crimes; rumoured crimes. They desired to pin their grievance upon somebody; and here, luckily, was the *Austrian*: that country of her birth an enemy of France for so long. No marriage could reverse the ancient bitter enmity.

"Madame, what are you planning now?" she laughed, trying to lighten the atmosphere, for how *did* one survive the experience that was hers right now?

"Me?" The queen smiled angelically, a look of innocence spreading across her still beautiful face. "But nothing at all *mon amie*."

Angelique laughed. "But that goes without saying, except to pressure Leopold into affecting a European Congress to settle affairs of France?"

"Ah! That of course does go without saying! But I do not seek war, *mon amie*, only that which its *threat* can achieve. That and somehow, whilst the nobility are in fear of a Republic, marshal them to support us. You know, before 1789 they had far too much power and that was our undoing. That was how this whole diabolical thing got off the ground. Hiding behind national unrest! It had nothing to do with a starving people and bringing back the only national parliament to deal with it. The States-general was simply a swift launching pad for their own desires. Indeed they cared not a fig for the people! In point of fact, they secretly fear them. Everyone does so. So while they try to bring *us* down, they try to keep *them* underfoot! Even Poland, with its recent Constitutional establishment, dare not elevate the peasants."

"Then Madame, use the émigrés: they be extreme royalists. And *mon père* says that regimes may come and go, over the centuries, but his property be his by the sweat of his family and indeed all who worked to make it so. And that the émigrés, with enough proof that they will regain their properties, would be a formidable force."

"Does he so?" The queen's expression softened for a moment. "Your *père* be of a rare breed."

"Use them Madame, for it seems to me that you be between the devil and the deep blue sea: the Constitutionalists or the émigrés and their foreign aid. And surely once off the ground, Leopold <u>will</u> throw his support behind the move?"

"The grim truth is that Leopold is more interested in restoring his own dominions of Hungary and Belgium, than helping his sister."

"But surely the foreign Princes see that the republican threat can spread to them?"

"If they do then I witness it not, although Leopold *does* say that he has sought the alliance of Frederick and William and made peace with the Porte at Sistova. And here they apparently signed a declaration of readiness to undertake armed intervention in French affairs."

"I see…I think…but why then do we see it not?"

"Some evidence of the intervention? They are waiting for other European powers to join them. That was the provision; that they only act if all other European sovereigns join them. Always there is the 'provision'!"

"And England?"

"Pitt has already refused."

"And the King of Prussia?"

"Oh, a violent hatred of the *principles* of the Revolution; but again, affairs of Poland and a distrust of Austria keeps him at a distance from French affairs."

"So: all make affectionate noises toward France but are very busy with personal affairs."

Marie Antoinette looked at Angelique and neither had the need of further words.

Barnave, the new friend of the queen, gazed at de Quatreaux speculatively. "You know *mon ami*, as I see it: two particular conditions have resulted from this cursed Revolution."

De Quatreaux raised his brows in humour. "Only two, Barnave?"

"Well, two major ones: One, the destruction of an obsolete and arbitrary regime: not all was bad. The other: the enthronement of the nation in place of the king, more or less."

De Quatreaux simply looked at him, took a sip of his burgundy and remained silent.

"And these are now compromised: by two more aspects of the fight for liberty.

*One*: the *speed* with which the Revolution has raced, clod-footed, over difficult and unforseen issues. Even Mirabeau said to me one day: 'Barnave,' he said, '...the beginning of this struggle for liberty, from the first meeting of the States-General, shall be disorganized and confusing, with radicals duelling across the floor with nobles. Perhaps it shall go too far too soon: a tidal wave effect at that point but then will come the second wave of change: the after wave. And *this* should go a long way to establishing its right of passage. Then will come the third wave and we may look forward to this, for here we may establish the new Constitution. But this should be a *gradual* process, *mon ami*, over say ten years or even twice that.'" He paused, gazed at the floor a moment, and then continued, "But for once Mirabeau was wrong! That estimate has been compressed into two years only. *That* is the problem! France's changing times are a tornado still not spent and trailing dangerous flotsam. Where that flotsam lands and what damage it will do, threatens everyone."

"And the other aspect: Barnave?"

"The *completeness* of the break with the past, including all that was good and solid; replacing it with a shallow-minded bourgeoisie. The people are now about to overthrow the new privileged class, of new wealth, with *another* revolution: that of education, talent and virtue! It leaves one gasping!"

Thus, in a state of domestic chaos and foreign threat, the National Assembly dissolved itself and convened for the first sitting of the new *Legislative Assembly* on October1st '91. This new body, comprising a reduced number of deputies, 740 as opposed to the original 1200 of the National Assembly, contained now no partisans of the old regime and no reformers with aristocratic tendencies.

The *right* now comprised constitutionalists, who nevertheless still sort to maintain the king. These could not envisage a purely democratic France and maintained a drive for a constitutional monarchy based on the foundations of the old regime.

The *left:* the vanguard of the Revolution, vied for a democratic government and abolition of the *Monarchy* but not of royalty. A group of young men, the *Girondins,* remarkable for eloquence and talent, sat on this side of the house. These were from Bordeaux, in the Department of the Gironde and did not seek to exile the king.

The small faction, within the *extreme left* now became, from its vantage point in the highest seats at Assembly, the *Montagne.* These were *fervent* democrats and republicans: inheritors of Voltaire's scorn and hatred of Catholicism, Robespierre their leader.

And so was born, at about this time, the party names within this evolution of political parties: the Girondins and the Montagne, to be frequently shouted abusively across the floor. Brissot, now with a seat in the house, belonged to the Montagne. His journal, the *Patriotic*, became the recognized organ of their party. Their attitude was one of aversion and scorn toward Louis and all that he had stood for but also one of nervous wariness; of the consequences of his treachery.

Catholicism was the first issue facing the new Legislative Assembly and the *right* sort to leave things as they were, on the grounds of religious liberty. But the *centre* voted with the *left* and a decree was passed depriving non-jurors of their pensions and their right to officiate in public.

Louis, however, though his reinstated position was now very weak, still had some powers of veto and would not sanction such. The Catholic mass continued to be celebrated, by non-jurors, under military protection of the National Guard. Soldiers lined the streets surrounding the churches, their internal and external walls, and the aisles of those holy buildings. To pray to one's God had once again become a dangerous affair.

The second and no less important issue before the government was the policy relating to the émigrés and foreign powers, especially those along the Rhine. Rulers of small border-states gave aid to these emigrants in arming against France. Here the Princes of State owned the worst governed territories in Germany and feared the contagion of the French Revolution infecting their own subjects. They prepared for war as they waited the French decision regarding the émigrés.

The Legislative Assembly, however, had declared its aversion to offensive war, authenticating such statement by limiting the army to 150,000 men. But the flight of the king and the drawing together of Austria and Prussia gave rise to uneasiness. France now added another 97,000 men. The degree of the Assembly's fear of these émigrés expressed itself in a new decree. This, soon issued, condemned to death all Frenchmen, whom, if after one year, remained still beyond the frontier and armed against their country. Any émigrés after this decree, warmonger or pacifist, would be treated the same.

Louis, however, with his remaining powers of veto, refused to sanction the decree, thus once again drawing suspicion to himself and reopening the whole can of worms of his continuing treachery. Realizing this, he followed up his refusal with an invitation to his brothers to return to France. 'The Revolution is now over,' he wrote, 'since I have now, on September 14ᵗʰ 1791, accepted the Constitution.' Both brothers categorically refused, resulting in the effect of a declaration of war between the émigrés and the Revolution. This made them traitors of the State.

Louis' acceptance of the Constitution, however, was received with relief: by those European sovereigns who had joined Leopold's European Congress, regarding active intervention on Louis' behalf.

"Now that acceptance *had* to be painful! Poor Louis," remarked a colleague at a meeting extraordinaire of the congress, standing alongside the old Austrian Chancellor: Kaunitz.

"But he *has* resolved the issue," muttered Kaunitz. "Thank God... it did threaten an insolvent problem!"

De Quatreaux finished reading the parchment in his hand and looked at Trifane. "Well, seems we must hurry things along a little. You have your er... foreign affairs in working order?"

"Almost: a delay in a couple of titles but the worst come to the worst, I could survive. The security of some property here is the stumbling block and I am damned if I shall leave it open to confiscation. They have already stolen enough from us all."

De Quatreaux stared at the fireplace before him a moment and then said casually, "But in essence, eventually, you would of course be in a similar position to the one here?"

Trifane gazed at him a moment and then responded calmly. "By the time I have finished, no future wife of mine shall feel the difference; excepting in that she may feel colder in England or must learn the Italian tongue in Turin."

"Ah. That is good then," de Quatreaux tossed off his glass of burgundy.

Trifane looked at him. "Monseigneur, be it so obvious? I thought to cover it rather well."

De Quatreaux chuckled. "There be no fool like that of one caught in the bonds d'amour."

"Then I must work the harder: I cannot risk her neck along with mine by being a fool in love."

"You worry about the royal flight? It be covered, Trifane; there were no names to *that* one."

"No, I know that, but there are those who may have seen me at Chalons. However, mayhap the coming war occupies their full minds now. The Assembly's threat of attack against the Austrian Empire, unless they disperse the bands of emigrants along its frontiers, is I fear, about to become fact, not so? What says Louis?"

"Ah yes. Louis may yet rule, he thinks. But best to have a foot in many camps these days. As to other plans, you trust Pontisqieu?"

"I do; decent fellow. I knew him vaguely at law school but lost contact when I had to abandon any aspirations that I may have had in that industry when *mon père* died and I had to return. He is the only one in the legal area, of a position to cause the switch, of papers, anyway."

"What caused his swing?"

"Over to royalist? He was never anti-royal anyway but is a lawyer after all and was ardently in favour of liberty: the true idea of liberty, for *all*: the peasants his passion. He did after all work with them a lot: witnessed their cruel suppression, unfortunately delivered by our Estate. But then he saw Robespierre's plans and that man's great long lists of names for nothing less than extermination: merely to ease the problem of property confiscation, you understand; then to be dispersed to the Bourgeoisie. He saw it quite by accident, was enough to turn any man's stomach. He decided that the old stability with all its faults be far preferable to this mayhem that can only get worse. He could not support the Revolution any longer. Swung him clean around, did not want to attach himself to, quote: a bunch of conniving foxes, completely mad individuals and outright idiots!"

"He has a copy of that list?"

Trifane grinned. "Yes, but in his head. Memory! I have heard of such people but this is fantastic. Never makes a mistake."

"And you really do trust him? It is of the deep instinct that I speak, for nothing else is as accurate, no matter the evidence stacked otherwise."

"I do," reiterated Trifane. "Besides, he has feelings, and quite deep I believe, for your daughter."

"Ah, then indeed he shall work against all that may adversely affect her. Good." De Quatreaux was quiet for a moment and then rising, moved towards the door, "We must pay a visit to our friend Anton. Tomorrow is convenient?"

"Yes, tomorrow be convenient." Trifane also moved towards the door.

"Oh: and one more thing, Trifane."

"Yes?"

"My blessings!"

Raoul felt a lightness of spirit suddenly; his step lighter than it had been for a long time, for de Quatreaux gave more than his blessing: somehow he managed to convey hope.

♣

War, declared by France on Austria, Friday April 20ᵗʰ 1792, brought Francis of Austria his advisors, in haste.

"Your Majesty, Leopold would perhaps have advanced conciliatory meetings first."

Francis looked at them. "Leopold is dead."

"Yes Sire, but I feel I must inform you that he would have tried to avoid a rupture, with your aunt's adopted country."

"How? And to what point," responded Francis. "Marie Antoinette's treatment by the French requires revenge to say the least! And the new French ministry declares war, therefore war they shall have! None can ignore the gauntlet and keep face!"

"War against you as king of Hungary and Bohemia, Sire; and Dumouriez' first attack shall come across the Belgium frontier, we believe."

"Let him attack!"

Angelique, quill pausing, lifted her head at the opening door. "Francois!"

"Ma soeur!" He moved forward to hug her as she rose and moved around the desk, "It is but a brief visit... in fact, I must almost immediately report for duty."

"Ah... I perceive I must not ask... secret army business!"

"Secret war business," replied an older and grimmer Francois. "And an army not ready!"

Angelique gazed at him, in compassion and fear, for Francois, as a dashing military figure, was now Francois the real soldier, in real active service, at real risk and the thought did not enamour itself to her at all. "Certainly a war with Austria whom has *Prussia* as an ally, appears not a wise move... but is the army really in such bad state?"

She pulled the bell-rope for drinks as Francois cast himself into a chair.

"Oh yes... the state of our fortresses are appalling as is the lack of military organization."

"That bad?" she asked in sympathy.

"The fortresses would not keep out a rabbit. As for the military... hundreds of officers have resigned, deserted, or been driven away by their men. And under-officers are elected out of rank and they advance according to length of service, not ability."

"So a soldier of ten years service but without brain could advance to officer-ship! And so what *do* you have to work with?"

"Of the total 150,000 troops of the line... 50,000 have yet to be recruited. And the 97,000 volunteers, for the most part, are untrained and unarmed."

"Perhaps it is as well, they might shoot one another... and the Minister of War?"

"Narbonne has worked hard but because he is friend of Lafayette the king has dismissed him! I like Louis and understand his motives for many things, but *this*?"

"And the attitude of the new Assembly?"

"Oh, eager in their support for war of course, but the increasing bitterness of party strife within the Assembly has to be seen to be believed. Spreads like oil on water and flows on to the army: spreading distrust and shadow jumping."

"And the man who most represents this prevailing distrust be Maximillien Robespierre! Though I cannot attend, I can guess."

Francois frowned. "He be a dangerous rat, that one: none more so than the man of purity and virtue."

"Yes. But he is not a member; excluded from the legislature on account of having been a member of the last Assembly, so how can he really be an influence... through his club?"

"Yes. As the Assembly becomes less constructive, the Jacobin Society dominates and is becoming more and more the unofficial Opposition; matters debated in the club direct results in Assembly. *And* he is making himself the people's idol: his oratory conveyed through the peoples' public gallery."

Henri arrived and received orders for refreshments and turning back to Francois, Angelique frowned in thought. "But can Robespierre really direct from such a remote standpoint?"

"He is brilliant at it! Robespierre the incorruptible, the wise and benevolent, 'without the least desire for wealth and rank'! Always respectable: the catchphrase of the lower and middle classes. But also he is now the proprietor *and* editor of the journal: *Défenseur de la Constitution*. The prestige of the Jacobin club increases as the Assembly declines." He chuckled suddenly and Angelique raised her brows.

"The Assembly in session... went the other day; good for a soldier to see exactly where his fighting orders really come from."

"I doubt that, but I should like to also see it. There *are* ticket-holding seats in the public gallery, for women, I know. Free ones even."

"You go there and our esteemed *père* shall flay you to within an inch of your life. And what's more I should not blame him."

She laughed. "It cannot be that bad!"

"You would not come out alive. The public gallery is occupied by the lowest of the low, mostly women, the like of which even I have not seen, in all my military experience."

"How many women *do* you see?" she murmured. "But do go on."

"The President sat on a high platform, protected by two ushers by his side; just as well or he'd have been lynched long ago and spent his time shouting 'silence'—the ushers following his lead, creating a booming, repetitive echo effect throughout the day. Reinforcement ushers, four more, in crisp black robes, wigs beautifully curled, and carrying gold swords, marched continuously up and down the free space also calling for 'silence'. But this was no easy feat, you understand, for the free space was blocked by the coming and going of the deputies, some straight off the street, booted and spurred in travel dress, shouting and calling across the hall, coughing and spit...er well never mind...but the scene was one of total mayhem. The whole while, the *claqueurs* continued unabated. The president soon lost his voice and resorted to continuous bell-ringing."

She stared, waiting, then. "That's it? But somewhere in there, be speeches and votes, must be, for we read of the results."

"Ah yes and *how* this is achieved be diabolical! The Jacobins…"

"Robespierre."

"That's the one!  While a deputy struggles to put up his reforms within this chaos of interruptions and shouted abuse: the extremists (Robespierrists) put up one of their friends with a well-rehearsed speech, in the middle of it all. Whilst the other speakers are still speaking, they call for a vote the minute he sits down."

"*Mon Dieu!*"

"Talent of a genius!"

"What is he *really* like?" She felt a sudden inexplicable sliver of ice slide down her spine.

"*You* will never meet him, but: discontent, always suspicious of ridicule, consumed I would say, with the burning ambition, that some small men own, to play a big part."

"So what is it that draws the adulation of the people, for it is not only from the lower classes but also the bourgeoisie—charisma?"

"That, but majorly flattery, clever flattery: he puts himself forward as the special representative of the people; constantly hailing *their* 'goodness and wisdom' until in the end they really believe that it be *they* direct the changes… this is his magic. His solemn, carefully composed and well-practised speeches, he delivers in carefully enhanced quality of speech and voice: really impresses them. Added to that is his trick of impressionism: never falters, offering great promise; and comforts as does a compassionate priest but most of all, the touch of aristocracy to his dress and manner. *Always* impresses the bourgeoisie, that… though they outwardly scorn it! Learnt very well… all of it!"

"The perfect impersonator… and that is enough to harness a people."

Francois shook his head, frowning slightly. "But no.  Almost but not quite: the real talent lays in the touch of the genuine, I think, in that he actually relates to them, is in complete sympathy with them, and comes of a background born *of* them.  *That* is the cream on the cake; *that* harnesses the people, cements his absolute success. They understand him, as they do not us. And he them: and so he knows how to play them.  It worries me; I get the feeling of 'great men' of the past who have ended in actions of wholesale slaughter. Because their zeal, born of insanity, grows beyond control! Like those other men of antiquity, he has made it his mission to save France from the dangers he now sees surrounding it."

"His real supporters?"

"Desmoulins for a start; followed by agitators and adventurers, of the lowest types: their sole purpose to pave a way; for their own rising star. However, of prime importance, right now, is Servan's proposal for an armed encampment outside Paris: for its protection.  But the Assembly does not like this and has decreed the formation of 20,000 volunteers, supposedly to meet in Paris for the 14th July celebrations; that damned…sorry…day of the Bastille, their real aim to have mastery over Paris, should the allies show up."

"Another 20,000 volunteers… have we any citizen *left*, upon which to call? But surely this be no more than an armed demonstration—and they be illegal, I know."

"The municipal is half-hearted about offering resistance; Mayor Bailly is gone, a Girondin, Pétion, replaces him and half the new members that have been re-elected are mostly ultra-democrats. The emigrants have lost all now: property impounded; placed under the charge of some administrative body and their revenue confiscated by the state."

"Huh, huh: and the bad news?"

"For Paris: the loss of Lafayette; I know that you and the Queen do not trust him but Emile seems to think him essentially all right and Raoul treats him with cautious respect. But he is an excellent man in the field and now he is to command the eastern frontier, leaving the National Guard to be guided by the city wolves."

Angelique opened her mouth only to close it as the door opened and Emile entered, ushering Rochelle before him, followed by Henri carrying the refreshments. "Francois! What are you doing here? Should you not be preparing another attack on Belgium or some such?"

Francois grinned and, moving forward, bowed and kissed Rochelle's hand. "Mademoiselle! Beautiful as always! How goes the wedding preparations?"

"That's female department, Francois; come sit here, Rochelle, and tell me what goes forward in your house! You have news from England?"

Emile grinned, hugged his brother, and took a chair opposite Francois, across the fireplace, as the ladies retreated to the window embrasure.

"Bit of a debacle eh? *I* thought that Dumouriez made a good call," said Emile as he settled himself, reaching for the claret placed at his elbow.

"Should never have been so. Dumouriez *did* make a good call; striking at Belgium, with Prussia not yet really properly mobilized and Austria not intending to fight until midsummer, waiting for the harvest of course, to provide subsistence for the men."

"And the death of Leopold left the throne in young Francis' hands. How did it happen... the fiasco?"

"Dumouriez despatched two columns to begin the invasion; one under Theobald Dillon to advance from Lille on Tounai and the other under the Duc de Biron, advancing from Quiévrain on Mons. But this was met with disastrous check and we fell into immediate disarray, with men and officers deserting and Dillon's men even murdering their general: should have stayed in his native Ireland! Rochambeau, Commander-in-Chief for the area, has resigned as has, I think, de Grave."

"Why is the army so disorganized... indiscipline of Revolutionary rank and file?"

"That... and the loss of so many of our most competent officers by emigration; disorganization by so many recent half-baked reforms; and of course war office mismanagement: a thousand reasons but mainly the impossibility of the rabble."

"It's really bad?"

"Worse! There is a jest going around that the men actually take a vote on whether or not to obey the officer's orders. It would be funny except that it is real."

"I read Dumouriez' report; shortage of men and material, officers and staff sold out to the enemy, complete disproportion between the aims and means of the campaign, a third of the officers throwing in their commissions and another third threatening the same. Plague could not have been more contagious apparently." Emile looked at his brother in compassion. "It should not be like this. It is a very great pity that you must serve under such conditions."

Francois shrugged. "Someone has to."

Wednesday June 13$^{th}$ 1792 saw Louis in consul with Roland, Servan and Clavière the minister of interior, war and finance.

"But Sire, you *must* sanction these two decrees, pertaining to the non-jurors and the 20,000 volunteers," said Roland, unwisely allowing emotion to take control.

"I *must*?" The king appeared suddenly taller, his features carved of stone, his voice flat. "I will *not* be *used*: to give weight to their heinous movements."

"Ah well, Sire, I do not know that it be that simple. You see…"

"Enough! Ministers, you have badgered me enough. I will not tolerate it. Go!"

"Your Majesty? Ah, hem… yes Sire! We shall return on the morrow?"

The king did not turn from his stance at the window and his voice was calm. "Forever."

Thus Louis dismissed the three ministers from office, effectively dismissing the Brissotin government.

Dumouriez, brilliant soldier and minister of foreign affairs, quarrelling with his colleagues on this issue and supporting the king in his stand, found it prudent, two days and two visits by strange men later, to resign his office in the face of enormous Assembly hostilities. He smiled grimly as he left the Assembly for the last time. He was damned if he was going to retire quietly to the country as had Séiyès and others of his disillusionment. He was a military man: he began to plan.

A further three days produced a letter from Lafayette to be read in the Assembly, denouncing the Jacobins as the author of all disorder. Calling upon the Assembly to maintain the authority of the crown, he threatened that his army would not submit to see the constitution and the king violated. This wedge, suspected to be of Louis and Lafayette's creation, now strengthened the division between the Revolutionary Constitutionalists and the moderate left, the Girondins.

The dismissal of the three ministers caused the gathering of a great crowd of people. Wednesday June 20$^{th}$ they massed yet again, under the leadership of Santerre, a butcher, to march to the Assembly. Now, thankfully, their march was only to the Tuileries, not the long trudge to Versailles. They came from Salpetière in the southeast, men marching of the Observetoirs and Montrieul sections. From the east: Place de la Bastille, came the Quinze-Vingts of the *faubourg* Saint Antoine and from the *faubourg* Saint-Marcel, the Gobelins. They met at the Hôtel de Ville and there swelled to twenty thousand in number as they surged westward along Rue Saint-Honoré. Again they carried pikes and sharpened poles, singing and chanting as they marched toward the Assembly, accompanied by several battalions of National Guard.

"*Mon Dieu*! Rochelle, come see this!"

"Ange, they have been a-marching since 1789 and still they love the cut and thrust of anarchy. Nothing shall cure them. No matter who is in charge… they just march!"

"Yes, after long subjugation they love the power. But what goes forward I wonder?"

"Emile tells me to beware of this, another insurrection, regarding Louis' dismissal of the three ministers, I believe. And you know... sometimes I wonder about him..." Rochelle stayed her tongue, feeling wretchedly disloyal but glancing at her friend, she detected a gleam of understanding.

"Rochelle, *ma chérie*... sometimes it seems things could be different but then none of us can possibly know what terrible impositions he labours beneath... what pressures, threats, he battles. He must be torn into small pieces, trying to hold France together: with his few pathetic powers of veto! Everything he does must have concrete reason... we just do not know what it is: that is all."

They stared down into the street and Rochelle turned to Angelique. "Yours definitely is the best vantage point to view the Revolution. Just think what you would have missed had you been housed some place far from here: your writings not half so colourful!"

Angelique stared still into the street. "I do not write."

"But of course not *mon amie*. You simply fiddle around with poetry... but what poetry!"

Angelique gazed down again into the raucous street scene. "The queen's life is at risk during such madness. Look, they are heading towards the Tuileries."

Rochelle watched for a moment. "No, they turn towards the *Mènage*... the Assembly."

"And then to the Tuileries; you'll see."

The swell of people sang and danced as they went; for their excuse to avoid the illegality of their large public gathering was that they came to celebrate the Tennis Court Oath and plant a tree in memory of that day. At the head of the column walked a small boy, proudly carrying a young oak tree. They had no real worries, however, as the Assembly, believing the dismissal of the ministers to be proof of their worst suspicions, took no measures to prevent the insurrection. Thus they flowed along the street to the Assembly room, and a deputation read the address, demanding the recall of the ministers.

"...for how is it that the executive powers of the traitor king can overrule the arbitrary powers of the Assembly? We demand our ministers! Give back our ministers. We shall not leave until you do so!"

The *left* and the gallery cheered this speech but then someone muttered that it be the king to whom they should address their grievances. The mob left the Assembly and broke through the iron gates and into the Tuileries gardens, flowing around the riverside to the courts at the back of the palace. Here Santerre trained his guns on the *porte royale*. By this door the mob entered the palace, plus another giving entry to the Feuillants and another into the Palace Louvre, all left treacherously open.

The royal family, expecting attack, had strengthened Palace Guard and also armed nobles and men of the royalist section of the *Filles de Saint-Thomas*. At four in the afternoon they heard sounds, familiar to them now, of shouting and smashing down of doors, then the tramp of feet upon the stairs.

"*Mon Dieu! Dé-ja vu,*" exclaimed the queen as she listened.

"October 5$^{th}$ Madame," nodded Madame Elizabeth as she gathered the two children together and then spoke to them: "Be not afraid, the people be angry and rather stupidly attack us. But we shall be safe."

"*Why* are the people always so angry, Tante Elizabeth?" asked Marie-Therese, but her aunt hushed her as they listened to the progress of the feet outside their door.

The king in his apartment looked about but there was no escape as they rushed into his room, shouting.

"Down with the veto! Give up the veto! Ye have no right to any veto now!"

"Recall the ministers!"

Protected as he was, by his bodyguard, he was nevertheless forced into the window embrasure and from here calmed the mob but insisted that he stood for his rights; as valid as theirs, under the Constitution. They paused: their weapon turned back on them.

Finally after several hours the Mayor, Pétion, not risking his popularity before this, entered the scene and moved the crowd away. But not before they broke from here and entered the room containing the queen, Princess Elizabeth and the two children, now backed behind a solid table. Here the Royals faced with amazing dignity the insults and taunts flung from the seething mob: that dignity once again halting the tide of hatred and fury, for the people understood it not. Here surely lay a mystery of latent power, a surreal power; a power that must be crushed. The National Guard finally achieved calm by about ten o'clock that night, June 20$^{th}$ 1792, at which hour Pétion sat down to write a missive demanding an increase to the garrison at Tuileries.

This new insurrection, and connivance of municipal authorities, angered the constitutionalists and also brought Lafayette now to Paris and the bar of the Assembly. He demanded the king's protection, a point of honour with him to shield the Monarch from harm. New projects of royal flight were now formed but died stillborn.

Trifane sat drinking his coffee, the fourth cup, as he watched the comings and goings of the *Palais-Royal*, lifting his head from the *Patriotic* from time to time, then stood and smiled his welcome as Pontisqieu arrived, returned the bow and slid into a chair.

"Do have some coffee, my friend."

"No… I already have, thank you."

"Then have more. I cannot take another sip; though it be very *good* coffee."

"Ah yes; my apologies, took longer than I thought it would."

"But you managed to use the upheaval?"

"That I did. Robespierre moved right across the building to watch the insurrection at Tuileries. Never thought to see an insurrection of such benefit," replied Pontisqieu, receiving the cup from the proprietor. He poured from the earthen jug and taking a sip pulled the paper, casually spread upon the table, towards him.

He read for a moment and then closing and folding it over, handed it back to Trifane. Raoul did not open it again but casually laid it aside, to be carried home when he left.

"I do not have to ask of course." He spoke softly, although no other person stood near.

Pontisqieu glanced at the paper. "No, it is done: transfer papers, deeds, all locked as securely as is possible today."

"It is no mean feat and the risk high. He is a courageous man, your cousin."

"And an enterprising one; but it be yourself that take the risk, your châteaux and estates now under his name. But no, he has no fear, that one. The driving force of course is the rape and murder of his wife and daughter by Robespeirre's henchmen. All will be safe *mon ami.*"

Raoul smiled faintly. "The recompense, should I stay alive and eventually return, shall be the estates south of Paris. If I do not, then he is an even luckier man."

"Many an estate has changed hands in stranger manner these days!"

"That is so. Keep talking; one of St Just's men is approaching, though he knows not that I know...who he is."

"Ah, then that be why I feel the ice slide down my spine," breathed Pontisqieu softly.

"Rest assured Henri, you are not worth the killing; they want bigger fry."

"Well, my thanks for that very doubtful compliment. You on the other hand are no stranger to them and, speaking of which..." Here he paused, brows rising and turning his head slightly to watch a man pass close by and then move toward a doorway, "...there goes a stranger of interest...and puzzle I believe."

Trifane turned his head to observe the stranger but saw only his disappearing back.

"At the *Jardin des Tuileries* yesterday, after I left the ministerial building, I bumped into an old friend from university, also caught up in the whole messy affair. No one could move in that maelstrom. He had in tow a person whom he seemed to hold in great respect, though this person did not appear to be at all well educated. However that he was of the military was very evident."

"This has a point, Pontisqieu?"

"Indirectly: he was foreign, although Corsica now belongs to France. He held back not at all from his opinions, regarding the rioting mobs before us, declaring that, should *he* be king such a thing would never happen! Had the most intense, glittering, piercing eyes that I have ever seen. And a demeanour resembling a sleeping force, such as that of a building tidal wave or some such; but yes, it was the *eyes* that shall remain with me."

"He did impress, you I see. Not without reason I imagine... a hypnotist?"

"Ah, that should not surprise me but his close link with Robespierre startled me. His name was... Bonaparte; yes, that was it, of Italian parentage. Italian nobility in fact, I vaguely recall. Now Robespierre mistrusts Italians, and of course all nobility, and yet he invited Bonaparte into the Jacobin fold, so my friend informed me."

Trifane shrugged. "Yet another budding Robespierrist!"

"Hmm... he was *intensely* interested in the goings-on of Paris."

Trifane stood, now that the St Just spy was gone, tucked his paper beneath his arm and, lifting his hand in casual farewell and dismissal of the stranger Bonaparte, walked away, leaving Pontisqieu still pondering the strange, piercing eyes.

Now, the possibility of the allies reaching Paris by midsummer 1792 was very real. 80,000 Austrian and Prussian troops massed on the Rhineland border and opposing this were the mere 40,000 French troops; at Metz and Sedan, half of which were raw recruits.

That this army was in no fit state to repel the enemy, the country was aware, but it was also apathetic, growing tired of the Assembly's eternal wrangling and disorder, lack of concrete progress and the willy-nilly dismissal of ministers. Honest and patriotic men were retiring to private life and to counteract this disinterest the Assembly issued a public proclamation; to the effect that the country was now in grave danger.

The sudden and lively resurrection of those waning interests, however, so intensely desired, was caused not by the proclamation but by a manifesto: the Brunswick Manifesto. Drawn up by the emigrants, this was published by the Duke of Brunswick, Commander in Chief of the allied forces. These powers required France to submit unconditionally to Louis' mercy and all who offered resistance were to be treated as rebels and suffer military execution should harm befall the king.

The Jacobins openly recommended the immediate deposition of Louis. Those of the Assembly that shared this opinion were the members of the extreme left: the *Montagne.*

In the house of Roland: the dismissed Girondin minister of the interior; projects were discussed for defence of the line of Lior, in the case of the Allies reaching Paris. Madame Roland, talented writer who directed her husband's actions, became the centre of a circle ready to aid and abet the destruction of the throne. However, other leaders of the Girondins would not comply; and offered Louis the chance to restore the ministers. He refused, leaving these loyal royalists throwing up their hands. An insurrection was planned and the proclamation of danger to the capital was now utilized: to retain some of the thousands of volunteers massing for the front, for use in this plan.

Paris was again armed against the throne and the constitutionalists. Roland's friend, Barbareaux, organized and sent up a band of 600 men from Marseilles, singing the rousing new song *Marseillaise*, as they marched. Following this example, workers came from all over France, recruited from the network of Jacobin clubs of villages and towns.

At this point these massing revolutionaries, the Paris sans-culottes, and country peasants, became known at last as the *Fourth Estate*. These were whipped into a frenzy of hatred by the militant; incited and controlled by the lawyers Robespierre and Danton and the journalists Desmoulins, Hébert and Marat. Every Paris section now had its own cannon and a special body of cannoneers. The terrified Assembly made no attempt to suppress the riot but acquitted the popular Lafayette: now on charge of treason on grounds of intimidating the Legislature, according to the *left*. The vote was read, on the eighth of August, as a refusal by the Assembly to pass sentence of deposition, on Louis. The following night, August 9th 1792, concrete plans for the second insurrection began.

Mandat, the new Commander-in-Chief of the National Guard, an energetic constitutionalist, had taken measures to ensure that Tuileries was well defended. However, with Tuileries in their sights once again and perhaps the final deposition of the king, the unscrupulous conspirators outsmarted him and the centre of operations began, once again, in the faubourg of St Antoine.

# CHAPTER SEVENTEEN

## Tuileries. Prison Massacres. Death of a soldier

## 1792

Angelique sat before the large mahogany desk in the reading room, frowning over her scratched and scribbled work; the more crossed out than was legible. She heaved a frustrated sigh, scrunched up the offending work, and tossing it to the floor, reached for another clean sheet.

Marie-Therese, plying her needle to the fast developing and colourful piece of work, now placed the frame on the side table and moved to pick up the offending ball of paper. "You *know* that you should burn these, my dear."

She tucked it into her workbasket to be carried upstairs, there to be converted to ash in her *chambre* fireplace.

Angelique paused her hand and laughed. "If anyone, and I cannot for the life of me see whom may wish to, finds them, they shall have a fine time trying to read them, for I cannot myself decipher what ideas I may have had. Besides, it be *poetry*."

"Subversive poetry *Chére* and you *know* that the Comte has forbidden it. He be the one from whom you require protection!"

Angelique leaned back in her chair and laughed. "My cousin, you worry excessively. Besides, he be away most of the time and forgotten such by the time he returns."

"Monsieur le Comte never forgets. However, I feel it be time to retire my dear; are you coming?"

"In a short while but do not wait for me. I get carried away sometimes and, after all, one cannot exercise these days so the need of sleep be minimal."

Marie frowned. "Personally, I do not trust the new coffee that you consume in the evenings, my dear. For *there* be the cause of insomnia; not the lack of exercise, which I doubt very much to be of any benefit at all, even though it is... was, all the crack."

"Marie, would you rather that I sat here drinking burgundy instead?" chuckled Angelique. "I be quite willing; in fact it does surely set the imagination free."

"Now that you be in one of your impossible frames of mind, I shall leave you. I wish you a good night."

Maire-Therese packed up her embroidery box and left the room, closing the door softly. Angelique continued to lean back in her chair, her mind flowing in all directions at once: flowing to ideas old that required work, ideas new that spilled half-baked onto the paper. It then turned threateningly towards Raoul, of whom no one had seen for some considerable time. But she knew from Emile that he be in Paris. She veered away from fruitless and depressing thoughts as to why he did not call any more and forced her mind back to her work of the moment: the political parties and clubs of the *Palais-Royal.*

The night was quiet, eerily and unnaturally so; no drums or tocsins, the watch calling: 'All's well! The clock: two hours past midnight.' Paris slept or so it seemed as she rode the tide of inspiration, her concentration of a strength that blocked out time and place, entering the vacuum that left one wondering on exit, for a split second, just where one was.

A sense of invasion, rather than the slight noise, brought her back to the present. Sitting very still, a chill running down her spine, she heard it again, right behind her.

Did one freeze and wait, lulling the intruder into a false sense of security, or suddenly dive sideways: swiftly, before they had time to plunge the knife. She deeply regretted that she had not her silver mounted pistol with her and made a mental note for the future. But it was too late now for knives or pistols out of reach. These lightning thoughts had only just evolved when a voice, familiar but puzzling the memory, sounded softly.

"Mademoiselle Vermont: do not take the vapours I beg of you...'tis only me!"

Taking a deep breath; at least he knew her name, she turned to find a person that she had not seen before: bewigged, be-whiskered and dressed in dark travel clothes and carrying a small oil lamp. It was not this, however, that held her spellbound. Behind the gentleman, a panel of the wainscotting slid soundlessly back into place.

"Monsieur? I feel that I know you and yet... anyway, I do not take the vapours!"

He laughed and it was then that she recognized the voice. "Why Count Fersen, I *should* have recognized you from the word 'vapours'! But I can guess what this be about and am enthralled that our tunnel really be connected to the Tuileries."

"In a roundabout way: beneath Craufurds house. I am sorry to startle you Mademoiselle, but I misjudged a fork in the tunnel and had no idea that I should pitch up here."

"Ah, but it is no problem," she replied as he went to the window to check the street below, then the door, passing out to gaze down into the hall for lurking servants. On his return she continued. "My cousin has retired as have all the servants, though I do believe that Henri lurks in the kitchens waiting my call should I need anything. An excuse, I believe, to obey *mon père's* orders to watch over me! But you may trust him."

"I may trust no one," he responded softly as he then set about peeling off his beard. "Hence the disguise and tunnel travel... to avoid notation of comings and goings to and from Tuileries, of persons carrying information and, er, devious ideas and plans!"

She watched the transformation in fascination. "Of escape. So you got lost?"

"The tunnel splits many times but I thought it went only thus far east to Craufurds house. That some off-shoots veer off toward the Seine I do know."

"Ah yes and *under* it, so I believe, to exit at the Notre Dame."

"Inside or outside?" he laughed.

"Why, I do not know if there be one on the outside but one *can* emerge behind a small alter of the Holy Virgin!"

"Then one would hope fervently that there *is* an outside one: embarrassing to pop up, as would a gopher, in the middle of the mass."

She laughed, blithely accepting this form of entry into her house, of a man who should not be there at all, particularly at late hour and alone. "But you do us a service Monsieur! We did not know of this particular entry to the tunnels. We only knew of the priest hole in one of the bedrooms; which then leads to a tunnel I think, mayhap this tunnel. But tell me, is all as well as can be expected at the Tuileries?"

"When I left, Louis and 'Toinette were wrangling with Lafayette's plans of escape."

"Oh? He is back from the front?"

"But yes, came to Paris in a hurry to demand punishment of the organizers of the outrage at Tuileries; to offer his services to the king and queen and to appeal to the patriotism of his old comrades of the National Guard!"

"And *can* he do anything?"

"I believe so, but the king rejected all that he had to offer. But they must get themselves *out* of France no matter the means. The time of prevarication be gone but to convince the king of such be impossible. I do not know of another soul that knows the constitution backwards and actually *lives* by it, as does the king. He be the only person left alive to observe its laws and sanctions. Is that not *the* most *ironic* thing ever heard of... in this great upheaval? But the queen, in her hatred of Lafayette, prevented him from addressing the National Guard."

"But...why?"

"I can only assume that, despised by the aristocrats but *hated* by the Jacobins, Lafayette was seeking an excuse to go over to the country's 'enemy'... the Jacobins the more fearsome; and she saw this."

"But then they could use that surely?"

"She feels that all who attempt to save them now have their own agenda."

"So what drove you from the queen's presence... surely not Lafayette?"

"But yes, for the queen be not the only person that trusts him not and I was in this disguise when he arrived. I stayed a while, but have you ever been in company where it be prudent for you to say naught, even though you feel that all around you are ill-guided? That he did not recognize me was evident but if I spoke..."

"I myself only recognized you by your laugh. So do remember to not laugh the next time you travel incognito to Paris—so what now?"

"My last visit to the queen has left me bereft. I shall go now back to Hôtel Craufurd and then home to Sweden. I can do nothing more here."

"But you shall not do so this night. Come, I shall show you to one of our guest rooms."

The Count de Fersen agreed, the hour so late that he knew Craufurd would deem him to stay at the Tuileries and was led by Angelique to the back of the house; where his thanks were kindly cut short and he turned into the guest quarters with gratitude.

♣

Lafayette returned to the front in despair and sent the Assembly a final letter of his political testament, in which he declared that he had never changed his principles. He still believed in the principles of the American Constitution and always would. But within France, he said, that could only be effectual with the addition of the hereditary executive power of the king. The queen was brought to review her suspicions of Lafayette.

Within six weeks of this event, Marie-Joseph, Paul, Yves Roch, Gilbert du Motier, Marquis de La Fayette, following Dumouriez' refusal of his orders' to march on Paris, fled to Liège. He was arrested: by the Austrians, whilst crossing the border in flight to England: having been declared a traitor, along with four other members of the Constituent Assembly fleeing with him. He was thirty-five. Here, at this time, ended his much applauded, long and brilliant, military career, both within America and France. This be-medalled soldier had given his all to the idealism of liberty and equality of man: of all men, and in particular, of all three estates of France.

♣

Robespierre, trim and smelling cleanly of soap and starched linen, stood at the window and watched the noisy streets below. He was convinced that it was at last time to come out into the open and call for the deposition of the king; thus summoning a National Convention. His smile was pure ice as he laid his plans.

For weeks, leading up to this point, popular anger of the people was concentrated on the court, the emigrants and foreign powers. The leaders focused on the Brunswick manifesto of Aug 1$^{st}$ 1792, to keep that anger burning. It worked: achieving the image of a nation at war pulling together. Thus far, the war was concentrated far away on the frontier only but still the country was declared a nation under arms: the very term sufficient to raise the level of panic yet again.

Lazare Carnot stood at the lectern. "We are a nation at war, gentlemen. The people are in extreme danger." He turned to the public gallery. "From this moment, *every* Frenchman is a soldier; for our war resides here in Paris as well, my friends, and we must do our part to assist those brave soldiers in action. We must therefore carry defence weaponry at all times, namely that of the pike, in the absence of anything better."

These were then manufactured rapidly and distributed to all except traitors, vagrants and beggars and the elderly, who, it was said, would quite possibly collapse beneath the weight. This statement incurred the wrath of many fine old warriors.

To add strength to the panic, the focus returned, never very far removed, to the treachery of Louis. Fighting for his life, he had tried to deny the Manifesto, declaring his faithfulness to the constitution. The Robespierrists, however, and indeed almost the entire population, were now once again stimulated to the preservation of the nation, which could not be achieved while the king still lived.

Forty-seven out of the forty-eight sections of Paris now called for the forfeiture of the throne and the summoning of the National Convention. The move of the Jacobin party's game had been made: Robespierre's position more powerful than ever.

All the fateful night of August 9<sup>th</sup>, 1792, the sections sat in consultation over this issue, by now nothing left to debate, except to reassert the Constitutional Right of Insurrection and re-enthronement of the people. Thus the *Insurrectional Commune*, comprising twenty-eight sections, was born: but had little more to do than sanction the preparations, already long-organized by the committees, for the coming insurrection of August tenth, 1792. Many believed that Louis must be taken: alive, to stand trial, then executed.

The Municipality sat in session at the Town Hall until three in the morning: including the old, the new, the legal and the *Insurrectional Communes*. Louis must be taken immediately. Whilst the illegal body organized the attack on the Tuileries, the legal body disorganized the defence of the palace by recalling the officers in charge. This occurred quietly and then attention was turned toward the most dangerous fly in the ointment: the 'royalist' Mandat, Commander in Chief of the moment, of the National Guard. This command of the Guard had been, since the decree of February 10<sup>th</sup> 1792, shared by each of its six *chefs de legion* (battalion commanders), serving two monthly periods. Robespierre suspected, correctly, that the '*aristos*' as the nobility were now known, were making great efforts to monopolize this position. Mandat must go. He gazed now at the nervous company, speaking softly. "Where *is* he by the by?"

"Mandat? At Tuileries!"

"Recall him!" The voice was acid, infecting, as was designed, the rest of the nervous company this night.

It grew late and all agreed.

Tuileries, in the middle hours of this night, basked in a rare peace, as Mandat sat in consult with the king. "Sire, it grows late, the hour after three I know but I feel that if you do not..."

A quick knock at the door brought a page, bowing low. "Excuse me Your Majesty, but..."

Louis gazed at him, brows raised. "I did inform you, did I not, that I was not to be disturbed?"

"Yes Sire, but it be urgent, Your Majesty—a message for the recall of M. Mandat to the Hôtel de Ville."

Louis looked at Mandat and sighed resignedly. "What *now* do they want?"

Mandat took the missive, read and stood, bowed low to the king and said, "Sire, seems I am summoned from the palace for matters most urgent..." He frowned, deciphering the message again. "...though it be unclear the exact nature of the urgency!"

Louis stood, stretched his back and turned. "It could be any dashed thing! It grows late anyway, Mandat. Thank you for coming. Call again at eleven... this morning."

Mandat bowed low. "I shall be here, Sire."

"Oh, and Mandat," the king's voice followed him to the door.

Turning, he gazed in inquiry.

"Watch your back, down there!"

Unaware of the Town Hall proceedings this night, grumbling about the late hour of recall, Mandat left the Tuileries. His carriage rumbled along the Rue St Honoré, twisted and turned some more and then arrived at the Hôtel de Ville. Stepping down from the carriage, he turned to be confronted by three strong and heavy citizens.

Startled, he gazed in alarm, sensing some impending doom. "But what is this, Citizens?"

The apparent leader of the trio did not answer. He nodded to the other two and Mandat was frog-marched away, around the corner of the building. Here he was swiftly and silently murdered, meeting his maker without ever understanding what had happened.

At six in the morning the *Insurrectional Commune* informed the Municipal body, in writing, that they had decided upon the Municipal's suspension. The Mayor, Pétion, would be retained, as would his deputy, Manuel the procureur, Danton the leader of the extremist Cordeliers' club and the administrators in their executive positions. Within an hour of this, the attack on the palace began.

Tocsins suddenly severed the quiet within Tuileries. The queen lifted her weary head; the megrim still not totally abated. Her senses swam on a wave of nausea on the movement and the hot pokers behind her left eye continued their torture. She glanced at the clock: it was almost seven of the morning. She pulled on her gown, slowly, and went swiftly to the king's apartments; holding her head as steady as was possible and walking lightly.

"What *now* Louis?"

Louis, having not bothered to retire following Mandat's exit, gazed down now from his window. "Do not worry too much *ma chérie*, I was made aware of this threat of insurgence. 900 veteran Swiss mercenaries in addition to the 900 gendarmes, 2000, give or take, National Guards and 2500 Chevaliers de Saint Louis be in place for our defence; along with other royalist volunteers."

The queen, hand to her head against the throbbing there, performed a quick calculation. "In excess of five thousand men: they *should* be able to defend the palace but I grow distrustful of everything these days, Louis!"

Unknown to them, however, was the serious shortage of ammunition, a grievous oversight: the culprits later untraceable.

The first bands of insurgents appeared as they watched. The queen raced back to her apartments, subduing the urge to throw up by sheer will and ordered the dressing and readiness of her children, then dressed hurriedly and returned to the king. The noise increased to deafening proportions as the battle grew fierce and soon it became evident that of the Tuileries defence, only the Swiss could be relied upon.

"Louis! This is disastrous! What now. *Mon Dieu*, they are going to murder us!"

"Calm yourself, *ma chérie*, none would dare."

The queen obeyed: not necessarily Louis but definitely the megrim. Each time her voice and anxiety rose so too did the intensity of the pain.

The page entered again and before he could open his mouth the Attorney General of the Department of Paris, Pierre Roederer, pushed him aside and addressed the king.

"Your Majesty! You *must* flee: before you are murdered. Please Sire! Just go!"

"I will not be intimidated by a mob!"

Louis strode to a vantage point and stood facing the National Guard, attempting to speak. The queen, pressing her hand hard against her temples—it somehow helped—grabbed him by the arm as they turned their cannons on him. "Louis! *Come*! To the Assembly! *That* is their so-called seat of justice, of fairness! This they *must* uphold… or appear very foolish!"

The royal family ran across the gardens—the queen pausing several times for one second to vomit—to the door of the Assembly, her insight invaluable: this was the only faint protection available to them. The noise of the guns and cannons thundered around them as they ran. This was terrifying enough; but the palpable hatred of the Assembly, on arrival, was worse.

The king and queen, the king's sister, Elizabeth and the two children, Marie-Therese and Louis-Charles, now sat listening in one of the press boxes whilst the deputies discussed what should be done about them. The queen's face was remarkably white, her temples pounded and dizziness caused her to sway a fraction but this she controlled by iron will as she swallowed back further rising bile, thanking, for the first time ever, her severely disciplined upbringing.

During this time the Swiss and the gendarmes, in the first phase of the fighting, had managed to clear the carrousel behind Tuileries. In the second phase, however, they were pushed back into the palace. The third, due to the king's relayed orders to them to lay down their arms at once, in event of civilians being present, saw their slaughter.

The Tuileries became a bloodbath: guards and nobles chased up onto the parapet, fighting to the last. They fought valiantly but were outnumbered and stabbed, shot or killed by sabre. The dead and dying, flung from the windows, landed at the feet of the mob women. Pouncing upon these in glee, they finished the job, screaming and laughing in macabre satisfaction as they disembowelled and decapitated the bodies.

Madame de Tourzel, the royal governess, ran until she became as disorientated as the queen had on her exit of the Tuileries, during the royal flight to Varennes. The vast rabbit-warren building exhibited a famed maze of narrow passageways and wide corridors; that not one person had been able to easily defeat. Rounding a corner she saw three guardsmen ahead and glancing frantically behind saw four more. She was trapped. She stood and stared, holding their gaze, tall, erect and dignified, though this illusion was destroyed, should they see her trembling hands. She shoved them, clenched now into fists, into the folds of her skirt: bluff had saved many a life; so the history books attested.

"Kneel, woman!"

Face calm and devoid of expression; she remained standing. The infuriated guard forced her to her knees and placed the sabre to the back of her neck preparatory to taking aim. Feeling the cold steel against her skin, she prayed to faint; bluff was not going to work this time. The next instant, she almost laughed in total hysteria when a voice sounded from behind.

"Stop… we do not kill women or children!"

Now a prisoner, she knew that it was but a little time before she was executed anyway. The hysteria bubbled forth again. She swallowed hard and walked with her captors, maintaining a dignified air by focusing upon her footsteps only, as they prodded and shoved her. Focus: focus on something mechanical. Footsteps: that was the thing. One two… three four… fifteen, twenty… sixty-six, turn. New corridor: one, two… and so it went for a seemingly endless time-span.

All dressed as nobles were hunted down and killed, the not quite dead bodies hacked to pieces, entrails spilling, as the sans-culottes vented whipped up fury. Some Swiss managed to escape into the Assembly but were dragged off to the Hôtel de Ville and there put to death. Others retreated to the Tuileries gardens but of the 900 Swiss 600 were killed and of the king's men 800 were lost, totalling 1400 men. Of the insurgents only 376 died: the revolutionaries had won.

Tuileries ran with blood from the 1,776 scattered bodies, lying where they had fallen and horrifying all who saw it. To Robespierre however, it was a glorious event, his flat, gentle smile increasing as each fresh set of figures were brought to him. His immediate insubordinates gazed at him in concealed horror.

*"Citizen...* there be many of our own though!"

His smile further increased; a gentle, pious, fanatical aura surrounding him, further deepening their horror. "Their souls shall rest as heroes in the heaven of martyrs."

The queen gazed about at her family, comforting and reassuring the children, glancing from time to time at Louis and Elizabeth. The small private journalists' box, within the Assembly, was their refuge. Ten feet by ten feet in dimensions, with a barred window over the gallery, it gave rather the opposite effect: that of a prison cell with no escape. In this she was correct: there was no way of leaving. They had nothing to eat or drink, if indeed they could have stomached anything and her appeal: for the children's needs, were met with mirth and scorn.

Throughout this massacre, the queen's jewellery, trinkets and clothes, were paraded before them, along with heads on pikes. With mute face she ignored them all. Louis sat with bland features, again puzzling his tormentors. In reality his mind was far from this place, travelling the road from 1789: in bemused effort to seek some sort of sense to it all; some hint as to where he had gone wrong, what more he could have done. He failed.

Thus they were held for two days, spending uncomfortable and sleepless nights at the neighbouring Feuillants. They were then, under Robespierre's direction via the newly formed Paris *Commune*, sent to Temple: a former medieval fortress in the east of Paris, close to the Bastille.

Marie Antoinette gazed without expression at the approaching Temple. A thin ironic smile then crossed her face. She should not have complained about Tuileries, as her more serious husband had said. There were indeed worse places and here was one right before her: the large twelfth century building, belonging to the Monsieur le Comte d'Artois.

Heavy gates led into the courtyard and behind the high walls there existed a small city within a city. A complex of lodgings and passageways had developed around the old fortress. The Great Tower, however, dominated the entire scene. Tall and sombre, its blackened windowless walls lent a dark, menacing and foreboding air to the whole affair. It rose 60 feet in height, topped by towers and turrets beneath a pointed dark roof. From the north turret it was possible to gain entrance to a second tower, the Little Tower.

The queen followed the silent guard through a series of vaulted corridors and passageways. Climbing up steeply winding stone steps and then finally a wooden staircase, she continued behind the guard, another closely trailing her. Arriving at a sturdy, nail-studded, wooden door, the guard opened it with a large iron key. Marie Antoinette was shoved into a small, sparsely furnished room containing two folding beds.

"This be the Little Tower," the guard told her. "You can never escape from here!"

She smiled politely. "Thank you. I do like to be well orientated."

The guard lifted his brawny arm high, to descend toward the queen's head but his companion leapt forward and cried out, "*No* Citizen...'tis the Queen!"

The hand, already on the descent, connected with his head, spun him round, and flattened him against the wall.

"You *know* that we no longer refer to them as royal! They be Monsieur and Madame Caput! Remember that if you do not wish to swing for treason!" The guard turned back to the queen. "And *you* will be beaten like any other prisoner, for insolence! You would do well to remember that!"

Try as she did, she could not drop her eyes to the floor in servile manner: not to this arrogant and obviously brutal man. To the Pope yes, to her husband yes, to other monarchs yes, and to martyrs and the nuns of the orders, yes, but to this monster of revolutionary France: *no*. She glanced away however and nodded politely. The junior guard, returned now to his feet, was impressed: the queen would learn quickly. He was glad for her and catching her swift glance of gratitude, gave a faint nod and followed his superior out of the room.

Left alone, she listened to the various noises echoing from the guards occupying the room next door. Trying not to look at the age-grimy walls, she thought about the Knights Templar, wondering whether any had occupied this very room. She asked, on the next day, of the whereabouts of the Princess Lamballe and Madame Tourzel but was refused an answer. They were in actual fact also confined then escorted to the prison of La Force.

The mob, owning a wonderful ability to destroy, could never reconstruct and the ones left to attempt this were the sixty or seventy commissioners who had disbanded the legal Municipal Council on the night prior to the insurrection. These commissioners now became known as the *Commune of Paris* or, the *Insurrectionary Commune*. Here resided supreme power. Within this new establishment were the newly chosen Robespierre, Hébert, Billaud-Varennes and others of mixed morals and principles. Of the new members, many were pure ruffians and these came to the front noisily, pushing the better men to resign, stay out of sight or prudently cross the frontiers.

The ministers were now disobeyed, the Assembly threatened, public property plundered, great numbers arrested and liberty of speech suppressed. Constitutionalists kept away from the Assembly and laws were passed that hitherto had been rejected by the large majority.  Non-juror priests were required to leave the country within fifteen days or face ten years imprisonment.  Emigrants' properties were confiscated and offered for sale.  Administrative bodies were authorized to issue warrants of arrest against persons suspected of political crimes.

These events proved one change too far however and the tide now began to turn. This tough, new, Reign of Terror now began the very downfall that the Jacobins had sought to prevent with their stringent new laws and policies.

The Assembly was not alone in their resentment of the Jacobins' ascendancy. The people had taken part in the massacre to destroy the throne: but not with the intention of replacing it with another and far more barbaric regime, led by the now feared and hated Robespierre and Danton. Thus, with the object of obtaining political supremacy, an atrocious new scheme was devised by these two and their supporters. In this, the advance of the enemy, on the war front, assisted.

Discussing this issue, Danton now looked at Robespierre. "Coblentz has surrendered and Verdun besieged: after fifteen hours of bombardment and part mutiny of the French garrison there. The commandant has blown out his brains by the by!"

"Which places the invader within 140 miles of Paris," mused Robespierre, ignoring commandants' suicidal tendencies.  "Dumouriez, commanding in Lafayette's place, is at Sedan with 20,000 men and Kellermann at Metz with another 20,000." He paused, frowning slightly. "These must be united, *below* Verdun, if we are to prevent a way open for the enemy; to Paris."

"To rescue Louis: the first of their motives."

"The sooner we execute that cunning fox, the better."

Danton smiled but only said, "We require another large body of armed men to send to the frontier. Leave it to me."

Danton now devoted himself to the task with vigour and passion, sending untrained volunteers to the front at the rate of eighteen hundred per day.  Also, on his proposition, it was decreed that Commissioners go from house to house to make inventory of household arms, horses and carriages, carts; anything that could be sequestered for the war effort.

Paris continued in ferment, church bells rang incessantly and the now tattered red flag of national emergency flew once again on the Town Hall. All had lost count of the times it had been raised since 1789.  Every day the volunteers marched away to swell the chaotic mobilization at Chalons, Soissons and Rheims; accompanied by their musket carrying and songful women to the Barriers and beyond.

Sunday 2nd September 1792, the news of the fall of Verdun to the Prussians reached Paris, creating further chaotic panic. The Commune took advantage of this event and at once closed the barriers to the city.  Signal guns were fired, the Church bells set ringing and arrests affected of many nobles and constitutionalists. Front doors of many more were plastered with threatening cartoons and freshly killed animals' hearts left on doorsteps, symbolizing the *cœur d'aristocrate*, soon to be as dead.

"The tocsins sound the alert against the enemies of our country!" cried Danton in the Assembly. "But they are not *all* outside the walls of our city! With every mile that the Prussians take, the counter-revolutionaries *within* our borders grow the more confident! Look to your neighbour, friends; to the *ci-devant* nobles, *all* nobles, refractory priests and any remaining foreigners; for here you find your *real* enemies! Hunt them out friends... these are your real threats to our capital!"

Taking their cue from this, the speakers in the cafes lifted their voices in echo of his every word, spreading panic and inciting slaughter and mayhem.

On the order to hunt out the enemy within, rumours spread as a wild raging fire and soon that of a royalist rising, within the choked prisons, ran across Paris. The tocsins rang out; had they ever really stopped, thought Angelique, as the feet tramped and the guns fired.

"When do they cease? When does common sense and humanity intervene?" asked Madame Bayette, ringing her hands. She shuddered at the rattle of gunfire close by. "*Mon Dieu...* where be the Comte!"

"Please... be calm Madame," replied Emile. He peered through a crack in the drawn curtains. "They have missed our hôtel... and gone on."

"Why?" asked Rochelle.

Emile turned to her a brief moment. "Who knows why... but you... all of you shall retreat behind the 'Fersen' panel, as Ange calls it, should they look like coming here. You go to Craufurd's house and should they then reach that area you all, including the Craufurds, return here, as the tide sweeps on. That be an order... and reciprocal with Craufurd," he finished, then gazing at Angelique's rebellious face, "The three minutes be *mine*!"

She laughed suddenly. "But we do not *know*. I believe them to be mine."

"The birthing papers say otherwise *ma soeur*."

"A fraud!"

"Well... how would *you* handle it?"

"I must admit that you be correct, for there be not just you and I to consider."

"Thank you! And we cannot underestimate this new wave of violence and hatred toward us. They really *believe* in the royalist rising within the prisons. How they are to do it is beyond me," he paused thoughtfully, then, "You know that the main business of the *First Vigilance Committee* was to fill the prisons..."

"With us!" cried Madame Bayette. "When we have done *nothing*!"

"Yes, with us," replied Emile gently. "And I hate to think it but I believe that now the main business of the *Second Vigilance Committee* be to empty them."

The Comtesse stared in horror at the implication and then laughed weakly. "But you jest! Oh, do not do so under these conditions. There *is* no *Second Vigilance Committee*!"

Angelique glanced at him but a moment, knowing that indeed there was: and its ethics left much to be desired. She watched him move suddenly to the door and said, "You *go* somewhere?"

He frowned. "I must see Raoul."

He turned, hand on the doorknob, but Rochelle was there at once, her hand on his. "Emile... do not go out there... *please!*"

"Worry not *ma chérie*, I go via Craufurd's house." He spoke so softly that only she heard and stepped back, a little comforted.

The hatred, hardly in need of Hébert or Desmoulin's media stirrings, reigned fast and furious. Twenty-four hours later, rumours swept Paris of an authenticated aristocratic uprising within the prisons. With the bells ringing and Danton's continuing incitement of citizens to enlist, bands of assassins, hired by the *Insurrectional Commune*, entered the prisons. These now overflowed with both nobles and constitutionalists. The assassins massacred all of rank and some of no rank at all. This work was not random but carried out under the express direction of the *Commune*. The slaughter began seemingly by accident, with the transport of twenty non-juror priests, carried in four carriages, to the prison at the *Abbaye* of *Saint-Germaine-des-Près*.

Emile had indeed been correct in his assumption: the new *Second Vigilance Committee* had met that morning at the Mayor's official residence. An enthusiastic armed crowd escorted Marat, 'the friend of the people,' there from his section, the *Quatre Nations.* In the afternoon, the four carriages set out, on the journey of about half a mile, with no escort: a sure invitation to attack. On arrival at the prison, the priests were dragged out and set upon. The twenty priests were swiftly slaughtered.

The psychological barrier, Marat's worry, to wholesale slaughter was now broken. From this point on it became an easy matter for the frenzied mob to break into the prison and murder all priests and nobles therein. Artisans, businessmen and anyone of lower rank than that of a noble residing there were spared: separated from the nobility some days earlier under the express order of the Commissioners to protect any debtors and civil charge prisoners of the lower classes. In addition, Desmoulins and Danton had arranged for the release of their own protégés prior to the 'spontaneous' prison slaughter.

A brief pause of some five to six hours now ensued, during which the Assembly was asked to send some of their own members to control the situation. This they did but the murderers ignored these.

From *Abbaye* the self styled executioners moved on to the Carmelites, killing all the priests there. Of the other prisons, none escaped the attack, the wave of genocide moving rapidly on to the *Châtelet, Saint-Firmin, La Force*, the *Bicêtre*, the *Bernardins*, the *Conciergerie* and the *Salpétrière*, in which women and their children fell before the madness. The original motive forgotten, boys and girls at the reformatory of *Bicêtre*, were murdered by the hundreds. At the *Salpétrière*, prostitutes and petty thieves joined the lined up dead.

A little more finesse was attempted at two of the prisons: a dozen individuals at the *Abbaye* and *La Force*, set themselves up as judges, with a president at their head. Some form of judicial procedure did ensue but beyond that the outcome was the same.

Each prisoner was called, asked one or two questions, and then ordered to the *other* prison: correspondingly *La Force* or *Abbaye*, a sentence known by the executioners, of death. As these passed through the prison gates, the executioners stationed there, rained blows upon their heads. The corpses piled up.

These executioners were not sans-culottes but middle-aged tradesmen and ex-soldiers and consisted of carpenters, bakers, watchmakers, retailers, businessmen, fariers, clothiers and others of varied occupations. They were provided with alcohol by the Section and promised twenty-four livre on completion of the operation.

The September Massacres of '92, operational in the eight prisons, went on continuously day and night for five days, ($2^{nd} - 7^{th}$). This occurred with no action taken to stop the butchering: ministers and deputies fearing the turn of the wheel against them and their families, for they had no military force on which to rely. Santerre, now commanding the National Guard, obeyed the *Commune*. The inhabitants of Paris remained perfectly passive; their objective achieved. A circular, signed by Marat of the *Comité de Surveillance* and his colleagues, was sent out into the country, inciting its people to wipe out the traitors: the nobles, their families and all connected with them, no matter their class, rank, profession or religious station. To work for the nobles was also to support them. Prison carnage did not stop at Paris, taking place also at Versailles, Rheims and Meaux.

At this point Danton, the new Minister of Justice, overshadowed his colleagues as completely as had the *Commune* over the Assembly. They met in his house; he directed their very new and faltering steps, organized the national defence and set the foreign policy. His real office, however, was as liaison officer between the Assembly and the *Commune*: the government and the people. From this post he resigned, however, to take his seat in the *Legislative Assembly*, which had now given place to the new *Convention* on September 21$^{st}$ 1792. Immediately the abolition of the Monarchy was decreed. The following day was recorded as the first day of the French Republic. One week later the deputies arrived at Temple to announce these moves to the king.

Jean-Rene Hébert, now a powerful voice in the *Commune* and as deputy *Procurateur*, insured his presence at this historical moment but was disappointed, then infuriated, by the lack of emotion exhibited by the royal couple.

The king glanced up at the entry into the room of the official party. His heart sank but he did not blink or even glance at the queen; focusing his eyes on his book.

The proclamation was read, with all pomp and ceremony; the speaker flanked by police and guards and important Convention members. The king, contrary to his usual extreme politeness, continued to read Hume's 'History of England'. The queen, following his lead, continued to apply very fine stitches to her embroidery, without the slightest tremor of her hand. Hébert knew, because he moved closer to see, wanting to strike the work from her. He vowed from that moment that he would see them dead, for no greater reason than that of pure jealousy and hatred. This born of fear and envy, for he knew that no matter how long he practiced, he could never achieve that air of total unconcern, belonging to the aristocracy. That it was born of extreme courage, of the strength that gave the ability to coolly endure humiliation, to laugh in the face of death, to calmly approach the guillotine, he could not comprehend. That these attributes were mandatory, hammered into each aristocratic child from the cradle, he did not know. That such attributes were the very bone marrow of their existence, he would never understand. His lack of understanding on this front drove him at a later date to agree with Robert Saint-Just; in that the Monarch 'should be executed out of hand with no trial, for simply put: Louis was never a commoner, no matter the Assembly's efforts to turn him into one. He was a king, would ever remain a king and now kingship *itself* be a crime.'

The constitutionalists were now gone or at least stayed away, leaving the Girondins: originally the 'moderate' leftists, as the new *right* of the Assembly. Thus was established, at this time, a totally 'leftist' government: of varying degrees. The Girondins then sort to bring justice to the organizers of the prison massacres with the promise of a court marshal but then delayed the decree: to focus upon the destruction of the rapidly ascending Jacobin led *Commune*. This took precedence over all else.

The war situation for France, during and after that bloody first week of September in Paris, was critical. The Prussians, under the Duke of Brunswick, crossed the frontier into France and occupied the two crucial passages of the river Meuse: the towns of Stenay and Verdun, on the direct roads from Trier in Prussia, to Paris. In doing this, Brunswick split the French army of Dumouriez to the northwest at Sedan, from that of Kellermann at Metz in the east. Ahead lay a direct road to Paris.

The Duke of Brunswick stood high on a hill and gazed south. "The only obstacle now between us and the plain of Champagne and then Paris, is that," pointing to a thickly wooded line of hills separating the Meuse and the Aisne rivers. "The Argonne." A cautious commander, by result of hard experience through the Seven Years War, he liked to move slowly. "But with 80,000 men I do not think that we can maintain communications *and* hold Paris in safety."

The King of Prussia reined in his impatience, to listen politely to Brunswick's reasons. "You are suggesting?"

"That it be better to hold the fortress of Meuse: and wait till spring for further operations."

The King of Prussia, fighting alongside the general, was eager to push on to Paris and the rescue of the royal family. "The royal family be dead by then."

Brunswick, startled, turned to gaze at him. "Regicide? They wouldn't dare!"

The King of Prussia grunted. "Just you watch them. Under Robespierre's influence they will do anything."

At the fall of Verdun, Dumouriez still held his French troops at Sedan, close to the Belgium frontier and Kellermann his at Metz, near the Prussian border. Verdun, held now by Brunswick, lay more or less south, behind them, on the road to Paris.

Seated on a sack of horse fodder, Francois spooned the tasteless, grey gravy mixture into his mouth, as he thought about what his commander, Dumouriez, might do next.

He glanced up at Devereaux, appearing with a wooden bowl containing the same watery stew in his hand, and said, "So Brunswick is now between us and Paris, Dev, while we sit at Sedan!"

Devereaux seated himself on a water barrel. "What think you, Vermont? We chase them all the way to Paris?"

A messenger approached at that moment, saluted and handed Francois a scrap of parchment. Francois read. Devereaux, exerting strong discipline to ignore the taste, continued to eat the grey slops and waited.

"Dumouriez has decided to move south and unite with Kellermann the other side of the wooded hills, in the path of the allies," he grinned.

"Between them and Paris...and then drive them back? It *should* work: all being well."

"And Kellermann being on time!"

Dumouriez, marching the French troops south, now occupied the Grand Pre, the central of the three passages through the Argonne. Here, about equidistant from Stenay and Verdun, he met with Prussian attack and was driven from his position, as Brunswick advanced. Dumouriez rallied his men in the plain and made a stand near Sainte-Ménehoud. Here, Kellermann and his forces joined him from Metz. The French, under these two renowned military leaders, were now a formidable force.

The allies, however, on their descent into the plain, had managed a position between the French army and Paris. The Duke of Brunswick, far from being jubilant as were his Prussian soldiers, frowned in worry and concentration: this created a sticky dilemma for him.

Francois, sitting his horse atop a small rise, gazed over the French forces. The weather was very wet, the roads almost impassable, causing great difficulty in supplying the invading army with bread, but this, he knew, was not Brunswick's major problem. What to do next was. If he moved forward now, to take Paris, he then must battle the descending, and very revengeful French army, arriving from behind. Francois shuddered; Paris would rest in a total bloodbath. He turned as Devereaux arrived, saluted, and relayed his news from behind the enemy line.

"Apparently, the placing of Prussian garrisons by Brunswick, at Longwy and Verdun, together with fever and dysentery, has reduced his effective force to 40,000. He cannot push on to Paris, leaving the French army behind him... unbeaten, that is."

"Ah, as I thought Dev. So what does he do, turn back to fight us? Render us incapable before going on?"

"That is what I would do, certainly, and it seems that the King of Prussia is keen to fight, but the Duke persuades him against it... and in place of wasting troops storming our French positions, he proposes to open cannonade on Kellermann's forces."

"They are still in position?"

"Stationed on the heights: near the village of Valmy: in advance of us."

Francois glanced at his old friend and smiled. "Good work Devereaux. You have the courage of a lion. Dumouriez must have been pleased."

Jacques shrugged, turning red. "You have been in it longer: so 'tis none to match yours!"

Francois shook his head, grinning. "I shake in my boots every time! So... Dumouriez will want us to support Kellermann: at Valmy, I think."

Devereaux nodded. "I think so. He will send orders within the hour."

The battle of Valmy, September 20th 1792, small though it was in the history of warfare, proved fast and furious, taking the Duke of Brunswick by surprise and soon the bodies began to fall. The French, he had been told, were an ill-disciplined and untrained mob but the young recruits stood the fire so well that he was forced to fall back a little.

Absently, Brunswick stilled his mount as it pawed the ground lightly. He gazed straight ahead. Taking stock now, he realized that his mistake lay in disbelieving the discouraging reports from his Chief of Staff, Massenbach. He had not believed that the mish-mash of half-trained French volunteers could stand against his regular troops.

He turned to the man beside him and ordered the assault.

"But...but...they have 50,000 men!"

Brunswick turned and the man caught the full fury within the glance as he said, "Attack!"

The Frenchmen on the hilltop did not budge, meeting Brunswick's Prussian advance with answering volleys and shouts and cries of 'Vive la France!' and 'Vive la Nation!'

Exhausted but undaunted, Francois urged his men forward and soon the Prussians could get no further than halfway up the hill: the Duke's infantry struggling to make headway against the French musketry and devastating fire of the royal artillery.

"Forward! Forward!" shouted Francois, leading the way. "We have them on the run. "Go go go!"

He charged his mount forward again, into the milling mass, the noise and movement swirling around him as he swung his sword arm, slashing to left and right, convinced that they were winning. He was correct but at a cry from Jacques Devereaux he twisted in his saddle to confront an upward thrust of a sabre and then hit the ground with a thump as his horse was shot, simultaneously, from under him.

Reaching for his sword lying on the ground and scrambling to his feet, he shook his head to clear the haziness from the fall. He bent to his horse and saw that he was very dead. The rattle of musketry fire and the boom of the cannons echoed in his head, as the bullets now flew past and over him. Bodies fell to the left and right but he did not have the time to look at them as he fought on. His sword arm grew leaden but he forced it on, stumbling over the dead and dying. Tripping against an upthrust boot of a fallen body, he pitched forward, thus narrowly missing a descending sabre. Amid this mayhem, the entire world suddenly blew up before him. It turned upside down, flying clods of earth smacking into him; then righted itself. The sky: moments before dark with rain, now showed a soft white light, increasing in strength by the moment. A puzzling stillness and quietness surrounded him. He tried to shake his head; had they defeated them so soon; so completely? Where was Dumouriez; where was Jacques? He had to find his childhood friend; this was his first active commission. He owed him his greater experience as protection. He opened his mouth to call but it filled with a warm, salty liquid and he choked in the effort. He tried again, but no sound came.

"Francois! Francois! It's me... it's alright *mon ami*, it's alright!"

"We defeated them?" he tried to ask but could not get it out and then knew that they had not as yet, as his vision cleared for but a moment and he witnessed rushing uniformed figures, muddy and bloodied. Soon, however, they were gone, permanently, as the kindly blanket of white settled over him. The air was warm and peaceful and he felt a gentle lifting, as his eyes reached into the soft white sky that should really have been dark and dismal with steady rain. The white grew brighter—and brighter: a figure began to form.

"Mère?" the faint sound was almost inaudible but Jacques caught it; then the body in his arms grew limp and heavy, the eyes glazed.

Jacques, tears pouring down his cheeks spun round in raging hostility, as a rough hand jerked him to his feet. "Get off me!"

"You want to *join* him? Leave him lad... he's gone! He's gone I tell you... get thee to the flank: they are on the turn! Go boy...*go!*"

Jacques stared, a bullet whizzed past his left ear, the buzzing hum mimicking a bothersome bee; at least, he assumed it a bullet: surely bees would be far from this field of carnage. His mind played with the conundrum.

"Boy, if I have to knock thee out and carry thee, I will!" shouted his benefactor, jerking him up with one arm, his sword arm swinging forward with a ring of steel on steel.

Jacques lost some of the glazed shine to his eyes and, turning, followed him.

The battle of Valmy was over, the small area now covered with the bodies of the dead and dying: the losses not large; no more than 500 men counting both sides. Brunswick, leading the Prussians, began to retreat, no apparent match for the mad and desperate French. Fighting on their own ground for more than just a war, these had battled with an energy that defied simple national defence against a foreign invader. The French were fighting to protect France. Protect her from within and without; each blow rendered with a pent up, fostered anger and bitter impotence that had been boiling for the last three years. For the decades and centuries before that: for harnessed here, within the fighting French, was a rising power, drawn on by the growing light at the end of a long, long tunnel of oppression. This was the inexorable, indefinable power of pure intent to exit that tunnel; that the Duke had not understood.

Back in Paris, the day of the Valmy victory, September 20th, also marked the birth of the 'New Assembly': the Convention. Elected beneath the shadow of the 'First Terror' it met at Tuileries and on September 21st its second day of existence, declared the monarchy abolished. Four days later, beneath the direction of Robespierre, the Convention set about creating a new constitution for France.

Angelique stood in the wide entry hall pulling on her gloves, her cousin hovering behind. "Do you think that you should go, my dear? I be convinced that the Comte would not allow it. Please do give it some thought. What if you get out there but the barriers are closed on your return?"

"Then I return to Temple. I am sure they would find no trouble giving accommodation to yet another aristocrat."

Marie-Therese shuddered. "Do not! How can you be so flippant?"

At this moment Henri entered to say that the carriage was ready: a carriage now minus the coat of arms emblazoned on its side. A clanging bell, followed by a thumping on the door, halted him. Moving forward to open it he found Rochelle on the steps.

"Rochelle! My dear, what is it?" asked Angelique.

"Ange! Please, I must see you... but I see that you go out. Not wise, my dear."

"Precisely what *I* have been trying to say," said Marie.

Angelique turned to Henri. "Tell the coachman to wait a moment please. Come Rochelle," then led the way up the stairs to the small salon on the first floor and seating her friend there perceived that all was not well. "Come, tell me, my dear."

"I have just recalled that I must see the housekeeper. I shall return to say goodbye my dear," interjected Marie.

Rochelle turned to smile at her, watching her leave the room and then, "She doesn't know that it shall be her last for a while."

Angelique waited and Rochelle finally turned and took her hand. "*Mon amie*, I am leaving you all."

"What?"

"Ange, I go home; at least to my English home. But I cannot wait to get back and be with you all again, for surely this mayhem cannot last."

"Ah, the wedding...we anticipate it with great excitement. But is your *père* here?"

"Yes. He arrived last night and we go...now."

"So soon...but why the rush?"

"*Mon père* has information that he will not share but he be in an urgent hurry; wanted to go last night and I am to tell no one but I could not go without telling you! The barriers are down and he says that they will close again at any moment."

"But 'Chelle, one can still get a pass, I believe, if you are English."

"He does not trust *any*thing! We go, as a tailor and his seamstress daughter."

"And *Emile*?"

"Yes, he knows apparently and rides across country to meet us half way to the port. I do not know more. Selfishly I hope that he travels with us all the way to England. Hopefully the thought of me sailing away shall persuade him! *So* selfish I know but cannot help myself."

"Calais?"

"No. Harve; a small boat awaits us there. English... and that is another thing: the English are very close to joining the Prussians. It is to prevent becoming a prisoner of the French within those facts that he takes me out of the country. He wonders that they have not already used such as excuse to imprison one more '*aristos*'! A *foreign* aristos!"

"Well, we shall be there for your wedding. Do not you dare go ahead without us."

Rochelle laughed and hugged her friend of very longstanding. "We shall wait!"

A tap at the door caused interruption and on calling 'enter' it opened and Henri stood there, ushering in a very tall gentleman in English travelling dress. "Ah, thought I may find you here my dear," he said to Rochelle, "*though* I forbade you to leave the house."

Angelique was on her feet and moving forward, speaking in English, "But how delightful My Lord, your daughter could not leave without saying goodbye surely? Please you must forgive her!"

"Now that she retains her head on her shoulders I suppose that she be forgiven. Anyway I had the intention to call here as I returned home. You must go with us, my dear."

"But, sadly, I cannot. My father… Emile…"

"It was Emile's suggestion. Your father is incommunicado at this moment."

"Do we not know it! But much as I appreciate your concern, I must stay here. I cannot, indeed will not, leave without knowing my father is safe. He may have a need of me. On his return, I may think of it again."

"No you will not," laughed Rochelle, "And indeed neither should I but for the wedding preparations. I must be there soon anyway or nothing can go ahead."

"You go, my daughter, because I say so." The earl's voice held a hint of ice.

"Yes Sir."

"Come Rochelle, we must delay no longer." The Earl turned and made his bow to Angelique, then taking her hand in his and gazing down at her a moment, said, "My dear, I have no power over you but wish, in the absence of your father, that I did. You are the daughter of one of my oldest friends, *though* he be French."

She laughed in delight. "You have no idea how many non-French people say that!"

"Yes well, your mother also was a childhood friend of my sister and so my friend too. As such I believe that I have the right to overrule your decision to stay in France at this very dangerous time. I feel her presence now… urging me."

She smiled. "Sir, I can see your dilemma but I will not go."

He stared down at her. "My dear, I can then only assume that your feminism and youth obstruct any sensible thinking. If I were your father I would not consider your refusal but bundle you into the carriage: now! However, that hypothesis falls apart on the very fact that I am not, unfortunately, your father. Come Rochelle, we must go now."

"Ange! My very dear friend, I shall see you at the wedding." Rochelle hugged her tight but Angelique insisted on following them to the hall below for a final goodbye; then, running back up to the salon, watched them from the window.

She leaned out to see them disappear around the bend and stayed there some small time: crushing as best she could the desolation and loneliness swamping her soul. Oblivious to the street activities, she pondered the times that made flight from France so necessary for so many just now. She thought about her sister and brother-in-law and their children and was glad that they were safely tucked up in Italy, but of her brothers, and most of all her *père*, she worried.

Henri entered. "Madame…"

"Oh Henri! I am so sorry, be pleased to house the carriage and stable the horses now: events have changed my mind."

"Yes Madame."

She returned to the window: as if that move would bring back her friend. She stayed a moment; then about to turn back into the room she glanced down to see a *pots-de-chambre* stop at the door and the Comte stepping down and up the steps.

She ran again to the hall below. "*Mon Père*! You have just missed the Earl and Rochelle!"

He held her a moment, feeling her relief at his return; then, arm around her shoulders, moved upstairs and to his library. "My dear, I must bathe. No matter the hour: the journey was frightful. Tell me all about it later."

"Ah, then it was also a dangerous journey!"

He raised his eyebrows slightly but would not humour her and then Henri knocked, and entered on call, to announce a visitor of the military.

"Ah. I am expecting him. Bring him up, Henri."

"Monsieur, it be a message only but he will not entrust it to me."

De Quatreaux raised his brows. "Then it be not he. I will come."

He left the room, then returned with the sealed missive, balancing it on his hand for a moment.

"Monseigneur?" Angelique looked at the parchment, her knees suddenly weak. She sat down, her senses screaming at her inner mind. A solid lump of lead sat in the pit of her stomach, the very core of her being heavy with a sense of absolute knowing. "Is it…is it…?"

He broke the seal, read a moment and then she knew. "It be Francois… yes?"

"Yes. He was killed at Valmy." He added, inconsequently, "They won the battle."

"Could they be wrong?" she asked faintly, "About Francois, I mean?"

"No. This be from Devereaux. We shall hear officially soon, no doubt, but he says that he was…er, with him, at the time."

She watched her father's iron will at work as he folded the missive and placed it in his inner pocket, his expression a mask of cold efficiency as he sat down suddenly. He gazed at the floor absently for some time, blind to the world and she moved slowly to his chair, then sank to the floor at his feet, placing her arms and then her head gently on his knees. Something from ages past seemed to pour forth as she remembered doing this long ago, on the death of her *mère*.

He did not see her or feel her. That too had happened. She stayed there a long time and that too had happened. Eventually he roused and glancing down, placed his hand on her head, stroking her golden-brown hair, stroking it for a long time and that too had happened. He said nothing. Again, there was nothing to say except to decide the mechanics of the event.

"I must go *mon enfant*, to the field at Valmy and bring him back. I will *not* have him buried in an unmarked mass grave in some far-flung field. He shall be buried at Quatreaux." He glanced at her now as she stared up at him with dry eyes but the deep pain there smote him. His lips compressed, drawing down at the corners, to stop their trembling and his face assumed a harshness of expression in the effort, resulting in the haggardness that was the penalty of an older man pushing himself beyond endurance.

"You must rest first, *Mon Père*. You are exhausted from your journey... after all..." Her voice faltered. "...he shall be going nowhere. Besides, you arrived incognito, apparently, otherwise why the *pots-de-chambre*? Should you be seen?"

He felt the pure concern for him and spoke gently. "*Mon enfant*, to be seen now shall cause no comment. 'Twas only where I came from that was cause for concern. I will bathe, eat the necessary amount for the energy required and set out again tonight. And you," he paused suddenly, "where is your cousin?"

"She left in sensitivity of my goodbyes to Rochelle and her father. She does her best at the function, which you gave her but cannot mourn someone that she saw briefly."

"No, but I expect her to support you through the next days that I am away."

She gazed at him, wanting to comfort him. "We can be proud of Francois, *Mon Père*."

He raised his brows. "But of course. He is... was, a de Quatreaux!"

"But he was fighting a war in which he had no say... for love of France." As always in times of deep emotional distress, the bizarre humour came to the fore. "You could have begot a son of er... say, Lareaux's calibre!"

The Comte stiffened and raised frigid brows almost to his hairline. "I could? *Never!*"

She choked back a hysterical laugh, felt the tears form in her eyes but he did not see and left the room. She wanted to run after him: erase the pain she had caused but she stood still, felt the tears run the length of her face; then, wiping them away in sudden and unprecedented fury, turned and strode to the library. Frustrated by her own inability to control this wretched misplaced humour, rage tore through her soul: at her own stupidity. She dropped into the chair before the desk, paused, dashed at her wet cheeks with the back of her hand and taking up the quill, dipped it in the ink and wrote furiously; verse after verse, concluding:

> 'And this once fair Land,
> Shall not be free...
> Until the Jacobin lay dead,
> To the very last one,
> For it be they that tread...
> The road to riches,
> On the blood of the innocent,
> On the death of a nation;
> And for this my brother,
> I take up my sword: the quill,
> And strike my blow in revengeful ink,
> For you, beloved Francois,
> For France,
> For the massacred innocent...'

She could see no more: the tears blinding her now: racing torrents coursing her cheeks. The quill dropped, blotting the parchment, as her rigid discipline crumbled. Her body shook uncontrollably as choking sobs clogged her throat; and her chest tightened to a solid block of heavy, constricting pain. She dropped her head onto her arms resting there upon the desk, silent sobs wracking body and soul to a depth before unknown. The candles flickered on, continued thus until a small pool of liquid wax snuffed the last of the light in that room. She lifted her head at last and simply sat within that dark silence: within a vacuum of total emptiness. She did not hear her father leave the hôtel.

# CHAPTER EIGHTEEN

## Death of a Bourbon – Jan 21ˢᵗ 1793

### Soldier be Proud

'Low, 'pon soft summer breeze doth float
Oh chill of soul: faint beat of marching feet,
Drawn on by drummers' invoke,
And: foreign marching song.

Nay; be not fearful or tocsin ring,
Crying its clarion call,
Of imminent enemy assault,
For the danger doth lie within.

It comes: darkest night of all,
When none shall sleep,
And a river of blood shall pour,
As they cry their innocence.

Our beloved Francois be proud
Your death wreathed in honour and truth,
Your courageous song forever heard,
Though perfidious, heinous plots abound.

For us remaining, brothers and sisters all,
May our vengeance in glory be writ,
And shame to our enemy strong,
For of self-same blood are they.

Beloved France,
Why divided so, be we?
Why greed and power must wrench asunder?
Our country: in red blood plunder?

> French men and women do pull out,
> From darkest iniquity,
> From pitting Brother against Brother,
> In lancing fury: and bitter dissent.
>
> Francois, so tall and straight,
> Now scythed to join those compatriots,
> Of courage and...

The quill paused, wavering in agitated manner above the parchment: honour? No: a better word must be found. A word encompassing all that he stood for, suffered for, died for; that *they* all stood for; the uncountable dead of France. Death by blood; rivers of blood: painting hillsides, staining pavements. Blood of the Sacred Sight; had this been its warning? Bloody death, stark and cold: sticky, congealed ashes of yesterday, no glory; no honour. No fanfare of triumph, even for the victor. Death: icily marching with inexorable feet, drumming, herding, relentlessly pursuing; racing across battlefield, village and town square.

She shuddered and drove herself into that vacant, unfeeling place. But that place led not to peace but to others, others of France, of foreign soil too, of alien race and doctrine, strings of fate linking them all, breaching culture and belief: to the loss of a loved one. Faces, wracked with pain of heart and body, drifted past her, appearing and disappearing. Oh Francois! The tears threatened. She forced a rigid control. No time for tears now, time only for: for what? The Lord hath no place for revenge: but the Lord had left France long since. She drove her only sword: the quill, on; the word treason scornfully banished.

Her brain turned: to that figure that had honed her very being, De Quatreaux. De Quatreaux would not grant time for such self-indulgence. De Quatreaux would extract revenge upon the heinous imbeciles that wrenched France asunder. On those that tore the deep foundations and superstructure of a superb race and culture apart: not as a surgeon's healing knife, to excise the rot and decay, then heal from the bottom up. But as a pirate's hacking cutlass, crudely seeking riches and self-gain: trailing pain and spreading disease, deep within the countless wounds; climbing over the wounded and the dead, on their ladder to supremacy. The image of her *père* turned her tortured but crystal clear mind again. This time to the early days: of sun and roses, lace and winter fireside, of dear, beloved *mère* taken so suddenly, of vanilla, rosemary, cloves and lavender, of Fanchon and Isobelle, of ponies and Marcel. Beloved Marcel, magical Marcel: drawing child-soul and equine-soul to one shared space; a space of simply 'being', of existing, melding together. This had been the key; *he* had been the key, to her standard of horsemanship that was beyond excellence.

Angelique, quill paused and very still, gazed into space as her thoughts turned to these old days of jest and laughter, even well into the Revolution but now, almost four years on, life held fragile hope of such joy again. When Francois had stated categorically that they would beat Brunswick and his army, he had been correct but had not known that that victory would demand his own life at the battle of Valmy. Or had he? Every soldier must know; live daily with the invisible ghosts of himself and his enemy. Survival rode on the toss of life: one died or the enemy did: no time for niceties or beg pardons; the crush of seething, humanity resembling that of an over-popular fairground but here one killed, or not, on the colour of a uniform. If death was to descend upon oneself then let it be with honour; if the enemy then please God let one's stroke be swift and true, that was all that a soldier asked of his personal angel. If indeed there was enough to go around: perhaps they had abandoned France altogether; her treachery, brother against brother, too heavy, dark and dense for their survival, this close to bloodied France.

♣

Jacques Devereaux trudged unseeingly through the mud and mire, stumbling over bodies of animal and man, not even noting the malodorous air that he breathed. Within ten days of the French victory at the battle of Valmy, the retreat of the enemy had begun and continued unopposed. Ten days since the loss of Francois. Ten days of automation of brain and body. How to face the de Quatreaux'? He had sent a despatch to their hôtel but knew not whether they had received such, possibly not: within the ruling mayhem. He moved with his regiment; the French troops following slowly behind the enemy, rather than vigorously pursuing. They trudged the road littered with dead horses and dead bodies of the not yet buried, the wet and the stench adding to the miseries of dysentery and hunger. They had all grown thin, escaping none of it but learning to control the griping pains of the dysentery. He smiled grimly: perhaps it was as well there was no food: his burning gut would throw it back anyway. He tilted his fevered brow to the cooling drops of falling rain, then glanced about, certain that there could not be more miserable victors anywhere in the theatre of war. Perhaps Francois was well out of it.

The evening halt called, Jacques eased the load from his back, dropped the bundle to a dryer patch of ground and set about organizing his men to camp for the night. He gazed about as they set to the work, watching their slowed movements: the energy rush of battle-survival now gone, they could barely move. He glanced up; hoping for a night dark with cloud: it may bring sleep the more quickly, annihilating the hunger pangs. But then came the haunting dreams and the grief; hanging there as a dark curtain, waiting, ghoulishly, the long hours of the night.

The camp was settled, uncannily quiet. The full moon rose, then arrived a dark bank of cloud and Jacques, to keep his mind busy, calculated the days and weeks since the Valmy victory: not quite a month had passed and tomorrow would see the enemy again beyond the frontier. Brunswick would not be a happy man. Would Dumouriez push after him, beyond the French frontier? He thought so, sighed and rolled over, the movement confusing the rising cramp of his lower belly. It stayed its upward route, settled, then twisted sharply, to carry on with growing intensity. He gritted his teeth against the intense pain.

♣

Jacques Devereaux had been correct about Dumouriez: now supreme commander of the French army, he crossed the Belgium frontier. A month later he took Jennappes and eight weeks later Namur, converting the invasion into conquest. In the south, Montesque occupied Chambery and Nice.

Within the Assembly, the Girondins were jubilant; planning now to set Europe ablaze with revolution and all seemed to be in their favour.

"We must push our frontier to and beyond the Rhine, gentlemen! And free the people both sides of the Pyrenees… not until then will our liberty be established!"

Roland raised his brows. "Brissot… you are extremely confident. What does Dumouriez say on the issue?"

"He writes Kellermann that we must work within the interests of the Republic, winter beyond the border; to alleviate the cost to France of army support and be ready in the spring to march north."

"Ah yes, but what *will* they forage through winter?" responded Roland dryly. "However, what does the Convention care? Let them march, by all means: run even! *Away*; and as far and as fast as possible: before they turn and cut *our* throats. They are a volatile lot, with little discipline: blowing with the winds of ill-gotten gain."

"They shall never do that while the wind blows from a foreign enemy," said Brissot.

"But not even *you* know the coming direction of the wind, Brissot!"

The advance continued and by October the army of the Rhine occupied Speyer, Mainz and Worms and by the end of November the frontier districts of Porrentruy and Delemont became the French department of Mont-Terrible. Everywhere Europe fell before the marching volunteers of the New French, overturning now their old image of ill-disciplined rabble and everywhere the Declaration of the Rights of Man was overshadowing the divine rights of kings. European monarchs no longer smiled at, or derided, the chaotic events within France; all now viewing the Revolution very seriously.

Until this point in time, the Girondins and the Jacobins were both unanimous in their belief in the war, the Republic and the Convention, but there their similarities ceased. Where the moderate Girondins still believed in a template cut from parts of the old regime, the Jacobins had almost no respect for tradition, or even respected and proven policies, and were eager for ruthless and often barbaric experimentation.

As the quarrel between the Girondins and the Jacobins developed, they grouped themselves the more to the right and the left of the President's chair than ever before. Or, as was noted: the 'moderate left' to the 'extreme left'. From this, the extreme Jacobins established themselves the more firmly as the Montagne.   From the opening of the Convention, irreconcilable hostility was declared between the Girondins, 'the Plain', and the Jacobins, 'the Mountain'. Though they did not yet know it, here began the insidious fall of the Girondins: eventually leaving the field clear for total supremacy of the extremists of the left: the Robespierre-led Jacobin *Montagne*.

To secure the independence of the Convention and supremacy for their own party, the Girondins sought to bring to justice the authors of the September Massacres, (of prisons) and to destroy the ascendancy of the Jacobin-led *Commune*. The stain cast on the Revolution by this event they resented keenly; and strove to prove to Europe that it was the work of a few hired assassins. Not, as the deputies of Paris claimed, the rise of the people of Paris to take revenge on the 'traitors' of the nation.

The Girondins were in the right of the matter but the *Commune* ruled the capital; and had in its pay strong bands of thieves and assassins. The *Départements* had taken no part in the massacres; but had also not intervened, intimating acceptance. Primary Assemblies across the country were all but deserted, as each waited the outcome before committal. Numbers were further reduced by the massive recruitment to the army.

Under this heavy mantle the suppression of criminal bands, by the Girondins, was especially impossible as these thugs ruled the city, through the communes and sections. Therefore the Girondins wavered and then did not attempt to break the power of the *Commune*. As a party they did not inspire confidence and were constantly divided in opinion among themselves. Their gentle and rather reclusive chief orator, Vergniaud, though extremely talented, was reluctant to face the volatile issues of the day. The Girondins, therefore, were not able to bring a working majority to the Convention.

The threats of the Girondins, to bring the *Commune* to justice, now degenerated into a full attack on the two most powerful and prominent men of the left, Robespierre and Danton. These were soon accused of conspiring with Marat—one of eleven men controlling the *Comité de Surveillance*—to form a triumvirate, and Robespierre of dictatorship. General charges of this sort, however, could not be substantiated and were easily repelled. It became impossible to fix firm charges of the massacre authorship upon Robespierre and the matter was eventually dropped into the abyss of the three monkeys.

Watching this heated argument across the floor, de Quatreaux drew his own conclusions. The *Commune* was no doubt immediately responsible for the prisons massacres but to prove it, impossible. He had no doubts at all that the entire uprising had been the brainchild of Robespierre, Danton his tool.

De Vries leaned close, his voice low: "Danton? Leader of the flock: right up there behind him."

De Quatreaux smiled grimly. "But not a member of the *Insurrectionary Commune*... leaves him clean. Although as Minister of Justice at the time, he made no effort to stay the assassins' hands."

De Vries frowned. "No written matter, no signature and no proof that it was he who gave the order for the bloodshed. Officially, he is no more responsible than Roland. As Minister of Interior, can guilt be fixed on him?"

De Quatreaux shrugged, waited as someone pushed past, then, "But listen to the mutterings, *mon ami*! *Danton* is the running favourite: crime does not revolt him; he is corrupt, already bloodstained; and clever."

"The latter accolade just may save him: clever enough to not allow personal animosity to tinge his defence speeches."

"Rivalled only by Vergniaud: thank the Lord the Girondins still have *him*. *Now* listen to them! Guilt or innocence; to live or die: balanced on a play on words, no more important than a boxing match... amazing!"

"More amazing that Danton has the benefit of defence."

A leaning neighbour brought a silence between the two friends.

The Convention room soon showed endless contests between The Plain and the Montagne: the Montagne slowly gaining strength. The Jacobin supporters in the gallery applauded the speakers of the left, and hooted those of the right, with the support of armed mobs, threatening insurrection unless their demands were met. The vote almost always went their way, by threat of armed insurrection.

On an international front the Convention wished to spread the revolutionary principles across the frontiers to decrease their financial difficulties. To do this, the annexation of conquered territories was necessary: to carry out there, the changes already brought about in France. Confiscated church property in these newly acquired lands would become national property and the possession of new securities would raise the value of the *assignats*. All haste was made on this front and was welcomed in some areas, namely Savoy, Nice and Liége. Within Austria and the Netherlands, however, the clergy and aristocracy owned much influence. This gave them the ability, within their new theatre, to discard Austria but remain independent of France. The Convention accordingly hesitated to decree these two in union with France. Their attempts to unite Belgium also produced resistance from England. Dumouriez suggested an independent Belgium Republic but this idea was repelled as strongly as the annexation of that country to France. Thus England and France sat on the edge of war, as the debate raged back and forth in the Convention and dominated every home of every social stratum.

♣

"What say you?" asked Montmaire of de Quatreaux as he shuffled the cards absently.

His friend reached for his wine and took a sip; then, "War with England? The Convention should never have proclaimed the free navigation of the Scheldt. England will surely declare war now. I cannot see any other result."

Montmaire dealt the cards and then picked up his own hand and fanned them out. "I agree. Liberation of the Scheldt is in the teeth of the treaties signed by both countries." He frowned. "The Convention, of course, desires nothing less than to carry out immediate annexation of Belgium and then invade Holland."

"Fools! But the Girondins desire only peace with England and withdrawal of Prussia from the coalition... and Pitt still strives to avert a breach with France. But whatever happens, all shall be overshadowed by Louis' trial. The Girondin Convention will not now be able to save him from the brutal hands of the Jacobin *Commune*."

Montmaire raised a brow. "Will they dare, though?"

"The only deterrent, a vengeful foreign army in support of the king, is now gone."

Montmaire frowned. "Imbéciles! Treason, I suppose."

De Quatreaux laughed suddenly. "The catch-cry of the century... *easily* fixed. They set the nation in the place of the King! Therefore it stands that any conspiring of Louis' against this debacle called a regime, be treason. Retribution is at hand, *mon ami*. Demands for his trial are coming in from all over the country."

"Surely there remain *some* scruples against the atrocity of regicide?"

De Quatreaux smiled grimly. "They shall be quashed by the Jacobins: not in the least squeamish."

"But... execution of a *Monarch*?"

De Quatreaux' expression was cynical. "None have any doubts as to his guilt, need only be that of being a king, few that the penalty be death. You wait and see. The English did it on less provocation."

"But the English are mad," dismissingly. "One should have thought that banishment or captivity until the end of the war would suffice."

"The ministers would agree. To hold the sword over the monarch's head would put pressure on Prussia and induce her to abandon alliance with Austria... in return for liberty of the royal family. But the members of the *Montagnard* seek his life, as proof of their passion for equality. Danton wants to cast in the teeth of Europe, the head of a king."

"A considerable gauntlet for battle."

"No denying *that*. But also the Mountain needs to keep the sans-culottes on the boil. Their attention span be that of a child and what better way than the execution of a king. As Hébert says: *they* be the killing machine of all their enemies but must be continuously stimulated. What better way to do that, than by periodic executions of the *Famille Roi* and aristocracy." De Quatreaux fanned the cards out in a perfect arc and then, taking them up and reshuffling for a moment, dealt a new hand.

That Louis was guilty, of ever mounting crimes, his apparent simplicity now seen to have long covered a double game, was a foregone conclusion. The only question left: what sentence should now be passed upon him? The Montagnards and the *Commune* demanded his head. The moderate Girondins hesitated, none more aware that the feelings of the majority in the provinces were different to those of volatile Paris: in spite of all the propaganda they retained an image of a crown at their head; found it impossible to envisage otherwise. This became the subject of fiery debate and party conflict. The Mountain set in motion all the machinery it could find, to intimidate the Convention. The *Palais-Royal* clubs were in uproar, crying for the 'tyrant's blood'. The ignorant of the populace were again taught to believe that the king's existence was, in some occult manner, responsible for the existing high prices, instabilities and continued famine.

Robespierre's party exerted every nerve to incite the Convention to execute the king. Exhibits of injured persons from the insurrection at Tuileries were brought in to the public gallery and the king accused of the most nefarious crimes. But worse: the discovery of an iron chest containing incriminating documents now sealed his fate.

Robespierre, master puppeteer, stood still and erect at the tribune. He paused until the noise of his puppets abated. Waited further: until total silence reigned. Only then did he speak.

"Louis declared war on the Glorious Revolution! He has been defeated! His life is forfeit. The only duty of the Constitution is to judge him here and now! *Il faut le condamner ser-le-champes à mort, en vertu d'une insurrection!*" He ceased abruptly, left the audience silent for a moment and waited. The cheering rose to the heights of the vaulted ceiling. He waited a further pregnant moment after the last sounds died into perfect silence, then continued: "Away with the moralistic prejudices of the old regime. A trial will merely be an opportunity for royalist propaganda! And remember: your primary duty is not to pronounce a sentence for or against this man but to ensure the public safety—to protect a nation—*from* this man's treasonable actions and possible future plans!"

He sat down again as the roar vibrated off the high ceiling once more. He smiled sardonically; it took so little to stir the mob.

Louis Lindet then stepped up to the tribune, for Robespierre was not the only contender to the dizzy heights of fame within the Convention and he had, after all, in his possession the report of the commission.

"The king's every step," he said, "has been in resistance to the Revolution. In '89 he tried to treat the Assembly as his predecessor had treated the *parlements*: until the fall of the Bastille drove him to dissemble. He has vetoed the charters of the Revolution: until the October 5th insurrection forced him to surrender. In '90 he still carried on counter-revolutionary intrigue through Mirabeau and Mirabeau's agents. In '91 he planned the flight to Varennes whilst professing fidelity to the Constitution... and his true aim of civil war was proved by the Brunswick manifesto. He encouraged counter-revolution at Avignon and Arles and used the Civil List to buy votes and finance the emigrants. In '92 he encouraged his ministers to neglect the army and navy, then assisted foreign invasion by vetoing the Paris camp; and, finally, he plotted to overthrow the very Constitution, previously used as a cover for his counterrevolutionary intrigues."

Lindet sat down amid further applause, almost equal to that offered Robespierre but had little time to bask before demands, of proof of his statements, were heard.

"My proof lies within the Iron Chest."

"Explain please; the Iron Chest," cried a voice from across the floor.

"The locked 'Iron Chest' full of incriminating documentation in the Monarch's hand, found in Louis' apartments at Tuileries. Believe me, there be plenty!"

At five o'clock the occupants of Temple were awakened by cannon fire across the gardens and the beat of drums. The *generale* was then heard, echoing around Paris. They had come to take Louis Caput.

The closed carriage stood rocking slightly, behind the restive horses waiting impatiently for the order to move out from the inner gates of the Temple prison, the coachman holding them firmly. "Watch that leader," he called to the postillion, "They are fresh this morning!"

"It be seven o'clock already... what keeps them?"

"Our passenger be not accustomed to early hours!" replied his superior cynically. "But he soon shall adjust. They all do. Had he the time, that is."

"You mean the *king*? We drive the king? Well I never did!"

"You shall address him as *Citizen* now. Do not be forgetting that. It be Robespierre's express order. We are all the same now; all equal in the eyes of the Republic."

"Does that mean I can wear fine clothes now? Buy a hat and cane and walk on the sidewalk?"

The coachman smiled cynically. "Should you be able to afford them... and can hold your own against the *new elite*... the newly wealthy." He ceased as the king exited the dark doorway and, closely escorted by seven guards, crossed the courtyard and entered the coach.

Louis sat back calmly in the dim interior, dressed in a plain olive silk coat and dun coloured breeches, and brought from an inner pocket a small volume of poetry, by the very new, young English poet, Wordsworth. With no idea where he was going, he simply waited, showing no surprise when they arrived at the Tuileries and he was ordered out.

The President of the Convention made his announcement. "Louis Caput, the French people have accused you of having committed various crimes to re-establish tyranny upon the ruins of liberty."

A long list of treasonable charges was read out, including the fleeing of the country, in order to return as conqueror and firing upon his people on three occasions. He bowed, mentally, now to his wife, as he listened calmly to the continuing list: she after all had been correct in her statement: 'They shall accuse you of firing first whether or no you do so!' But his conscience was at least clear: he had never fired upon Frenchmen or civilians.

He was questioned for nearly three hours at the bar of the House: the deputies reminded solemnly by the President that the eyes of Europe were upon them. They listened silently for once, while he put Louis to a series of questions based on Lindet's report; it in turn based on the Iron Chest information.

"Why oh why does he not dispute the Convention's competence to try him?" whispered Beaumont in de Quatreaux' ear.

"Charles of England did that; with rather poor results. No, he will skate."

"Look at him! He had no idea this was to take place. Or indeed any idea of the questions! He has no counsel to assist him. He is obviously totally unprepared. The heinous...!" Words failed him.

"What did you expect, *mon ami*, from this barbaric mob?" De Quatreaux' voice was low and vicious but not low enough. A neighbour glanced at him with interest.

Louis XVI of the Bourbon rule of France, now addressed as Louis Caput, sat patiently silent in his wooden chair. He asked for nothing at all: though the accusations were too long and involved for a simple, negative or affirmative response and time to consider denied him. His simplicity was disarming but those intimates that knew him well knew that his intelligent brain operated rapidly behind the placid features of his kindly face and myopic eyes.

"And now *Monsieur* Caput... your involvement with Mirabeau's counter-revolutionary intrigues, the details of which have just been outlined. What say you?"

"I have forgotten all about it. Indeed did hear something trivial by second hand information at the time I believe but was unaware of any intrigue."

"Oh I see. So the fifty or so notes despatched by Mirabeau to you every four or five days until mid-November '90 and then only a little less frequently until February '91, were a figment of our imaginations? You deny that these were kept in the Iron Chest?"

"What Iron Chest? I know of no Iron Chest."

"Come now! Do not waste our time. The Iron Chest found in your Tuileries apartments following your capture and confinement at Temple! The evidence found herein, of your intrigue against the Convention and the nation, is overwhelming. Even the constitutionalist Lafayette writes of his plans for your re-enthronement!"

"I have no knowledge of any chest, 'iron' or otherwise."

"Then you also deny these: your signatures? If you look closely you will see that indeed the whole is in your hand... is it not so?"

The sheaves of documents were handed to Louis. He took them in a steady hand, glanced briefly at them and then handed them back. "I have never seen them before."

"I see. Then let us move on by all means. We shall return to the Iron Chest, make no mistake. Now to the shedding of the blood of loyal Frenchmen: You deny that too I suppose?"

"Yes Monsieur, I do! I have never shed the blood of Frenchmen! The very fact that I have not; be evidenced by the outcome of every attack upon me at Versailles, Tuileries and many other occasions! Always, I ordered to hold fire, *because* Frenchmen were within range."

De Quatreaux and Beaumont watched as Louis pulled himself swiftly together again but it was evident to all, that this last injustice had wounded him deeply. He was asked a further myriad of questions and then taken from the House back to Temple. On his exit from the House it was eventually decided that he did after all warrant some sort of counsel to prepare his defence.

Louis chose two of the oldest and most distinguished members of the Paris bar, Guy-Jean-Baptiste Target, who declined on the grounds of age and infirmity, and Francois-Dennis Trounchet who did accept the onerous and extremely dangerous task. Marlesherbes offered his services in place of Target. The king had no lack of support, now that the emotional threat of Regicide appeared imminent. Many offers generated from beyond the frontier, even to the point of the Comte de Rofignat writing from Madrid to offer his life in the place of Louis'. That he was far enough distant, to make the offer, afforded the king some cynical amusement.

The avalanche of seditious and treasonable material collected against the king, soon caused a mountain of work too heavy for the two counsels. They invited the help of a younger man, Raymond-Romain, Comte de Sèze. The Comte was a Bordeaux barrister, known to secure the acquittal of royalists suffering beneath heavy charges of treason. He was to make the king's formal defence on the 26th December 1792: the king's, second and last appearance at the bar of the Convention.

Sèze now gazed at his king. "Your Majesty, the defence shall fall under two heads."

"And they are?" Louis sat in his cell-like quarters listening, neither interested nor disinterested, simply silently bemoaning the fact that the Queen had been prohibited from visiting him at all prior to the trial. Her more cunning and energetic brain, seeking every avenue possible for his acquittal, must be kept isolated from him. That she had her means of communicating with him secretly, was deeply suspected and an extra guard was placed outside both doors, the number of guards in the guard room next door now increased to forty at any one time. Every article was inspected for notes, every bread roll torn open, every piece of meat carved into tiny pieces, every container of wine poured and repoured, every serviette held up and studied against a strong light.

"One: the legal argument that your trial is definitely unconstitutional and the other; the historical argument to refute the charges brought against you, Sire."

The king smiled sardonically. "If you wish to keep your head upon your shoulders, do not call me 'Sire'. They call me Caput. Though why is beyond me; for though they be mine ancestors, a Caput has not been around for a very long time... mid 900's I believe."

"You shall always be my king, Sire, whatever they try to do and shall address you as such. Now, we have only ten days in which to do this so we must get through as much as possible, so that I may form your defence."

"Very well then, let us proceed—but let me say this: I will not allow any appeal to the emotions. That is for cowards: the truth and nothing but the truth, Sèze. Form our defence on the facts; which *be* the truth."

"But Sire, the legal system has nothing to *do* with truth... you *know* that."

"The facts: nothing but the facts, Sèze!"

Sèze swallowed a sigh and continued, "The first instance be that of your inviolability. You never did abdicate, under the terms defined by the constitution and therefore remain un-indictable. Now for them to say that you were judged by the nation on August 10th is insane! You did nothing more than defend yourself against armed insurrection, *with* the voluntary concurrence of the municipal and departmental authorities and the help of the National Guard. You also capitulated, in order to avoid bloodshed, before a shot had been fired. Also, if they wish you to be judged as a mere citizen, where are the forms of justice? The Convention is not a court! Your accusers cannot also be your judges! But it should not come to that, Sire, the August 10th incident was inspired by Danton, with the intention of using the attack on the Tuileries to draw your response of defence, and then blame you for the dead."

"And he succeeded."

"No Sire. He succeeded in twisting the truth of the event."

"Just so, Sèze, *mon ami.*"

It was the day following Christmas Day and the King's Counsel put forward a keen argument. When they had left the House along with the king, some deputies urged immediate verdict but the majority hesitated and voted for further consideration.

"You wait and you lose!" urged St-Just with heat. "Do you not see... they play for time!"

"But it be a weighty affair, Monsieur," responded another from across the floor. "We are judging the last king of the French... and as such the National Convention shall enter into the European fields of fame."

"Just so: let it be the sooner than later, before he slips through our fingers yet again!"

His opponent drew a sharp but controlled breath at this. "Then let there be no cause for a slur to be cast upon our good French name. The verdict must be just and *that* should take some deep considerations."

The Convention was persuaded: there now appeared no reason for the sudden hurry. The king was secure, as was their undeniable proof against him. This allowed Buzot to start a Girondin attempt to postpone a decision and to disown responsibility for it. He argued the point that in any settlement of a Monarchy, the country as a whole should be involved with the final outcome. De Quatreaux wondered that he did not call for a bowl of water and towel. A week of debate upon the use of a referendum ensued. The Girondins hoped, and the Jacobins feared, that a latent royalist uprising in the country would prevent the deputies to carry the trial to its now driven end.

♣

January 16<sup>th</sup> 1793 dawned cold and crisp and Angelique shivered at the lack of heat from the half-hearted fire in the dining-hall. It was only seven o'clock and had been lit but a short while. She turned to de Quatreaux at the breakfast table. "You go to the Convention today, *Mon Père*?"

He glanced up from the carving of his ham. "If I do not then my name shall be posted, yet again." He smiled grimly with ironically raised brows. "Yes, I shall go; and attend another farcical hearing."

"What did they decide yesterday?" asked the Comtesse Bayette.

"To vote today: on Louis' guilt or innocence. Next: on the decision whether or not to refer that decision to the people... and last but not of course least; that exciting, stimulating feature of the whole affair: the punishment of Louis."

"The votes?" murmured Marie softly. "Any security there... a show of hands perhaps?"

De Quatreaux laughed suddenly. "Should we be so lucky as to strike such good fortune. No, my cousin, vote is to be given, by each individual, aloud from the tribune *and* his reasons for his decision. Each voter is to be registered and his vote recorded of course."

"I see, and if one was absent?"

"Then it be expected in writing."

Angelique tried to hide her anxiety as she asked, "And if one is beyond the frontier?"

He smiled very gently. "*Mon enfant*, those beyond the border are all considered treasonable, regardless of their reasons. But Emile shall be safe... as will Trifane. Their names did not cross the frontier."

"And support for Marie-Antoinette? Could I er... go to her do you think?"

He gazed at her in perfect stillness. "*Ma fille*; I credit you with more sense than to even ask such a foolish question. The barriers are closed by the *Commune* for the voting anyway; Roland is almost hysterical about the issue."

"He suspects another massacre?"

"Yes *mon enfant* and so you, all of you, shall remain here and close to the panel and the tunnel. If necessary you all go to Craufurd's house. For such reason Madame Bayette stayed with us last night. Should a raid on nobles' homes commence, following judgement on Louis; you go. You do not wait for me. All be in readiness. Do I make myself clear?"

"Yes Seigneur!"

The Convention pronounced the king guilty of treason against the nation. Of the 721 deputies, 361 voted immediate death penalty, 72 for death but with demand for a delay of execution, 288 for imprisonment or banishment. The 361 votes for immediate death were in the majority by one and the voting did indeed take place aloud and at the tribune. The procedure began at eight o'clock on the evening of the sixteenth and lasted until the same hour of the seventeenth, the galleries and corridors of the House occupied throughout by armed adherents of the Jacobin-led *Commune*.

The public galleries were now crammed with foreigners, sightseers and people of every class. A constant flow of ices and sweat-meats, wine and liqueurs supplied the ladies and gentlemen there: all conversing in social fashion, some counting the votes by pricking cards with hat pins, or knotting threads as they crocheted or created lacework.

Tired deputies, who had been at the Convention since eight o'clock on the morning of the 16th had to be woken to vote and did so at last; and scrutineers could be seen slipping away a vote here and there, scrubbing out one here and there. The neighbouring coffee houses were taking bets and the scene throughout Paris was one of general entertainment.

Much more was at stake, however, than the mere life of a deposed king. The outcome would determine the immediate fortunes of the two political parties and the ultimate fate of the seven hundred or so voters, for years to come. A fresh and final vote was taken two days later and the majority was swollen by 60: for immediate death.

Louis heard, on the afternoon of the 20th January, that his execution was fixed for the next day. It was Marlesherbes, the loyal and devoted member of the King's Counsel, who delivered the news, meeting and telling first Hanet Clery, who fell back in shock. But the king heard with calmness and resignation, with no feelings of resentment or hatred, these emotions amply supplied by his furious and impotent wife, though her face too, was impassive when she heard the news. The news that the Duke of Orleans, now Phillippe Egalité, had voted death did however have an effect on Louis.

"Sire, we may yet come about. Let me rally a party and get you and your family out of here for the last time," said Marlesherbes.

"No *mon ami*, you are to be commended but such a move would compromise too many people and begin a civil war in France. No. This way they have what they have wanted for so long and only one dies."

The king did however request three days in which to say goodbye to his family and prepare for death.

The reply was firmly negative. "I am sorry, Monsieur Caput, but the extra time be not allowed: to say goodbye to your family certainly, under guard of course."

The king sent for his sister's confessor, the abbé Edgeworth de Firmont, a non-juror priest of Irish origin and prepared for immediate death. That night he said goodbye to his wife and children and told them to forgive their enemies, just as he had. The king and queen maintained a cool and calm exterior: heads held high in the presence of their enemies. Time enough for tears later, in the darkest of night, after the ordeal was over.

At six o'clock on the morning of Tuesday January 21st 1793, the king received communion from the abbé. Following this he sat in silence and tranquillity, much to the amazement, curiosity and of some—those guards that did not understand such emotional control—an impotent fury. At eight hours thirty minutes, he left Temple in a closed carriage, surrounded by troops, with Santerre on horseback, at the head of the convoy. Armed citizens drawn up along the sides of the road, two deep, prevented any attempt at rescue during the two and a half mile journey to the Place de la Révolution, previously Place de la Louis XV, where the guillotine now stood.

The constant beating of drums drowned any sympathetic cries and also the distraught voice of the Baron de Batz who, with a small group of royalists, called for volunteers to save the king as the carriage turned the corner of the Rue Saint-Dennis.

"*A nous, ceux qui veulent sauver le Roi!*" he cried, in frenzy now of anger and grief but the drums continued and the crowd watched as the carriage rolled forward. The Marquis de la Tour du Pin and his wife, along with other royalists, waited in vain for sounds of musketry fire that meant his Majesty's rescue.

A thick, cold, early-morning mist still hung over the Place de la Revolution and troops could be seen, through its gently swirling lighter patches surrounding the newly erected guillotine. Behind them a great crowd of Parisians waited, upon piles of leftover builder's materials and the terraces of the Tuileries gardens. Whole families waited, mothers and grandmothers and their children, some young enough to be still in swaddling cloths.

The carriage pulled in close to the steps and then remained still. So too did the crowd. There was silence. The crowd stood in perfect stillness. Louis spent his last five minutes in prayer and then descended from the carriage, took Edgeworth's arm and mounted the steps to the scaffold.

The drummers continued in rhythm but when Louis reached the scaffold he signed them to cease their drumming and said in a loud voice: "*Peuple, je meurs innocent!*"

The drums, at a swift sign from Santerre, beat again but the men who pinioned him heard him add, "I hope that my blood may secure the happiness of the French people!"

A moment later he was swung forward; the blade fell and the executioner held up his dripping, severed head for the crowd to witness. The ethereal silence of awe continued a moment; then a roar suddenly went up, amid shouts of '*Vive la Nation!*' Pandemonium broke loose and the guards struggled in fear and panic, to control the mob. Sitting at a small table to the side, an official noted the time: ten hours twenty-two minutes on the twenty-first day of January, seventeen hundred and ninety three. He looked at the words as the black ink dried, then placed a careful full-stop after the 'three': a full stop to the monarchy of France.  This then was it—the end of a thousand years of history; perhaps several thousand, he did not know precisely. He shook his head: it was too much to absorb, in reality.

There was little more to the scene, other than the obscene sale of his three-cornered hat with the tri-colour badge, auctioned from the scaffold. His hair and ribbons were sold by the headsman's assistant, as was his brown coat with the blue enamel buttons divided and distributed to the crowd.  All manner of artefacts were dipped in his blood as many danced around the guillotine singing the *Marseillaise*.

De Quatreaux stayed a moment only, nauseated by the scene before him. He gazed at the beheading machine and wondered how many more were to go beneath its blade. He glanced around and understood just why Robespierre had suggested this enormous square for the event: nothing beat it for spectacle; the large amount of space catering for a splendid audience. He smiled cynically at how far the man would go to keep the sans-culottes on the boil, then turned his horse and rode back to the Rue Saint-Honoré.  His face remained impassive but he could not eat dinner that night.

Louis was buried in the cemetery of the Madeleine on the same day as his execution.  The grave was dug to a depth of ten feet. Nothing could now resurrect a Bourbon King to the old French throne.

# CHAPTER NINETEEN

## Treachery and Arrest

Plots now abounded to rescue the remaining royal family and assistance was offered from within Paris, the Provinces and across the seas by émigrés and sympathetic foreigners. Prominent among these was Count Fersen and no small number of concerned English aristocrats.

Within France, many stomachs were turned by the regicide. Escape plans for the Queen were devised, in particular by Francois-Adrien Toulon and the royalist Chevalier de Jarjayes. Toulon, defence veteran of the storming of the Tuileries, planned with the help of the guard Jacques Lepitre, in charge of passports and barrier passes. Others offered to rescue the family separately, the children first: dressed as filthy street urchins, blackened sweeps' or lamplighters' assistants or white flour covered bakers' child-labourers. But Marie-Antoinette would not agree to any separation and so this and several other imaginative plans were abandoned. Count Fersen hoped fervently that the queen would not bow to fate, as had her husband, raised and nurtured in the old beliefs: that of the inescapable duty of a king or queen to suffer for his or her people.

In England, Lady Cowper continued her long campaign of financial support for the rescue of the royals. Lady Charlotte Atkins contacted royalist supporters and made arrangements to travel to France to visit the queen. General Francois Dumouriez planned a march on Paris and the proclamation of Louis XVII as king. Learning of these efforts, Hébert fumed within his columns, that France was as yet not safe and liberty be threatened until they, the royal family, all lay dead, his *Père Duchesne* devoting many pages to the issue.

European Monarchs now formed a coalition, joining the Austrians and Prussians against France. Aligned against France, now, were England, Spain, Russia, Netherlands and Sardinia. The French armies were forced to retreat as Austria overran Belgium, France's position collapsed in the Netherlands; and the Spanish invaded France from the south. The regicide had not been the Revolutionaries' best move.

Within France trouble again brewed in the Vendee, a strong Catholic region south west of the Loire, where forced conscription to the Revolutionary Army stirred a brutal royalist uprising, causing counter-revolutionary centres to spread rapidly. Growing food shortages and inflation prompted street rioting and Danton, author of the August 10th insurrection at Tuileries, now organized the creation of a special court with powers to try the political prisoners: the royalist sympathizers. Named the *Revolutionary Tribunal*, created March 10<sup>th</sup> 1793, this became a key instrument of the Terror.

"*Another* Terror?" exclaimed Marie, eyes locked on the *Père Duchesne* before her.

"No, no, my cousin, a continuing one," murmured Angelique, lowering her letter a moment and glancing up at Marie. "And Rochelle says here in her letter... now where was it..." She rustled the stiff parchment and peered at the fine print crossing and re-crossing the page. "...ah here it is: 'Pitt asks in parliament: is there any left to kill? The French have surpassed themselves this time!' And she goes on to say that 'as early as the news of August 10<sup>th</sup> Lord Gower, the English Ambassador, was recalled from Paris, and the new ministry of the French Legislative Assembly not recognized in Whitehall.' Did *mon père* say anything about that?"

"I do not remember. He tells so much that is amusing but of course keeps the most worrying aspects to himself. So thoughtful! But I do remember that the invasion of Holland would reveal an even richer bank than England."

"I do not call the withholding of vital information thoughtful, Marie; knowledge is armour. But all war is about money, Marie. Your bids for freedom, religious differences, liberations, old grudges between monarchs and such-like, be the foundation upon which they lay their excuses."

"But Cambon actually *states*," Marie poked at the paper with an angry finger, "that this is to be a 'Money War' and is now busy issuing more *Assignats* to pay for it."

"Well, I do hope that his investment be justified and that he can live with the fact of the growing number of dead soldiers!" Angelique frowned over the letter. "The English ambassador has been recalled. That be not so vital I suppose, as is not the fact that the horrid, oily French ambassador, the Marquis de Chauvelin was rapidly despatched from England, by an Order in Council on the news of Louis' death. Rochelle adds that 'here too he was well disliked and nobody listened to him'; I do not blame them! She goes on—'the ex-bishop of Autun, Talleyrand, has settled in London and continually bemoans his ex-communication and abandonment by his own family both sides of the channel.' Well, well! He did, after all, propose the nationalization of Church property back in '89! And she adds that with her 'poor but added input to the English font of knowledge of events French, the ladies of London, indeed much of England, are redoubling their efforts to raise funds for the rescue of the French royal family and aristocracy'. Goodness, she *has* been busy."

"Nothing of their war with us... I suppose that she must be cautious."

"Oh no, that does not seem evident, but this missive be old; held up I suppose by the ravaged towns and villages; indeed we must consider ourselves lucky to have received it at all. She only mentions the old news: that Spain, Portugal, the Empire and most of the Italian States were rumoured to have joined the coalition," replied Angelique. "But if she knows of Louis' death then she must know by now, that the Convention declared war on England and Holland immediately following its controversial decree; effecting the union of Belgium with France, in February. She does say that...'as Europe finally broke off diplomatic relations with France following the imprisonment of the king at Temple... they be even more adamant now, in the face of regicide, therefore an ever-strengthening coalition against France be inevitable and of course London has long since armed, equipped and paid much toward the coalition'." She paused again, frowned and then continued, "'And along with the Prince of Coburg they cannot lose. He is a brilliant strategist.' "

Marie sighed, laid aside the paper and took up her embroidery frame. "All this war. Is not the ridiculous Revolution enough? I suppose that is *why* they all jump on the bandwagon!"

A light tap at the door and Henri entered to announce Monsieur Pontisqieu. He bowed low to the ladies and took Angelique's hand as she moved forward in greeting, pleasure lighting up her face. "But Monsieur, what a surprise, you do relieve a monotonous day. We can still not go out quite safely, much to our irritation."

"Mademoiselle Vermont." He kissed then released her hand and accepted the chair, following Marie's acknowledgement. "You be as well to contain your irritation, for such conditions go on, in fact from bad to worse if I may say so. Please do not be tempted to travel the streets."

"But Monsieur, one would surely be forgiven for thinking all is over now, now that the king be gone and they have what they wanted? Not so?"

"Absolutely *not* so Mademoiselle... but you jest and I have come on a matter of some urgency to the Comte. Be he available to visitors this morning?"

Angelique looked her concern suddenly. "But no Monsieur, he is out at this moment; in fact, I do not know when he returns. Mayhap I can be of help?"

He glanced at Marie and she rose gracefully from her position by the window, shook out her skirts and made her excuses. Within a second of the door closing behind her Henri-Marie turned urgently to Angelique. "I know, of course, that I may trust you..."

"Ah, but you should not... not *anyone*... *mon père* is adamant about that; also Trifane. Does your message have anything to do with him?" she ended casually.

He smiled, hiding his own pain, for his feelings for her now ran deep. Trifane, of course, held her heart. She would be surprised, he knew, at his knowledge of this fact. His sadness deepened as he gazed at her, for his lack of birth placed her beyond his reach anyway, even had she feelings for him also. It was as well that there was pain on only one side he supposed. He shook his head now, saying gently, "No... but I do know that he shall return very soon; perhaps as early as tomorrow," and at her sudden look of concern, "It be quite safe at the moment; the war front takes all their attention. Besides, he is not a returning émigré but simply a returning traveller under another name. However, there are plans; and it be those that I wish to impart to de Quatreaux."

"Please, you may safely give me the missive."

"I know that but do not place anything in the written word these days, Mademoiselle," glancing at her desk, scattered with parchment and the new issue of thick paper.

She laughed. "Those are the mere, inferior, scribbled attempts of a poetic female, Monsieur."

"Beware their content, please Mademoiselle. They can read what they want into a household list of duties… or a grocery list. Your laundry record could get you executed!"

"They? You mean Robespierre? He is rising fast now: 'twas he that pushed the *Revolutionary Tribunal* and now the *Committee of Public Safety*."

"Yes… and St-Just and Couthon."

"The diabolical threesome: bringing down the Girondins!"

"Ah yes, they and …" He paused, hating to cause her added stress.

"Lareaux!"

"Ah, I did not quite know how deeply you held him in suspect, but yes, he is deep in there with them. I suspect that he be the culprit to supply de Quatreaux' name on the list."

"But *mon père* has always known his name to be up there with the recalcitrant nobility."

"This is Robespierre's list containing the names for immediate arrest. The names upon which they work incessantly to search out, or manufacture, proof of treasonable actions. I do not wish to distress you, but you should know that in every department property is being confiscated, people imprisoned and lives taken, in enormous numbers now, to fill the coffers! I beg pardon Mademoiselle, for speaking plain truth."

She stared at him, a sudden cold shiver travelling the length of her spine. "I do thank you for it, Monsieur Pontisqieu. That those in authority make use of such power for… for outright *theft*… is not new of course, but this collection of Machiavellian individuals are feasting on the carcase of their only support: their *country* and yes; our wealth. How have we come to this?"

"I suppose how it happened be complicated and a moot point now. It is more to the point to plan ways to combat such, as we feel the power enjoyed by the tyrant."

"Which tyrant?"

He smiled grimly. "Ah yes, not just Robespierre but also those of Saint-Just's calibre: taking all that he can, even ordering the municipal officers to take the very boots off the feet of the aristocrats. In Alsace, he took all Revolutionary Army supplies from the citizens of Strasburg. Although to be fair he also obtained state grants for the embellishment of Clermont, his native town certainly, and established a manufacturing factory of arms to give employment to destitute workmen. He is a rare breed of honesty and integrity; though severe to the point of pure fanaticism: where just as many shall die of course, for he calls for the execution of everyone that opposes the Republic."

"Yes, Monsieur Pontisqieu, these people reach far beyond those acting on impulse of mere greed: such as the *deputies en mission*, enriching themselves through their agents."

"But we digress, Mademoiselle; I came in search of de Quatreaux."

"But I do not know just where *mon père* be… oh, I do wish he would trust me more."

"Mademoiselle, I think that it be not a matter of trust but that of security."

"That is the same thing surely."

"No. I mean your security. If you know nothing then…"

"Then I am safe. I can look after myself, thank you very much."

He laughed suddenly. "Oh yes. But one small silver-mounted pistol is not sufficient protection against this mob. They deal in paper; paper bearing false witness to fake crimes!"

"You heard of my, er... altercation with Lareaux?"

"Oh yes and he, of all people, will not tolerate being a laughing stock: to be held off, indeed shot, by a woman! That is intolerable. Have a care there, please, Madame."

She smiled suddenly. "But Monsieur, to shoot him was the only thing to do. I only now wish that I had killed him."

"Then you would definitely be confined in the *Conciergerie* or *La Force*... not at the time, for it would have been viewed as self defence, but now they would slate it as murder."

She laughed it off with a jest. "Tell me, which be the better one; I believe that only the *Abbaye* allows prisoners to lie on mattresses, of only one truss of old hay certainly, but they also have no more than six to a cell... not so?"

"They are also allowed with their *soupe et bouilli,* a quart of wine per day. But you do not have a say in where you go."

"I suppose not, but they say the *Châtelet* be the one dreaded by the most hardened criminals. And five hundred persons crowded into rooms for half that number with not even straw to lie on. I suppose, on the bright side; the vermin are denied refuge."

"Mademoiselle, please be serious: the nine principle prisons are filled to the maximum again but still the public is not satisfied. Several Sections are demanding quicker executions."

"Oh, but I am serious... deadly! But what can be quicker than the guillotine?"

He frowned, then, "Another guillotine?"

She smiled. "Well, at least it is the method of execution with no stigma of dishonour."

"Ah yes, decapitation: once the monopoly of the nobility; regarded as a privilege... but now the right of the humblest *citoyen*."

"Ugh." Angelique instinctively placed a hand upon the back of her neck. "I cannot reconcile to this barbarous practice." She shivered suddenly. "It must be horrendous!"

He gazed at her a moment: a gentleman did not discuss matters causing a lady any discomfort but times were different now: knowledge was armour. "But no, rest assured," he said gently. "That style of death be instantaneous and painless, they say."

"Quote whom? Whom hath returned?" her tone was scathing.

"Those that have witnessed the executions say that the victims' faces bear no expressions of pain, only surprise, that is after the, er..."

"Their head departs from their shoulders! I still say the guillotine be barbaric. And Robespierre and his *Revolutionary Tribunal* will not allow it to grow rusty!"

"And another Committee: that of *General Security* now assists him in that duty."

"General; does that mean just what I think it means?"

"Devised for the detection of political crimes, and like the *Tribunal Extraordinaire*, it will exploit the people with only 'generalized' and 'circumstantial' evidence... and to convict with no appeal.  But the new *Law of Suspected Persons*, enforced by the *Revolutionary Tribunal*, is to be the more feared."

"But by whom?"

"The nobility, if they are wise. Urged on by the *Commune*..."

"Robespierre!"

"That's the one... the Convention is at this moment passing a vaguely worded law further empowering the *Revolutionary Committees* throughout France to imprison all nobles, relations of emigrants, federalists and other persons 'suspected' of ill-will towards the Republic. This one be the Grand Master of them all... any man or woman who, by conduct or even a look, expresses disapproval of the existing order, shall be cast into prison and consequently executed.  But worse: all persons bearing names of representatives of the 'past,' especially courtiers of Versailles, shall be automatically taken up. The choking of the entire scheme is slowing the process but it *is* proceeding: systematically."

"But that refers to us all!"

"Precisely... the legacy of the August 10<sup>th</sup> insurrection... is dictatorship by the *Commune*.  People do not seem to give this the attention that it deserves."

"*Mon Dieu* and I was beginning to think that it could grow no worse." She put her hands to her cheeks and stared down into the momentarily quiet street below and then, dropping them to her sides again, suddenly paled. "I do believe that they can round up the likes of us on at least two, even three, counts. And *mon père*... so openly anti-revolutionary!"

He gazed at her in deep compassion. "Four: your titles, your estates, relationship with emigrants and past connections with the royal family. And as to your *père*: they cannot wait to get hold of him. He must be warned. Of his friends, whom do you trust most?  I do not know how soon they plan to move but it cannot be far away... mayhap a sennight to two weeks. And I must leave tonight for the country. A client about to hang needs me."

"Then you must indeed go to him. Beaumont: he be his oldest friend." She stood and held out her hands. "Thank you so much Monsieur Pontisqieu. I must get my cloak and go to Beaumont's hôtel now."

"No, you must not: I shall do that for you.  If you assure me that Beaumont can be trusted then it is he that I find; this morning if possible. Please, stay safe."

Beaumont nodded goodbye to Pontisqieu, as that man bowed himself out in the wake of the butler and then sat again, sprawled out in his chair, glass in hand, his thoughts far away.  He could not however maintain this posture, every nerve jumping within his body. To kill further agitation, he left his residence for one of the select gaming houses still defiantly operating, where he at least could lose himself in deep play. He knew that de Quatreaux be absent from Paris at this moment but in deep caution he chose a gaming house less frequented by his friend.  He flinched at the term 'friend' but could not escape his thoughts. Where did loyalty and ethics cross the line? At the absolute mid-line, where honesty meets dishonesty? Loyalty meets disloyalty? But the luxury of choice was not his: the survival of one's family overrode that of a friend.  That he had already known the information supplied by Pontisqieu had been pushed deep out of sight: that man's visit serving only to heighten his guilt.

At the entrance of La Coste, he met Montmaire just divesting his coat and together they entered the gaming room.  Following in the wake of the new young page, they entered the room and he saw Du Toit and also de Quatreaux, already deep in game. Startled, he paused, just a moment.

"Hail Beaumont, Montmaire," said Du Toit cheerfully, as he spread the cards but then took them up again to reshuffle. "Just in time for play."

"Yves...Dominique," nodded de Quatreaux with a friendly smile as they stood to greet the newcomers. They settled again and de Quatreax unfobbed his emerald-studded snuffbox and offered it around. This accomplished, he leaned back and continued, "Any new news on the war front, Messieurs?"

"Dumouriez be in deep trouble," supplied Yves Beaumont, his voice steady and cool.

"Ah, but that had to be, did it not? After all, he returned from Holland resolved to break with the Convention; irritated with that body for not pursuing his advocacy of creating Belgium a separate state," replied de Quatreaux, studying his hand closely.

"But his expected victory against the Austrians," said Montmaire; "did not occur."

"So he cannot now dictate his own terms to the Convention and mediate between France and the allies, his plans all blown out of the water!"

"Defeat tends to do that to one, *mon ami*," replied Beaumont, managing now a casual indifference. "His first mistake, of course, following his defeat in Holland, was to offer Coburg, in negotiation, to march to Paris and place the Dauphin on the throne."

De Quatreaux stared suddenly. "In exchange for what?"

"Material support and, as a pledge of good faith, he was prepared to admit Austrian troops into Lille and Valenciennes, on condition that the towns were restored to France on the making of peace," replied Beaumont.

"Optimistic. And then?"

"The Convention, who had always mistrusted him, sent four deputies to summon him to Paris and he immediately gave them up to the enemy Coburg; as hostages for the safety of the Royal family!"

"You jest," laughed Du Toit now.

"Not at all *mon ami* but he underestimated his own rabble soldiers. They are strong revolutionaries and refused to betray France to Austria.  He in turn, had to run... and take refuge in enemy quarters: Coburg's."  Beaumont leaned casually back in his chair and surveyed the company, then turned as Montmaire spoke seriously.

"Dumouriez' treachery has sent the country into deeper violence of party struggle. The Girondins and Montagnards are accusing each other of being his accomplice."

"Danton is the culprit," said Beaumont now.

"You deem it so?" asked Du Toit.

"The grapevine says so! *And* that he plotted with Dumouriez, for the restoration of the throne. Bribed by Louis, and he misapplied public money and ordered the plunder of state property in Belgium."

"But Danton *could* not have calmly accepted these accusations," said Montmaire, "Though they *are* probably true."

"Oh no, he ranted and raved in counter-attack until Robespierre came in to rescue him with an entire list of worse crimes directed by the Girondins: against liberty and the Republic, ending in a suggestion that they send before the new criminal court Brissot, Vergniaud, Gaudet and Marie-Antoinette and of course the Duc d'Orleans."

"Then it is time to move to Lyon and such places," said Du Toit. "The Girondins there, so I hear, formed anti-Jacobin clubs. When *they* were closed they organized an attack on the Town Hall. Four hundred fell but the point is: they remained the victors."

"But the Jacobin revenge ran with speed and efficiency," grunted Montmaire. "Had to use the firing squad as well as the guillotine, trying twenty Girondin prisoners per hour. Not such a victory after all!"

De Quatreaux leaned back in his chair, rubbing the back of his neck theatrically. "Why do you think that most of us try hard to not attend the Convention these days, *mon ami*?" he said softly.

"You are willing for your name to be documented?"

"Of no use whatsoever trying to avoid it," replied de Quatreaux in a bored voice.

Beaumont felt a sudden chill and moved a little in his chair and then ceased as his old friend turned his head and bent an unexpectedly penetrating gaze upon him, eyebrows raised, and said softly, "A worry *mon ami*?"

"What? No, oh no, Vermont," he managed a laugh. "None more than usual, in this political clime: enough to make a saint nervous!"

De Quatreaux cast him a look of mild enquiry at the alien note in the laugh and then returned to his hand of cards. He cast one down and then lifted his head at the sound of his oldest friend but one, de Vries, from behind him. "How be your luck this evening Jean-Pierre?"

"Wearisome," replied de Quatreaux with a smile and moved to rise but de Vries pressed a hand upon his shoulder.

"No my friend, do not get up."

They settled once more and de Quatreaux lifted one finger slightly to the attendant footman and ordered more wine. It duly arrived and a glass was poured by a nervous page attending the footman and offered to de Quatreaux.

Without looking up de Quatreaux pointed to his new guest and the page bowed and begged pardon, offered the glass to de Vries and then refilled the rest of the glasses in order of importance, offering the last glass to de Quatreaux, the evident host. He stood back, holding his breath but no further rebuke followed. De Quatreaux even smiled his approval at the speedy correction and he beamed at his success. Slowly he was beginning to recognize the hierarchy of rank amongst the patrons of La Coste, listing off lengthy titles and giving them faces as he drifted off to sleep each night. He liked his job and refused to listen to his rabblerousing older brother. Of a certainty, there would not be the generous 'tips' from the new regime. And the man de Quatreaux he liked a lot: his backside and job saved by that man's intervention one evening some months previously. But it was more than that, the man de Quatreaux did not patronize; simply expected the closest one could get to perfection of service, as he himself strived to give, in his own life. These thoughts the page kept to himself: as with his juvenile political opinions: not that he knew much about it; except that it appeared prudent to walk the ever thinning line, poised to fall either way. A sharp mind and nimble feet: that was the thing to polish.

"You have just vacated Madame Vissauds' salon, Marc?" asked Du Toit, of de Vries who had lounged back in his chair declining a hand and all set to watch the game, then laughed. "There to gaze upon the new beauty of the Parisian salons?"

"Be a relief against the endless talk of war and politics I be thinking," de Quatreaux chuckled. "Of the new release of debutantes is she not... another declining tradition!"

"But yes... if you could but behold; the lady is *ravissante*," laughed Beaumont.

"Ah but I behold this card instead... and win," smiled de Quatreaux.

The game was at an end and Du Toit, one of the longest at table, yawned and pushed back his chair. "Tis enough for me, my friends. What of you, Jean-Pierre?"

His friend sat gazing with hooded eyes at apparently no person in particular but in reality he was scrutinising Beaumont: the man was uneasy. He sat a moment, toying with his dice box, then replied, "I think I may remain yet awhile. I have not seen Beaumont for a sennight or more. What say you Yves? Will you hazard a throw with me?"

Thus addressed, Beaumont could say no other than, "Aye... what you will. You throw?"

They played thus for a short time and then Beaumont, feigning tiredness also left the company, leaving Montmaire, de Vries and de Quatreaux to drink and continue play until the early hours of the next day. Beaumont also drank through the night: alone.

♣

Robespierre leaned against his wide solid desk; arms folded and surveyed Beaumont. "You are sure of this?"

Beaumont's dry mouth stretched into a smile but his eyes remained cold. "As sure as you of Danton's involvement. And I can add to that one's treachery; with proof of the spending, upon his private person, more than 27,000 livre of monies entrusted to him as Minister of Justice."

Lareaux turned from surveying the street below and gazed at Beaumont a moment and then at Robespierre. "I can back up that story... and that he is paid as a secret agent of the English government. He and Delacroix are believed to be the two real leaders of the new conspiracy to overthrow the Jacobins' monopoly of power."

"I was not aware that we discuss Danton," replied Robespierre in chilly, dulcet tones. "So let us return to de Quatreaux. Tell me again; are you able to furnish proof?"

"Dumouriez' letter mention's the gold from Louis via de Qautreaux... to support the new émigrés army," replied Lareaux, squirming beneath the rebuke.

"But is his *signature* there?" Robespierre gazed now at Lareaux in some contempt and that man coloured a little under the scrutiny, hiding his building fury. At least he was an open enemy of de Quatreaux and at last he had found a way to defeat and humiliate that enemy—and to gain his property into the bargain. This had been part of the deal. He had spent months and a small fortune in bribes searching endlessly for treasonable proof against his hated enemy and it had paid off, securing him a paper carrying power far beyond a mere birth certificate. But he wondered at the treachery of Beaumont: a supposed longstanding friend. Lareaux felt a silent scorn toward him: he could inflict pain on others, particularly women, in complete indifference and could annihilate an enemy—but never a friend.

"It is there Monsieur *and* on documents regarding forged *assignats*: by Calonne, operating out of Coblenz."

"Not Monsieur...'*Citizen*'! Get them for me."

"The letter *and* the documents, Mon, er... Citizen?"

"I own a severe aversion to having to repeat myself, Lareaux," replied Robespierre in acid tones; then, "I must have proof of his treason. He must be executed... first; then his family and associates."

He reached out and struck a bell. Within a second, no more, the attendant from without entered and stood silently awaiting orders.

"Go you now, send the chief of night watch," he paused, "with two security coaches and five... no, nine guards... to the end of the Rue Saint-Honoré, at the junction of," he paused again and turned to Beaumont, "he is still at the gaming house, La Coste, no?" and as that man nodded, "But if he be, upon subtle enquiry, left that establishment then they are to wait close by his hôtel and take him up there. He may return to one of his friends' hôtels of course... those of De Vires or Montmaire but *do not* go there. Wait close to Hôtel Quatreaux. Tell him to wait until dawn if necessary."

Panic now pounded within Beaumont's breast but the deed was done. Robespierre completed his orders for the capture and incarceration of Jean-Pierre Vermont, Comte de Quatreaux, under the *Law of Suspect*. The two wary companions in intrigue gazed at Robespierre and each suddenly felt the implacability of that man's total lack of emotion; knew that no one was safe from his power.

"Er... Citizen Robespierre; surely not his daughter," said Lareaux desperately.

Robespierre turned and bent his flat, emotionless gaze upon him. "Especially his daughter."

"But Citizen, she has done nothing, knows *nothing* of de Quatreaux' intrigues!"

"You will do well to calm those nerves, Citizen; and your passion. She is female. They breed. The daughter goes." He turned his back on them and moved behind his desk, frowning a little, then glanced up again at Lareaux, his expression one of cool contempt. "However, bring me *Trifane* and we *may* re-examine the matter of the daughter. You have material on him also?"

"Yes, of forgery, bribery and smuggling gold and silver out of the country. Also that of plotting: with the English spy to cause the rate of exchange to rise: to 200 *livre* per pound sterling."

"To discredit the *assignat* as much as possible; yes, I heard, but do you have proof of this connivance?"

"No Citizen, but I do have such of his joining M.de la Colombe... Lafayette's ex-aide-de-camp... in raising an army in the Auvergne, and to join in the fight for the restoration of the French Monarchy."

Robespierre stared at him for a moment. "Produce it."

He turned away from them, moving behind his desk and sat, pulling some papers before him. They were effectively dismissed and Beaumont suddenly felt himself to have a foot on either side of a separating iceberg. He controlled a shudder with difficulty, suddenly aware that selling one's soul to save one's family, and property, may not gain a lasting immunity. He shook his head at Lareaux who was about to speak again and guided that man out of the room and on to the street below.

They walked a brief period in company, although Beaumont could hardly be accused of being 'company' as they silently trod the slippery cobbled street. His mind ran over and over the same old route, never finding an answer, for there *was* no answer from within the clutches of a blackmailer. He had searched long and hard for anything; or anyone that may have known Robespierre in his past. And although the search for such a person was not difficult, to find embarrassing or incriminating evidence of any misdemeanours of that man, proved negative. Indeed, any information that may turn the tables proved illusive. The man really was a paragon of virtue: of the type that could order genocide in the name of God, or simple purification of the sunken, debauched country, that was France: as perceived by him. He sighed at the puritan cult that was Jacobinism and parted from Lareaux with a curt nod.

♣

Jean-Pierre pushed back into his chair and stretched; then, having drained his glass, looked across at his old friend. "It has been a long and enjoyable night, Marc, but here I must depart. Thank you for your hospitable company and pleasurable beverages."

"But the pleasure is all mine, *mon ami*. La Coste is enjoyable but no place, any longer, for private discussion and I feel that the time is approaching when each other's hôtels shall be the only venue for our gaming pursuits. Point of fact: the gaming houses have been dwindling for some time now."

"It appears that way, but I'll be damned if I will allow them to tie me to my home like a woman, Marc. I thoroughly agreed with the public protest by Desmoulin against police involvement in gambling affairs and venues."

"Ah, but even *his* amazing oratory failed. Robespierre shall destroy him, mark my words: he grows too clever by far. But *you, mon ami*: your stubbornness could be the death of you, my old friend... and lose you I will not! Do have a care."

De Quatreaux merely smiled, waiting.

Marc gazed at him a moment in uncertainty.

"Do open your budget *mon cher*! We know each other too well and too long not to do so!"

"Well, you should know that my wife's assault on the *Committee of Public Safety* has rendered her almost a Suspected Person." He paused at the raised brows. "Yes, my Claudette! She was warned. And, my pardon *mon ami*, but the tongue of your daughter also; be heard in the radical circles. It would be better that she was not quite so intelligent, but there you are... you get what you get."

De Quatreaux stared a moment then smiled grimly. "It appears that my instructions often go out the window: shall be amended!"

Marc shuddered suddenly, for Angelique, then, "Their power is strengthening, by the by, *mon ami.*"

"The C.P.S.? Yes I know: the original Girondin members all gone; the extreme Montagnards dominate every avenue of power now. The deputies have sunk into the position of nothing more than chief clerks of their respective Departments: while the *Committee of Public Safety* stands at the head of the executive government."

"And the *Committee of General Security*, for detection of political crime, have replaced, since the king's death, all 12 Girondins by 12 Montagnards."

"Their eternal struggle for supremacy becomes wearisome! But now, it grows late. I depart." Jean-Pierre rose and stretched his long, indolent body.

De Vries stood. "But you do not walk alone, surely? Allow me to call my carriage."

"*Mon ami*, we walked to here, from La Coste, without mishap, did we not? And the distance to my hôtel is half that distance, just a mere few minutes along the street, in fact. I should be home by the time your carriage arrived at your entrance."

Marc de Vries moved with him to the entrance hall and waited as the footman handed his guest his cloak and hat, a feeling of deep unexplained foreboding within his heart. He shook it off; the turbulent times were affecting him.

"One more thing, Marc—what think you of Beaumont this night?"

De Vries studied him carefully for a minute. "I know that he be oldest friend to you but... there was something uncomfortable about him this night, of that I am sure. The cause of that discomfort has me in a puzzle."

"Ah."

"Who holds what, over him, is a mystery of course, but I do believe that he has not only been in secret communication with Robespierre but also Saint-Just."

"You do?"

"You are not surprised, I see... but Saint-Just has stretched his long arm far across the frontier, in his fanatical purge of the army and émigrés and their contacts; setting the Representatives en Mission to watch the officers and Generals and *their*... er, contacts."

"Ah. To be expected of course... but my thanks for your concern, *mon ami.*"

The Comte walked with purpose but not with haste, the moderately high heels of his evening shoes slowing his dignified gait a little, mind on one friend in particular. His long black, rose-lined cloak fell from broad, fit shoulders, falling open to expose a plain black coat, breeches and waistcoat. He wore a cascading lace cravat still, but bowed to dangerous times by omitting the usual single diamond pin. He was fond of this trinket but not controlled by it: he could, in effect lose all and not be affected by that loss: he would simply begin again. He had done so numerous times. Now, aside of a heavy family ring that would not come off, he wore no other jewellery. Also missing was his light sword.  He cursed the times that prohibited a man from dressing as he had always dressed.  He remained, however, though modest, very elegant: no revolution could enforce otherwise.

The hour was advanced, the streets deserted but he walked casually, unconcerned and his waiting assailants expected little resistance, though they rather expected to see a slight stagger in the gentleman's progress.  However, soft living softened the man and the aristocracy were all the same: deep drinking, much rich food and a sedentary life, rendered most of them fair game: most.  The first to attack discovered otherwise as his seeking hands were suddenly gripped by the wrists with a strength that surprised.  Several wrist bones cracked suddenly, their owner staggering back, cradling them.  The second suffered a sledgehammer to his jaw that landed him upon his back, some feet from the Comte.  The third flew off the gentleman's hip and the fourth over his shoulder.

De Quatreaux straightened his cloak and continued, without even casting a glance behind, in leisurely fashion, on down the street.  He smiled suddenly; he was not so old after all.  The regular morning sessions, at the renowned and exclusive boxing school of Paris, were apparently to be recommended: the more so the secret, oriental self-defence school close by.  He flexed his shoulders: it felt good all of a sudden, to be alive.  Equally suddenly, he craved his estates and favourite hunter: the pull suddenly strong.

The next bend, turning into Rue Saint-Honoré, however, left him no fighting chance.  Here, lined up and blocking the street were two black, unmarked, closed coaches and standing in front of them two apparently important officials.  The narrow sidewalk held two guards holding firearms: pointed directly at his head.

De Quatreaux slowed his pace but did not need to look to know that behind him now appeared many more guards.  On the top of each coach sat two men, determinedly pointing a blunderbuss each into the street, right at his person.  He sighed tiredly, came to a halt, eyebrows raised in polite inquiry and waited.  Behind his apparent indolent attitude his brain did not have to exert itself to land the face of Beaumont.  He layered prophylactic ice against any rising emotion: time enough later for self-recriminations; and puzzlement over treachery of such proportions.  The present moment required his full attention.

"We are come to find Citizen Vermont," said the spokesman, moving forward.

Coolly he ignored the intended insult: the use of his family name by a stranger. "Then congratulations, you have found him."

"Citizen, you are under arrest."

"Just like that, eh? On what charge, Citizen, er... my pardon, I know not your name."

"My name is not your business, Citizen."

"May I know the charge then?"

"That is not *our* business; only to convey you to the Châtelet."

"Ah... and on whose orders?"

"Citizen Robespierre."

"But of course... and the grounds?"

"That is not our business, Citizen."

"But you must have grounds... or you cannot take me up."

"You be taken up under the *Law of Suspected Persons*, Citizens."

"Ah. Of course! Suspected of what? But wait, that be not your business, correct?"

"Citizen, you will be wise to say no more; you are surrounded by the National Guard."

Beneath hooded lids he glanced about, the coachmen and their lackeys did not desert their full attention upon him and the guards in front and behind had drawn swords now, as well as the pistols. In these nervous times they would, he knew, blast, or carve him into small pieces at the slightest provocation.

He laughed suddenly, in genuine amusement. "Citizen, I am delighted and flattered: so much for the capture of one."

"Laugh now, for you shall not be able to do so soon enough, Citizen."

The door of the larger coach was opened and, casting a sudden haughty look at the outstretched hands that then fell away, he entered, sat down and promptly leaned back, eyes closing, with a bored sigh. Within a minute he gave all the appearances of one quietly sleeping as though there was nothing better to do. The guards enclosed with him found it impossible to understand this attitude and waited nervously for an outburst of innocence or attempt to escape, but the Comte apparently slept peacefully, swaying in practiced manner until it was time to alight at the prison.

Watching this from a first floor window stood two men; one openly gloating, the other with the bland expression of total disinterest and this was true of his emotion: they had one more of the counterrevolutionaries in their capture: that was all.

"Execute him last!"

Saint-Just turned to Lareaux at his side. "Oh?"

"Yes! I want him to sweat and squirm every time the *tumbril* comes for the next collection for the guillotine!"

"Then you must be disappointed Citizen, for they do not."

"Do not...?"

"Sweat and Squirm: own fear. They do not comprehend the meaning of the word. They are born to courage. Courage steeped in obsession: the obsession of the aristocracy for such apparently mandatory attributes!"

"Then he shall *learn* fear!"

"Oh no: never." It was said in the expressionless voice born of a surety of knowledge.

Lareaux looked at him. "But of course he shall. Nobles are not *devoid* of fear. They simply be the more practiced at acting. I know! I am one!"

"But *not* a Noblesse de l'épée," murmured Saint-Just softly. "Or, more to the point: a de Quatreaux! He may be hated by many of the Revolutionaries but never disrespected."

Lareaux controlled his rising fury at the slight: indeed, his Grandfather though tied to the de Quatreaux' by marriage, had had to acquire his title from the king. "Pah! He is still human! And I have seen many crumble before the threat of the guillotine; if not in the first instance, then as the time draws nearer."

"But always of the Robe, my dear friend! Still learning: requires centuries of practice. Those of the Sword you shall never break. It be *required* of them; their very duty, instilled in them at conception, in their very blood. They are all quite mad of course: inherited... inbred. Just chop off their heads and be done with it."

Lareaux gazed out, his face bland; his thoughts black: he would search out Saint-Just's own background and nefarious deeds. Nobody offered slight to a Lareaux and escaped revenge.

♣

Angelique paced. Marie watched her and eventually, biting a thread and laying aside her work for a minute, spoke: "*Ma Chérie*, you shall not hasten his return by excessive physical activity. In point of fact, you be thin enough, so sit down, do."

"But Marie," continuing to pace, more slowly now, up and down in front of the windows, glancing frequently into the street below, "he did not say that he was going anywhere! I mean anywhere distant from Paris; for even should he absent himself for some few days, he does inform us of the approaching event, always."

"Not always *chérie*, there was the time…"

"Oh Marie! Spare me do; an account of the occasions that he has *neglected* to do so. I speak of these increasingly dangerous times. Even if we do not know where, we generally know that he *is* going. There be *something wrong*! Ah… this be intolerable!"

"Yes, but in such situation your agitation serves no useful purpose that I can see."

Angelique stared at her cousin's cool calm and suddenly laughed. "*Mon Dieu*, be you related to Rochelle by any chance?"

Gentle, well meaning but humourless, Marie gazed into space a moment. "Noo… I do not think so but then I do not know all of my mother's ancestors. There were of course the Dubois'. They lived much in Spain and therefore were not familiar to us, and then of course those across the border from there… in France certainly, so…"

"*Marie!*"

Her distant cousin and chaperon smiled suddenly. "There now, settle, my dear. Why do you not send for the nice Monsieur Pontisqieu? He may have heard of some event that be within the Comte's wide interests."

"I thought of it Marie, but the intrusion? The burden when he be so busy."

"But there appears not to be any one else: upon whom to call."

"I am deeply sensible of it, thank you. *Mon Dieu*, in the old days we were so many that they could not all fit into the large salon and the great hall had to be used; regardless of weather and the limited efficiency of the fires."

She sat down for a moment on a low stool, elbows on knees, chin in hands; where was Emile? Where was… but she could not, would not, go down that line of thought. The return of the vision, spreading of the blood, becoming the dark purple shadow, sent a chill down her spine and she stood up suddenly and moved to the mahogany desk. Here she took up the quill, dipped it in the ink and commenced scratching rapidly across a sheet of crested paper. She pressed the waxed seal a moment, rose from her chair and moving to the bellpull; gave it a tug and waited. Marie continued placidly with her needlework, selecting differing coloured threads and closely studying them, against the developing work within the frame. Henri entered and stood waiting his orders.

"Henri, I want you to delegate one of the footmen to your duties for a short while and take this missive to the Monsieur Pontisqieu. You know where he lives?"

"Yes Madame, but if he be not in?"

"Then find him. Do not return until you have done so please. He may be in his law office, I do not know: or at the Châtelet or the Palais de Justice."

"Yes Madame, I shall attend to it."

She watched him go out of the room and then moved back to the desk. Perhaps she could write; sometimes agitation was the forerunner to some of her best work but she found that she could think now of nothing but that which Pontisqieu may find. Her heart sank to join the leaden ball residing in the pit of her stomach. She was restless, unable to sit, think or keep her mind on one subject for more than a moment.

Watching her, Marie finally cast aside her needlework, rose; and going to the bell-pull gave it a tug. Angelique gazed at her in inquiry and was answered when the footman entered and was given orders for canary and sweetmeats.

Angelique laughed suddenly. "But Marie, the hour be only a little beyond noon: shame upon you."

"*Ma chérie*: *something* must be done about you."

Angelique shook her head solemnly. "But Marie, *canary*? Why not ratafia? It be even more insipid."

Marie gave vent to a desperate sigh and waited the footman's entry with the tray loaded with the requested fare.

"My apologies, but take it back, if you please… the canary… and bring *cognac*," said Marie firmly.

Angelique sat down at last, laughing and accepted a sweetmeat. "Do not say it: I shall be the death of you!"

"I need not. You just have," replied that stalwart, unimaginative woman, then, "*Ma chérie*; truly, you *must* discipline your sense of distraction. For the Comte, if nothing else but also… the troubles ahead shall require an iron constitution of the nerves, I think."

Angelique raised her brows. "You *do*? Whatever gave you that idea!" Then, at Marie's poker face, she moved forward, hands held out. "Marie, forgive me! My wretched humour… always warped and twisted under stress! I *must* learn to control it."

Marie took the hands, felt the fine tremor and smiled softly. "No, do not. It may one day be your only saviour."

"Or my death," muttered Angelique, but Marie had turned away and moved to the window at the escalation of street sounds. The tumbril traversing the street, however, held persons unknown to her. Uncharitably she let out a breath: while it held unknown persons, the hand of fate bypassed one. Immediately she prayed to the Lord Jesus for forgiveness and followed this with one Our Father and ten Hail Mary's.

# CHAPTER TWENTY

## Panic at Hôtel Quatreaux

Angelique struggled to contain her anxiety. That her father had lived his entire life in danger was no comfort. His children had long since wondered whether his apparent immunity against disaster had built for him a false sense of security. Certainly he would not ever underestimate his enemies, but had familiarity with risk and danger desensitised him? She turned to look at Marie, placidly plying the needle, with very fine stitches, to the work stretched within the frame.

Marie glanced up at the scrutiny and smiled suddenly. "Ma *chérie*, do not allow this affair to disturb your tranquillity. Your *Père* be of all men the most astute; and aside of that he is always in full possession of his enemies' moves and whereabouts and *that* is power of the ultimate."

"But Marie, does he *know* all of his enemies? In this age your best friend could turn traitor, though I find it difficult to believe of our own friends. But the bribes and blackmail grow to amazing proportions. And I do not think they all own the fortitude to withstand this fearsome *Terreur* wielded by that dratted man! He will not cease until we are all dead! The stronger the *Montagnard* grows so too does our danger."

"That may well be but you shall serve no purpose by striding up and down my dear. Come, call for coffee… but no; a calmative be in order; and if you will not take the vinaigrette or salts…"

Angelique laughed suddenly. "But Marie, I do not feel faint."

Marie looked thoughtful. "No, so I suppose more effective would be the Laudanum, but I do not recommend it, though *ma mère* used it frequently, poor dear, and that was her undoing I am sure. The English tea then must suffice."

Angelique controlled an impatient sigh, for Marie was doing her best to ease the building tension within her charge. She grew deaf to the rambling dialogue behind her as she watched the street below, her mind racing ceaselessly through every possible disaster.

The door opened and Henri stood on its threshold. "Madame, Monsieur Pontisqieu." Angelique moved swiftly forward, holding out both her hands. Pontisqieu bowed as he took them in his, gripped them for a moment and then led her to a chair. By this she knew, and waited within a vacuum of false calm; then marshalling her voice, spoke.

"Please Monsieur, do not wrap it up! What has happened?"

He gazed at her pale face and watched it grow parchment white as he imparted his news in the simplest terms possible. She sat there, silent; listening to the words as they came from afar and indeed she did feel, after all, faint. The room tilted and then settled. Fighting for control against a wave of extreme nausea, she tried to marshal some workable thought process but could not and gazed helplessly at their visitor.

"Monsieur... what on earth is to be done? My mind is blank. *Mon Dieu...* who betrayed him... but that be of no consequence now! We must act but how... what to do?"

"He has many friends that shall assist us and I go now to them."

"Yes, yes of course, that would be the best." She thought a moment and then turned towards him. "Monsieur, Emile is not available: I must send for Seigneur Trifane! Do you know of his whereabouts?"

"No Mademoiselle, but may find out through a mutual friend. Leave it with me... and do not worry; the trials are backed up to severe degree."

"Monsieur, a trial is the last thing that he needs!"

"Ah yes, but this allows us time to affect his er... rescue."

"Yes, yes, a rescue. But who on earth can *do* that?"

"We are quite a strong network, Mademoiselle." He paused, glancing at Marie, who now rose and brushed out her skirts but he motioned her to sit again. "Madame, do not disturb yourself: I go now and you shall hear from me, possibly by tonight. If not, then by the morrow at the latest."

The antique clock ticked loudly on the mantle, now showing twenty hours thirty minutes in the evening. Angelique and Marie sat at table: Angelique staring into space, noting vaguely the enhanced ticking within the silence. But as the hand continued to move, jerking forward on each sound, anxiety built. Time! They did not have time. Where *was* Trifane?

Marie, that remarkable woman of no imagination, finished the last but one morsel on her plate and lay down her knife and fork. "*Ma Chérie*, you do yourself and your *père* no service by starving yourself. Do try to eat. Whatever has to be done for the benefit of your *père* cannot be achieved if hindered by the vapours."

Angelique rose, without excuse or apology, and headed for the window once again, gazing far up the curve of the Rue Saint-Honoré.

Marie tried again. "My dear, this be a black hour certainly but just think, with one's back against the wall, one can only go forward. It at least cannot grow worse."

Just then an empty *tumbril*, returning from the Place de la Revolution, passed beneath the window and Angelique grew very, very cold. "Oh, but it can!"

Marie sighed and rising now from the table, headed for the door. "I must go fetch my embroidery, very beneficial in times of stress. You should try it my dear." She left the room quietly, leaving Angelique still standing by the window, lost in a dark swirl of fear, agitation and unbearable impotence.

Not many minutes later a decisive rap on the door preceded the entry of Raoul Trifane, stepping swiftly into the room and coming to a sudden standstill. He surveyed her, a moment, through narrowed eyes and then strode forward, taking both her hands as she moved swiftly to meet him. He gazed down into eyes dark with horror.

"Raoul!" The relief, though why so, she did not know: how *could* he know what to do, swept through her, leaving her knees weak, now that reaction began to bubble over.

He drew her against him, held her a moment; then, "Easy *enfant*... easy, extreme emotion never achieves a thing! Come, sit down." He indicated the chaise with one hand, the other arm still encircling her.

She leaned back against it and stared up at him. "I am truly sorry for calling you... I do beg your pardon... but you did say at one time, that I may call upon your services. That they were at my... disposal." She halted, unable to go on. She wanted to lean against him again, close her eyes and know that it would all go away. The fine-tuned tension born of quandary and inaction reached for the zenith. She cursed again the restrictions placed upon a female. She began to shake.

His grip tightened, one hand pressing her head against his shoulder, then stroking her hair as he spoke. "And I told you that I was serious, remember?"

His habitual tones of cool unconcern calmed her a little. She wanted to stay there forever but the tension within screamed for release. The tug of these opposing forces demanded action. She broke away suddenly and returned to pacing up and down before the window.

Understanding, he watched her for a moment; then, "Come *mon enfant*. You shall cause my head to spin," and taking her elbow he guided her to the chaise and sat beside her, where he could retain her hand until some of the tension left her; and then, placing it upon her knee, spoke softly, "You *know, mon enfant*, we *all* know... that this diabolical farce within France, be but a badly staged play... yes, yes, not very original: personally, *I* prefer, for these farcical times, 'puppet show', directed by Robespierre: and though he is a master puppeteer, *we too* own characters on that silly stage; and so..." He paused, alarmed at her change of colour, ready to catch her.

Suddenly, on the word 'stage', the scene of bloodshed was before her again, holding her mentally and physically frozen, unable to longer push it away, the deep, dreaded knowing settling in the pit of her stomach as a lead cannon-ball. The room swayed, the wall opposite her tilting inwards, she focussed on the clock: time, every moment precious, no time for histrionics. Her old friend: warped humour, surfaced at last.

"But Seigneur Trifane, I do not wish *mon père* to be a *headless* character!"

"And so," he continued, in cool even tones, ignoring now, even the beaded sweat on her forehead, "*We* write the next act. Now, I have sent a missive to Emile. Yes, yes, I know the dangers attached to his return, but not to inform him would lead to *my* demise. At his hand!" He smiled gently, observing her slow recovery. "But seriously, the risks are small. He is a returning traveller, not an émigré to be punished by guillotine. And we none of us, travel or indeed do *any*thing, under our own names: any of them! As for the immediate future of the Comte, there are many that will assist us in his rescue. Try not to worry."

Her equilibrium gaining strength now, she stared at him in disbelief. "Not worry Monsieur? But of course I shall. 'Tis the waiting; the inaction, that destroys the nerves. However, I shall retrieve mine in but a moment, believe me. I do not require the Laudanum, only some plan of action!"

He leaned back and laughed suddenly and the tension eased a little. *"Mon enfant,* there be none like you! Now, do not try anything yourself. I am aware of the difficulty this poses for you in particular but, while I plan with others, please remain invisible."

"Oh worry not. I am fully sensible that they shall pounce on the slightest excuse to confine myself also and that would not assist *mon père* in any way."

"Quite apart from the, er… inconvenience to yourself!"

She smiled wanly. "If it would serve to extricate *mon père* then I would go willingly."

"Ah, but then we should be obliged to rescue *you.* A far more difficult task I assure you." He paused, rose and moved to the fireplace, leaning broad shoulders against the mantle, gazing at her a moment. "You would be best out of Paris, in point of fact, but I suppose it would be useless to try to persuade you? Yes, I perceive that it would; the de Quatreaux stubbornness renders that line of direction null and void… if indeed it could be achieved! But we shall not discuss that just yet. I shall place a guard outside you hôtel at night. Do not trust anyone of your staff."

"But I shall have to trust Henri; he knows so much already."

"Do not, please. Even amongst our own there are traitors, let alone the staff, no matter their length of service. The persuasive methods of the *Commune* never fail."

"Who amongst our own would betray *mon père*, Seigneur?" she asked now.

"Ah, do not go there, *enfant.* It is not known but I shall find out. Be sure of that."

"I know of none that could be of such a despicable character."

"Leave it! And give me your promise, or I shall be compelled to abduct you. And do please remember, that I am aware of your ability to defend your person under such circumstances, and shall be prepared." His grey eyes glinted with humour and she smiled at the memory but could raise no response.

He moved forward, took one of her hands in both of his, gazed at her a moment, then lightly kissed it. "I must away now. Try your best not to worry *mon enfant.* I shall see you no later than tomorrow evening. Should you need me at any time of day or night, send a message via the 'guard' across the street from your front entrance: he shall appear dirty and unkempt: dressed as a sans-culotte."

With that he was gone and Angelique, smiling weakly at the fact that he may trust but she may not, removed from the salon to the reading room. Here she wrote furiously and paced when inspiration deserted her. Wrote and paced, paced and wrote. She studied now, seated at the desk, the words of an older verse, written some few months ago:

> 'Where gone: beloved Paris?
> Her beauty; her romance,
> Gay music and perfumed flowers,
> Laughter and dance,
> And filled café's spilling,
> Across summers' shady sidewalks!
> All is gone; all is dust.

> Search not among the ashes, my friend,
> And cast nostalgia to the wind,
> Better to tune thine ear to the Tocsin's ring,
> The beating of the drum,
> And the tramp of patrol feet,
> Down darkened unhappy street,
> Presage of myriad menace....'

She tried to complete it. Nothing came to mind. She screwed it into a ball and threw it upon the floor in frustration, for France had gone very far beyond simple 'dark and unhappy streets'; and the Jacobin government would stop at nothing to win the foreign war and bring the internal rebels to heel. She drew a new sheet of parchment forward and began to update her *'Chronicles of France: Under Revolution'*.

Her quill flowed unceasingly across the page. France now faced war on three fronts; the foreign enemy in the east, a Catholic-royalist battle raging in the west and a federalist enemy in the south. Added now, according to the *Père Duchesne*, was a fourth, the rising in the northwest. And from Rochelle's contacts she also knew that England had given financial support to Holland, Russia, Sardinia, Spain, Naples, Prussia, and Portugal. France, it appeared, had no friends left in Europe. Perhaps the invading armies may just put the Dauphin back on the throne, with a return to at least a monarchical constitution.

She stood, eased her aching back and dwelt a moment upon her treasonable thoughts: how could one be brought to this, the desire for the ruination of one's own country. But she knew that it be such men as Chaumette and Hébert that she held in disgust, not her countrymen. For such as these were not countrymen: where they belonged she did not know but denied them ownership of the warmth and generosity that was the French soul.

She returned to the desk and took up the quill again. These despicable two, had both been men of the *Insurrectionary Commune*. The *Commune*: that had attacked Tuileries in '92; and driven Louis to shelter in the Assembly rooms. Following this, they had taken the influential positions of law officers to the new *Commune*.

Since this time, extraordinary outbursts of cruelty and fanaticism could be traced to them, along with their successful attempts to destroy all superiorities of intellect and place all men on the same level. The latter sentiment not a bad idea in itself but to do this they did not seek equality by raising the lower, through means of solid education and lifting the standard of living, but by degradation of the higher. Jealousy within the middle classes ruled. She paused a moment: the bourgeois would always answer the urge to climb, for he had reached that place of vision. From here he could see a possibility of reaching 'the top'. And what better foot-leverage than that of the unsuspecting sans-culottes: believing totally that they themselves be included in his plans. Continuing serfdom was a very necessary prop to the new 'privileged' orders of wealth and political supremacy.

She paused, as Danton now infiltrated her mind. Danton: both the strong man of the executive council and the Prosecutor-General of the *Commune*, author of the First Terror, and the leading spirit in the national defence; with his eternal cries for greater 'daring' in the purging of France. It had been *his* voice that had cried aloud and fanatically to the Council, that the 10th of August attack on Tuileries and the *Famille Roi* had caused a clear and undeniable division of France: the people were now either republicans or royalists. Therefore, to assist the Glorious Revolution and frustrate the designs of the royalists, terror, real and organized, must be driven into their hearts. Following this, all relatives of émigrés were swiftly declared hostages of the State and non-juror priests imprisoned.

Superiority of wealth was high on the list of those to be brought down. Capitalists, bankers, speculators and large landowners were classed along with the federalists, the moderate Girondins, nobles, priests and royalists, as enemies of the Republic.

Intellectual superiority and culture became a crime, and working alongside Robespierre, Couthon and Saint-Just, was Hébert and Chaumette, outstripping even Robespierre in clinical harshness. They proceeded now to destroy the very foundation of France. *Anything* that bore traces of having been produced beneath a monarchy was destroyed; valuable books, statues and works of art: everything that gave evidence of decent living, irrespective now of class. Ignorance and rags were put forward, as in themselves giving claim to respect and the term 'sans-culottes' seen as the epitome of patriotic evidence but as symbol only: to actually improve their standards not part of the plan. She continued to write; the parchment taking the brunt of suppressed torment.

All was quiet; the streets below empty of the raucous daily sounds, the fitful moon flitting occasionally through a light cloud cover. A wax candle sputtered as it commenced dying in its holder but this did not intrude upon her concentrated mind. She wrote on, lost in the deceitful world of man's evil against man. All evil beings, she decided, pausing to rub her aching wrist, should be put to the sword, along with those simply garnishing their own plates. She smiled grimly at the contagious nature of violence. If she wondered at herself before, she now had no illusions that she could quite easily and without guilt of any kind, destroy those responsible for the genocide of France. Did that make her as evil as the heinous authors of this monstrous upheaval? Was 'good' or 'evil,' nothing more than a matter of which side of the fence one sat?

The night watch called the hour and that, unusually for Paris, all was well but she did not hear him. A faint unusual sound did however send a warning bell to her subconscious and rising from the depths she lifted her head and listened, a freezing torrent suddenly coursing her bloodstream.

It sounded again, from without the door. Chilled now to the core, she lay down her quill, slid a draw open and reached in; then rose. As a silent shadow, she moved softly, lightly to avoid creaking floorboards, through the low, flickering light of the dying candle. She arrived at the door onto the wide landing. Leaning there she listened, sure that her thumping heartbeat could be heard. Nothing further sounded from without and cautiously, holding the small silver mounted pistol, she opened the door. Hand still on the knob, she moved silently out. The upper landing was devoid of human life. The hall below was deserted, but as she peered down into the ill-lit recesses, a faint swish of skirts came to her ears. Nothing could she see, in the shadowed abyss, but the sound was undeniable; one that any female would recognize.

She turned suddenly and went back into the reading room and across to the window. Peering down into the street she saw no sans-culotte but three National Guard. She pulled back. Retrieving a taper, for though its light was inferior to that of a wax or tallow candle, it would not smoke: fumes would alert any roaming vigilante. She headed up the stairs, catching up her skirts in one hand to prevent the swish of her own dress from causing her detection. Up to the second floor, pausing frequently to listen, the hairy fingers of fear and anxiety brushing with cobweb lightness, her heightened senses. She moved on, trying not to jump at every leaping black shadow, from the remaining candles flickering and flaring occasionally in every second or third wall bracket. She continued on to the third floor. Here she located the short narrow wooden flight of stairs to one of the attics. All was very dark now, the last of the wall brackets several yards away. She moved silently through the door and paused; peering back into the void of the narrowed stairwell just here, but she could detect no movement and no sound reached her.

Closing the door, she kicked the long roll of draft-excluder against the crack beneath it, fumbled for the flint, lit the taper and stood it in an old tooth tumbler. The next few minutes were spent rummaging in the dim recesses for the stored trunks. She pulled out linen, pillows and blankets stored there: to be dragged out only when the hôtel was so filled with visitors that they used up the below-stairs supply. She felt a tug of nostalgia; it would never happen again. Here also, within other stored trunks, were cast-off ball gowns, eveningwear and spare servant's clothing. A full livery for a footman, including a wig and silver salver, had been squeezed on top of the bed linen. She paused sadly: Fanchon's 'town clothes' rested there also. She extinguished the taper and left the attic storeroom, moving back downstairs only as far as Marie's boudoir. Opening the door she tiptoed in, dumped her load, and wakened Marie gently.

There was nothing, thought Angelique humorously, to beat the prosaic, unimaginative mind of the stoical temperament. She could after all, Rochelle aside, not find a more suitable companion to ask to join her in the tunnels below. Marie took it in her stride, agreeing complaisantly that it would indeed be for the best for them to spend each night within these pitch-black and possibly cobwebbed confines, commencing of course in the middle of this night. The only cause for a slight, forgivable, hesitation, that of the rats that must also reside there.

"It is the rats, Marie, or the guards of the Conciergerie."

"Ah yes; well, I daresay the rats be actually quite nice, once one gets to know them. And they could be useful: warning of enemy approach long before *we* could hear them! "

"Well *ma chérie*, you shall have your chance to create an alliance with the rodents. I propose that we locate the small hollowed out alcove just beyond the second bend of the tunnel, heading towards the Seine, for it is elevated by some several steps and has a low wall of concealment. Not that the traffic will be heavy!"

"You *know* your way about this mythical tunnel that has been a jest within the family?"

"Emile and I explored it one day, following Fersen's sudden appearance into the library."

"And does it indeed travel under the Seine to the Notre Dame?"

"It does."

Marie looked thoughtful and Angelique chuckled softly. "I know that look, cousin. What bee resides in your bonnet now?"

"'Tis naught, but... well, be it of *use*? I feel that all is not that easy, for the Notre Dame be located on the Ile de la Cité. One then owns the puzzle of exiting *that* island."

"Worry not, Marie, I believe that Emile and Trifane have the plan arranged from that point onward, should we require it."

"Ah. Then all is well of course, providing they are in our company at the moment that necessitates our use of that plan." Marie paused beneath Angelique's threatening glance; then, "If the linen be missed..."

"Shall not be, Marie. That is why I stole from the attic and not the linen press, though of course should our beds be found to be empty then questions shall be asked. We must be back before the *femmes de chambre* rise for the day."

"And we *Suspected Persons*. Now why would they draw that conclusion?"

Angelique stared: Cousin Marie had a sense of humour after all. "We will be watched: by which servant we shall never know of course but must change our routine of access each night. Come."

But Marie paused again and Angelique sighed, stood still and waited.

"*Ma chérie...* can they not just as easily come by day?"

"Ah. Yes, Marie, but then we shall be awake and alert. Sleep tends to cause one's lack of defence. Unless, of course, you wish us to sleep in shifts? But I warn you... a stealthy shadow; a swift hand to the throat... and the 'watch' may lay dead!"

They moved silently along the corridor to the gallery, carrying their bundles, rolled in the middle of which lay tapers, holders, flint and a few personal items. Avoiding boards that creaked, Angelique led the way; certain that spies lurked everywhere.

A sound came to them from far below: possibly the rear entrance. They stopped, hugging the wall, then jumped. Startling in its loudness now, the sound of boots and unconcealed voices rose to the gallery. Angelique drew a sharp breath.

"They shall be abed: to the boudoirs!"

Angelique and Marie raced along the gallery. Using the shadows to avoid the faint light from low burning wall brackets, they slipped around suits of armour, exited the gallery at the far end and ran down darkened stairs to a small room holding disused furniture.

Marie paused, gazing at Angelique. "Can we get to the library from here?"

"No!"

They peered at each other, listening to the tramping feet climbing the main stairs. Angelique frowned. "They are very sure of themselves or they would be running... therefore, all hopefully will be heading for the sleeping quarters. Let's go!"

She turned and slipped back up the stairs, entered the gallery just exited and stopped to peer along to the library door and down the stairs. Inching silently forward she peered through the balustrade. She could just detect a faint shadowed head in the hall below. Servant or soldier, he stood very still. The last of the wall candles suddenly flickered and died, leaving the gallery in total darkness.

"The best opportunity we shall get!" she murmured beneath her breath. "Quickly!"

They moved swiftly, feeling the exposure acutely, then slid into the library. Angelique leaned against the door, listening a moment, then rocketed toward the panel as a clear voice called up the stairs.

"Monsieur! The library I think!"

A muffled answer came and Angelique fumbled for the carved motif, praying that it would open without problem. Locating it, her hands shook as she applied the pressure. Glancing around, she almost laughed: Marie simply stood, clutching her bundle, waiting calmly. Suddenly, her hands steadied and she focussed on the motif.

Voices sounded along the gallery. "Where is the library, woman?"

The panel slid open as the library door surged inward, admitting an unknown number of soldiers and agents of Robespierre.

"Quickly girl... a candle: it is dark as a cave at fifty feet! Move it!"

"Yes Monsieur." The kitchen maid, that Angelique now recognized, fumbled towards the table holding the candelabra, tripped over a pile of books left on the floor by Angelique that evening; then righted herself.

"Girl!" roared the man, "Do you work here or not?"

"Yes Monsieur... but in the kitchens!"

"*Citizen*! Nobody holds rank now! Learn that!"

Yes M...Citizen."

A candle glimmered, its first shaft of light waving ineffectually, pouring smoke a moment as the panel slid its final inches, to close soundlessly within the shadowed darkness. The guards looked around. The room was empty. One moved to the window. It was locked. They searched but a few seconds, behind heavy furniture and drapes.

"You are jumping at shadows girl!  No one entered here!"

"I thought I heard the door close, Citizen."

"Thought is not good enough...'twas the wind. Where else could they be?"

"Gone to Madame Bayette's hôtel, perhaps..."

250,000 men now stood under arms. 550,000 were required, preferably three quarters of a million, but at least another 300,000 must be recruited. All National Guards between the ages of 18 and 40 were requisitioned and every department had to furnish a definite contingent. If the voluntary system failed, then conscription was resorted to.

The Convention now, in order to bring local authorities under immediate control of the government, took direct part in this administration and sent deputies into every department. These men were authorized to take all measures necessary for the levy of recruits and providing supplies to the armies.

The deputies then established special committees to act as their agents, compelled the sale of corn, horses and arms and dismissed administrative officers held in suspicion of anti-republicanism. Furthermore, *deputies-en-mission,* were increased: responsible only to the *Committee for Public Security* and sent into the armies to keep watchful eye on the conduct of generals and officers.

As the situation grew more perilous, legislation grew increasingly more harsh and tyrannical. The Convention, enraged and frightened by the French defeat in Belgium and the simultaneous royalist Vendee uprising, now struck at random, regardless of innocence or guilt. Those who instigated resistance to the recruitment of the armies were punished by death. Recalcitrant non-juror priests were banished to French Guiana. Returning, previously banished, priests were executed within twenty-four hours of their entry into France.

The Legislative Assembly had rendered it a crime to quit the country and had confiscated all property of emigrants. The new Convention now laid a firmer grip, by banishing them forever from the Republic of France and forbidding them to return, under penalty of death. No exception was made for exiles not intending to fight against their own country: merely leaving because their lives were in danger and no account taken of age, sex or circumstances.

The rise in figures of escaping aristocrats now caused some frustration to Robespierre. He gazed grimly now at Saint-Juste. "All émigrés, recorded in the passport offices, shall be listed. Make sure they are posted at frontier crossings. Take this list of suspects as well... under *any* dashed name *they* will be! Ensure Trifane, and Vermont, are at the top. I am certain they will return: if they have not already done so."

"We need proof of their emigration to confiscate their property?"

Robespierre smiled thinly. "Oh no. I merely want their heads. Trifane does not own any... now. The Vicomte either."

Saint-Just grunted. "In another name of course: could be anybody!"

"A peasant even."

Saint-Just stared. "How so?"

"Trifane's estates sold for one livre."

"But he *cannot.*"

"There be no legislation to demand set price, Saint-Just."

"But *why*? It does not make sense to lose money!"

Robespierre's face remained expressionless. "To annoy me. An unfortunate mistake... I shall now hunt the entire planet to find him!"

In the midst of the multi-faceted, internal strife and defence preparation, the Convention focused upon the forming of a new constitution. The Girondins sanctioned decentralization, free trade and popular election. The Montagnards claimed that free trade, against the will of their supporters, must lead to the overthrow of the Convention. To them, decentralization meant France would be without an effective government at a critical time: a time when a powerful foreign coalition was forming against her.

The moderate Girondins now denounced every policy of the extremist Montagnards, with a fervent indignation. Support, however, was nowhere to be found. The middle classes were alienated by the death of the king; the lower classes by the ever-rising costs of food and goods and the continuous recruitment of their menfolk. More heinous, however, was the Convention's indifference to the Catholic faith and now the persecution of the priests created unexpected hostilities from all walks of life.

Financially, in spite of the sale of almost all Church lands and confiscated émigrés properties, the Convention remained no better off. It had no credit and taxes were still only partially paid. The situation was now far worse than it had been under the old regime. Therefore it became necessary, to cover war expenses, to yet again issue new *assignats* and the paper money fell rapidly in value. Now they could be exchanged for half their normal value. This depreciation of the paper money inflicted great suffering upon the men relying on wages, adding to the misery of continuously rising prices.

Men of Anton's calibre and determination fought hard to build their cache of metal money. Seated now at his desk, above his cellar, Anton desperately tried to evade the assignats. He looked at his guest. "Silver or indeed gold be the only trade, *mon ami*! If you do not have it," he shrugged, poking a finger at the pile of *assignats* on the table, "I am not alone. All persons dislike holding on to these *assignats*. We sellers press for coins in exchange for our wares."

"And we buyers press to offload our *assignats*. Will you not take just a few? Half-half? No? Well, you do know, *mon ami*, that trade is deserting Paris."

"The city of paper money," chuckled Anton. "That is why I go to the countryside: greater ease of procuring gold and silver. You give me such or no deal. My wine is pure gold! Gold for gold: a fair deal."

They struck a reasonably fair deal and Anton poured wine. They drank and then, showing his client out, he went below to the cellar, locked the door and entered the secret chambre, there to hide the contraband.

Bread, vegetables, meat, fish, wine and wood, lamp oil, leather goods and clothing; in fact, mostly all commodities trebled in price, corn growers hoarded their crops and fowl, goat, sheep and cattle were rarely seen at market. Those playing the dangerous game of shifting animals and birds backwards and forwards between neighbours at census time, abandoned this as brother increasingly reported on brother. *Real* want; in the true meaning of the word, prerogative of the poor was now felt amongst the remaining upper classes. Those with money laid it up in store, or sent it abroad, increasing the scarcity.

The capitalists, speculators and wholesale dealers blossomed: making deals with the government or foreign countries, and black market profiteers experienced a very rich harvest. The State, however, lost, for while its revenue was received in *assignats* at their nominal value, it was forced to find hard cash for its purchases. How to raise the value of paper money, *and* lower prices, became the Convention's greatest headache during the spring of 1793. The solution then found was simplicity itself: those exchanging *assignats* for gold or silver; speculating on price variants, or holding goods back from sale, went beneath the guillotine. A special tax for the supplying of Paris with bread was implemented and a forced levy, for the maintenance of the war, imposed upon all wealthy citizens.

Plotting continued, now openly, for the final expulsion of the Girondin Deputies from the Convention. Special Revolutionary committees were also set up to enforce the policing of foreigners. These foreigners, it was declared, supported the Girondins accused of seditious activities, to assist the coalition of eight European states now succeeding in their war against France. Every section in Paris contained a *Revolutionary Committee* usurping the functions of all other committees.

Nobles and ecclesiastics were excluded from the committees: ruffians and dissolute characters offered these places. The *Commune*, under the leadership of its new mayor, Pache and two of its law officers, Chaumette and Hébert, set itself at the head of this movement. These two then directed all actions taken by the *Commune*: that powerful machine overshadowing the Convention. Robespierre, watching their every move with secret hostility, perceived that it would not be long before Hébert's increasing control over the *Commune* would become a threat.

Undisguised support for the Revolutionary committee within Paris came from, among others of the Montagnards, Robespierre, Marat, Collot, d'Herbois, Chabot, Tallien and Desmoulins. The *Committee of Public Safety* looked long and hard at this new usurper and decided only to moderate its violence, if indeed they could.

The moderate Girondin leaders, now under attack, stood no chance, their enemies turning popular opinion against them by accusations of exciting civil war, being Federalists and plotting to destroy the Republic of France.

The Jacobin's moved with speed for the expulsion of the moderate Girondins: essential, they said, for a free and effective functioning national parlement. Only without them could the Glorious Revolution continue on its proper path to lay the foundation of France's true destiny. Plans were laid and consolidated. A list of twenty-two Girondin deputies was drawn up: the accusation that of felony against the sovereign people; of causing counterrevolution within the government and the National Convention. There, however, the Jacobins paused, the *Commune* not yet ready for the final attack.

The moderate-left Girondins, using this period to advantage, pressed their counter-attack: on the continuance of Jacobin-led insurrectional meetings with the connivance of the city police. Led by Maximin Isnard, chairing the Assembly from May 16th to 30th, the Girondins decided to suspend the municipality: as the Minister of Interior appeared powerless to enforce order regarding the insurrections. A more subtle action was eventually agreed to: that of a '*Commission Extraordinaire*', of twelve members set up to investigate recent proceedings of the *Communes* and sections.

Three days later the Commission of Twelve ordered the arrests of the insurrectional ringleaders, Michel Marino of the police department, Varlet of the Post Office, Brichet, and Hébert, *procureur* of the *Commune* and editor of the *Père Duchesne*. These had refused to submit their minutes to the scrutiny of the Commission.

The resentment within the *Commune* on these actions by the Girondin leaders resulted in swift vote within Assembly: the Commission of Twelve was dissolved and the three prisoners released. An insurrection against the Assembly Girondins, with assistance of the newly fired-up sans-culottes, got swiftly underway. The sovereign people, asserted the Jacobins, must reassert their rights against counterrevolutionaries within the government.

The heavy oppressive ever-watchful atmosphere that was Paris, now slipped once more into its opposite personality; that of excited, fearful, bell-ringing, drum-beating action, as 2$^{nd}$ June 1793 dawned a clear hot day.

The Chamber was in tumult: Girondin deputies shouting the illegality of the dissolution of the Commission of Twelve, the Jacobins countering these attacks with hostile force, the public gallery noisily adding to the mayhem. The new Convention premises, now removed from the Mènage to the Palace of the Tuileries, housed, in the spacious hall, over a thousand persons. Into this surged the insurgents, demanding, with threats, the arrest of the leaders of the 'right': the moderate left Girondins.

"Down with the Girondins!"

"Arrest the Girondins!"

"'Afore they bring us all to ground!"

"Arrest! Arrest!"

The deputies attempted to leave hurriedly, fighting their way through the press of hostile humanity, but all exits of the palace courts and garden were closely guarded and passage refused.

"Capture the Girondins!"

"Let them not escape: implementers of the Commission of Twelve!"

Suddenly facing cannon; brought to the doors for the occasion, the Girondin deputies were forced to return and a decree was immediately issued for the house arrest of thirty-one of the leading Girondins. The last of the death throes of the moderate-leftist Girondin political party, a very necessary balance, for the radical 'leftist' Convention, was now complete and finally it lay still. The dramatic Jacobin-led *coup d'état* had succeeded; the Convention now dominated by Robespierre's extremist Montagnards.

At about the time the Girondin party began its desperate fight for survival with the instigation of the Commission of Twelve, it became evident that the Dauphin, Louis-Charles, was openly recognized as King of France: by England, Austria, Portugal, Russia and America. Fear of a restoration, as had taken place in England of Charles 2$^{nd,}$ created paranoia. Inside France the nobility, the clergy and even many commoners recognized Louis-Charles as monarch, representing a real danger to the leaders of the Revolution. The murder of a child, however, could not be countenanced. Those owning no problem with the issue also held back: fearing the ire of the rest of Europe. But he was too young to be tried and executed; therefore was separated from Marie-Antoinette and placed in solitary confinement, still within the Temple. The dark, filthy, vermin-infested, bare cell held only a cot, wooden table and one chair. Antoine Simon, an ex-shoemaker and sadistically brutal man, became his guard and tutor.

Antoine stared at them, at those superior leaders of the *Commune*. His alcohol-dulled brain sought clarification as to just what they wanted done with this boy spawned of Louis Caput.

"You wish for him to be poisoned? Killed? Tortured? Rendered insane? Or tame him to the sans-culottes way?" he grinned, cunningly. "Me thinks the latter the more fun!"

"Just get rid of him: we are not involved!" came the swift reply as it suddenly dawned that this man's bordering insanity could be used as a scapegoat. Antoine Simon, therefore, had full, unrestricted reign over the care of the dauphin.

A pattern of abuse began and grew increasingly abominable over time. The gentle and intelligent dauphin, born at Versailles so short a time ago, was slowly turned into a wild and uncouth child of the meanest streets of Paris. He survived the torture and crudities simply because his body, surprisingly, was not yet ready to die. He was nine years old.

With the growing public concern regarding the prince, it was now time to whip up the fury of the people: to resurrect the past iniquities of royal life, past iniquities of the queen. The Comte de Provence, now calling himself the Regent for the young Dauphin, was declaring from across the frontier, that he would restore Louis-Charles as Louis XVII, along with the Catholic religion and a Bourbon constitution. Emigrants and secret agents were rumoured to be busy urging foreign courts to intervene on behalf of the royal family once again. The Temple buzzed with rumours of cipher communication and legends of escape. The profit-making pamphleteers became frenzied once again in their foul work against the queen and the daily papers of Hébert's *'Père Duchesne'* and Desmoulin's *'Revolution's de France et de Brabant,'* competed unethically and ferociously with each other on the subject.

Over and above the problems of an embattled Girondin/Jacobin Convention and sudden attention to the plight of Louis Charles, the summer of '93 brought new fears for the Revolutionary government: that of a ring of opposition tightening around Paris. The Royalists were also raising the standard of revolt. The west was ablaze. Royalist uprisings abounded in Normandy and Brittany and further down the coast the Vendean insurgents still rumbled and were strengthening. Reinforcing this were the new rebelling centres of Limoges, Toulouse, Bordeaux and Deux Sèvres.

The forced levy of soldiers and the banishment of their priests was the immediate cause of these countryside insurrections. In these wholly agricultural areas the people were strongly conservative. Here, nobles and their tenant farmers lived in personal and friendly contact. The peasants' hostility, on attempts of the government to deprive them of their faith and destroy amicable and lucrative relations with their landlords, came as a shock to the ruling government.

With all soldiers serving on the frontiers, there remained no means to control the new rising populace. The countryside was almost impregnable; the interior, the *Bocage*, hilly, thickly wooded and intersected by deep ravines. Roads and lanes, connecting the remote villages, ran between thick furze and broom bushes, impassable to carts and canons. Here the Vendeans hit and then disappeared. These difficulties, faced by fighting Republicans, were increased along the seacoast by great stretches of marshland and wide, deep, draining ditches. Here the Republicans experienced heavy defeat, against insurgents comprising tough land labourers, brigands, poachers and smugglers. Thorough and brilliant marksmen, these conducted a successful guerrilla war through this wild countryside.

The Vendeans won repeated successes, fighting with religious ardour and following their leaders unto death, the non-juror priests offering immediate entrance into heaven for those that fell. The government had blundered badly by its attempts to render Mother Church a state-owned business. All could be taken from the peasants and still they would hesitate to rebel against authority; but take their faith and they would metamorphose into a violent, indomitable force. In the south, Marseilles, Mímes, Toulon, Grenoble, parts of Provence, the Rhône Valley and Lyon, were in successful rebellion.

While these anti-government triumphs were being enacted, the Austrian army threatened Paris from the north, down the valley of the river Oise and river Maine and on July 26 the important frontier stronghold of Valenciennes, north of Paris, fell into Austrian hands.

The Montagnard soon received intelligence on the coalition's beliefs: that of French government's imminent collapse. The Terror increased; the reins in the iron grip of Robespierre, the incorruptible. The Montagnard now put at the disposal of the armies, the entire resources of the country: revenue, stock, capital and labour.

In the spring 1793, in effort to prevent further sliding of the economy, a maximum price of corn was fixed but variable within different departments and to be sold only at fairs and markets: this trade supervised by the municipal bodies. Soon most raw materials also became subject to the *Law of Maximum*. Corruption thrived within these parameters, as it did regarding nearly all articles of consumption. Counteracting this, in order to prevent hording, traders were required to post, above their shop doors, lists of all articles in stock.  Raids began for the unlisted and hidden goods and death ensued for those caught in this practice.  Within the private sector, anyone with even a small amount of money: from nobility, upper middle classes to the *Petit Bourgeoisie*; set up their circle of secret contacts and suppliers. Cellars and dungeons, priest holes and attic hideaways, bulged with an enormous array of goods. Death penalty was therefore extended across the board, for all citizens thus occupied.

The practice of supplying the army through contractors was now abandoned. All supplies to the armies were now requisitioned; their owners (of supplies) forced to sell through the government at maximum price and were paid in *assignats*. Deemed a capital offence to refuse this method of payment, for anything, those of Anton's calibre began to accept more and more of these worthless pieces of paper, as trust disappeared between old business acquaintances.  Better a worthless piece of paper than provide entertainment on Revolution Square.

Financial and commercial companies were now dissolved, the investment of capital in foreign countries prohibited, the Exchange closed, the export of all French articles of growth and manufacture forbidden and the possession of foreign articles declared a crime, no matter the date of purchase. Capitalists, Bankers and Merchants now engaged in foreign trade, were declared enemies of the state and subject to the law of treason.  Fines, property confiscation, imprisonment and execution enforced these measures: sometimes all of the above. These methods of control succeeded. Property was seized and dispensed rapidly to the highest bidders, the prisons overflowed and the guillotine ran non-stop.  Place de la Revolution was packed each day: the Jacobins stopping short only of entry ticketing at the barriers and this only because of Robespierre the Incorruptible.

As the cooling autumn approached, the Jacobin government now staged a great political trial of the house-arrested Girondin leaders: to consummate and celebrate the overthrow of Girondinism. The trial procedures—beginning October 15th 1793 and simultaneously to that of the queen—proved barbaric in the extreme: for simple justification of execution and, as intended, brought back to the boil the revolutionary fervour. Many of the charges could not be considered applicable to the prisoners. This however was of no concern: the chief witnesses always the political opponents of the accused men: just as the judges and jurymen of the *Revolutionary Court* were tools, or accomplices, of the *Commune* and committees of the government.

A trial of a party now evolved; using the accused twenty-one men eventually brought forward for interrogation, beneath the public prosecutor, Fouquier Tinville, acting now under the express instructions of the *Committee of Public Safety*. If it could be shown that seditious opinions were characteristic of the 'party clique,' to whom they belonged, then a presumption was made that they were individually guilty of seditious acts.

This mode of thinking escalated. Soon, an association at any time during one's career, with any person now declared a traitor, was equally damaging. A plea that that person had been a loyal Frenchman at the time of acquaintance made no difference: he was a traitor now, albeit a headless one, therefore so too was the defendant now a traitor. Two persons heard speaking in treasonable accents, caused every person known to them both to be also imprisoned. The net grew so wide and so fine of mesh that no accused person could escape. Documented evidence was produced from as far back as the first year of the Revolution and beyond: a time when Sieur Goisset and his gang, the spies of the new and enthusiastic *Commite des Recherches*, mingled discreetly amongst the crowds of the *Palais-Royal* arcades. Here they recorded a look, a remark and that windfall; the indiscreet statement made out of pure frustration, easily read as treasonable intent. Thus the time spent in these arcades by Emile and Trifane: spying out the spies. Such double game became extremely dangerous however, until they abandoned the practice at the time of Louis' execution. Not however before Beaumont was witnessed speaking with Sieur Goisset. But they assumed, unfortunately, that he played the same game as them.

The farce of trials continued. The prisoners must be seen to have their defence under the Glorious and honourable Republic: even though their guilt was ascertained simply by being a Girondin. But a trial of the whole Girondin party brought about charges ranging across the political field and dating from 1789 to the final 'crime': the formation of the *Commission of Twelve* to investigate the actions of the *Communes*. It soon became evident, therefore, that this could evolve into the longest trial in the history of France. Finally, the Public Prosecutor Fouruier-Tinville, appealed to the Assembly.

Standing at the lectern he gazed around. "This trial has no hope of drawing to conclusion, citizens, with each prisoner prolonging his defence, dragging us through a lengthy history of the early beginnings of the Revolution! Each weaves a web of false trails, dead-end evidence, brick walls and misty facts, trailing without trace into a foggy horizon where no man can follow! We must act to prevent him from so doing! A court cannot remedy this state of affairs... but the Convention may perhaps do so!"

"A decree then: shortening the defendant's time of trial to three days only," responded a deputy. "After which the president may close the trial; if the jury agrees that they be sufficiently enlightened to the defendants' guilt."

After little debate, the decree was immediately passed.    All the accused Girondists were found guilty and went from the court to the guillotine, amongst them Verniaud, Brissot and Gensonné. On their way to the Place de la Revolution they commenced singing: '*Allons enfants de la patrie, Le jour de glorie est arrivé*', the already famous *Marseillaise* 'song of the people' and continued throughout the executions until the last head fell: underlining their faith and loyalty to France. The notary at his desk, to the side of the guillotine, calmly noted that it was the 31$^{st}$ day of October1793 and proceeded to list the names.

From this time forward, a number of victims, some distinguished, others obscure, belonging to all parties, went every week to the Place de la Revolution. Amongst them were the gentle and pious Madame Elizabeth, the king's sister, the former Mayor of Paris, Bailly the astronomer, Barnave, Madame Roland—champion of *le peuple*—and Phillip Egalité; the former Duke of Orleans. Voting with the people for the king's execution, apparently could not atone for the crime of his birth into the nobility. Of other prominent remaining Girondins, Cambon was shot down in a village refuge; Condorcet found dead in prison of unknown causes, Clavier stabbed himself to death and Lindot apparently shot himself. Many took to the Pyrenees, the forests and the villages, but the countryside was on the alert and most of these captured and dragged to the guillotine. It was stated Pétion and Buzot, hiding in a forest, apparently shot themselves, or each other.  Salle and Gaudet, found hiding in an attic near Bordeaux, were executed, as was Birotteau. All of these guilty of one crime: being a Girondin.  Roland, the former Minister of the Interior, was found in the countryside: stabbed many times, by his own hand.

Stunned, the near-relative gazed at her tormentor: "You say *what*?"

The bearer of these tidings wore a wooden face. "He committed suicide, Citizen."

"Indeed! Then he did own phenomenal fortitude!"

"But here, Madame; is his suicide note."

She took it, glanced at it, then handed it back: of what use now, to enlighten the poor messenger that it was not his handwriting. She wondered why they had bothered.

Of the sixty-three leaders of the Girondin party, only twenty-five survived the Revolution to die of natural causes, a much-coveted experience, within revolutionary France.  Thus the final demise of the moderately left Girondin political party: leaving the way clear for the 'Montagne'. Nothing now could balance the extremist, Robespierre-led government.

At the beginning of the Girondin trials—early October 1793—Robespierre had put to good use the resurrected lust for blood within the sans-culottes.  About to intensify The Terror, he brought back past royal life to whip further that fervour and hatred. His position on the *Committee of Public Safety*, he knew, would empower him to crush the enemies of the State: the Girondins and Royalty, once and for all. Together with his allies, Saint-Just and Couthon, Robespierre now held the balance of power on this committee.  Remaining clinically incorruptible, he believed in the power of a political system backed by Terror, but death only to the peoples' enemies. Saint-Just, however, determined to exterminate everyone opposing the Glorious Revolution: in particular those of deep religious convictions.  He now set the sans-culottes to destroy the Tombs in the Church of Saint-Denis: and all ancient tombs that could be found. Their looting and destruction now sanctioned, they required no championing.

Whilst St Just was thus occupied, Robespierre, busy organizing and supervising the Girondin trials, prompted Hébert to stir once again the hatred of Marie Antoinette. Her life had been long sought by the Hébertists; by the whole population of France, in fact: at least, the woman they had been taught to hate. The Marie Antoinette image that had been fed to them was so far from the truth that it entered the realms of mythology. Her trial was arranged.

Shut off from all communication since the fall of the throne, she was suddenly informed of her fate by her removal from the Temple to the Conciergerie. Sitting on the Il'e de la Cité in the middle of the Seine, close to the Palais de Justice, amongst the Revolutionary and other courts, the Conciergerie was known as the anti-room to the guillotine: the *cour du mai*, holding the tumbrels that then travelled the Champs Alysses to the Place de la Revolution.

At 0800hrs Monday 14th October, a preliminary examination of the queen was held at the Tower, before the *Revolutionary Tribunal*. Her inquisitors: Armand Martial Herman, Tribune President and Antoine Fouquier-Tinville, the Public Prosecutor. They could not, however, shake her composure or trap her into admission of guilt. Her manner always dignified and polite, she managed to parry their question without accusing her inquisitors of any of their own very real iniquities: such accusations of any good republican considered an act of treason. Parrying the many set traps, she successfully ran the cleverly designed gauntlet, leaving her accusers frustrated and even more determined.

October 15th 1793, Marie Antoinette stood formal trial at the *Grande Chambre*, before five judges and a jury of twelve men, all eager republicans; hand picked by Robespierre. Here she heard the lengthy indictment: accusing her of the treason of conspiring with her Austrian brother against France, influencing Louis to veto decrees of the Assembly and manipulating him against the people. Also of organizing counterrevolution, maintaining secret relations and correspondence with the enemy and numerous other conspiracies: including instigating the flight to Varennes and sending millions of *livre* to Austria. The list went on but these considered enough to incriminate her.

Marie Antoinette gazed at the witnesses against her. They were all stooges of the revolutionary government she knew; and to these she listened without a word. She looked at them, at the very scene: this surely was a badly staged comedy. She smiled inwardly, grimly: she too could act and rather well. Her skill, once embarked, outshone theirs' as does a sky on a clear night after that of a dark and stormy one. She replied firmly to the accusations made against her and by her composure and dignity won murmurs of approval and applause from the hostile crowd gathered for the spectacle.

The shock accusation, however, proven by the childish signature of her own son upon papers claiming incestuous relations with his own mother, caused her temporary loss of control. Nothing had prepared her for this: not for a second had she the imagination to even guess at such fabrication as this. She swayed on her feet, her face white and expressionless. Collecting herself a little, she turned to gaze at her enemy: Hébert, editor of the *Père Duchesne* and creator of the web of lies and deceit and unbelievable tales of horror about her. These included even that she ate the children of peasants on frivolous dare. Such stories had endlessly spewed across France in the form of cartoons, by brochure and pamphlet. That he had masterminded this latest obscenity she had no doubt and there was of course, here, those that knew it to be so. But now she was defeated, for there was no fighting such depths of depraved manipulations. She stared silently at him across the room, with nothing to say; whatever she said would be misinterpreted to their advantage.

Apparently struck dumb she was brought back to the present. "Well Madame? How do you plead?"

"I have no knowledge of these accusations."

"How do you plead? You are required to answer."

"If I have not answered, then it be because there *be* no answer sufficiently strong: a simple 'no' lends itself to disbelief. All would refuse to answer such a charge against a mother." She turned to the audience. "You that are mothers: could *you* bear such an accusation? Could *you* fight such vile and debased accusations, involving your beautiful, beloved children? Have a care, mothers of France: absolutely nothing remains sacred."

The following disruptions brought the trial into suspension for some minutes; however, the long years of scandal sheets listing her iniquities held sway and they swung back, lusting for her blood. She was found guilty by unanimous vote and to be guillotined.

Nothing prepares one for the final blow, even though such has long been anticipated, but shock sometimes assists one, by stealing all emotion and thought. The next wave, however, that of reaction, races in on the heels of that false calm. If one is lucky, then that wave takes a little time to reach one's consciousness, allowing the body and mind to conduct normal activity and thought. Whether or not that had occurred within the queen none would know. She did remain stately and dignified and gave not one moment of victory to her persecutors by means of emotional exhibition, no matter how slight; but the pain of separation from her two remaining children could not be overcome. However, even in this, of outward display there was none.

She was taken in the tumbril, to the Place de la Revolution. Hands tied behind her, she swayed gracefully within the gentle movements of the slow-drawn cart— slow to gratify the staring citizens of Paris but also because the crowds did not allow any speed of progress. Her courageous endurance, however, and noble resigned manner in which she met her death, won grudging respect from the mob. An ethereal silence fell, as she stepped from the tumbril and then, politely refusing the guiding hands, mounted the steps in sedate and serene manner. A dais plank, following the top step, was a little uneven; causing her to stumble, lose balance and step upon the foot of a guard.

"I am so sorry," she said softly, glancing up at him automatically, her gaze gentle with genuine apology.

The guard stared into her eyes; stunned by an aura of gentleness, and yes, purity, surrounding this woman so denigrated, hated and reviled. Though he did not own great intelligence, the remainder of his life was so affected by the encounter that he turned away from self-seeking, raw and crude Paris: entering his native countryside, there to burn his guard uniform and eventually die a market gardener.

Sixteen days prior to the execution of Girondin leaders, following their drawn-out farce of trial, Marie Antoinette died by guillotine, October 16th 1793.

♣

Emile sat forward in his comfortable chair and pulling his intricately carved snuffbox out of his pocket, flicked it open and offered it to his friend. "What think you of Beaumont? Be he guilty of *mon père's* arrest?"

"Without a doubt: he has not been abroad since de Quatreaux' arrest and they say that his health be not salubrious and he be sunken in torpor." Raoul took a delicate pinch of the fine tobacco.

"He be a damned sight more sunken when I get my hands on him; to the depth of six feet... point of fact.  Charlotte Corday does not have a monopoly on revenge."

"Ah yes... I heard about that... poor Marat!"

Emile cocked an eyebrow. "*Poor* Marat?  He be second only to Robespierre in sheer, unadulterated brutality! But no, on second thoughts... he is in fact worse. Robespierre... though insane, is incorruptible. End result the same, of course."

"But in his *baignoire*?  Can you imagine your last breath in your *baignoire*? But just why did he simply lie there and allow her to stab him, by the by... modesty?"

Emile smiled faintly. "*I* heard it was the oatmeal!"

Trifane stilled his hand hovering over his snuff box. "The what?"

"Oatmeal... for his skin disorder... slippery as all hell apparently, couldn't fight back... his bathrobe simply slipped against the tub sides!"

"*Grand Dieu*... must remember never to use the stuff!"

"Whatever it was that aided her, she got her revenge." Emile's smile was grim.

"Eye for an eye?"

"'Tis something that he certainly understands."

"Beaumont?" Raoul eyed his friend in compassion. "Easy *mon ami*, he be an older man, you cannot touch him. Duelling etiquette will not allow it."

"Can I not? Just you watch me."

"But you cannot prove a thing."

"No? He played at La Coste with *mon père* the *very day* that Pontisqieu passed his message. All at that table swear that he said nothing. Both he and Lareaux, they both shall go, one day soon.  I shall not rest until justice be done!"

"He shall deny that Pontisqieu was ever at his house. And Lareaux be mine. But enough." Raoul went softly to the door, listened a moment, then whipped it open. The hall beyond lay deserted. He closed it and returned to his chair. "Clear. All is ready?"

"All from my department... and you?"

"Ah yes, de Quatreaux arrives back at La Force at midnight but we cannot operate until the change of guard, by new recruits, midday next day."

"Are we ahead of their constant moving of him *this* time?"

"We are, thanks to Pontisqieu. He has my complete admiration, that one." Emile smiled grimly. "Hate to see him go down *mon ami* and the risks are monumental."

"He is a cool individual. He believes Robespierre does not suspect, but is ever vigilant."

"Then all goes ahead. We cannot slip up this time! This be it. You trust Anton?"

"I must, we cannot do it alone. We need his wine shop premises, and his friendship with de Quatreaux seems to have transcended all social confines."

"Ah yes, *mon père* has the trick of that particular magic."

"I believe it to be a genuine feeling for anyone that he likes."

"Oh yes. He be a law unto himself: societal mores and laws totally ignored."

"And besides, you reside below Anton's wine shop, and you still live."

Emile grinned. "Ah yes, but I pay him well for that malodorous rat-infested hell-hole."

"Emile, *mon ami*, still he be a very decent man. I welcome him any time."

"I must enlighten him of your feelings, *mon cher*," chuckled Emile.

# CHAPTER TWENTY-ONE

## Guillotines and Tunnels

The two sans-culottes, dressed in muddied boots and bedraggled cloaks, moved towards the gates. They glanced hesitantly to left and right as they drew closer, their mien a mix of the old humble attitude, tinted with the newborn arrogance of true revolutionaries. The duty guardsman yawned, straightened; and moving forward, searched them briefly. Glancing at the general pass held by the lowest echelons of society, he waved them through into La Force courtyard. They crossed this to the century-box against the inner wall: tall, dark and windowless. Here, they showed their special access passes, stamped '*Pour le Prison*' and documents requesting to visit Prisoner 225, Citoyen Louvois of 'D' block: cell 15. Those documents in the name of de Quatreaux: prisoner 228 remained in Raoul's pocket, until they reached the cell.

After studying the passes, a red-faced individual with bulbous nose opened another iron-bolt studded wicket and they passed into the dark, dank and noisome prison buildings. They crossed the stone-flagged floor to a large guardroom. A man, dressed in a dark cloak with drawn hood, stood waiting at the desk with his back to the entrance. They stood in line: waiting the guard's perusal of the man's papers. At last he nodded, handed them back and said, "Follow that guard."

"*Merci*, Monsieur."

At the voice, the two sans-culottes froze; then one turned away in a sudden coughing fit. The other bent toward him in brotherly solicitude, as the nobleman turned from the desk and passed them without a glance at the sans-culottes. Marc de Vries followed the guard.

After several minutes of being ignored, they were beckoned forward and their proffered paper, showing the name Louvios, checked against a register. A curt nod indicated acceptance and an idle guard summoned forward.

Taking a set of keys off a hook, this individual said one word: "Come."

In this man's silent company they continued on, through many sets of locked doors into the inner depths of La Force prison. Reaching the last grilled door the guard nodded ahead. "There shall be nothing now between ye and cell fifteen."

He turned and left them to continue the convoluted route through the twilit dank corridors and staircases of the grim building. They passed some few guards and officials as they scuffed along but were ignored.

Finding a momentarily empty stretch between cells, the two silent sans-culottes swiftly divested their cloaks and grubby red caps and stuffed them behind empty water-barrels against the wall, disturbing several very fat rats there. Two guards now moved arrogantly and purposefully along the passageway. Some minute or so later voices could be heard and they glanced at each other.

Voice almost inaudible, Emile leaned toward Raoul: "What is he *doing* here?"

"Pray not to visit de Quatreaux! He is, thankfully, astute and will take our cue. But everyone has family of some connection imprisoned now! Play it by ear!"

Rounding the corner, they perceived the guardroom at the junction of two sections. The low-vaulted, malodorous room contained only two guards. A swift glance into the large cell to the right showed some few visitors but no sign of De Vries. One of the guards was slouched at a desk, an open register before him, the other seated on a stone bench, lounging back against the grimy wall; giving all the appearances of one in a comfortable slumber. The jaundiced guard glanced up casually from his register at the approaching figures and then straightened suddenly. He pulled a watch from his inner pocket and glanced at it; the new guards were early. The new guards waited: hopeful the Jacobins' restoration of the state of prisons to the vicious seventeenth century control, would keep him from questioning this too closely. Those who incurred the serious displeasure of the Committees, *any* Committee, were in grave danger of imprisonment and or execution and who knew just who these two might be: spies roamed everywhere. He kicked sideways at his colleague who then woke with a small snort.

"Do not disturb him, whatever you do, Citizen," said Raoul sweetly.

The desk-bound man sat a little straighter and reaching out to take the proffered papers from Raoul said mildly, "A little early are ye not?" staring at the transfer papers from a high authority with a puzzled expression.

Raoul moved quickly into speech, before the puzzled expression turned to one of suspicion. "Early? We are not the change of guard. We are here to collect prisoner 228. Come, the necessary La Force exit papers, if you please." His voice changed to one of stern rebuke. "And *stand* when addressed by a superior officer... the old regime may be gone but you would not offer such rag manners to an emissary of Citizen Robespierre, I be thinking!"

"Emissary?"

"Exit papers?"

The guards shot to their feet, the one swaying a little. These before them were not your usual guards of the La Force and the mention of Robespierre caused a chill of fear. An observer would find it difficult to say who was the more nervous of the two parties. The advantage, however, for the moment lay with the impostors: they were not puzzled. The fear of the regime could be felt within these two and Raoul pressed his advantage.

"That you must issue... *imbecile:* for his release from your custody to mine, come man... we be short on time!" Raoul held his breath, hopeful of his attitude of superior rank and uniform carrying him through. He used the word '*tu*' in the sans-culottes accents, in place of the more formal '*vous*'. Added to this was a nice touch of lower bourgeoisie cadence: giving the appearance of one elevated to higher position by the new regime. His own manner of speech and accent however, would creep through, should he be forced to converse for very much longer: no matter how long and hard he had practiced.

"We have no news of this, Citizen!"

"Of course you have not: it is urgent. Does the document not say 'special release'? Is that not Robespierre's signature?"

"That is so... but..." He glanced at the name on the fake documents again, then ran his finger down the register, searching. His comrade, reeking of stale wine, stared at them. He remained silent and watchful, a dull suspicion growing in his eyes but the effort of thought required to illuminate that suspicion proved too difficult. His position as guard, however, was almost as precarious as that of the prisoners. He leaned forward and pulled the Anton devised fake papers towards him, squinted at the name and compared it with those on the D Block prison register. Of this, some he could read, others not: his illiteracy overcome by ordering a literate prisoner to read the rollcall.

He struggled with the spelling of the name de Quatreaux, then beamed triumphantly. "But he be gone, Citizen."

The first guard confirmed this now upon the exit register.

Raoul felt the ice travel slowly down his spine: "What mean you...gone?"

"He be gone when we comes on dooty Citizen: the soft spoken and polite one; but deep down: haughty as all hell, I be thinking!"

"Where did they take him? Come Citizen, the Governor awaits."

"To the Conciergerie," he grinned suddenly. "Mayhap already to the guillotine, Citizen!"

Raoul dared not glance at Emile's wooden features. Born of the Sword, his childhood conditioning and discipline would hold him in check but for how long was the question. Labouring beneath the bitter fury regarding Beaumont's treachery, Emile had shown signs of building tension for some time now. That his *père* be consequently handed over to the Jacobins was insupportable; but that the traitor had been such a long-time friend beyond the imagination. Within the short but agonizing wait, necessary during the planning of this rescue mission, he had been busy. Acquiring information, uniforms, passes and other fake paperwork required concentration. Added to this had been two failed attempts to do this very thing: spring de Quatreaux. Any faint facial expression or impotent fury in his eyes, would now undo them. Already the guards stared suspiciously at the two superiors who were now appearing to lack credible knowledge. Emile maintained his cool exterior, however: face calm, demeanour polite, he swung to Raoul, brows raised.

"Seems Citizen, that we are in the wrong place." He turned back to the two guards and almost bowed, controlling this just in time. "Our papers, please, *merci*, Citizen. We go now, to the Conciergerie!"

Watched by the two faintly frowning guards they retraced their steps, turned the corner and many more and at the point of the barrels retrieved their cloaks, including the spare one that was to have been worn by the now absent de Quatreaux: that strict, unbending disciplinarian, beneath whom all, servants and family, felt safe and secure, especially his daughter. Raoul cursed the Revolution. Anything that caused his lady's discomfort brought on his ire. This deepening feeling outranked any fury at the loss of certain properties to the various *Committees*, sequestered for the benefit of the *Armée Révolutionaire*. He had snorted in disgust: this 14th Armée comprised the toughest, meanest specimens of criminal humanity from the *egouts* of Paris.

The return journey differed only in that they had no escort and were let through each locked grill by rattling them and calling and then waiting the guard of the section to open it. Once outside the La Force prison they quickly sought the waiting horses.

"Seigneur?" the groom held the three sets of reins, "The prisoner?" His voice was low, for although traffic was light just here, other animals were tied to the post rail and other grooms lounged about, laughing and talking.

Raoul cast a hasty glance at the girth and stirrups of his animal and sprang up, the mare sidling and fidgeting to be gone. "*Citizen*, Beauvois!" he hissed, then, "Sell the spare horse... keep the money! And you have not seen us this day!"

"Very good Monseigneur."

Emile, mounting his horse also, groaned softly, "*Mon Dieu* man... and you Anton trusts!"

Raoul and Emile left the apologetic groom, their mounts leaping forward at a touch and they rode towards the Champs Elysees at a steady gallop. They rode thus for some five minutes or so, weaving through less populated side streets but then had to slow for traffic, pedestrian and equine: carriages, *pots-de-chambre*, produce carts, closed travelling coaches and clusters of pedestrians: there be safety in numbers.

Emile, moving up close to Raoul, spoke in savage undertones. "Who *told* them?"

"Ah, leave it, *mon ami*. You will never find out and it may have been pure co-incidence."

"For the moment, yes, you are in the right of it, but when this be over? *Then* I shall find him." He rode on, thinking; then, "Pontisqieu? I am reluctant to believe it but..."

Raoul turned toward him. "If you persist in this then Anton also be suspect."

"No! I will not have it."

"Likewise: of Pontisqieu."

"But we know him not so long, Anton, almost twenty-five years."

"Longevity of friendship is never an assurance these days; you should know! But Pontisqieu: he is discretion, be assured. He is deep in love with your sister, *mon ami*."

Emile turned to stare. "No! The poor dog!" He gave this some thought and then, riding up close to Raoul again, "Direct to the Place de la Revolution, think you?"

"Yes... our papers will not hold water at the Conciergerie."

"Of course... where are my *brains*?"

"Your brains are fine, *mon ami*," replied Raoul in deep compassion, "just desperate."

"Place de la Revolution then. If he is not there... then we wait en route. Dépêchons nous!"

♣

Marie gazed down into the Rue Saint-Honoré, just as a tumbril turned the corner and trundled along, beneath their window. "Oh dear, there goes another. I cannot watch."

But she lingered, owing them at the very least, she supposed, prayer and spiritual support, no matter it be unknown to them or they to her. If they could ride those malodorous carts in such stalwart fashion, then she must discipline her selfish sensitivity at the thought of the guillotine.

"Marie, the executions shall continue until something or someone brings them to a halt. And that shall not happen any time soon. Not while *Robespierre* holds the reins."

"Well, I suppose if they must lose their heads, they do it with pride," replied Marie.

"That of course is a tremendous advantage."

"But of course. We all die some time. This way at least one has centre stage and the history books shall record all."

"Yes, and just think, that stage has an audience of 30,000: and the *tricoteuse* counting... so the mathematical records of it shall of course be accurate!"

Marie missed the irony. "Well it *is* a spectacle and of the tricoteuse: there always were and always shall be such people. Not so long ago they sat in hired windows; to watch the Damien tortured to death in front of the Hôtel de Ville. At least the guillotine is merciful... so it is said!"

"Mechanized execution does not turn judicial murder of political enemies into a virtue, Marie. And I for one shall not put it to the touch. I be quite happy to forego the infamous ritual and can survive without mention within the history books; that the victor writes!"

Marie turned to gaze at her. "You are, I think, fond of your head?"

It was a poor attempt at humour but at least caused Angelique to smile. "Perhaps I am a little self-obsessed, but yes, I like it, preferably upon my shoulders."

"Do not worry, cousin. I shall not allow them to execute you."

"My heartfelt thanks, Marie, but pray do consider, should they execute *mon père*, then I shall be next."

"No, no. Emile be next, with his er, secret business across the border."

"But they cannot find him. *I am here.*"

"Know what I think?"

"You are about to tell me I fear!"

"They shall not sweep you up in their infamous net: Monseigneur Trifane shall not allow that to happen." She paused, a tiny smile at the corners of her mouth.

Angelique felt the colour sweeping up and over her face. "You mistake Marie, indeed he has not said... there is nothing... between us!"

Marie smiled knowingly and, allowing time for Angelique to recover, turned once more to stare down into the street at another tumbril and shuddered, "Perhaps God wants to end it all."

"Not God. *Robespierre.* His net spread wide, none can escape it, I begin to think."

"But no *ma chère*. Be of stout heart, our escape plans still stand, do they not?"

"Yes Marie, but once outside Paris, the dangers shall be threefold of a year ago."

"I do not pretend that it shall be comfortable or to foresee just what measures your brother and Trifane have in place, but rest in their superior intellect."

"Oh Marie; Olympe de Gouges would wring her hands over you."

"That may well be, my dear, but could *she* arrange safe route out of France? I believe Emile and Trifane *will*."

Angelique looked serious suddenly. "I hope so, but the countryside will be fraught with obstacles; scarcity of animal feed, bad roads and inferior equipage." She paused. "And the towns and villages must be avoided: every single man knows every other and the network of communication between villages amazing... and swift!"

"But the villages are necessary: how else to obtain food and water?"

Angelique shook her head. "A universal vigilante exists within all towns and villages: patrolling day and night. Every barrier, every taxing house, every hostelry and posting house now own cannons, guns and 'missiles', all pointed and ready; their guards with swords drawn! All travellers are halted: and thoroughly examined from every angle. They are cross-questioned; papers are inspected, checked and rechecked against names on lists, issued by that horrendous machine called the *Commune*. They pull off wigs, tug at beards and moustaches and thump chests of the gentlemen for evidence of er... bosom! They check even the horses' leathers... and underbellies! And do not think that one may breathe easy once past these barriers, for often one is pursued or entrapped apparently: following some person's sudden and imaginative illumination!"

"Where acquired you this extensive knowledge?"

"Francois. He said that he was stopped thirteen times, on one journey back to the frontier; and once escorted back to a guardhouse full of rough and filthy, Phrygian-adorned peasants, claiming his uniform to be a disguise."

"But he was a soldier of the army... his papers... his uniform!"

"Just so: but they are mostly illiterate and to try to convince the drunken patriots of anything at all be impossible in this climate. For such people he died. But I cannot blame them. They are *educated* to hatred. Those educators I *do* want to kill! Now I must go find more paper, Marie. For me, to write be the only relief: and now I can add that it was the bankers who pushed for war: more profitable than peace! According to Olympe... no, do not look at me like that! She has written proof!"

Marie could find nothing to say to this and watched her leave the room. She was about to desert her post at the window when another tumbril entered the far end of the street; they were coming at half-hourly intervals this day. Something kept her there, watching the horse moving at a slow pace. The pedestrian traffic stood still and silent, as happened on the passing of a funeral cortege; and she supposed this was appropriate, really.

Marie suddenly stiffened; staring in shocked disbelief and then did a very un-Marie like thing. She fainted into a state of cold unconsciousness. Angelique, re-entering the room some few seconds later, halted and then moved swiftly to her side.

"Marie! Goodness... what be the trouble? Wake Marie..." She shook her and slapped her face hard, to no avail. Moving to the bell-pull she gave it an urgent tug and ran back to Marie prone upon the floor.

Henri appeared, took in the scene and bowed himself out again with the words, "I shall send for her *femme de chambre*, Madame."

"Yes do, Henri, and tell her to bring the vinaigrette and some feathers to burn. Oh, and fetch some cognac please."

Henri disappeared, reappeared several minutes later and transferred Marie from the floor to the chaise. Following this the *femme de chambre* arrived and took charge, rubbing hands and feet with lavender oil and waving the vinaigrette beneath Marie's nose, but it was the odour of burnt feathers that finally brought a groaning Marie to her senses.

"Oh…ugh!" She struggled to sit up and then choked upon the brandy poured down her throat by the enthusiastic Henri. She gazed around and then, seeing Angelique, stared at her in sudden dismay. "*Chérie*…your *père!*"

Angelique felt the energy drain from her entire body, her fading limbs suddenly prickling with pins and needles and she had to sit. She struggled to her feet and waving vaguely towards Marie, told the *femme de chambre* to attend to all that was necessary. She then motioned Henri to follow her and left the room. Giving him instructions to quickly bring round the light town carriage, she ran straight to the attic. Here she rapidly struggled out of her dress, donned one of Fanchon's oldest sets of clothing and headed down the stairs again and out the front entrance, the hood of the old cloak pulled over her head. The carriage was just pulling up.

The sounds of the howling mob rose in a crescendo: in response to the figure upon the dais, working the crowd against the prisoners climbing the steps to the scaffold. She drove her numb and shaking legs forward. She had left the carriage with a frightened coachman and groom at the entrance of the square and forced her way through the crush on foot. It seemed the whole population of Paris was here. Stretching and straining to see the occupants of the tumbril, she wove her way inch by inch forward.

''Ere Citizienne,' 'easy girl,' 'wait your turn!' 'we was 'ere first!' and like statements she ignored until she reached three deep from the foot of the dais. The mob, many taller than her, some with children perched upon shoulders to gain better view, blocked her vision, but she had a split second glimpse of the board swinging forward.

The eerie sound of the sliding blade through the air cut through the sudden awed silence that always accompanied every execution at this point. As it thumped to its final destination and the head, with a softer thump, landed in the basket, a deafening cheer rent the cool, still air. She fought to hold on to consciousness and her stomach contents as the ground pitched beneath her feet. Concentrating fiercely to remain upright, she locked her gaze on the dais: to witness a dripping head held up before the crowd: the head of Jean-Pierre Vermont, Monsieur le Comte de Quatreaux. Her legs apparently turning to water, Angelique crumpled to the ground. Surfacing groggily, she sat up and then, head swimming again, lowered it to her knees.

Sitting there amongst the dancing feet and echoing noise of the barbaric crowd, she fought to hold to her senses and stomach contents: fought the waves of nausea, swallowed the bile rising to her throat. Sweat poured, soaked her dress and the grey veil of faintness threatened her again but it must not happen: *Père* had trained her better than that. What would he say to such faintheartedness: nothing must humble her amongst this barbaric mob! But no, he could not say anything to her now: but was that really him? No, no; it *could not* have been. Struggling to her feet and fighting through the deep ravines of shock and hysteria, her control slipping, she stared ahead and saw again: de Quatreaux' head. Suddenly, she recognized a hated figure astride a large mount: watchfully scanning the mob. The tenuous vacuum of mental no-man's-land dissolved and she gave vent to the long-built fury, boiling within her from the time of Fanchon and Isobel's death. The horseman was Saint-Just. Another sat his animal at a point west of the dais; others were posted at intervals around the guillotine and outside of these, two rows of soldiers formed a square around the dais, holding back the mob.

Gaining her senses fully now and driven by grief and fury she surged forward, pushing between two restraining soldiers who grabbed her by the upper arms. Pulling them with her, suddenly exhibiting the strength of the raging demented, she surged forward to the foot of the block. Intent upon retrieving the head of her father, she reached up to the attendant there whose job it was to place the head with the body. He gazed at her a moment, casually holding the head by its hair, waiting for the storm of tears. Behind her was a dirty, toothless, grinning sans-culotte, and the head was tossed to him. It became evident that this one was to be screwed upon a pike to satisfy the bloodlust of the mob: as the interest lulled a little, the offer of a head did the trick.

"No!" she screamed, "No…you bestial beings! Worse than beasts! They do not sink so low! That man has no crime! He has done nothing to you! He fed you… *protected* you… loved you! Ask *anyone* at Quatreaux village! Ask *all* at that village!"

She choked back a sob rising within her throat, aware only of the screaming grief and fury within her incoherent brain. Nothing could have stopped her.

Saint-Just turned his head, searching out the voice below. "Whom do we have here? Yes, you! Do you challenge the wisdom and justice of the great and honourable Revolution?"

"Wisdom? *Wisdom? Honourable*? You call the murder of thousands of innocent people, *honourable*? Even the 'Fourth Estate'… now go beneath, that… that…" She could not even glance at the blade: waiting high in the air, mercilessly, bizarrely: hungry.

"You refer to *class*, Citizienne? But it is abolished! Oh so careless! You have now *really* sealed your fate."

Horse and man were now close to her and he recognized her not but a noblewoman she surely was and as such it behove him to hand her up to the bloodlust of the mob. Nothing could have been more propitious; they grew speedily bored with regular executions. "So… are you aware, *Citizienne*, that to criticize the Supreme Revolutionary Government be a treasonable offence? But of course you are; and no one speaking such treason escapes punishment." He raised his voice. "What say the people? Be she guilty of treason?"

"*Yes…yes…yes!*"

"Treason! Treason! Treason!"

"Does she suffer the punishment of the guillotine for this treason?"

"Yes, yes, yes."

A thousand near voices cried, "The guillotine! The guillotine! The guillotine!"

The crowd went wild and wave upon wave of applause rippled across the packed square, those on the outer environs wondering but the sound was infectious and so they too cheered. The soldiers shifted nervous feet, the mounted guards gripping the reins to control bridling horses. Saint-Just shrugged and turning away in bored fashion indicated the guardsman to take her. A roar of applause went up.

These were the sounds to greet Raoul and Emile as they entered the Place de la Revolution, struggling to thrust their horses through the milling mob. Raoul, fearing the worst, urged his mount on, causing hostile eruptions around him. Emile, a little way behind him, struggled to cut a swathe through the dense humanity.

Raoul, first to see the head upon the dancing pike and simultaneously spotting Angelique, standing upon the top step, turned and called urgently to Emile: "Go *mon ami...* go! It does not require us both here, our friend Saint-Just be here!"

Emile must not be recognized and two could not do more than one amongst these thousands: this would be a battle of minds now. He dare not say more, for fear of alerting the crowd and forged on towards the steps, pushing through the reluctantly parting mob.

Emile, not understanding but recognizing the urgency within Raoul, made to turn his horse but the milling crowd was too dense, and glancing back to shout to Raoul, caught sudden sight of Angelique being strapped to the wooden board. He gasped and shouted to Raoul: "What the *devil*?"

The board was tilted forward to the horizontal; the attendant pulled aside the long hair and lowered the neck-board into place. The signalman lifted his hand, then paused for effect. He got it. The roaring crescendo just then precluded any communication between Emile and Raoul: now close to the foot of the guillotine. Raoul nosed his animal forward, pushing and urging until he arrived a few yards from the scene before him. He lifted his hand in staying motion to the signalman. Puzzled, but brainwashed in obedience to authority, the man automatically lowered his hand.

Sitting very still now astride the horse, both hands lightly holding the reins and resting upon the pommel, he addressed Saint-Just. "Pardon for that Citizen, but I feared for yourself... correct procedure must be followed I think. What's about with yon wench there?"

Saint-Just paused; just a fraction at the faint underlying authority in the voice, then shrugged. "Treasonable speech. She goes."

"But what did the lady say, Citizen? I gather said citizen," pointing to the head upon the pike, "be connected to her?"

"Turns out, her *père*," Saint-Just spoke briefly and in bored fashion, not recognizing Trifane from the many parliamentary sittings and Raoul let go his breath, just a little.

The horseman raised his eyebrows gently and smiled benignly. "Then Citizen, might I suggest that some leeway be granted? After all, a lady be weaker than a gentleman and cannot master her emotions as can we."

A roar of applause rose from the men in the immediate vicinity. Angelique did not help by exhibiting a look of scornful disgust, even from this perilous position. Raoul would normally have smiled at this but far removed now from humour, his heart contracted painfully at this display of courage as his mind worked swiftly. His desperate panic for her held him very still, barely breathing. He prayed for her continued state of shock—induced numbness: suspending her from grief and now, surely, terror; prayed that she would hold to anger and hostility. He prayed very much harder that the 'blade-man' did not grow impatient and release the rope holding that blade suspended.

"Me thinks," he continued before Saint-Just could reply, "that in all due respect, Citizen Robespierre would wish for pure justice. After all, is that not what our Glorious Republic is all about, Citizen?"

"Indeed it is Citizen, justice that was never granted *them*," indicating the mob, "by these," now waving to the lined up headless bodies.

"Ah. Just so, and is not our beloved Republic risen above such tyranny, my friend? Are we not more humane than those that have blighted our past? Is this not what we wish to portray to the world?" He paused and a cheer rose from those within hearing. "Perhaps a little clemency is in order for the lady... to exhibit our great and honourable justice?   Can we afford the world to witness inhumane treatment extended to children grieving for their freshly... er... despatched parents?"

Saint-Just shrugged again. "I grow bored Citizen; the crowd have judged her. She goes."

"Ah yes, the crowd... and they are owed vengeance against those from the old superior classes of course; but has she passed through the courts of Citizen Robespierre... the incorruptible, the magnificent monument of *true* justice? Everything must assuredly be done in proper order, the *Jacobin* way! If not," the stranger shrugged and Saint-Just grew wary suddenly, and began to wish that he had not attended this day of executions; his first and last experience at the guillotine but to see de Quatreaux off personally had been his ambition.  However, the man before him appeared to own a heightened knowledge of the law.  He paused suddenly for Lareaux had, he knew, unearthed secret documents held by Robespierre in which he, Saint-Just, featured as one to be noted.  Noted alongside Danton, for investigation: the two of them, stated the document, were growing far too headstrong and powerful. He did not need further criticisms to be added to that damning report. The time was not ripe yet to push his agenda. He glanced again at the humble, sans-culotte that was obviously not a sans-culotte: Robespierre's secret agents were everywhere. The man sat calmly on his stead as if he were simply waiting for the hand of fate to decide the issue.  He was obviously not related, or connected in any way, to the culprit.

"This time Citizen, I allow clemency," he shrugged; he could pick her up anytime. "But you, Citizenne," turning back to the dais and addressing Angelique's head in the stock, "will be wise to hold your tongue." He motioned to the attendant. "Release her."

Angelique reverted to the upright and now, released from the hinged board, fought for consciousness as the blood rushed to her feet; forced forward legs that accurately mimicked half-set jelly. Eyes cast down, she left the last step to find a hand held out. It was a hand fringed by a dirty sans-culotte sleeve and she gripped it gratefully, but on extreme pressure from the fingers of that hand she glanced up and recognized her twin. She controlled a gasp, quickly dropped her eyes and allowed herself to be led to the cloaked and hooded horseman who had been her champion.

Emile's voice, roughened with emotion, spoke harshly. "Come Citizienne, you shall require the assistance of a strong animal, following that ordeal. Up you go!"

He had stayed behind Trifane throughout the interchange, inconspicuous, hood drawn, in taut readiness: should Saint-Just win the battle: if his twin died, then so too would Saint-Just. He now bent and cupped his hands and as she automatically placed her foot in them, threw her up in front of Raoul. Releasing the reins of the other animal to Emile, Raoul caught her and drew her up, settling her in front of him. Suddenly she did faint, sagging back against her rescuer, his arm a band of steel around her waist, as he turned the animal and nudged gently through the still deeply suspicious crowd. They felt cheated and were slowly plying their brains to the problem. The time to exit that place of horror was short.

Emile mounted his animal again and slowly, carefully and watchfully, they made their way through the silent mob, nosing forward, eyes fixed above and beyond the stares of the crowd. The next victim, a grocer innocent of the charge of hording, and protesting wildly, soon claimed their full attention. Within this narrow window, the two horsemen made their way unmolested towards the exit and the Rue Saint-Honoré.

Angelique, reviving slowly, was tempted to sink again into oblivion. She could still taste the fear in her mouth and throat; a taste that only those experiencing situations of extreme danger could attest to. It had a taste all of its own, likened to nothing else upon the face of the earth and, once tasted, never forgotten. Pins and needles still prickled her hands and feet but she did not faint again.

Finding her voice now she offered a simple, "*Merci.*"

"Ah… you recover, Mademoiselle." His voice deliberately cool, he launched into light dialogue: grief had no place in the scene just yet. "That is good: for to hold erect a limp form, upon a horse, is no easy task!  It seems you cannot keep your person safe, Mademoiselle."

She struggled to speak but her voice was gone; then, hand to stomach, "I feel sick."

"Discipline: *mon enfant*! Discipline: sprayed stomach contents could anger the crowd."

She twisted to stare up at him. "But of course: *discipline*… just like… that…" Her voice failed, eyes suddenly brilliant with tears, much to her fury and mortification.

"Easy *mon enfant*; easy. 'Tis no time for emotion, though I quite see that the retaining of your head, following that very unwise escapade, *would* bring one to the point of tears."

"Oh, I rarely cry, Monsieur," furiously, then choking back a sob, "I wanted his body! Oh Raoul… I cannot bear that he be tossed into a communal grave! That is what it was all about. I wanted his body… his… his head… oh *Mon Dieu*: the blood! But they…they…"

Her unconscious use of his name went unnoticed as he replied bracingly, "Ah, so. But of course, his body: though it is of no use now. You would throw away your own life for an ancient ritual of burial. Come Mademoiselle, these times allow not that privilege now."

"I do not give a straw. I do not care any more about anything!"

Throat tight, chest a hard lump, she fell silent, unconsciously leaning back into him, feeling his warmth and protection as the horror of the last minutes washed over her again. The nausea returned, sweat poured. She shivered and his arm tightened.

"Steady *ma chérie*," he whispered softly and that was enough.

She twisted and looked up at him, empty suddenly of all emotion. She puzzled this abrupt change but knew only one thing. "Ah Raoul, I do not care what happens now." His eyes were brilliant as they gazed a brief moment into hers. He had to keep her talking; keep her brain busy: keep her in that static vacuum, into which, he could see, she had slipped. Here, within this crowd the spectacle of her complete breakdown would dissolve the grudging respect of the mob: the mob that would kill without a blink.

He spoke softly, mouth close to her ear as she leaned back against him: the curious and volatile crowd seethed close around them now. "But you simply have not sufficiently thought it through. There be an ancient Arabic saying *mon enfant*: 'to truly live, one must almost die'. Therefore it stands that you must wish to truly live now. Not so?"

"Facing that...that...*machine*... only the thought that I was joining *mon père*, registered and that, I did not mind. I clung to it: I was going to see *mon père* again. But I believe you are right: when I did *not* die... then I think that I decided that perhaps it was better to live after all... until now of course: *your* anger towards me could be worse!"

His eyes blazed now: and whispering in fury, "For tempting the fates within these insane times of ours! You *knew* the madness of confronting Saint-Just ... of all people! You *must* bring to heel your impetuosity, Mademoiselle! I do not *care* the circumstances, we none of us can *afford* to succumb to mitigating circumstances!"

"I am sorry for your inconvenience, Monseigneur!"

His supporting arm tightened again, giving a lie to his rough voice and harsh words. She felt the warmth and hard leanness of his body against her back and wanted to snuggle there forever; close her eyes and mind to everything and allow the animal to carry them on and on. But the crowd thinned suddenly as they exited the square then they were soon upon her carriage. He handed her down to Emile who had slipped from his mount to assist Angelique to the cobbled pavement. His face was grim, the pallor there grey-tinged with shock and grief. He too battled deep nausea; sweat beading his brow.

"*Ma Soeur*, go home. I shall contact you tomorrow."

"No you shall not. No one recognized you back there, or you would not be here now! But to Anton's you shall go... now!" Raoul's voice was low but harsh.

"A trifle patriarchal, aren't we?" Emile stared at his old friend and then, realizing that his own cool control, born of suspended belief and grief, fostered by action, could break at any moment and without warning. "Oh very well then, but we must get her out. Robespierre *will* have her head *now*."

"Not if I can help it," responded Raoul firmly. "And I believe that your sister is anguished enough this day. Saint-Just will not tell Robespierre of these events. Go home *mon enfant*, and sleep this night behind the panel," he said now, gently, to Angelique. "I insist."

"We have been enacting that precaution, for some time now, Seigneur Trifane."

"Then my mind is a little relieved. I shall call tomorrow. Lucien shall be outside your hôtel tonight."

Emile frowned. "Should she go home though?" He glanced at the groom and coachman and, lowering his voice, stepped close to Raoul. "Would it not be better..."

Raoul shook his head. "No...*mon ami*...we are watched for just that: she goes home. Later tonight..." He paused, certain that he was right and gazed at Emile in deep compassion. "Trust me please, *mon ami*, I be slightly the more rational than you... at this moment!"

The steps were put up, the carriage door closed and Angelique leaned back against the satin squabs, the palpable emptiness of the mind a curious phenomenon. She puzzled this a moment and then realized that it was better to cry after all, for of this incredibly tight pain banding her throat and chest and fogging her brain, there was no relief. Raoul followed the carriage and watched her safely into Hôtel Quatreaux.

♣

Hôtel Quatreaux,
Rue Saint Honoré,
Paris.
Frimaire AN 2 (New Republican calendar!)
November, 1793: for your edification!

'My dearest friend, Rochelle,

Can anything be more ridiculous than this new Revolutionary Calendar with which we all battle: the first year of the Republic be passed, the second commenced on September 22 '93: day one of the new-year! There is no Christmas anymore and no snow bound beauty of the new-year. But hopefully the impossibility of this incredible innovation will be outlawed before much longer.

You will wonder, my love, at the frivolity, (a savage frivolity of extreme dimensions at this moment), beginning this missive when I give you news of yr beloved Emile, (rest assured; he be well) and our beloved *père*: but please try to understand that none of us can afford the time for the expression of grief at this moment. And as you are aware, mine own defence lay within the quill and a very crooked humour: so long as I can still laugh then so too can I still stand. With these weapons, the quill and my humour, I am able to lose myself in pouring forth the great anger from within my soul. And yes, people look at me strangely, who witness this display of humour that is not humour!

I hesitate to destroy yr serenity, *mon amie*, but you must know that *Dearest Père* died beneath the guillotine today. I know of yr deep affection for him and am grieved that I can give it you no easier. For me it is not real, even though I witnessed the horrific event. But the body appears to react whether or not the mind does. I have at last ceased the periodic loss of stomach contents that has continued for many hours; and now write: somewhat shakily—but the cognac helps. Please forgive me as you struggle with the scrawl!

*Ma chérie*, the numbers travelling to that destination daily now is astounding. It seems there is no stopping the monstrous, heinous Jacobin government, following the annihilation of the Girondins.   And there be many, many more than the documented 21 persons on that horrendous day. The dear gentle pious Madame Elizabeth, the grey-haired and well-meaning Mayor of Paris, Bailly though I always did suspect him against the king and she that inspired the Girondists: Madame Roland! Also was Barnave, whom you shall remember as Mirabeau's rival for popularity within the Constituent Assembly, and *Orleans*. I even feel sorry for that fool now; evil though his reputation was.

Those prepared to shed blood like water and openly admit to placing *Terror* on the order of the day, now recognize no limitation to their power. Our two great enemies be, in general opinion, those of Hébert and Chaumette, who entertain no scruples to continue the slaughter and whip up the poor, uneducated sans-culottes into cruel and bestial desire of mob mentality; that of more and more blood. I would not have believed even one month ago, that there be any one person to outstrip Robespierre in this—but am coming to see that he be actually sincere within his driving passion for cleansing France of all that reeked of corruption and immorality and the degradation of the lower classes. To do this by the degradation of the upper classes was not his aim but when this evolved he did not care—so long as the scales were reversed and the French blood 'purified'. The only problem with this of course lay in the system that he has created wherein many, many souls become ensnared that be guilty of no crime at all. And he is now seen by more and more individuals to be entirely insane. I say that in the true sense, not one of satire, and believe that the table shall be turned some day upon this coldly cruel and oh so virtuous, incorruptible tyrant.

On the subject of Catholicism, the Hébertists, following the atheistic and materialistic doctrines circulated by Diderot and other philosophers of like ilk, are now denying the existence of a personal God and the immortality of the soul. Random theists and sceptics, following Rousseau and Voltaire, regard the Catholic faith as pernicious and degrading but thus far they hold themselves in check regarding its suppression. Hébert and Chaumette cleave no such scruples to their breasts! Morality and Reason are alone declared fit for veneration. The worship, to replace the Catholic ritual, is to be one which, refusing recognition of a spiritual world beyond the sphere of human knowledge, glorifies human nature and material objects in the virtue of reason.

*Reason*! Hébert wants that the *people* shall be our God: no other Church or Temple than that of Reason, no other worship than that of liberty, equality and, here is that word again, fraternity! What could be further from 'brotherhood' than this new debacle called a Regime! The suppression of Catholic worship is begun now in the true sense: churches can be destroyed, priests murdered but the *essence* of religion has always survived—but now that very essence is attacked. Constitutional priests are told to marry and abdicate their functions. Those that refuse are imprisoned and then guillotined. Catholic worship is prohibited. Every sign of religious mourning is abolished.

The Convention, now totally Jacobin, gives official recognition to this new worship. The archbishop of Paris, Gobel, attended by his chaplains, was forced to give official recognition to the new worship. Every day the revellers visit the Convention, there to deposit their spoils from raided churches and denounce the maintainers of the Catholic doctrines. And finally there is to be a festival in honour of the God, Reason: to be celebrated in the Cathedral of Nôtre Dame. A mountain of garishly painted wood is erected in the choir area and a sans-culottes woman shall sit there, dressed in virginal white, a pike in her hand and Phrygian upon her head. All civic authorities are to attend and a procession shall march, accompanied by music, carrying this Representation of Reason, the girl, to the Nôtre Dame, which shall then be declared the Temple of Reason. I rest my case! From this time the Churches of Paris shall be either closed or used as meeting places.

I must end this missive, for though the cost per weight, equalling not more than one denier, be not a problem, its density of parchment may alert suspicion. My love to you and yr *Père* and yr remaining family and believe me that yr Emile does quite well under the circumstances and shall be within yr country soon I be sure! Hopefully we shall all be present for yr marriage that you must now be anxious to execute—for once he is yr husband, Emile shall no longer own the freedom to risk his life on these fatal shores. Not of course that that fact shall hinder him: he is a de Quatreaux after all.

My very great love to you, *ma chérie* for such friendship be precious to us across the channel. I go now, afore mine tears besplotch this missive beyond yr ability to decipher it! Thank you for listening: the relief, for me to 'pour forth,' is without measure.

Angelique.
@ 2200 hours 12: this twenty-second day of November, 1793.

Postscript:
Rest assured: Emile does not reside with us at Hôtel Quatreaux but be well disguised.'

She raised her head and found herself on the edge of the abyss of a dark world: that of the black shadows of the mind. Hurriedly she busied her hands with the sand brevette, folded and sealed the parchment with a smudged de Quatreaux seal, addressed it and then began again with a missive to her sister Clarisse.

A candle sputtered in the candelabra but she did not hear it. Ally cats screamed in fight in the street below but she did not hear them. She picked up the quill, reached for the small knife and sharpened the point again. Drawing a new sheet to her, she dipped the quill into the black ink and commenced again, this time to Clarisse. She wrote a while and then, gazing a moment into those dark shadows that now swirled around her, continued. The room was silent but for the scratching quill, as she sat lost to time, place and event, rapidly covering the sheet before her.

'And now dear sister, I am moved to impart news of the provinces; for while this be depressing in the extreme it does serve to comfort me that you be well out of France.

While the strange scenes of disorderly meetings within the Churches, of haranguing speeches and songs in praise of Reason, Liberty, Equality and Fraternity, carry on within Paris, the wars of the interior continue as fiercely as ever.

We could have experienced, *ma chérie*, some degree of success within the provinces had the allies; deferring invasion whilst awaiting the next campaign, assisted the Royalist Insurgents within France. England could have perhaps assisted the brave Vendeans and Austria those of Lyon; however, they did not and that was that; Lyon Royalists, following long and courageous battle, surrendered to the Republicans. Toulon helped itself by admitting an English and Spanish fleet into its harbour and has managed to hang on thus far against the French Republican Army. Mayhap it will be defeated soon. On reflection at this point I am brought to the incredible fact that I be supporting the *enemy*. Where does this lead me? But I own no guilt on the matter!

The Convention passed a decree, enforced by the *Committee of Public Safety*, ordering scorched earth policy and making prisoners of the women and children. I suppose we have evolved a little. They could of course have murdered them as in the old days but this method of burn and starve the country out be as heinous.

The Republican generals are now apparently incompetent, though whose opinion be this is unsure. The *Commune, C.P.S.* and the Montagnard are all, through the wretched *Deputies-en-Mission*, contending with one another. All giving differing directions to Generals and so mayhap work in our favour as even greater confusions reign.

Following their earlier successes, the Vendeans now suffer terrible defeat and deprivations. They fought furiously and bravely but faced by several thousand Republican troops of the line, who penetrated the heart of Upper Vendée, they could do nothing but retreat. This was accompanied by a host of non-combatants: the elderly, the women and the children, burnt out of their homes and villages. These poor souls, hounded by their own countrymen, were forced on to the Loire and made a stand at Chollet: to experience fresh defeat and the battle degenerating into fighting across the river in boats. Most of the chiefs were by now dead or dying and one brave La Rochejaquelein, a very young noble and an even braver peasant, Stofflet took command. They were, however, compelled always to move on, through scarcity of food, and arrived in Normandy. Here they were hopeful of occupying the port of Ganville and receiving support from England. However, whether or no they would have, be of no import now, for they had no siege equipment and could not take the fortresses. The fighting men grew weak, through food scarcity; and the sufferings of the wounded were intense. The Republicans then massacred every man, woman and child left behind. They massacred their own blood, *ma chérie*. The defeated Vendeans, who could have been sent walking back to their districts; were placed upon rafts on the river Loire and those rafts then sank. This fiendish act was repeated upwards of a dozen times, so we hear. I stand corrected on my previous comment! We are not at all evolved.

While this continues in the west, scenes of Terror continue in the *Departments* throughout France. The will of the *Commune* be law and the *Deputies en Mission*, joining the Hébertist faction, exercise uncontrolled power over the properties and lives of all. New laws, taxes, fines and criminal courts are launched every day. One would be forgiven for thinking that nothing more could be invented but one would be sadly wrong. There is no end to their fiendish imaginations.

The Deputies now have slavishly serving them the *Municipalities*, which are repeatedly reconstructed. The men of these committees are drawn from the most fanatic, cowardly and worthless men alive. On their bidding many thousands are flung into prison daily, often with no pretext at all and there be no discrimination between sex, age or rank.    Added now to the list of criminal offences be: relationship to an emigrant, similar name will do, earning a wage of more than 50 or 100 livre per year and being a fanatic—of anything. Those in possession of metal money and those unable to pay taxes (randomly set) bear the added burden, over and above imprisonment, of revenue confiscation. And let no person imagine that he may live as quietly as possible and thus avoid trouble, for then he is imprisoned for 'doing nothing for the Revolution'.

I could fill pages but I feel your tears, ma chérie. Suffice to say that there now be no less than 178 Revolutionary Courts and executions continually take place; often following no form of court appearance whatsoever. Sometimes when they do operate, these courts pass several hundred judgements en masse.

I shall not sadden you further, *ma soeur* of such deep, deep faith, by expanding on the subject of Catholicism. Suffice to tell you that the Hébertist Deputies, within their efforts to de-Christianize France, are now creating great bonfires of religious books and relics. Vessels used in the chapel of the Town Hall are sent to the mint and the alter-linen is to be made into shirts for the soldiers—perhaps they shall be protected: by such holy coverings. The churches themselves are not to be higher than any other secular building—hence the tearing down of many spires. The world hath gone mad!

At Vitry-sur-Seine, stands on the alter busts of Voltaire, Rousseau and Marat and hymns are still sung; *patriotic hymns* in glory of the Nation. Oh, and the Rights of Man recited as daily prayer. At Harve the publication of Romme's Revolutionary Calendar was made cause for further celebration. At Reims, upon the pedestal that once held a statue of Louis XV, the sacred *sainte ampoule*, was broken into tiny pieces.

Chaumette himself took part in the destruction of the reliquary of Sainte-Geneviéve and the holy oil flask at Tours. He then, just this month, encouraged the archbishops, Gobel and Lindet and constitutional priests to publicly renounce their orders. Scores of constitutional priests are being guillotined for their refusal and Sunday observance be prohibited. On the first day of the new week of ten days, observance must be made by feasting in the churches of France, to honour Reason, Equality and Liberty. Any person absent from this rite shall be taken up under the *Law of Suspected Persons*. I refuse to go, therefore rank high on that list: as did our *père*. I am beyond fear, a dangerous state in which to be I know, but as I now see he was. One is so repulsed by it all. The government *ma chérie*—believes that all this is in the public good and that by such measures alone shall France be saved. But there: I said I would not expand on this: my pardon.

But how does an entire country bow to a small minority of men: corrupt deputies who sit on the Revolutionary committees and act as judges in Revolutionary courts? It remains a puzzle to me I must confess. I long to turn the guillotine upon *them*! This be very un-Christian of me I am aware and our beloved Jesus would preach otherwise, but *He* is not here and one is eventually brought to this stand. As to turning the other cheek; look where *that* got *Him*. *Ma chérie*, forgive me—my humour, extremely warped these days, be my only survival weapon! And yes, I do know His real meaning: that of passive resistance—but *continued* unstoppable passive resistance, hence the 'other cheek'. But, though He is of course right, passivity is far from my soul at this moment. I hope that He may forgive this confused and revengeful soul.

I end this with a sardonic twist; the now freed peasants are become conservatives and are fighting the very people that caused their 'freedom', for their lot now be one of taxes, taxes and more taxes, battles with maximum prices, a total absence of a labour force and roaming spies of deputies hunting flimsy reason for arrests. But it comes too late: the Hébertists have succeeded in ruining the wealthy, from all walks of life, and failing to benefit the poor: my poor, poor dear France.

Ma chérie—I go now with lightened heart in the knowledge that you and yr family escape all of this. Stay safe.

My beloved, gentle Clarisse, I bid you farewell: my deepest love and prayers, to Stanilaus and children and yourself.

Angelique.

Postscript:—you will not, I know, read past the first few lines of this missive—may never read it all but to write my only solace: though the lessoning of that tight band of the chest is but brief—my apologies; and my heart-felt thanks, my beloved sister. You will no doubt receive official notification of *Père's* demise. *Au revoir, ma chérie.*

She finished the sealing of this missive too, addressed it and then sat staring ahead into a darkened corner of the room. The writing *had* relieved a little the frozen, solid lump banding her heart, but its return caused her to reach again for the quill. This time she pulled forward her recent works but as she flexed her muscles and straightened her back, Marie entered the room. Clutching her gown around her, candle in hand, she wore a worried expression upon her face.

"My dear, it is but a few minutes to midnight; and I grew concerned. Please do come to bed. You know that you promised Monseigneur Trifane that you would observe great care following…after…"

"Following my indiscretions at *père's* execution, Marie? Yes, you are in the right of it, but I am so tired that I cannot sleep and that feeling of ants crawling and biting their way through my body is strong."

"'Tis the agitation, frustration… denied grief, dear one. Come: try to rest. I have a posset for you below."

Angelique smiled wanly. "But *not* the laudanum, Marie, even now?"

"*Especially* not now...*ma chère.*"

"Ah yes I see. But you have no worry of my developing an addiction to the opiate. My only desire; only obsession... only comfort... shall be the demise of the persons responsible for *mon père's* death. And if I develop an addiction to that sentiment then so be it."

Marie gazed in complete defeat, for there was no comfort to be offered one under these appalling circumstances. She led the way and they descended into the bowels of the earth.

Angelique rolled over for the umteenth time and lit a candle. Marie lay prone and slept heavily. She wondered just how she could. Grief aside, to sleep within this surreal place imitating the underworld of Hades, was beyond Angelique. She sat cross-legged on her padded quilt, staring at the leaping shadows from the flickering candlelight, eyeing off yet another rat, daring him to surmount the barrier. No sound penetrated into this section of the tunnel; into any section she supposed, but the silence was ethereal. She wondered whether Robespierre's secret police had called yet upon the Hôtel Quatreaux. She discovered that she did not care. She snuffed the candle and idly absorbed the total density of underground darkness, fearing the deep abyss of grief. She closed her mind. But ruthlessly, moving swiftly, defensively, beyond the immediate past, her mind slid down the road to childhood days, days when Fanchon had tried in vain to halt her 'flights of fancy', 'imaginative journeys'. Days when she had followed Fanchon about the château, assisted her with the drying and hanging of the herbs and confided that she had only to close her eyes to slide down the familiar shaft that was her central self: arriving at that place of white light. Here the twelve gleaming white steps—she had counted them—led downward yet again to the edge of a deep still pool. From the pool a path led through a forest of natural wonder and light and wandering this pathway she would be confronted by many people. They had begged her not be fearful, for they were only there to assist her in her search. She had confided only once in Fanchon: that woman's terrified anger and offer of life-threatening punishments, if she so much as spoke one word of the incident, silencing her completely.

She tried again to reach that place of great peace. Again and again she tried and then, frustrated, lit the candle, and ascended to the panel that opened into the library. Here she gathered up writing materials and then, turning to leave, noticed an old piece of unfinished and forgotten prose. She pulled it toward her and read it, noting the antagonistic, anti-Jacobinism slant and drew an angry breath: it was not half antagonistic enough. She picked it up to take with her but suddenly, out of nowhere, a new verse, struggling to be born, arrived in a rush. Dumping her material she sat suddenly, crookedly sideways on the chair and pulled paper and ink toward her. It would take but a minute. The quill scratched rapidly across the parchment, hatred and fury pouring forth.

Angelique wrote furiously, her concentration of a depth that excluded the known world. She had no body, was deaf and blind to the physical world. Her awareness travelled only the mystical world of whirling inspiration, of bright colourful scenes of yesteryear, vying with the dark depths of depravity and horror of the present. Struggling again and again, to reach that flat plain of exquisite clarity of thought, for here, unimpaired by emotion, intellect even, the words would flow. Now she was almost there, almost but not quite, for the racing words trailing the black ink were still of her choosing. Many words were swiftly scored through: to be replaced later. Later when time was easy, she could ponder them. At last the flow began and now she wrote the driven way, always fearful that the speed of the flow would increase beyond that of the ability of the hand to move the quill: for the ethereal thought forms wafted and drifted often on the edge of the subconscious, appearing and disappearing through that permeable wall. Here, within this void of stillness, the conscious mind reached desperately to grasp, clutch and hold, in frenetic desire to retain the thought before it disappeared forever; for once gone it could not be recalled.

Thus employed, she did not hear the slight sound of the door opening a fraction and so wrote on, unaware of the stealthy movements within the hôtel, wrote on until she reached that Elysian Field of no pain, of lightness of being, a place only once before discovered. Discovered in a time following the death of her *mère*; the depth of grief causing an expansion of her earlier and lighter experiences of the 'forest path'. A time when she had had need of strong emotional control in the public face and had deliberately pushed her mind out into the world of nature. Standing there, her mind had left the crowded room and chattering people. Had travelled the forest path, sinking to the earth at the bole of a large tree, sinking further into the soft rich chocolate earth; becoming the earth: feeling the soft moist crumbling state of self: *becoming* the soil. She *was* the living, crumbling, encompassing soil, linked in a communication of web-like structure: with all that surrounded her, with the very universe, with no need of thought, emotion or intellect; she just 'was'. An effortless flow of 'dialogue', of receiving great knowledge, commenced between self and the trees, rocks, sky and the warmth of a loving energy permeating it all, as a soft summer breeze. And then, suddenly, her state of being, of existence, was warm, light and pliable; silly and inadequate words but the only ones that her mind had found to describe the ability to stretch and shrink, stretch and shrink, as far or as little as she wished. Here she witnessed the vast web of connectedness, everything to everything: no thing stood alone.

She sat now in a state of static immobility: hand paused halfway across the paper, quill resting loosely between her fingers, staring ahead for some few minutes only, for where Angelique had gone there be no restraints of time. Behind the static face the mind rejoiced: she had found the 'place' again! And so; just as she had not heard the Jacobin spy at the door, she did not now hear her return, this time with Saint-Just's agents. There were six of them, four standing in front of the desk, two behind, as she returned to the present at the sound of the harsh voice. Her thumping heart, at the suddenness of that return, not the sight of the enemy, thrust against her chest wall in bounding leaps. Her breath caught in her throat and the room receded. Her mind begged to stay there, in that white no man's land, but the harsh voices were recalling her again.

She gazed now at the enemy surrounding her as she sat at the desk, suddenly acutely aware and alert, deeply sorrowful that she had committed the unforgivable: that of laxity of surveillance. For herself she did not care; however, she had discovered long ago that one be never free to act to please oneself, for there were always those that would be hurt by those actions. In this case Marie, who would be distraught and her brother, who twin-like, would grieve the deeper. She did not allow Raoul even to the perimeter of her mind.

A voice, harsh and booming against the silence, spoke, "*Citizienne?*"

The man frowned at her vague expression and lack of fear and glancing at his colleagues took her by the arm and shook her. "Citizienne! I said that you must come with us!"

She gazed down at the hand; spoke softly, "Monsieur! Unhand me if you please. It is obvious that I cannot affect an escape."

But they were taking no chances and so with one either side of her, taking an arm each, she was brought around the desk. Here she turned toward one and spoke quietly.

"Monsieur, you must observe that I be not dressed…"

"I do," he replied. "The Revolution does not seek to humiliate its citizens! But it *does* insist upon proper address, *Citizienne*! Please do not address me as Monsieur!"

She was allowed, under escort, to her boudoir to dress, in the presence of three guards.

# CHAPTER TWENTY-TWO

## The Rose and the Vine

Robespierre glanced down at his desk; to the lists of those appearing before the Tribunal on the morrow and smiled grimly, then looked up at his secretary. "Yes Citizen, these are all for the morrow. Get them to the prisons afore midnight."

His assistant looked again at the lists. They grew longer each day and each evening they were sent out to the various prisons, there to be read out by the gaolers of the cells and sections holding those persons. As each name was called, that person stepped aside to a designated spot, isolated from the rest of the prisoners by order but also by superstition. If one shunned the area one might avoid the hand of fate.

Sometimes mayhem would reign a moment at no response to a name thus called, until the guards remembered, were convinced, or found out, that that particular person had died, had already been executed or whisked away. The crowded, vaulted anti-chamber, and cells, would be thoroughly searched anyway, until the guards were eventually convinced that these were not lurking still within the shadows. At last, the roll call would continue, until the last name for the morrow's execution was called. This was not mentioned but everyone knew that the word Tribunal heading the list was a misnomer: these were not even for trial. Tearful farewells were affected through the grates and grills, prisoners crowding against their cell fronts to witness the next batch as they passed by, calling words of comfort. Many of these owned no more crime than that of their birth-lines and many were not even nobility: but did own land or businesses, or worked for, or were involved with, the nobility in some way.

"And the girl, Citizen... the girl Vermont?" asked Roublét, glancing covertly at the neat pile of parchment, covered in black ink scrawl, as if written in a hurry.

The man before him continued to gaze out of the window at the early evening; watching the lamplighter going about his task, a small boy trailing behind, carrying the end of the ladder. "It be safe to send her before the Tribunal," he smiled grimly and turned back toward the desk, indicating with the sweep of his hand the material under discussion. "Nothing can cause her acquittal, with that lot."

He walked toward the desk, reached down and picked up one of the pieces of paper and held it out to Roublét. "*This* can be attributed to nothing but treason."

Taking it hesitantly, Roublét read:

*The Rose and the Vine*

May Odin's army,
And Solomon's wisdom,
Go with you, my brother, my sister,
Forget not the grace of the *Rose*,
Or the strength of the *Vine*,
These too, shall bear you through.

For this dark night,
Be not o'er,
For me or for you,
Til justice be done,
Upon this wounded
And bloodied land.

Til the Jacobin lay dead,
To the very last one,
Til those rampant Machiavellians,
Spawned of Hades loins,
No longer inflict
Their heinous wounds.

Til this tortured land,
Knows peace and prosperity anew,
Till the spreading red,
Be none but the glow of the *Rose*,
And the bonds so tight,
Be none but the entwining *Vine*.

"Be it hers though, Citizen? Mayhap it is de Quatreaux' and he already be dead!"
"It be her work, of that there be no doubt. But we keep her alive yet awhile."
"Citizen?"
"It may be a code. It goes to the decoders on the morrow *and* these others; the indecipherable scribblings, may also lead us to her brother and one Marquis de Savieur. Following all avenues of investigation, then, *only* then, she may be executed."
"But surely we can arrest him on emigrant status; the brother?"
"He never did emigrate; however, that does not matter, the jury shall execute him anyway. He has been out of the country and that be sufficient for them but his

whereabouts is what I want from her. He is in Paris, that much we do know. If her torture does not produce his whereabouts... then we think again."

"Er, regarding Savieur, Citizen, I thought that you had material relating to his foreign activities?"

"Also did I. But that fool Lareaux could not bring me proof after all but it shall be forthcoming. Of that I shall make certain. Go now and ensure the delivery of the prison lists before midnight."

Roublét gathered up the necessary papers and casting one doubtful glance at his superior, glad to be exiting the heavy but eternally chilly atmosphere of the room, passed through the door and closed it quietly behind him. He was growing sickened by the daily sittings of the dreaded Revolutionary Tribunal; with its five judges and juries determined for the blood of the aristocracy; any blood for that matter. It did not matter any more, so long as the defendant ended his day beneath the guillotine: to prevent any person slipping through the net. He could be a good chandler, a baker, trader or a rope maker, with roots steeped in peasantry. But if he offered apparent or imagined disruption to the cause of the Revolution, or conversely, offered nothing at all to assist same, then he would be judged guilty. The jury and the audience, red-capped and from the lowest echelons of society, indivisible: for the jury did not move without the approval of the audience.

Emile's face was grim. Raoul's, if at all possible, grimmer, as they sat at the table below Anton's shop; varied papers and parchment, barrier exits and passes scattered about them, along with passports and travel documents. Raoul picked up Angelique's passport and absently gazed at it, turning it over; his vision vacant and far away.

"Anton... we have need of something very strong... for the sleeping draught."

Anton did not glance up from his work upon one of the forged papers. "How much so?"

"Infinitely so; something that mimics death... within minutes of swallowing."

"Ah. Then you are in luck, I think, my cousin. *His* cousin: twice removed I think, can supply such a one."

"Unless it affects his work," replied Raoul; his voice cool and unemotional as he continued, "I do not care if he be removed to the other side of the planet, just get it. And it must be effective; no wrist pulse, breath so shallow that it appears non-existent."

"That can be arranged, Monseigneur. There be of course a risk, you understand. Ah yes. I see that you do! And just who..." Anton began humorously. "Ah. Just so, not my business... but the weight and build of the man *would* be my business: at least that of my cousin' cousin... the, er one..."

"Twice removed," nodded Emile sagely then frowned. "Or would that be thrice?"

"...for he be the one to procure the contents, and measure out, the posset."

"Approximately, 110 livres or 48-50 kilogrammes, slight build. Also be necessary a doctor's bag; with certificates of death and whatever other paperwork a doctor carries."

Emile gazed steadily at his friend. Once the plan for Angelique's rescue was resolved, and this time there would be no room for failure, Raoul would seek out Lareaux and possibly Saint-Just and his vengeance would know no mercy. He smiled grimly suddenly, for Raoul would not be the only one on a cold mission of revenge. He himself could not wait to get his hands on Beaumont. He turned in his chair now to study his friend's cool remote expression.

"Trifane, it seems a little risky, not so? It may well kill her."

"If it does, then I shall remove the cousin a fourth time, permanently," replied Raoul calmly. "You had better ensure his knowledge of this aspect, Anton. And there be no other way. We cannot pose as guards again. The priest idea may have worked, though it is an old trick, but now they are banished. Visiting officials? Too risky... so... think you of a better plan, *mon ami?*"

"Noo... but still I do not like it."

"I am not thrilled myself, Vermont, but it should work. Anton..." Raoul turned to the wine merchant cum locksmith, clock maker, forger, jack-of-all-trades. "We require a corrupt turnkey... and guard."

This remarkable man, without looking up from his task, gave a fat chuckle. "They all be *corrupt*, Monsieur! It all depends on how much you pays 'em as to how far their corruption goes."

"As much as it takes."

"Ah, then in that case it be no problem. Two guards that I know are anxious to be anchoring in safe port across the frontier afore much longer."

"I see. You trust them?"

"No. But they carry no love for Jacobins." Anton picked up the Belgium title deeds, claiming small land holdings. "These shall buy more than their loyalty, Monsieur."

Raoul glanced at them and nodded. "They are to be used only to good purpose. You be the judge, Anton. Mayhap they shall accept the gold."

"Metal money be too risky; begets the guillotine nowadays, Monseigneur."

"To some it is no worry: they have their methods. However, hesitate not, if the land would seal the deal... and their mouths."

Anton smiled faintly, then, "The Conciergerie, definitely?"

"That is the one. And one more small matter further..."

"Not any of your requirements are of small matter, Seigneur, however..." Anton sighed resignedly.

Raoul looked up from his endless signature practice; that of a known prison doctor. "An undertaker's... no, too presumptuous... a hospital, stretcher."

"And I the stretcher bearer," murmured Emile.

Raoul gazed at him a moment then slowly, in thought. "The *terrified* stretcher-bearer. Face muffled against contagion; in fact, now it comes to me. Anton?"

Anton paused in dread anticipation of further bizarre objects to be procured for this insane excursion then directed his bland, questioning face towards Raoul.

"Ask your *'cousin'*, the one so many times removed you understand, for some juice of the stinging nettle; or a similar substance."

"To cause the welts upon the skin?"

"*Now* you comprehend brilliantly, *mon ami*," responded Raoul calmly.

"In a face cream it shall be. Yon prisoner *is* female I take it… at that weight. Your wish my command, your gold and or land, shall buy you cartloads of the irritant if you so wish." Anton sank once more into his task before him and Raoul suddenly rose.

"Anton, we require maps, if they may be found, of France's worst terrain."

"The army controls all roadblocks," replied Anton, head still bent over his work.

"We do not travel the roads."

"The maps you shall have."

"Cattle?" asked Emile now. "Still your valet?"

"No change there. He has bought the inferior animals for exiting Paris. He also has transferred mine from the château to our first post. Their thoroughbred status may draw attention but we desire their strength. I have asked them to be left ungroomed these last months: looking suitably shaggy now. I do not intend being observed but if we are, we shall be in need of fast horses, also capable of long endurance for the lands we travel shall be rough in the extreme, with no tracks or trails… and little food."

"And the Trifane cattle are the fastest in France. If not Europe," said Emile with a faint smile, his mind travelling retrograde to better days.

"No. De Quatreaux had that reputation."

Emile was suddenly motivated to be gone: Beaumont would not keep forever. "Trifane, I have a small matter to attend, we meet again, as arranged. No changes thus far?"

"None *mon ami*," replied his friend softly. He did not attempt to dissuade him from his deadly course. "You have need of seconds?"

"Dev shall oblige, *merci mon ami*: he be returned briefly, taken leave, in order to secure certain properties."

"Have a care then."

Anton, now that his guests were hatted and cloaked in shabby, peasant attire, rose from his seat and left to check the exterior for danger.

Emile watched him go, then, "The doctor, *mon ami*… he be safe?"

Raoul, practicing once more, from the standing position now and leaning over the table, finished the signature with a swift flourish. "As can be: he does not get the signed titles until the operation be over by three days."

"And making himself scarce after the switch… you for himself following his call to the Conciergerie, he does not stupidly spend the evening with friends…hmm?"

Raoul smiled coolly, strapping on his scabbard. "He dons the incognito attire… beard and all and visits the museum… under an alias!"

Emile eyed the small-sword scabbard. "You er… intend to duel *today*?"

Raoul shook his head, smiling grimly. "No, the more evil the person, the higher the etiquette: he must state the day, and weapon of course, but some instinct warns me… strongly. Besides, would *you* confront Lareaux, naked of a weapon?"

"*Never*… but have a care, *mon ami*; random body searches courtesy the *Marchaussie* have increased: patted, poked and prodded at length myself, t'other day!"

Raoul shrugged. "Dressed as to your station that day though…they are not searching sans-culottes."

"Well yes, but you know you do own a distinctive walk, *mon ami*."

"Oh? Still? More work on that then!" His shoulders slouched, he lowered his gazed to the floor and affected a limp, causing Emile to grin and shake his head.

Anton returned, ushered them up to the cellar level and then through the wine shop and out a rear door to the laneway beyond. He returned to his tasks, a deep unease within his chest, but then this was not new. The actions of those he assisted in this insane France never failed to produce such angst for they were good men, all of them and France was losing them to foreign climes, or Madame Guillotine. He sighed, took a pinch of Trifane's finest snuff and settled again to concentrate upon the papers before him. At journey's end he should be able to buy his own estates. He pushed the shadow of the guillotine aside and focused upon those pretty estates on the banks of the Loire.

Yves Beaumont, Comte d'Arteaux, sat in his library, open book sliding now out of his slackened grasp, sliding until it landed on the floor at his feet with a soft thump. He did not hear it, his glazed eyes and flaccid body evidence of his complete torpor. His worried staff, those that had been long in his service, glanced at each other. Gossip about him in the kitchens below was rife, as they anticipated his next move, ceasing this speculation only on the arrival of Bellier, the butler of several decades. This man would not tolerate anything less than perfect service to the man who had been his master but also benefactor from an early age. Many youthful escapades had been resolved by the Comte's timely and often generous intervention. Bellier's loyalty was total. This would eventually lead him along the heavily trodden path to the Place de la Revolution.

He now answered, with calm and stately grace, the insistent tug on the door bell-rope. The clanging of the bell continued until he opened one of the heavy oak doors to Monsieur le Comte de Quatreaux. The new Comte de Quatreaux: all had heard of the elder Comte's demise at the hands of Robespierre. The visitor, however, knew better the real cause of his *père's* demise and greeting the old butler now, known to him since early childhood, moved past him into the entrance hall.

Bellier bowed politely then reached, with bland expression, for the disreputable cloak, hat and gloves. "Monseigneur, it be very well to see you back in Paris. Yon master requires some cheering, that he does."

"Not well is the Comte? Well, well. I dare say I shall be able to stimulate him a little."

"If you are able then it will be more than any one of his friends could do. He will not eat, or sleep: sits in the library day and night, drinking heavily, sometimes pacing but now even that has ceased."

"I shall see myself to the library then, Bellier. I know the way."

Emile strode to the foot of the stairs, mounted these two at a time and walked along the gallery to the library. Entering, following a rap on the door, he paused a moment, adjusting his eyes to the gloom of the room. The heavy brocade curtains were drawn, shutting out the remains of the day's light and no fire flickered in the grate yet. However, the man slumped in the chair did not appear to at all feel the chill of late autumn. To a stranger even, the signs of deep lowness of spirit would have been evident at a glance. Emile stared, barely recognizing the once urbane, impeccably dressed nobleman of the court of Versailles; of the hunting rituals of Quatreaux and Beaumont estates. He watched a minute and then spoke and had to repeat himself in louder tones.

"Seigneur Beaumont: it is provident that I find you at home!"

Beaumont looked up suddenly, struggled to emerge into the present and rose unsteadily. It was an old man that now stood before Emile, a fact doing nothing to soften his heart.

"De Quatreaux!" Beaumont struggled over the name. "You return. It is good to see you."

"It is? I should have thought otherwise, *Monsieur*!"

"Come sit, some claret? I suppose it be early for burgundy yet... though the time?" He paused and turned his bloodshot eyes toward the clock upon a side table, and appeared startled to find it well past the fashionable hour for burgundy.

"I shall not sit, Comte, or drink, thank you. I come only to gain clarity of events just gone. In relation to *mon père* you understand," replied Emile softly, his eyes hard and cold. "Would you be a-knowing, I wonder, just how he was picked up by the *Commune* so easily? How the information on him managed to find its way to Robespierre's notice?"

Beaumont seemed to regain some of his old sangfroid and stood erect now, gazing at his oldest friend's eldest male offspring. "But you obviously know, *mon ami.*"

"Do not call me friend, Seigneur. For if it be yourself that be deeply embroiled in this matter then I am come to challenge you. Simply name your friends, Seigneur, if it be true."

Beaumont gazed at him sadly a moment, then, "Ah, but you do not know of the threats to mine own family. However, I did act in weak fashion certainly, unforgivably so."

"*Weak? Weak?* Be that *all*? And you *mon père's* oldest and most trusted friend? I cannot neglect the defence of his honour, Monseigneur!"

"I quite see that and you are in the right of it. Honour must be satisfied. Du Toit shall act for me. Here; in the long salon; we cannot exit Paris now."

"You be correct, of course. The reason for a barrier pass: that of duelling could cause a problem: tomorrow then, at the hour of, say, four? Before the house stirs, you understand."

"At four."

"Name your weapon, Monsieur."

Beaumont bowed with exquisite grace. "Ah, sword, be the appropriate one, me thinks."

"Indeed it is!" Emile returned the bow, then turned and left the room abruptly. He moved slowly now down the stairs. He was breaching the rules of respect within duelling etiquette in challenging an older man but knew that he could not live with himself if his *père's* death lay unavenged. He could see no other way. To behave in the same fashion as had that man toward de Quatreaux was an easy alternative: for he had solid proof of Beaumont's involvement in many 'treasonable' transactions. This despicable action however was unthinkable. Besides these facts were most likely already known by Robespierre, whom then had held it over Beaumont: to get to de Quatreaux. He reached the foot of the stairs and crossed the great hall, turned his back to Bellier, who dropped the disreputable cloak over his shoulders with a pained expression; and then turned back, holding out his hand for the grubby hat.

"Bellier, you have been a good man. I have known you long and I want you to know..."

A muffled retort sounded behind and above them, bringing Emile's speech to a sudden halt. His hand, now holding his hat and gloves froze and he stared at Bellier, who stared back. Of one accord they both turned and moved swiftly to the stairs and ran up these, Emile reaching the library door ahead of Bellier.

He opened the door slowly, in which time Bellier had caught up with him and they stepped into the room together, eyes drawn to the fallen body of d'Arteaux upon the floor. What was left of his head required immediate covering and Bellier quickly threw his own kerchief across what had once been the face of his master. He was pale and shaking and standing up again felt his legs trembling.

He glanced at Emile and started at that man's grim expression. "What's to do, Seigneur?"

Emile stared a long time at d'Arteaux then brought glazed eyes round to Bellier. "What? Oh, do whatever you think fit, Bellier. Call Du Toit; he shall know."

With this he turned and left the room; ran lightly down the stairs and entered the street below with sudden energy. He did not feel cheated. He did not feel anything. He thought of his *père* and did not feel good about Beaumont's death: this had not been the clean duel required to avenge the crime. He returned to Anton's wine-shop. Pulling a bottle of cognac from the cellar on his way through to the underground haven, he checked all vantage points and then disappeared behind the Persian wall hanging, closing the door softly behind him. The candles still flared, there upon the rough wooden table; and sinking into a chair he poured a short glass of the fiery liquid and tossed it down his throat: then another. Next on the agenda: Angelique and then England and his beautiful Rochelle. The estates there, that he had bought from the impoverished, alcoholic gambler; a young peer of the realm, would be home for the rest of his life. Mayhap it mattered not where one lived when one had the luxury of a beautiful and loving woman for a wife. It beat an arranged marriage: that was certain. He still experienced a problem, however, wrenching his mind away from Château Quatreaux and all that was, had been, beloved France. He cursed the Jacobins, the Revolution and Beaumont for having the last word and drank some more: only later did he realize that Beaumont had actually released him from the necessity of breaching the duelling laws.

Whilst the Hôtel Beaumont echoed with horror and confusion and Bellier received his orders from Monseigneur Du Toit, Phillip-Jean Bernierre, Comte Lareaux, a little further down the Rue St Germaine, was entertaining himself by holding hostage one of the Tribunal victim's daughters. She stood now, trembling and staring from the corner of the long grand salon, twisting her hands together and endeavouring to control her erratic breathing. She was very young and very beautiful but only one woman's beauty could hold him enthralled and she was now a resident of the Conciergerie. Of greater value than beauty, however, was the great properties and revenue that would come to this girl with no brothers, upon the death of her parents. The Revolutionary Tribunal was slow, certainly; but it worked.

She gazed at him now as he stood with his back to her, tall and extremely handsome, elegant of dress and smooth of manner and wondered how such an apparently attractive person could manage to send shivers of horror and revulsion through one. She watched him pouring a deep red wine into a large glass. He picked it up and taking another glass, of ratafia, turned and advanced towards her, holding out the second glass.

She stood rigid. "No thank you Monsieur. I do not drink."

"Ah, but of course you do, my dear. I have witnessed it myself, at Versailles. Take it, do. It shall ease the nerves."

She turned her head away and put her hands behind her. He smiled gently and engagingly but those unblinking coal-black eyes remained cold and glittering. "Come Mignon; sit down, my dear; it shall be a very long evening upon your feet."

"Monsieur, I do not intend to stay."

"Ah, but you know you have no choice. 'Tis too dangerous to travel alone these times and in those clothes," smiling at her exquisite la mode gown, "you would not stand a chance against the rabble out there, *ma chérie*. Besides, you are to stay here this night. Did I not tell you that, no?"

She tried to suppress a shiver, failing completely when he placed an arm around her waist and guided her to the sofa before the fireplace, but she would not sit and, short of an embarrassing struggle, he could not force her. He watched her sidestep the sofa and move away several paces and then turn to face him. He smiled at her courage, for she now appeared even younger than he had at first thought. He settled in to enjoyment: for courage in the hunted served to heighten the excitement in the hunter.

"Monsieur, if I am to stay, then please: conduct me to your housekeeper. I have had a long day and do protest I am extremely fatigued. Everything else must wait the morrow."

"*Ma chérie*," he sighed in bored fashion, "I would oblige you with the greatest pleasure on earth, always supposing that I possessed one."

"Then I must presume you to have at least a maidservant, Monsieur. I beg to be conducted to her."

"In good time, enfant, but first, come." He took her hand in one of his that showed its steely quality when she attempted to pull away and led her once more to the couch. "Be pleased to observe; that before you stands the means to sit!"

"It be a waste of time, Seigneur. I am not staying."

His grip converted to vice-like quality and she sat.

He nodded. "Wise at last, my dear. Now I have several things that I wish to say to you. Some should please you, some may not, but please do not interrupt."

"If I am to stay, then I would that you reserved whatever it be until the morrow, Monsieur." She stared straight ahead, managed a yawn and drooped her shoulders.

"But so fatigued...*and* so cold, *ma chérie*," he laughed.

"I am not likely to differ, at any time Monsieur, and your familiar address insults me."

Lareaux sat gently beside her on the couch, one arm flung over the backrest, fingers trailing, just touching the smooth white skin of her shoulder, trailing, caressing. She controlled a shudder and stared ahead.

He laughed suddenly. "You think it worthwhile to anger me? I assure you that it is not. But if you concede to run in my harness, then you shall have everything that you could wish for."

She stared blankly. "How? Not that I ever, *ever* shall bend to your insane idea, whatever it may be. It must be nefarious, of course, to involve my abduction."

"How? Why, by marrying me... tonight."

Very white and shaking now, she made to rise but the grip on her shoulder became a vice; forcing her to remain seated.

"Then it shall be *I* that give *you* everything. That shall never happen. You waste your time!"

"Think, *ma chérie*."

"I have no need of thought. I would rather die!"

"Very possibly... that can also be easily arranged." He smiled in bored fashion again. "Come, have done with this bickering. You have no choice. Think girl, better to marry me in honour than to... well, I leave it to you... by tomorrow morning you shall be ruined."

"I do not give a straw. Married to you would be greater ruin!"

"You think to insult me? Not wise, my dear, and the ruin; the death mayhap, of your parents shall be the price of your freedom. The tricoteuses wait: counting their stiches."

She stared at him, the room swayed before her as those hypnotic eyes held hers in calm and gentle amusement. The man was assuredly mad. She took a long overdue breath and, so suddenly that his hand fell from her shoulder, leapt to her feet and ran to the windows. He watched her and then rose and followed her casually, for the widows were locked against street riots. He caught her around the waist as she struggled with the latches and then, with cold intent, spun her around to face him, pushing her back against the frame. She had but a moment before he bent his head and kissed her. The strength of his arms prevented her escape, her total loathing of him causing the faintness to steal over her. She fought it and began to struggle.

He lifted his head at last: "You had best give in, Mademoiselle. You shall not escape..."

"Ah, but then neither shall you, my evil friend." The voice was level, cool and bored.

Lareaux let forth an oath that no lady had ever heard before, as he released her and spun to face the intruder, a sword's length away: cold vengeance in his very steady gaze.

"Release her, Lareaux! Do not feint... I perceive your sword by the fireplace: oh so careless... in one who surely must always watch his back."

Mignon, unable to properly comprehend this last minute rescue, stumbled towards him. She vaguely recognized the gentleman from occasional social events: their families, though of the same social strata, did not always move in the same friendship circles. She did not know his name but that he be her knight at this moment was enough for her.

"Thank God... oh thankyou, Monsieur!"

Holding Lareaux at point, he took her hand in his; a hand so different to that other and, walking backwards, led her to the door and pushed her through. "Go to the small salon. There is a fire in there and a couch. I visited this house often; afore Lareaux picked it out of the confiscation bin. Rest there until I come for you. Go! Do you hear?"

His eyes never left Lareaux'; his powerful vengeance holding Angelique's 'cobra' stilled a moment. Mignon moved with alacrity now and he closed and locked the door behind her and pocketed the key, his eyes still locked on Lareaux.

"This *is* an unexpected pleasure, *Monseigneur*," Lareaux drawled, an unpleasant accent on the title of address. Turning his back—Savieur was the type of fool that would not strike from behind—he moved towards the fireplace. "I'm afraid I cannot let that go, Savieur... the girl was mine! A duel must sort the matter... now!"

Raoul smiled grimly, "Take your time, do."

"Ah, but mine impatience overwhelms me!"

"Likewise, Lareaux: in fact, I have waited too long it seems."

Lareaux bent to tug off his boots, remove his jacket and tuck up his ruffles, one eye on his visitor, and Raoul knew that the 'cobra' would not allow himself the time to do this. Laying his sword gently on the table, inches from his hand, Raoul swiftly performed the same ritual, finishing at the identical moment to his enemy. Lareaux then turned; and pulling the sword from its scabbard, sliced the air a couple of times.

"Too long you say?"

"To avenge Mademoiselle Vermont; of your heinous abduction of her: and even more evil intent on that day. And as for de Quatreaux, had I taken you out sooner mayhap he would be still alive. For that I shall not forgive myself. For it was you that furnished Beaumont with his armoury of weapons against de Quatreaux, isolated from himself: to satisfy the blackmailing Robespierre. I am afraid that that was completely unforgivable. And now, there lies beyond that door further proof of your despicable and unforgivable behaviour toward a very young girl of quality." He shrugged. "There is nothing for it, Lareaux. They must be avenged. All of them... so I accept your challenge!"

The room held a quiet, waiting silence. "I am entirely at your service, Savieur!"

Lareaux measured paces and then returning, without the mandatory 'On guard!' suddenly moved straight into attack, lunging in quarte and there was no sound but the ring of steel upon steel. Thereafter there was circling, lunging and recovering, countering and delivering until Lareaux delivered a lightning riposte en quinte. Raoul parried lightly in tierce and chuckled softly and humourlessly, his eyes an icy slate grey.

There was no doubt that Lareaux' reputation of swordplay was not exaggerated. He was indeed brilliant but Trifane trained every day, though he did not flaunt this as he felt his way, observing his opponent. A number of times it seemed that Trifane would be run through, his enemy using always the element of speed and surprise. But this began to develop into a pattern: something that Trifane had waited for, assisting his anticipation. The deadly intent on both their parts was never in question, but Trifane, developing an uncanny instinct, especially for his opponent's method of feint, began to anticipate almost before his opponent decided himself upon his next thrust.

Lareaux thrust now with vicious strength and accuracy but his sword tip met only with cambric shirtsleeve. Raoul retired his foot swiftly and nimbly and parried and reposted with straight thrust, wrist held high, before Lareaux could recover. They danced back and forth the long salon for some time and now the breath was coming in small gasps from Lareaux but Trifane managed to contain his breathing discomfort for the moment. Physically he was on a par with Lareaux: both were neat, precise and quiet, both owning a nimbleness of wrist and using, thus far, quickness of spirit, rather than muscular vigour. Both fought with the small-sword of Versailles pattern. Psychologically he was slightly ahead. And on an almost ethereal level he floated in a cool, clear realm of ancient spirit knowledge: he meant Lareaux to die: but for legitimate reasons. Lareaux had to pay—honour must be satisfied: lending the advantage of a clear untroubled conscience to Trifane. On the other hand, Lareaux' desire for revenge was based upon envy, hatred and a deep desire to kill all above him, especially those that obstructed his path. These dark swirling emotions became a hindrance: until he entered that cool and welcome arena of pure insanity. Then they became equally matched.

The only sound in the room now was the small gasps from Lareaux and the dull thud of stockinged feet. The voice of his old tutor sounded in Raoul's head: 'Anticipate your enemy, be there before him, but above all, care not whether you live or die, for he surely shall and therein be your unassailable advantage.'

The blades clashed and ragged breathing sounded now from Lareaux but also from Trifane there came the beginnings of grunted gasps on occasions. Now he lunged straight at his opponent's breast but Lareaux disengaged over his wrist and parried with ease and dexterity. The dark, unblinking cobra eyes glowed and sparkled with the lust to kill. His enemy's remained cool and steady, with no less desire to end the life of his opponent.

Lareaux, moving accurately and deliberately, always covering his body but never wasting a fraction's space or energy, seemed tireless; but Trifane parried with the swiftness and lightness of a jungle cat. He feinted suddenly inside Lareaux' arm: deceiving that man's parade of tierce, forcing him to fall back a pace, parrying quarte. Raoul changed quickly to quarte also and the blades rang out as they crossed: Lareaux' running the length of his opponent's arm. A red splash lay on Raoul's cambric shirt at the shoulder.

Trifane reeled slightly but controlled his gait and only said, "On guard!"

Lareaux, no intention of observing duelling etiquette, fought on, his eyes almost shut, his breath coming in gasps again, his chin thrust forward and his mouth a grim line. Suddenly his opponent's blade ripped open his shirtsleeve, a steady trickle of blood now running down his arm. He took no notice and fought on; countering Trifane's thrust so deftly that that man staggered back, a sudden and copious blood loss causing the swirling within his head and parchment hue to his now wet skin.

Raoul regained his footing somehow and steadied himself, recovering his guard but his point was no longer so purposeful, his vision blurring periodically. He knew that he had to either finish or be finished: knew also that the victor would be he who held the deepest desire, and strongest reasons, for his opponent's death: that this far outweighed mere instinct for survival. He parried again and they moved by inches toward the windows, fighting faster and faster now. Suddenly through the barrier of pain and exhaustion, a surge of seemingly supernatural force drove him on, flowing coolly through his body. He could feel it, uplifting, weightless, as his feet leapt from place to place, nimble and sure, in a last unbelievable push for supremacy. He flew on the sudden rush of last-ditch energy; that would of course be short lived. Lareaux knew it and lunged suddenly. Thus it was that, with his back to the window frame, Trifane also lunged: a split nanosecond after his opponent, parrying Lareaux' blade as it came through, passing on with not the smallest check, to the heart of his enemy. Trifane had fluked a coveted time-thrust. Others, that knew his swordplay, would have dissembled: Trifane had exhibited swordsmanship of the highest order; 'fluke' did not enter the equation. Lareaux stared in disbelief a long, long moment and then crumpled to the floor as Trifane pulled his blade free. Trifane also reeled in disbelief: he had feared, within the split second of his counter-lunge, the coup-double.

Raoul, bent over and panting now, leaned both hands on his sword; the tip embedded a millimetre in the wooden floorboards. The sweat dripped from his chin, blood from his shoulder and a grey mist descended around his head. He moved sideways to lean against the wall then slid gratefully to the floor there. A persistent knocking penetrated the mists. He listened vaguely then: the girl; the girl was at the door. He called a husky come in and then remembered. He pushed himself to his feet and moved across the room, his limbs completely without feeling and wobbling as half set jelly. In slow motion, forcing his limbs to obey, he searched out the key from his jacket pocket and unlocked the door. Mignon stood there, staring at him and then moving quickly into the room, closed the door and caught him as he reeled, ignoring the transfer of bloodstains from his soaked shirt to her dress.

She was extremely level headed for one so young but then he supposed hazily that all youth growing up in the current French environment would be so. She was also strong for one so small and half dragged him to the couch where he collapsed but managed, in husky voice, to say, "You are safe now. I shall see you to your home."

"Not yet awhile: Monseigneur."

But he insisted, and regaining his breath within a minute or so, shoved his tightly folded waistcoat as wadding against his shoulder wound and attempted to drag on his jacket. Mignon stopped him, gazed around, then, striding to the mantle, swept the artefacts there to the floor and caught up the long linen runner. With this she bound tightly his shoulder wound, pressured the waistcoat into position and then assisted his good arm into the jacket. He struggled with his boots, surprised that the one arm appeared reluctant. With Mignon's assistance they managed to push his feet into the resistant boots and finally he stood, no longer swaying; and gazed down at her.

"Now young lady, we must see you home with no witnesses. No, do not look over there, he is truly dead and so you need worry no longer."

"But Monsieur: what must we do with him?"

"Do with him? Why, nothing. What should you like to do with him? Feel free, Mademoiselle. The decision be all yours. You be owed that."

She chuckled softly. "Monsieur, I want nothing more than to get out of here and away from him."

"Then say no more... let us depart, Mademoiselle."

"But did *no* one see you arrive, Monsieur?"

"Not a soul, Mademoiselle. I hold a key. I once visited this house often but now of course it be sequestered to our evil friend there. I assume that his particular species of vermin send their servants to bed or home when they entertain a lady... there were none apparent as I entered." He glanced at her suddenly. "My pardon, mademoiselle, I appear to have been uncommonly self absorbed. Did he harm you in any way?"

She chuckled again. "If he did so, you cannot kill him again Monsieur."

Trifane looked over at Lareaux' body thoughtfully. "Oh, but there must be a way. I am sure that I could find it, if I tried."

"No Monseigneur, he did not hurt me, not really."

"I see. Then those bruises, already beginning to show, were caused by your own carelessness against his hands?"

"Oh, that be naught, Monsieur It was the terror of being captive that I found difficult to combat."

Raoul looked grim, his mind travelling to Angelique and another of Lareaux' attempted abductions. "He shall never terrorize any one again. Come, my name by the way be Trifane. At your service, Mademoiselle." He grinned weakly. "We seem to have done that a bit late."

"And mine Mignon. Mignon de Ville. Monsieur, he threatened the life of *mon père*. He says that he faces the tribunal. Do you think... would he not be in prison if that be the case?"

"That is so, *mon enfant*. But we must warn him. Now try not to worry: first things first."

He opened the door, without a glance in the direction of the inert body lying there in a surprisingly small pool of blood, and led the way down the stairs, searching out dim recesses; but no sound of life ensued and together they crossed the hall. Raoul picked up his dark cloak and dropped it around her shoulders, gathered his hat and gloves and they exited the hôtel, two silent shadows keeping close to the shadowed walls.

Light traffic still traversed the streets though it grew late now but these were intent upon nothing more than reaching their homes and firesides: winter tended to cool the revolutionary zeal. They managed to find an empty *pots-de-chambre*, its owner happy to collect an unexpected fare on his way home for the night, averting his gaze from glimpses of the high quality of the lady's dress: it was best at times to play it both ways. They both squeezed into this and Mignon arrived at her entrance not many minutes later. He saw her in to the protection of the butler and promising to call upon her paternal parent at the first opportunity, headed in the direction of the lower end of town and a certain wine-shop to be found there.

Raoul pushed aside the Persian wall rug and silently entered the room beyond. Emile was nowhere to be seen but on entering the second room through the revolving wall panel he found his old friend lying full-length upon his bed, staring at the smoke-stained low ceiling.

He squinted up at Raoul's entrance. "What's about?"

"Your story first," replied Raoul and, having noted the half-empty bottle upon the table without and now his friend's befogged state, turned his back and began to divest himself, not without difficulty, of his outer clothing.

"My catalogue of this night's events be surprisingly short, *mon ami*. Beaumont blew out his brains. That be all: nothing more to do... let us now exit this monstrous place."

"I could not more agree but we have one more chore to attend."

"Oh? A chore? Angelique a *chore, mon ami*? To you? Never!"

Emile sat up. At least that had been his intention but suddenly the walls of the room leaned in and then righted themselves again: almost. He stared at this phenomenon a moment, in puzzled mien and then fell back against the pillows, a random thought occurring, "*One* more, Trifane? Singular?"

"The number one usually denotes the singular."

"Pleased you explained that. Then congratulations be in order! Or did thee too witness the blowing of the brains?"

Trifane, now occupied in tending his wound: pressuring the wad of sad waistcoat against the clean gash, smiled. "Not at all. Lareaux was despatched by, er, mine own hand."

Emile nodded sagely. "Ah. Picked up your seconds on your way, did you?"

"I did not have any."

Emile attempted, gingerly this time, the upright position and turned to look at his friend. "But no..." shaking his head now, once only, "no...shall not believe it of you *mon ami*...stickler for the etiquette...that's what you are."

"I did not go there to fight but to arrange the time, place, seconds and choice of weapon, but found him so engaged in foul play that I had no choice... aside of which he then challenged *me*: followed by an attack which omitted any duelling courtesies!"

"Ah! So, the world does breathe cleaner air now... and *mon père* be completely avenged." He paused, frowning reflectively. "But death be not enough. Is it not so?"

"It be all that be available to one, upon this planet, *mon ami*; so do try to make the best of it. You may chase him again in the afterlife if you so wish to waste your time."

Emile chuckled and turned gingerly again to look at his friend and at last perceived his weakened state.

"*Mon Dieu*! Why did you not say something! But that requires attention, so it does."

"It be but a graze; no major vessels or ligaments. Clean water and some spirits shall suffice."

"Allow me, Monsieur." Emile stood, smiled at the success of this difficult feat, then left the room to find the necessary items for the treatment of Raoul's wound. Reaching the stage of pouring the raw alcohol into the wound held wide open, his friend shook his head.

"I shall attend this; thank you."

"But not at all, my friend: vengeance be mine! I am *owed* this. From a time well remembered. You poured *hot* alcohol into me."

Raoul grinned "We were very young and the fashionable theory of heat to prevent complications was just emerging. And the head groom did not include the fact that mostly it was done when the patient was unconscious... which of course you soon were. But you must admit, there followed not the slightest sign of that mysterious but fatal complication: the reddening of the wound. I did you a very great favour, *mon ami*."

"And my manners and gratitude would be sadly amiss an I did not return the compliment. Give me the bottle!"

"What... and no wedge to bite on? But you are inhumane, Vermont! *Inhumane!*"

# CHAPTER TWENTY-THREE

## Lady's Slipper & Skullcap

Angelique paced, slowly now, her skirts brushing the unswept stone-flagged floor. Her shawl, caught in her elbows, trailed below her waist; the warmth generated by this activity, sufficient for personal comfort. She did not pace alone. All the new arrivals paced. The gamblers within the male fraternity laid their bets on which would stay the longest. Handicaps were laid, favourites announced and people waited anxiously. The money was not important. The mental activity was. They gambled their fortunes, their estates and châteaux. This way they retained their hold on sanity, denying that those possessions were already in the hands of the revolutionary government.

Angelique ignored them as she paced. She supposed that everyone travelled the worn road of hope, then anger, then plotting and planning, vengeance a most powerfully sustaining factor. Primeval emotions, ancient roots of mankind, sat only too close to the surface; the extreme fragility, of the veneer of 'civilized' societal trapping, no deterrent. Had she the chance, she would drive home the sword with a precision born of pure hatred and bitter vengeance, directed at the person or persons directly responsible for the death of France but more violently: of de Quatreaux. She tried to analyse this, not even sure who it was that had betrayed her father but someone must pay: she would deal with the confessional later. She paused: even the Church could not override these feelings. Suddenly an understanding of the sans-culottes entered her mind, leading to a deeper compassion: theirs had been a long, long growth period. Their hatred she could accept but never the Machiavellian monsters orchestrating mayhem and wholesale murder, in the *name* of the sans-culottes but grinding them also, underfoot.

She continued to pace. One two three four five six, turn, one two three four five six turn: the square complete; pace, turn, pace turn, on and on. Past childhood events ran by her conscious mind, crystallised and taunting in their beauty and colour. Days at Château Quatreaux drifted past her: running through the dappled light of the wooded hills, beneath the summer sun, fishing with her brothers in the slivery stream, falling in and returning to be scolded by Nurse. Gathering lavender with Fanchon and skating the frozen duck-ponds in winter. Sleigh rides; and riding beneath the guiding hands of the first groom, Michel, shaking free from his supervision and galloping breakneck across the estates. The festive season hunt flashed before her and then came, as always in times of stress, the flashing insight she had had on the last of these festivities then the blood of the kill, the darkness, the horror, her *père* and—a face: now was added a floating, unclear face. She strained, the cell sounds receding, her mental 'eye' reaching again, straining to clear the mists, then failure. Stretching out again, yes, there it was, becoming clearer now. Before it pushed an aura of extreme sadness, then the darkness cleared: Beaumont? Startled, she focused again upon that face, gentle, thoughtful, wavering before her. No! Surely not: she was going insane; and then came the hand raised in anger, the third finger wearing a heavy signet ring: Emile! Startled back to the present, she gasped aloud, heart pounding. Aware suddenly of the noise filled cell, she swiftly reined in her demonstration of emotion. But no, it could *not* have been Beaumont, that genial, laughing man: most supportive friend to her father. She paused and saw again Emile and suddenly contracted, twin like, his fury and vengeance. A sudden sound, of a fallen chair close by, brought her back to the present. She returned her attention to the occupants of the room. Each and every one of them was experiencing grief, fury and most of all disbelief, though none were by any means naive. The revolution was heading into its fifth year but until it touched one personally, there remained the hope, as with all discomfort and tragedy, that it would somehow bypass oneself. Not an unreasonable desire for the people surrounding her now. All had committed no other crime than ownership of undeniable birth lines; or some faked evidence of supposed treason against the Jacobin government. All had owned property or banking balance weighted by gold.

She moved past the table now, the ladies seated there embroidering, mending, writing letters to their remaining families, though it be anybody's guess whether these reached their destination or indeed that the recipients were even alive still. All communication was of course, read by the guards and so if one was wise one picked a guard evidencing poor literacy at rollcall. But Angelique had no one to write to. Hopefully Emile and Trifane remained undetected by Robespierre's secret agents and she would not risk the life of poor dear Marie, or Madame Bayette: poor dear Madame Bayette. And then there was that other kind and generous being of their acquaintance, Pontisqieu. She wondered at his growing involvement in the counterrevolutionary cause and could only suppose it to be due to his friendship with Emile and Trifane.

"*Ma chère*! Do rest those restless feet! You must relax a little if you wish to survive this experience," said Madame de Brionne gently. "You shall wear out not only your physical energy but also that of your mind."

She turned and paused behind this very large lady as she sat embroidering and thought suddenly that all very large ladies seemed to possess a generous nature. Nothing appeared to disturb her sensitivity. "Madame, how do you do it? Remain so calm in the face of what we face each day?"

"*Each day mon enfant...* that be the essence... every day I do my best for one more day," she replied gently, then looking up at Angelique, "Come child, you suffer greatly the loss of your *père* but he does go into the next world knowing that he did his extreme best. Never can it be said that he did not pursue the course of truth and justice in the true sense. His assistance to others outweighs all other noblemen. This I know through mine own husband." She said it quietly, with no bitterness at his demise.

Angelique placed a spontaneous hand upon her arm, and that woman, chin, several chins, quivering, shook it off but she was not offended; she understood. "I shall have something to say to Robespierre should I ever have the pleasure of being in his exalted presence!"

Madam de Brionne blinked hard, dispersing the threatening tears. "I think it better that you do not anger him."

"I am not afraid of him Madame."

"You shall tell him this?"

"Most certainly I shall and other bits of information for his edification."

"Then, should it occur, this should be a most interesting meeting but to what cost: for it can only end in your final curtsey: to Madame Guillotine."

"But Madame, I see no other outcome, for any of us."

Madame de Brionne smiled ruefully. "But you mistake the one called Robespierre... he shall not care whether thee be afraid of him or not. To exterminate, the quickest and purest way possible, all that he imagines despoiling France, be to him all that matter."

The day drew to an end at last, the women preparing as best they could what food had been sent via visitors, the central table now cleared of all evidence of previous works of mending, embroidery, lace-making, drawing and writing materials. Angelique took no part in this, avoiding for others the embarrassment of not being able to offer her a share; there was so little. She could not stomach the prison swill and old, green/grey bread and so stayed apart. Her body could not have reached of course, in so short a time, the state of being that prefers prison swill, a scurrying cockroach even, to starvation. Madame de Brionne, making space for the bread and large tureen, glanced up at Angelique, now sitting upon a stone bench against one wall. Her gaze shifted suddenly, to a neat, conservatively dressed gentleman being escorted into the cell. He had the look of a lawyer and paused once the gaoler had ushered him in and locked the wide grill behind him. He gazed about for a moment and then moved purposefully toward Angelique as she sat reading the small book of prose handed to her by an elderly lady leaving the cellblock for the last time.

"Mademoiselle Vermont: I am pleased to find you apparently well."

She started at the familiar voice and looked up, her eyes widening.

"No, do not appear to know me too well, I beg of you... we do not need the guard hovering close to hear our conversation! I have but a few moments afore he returns... at which time I make it obvious that I am here only to discuss your defence at the Tribunal. So please just listen."

"But Monsieur Pontisqieu," she said softly, "It is so refreshing to see you, believe me. I cannot *but* be happy to see you."

"Then conceal the fact, Mademoiselle. I am come bearing gifts of er," he paused to glance about, then placed the basket beside her and opened the lid. It had been searched minutely but none in the guardhouse could find aught wrong with its contents. "I have here the obvious gifts for a lady confined to prison but also, most importantly, the vinaigrette bottle."

"Vinaigrette?" she echoed, laughing suddenly. "Why does every one insist I should benefit from such? I think that I did mention, some time ago certainly, during the street riots was it not... that I do not faint! Or was that to Trifane... no: it was to Fersen!"

He gave a small smile in response. "But this is for your megrims. I know that you suffer such, frequently; and the current fashion be to take it on retirement. Do not forget: on retirement; in order to gain relief and a good nights' sleep."

"*Megrims*? But I do not... oh... well yes of course; my megrims be of a particularly violent nature of late. Tell me, how does vinaigrette cure such?"

"Mademoiselle, continue so, for it appears well that we simply converse thus lightly but I be deadly serious when I say that it is to be taken immediately afore rollcall: *this* night."

She stared. "*Taken*, Monsieur Pontisqieu?"

"Yes Mademoiselle, you *must* remember to do this!"

She gazed at him. "You are quite sure about this, Monsieur?"

"I am! Very definitely; your life could be said to depend upon it!"

"Then I shall be obedient to your wishes, Monsieur." She had a sudden thought and chuckled. "*All* of it? Forgive me, but you see, one does not usually *drink* the vinaigrette... one, er... usually sniffs it, through the nose you understand."

He smiled faintly, heart contracting at her incredible courage. "This one is drunk. The top unscrews. Take all of it. And," he glanced over her shoulder and fished in the basket, drawing forth a small oval, metal container: green based decorated in pink flowers. "There approaches the guard so I must hurry." He pulled out a sheaf of papers from his leather satchel and shuffled through them until the guard wandered away. "Now, apply the cream generously to your face, neck and forearms immediately after swallowing the vinaigrette. It may sting a little."

The guard was approaching again. Pontisqieu smiled and bid her farewell. He followed the guard, leaving her holding the green, metal container of possibly not so beneficial cream; a sense of cold loneliness swamping her, suddenly, at his retreating back. He passed the large lady and had noted, on entry, her concerned attitude toward Angelique as she had sat reading. He now took a gamble and bowing briefly and apologetically indicated that he would speak with her. The guard shrugged but stayed close.

"Citizienne, forgive my impudence but I would that you looked out for Citizen Vermont. She has no one, you understand."

Madame de Brionne smiled her acquiescence and nodded, her eyes signalling that she understood. "But assuredly Citizen... poor lamb."

Monsieur Pontisqieu nodded his thanks, controlling a smile at the description; no one could be less lamb-like than Mademoiselle Vermont and turning, left the cell without backward glance. Madame Brionne was left mulling over the extreme depth of appeal, within the steady eyes. She did not know what went forward but would remain alert.

Angelique, eyes following his exit, guessed that the contents of the small vinaigrette bottle would cause drowsiness, mayhap even vomiting. Did they have an infirmary within the prison, from which she could be snatched? She had not heard of one and could not see that the current regime would be concerned with prisoner welfare; if they died then all the less to manage. She did not know what her brother and Trifane had planned but she was prepared to assist in any way that she could.

Dinner was over, such as it was, and it wanted a few minutes to rollcall. Heart thumping already, Angelique moved slowly and casually toward her patch of bare floor within the cell, having refused the straw, kindly proffered on her first night, by Madame Dupont, sleeping alongside. On her other side slept Madame de Brionne, though none slept too much it was true, due to this woman's constant scratching and tossing; courtesy the lively inhabitants of the straw. Here she opened her basket, took out the small glass vinaigrette phial and removed the stopper. With back to the company, she tipped the contents into her mouth, swallowed and then grimaced. She would repay Monsieur Pontisqieu one fine day. She replaced the phial in the basket and then proceeded to apply the cream as directed. There occurred a faint stinging and itching but nothing of note. Having complied with his orders, she replaced the tin of cream, then picked up the third gift: a book of verse and perused it. After a minute she returned it to the basket, sat this on her 'sleeping patch' and made to move out to the anti-chambre where she could see the guards preparing for rollcall, list in hand. See vaguely, for her sight appeared to be impaired suddenly, the walls of the cell dancing up and down and her legs comprising blancmange. Darkness descended as she crumpled to the floor, hoping that the men in her life knew what they were about and then all was warm and dark; the sounds around her coming from far away, then fading to nothing.

The role call neared its end until the lack of response to one name, caused concern.

"Citizienne Vermont!"

The still and silent prisoners remained still and silent.

"Citizienne Vermont I say!"

Several prisoners shuffled their feet, glancing at each other and then, to allay their ire, which would then be projected onto the unfortunate Citizienne Vermont and then the rest of them, Madame de Brionne spoke up suddenly.

"I believe that she was feeling unwell, Citizen—I noticed her lying down earlier," she said and turned to glance back into cell 14.

The guard grunted and sent a man to investigate and stood waiting, his thumb on the spot of the last name called while the rest stood very still. They waited and then a cry from the cell had everyone turning to stare.

"Citizen! She be not ill. She be dead!"

"No! I shall *not* have this in my section: *how* dead?"

"Very dead: Citizen!"

The guard rolled his eyes. "How is it that she *be* dead?" He dropped his list onto the table and left the anti-chambre to investigate Angelique: prone and inert. He felt for a pulse: it was absent, her skin moist and cold. He placed his fingers beneath her nose, then leaned forward and placed his cheek there. She was not breathing. He straightened, rose and signalled his junior to his side, gazing down at the prisoner; her skin a strange colour; face and neck ominously mottled.

"Take her out of here. Place her upon that stone bench there. And then continue the rollcall."

"But Citizen, I cannot read."

"Use a literate prisoner. I must go report this and send for the rostered prison doctor."

"Doctor? But she be dead Citizen... I *saw*... and you just said so!"

"*My* pronouncement be not sufficient you fool."

"Ah, er, Citizen, be it not the duty of the junior guard to deliver messages?"

"Very well Dumas, but in this case, the name of the reporting guard shall be on the doctor's report to those far above us. If you are willing to face the extreme ire of one Robespierre or worse, Saint-Just, for losing *this* one of special notation, then proceed. Better men than I have been executed for dereliction of duty and to lose a prisoner in such a way; depriving the *Revolutionary Tribunal* of its satisfaction can only be interpreted as dereliction, I do believe."

"Mayhap it be better that you go then, Citizen." The guard gingerly picked up the limp and 'very dead' Angelique, endeavoured not to touch any bare skin, moved through the cell to the anti-chambre and dropped her upon the stone bench.

The night was dark, the moon many hours from rising. The heavy clouds, of early winter rain, hung over Paris. The streets just here were now empty of all life excepting for the homeless and the skeletal canines and waif felines. But still the coach driver kept his eyes moving across the immediate area, though of street urchins he did not expect; there were no sheltering doorways. The dark, closed coach stood just to the right of the prison gates, a black shadow against a black wall, with its heavily caped and hatted driver seated huddled against the cold. He hoped it would rain, for the slanting driving rain would offer further deterrent to dangerous vehicle checks just outside the prison. Thus far they had avoided the watch. He glanced often through the iron gates and across the courtyard to the dimly lit wicket, as did his passengers within.

At last the wicket opened and a guard and turnkey came striding out. They both crossed the courtyard and the turnkey unlocked and opened the gates. The guard spoke to the occupants of the coach through the window and then disappeared into the darkness and the coach was motioned through the gates, the turnkey relocking them again. They rumbled across the stone-flagged courtyard to finally stand to the left of the wicket. Through this the two passengers, the doctor and his attendant, disappeared with their escort.

Within the prison they moved briskly through the corridors and passageways, following the silent turnkey who sanctioned their presence at each checkpoint and rattled the keys at each grilled gate. The attendant carried the stretcher beneath his arm; the two rails, fed through canvas envelopes, collapsed together.

Reaching the anti-chambre to cells 13 and 14, they dumped the stretcher against a wall and the doctor moved to the guards in the guard room, not even glancing at the stone bench where lay a figure covered entirely with an old blanket.

"You have a man down, here?"

"Woman, Citizen," answered the guard and stepped back from the doctor.

The doctor raised his eyebrows in cynical fashion. "I am only *le docteur*, Citizen. You act as if *I* had died *and* of something foul and mysterious!" He wondered for a moment whether he had overdone his act but the two guards were obviously terrified.

"Citizen, she be mighty ill afore she died. The plague be my punt."

The doctor frowned. "Come, come man; that be over long ago. It only descends upon us every hundred years or so."

"The pocks then: she lies there… yon stone bench."

The good doctor almost choked and stepped toward the body. He pulled the blanket away from her face and stood back. The patient had clearly been very ill and it was evident that her complaint could be contagious. Her face was very white, where normal skin could be seen. This however was limited, for the welts and blotches—dark, angry, red blotches, each centred by a large yellowed blister— almost covered her entire, swollen, face and neck. Curiously these stopped just below the throat, in an uneven line. There was, on examination, no pulse and no breath. Her skin was cold to touch and clammy and the doctor experienced great difficulty controlling his panic. He finished his brief examination and turned to the two guards standing as far as was possible from the 'dead girl', watching with more than usual curiosity, holding cloths over their lower faces.

"Come, you two, help my attendant: to place her into a shroud." He caste a look at the senior of the guards. "You do *have* such here? For contagious diseases… yes?"

"Er… yes, Monsieur *le Docteur*… somewhere in those cupboards."

He unearthed a stiffly folded and dusty canvas and handed it across.

Monsieur *le Docteur* watched them a moment; then said, "Place her on the stretcher."

Ignoring them henceforth, he moved to the table in the guardroom and sat down to write out the document of diagnosis and then two certificates of death, dated and signed each with the much practiced scrawl and returned his attention to the guards.

"This be your copy, though things change so rapidly, that I do not know from one moment to the next whether this or that document still be necessary," he said in irascible voice. He waited.

"Citizen, 'tis this one that we need, we *did* need the other," pointing, "but no more so… dead is dead!"

The doctor packed up his satchel, turned towards the bench and nodded. He followed his attendant and one guard carrying the stretcher, to the exit of the anti-chambre. Here he stopped them and placed his satchel on the foot end of the stretcher, held by the guard.

"Citizen, you have no need of accompanying us: you could be correct about the contagion."

The guard made mild protest. "But Doctor, perhaps I should…"

"No, my friend, you stay here, where it be warm. And scrub that bench thoroughly with strong alcohol. The turnkey shall be our escort."

The turnkey, thus far ignored, agreed, adding that he would be going off duty; therefore it was no trouble to escort them to the prison courtyard.

The cadaver, now residing within in a long canvas envelope, lay still: as expected. Only the doctor's attendant worried at the possibility of it suddenly moving in effort to gain air; should it regain consciousness. The doctor worried more that it would lie still permanently: the signs of life had been so very faint. The panic within threatened to surface as he walked, crushing the desperate urge to lengthen and hasten his stride; eyes locked onto the canvas enshrouding Angelique's head: a necessary procedure of authenticity. Emile had wrapped it as loosely as was possible without arousing suspicion but the air there would not last long.

Unconcerned, the turnkey continued along the corridors, nodding to other traffic: guards and prison officials, arriving or exiting the prison for the night. They followed him. A damp chill settled around them. The long, dank, noisome passageways were now dully lit by the wall brackets; shadowed corners rustling with emerging rats now that night had arrived. The cadaver remained still.

Arrived at the exit to the prison courtyard, the turnkey approached the guardroom. Several individuals sat about: drinking forbidden alcohol and munching on dry bread and cheese. The turnkey checked his stride a moment; then, not even glancing at those he escorted, addressed the foremost: "Citizen! You be early. Or else we late... where be Poitier?"

"Sent off on an errand but he warned us of your arrival and that you take this one with you... something about a broken wheel on the prison hearse. I am Vesoullé, replacing him."

Raoul and Emile, still holding the stretcher, froze: the bribed guard, to pass the 'body' as deceased at this checkpoint, removed? They stood, apparently in bored fashion, as the turnkey produced the necessary release papers for one Angelique Vermont. The noisy chatter had subsided to the odd comment. Now it ceased altogether as Versoullé took them, glanced at them and placed them on the desk. Some drew back in normal superstition, casting furtive glances at the shrouded body. The doctor and his attendant remained static: weapon-less for the search on entry meant unarmed combat, should an opportunity arise. They waited, holding the stretcher.

"Put it on the bench there," and as they obeyed, "Step back by the wall... over there."

They obeyed again and Versoullé moved forward; waved a hand at one of his subordinates. "Unwrap the cadaver."

Two guards stepped reluctantly forward and hesitantly tugged aside the canvas shroud, this procedure dragging a thick swathe of curling, tawny hair across Angelique's face. Versoullé stepped up to the bench, gazed a moment then looked at the doctor.

"Check her again!"

Raoul stepped forward and checked her breathing, picked up a limp wrist, held it a moment, dropped it, placed a hand just below the jaw-line a moment, then stepped back and nodded. "You wish to check, Citizen?" indicating the wrist, lying across her body. He held his breath: though there be no wrist pulse, he did not want a closer inspection.

"She be dead?"

Raoul nodded again. "As the documents do ascertain."

Versoullé shrugged, walked to the wall and picked up the bayonet leaning there, then approached the dead girl.

"No!" the cry was a reflex: nothing could have prevented it; and nothing could now retract the urgency of tone.

Versoullé halted and turned to the doctor, brows raised; a faint smile settling across his features. "So the cadaver is known to you... Monsieur *le Docteur*... a relative? Sadly I must ensure her death be authentic... procedure, you know. You have no idea of the tricks pulled within escape efforts these days. They soon jump with a prod from this. Do not look."

He lifted the bayonet but recovering swiftly, Raoul moved forward, to stand between Versoullé and the stretcher, smiling calmly now. "No Citizen, she be not from my family... and you surely must ensure *some* authenticity of death, that be the requirement... but do you really want to expose everyone; by opening the body?"

The brows lifted again. "Thus releasing the fumes of disease? A poor effort, Monsieur *le Docteur,* to explain away your panic."

"Pardon Citizen, but my 'panic' was well founded; you see I am the one that must handle her! I do not wish to carry *this* to my family: my youngest is sick and therefore already weakened and at risk. Please look at this." Raoul's tone hinted impatience.

He pulled the thick swathe of tawny hair from across her face to expose features that even Emile had trouble recognizing. The bloated blisters now extended to join each other. Her eyelids were so puffed they would require the fingers of both hands to open them. Some blisters exhibited the skin so taught across the surface as to split, a watery, yellow exudate oozing out. The gasp came in unison. The room stilled. Raoul ran two gentle fingers across a blister and held them up, moving closer to the company that they might better see the repulsive substance. He extended his arm, moved closer. They backed up, staring.

"Citizen," he approached Versoullé, offering better view of the fingers, "I *must* consider a resurgence of the plague... the colour of the pus is typical."

For a moment he feared he had gone too far but Versoullé could now do no other than allow them through: neglecting to report an outbreak of plague before it claimed a victim, and caused a possible panic, would entitle him the privilege of the guillotine. He stepped back from the fingers, shuffled the papers, retained those for prison records and held out the remaining ones, at arm's length, to the doctor.

"Go!"

The turnkey, standing in bored silence the whole of this episode, now turned and moved indolently to exit the room. The doctor calmly placed the sheafed papers back in his satchel; locked it and placing it at the cadaver's feet, picked up his end of the stretcher.

They made their way to the wicket and the turnkey waved them through and slammed the door shut behind them. They were alone, but trusting nothing, Raoul indicated that they drag the stretcher none too gently into the closed coach: identified as belonging to a doctor now quietly enjoying the interesting items of antiquity within the museum. The coachman, standing by, pulled the poles free of their canvas envelopes and stored them behind the driver's seat. The attendant settled himself upon the opposite seat and the coachman put up the steps, closed the door and returned to his driving box. The black coach moved off across the courtyard, exited the gates now unlocked by the turnkey and drove off into the dark Paris night. Emile leaned back against the backrest and remained silent after one query.

Raoul's voice was grim as he answered, "Her heart beats... just! I shall kill Anton's cousin!"

"Thrice removed," offered Emile helpfully, "though I feel it be more than that." He frowned. "Twice from his cousin and then that cousin twice times removed..." He shook his head. "Something wrong there... but yes, it be four times. But kill him by all means."

"Slowly!"

"What did he use by the by?"

"I do not know, aside of the lady's slipper and skullcap. They be sedatives only and *could* not do this."

"You did ask for it. For the appearance of death, *mon ami*. Possibly hemlock be added. That could do the trick. Or *mayhap* some Monkshood; now *that* slows the heart rate and breathing. I remember when I was quite young... the gamekeeper you know..."

"If you cannot offer accurate and encouraging knowledge then I would appreciate your silence."

"But I think, *mon ami*, if..."

"*Do not*, whatever you do Emile... think!"

Emile subsided. Somewhere deep inside he knew that his twin would survive. Granted: her complexion may never be the same again. He suppressed a grin; Raoul's sense of humour was sadly absent. He sobered however, as his mind turned toward Rochelle, knowing that should it be her lying there, he would be distraught: with a concern far removed from that of sibling to sibling.

Angelique had died. She had died and descended into hell. Of this she had no doubts at all. Only in that place so named could one feel this foul. She felt deeply for the Lord Jesus. It was no wonder at all that *He* only stayed three days; in fact how he had survived that length of time she could not understand; but then he *was* the Lord Jesus. The mists, nay, choking fog, returned and she could hold this thought no longer; then they shifted again, swirling around and around, causing that certain imbalance that created the vile, nauseous dizziness.

She retched, and felt the arms beneath her shoulders and a soothing voice, a hand sweeping back her hair and holding it behind her neck as she retched again... and again. Now she knew that voice from someplace; had he accompanied her: to hell? She must thank him; only a very good friend would do that. But then there was another voice from far away and this one she knew well. Her mind, operating over and above the retching and wracking agony deep within her stomach, travelled back to when she had greedily gobbled the berries before her brother could reach them. He had fed her green ones: it had been payback but then this very thing had happened and they had all thought that she would die. She frowned, she obviously had not: for *this* be that experience. She saw the château now, upon the hill, beneath the hot summer sunshine, felt the soft green grass beneath her feet; mayhap she was being transferred to heaven after all but then came the cold edge of the china vomit bowl, beneath her hot chin and Fanchon forcing a jug of salted water down her throat. Someone was doing it again for goodness sake but it was definitely not Fanchon and this tasted worse than plain salt water by far.

The voice from far away, the one that she recognized which was in actual fact only across the room, spoke again. "You think more, *mon ami...* while she be a little more conscious? Can one overdo the ephedra, I wonder?"

She cried out, "No, you beasts... not more... *whatever* it is that you be doing to me!" But they did not hear her. The sound did not leave her throat even.

Then the other voice sounded: the one above her head as he held her so tenderly but she faded a little at this point and could not hear distinctly his words. Words from the voice that was familiar but remained illusive of identity; the one filled with warmth and tenderness when it spoke to her. She puzzled again, retched and puzzled no more. She sank back into the soft black, velvet cocoon. This was a good thing; a very good thing for here, only here was there respite from the wracking waves of abdominal cramps and that vile, indescribable pre-vomit experience. Luckily she was blissfully ignorant of the greater of her problems, for had she been aware of her appearance; she would definitely not have survived the mortification. Tangled and sweat drenched hair, the stench of vomit and fever ridden body odour, that surrounded her, plus the state of her facial skin imitating one afflicted by a severe case of cow-pox, did not add to one's charms. The humiliation would be unendurable.

For this reason Trifane did not attend her further, following her awakening from that experience into a saner and definitely more stable world. He had enquired of Anton the availability of a woman to attend her but that man, unmarried himself, did not trust the introduction of any extra person to their plans; especially a female.

"They be mighty fine in the kitchen, Monseigneur... in the procurer's house, *magnifique* and in the cot as one's wife I imagine, with the right one certainly... but unless blind and deaf ... *and* mute, do not trust them!"

Raoul glanced at Emile with humour in his eyes and acquiesced. "You be in the right of it, Anton. Then there be nothing for it but to acquire the services of her own companion."

Soon Marie arrived, brought to Anton's hidden quarters below the cellars of the wine shop. She took this in her stride, showing no shock on sight of her charge. Bathing and tending her, soothing her agitation, she pampered her with oatmeal scrubs and lavender oil massages, washing her hair and brushing it until it shone in its old manner. For Angelique's face she had brought fresh chickweed, the aerial properties crushed and ground and added to a soothing cream and applied it directly to her skin. The root she crushed and mixed into a concoction to be swallowed; its purpose to cool the remaining fever in her charge and boost her malnourished state: following the prolonged vomiting and prison fare. This was followed by a tincture of cleavers, yellow dock and figwort; made into a concoction and offered her charge thrice daily. It took Marie some little time to entice her to drink it but she succeeded in the end.

Angelique improved as the hours continued and the poisons left her system; the nausea abated and the cramps disappeared. She was a little weak but that was all. Finally Marie sprinkled the air with a mix of rose water and lavender oil and scattered rosemary and other herbal leaves across the floor. Refined rosemary oil she also administered to her patient as a carminative and anti-spasmodic. Following this she waited a little and then offered a little clear beef soup, which her patient could, surprisingly, swallow without return of the nausea. Marie then settled her back into clean sweet smelling linen, brought from Hôtel Quatreaux, plaited her tawny hair in the French way and tied the end with a satin riband.

"There! You be as good as new. I suppose you do not require a sedative?" she caught the look from her charge and laughed.

Angelique gazed at Marie. "Marie, I have much for which to thank you."

"Ah, it be naught. I must go now, dearest one, for I cannot afford… we none of us can afford for me to be absent from the hôtel for long periods of time. Now sleep; for you have little time left to regain you strength."

"But Marie…"

Marie put her finger to her lips and slipped out of the room, closing the door quietly behind her. In the outer room she approached Raoul and curtsied gracefully. "Monsieur, she be well now. You may see for yourself."

He looked down at her and smiled. "Madame, I owe you a great deal… *one day*…"

"Yes, yes, but here I must depart I think Monsieur, it must be growing late and I am known as an early riser. I must be there to direct the staff, though goodness knows why… there be no family left there now… and how long they will stay now that the Comte is gone, is another matter. *I* cannot pay their salaries."

"Come then, I shall escort you back. But worry not; it was de Quatreaux' habit to pay them up front; to the length of a year, I believe. As to your future… should you wish to return to your home in the south then I shall ask Monsieur Pontisqieu to arrange safe journey for you."

They left the room and silence descended. Angelique slipped back into a deep slumber but it was the slumber of a recovery; the deep untroubled slumber that healed. She did not hear her brother and Savieur return to the room next to her and settle to the task of decision-making.

"It be urgent *mon ami*, already time be pressing," said Emile to Raoul as that man paced slowly across the small space between table and door. "The sooner the better. We go in two different and separate conveyances. Anton could not arrange the coach in time, not without arousing suspicion. Come man, she shall be fine!"

Raoul gazed at Emile. "I myself have never prayed, considering earthly action, in the interests of self-preservation, be the more effective in times of danger. But now *mon ami*, you had better pray that you be correct. I will not risk her safety. Not after what she has been through thus far. That *I* have put her through."

♣

It was late afternoon but one would not know this within the darkened rooms below the wine cellar. However, at this moment the outer room contained only Angelique, who sat at the table studying the passports and barrier passes and then the pile of old, threadbare and stained peasant's attire that had been delivered by Anton earlier that day.

She glanced up apprehensively as the door suddenly opened and Monsieur Pontisqieu entered quietly. He let fall the wall-rug and closing the door softly, placed a finger to his lips. She remained silent.

"Mademoiselle," he whispered softly, "Without, there be agents of the Tribunal. They know nothing of your presence but question Anton's bookkeeping and his profits. Now come, back into the bedroom and remain silent."

She nodded and together they scooped up every vestige of paperwork and personal belongings of the residents and then manipulated the revolving panel and stood in total darkness, ears to the wall but no sound eventuated. No shouting, running feet or tramp of guards could be heard and after what seemed a very long time Pontisqieu whispered softly in her ear that he would open the panel. At that moment however they heard the sounds of a thorough search of the room beyond and Pontisqieu froze his actions. They held their breath and waited but the revolving, seamless door behind the wall hanging was not discovered. A moment after the noises abated, he softly opened it and slipped through. He returned after some few minutes and called her through.

"Mademoiselle, you go now. Anton remains: they could not indict him. He clears the way and be adamant that you now no longer be safe here: even though they were satisfied there was the only one hidden chambre... supposedly for his documents and personal items. Come—into the country girls' attire... we go before they make a surprise return."

She did not question but obeyed and slipped back into the inner room and soon emerged again. Now stood, in her place, a downtrodden country wench, dirt smudged across her face, a dirty red bonnet covering her head the only splash of colour.

He smiled. "Very good! Now double check please; passport, exit permit, barrier pass, basket with basic victuals for the journey and another carrying that broken boot and mending needle and thread. It be better that you be occupied while I be questioned."

"You... Monsieur?"

He smiled again. "Yes 'tis I that you travel with, in my cousin's produce cart: leaving the city at the end of the day, to return on the morrow with fresh produce."

"I comprehend...er...nothing Monsieur."

"No, but you shall. First, you must call me *Citizen*. Begin now, if you please!"

"Yes Citizen."

He smiled suddenly. "Very good Citizienne! Now you sit in the cart, upon a vegetable crate, amongst the old cabbage and other vegetable leaves. You are preoccupied with the boot. I shall demonstrate in a moment just how it is to be mended. It be very tough leather to work on and so you shall quiet naturally be wearing these."

He produced a pair of rough and hardened leather gloves. "They be too large for you but that be all to the better; peasant girls do not own small and dainty hands, neither be they white and unsullied."

She accepted this, pulled them on and took up the basket. Her shoulders slouched, causing the dark and heavy cloak to trail the floor and she lowered her eyes submissively.

He laughed suddenly. "Excellent! How do you achieve such marvellous impersonation?"

"My brothers and sister and I spent many long cold winter evenings performing plays, Mons...er Citizen... and learned the trick of slipping into a character's head."

"Ah. Little did you all guess how grateful you would be now, for that exercise— now come."

"Excuse me, Citizen, but will they not know *you* dressed like that?"

Ah but I *am* me. I do not change; for you see I am well known and at present well respected. I am the great lawyer that puts away the nobility."

She stared and he laughed again. "No Citizienne. I do not cause good and faithful Frenchmen of the nobility to be executed but that be the reputation that I have been at great pains to promote... by denigrating such; in my defence of poorer folk."

She stared again, hard.

"No Citizienne, I do not lie.  But yes, *some* nobility, who have wantonly murdered both before and during the Revolution and are thoroughly bad lots, I *have* prosecuted; and by chance this promoted that image and these, believe me, deserved to die."

"Citizen, you are very clever indeed and..."

"Devious?  Oh, but I agree thoroughly.  One must, these dangerous times, lead a double or even treble life to survive, Citizienne.  Now, so that you are not surprised by a trick question, listen well.  Firstly, as I have said, I am who I am.  I do have a cousin, of the farming branch of my widespread family.  He does indeed own a market garden and does indeed travel into Paris each day with produce for the markets.  The cart and horse be indeed his and I do indeed offer to return that cart to his home village and return with it filled on the morrow.  The reason for this be his unexpected delay within the city and I owe him a favour from long ago. Tomorrow he shall be free to travel of his own accord."

"Does he really stay within Paris?"

"Oh yes. Everything be authentic, Citizienne. The tax collectors you see; accuse him of avoidance but I have arranged for him to oblige a certain individual within that authority and in return he will go free. But that man cannot be reached until the morrow."

She laughed suddenly. "The poor man. Is it er... true?"

"The avoidance? Oh no, but a whisper here, a word there and the trick is done; though over *that* I do feel slightly guilty. This is how the whole of France works now.  Happens every day at the markets; if one be able to get to the markets and away again without harassment, courtesy the tax collectors, then one be doing well."

"I see. Then he himself believes the accusations?"

"Sadly he must. I cannot afford to enlighten him."

"Then after I am, er, deposited—and I am loath to ask *where*—you return to Paris to carry on as per usual?"

"That be the plan. All be genuine: we cannot chance any holes found within the fabric of our story. We be safe: for even if they suspect, all is authentic. Only the barrier be fraught with a small amount of danger and that only because they do not trust anyone or anything, to say nothing to the government bonuses to ensure vigilance."

"Citizen... just a small matter, you understand: but who then, am *I*?"

"My female cousin: said market gardener's sister. Oh, and you be mute... all clear?"

She resorted to simply staring again and he smiled then grew serious. "That be also true. Not long ago, she would have been disposed of by her very own father, as you well know: for no one could afford the stigma of any peculiarity within the family blood. The only mistruth be that of the switch: you for my mute cousin. But you be of same colouring, same build, something the same of features."

"It seems that I owe you a great deal... again."

He shrugged it off. "Come, we have wasted too much time already."

Angelique paused a moment, a worried look on her face.

"And now?" he smiled.

"Monsieur... Marie! She has been so good to me... how can I leave her?"

"Savieur and I have that arranged... after you are all gone... should she actually wish to leave France. I doubt this, actually, and she be in no immediate danger. Now... let us go!"

Quietly, without a possession of any nature, they left the haven below Anton's cellars. Angelique pondered the escape plans she and Rochelle had laid, as she moved now, head down, eyes on the cobbled stones of the rough street surface, face averted in demure fashion from any curious eyes. Plans including family jewellery stitched into hems and personal papers in saddlebags. She smiled faintly at their naiveté, as she followed in servile manner, Citizen Pontisqieu, to the back of the wine shop and traversed some hundred yards until they came upon a mangy horse of doubtful pedigree, harnessed to an old produce cart, smelling of rotting vegetable leaves. With Pontisqieu driving, they moved off into the darkening late afternoon: winter approached but a greater chill than that presented by the seasons, settled over of the soul.

# CHAPTER TWENTY-FOUR

## In the Lap of the Gods

"So! You Citizen! Yes, you there in the *ancien* cart!" The barrier guard walked around the cart, "*You* do not grow the vegetables for a living."

Angelique held her breath, staring at the uneven boards at her feet; then realized that there was no more complete cover than that of offering suspicious circumstances, which could then be explained away totally.

"But you deny that this be a produce cart, Citizen?" Pontisqieu did not attempt to hide his educated accent: belonging to the most prestigious law school.

"Come, come, Citizen, you cannot fool me that you be a farmer of the cabbages."

A modest, disarming smile shone forth. "Oh no Citizen, my apologies for the misrepresentation: I am not the farmer of vegetables. That is my cousin. I simply do him the favour of returning his cart and sister, *for* him."

"Ah of course, I see. Cousin: eh? Where go you then, Citizen?"

"To the village beyond the next, fifteen miles in that direction," replied Pontisqieu, pointing with his whip. "I escort yon girl there; she cannot travel alone these days, Citizen, and her brother needs to remain in Paris this night but the morrow's crop must be transported back to the city. We shall leave the village at dawn to do so."

"Papers!" The guard was growing tired of the smelly produce cart. He glanced at them and his eyes widened, for the name Pontisqieu was growing famous. The papers could not be more authentic. He then glanced at the girl in the cart, diligently mending a broken boot, finding the leather almost too tough to push the needle through. He glanced again at her well-thumbed pass.

"Ah, so Citizienne, you are Anastasie Piers?"

She looked up, bowed her shoulders towards him in assent, her eyes demurely lowered and nodded. The guard looked at her suspiciously.

"My female cousin be mute, Citizen. She be lucky to live of course... but soon such archaic practices as infanticide of the malformed shall be legally outlawed, not so?"

The guard remembered the story from his predecessor and, tiring of the whole, commenced waving them through but then appeared to think better of it. He nodded.

"And what Citizen, be the reason for the cousin's stay within Paris this night?"

Pontisqieu told him and he waved them through the Barrière Saint-Martin.

They moved off at sedate pace, Pontisqieu touching the underfed animal on the flanks with his whip but as he did so there was a shout from behind suddenly. Angelique froze and sat very still. Pontisqieu stopped the barely moving horse.

"Yes Citizen?" he turned to gaze back with limpid eyes at the approaching guard.

The guard came running the few yards to the cart and stood looking up into the driver's face. "Citizen, I have a matter that I would refer to your attention, if it be no trouble, Citizen. A, er…delicate matter, you understand."

"Ah, you wish me to represent you?"

"Would you, Citizen? I feel that you must be uncommonly busy but if you would, I would rest this night with relieved mind, Citizen, and of course your produce on the return to Paris shall be sanctioned without question or need of tax."

Pontisqieu glanced down at him in slightly bored fashion, ignoring the bribe, as would a good republican lawyer. "But of course, I always have time for good republicans, Citizen. Come to my law chambers on the morrow but two. You know my address?"

"But yes, Citizen, all know where it be that you work. *Merci*, Citizen."

The guard stepped back and they continued unhindered. Angelique, steadily plying her needle to the worn boot, did not lift her head. Even within the tough leather gloves, owning reinforced thumb and first and second finger pads, her hands were already becoming bruised and painful from the effort. She ignored the stares of the people lining the barrier entrance, face dropped to her work, mouth partially open and lower lip slack in concentration. Glancing back at last, Pontisqieu was obliged to quickly control a chuckle. He drove for some fifteen minutes and then glanced about; the road was empty of pedestrians and carts.

"Citizienne, if nothing else did it: it was the flaccid lower lip of yours that surely won the day."

She smiled suddenly and then tensed again as another cart approached from the opposite direction and waited its passing; then, "Citizen, I work very hard at whatever I decide to do. A fault of mine, I fear."

"Then it is a wonderful fault. Now we have but little light left of the day and I must get you to the rendezvous, after which I go quickly to return this animal and cart to ward off any further suspicion. The minds of these people are cunning in the extreme and never still but, to our benefit, rather slow: not because they are dense but because everything moves very slowly in the country. They have never been required to think on their feet, as must city inhabitants. Brace yourself: I endeavour to stimulate this poor beast to a trot!"

"Just one thing, Mons… Citizen: will Anastasie return on the morrow with you?"

"But of course. She did not come with her brother today because I begged him to leave her behind: as it was likely he would be kept in town by the 'tax tangle'; though I was doing my best for him." He grimaced. "I shall feel the guilt of my total deception toward him for many a long year!"

"My apologies, Citizen… but for me…"

Swiftly he intervened. "No, no, Citizienne, it be a pleasure… and no harm shall become my cousin!"

"But they may see the difference…between us: Anastasie and I? Be that not a risk?"

"Worry not, Citizienne, tomorrow be the change of Barrier Guard."

They settled in to a silent journey as the sky grew dark with the approaching night and gathering rain clouds.

The unkempt, dispirited horses dragged the mud-spattered plain black, closed coach up to the Barrière de Belleville and stopped. The driver climbed stiffly down to the road. He was obviously not young any more. Shoulders stooped, one arm held stiffly, his hair was almost white and his longish beard, not the thick dark growth of a young man but grey, wispy and straggly. He shambled forward on stiff and unsteady feet to present his papers and stood silent, waiting the pleasure of the Barrière guards.

The guards glanced at the vehicle then gave it intense scrutiny; one never knew just where these aristocrats thought of hiding these days; some even strapped themselves to the underside of the carriages.

"Name!"

The driver shambled closer and told him. It corresponded with the name on the pass.

"Open the door, Citizen."

"Er…you may not want to…"

"Did you not hear me Citizen? Open the door!"

The driver moved slowly, muttering to himself.

"What be that, old man? What say you?"

The old man spoke slowly and with effort. "I say that you mayhap not wish to breath the same air as my passenger, Citizen; he is right ill, Citizen, an' that be no exaggeration."

"Ha! Is that so? *Open the door*!"

At that moment however the passenger negated this necessity by thrusting open the door himself and retching into the dirt before the feet of the guard. The guard jumped swiftly back but not in time to avoid becoming splashed by the bile stained vomit. He stared and then looked up at the passenger.

"I'll *have* you for that, Citizen!" he shouted, then paused suddenly, as the previously gathering crowd moved back several paces, for the sick man did indeed appear extremely unwell. His skin was sweat ridden, his face blotched purple and red and exhibiting great, yellow-fluid-filled blisters. He was shaking as if attacked by the ague. He could barely stand, leaning against the doorpost and the driver moved forward to catch him in his arms as he toppled out of the coach, retching again and again.

"Come, my brother, you must lie down. Come, into the coach with you. Soon we shall arrive at that place of healing… then home to our beloved *grand'mère* who shall tend thee as only she knows how."

He glanced about and asked for help to get his sick relative back into the coach again but none would oblige. Hands were placed across mouths, feet shuffled away from the scene and women grabbed little bags of dried herbs, hanging from a cord around their necks and held them beneath their noses.

"You are travelling to?"

"To the healing springs: beyond the second village, Citizen."

The guard grunted, glanced at the ill man again. "They be sulpha ridden waters, that be all. There are no magical healing powers within them, Citizen."

"But we were told, Citizen…"

"Fairy tales: but go, on your way old man. If your horses be able to pull you that far… they be dead afore you arrive I reckon."

The old man, struggling slowly with his burden, lifted him into the coach and laid him on the seat; then, putting up the steps and closing the door, as slowly resumed his place on the driver's seat and the carriage rumbled away from the Barrière. The guards and audience watched it go.

"Citizen, be it a trick think you?"

"Assuredly it has been tried afore," replied his superior. "But nobody can fake that skin or that amount of vomit. Ugh! That was no faked illness. He will be dead afore long."

"Along with his 'orses," chuckled another guard.

Better pray to your patron saint… that the vomit did not touch you," replied his senior.

♣

The ancient horse of doubtful parentage was perhaps not so old, simply underfed and worm-infested, for he managed to respond to the touch of light hands on the reins and the cart moved far more swiftly than supposed possible. Angelique was growing tired: her limbs shook from the lack of sustenance and her body ached from the rigidity required to keep her balance within the moving and jolting cart. They travelled another two hours into early dusk.

They had passed through the first village with no mishap, very few villagers still out and about. Smoke poured from chimneys and doors and windows were sturdily closed against the cold and the Revolution. None moved about after darkness unless imperative, but Pontisqieu was ever vigilant. All villages set a watch for any sign of foreign travellers but the dilapidated vegetable cart, a common sight this close to the city, should, he felt, go unnoted.

Halfway between the two villages that he had mentioned to the Barrière Guards, Pontisqieu searched the road ahead for the fork that would lead them off the direct route to that second village. If pursued, then he hoped that the pursuers would pass on. The fork appeared. They branched off then stopped. Pontisqieu climbed down and, breaking off a furze branch, brushed the cart tracks from the ground. During this brief respite, the horse offered a firm dollop to Mother Earth. Using two broad leaves of a local weed similar to marshmallow, Pontisqieu scooped it up and deposited it on the cart.

"My apologies, Citizienne, but fresh dung can be smelled for hours… a definite clue."

She gazed at him. "Citizen, you are not new at this. How many people have you helped I wonder?"

He turned an innocent face towards her then climbed back onto the driver's seat. They moved on: via the rough, barely discernable exit, travelled a further mile or two and then turned down a small rutted track; again to the left, so narrow and disused that it was almost missed by Pontisqieu. They pushed through heavily wooded growth on either side of the narrow trail. Suddenly stopping and handing the long reins to Angelique, he leapt down to the dew damp ground and moved silently off through the low dense furze and broom bushes. The sky was black, the clouds obscuring any moonlight and no sound occurred. She sat still and listened to the silence, a thing she had not experienced since happier days at the château. It had a quality of its own, owning a sound of its own, undetected by the human ear, which sang to the soul. She shook off these nostalgic fancies and listened for Pontisqieu. He returned.

"Citizienne, here be the old cottage by the stream; the barn also be empty, burned practically to the ground. We shelter there to wait for your brother and Trifane. Come."

They walked now, following the tethering of the horse to a tree and rounding a corner in the overgrown path arrived at the cottage: derelict and completely obscured, even from the track. Poachers or vagabonds had used it in times of storm or rain and straw lay in lumps across the floor. She sank gratefully to the one chair and leaning to the window for what light could be found, lifted the basket to her knee.

"You shall require sustenance, Mon... my pardon, Citizen."

"No!" he replied quickly. "Thank you, I shall eat when I reach to village. Eat sparingly. Who knows how long your journey shall take."

"But of course. I am not hungry anyway." She closed the basket and slumped suddenly, her body still not recovered from her ordeal.

"Sleep a while Citizienne, you will need your strength. I shall keep watch. Please drink; and I shall refill you vessel from the stream."

She did as she was told and handing the stone vessel to him, kicked the lumps of straw together and lay down on her side for a brief rest. Her entire body thanked her for the supine position. Not meaning to do any such thing as sleep, she slid quickly into a light doze and awoke some time later to find Pontisqieu pacing. Rising, she joined him at the window and stood gazing out, pulling her cloak tight about her.

"What's about, Citizen?"

"Nothing, that is just it, but they shall be here soon no doubt."

"Please, you must not jeopardize yourself; how shall you explain your late arrival? You must go and leave me here. My brother must know the meeting place."

"He does, but I shall not leave you."

"Please Citizen, you must! You must keep to the story, so that even your relatives do not suspect."

He refused to leave her. The argument continued until Pontisqieu held up a cautioning hand suddenly and she stilled to listen. There was no sound; but a large, bulky, dark shadow moved suddenly out of the deep undergrowth, towards the cottage door.

A low call of a bird of the night occurred just then and Angelique laughed suddenly. In unladylike manner, she called back. She moved to the doorway to find Trifane there, arm beneath Emile's shoulders.

"Emile!" She rushed forward in concern. "Whatever has happened... are you wounded?"

Trifane chuckled. "Wasted sympathy Mademoiselle. He suffers the same agony that you did."

"Ha! So: my dear brother, now you know just what you put *me* through!"

"No...no, *ma soeur*... 'twas he that stands there! I swear 'twas! *His* be the idea, both for you and for me."

Trifane's smile could not be seen in the darkness but it threaded his voice as he answered:

"What a weak soldier of the counterrevolution *you* be *mon ami*. Your agony be but a touch of what your sister suffered: for she was administered the Lord knows what poisons by the villainous and secretive, greatly removed, cousin of Anton... and *then* the added insult of the emetic. But for you, only a *little* of the dried rootstock of the ipecac shrub... and you have to admit that it did work quickly. You heaved up your very boots to great effect."

Emile glared, then sinking suddenly to the floor, "But my face! Shall never be the same again. I shall have mine revenge, Monsieur," reaching to his side for his sword; then remembered that he could not wear it through the Barrière. "Name your weapon," he ended weakly.

Angelique chuckled but went to him out of pure empathy.

Pontisqieu stepped aside with Trifane. "No trouble?"

"None; but I think that we must continue on. We must reach the rendezvous for the horses. They cannot be stabled for more than a day and already we be late. But you *mon ami*... any suspicions? The slightest thing be important."

Pontisqieu laughed softly. "None: thanks to Citizienne Vermont's brilliant performance!"

"Not *too* brilliant?"

Pontisqieu heard the deep concern and fear and understood as only another man deep in love could understand. He smiled grimly into the darkness; his own icy coldness of the soul, and deep pain of hopelessness, he shoved even deeper into the recesses of his mind. He would deal with it all later; his life running in a direction far divided from these people who had become his friends in these bizarre times.

"No, definitely not: ask her sometime to repeat the performance; you will be amused."

Trifane gazed at him. "*Merci, mon ami*! Go now... be safe!"

Pontisqieu bowed briefly, straightened, saluted in a manner conveying good luck and farewell and left the room. They did not hear the cart move away and Trifane followed some few minutes later, escorting the siblings to the black coach some small distance beyond where the produce cart had been tethered. He assisted Emile up the steps and Angelique followed, wrinkling her nose at the revolting odour of stale vomit. She settled her brother along the seat opposite and then settled back in her own corner, leaning against the filthy remains of what had once been satin squabs.

Trifane put up the steps; then, gazing at her deep in the shadowed interior, smiled gently. "Courage *ma chérie*, we are all but on our way."

"Escorted by yourself and my brother, I shall have no need of such."

He laughed suddenly. "Mademoiselle, your faith be much misplaced. We be two of the most wanted by Robespierre. Within our company you cannot claim safety."

He closed the door with a dull click and returning to the driver's seat turned the animals, with difficulty within the dense bushes, and headed back up the track.

♣

Robespierre paced. It was the age of pacing. Pacing: that slow regular stride affected by those deeply agitated, according to the encyclopaedia, or suffering extraordinary tension, impotence, fear and fury. All of these emotions accompanied the current mode of living within France, the more so within Paris.

He paused at the window, gazing down into the noisy street below; the mob was rioting again and this time he knew not why. *They* most likely did not know: they never did; simply reacting to the stirring oratory of clever speakers. He would of course find out; nothing escaped him: almost nothing. At the present moment his own controlled fury focused upon the assumed escape of de Quatreaux, Savieur and Citizienne Vermont. Of this last there was no proof, for the prison doctor recalled the case; and the scrutinized signature to the papers definitely his. And why would he lie? But this he must establish afore much longer, for if he could prove her escape then the entire story of a strange disease, or new plague, descending upon the prisons, would fall: and the exodus of gaolers be amended. Also, of course, the good doctor would lose his head.

The girl was buried quickly: according to regulations for deaths resultant of diseases suspicious in nature. The papers to state such an event were unexceptionable. The body: exhumed on his demand, was of correct age, size, build and colouring. But Trifane had not been seen of late and Robespierre now awaited reports from his agents travelled into the country. De Quatreaux was supposedly not in France but had been sighted by more of Robespierre's spies. He had sent secret police to the Hôtel Quatreaux and the woman there, a cousin—lord, how many cousins the country of France housed—had been all grief and tears at the demise of her charge. She had also been packing to return to rural France and her family there. Her intellect was not bright certainly and it had been obvious that she had not been acting; besides, she was related to Couthon, in some oblique way.

He struck the bell now, suddenly impatient, a faint panic in his mind. His instincts were sure they were attempting escape. Lareaux' informant, a footman of the de Quatreaux household, brought in for questioning regarding Lareaux' sudden demise by knife or sword, also told of plans for this. He meant to have them: he thought again of the girl's poem and felt her hatred for the Jacobins, for the Revolution and for all that was not nobility. In this last he was incorrect but unwilling to admit it, even though his investigations had cleared her of all rebel subterfuge. Her family were counterrevolutionaries and as such they must all go to the guillotine. And what had happened to Beaumont? He frowned heavily: no matter the butler's witness statement, he did not believe the man had shot himself. No: the almost simultaneous death of Beaumont and Lareaux was too much to swallow as coincidence. A man now answered the bell and stood silently waiting for orders.

"Send a message to the ports and frontier posts to stop Saviuer, de Quatreaux and his sister."

"*All* of them, Citizen Robespierre... all the ports?"

"Not the south coast of course, they would never make it, but of the channel coast, definitely." He paused suddenly. "Also, the frontier crossing into Belgium and of course Italy; the de Quatreaux' have a sister there. Alert the villages surrounding Paris, to tighten their watch for travelling foreigners, giving them a description of course of the two men and *perhaps* a female. Go, hurry."

The plain, black coach rumbled on to the next village, slowing for this, and then they were through the empty square and out the other end, pulling up the slight incline then moving with more speed. They melted into the darkness, two dark horses pulling a lightly built black coach against an even blacker skyline. That skyline began to streak with slivers of dawn light however, following another hour, no more; and Trifane pulled a map from his inner pocket. Shaking it out, with one hand still controlling the horses, he glanced at it and then, pulling the vehicle to the side of the road, stopped and spread it out to the side of him; on the coachman's box. A low belt of the eastern sky was changing colours rapidly now and he studied the map frowningly.

The offside door opened and without putting down the steps Emile leapt lightly to the ground and turned to offer his hand to Angelique. They stretched their legs and backs and Emile announced his improved health.

"I am glad of that *mon ami*, for we soon reach the appointed place of the horses and we shall then be riding without respite. I wish to get beyond the villages that may be alerted to watch for us; and that means riding with very little rest for our horses; and riding through the night again," responded Raoul.

"That should put us beyond any suspicions of our illustrious Robespierre!"

"Nothing shall make us safe until we arrive at the port... and even then... when I see those white cliffs that be England, I shall still not feel at ease. Not until we be beyond the French fleet and my feet touch English soil. Never did I think to hear myself to say such a thing." Raoul shook his head. "The English! Our oldest enemy now proves to be our saviour. Not a new phenomenon of course."

Emile softened. "It be not so bad *mon ami*! Many English are now our champions. The English Lord... whomever he is... the one sliding into Paris and out again with one noble family or another, now be no myth. Many have reached England by his hand."

Raoul frowned in thought. "Code name... um...something *rouge*..."

Emile shrugged. "Yes, that one; the English attitude to us, it does change now. However, whilst Robespierre remains alive, we shall certainly be hunted and he *does* own a wily brain I do admit. In view of this: do we push on in daylight?"

Raoul gazed at the sky, heavy with rain clouds. "The disused tracks could be rendered impassable if that lot tumbles down... we need our horses. And we are late! They shall begin to kick up a noise if not fed. Yes, we risk it."

They pushed on, Emile and Raoul taking turns to ride up on the box and push the poor old horses, but thus far they showed no sign of faltering, their legs amazingly sturdy and untiring; so long as the pace was steady and they were not required to gallop. Raoul studied the map endlessly, leading them around towns and villages. Avoiding main roads, keeping to solitary lanes and narrow disued trails, ever skirting habitat of any kind, he bent always in the same direction; that of his point of rendezvous.

"Where exactly are the horses, Seigneur?" asked Angelique as she leaned across the tiny space between the bench seats to gaze at the map.

He pointed and she gazed for a moment; then, "But it be a little out of our way, not so?"

"My groom could not travel with the horses any further west than this point," pointing to a small mark on the map. "So we must go east here. And from this point on we shall be travelling cross-country, and so outstrip any of Robespierre's men. That was your worry, not so?" He leaned back and watched her, as she took the map from him and studied it.

"Monsieur, to which port do we head?"

"Dieppe."

She looked up and stared. "But do English packets call there?"

"Possibly not, the small issue of the war you know, possibly you have forgotten such. Quite understandable of course; after all, you have not been of the regular world of late."

"*Monsieur*, have you ever been in prison? I assure you that one's entire concentration be of escape, with no room for wars of any description, small or large."

His gaze softened as he replied, "No Mademoiselle, I have not experienced that dubious privilege." His expression grim now, he added, "But the man responsible for your incarceration be paid out in full, *ma chérie*, believe you me."

She was so startled by his tone of cold retribution that she did not notice the term of endearment; they both did not. "*Robespierre*? But how...?"

"'Twas not he alone... but I think his days be numbered; he shall not retain his power many more years, months even. However, we do not have even days to spare, in this country. It was Lareaux who received the full of mine ire."

"So *he* was the one? His the men who came to collect me? I was suspicious of such but could not be sure. What did you do to him?"

"Another time, *mon enfant*. But now the route: you see something wrong with it?"

She stared at him a moment and gave up any conjecturing and turned her attention to the map again. "Seigneur, if I was Robespierre, I would send out a missive to all the ports along the channel coast and northern frontiers... elsewhere, it be too far for escape."

"Yes, I agree, and for that reason we travel non-stop to Dieppe. We have the edge on any messengers, in that Robespierre cannot be sure. He must first ascertain that we are indeed fleeing the country and also you, do not forget, be dead. Also he had no *special* interest in you, other than your birth-lines."

She looked uncomfortable suddenly and he eyed her suspiciously then chuckled. "Do not stand on ceremony with me... open your budget, do. Something bothers you!"

"Um, well Monsieur, perhaps," she hesitated unwilling to show her guilt.

He laughed suddenly. "Come, better now than later. What have you done *now*?"

"Well *mon père* was adamant about a certain passion of mine and er... well..."

He groaned suddenly. "Not your picturesque and gifted writing?"

She looked straight at him and confessed.

"I see," he eyed her a moment. "Forgive me, Mademoiselle, I am sure it be brilliant; in point of fact it is said so and your fame was advanced by the dizzy heights of Versailles' approval but the thing now is... be these writings in Robespierre's possession?"

"Well, I do not know, but I was mid-verse when I was picked up and taken to the Conciergerie. Mayhap they do not. Mayhap they could not read, those despicable men that entered our hôtel that night, and therefore did not scoop them up. Certainly I did not see them do so."

"And the nature of the papers lying there, upon your desk that night?"

"Um...anti, er... Jacobinism: worse."

"So he will be absolute, should they be in his possession, in his drive to capture you." He thought a moment and then shook his head. "You be dead, would he believe otherwise I wonder?"

"No 'body', Monsieur; would cause deep suspicion."

"Oh, but there was one... buried with all due honours... all that a load of gold could buy!"

She stared again, hard, and he smiled and said, "For the privilege of switching identity for a brief period. That is all I shall tell you at the moment: except that no one, dead or alive, directly or indirectly, was hurt. Come, I must give Emile a break."

They changed drivers and Emile remained sitting up on the box with him, scanning the countryside as they travelled. Just before midday they pulled beneath some dense overhanging branches of a very large evergreen. Here they remained hidden and rested for the remainder of the day, the next stretch likely to be heavy with traffic travelling to and from the nearby large town. Emile unharnessed the horses and brushed them down, with an old brush found in the storage space beneath the box seat and then tied them to a branch. Following a brief respite in which the animals cooled, he led them down to the stream and allowed them to drink. They all did so and Angelique pulled out the basket and they ate a little of the plain fare provided by Pontisqieu.

"Now I know that their redeeming feature be durability: but *where* would he find ship's biscuits?" grimaced Raoul.

"I cannot imagine but lay you a gold louis that the tooth doctors promote their sale," replied Emile, breaking one across his knee with effort then stood up and made to move off. "Settle and sleep everyone. I shall take the first watch," he said now, "For we do not move I think, until the darkness descends again, agreed?"

They moved out again at eighteen hours, the shadows lengthening and darkening rapidly, the traffic non-existent. They travelled silently, following barely discernable trails and tracks that patterned the countryside of France. Keeping to the wooded hills as much as possible, they traversed the open farming lands with bated breath and a prayer that the moon stayed cloud-bound.

They arrived at the rendezvous at twenty-three hours fifteen that same evening, just a little over thirty-six hours after their danger-fraught passages through the Barrières. The black coach, near-invisible in the dense darkness, pulled alongside the barn and there, munching upon bits of straw in bored fashion, were three very strong and handsome horses, each tethered to a pole.

Raoul leapt down from the box and directed Emile in the backing of the vehicle into one end of the barn. The other held the tethered horses and a store of bagged grain, stacked hay and a quantity of farming tools and equipment. Emile then set about freeing one of the horses from the shafts then removed the harness, handing him to Angelique. She set about rubbing him down while he attended to the other. She then led them both to fodder and the water trough and tethered them also to a pole while her brother checked the contents of the saddlebags as Raoul finished saddling the three horses.

All in order, Raoul scouted the perimeter of the barn, stared a long moment at the silent and darkened farmhouse and then returned to hold out his cupped hands to Angelique. She could as easily mount alone but took pleasure in this small courtesy and placing her foot there, was flung up into the saddle. The entire operation, from their time of arrival, took place in total silence and very little time. Raoul tucked an extra chamois bag of gold coins into the coach pocket for his groom.

They left as quietly and invisibly as they had arrived, walking the horses past the house and into the lane beyond, their hooves silent on the soft dirt underfoot then they were out in the open and crossing fallowed fields, now trotting, now galloping.

Emile allowed his animal its head, taking the fore, Raoul and Angelique galloping shoulder-to-shoulder just behind and thus they sped over silent fields, dappled with the flitting moonlight. In such manner they traversed many miles, unseen and unheard, the pace too fast for any dialogue and Angelique was content for it to be thus: content to absorb the exhilarating sense of total freedom experienced by fast riding. Let it flow over her entire being in luxurious swathe, her entire body and soul moving ever forward: the past slipping away behind, further and further, until it became hollow mist, left hanging in some gully, drifting across a stream, dissipating, forever. Raoul turned his head to her once, smiling into her eyes. She smiled back, in sheer pleasure, knowing that it was false pleasure, a foolish sense of freedom, for there were worse dangers to face ahead than they had yet faced but for the moment, she revelled in the sense of escape and freedom.

They rode on, galloping, trotting and then reining in to a walk, resting their animals awhile then spurring onwards again. They travelled the road at times, turning off again and again to avoid a village or lone roadside cottage. Generally they tried to keep to the fields where no man would see them in the dark hours of the night, no person hear the sound of galloping hooves on hardened roadway. The wind tore at hair, flapping cloak-hoods behind shoulders, producing exhilaration as they made their mad dash for freedom; leaping the many hedges and low stone walls when visibility was good and crossing shallow streams gently by feel.

There came another spell of extreme darkness and they had yet again to walk their horses, for want of visibility, along a deserted laneway. The moon cleared the clouds again and showed the way clearly with ghostly light, the trees throwing weird shadows across the ground.

They paused a short time now; the occasional hoot of an owl and call of night birds clear in the crisp silence but all else was hushed as was the inner sanctum of a cathedral. A dog barked in the distance as, having watered the horses and themselves at the stream, they set out again, skirting the dark squat huts of a tiny village. A small animal ran across the path of Angelique's horse, causing it to shy and Raoul's hand shot out to snatch the bridle and she laughed softly.

"You have no need of fear for me Seigneur! I can handle this lovely mare!"

"I can see that: I have had ample opportunity to observe your faultless skill. But I cannot help myself. To protect you appears to be inbuilt."

Startled at these words she turned to look at him. The moon was sinking towards the horizon. Emile rode some few yards ahead: his, the chore of surveillance at this moment. The horses behind him grew close and Raoul glanced at her suddenly.

"Tired, *mon enfant*?" His hand reached out to touch hers a moment and she was amazed at the sudden flood of warmth washing over her at that small gesture of concern. Gracious it be a wondrous thing to be so cared for, though she knew that he would not tempt the Gods yet, by a declaration.

"Not I Monsieur. I have ridden much in my life and can never tire of it!"

"But not under such conditions, I be thinking."

She chuckled. "But one must never reject life's offerings; no matter their difficulties, all be life's lessons." She paused suddenly. "And sometimes a test of courage I be sure."

He smiled again. "Then you have no fears on that head! You pass with gilded laurel wreath and the victor's crown upon your standard... no Roman soldier could outshine you in degree of courage! Never have I seen you lose your head."

She laughed. "But no Monsieur, you have forgotten... sadly I *can* lose my head... thus far emotionally, only, thankfully: during my indiscretion at the guillotine! 'Twas your *own* level-headedness that saved me that day." She paused, thinking about the episode and then continued, "Perhaps it was simply denial: but I believe that I was so infuriated that no thought of the guillotine for myself entered into the equation. A bad fault I know: for *others* are always hurt in such unthinking bursts of self-indulgence. And *mon père* says... said... that it be my mother in me Monsieur: the impetuosity when stirred to anger."

"I meant lose your head in fear and panic. In anger, well that be another matter." he grinned, "that, of a certainty, requires further discipline...hard work for you!"

He reined in as Emile called softly from ahead. "A stop here I think. That barn there: tumbled down certainly by revolutionary activity but stashes of hay may be found there. Our saddlebags are growing low. And there be a pond for the horses. Wait here."

He trotted silently into the shadowed darkness and they waited, still mounted, listening to the sounds of rustling in the undergrowth. Soon he returned and waved them forward. They rested again, within the barn for an hour, no more, then climbed back into their saddles and continued on, scouting the countryside toward dawn, for safe haven for the daylight hours. Only by strict adherence to this golden rule had they evaded capture: for the *représentants-en-mission* roamed everywhere, maintaining daily contact with the government, the spies, the new *commission des administration civiles, police, et tribunaux* and varying other agents. All of this, in addition to the dangers of village and town vigilante, ensured extreme caution; and evasion of all humanity, within the escapees.

A cold efficiency now replaced the early chaotic heroism of the Revolution and Raoul did not know which was the worst to combat; on the one hand some anticipation could be relied upon, on the other, knowing the peoples' mood and mind was of a greater value. Either way, there was no substitute for acute alertness, heightened senses and the old adage of never, ever, underestimating the enemy; no matter how stupid he may appear to be. Underestimation of the enemy, however, was not a possibility within the three of them. But of sheer luck he held his breath: only the Gods controlled luck.

# CHAPTER TWENTY-FIVE

## 21 Miles of Foamy Blue

Travelling as silent shadows of the night, hiding and resting through the shortening daylight hours, the fugitives had managed to place the countryside of France behind them. The forested hills, deep ravines, rivers and streams, fallowed and grassy fields; and then the swampy coastal plains, striated with deep and wide ditches, had all held many dangers. Their success, thus far, they attributed to a combination of good luck and extreme caution. They had foraged what they could for their horses, to supplement the little they carried in saddlebag; and rationed themselves to the bare minimum.    Sheltering: amongst dense bushes, within deserted, war ravaged barns and limestone caves, had been the most difficult feat; for never was the protection total. The villages and towns they had skirted by night to avoid the vigilant watch; and the shepherds tending flocks on commons, curious about their presence, they had ignored; as would travelling locals. Republican soldiers on the march caused a detour of their chosen trail to the high shoulders of steep and boulder-strewn hillocks.  Here they slid into a sheltered valley high above the activity below. Waiting until they passed, they had then skirted their anticipated route by many miles; traversing the devastated scorched countryside, courtesy the Republican Army. This in itself was a feat not commonly won by fleeing citizens; for the army now numbered seven hundred thousand men under arms, a great number of which were scattered loosely across the country just here.  Small gaps only, between them, had to be searched out, anticipated or stumbled upon by the escapees.

These armed forces were now better trained than ever before. At cadet College, thousands of youths lived under canvas; undergoing a tough training regime beyond the normal: simple arms training, discipline; and to kill without emotion. Here they were trained to hate kings and nobility and taught patriotism and brotherhood.

Ahead of the escapees now was the worst and most dangerous period of their flight from the Revolution: the coastal vigilante, seeking reward for capturing escapees and assuring their own safety by this deed.  The hungry shadow of the guillotine, spread across the nation, must be fed: offered sacrificial victims, innocent or otherwise; so long as it was kept busy in the name of the Glorious Revolution and stayed its bloodied power just short of their own selves and families. The madness was not over: like a runaway horse, dragging its carriage behind, panicked and unstoppable, the Revolution was in dire need of something, or some one, brave and

356

strong enough to drag it to a halt. The Jacobins thought that they held the reins and had only to drag on these to bring it back under their control. Jacobinism however, was falling into the trap experienced by all dictatorships: that of despising the very people that had created them and using force and propaganda to then control and direct these.

The three fleeing the guillotine had now arrived at that point of their journey demanding extra caution; the final hurdle. They sat now upon their horses, atop a rise and gazed over the port of Dieppe, some five miles away. Somewhere down there, existed the infamous Barrière, most probably choked with early morning traffic for the market and the docks.

Emile gazed a moment. "We should separate, no?"

Raoul, also scanning the valley below, nodded. "The dockyard is my rendezvous point: regarding our passage. We are a little late, therefore I hope our vessel has been detained for some reason... in these chaotic days it be most likely so. "

"Ah, my apologies Citizen," offered Angelique to Raoul.

He shrugged. "I dare swear you could not have helped it," he grinned. "You *attract* trouble, so you do!"

Emile chuckled. "Do not stir my sister *mon ami*; she be saddle weary and may snap off your nose."

"Oh no, I am sure that he be in the right of it. Had I not become carelessly imprisoned we should not have arrived thus late," said Angelique sweetly but a sincere apology lurked in her voice: she had after all been careless of vigilant surveillance on that night.

"But if all our troubles be at the beginning, then that be a good thing," said Raoul gently, "and they know that a mission such as this cannot guarantee set time of arrival."

"But they will not wait beyond *their* convenience, so you had better pray, *ma soeur.*"

"It could have been any one of us, de Quatreaux! You in particular, own diabolical impetuosity."

Angelique started at the degree of cold rebuke in his voice, realizing the mantle of protectiveness for herself. This she had not experienced and now revelled in it.

Unmoved by the rebuke, Emile shrugged. "What to *do* with her is the thing now."

"We must leave your sister somewhere that appears nothing out of the normal," replied Trifane. "No sense in three of us going beyond that barrière, only to have to exit it again."

"The coffee room: of some small and unimportant inn on the outskirts... only thing to do with her," replied Emile.

"Yes, and just you and she approach it. I shall meet you at the barrier."

"I am still here, *Messieurs*! And can look after myself...*merci beaucoup*!"

Raoul gazed at her, a faint smile hovering about his mouth and she blushed. "Oh very well then, in doing so I have exercised some incaution on occasion and I agree: that be unforgivable; however, tell me if you dare, that you two have not been in hot water at *some* stage of your charmed lives: *especially* in the recent year or two."

Emile stared across at her in severe, patriarchal mien. "Never! Had we been so slack in our surveillance, we should now be explaining ourselves to *mon père*."

"Only if we could not outrun him up there... big place, me thinks." Raoul grinned. "Attend him not, Mademoiselle, he lies!  But any mistake now on our part certainly does not bear thinking about... so close are we. And as such we must be extraordinarily vigilant.  Emile, *mon ami*, not the coffee room but a bedchamber and booked for two... no three... days I think, placing her beyond suspicion. The coffee room could invite trouble."

"And how can such peasantry as us," Emile glanced at their clothing, "afford such?"

Raoul frowned. "Yes, but we cannot be that poor: with these animals; granted they be looking rough now but their pedigree remains visible."

"Stolen."

"No, no, we bought good reliable animals to withstand the long journey from Amiens. We travel from the north: and they may have *been* stolen of course or confiscated, who can tell these days, anything goes and to acquire property of the nobility gains respect and admiration. We come to Dieppe to find a relative, of the good Republican Army; not sure that he even be alive but we try."

"Who be the illustrious relative that we seek... a cousin, yes?"

Raoul chuckled. "Several times removed by birth but close to you, you understand." He turned to Angelique. "His name be authentic and he is dead of course but we be not yet appraised of this. If they bother to check, they will find his name there: among the slain."

"So appear suitably grief stricken as they inform us," murmured Angelique.

Emile grunted. "All the planning and preparation of useless information."

"Tiresome, is it not... the one hundred percent preparation: to ensure the vital *one* percent that will cover our backs; for we do not know *which* one percent that will be."

"Who is this illustrious cousin?"

"He be listed as dead in the field: Raynard Toulon. Now, I think that you must seek out one Michel Roublet, at the Naufrauge Inn on the waterfront.  Pay him the gold louis that we owe him. Then return as fast as possible to your sister. This way we save time and should be able to skirt Dieppe from here, then follow the coastline to the river mouth at le Trèport. Unless things be changed... let's go!"

They walked their horses down the slope to the small but busy inn at the bottom of the hill and some few miles from the barrière.  Emile installed Angelique in a room overlooking the back courtyard, then trotted towards the barrière.  The queue thronged with milling and impatient people. Irate farmers with produce for the market called out in disgust, the general atmosphere one of chaos.  Under such conditions, their passes were scanned briefly and they were waved through.

Angelique wrinkled her nose at the tiny room smelling of stale wine and unwashed persons. Exhaustion: from the journey and her 'illness' prior to that, swept through her body. She glanced longingly at the not very clean bed but moved slowly up and down in front of the window, assessing the activity in the courtyard below. Eventually the exhaustion claimed her. She sat in the chair by the window, determined to stay vigilant. Her aching body and limbs appreciated this brief respite and after a short time drowsiness assailed her: the hard, upright chair no deterrent. She battled it but under such conditions, however, with no stimulation, sleep will claim one for several hours. She eventually drifted slowly to the surface, fighting the heaviness of deep sleep, a sense of impending doom upon her. The pounding continued, raising her to full consciousness and a stiff neck.

Suddenly alert, she sat still. The knocking was repeated. To not answer would cause suspicion. She rose, staggering on stiffened limbs and glanced out the window: the drop was not impossible but the yard milling now with people. She unlocked and opened the door. The ample figure of the innkeeper's wife stood framed in the doorway.

"Come girl, there be men below, they must see you and shall not go until they do so!"

"Oh, thank you Citizienne, it must be to do with my missing cousin, Raynard Toulon, of the Republican Army, you understand."

"I do not know or care but you cannot stay here longer, Citizienne! Men indeed! I runs a respectable establishment I do. But it be something about yon horse out there."

Angelique went cold. She followed her down the narrow stairs to the courtyard, no way of escape presenting itself en route, and confronted the two gentlemen discussing her animal, tethered to a post-rail, just beyond a carriage and two.

They stepped forward; one on either side of her and speaking not at all took her by the arms and forced her up into the carriage. She did not struggle, yet, for the courtyard was filling now with interested spectators and not one would prove to be a friend she knew. A mild scuffle and a lynching would be enacted and over within minutes. With a word from the superior of the two, to the ostler to watch the horse until they returned, they set off. She did not even glance at them as she spoke to the elder.

"Monsieur, I cannot think what you would want of me," her voice and demeanour were appropriate to a person belonging to the third estate; however she immediately knew her mistake. She cursed herself as he gave a knowing grin. This came of sleeping! One's wits were dulled.

"No? Of what nobility do you belong then...*Madame*? Do not deny it; your horse be enough to hang you."

"It be not mine, Citizen..."

"All the more reason to hang you: *Madame*!"

"No, no. I mean that I bought it from a man..."

"Ah yes, they all be bought," he chuckled and gave the order for the carriage to move out. It wanted five minutes to sixteen hours and passing out through the courtyard, Angelique saw Emile enter.

He entered the inn and took the stairs two at a time but at the door of Angelique's room he paused; a large gentleman was just emerging and gazed blankly at him. It did not take long for Emile to decipher, with an ear to taproom gossip, the turn of events. Strolling out of the inn, he mounted casually, rode out sedately then galloped after the carriage, remembering it just exiting the courtyard as he had entered it. It had been travelling at sober pace and he had little doubt that he could overtake it, with five miles to do so, ample time. His mount had been rested while it waited his business at the dockyard and was reasonably fresh. He left the road for a short cut across the fields noted on his return journey, and gave the horse his head. How to take the carriage was a problem that he hoped would solve itself within his brain as he rode.

He passed the coach trundling along the road and swept further ahead, the animal covering the fallowed ground in long, easy, galloping strides. He continued on, recklessly leaping hedgerows and stonewalls until he arrived at a small hollow filled with furze bushes. Pushing through these, he entered the road at a bend and looked about. He backed his horse into those same bushes and awaited the carriage, straining an ear but hearing nothing, guessed the vehicle to be some minutes away. He did however hear a horse approaching at a steady trot and backed further into the covering bushes. It came on, steadily growing closer and Emile, peering through, suddenly laughed out loud: the problem of taking possibly four men; and swiftly to effect success, was now solved. He spurred his horse through the undergrowth and across the path of the great roan, belonging to and carrying, Raoul Trifane.

Raoul, with just enough time to abruptly rein in his mount, settled him, then turned to Emile and had the brief story from him.

He frowned a moment. "We cannot use pistols and more to the point we must prevent *them* from doing so. 'Twould attract the entire neighbourhood." He paused. "Must be at least two inside and two on the coach box, you said. You, I think, *mon ami*, ride alongside and take the two on the box: I shall enter the cab. Agreed? Or do you want to toss for it?"

Emile grinned, knowing Raoul's reason to enter the carriage. "Not a problem at all *mon ami*. Having dealt with the coach driver and his friend, I shall cut the traces and then head back for the mare."

Raoul stared ahead thoughtfully. "No. I disagree: the place shall be crawling with alert vigilante... expecting just that. Post haste to the rendezvous. We play for gold now!"

Emile laughed. "I begin to enjoy myself Trifane."

"Then do so with speed and wisdom; we cannot lose this game. If we cannot stay together in the event of some unforeseen event, then you know the place. If you be not there at the turning of the tide... I shall install your sister and come back for you."

"No need... but likewise, if you two..." He held up a hand, listening. "Yes, 'tis they."

They melted into the dense bushes, one either side of the road.

The carriage rounded a slow corner some minutes later and trundled towards the sharp bend. It was closed against the cold and nothing could be seen of the occupants. No other traffic showed from either direction. The afternoon was drawing in, the shadows long. At the bend the road impersonated a tunnel, through dense and dark bushes and overhanging tree branches. At this point, from either side of the green tunnel, there suddenly erupted two horsemen: one from each side. One moved swiftly alongside the coachman seated on his box-seat. He stood in the stirrups; then, his offside foot planted on the saddle for leverage, left his horse in one leap and mounted the box. He pulled a pistol from his side pocket and held it in a steady hand. The driver gasped and shouted one word; then all power of speech was cut from him by a knife-edge hand to his throat. As he tumbled off the carriage Emile leaned in to connect fist to the jaw of his companion. The carriage horses, rearing and plunging at the convulsive tug from their driver, jolted the vehicle in violent manner. It continued to plunge and sway, the panicked horses dragging it closer and closer towards the ditch. The rearing horse now became entangled in the traces as Emile battled with his opponent. Finally, assisted by the sway, giving greater power to his lunging fist, Emile clung to the superstructure as the man flew backwards off the carriage, hit the dirt and lay still. The other body remained horizontal further back.

On that one shout Angelique sat up, suddenly very alert. The two men started up and lurched toward the door in suspicious alarm, just as it was jerked open and a large heavily booted foot, swinging free from a stirrup, travelled with power through the air into the carriage. It connected with the foremost man's wrist, sending the now drawn firearm flying to the floor and carried straight on to the jaw. This man then slumped and the violent sway of the carriage at that moment catapulted him straight at Raoul, swaying in the doorway. Swinging away, one foot shoved hard against the door-hinge and a hand gripping the superstructure, he accommodated the travelling body through the door and into the road. Before he even hit the road, Raoul swung back into the carriage and followed without check, a fist to the jaw of the second man. He slumped to the floor in an awkward heap.

Angelique, now holding the bailiff's pistol, smiled and inclined her head. "Thankyou Monseigneur."

He laughed, reaching out a hand for the pistol. "No problem Mademoiselle! Practice makes perfect, you know."

"Well, I suppose in all fairness, I deserved that."

"But we have no time to waste discussing your incredible ability to attract trouble!"

Raoul, checking the slumped form on the floor, rolled back one eyelid and shrugged. "Out for an hour at least."

He ripped the curtain tie-cord from its hook and proceeded to tie the bailiff's hands behind his back. The other, together with a kerchief from his pocket, he used as a gag. Turning from this task, he mounted his large roan from the carriage doorway. She gazed a moment at the animal still standing alongside: only he could own such a well-trained mount. Raoul sat there, holding out his hand to her. Taking it she swung, using the carriage as foot leverage, up in front of him. Turning short in the roadway Raoul witnessed Emile finishing the last knot on the gag of the tied and trussed coachman. He then turned back to the still twitching and fidgeting horses.

He waved them on, "Go! You be two and heavier. I shall catch you. I want to check our friends on the road."

"Rope to secure them...?"

"In the box-seat, then I want to cut the traces."

Raoul nodded and kneed his mount. Cutting slowly through the dense furze they set out at a gallop across the fields, utilizing the shortcut that Emile had described. The Inn they did not want, but pass this they must: to reconnect with the road that led to the river mouth and the small smugglers' boat now waiting there.

They rode at speed for some time and then, darkness descending rapidly; Raoul slowed the horse to a canter, then a walk. To all appearances, some degree of safety had been achieved by dint of distance between themselves and the barrière and any pursuing men of the law or individuals from the inn now behind them.

Raoul shifted his weight a little in the saddle, but did not relax the arm girding Angelique's waist. "Quite comfortable there, Mademoiselle?"

"Yes Monsieur. I, er, thank you—again."

"Ah yes, and etiquette obliges me, I believe, to reply that it be 'no trouble at all'! However you realize of course that this be one of a few rescue operations required to keep your person safe? Just a small thought of course."

"My deepest apologies Monseigneur... I shall of course endeavour to bring my lamentable habit of attracting disasters under control!"

"Ah, but can you? Now there lies the question and it occurs to me that there be one way only to put paid to a seemingly recurring pattern of behaviour. Not that it causes any inconvenience whatsoever of course." His voice was low and soft, just in case, but the fields were wide and their horse's hooves silent upon the ploughed ground. There appeared no human about that could be detected.

"You speak, Monsieur, as though I actually *seek* these, er... unfortunate events!" It was difficult to voice outrage while one was obliged, if not to whisper, then at least to keep one's voice low.

"Do you not then?" The warm amusement in his voice threw her a little and she was glad that he could not see her face. "*Ma chérie*, should you ever manage to school yourself to the sedate and proper conduct expected of a lady of your station, inform me, do! So that I may prepare myself: for the shock."

She gave a deep chuckle now but ignoring this, he continued, "However such an event not being at all likely, I am afraid there remains only one course of action open to me... to resolve this issue of my being ever obliged to rush out into all manner of physical and political dangers to rescue you... and that is for you to marry me." He paused, she was silent; he could not see her face. "So that I may care for you in proper manner." Still encountering no response, he continued valiantly, "Now I am acutely aware that this not be the ideal proposal: that I should be upon bended knee within one of your salons, or before your brother, begging for the honour of your hand. However, this not being likely, or even remotely feasible, I inform you now, upon this magnificent steed, whom I know agrees with me... that you *must* marry me *ma chérie*... if only to preclude further and repetitive rescue missions." And with tone changing to mock severity, "There be a limit, so there does, Mademoiselle!"

He waited, the arm girding her waist holding gently now, aware that the entire journey, nay the entire year and more, had been one long grief and stress-ridden episode for her and he worried that, though couched in jesting terms, he had spoken too arrogantly.

"Oh well, as to that Monseigneur... Monsieur le Comte de..."

He stopped her speech by tenderly drawing aside her wind-tangled hair and placing a kiss upon her neck. Granted it was not upon her mouth but the effect was as silencing. He let her hair fall again and said, calmly, "I have wanted to do that for a long time! You were saying?"

Some seconds passed, within which time she struggled for control; then, "I dare say your wisdom exceeds mine, Monseigneur, but you must not feel in any way obligated... due to these unusual circumstances..."

He brought the horse to a halt, dropped the reins upon its neck and, gripping her shoulders, turned her to face him; as best he could upon the back of a horse. His face was very close as his eyes gazed straight into hers, alight with laughter but also something much deeper. "*Obligated? Will* you cease your infernal reasoning? I want you! I *really* want you! I *love* you!"

"Oh! Oh... well, in that case... why didn't you say..."

He took her face in his hands and again his kiss silenced her: this time with a passion that threatened to topple them both to the ground. The horse, however, stood still in very bored fashion, awaiting his master's directions, which in all probability would be given some time this night.

Raoul lifted his head at last. "And *that* also, I have wanted to do for a long time! But you were saying? In that case...?" But he did not wait for the answer: desire taking precedence.

Some time, minutes, or perhaps it was years, later, he lifted his head and smiled into her eyes. "Now where were we? Ah yes... you were saying?'

She smiled shyly. "I shall marry you." She lifted her hand to his cheek.

He caught the hand and kissed her palm, his eyes brilliant with laughter; then, turning her around again, nudged the horse to a walk. "Has any man ever, I wonder, had so much trouble wringing an answer from his love?"

She smiled and then shivered as she felt again the familiar sensation of creeping ice through her body.

His arm tightened. "What? *Ma chérie?*"

"I do not know; mayhap a strong mistrust of our luck holding. The thought of losing you fills me with terror, Raoul, and I have lost count of the number of times that I thought it would be so: indeed that you were *already* dead someplace!"

"And I you: when I heard that you had been taken to the Conciergerie I thought that my heart would cease its beating. Had anything happened to you *ma chérie*, I should not have ceased my vendetta until every last man responsible lay very still," he replied calmly and coolly and she knew that he spoke truth.

The sound of a horseman riding fast caught their attention and Raoul lifted his head then smiled into the darkness. "That be your brother I be thinking."

He turned the big roan and rode toward the sound.

Emile now cantered toward them. He pulled up at sight of them, the two mounted on the one horse almost certain to be Raoul and his sister.

He reined in and the two horses drew level. "My pardon Raoul, but I did scout to see what was happening at the inn and the uproar back there has to be seen to be believed. But also I overheard dialogue intimating roadblocks. Could not be for us for they could not be aware yet of the ambushed carriage. But we cannot travel the roads now. I wish that I could have taken the horse!"

"We make do with what we have. This large fellow can carry the two of us, your sister be a featherweight and we have only about fifteen miles, or less cross-country, to Le Tréport and the boat there. Come: we must be there this side of the turning tide."

Emile looked at his twin. "It cannot be comfortable for you, *ma soeur*, riding thus."

"Why Emile... concerned for my *comfort*? I am glad that I have a witness to this sudden and unprecedented brotherly affection."

He shrugged impatiently. "Well... for Raoul too... it is not easy to ride as such!"

The deep chuckle from Raoul caught his notice and he moved closer to gaze intently at his friend in the fading light. "Oh *Mon Dieu*! You do choose your time, do you not?"

Raoul assumed a haughty manner. "Whatever you refer to, de Quatreaux, must wait... we waste time!"

The night was very dark, fortunately on the one hand, for none witnessed their silent and swift passage along the coastline; on the other it caused some confusion of track and trail and much back tracking.  Eventually the river-mouth appeared, glinting in the breaking moonlight and the small 'fishing' vessel was there. It wanted three minutes to midnight, and the turn of the tide.

Angelique sat in the bow, adjusting from the motion of the horse to that of the boat, cloak around, hood fallen back from her head. The breeze was fresh and smelled gloriously of salt and weed and shoreline marine things. Raoul sat beside her, his arm around her shoulders.

Emile smiled suddenly. "Well Ange, here we ever return to England. If the old man could see us now! And speaking of he that must be obeyed, would *he* not give *you* the trimming of your life, my dear, were he here."

She smiled. "But Emile, he would understand as apparently you do not."

"Do you expect me to?" he grinned. "I am the head of the family now *ma soeur*... and must contemplate your just an' fitting punishment: long overdue for recent and recurrent scrapes!"

"You do, de Quatreaux, and you shall have me to answer to." Raoul's voice was cool suddenly.

Emile grinned. "Be that so?  Well as to *you* Savieur, you were obliged to seek *my* permission; afore you assumed the responsibility of my sister."

"I beg to differ. You see I had that, and the blessings, of de Quatreaux long ago."

Angelique turned her head to stare up at him. "No! How long?"

He smiled gently into her eyes. "Mayhap a year ago now."

"Gracious!" She leaned back against his shoulder again. "I do miss him so. Well, I suppose that at least he has the company of poor Beaumont now."

Above her head, the eyes of the two friends met in silence. Raoul pulled the hood of her cloak tenderly up over her head against the chill of the open sea wind, tucking in the strands of hair flying free and his gentle protectiveness overwhelmed her. She revelled in the new feeling of being totally cared for; of sensing his desire, the complete, enveloping desire: that born of deep, deep need to love and protect, to nurture and hold, thrill and satisfy. They had rounded the long headland and now crossed a stretch of open sea; and seen dimly against the dark skyline appeared an even darker hulk, that of an English vessel, awaiting their arrival.

Emile stood now, shoulder to shoulder with his friend, as they drew closer. Raoul with his arms circling Angelique standing before him, chin resting on the top of her head, calmly gazed straight ahead at the dark and heaving sea, beyond which lay their adopted country. He tried to resist the temptation to glance over his shoulder: that they had all reached thus far deserving of his full appreciation. He failed: turning his head to scan yet again the shoreline, but all was quiet and dark there. No guns fired, no shouts echoed across the water, no boat pulled out after them. He held his breath: so many times they had 'almost' won: de Quatreaux point in fact; Louis and Marie Antoinette and many others, in their hair-raising attempts to affect safe passage out of France for friends and countrymen. His arms tightened around Angelique: to manage the few that they had; and the three of them, he supposed was worthy of heartfelt thanks. She turned her head to look up at him, saw the pain in the depth of his eyes and returned the pressure. For the expression in her eyes, there were no words, even in the French language. He smiled gently, wanting to drown in the depth of feeling there and forget France. He hugged her tighter.

Emile caste him a sideways glance, longing suddenly for his very own Rochelle. He too felt the pull of the bloodied soil receding behind them: deeply enhanced by the reality that they would possibly never ever be able to return.

He glanced again at the face of his old friend and smiled suddenly. "Twenty-one miles of foamy blue *mon ami*! We are all but there." He then tilted his head to the decks high above as they came alongside and grabbed the rope ladder as it was flung down to them, swinging and swaying there. He paused a moment, alert, scanning, listening.

Raoul, waiting to ascend behind Angelique, grinned suddenly but his tone also was wary. "Caught in too many traps, old friend?"

Emile glanced again at the heads now appearing above them. "If there are French Republicans up there, Trifane... well, we deal with it... as always! I did not come this far to fail!"

Raoul glanced again at the vessel's name: '*The Lynfa*'. "You cannot get much closer to the English than the Welsh, *mon ami*." But he too listened for accents, reaching out his senses for the indefinable, for silent treachery.

From the deck, high above their heads, there floated down the sounds of English feet running, of English voices: giving commands, shouting responses; warm, rich and welcoming for every sailor loves to be a rescuing hero. And the romance developed now around the escaping French, from that awesome guillotine, heightened their sense of 'knights errant' to high degree. A cheery, round face appeared above the rope ladder and beckoned them up with a waving hand.

"Welcome, friends! Come, make haste, the white cliffs of Dover await thee!"

# The End

# EPILOGUE

(In honour of Anton: integral to our escape!) Anton Manor,
Breton,
Hampshire,
England.
Second July 1795

My Dearest Clarisse,

I write to share with thee my extreme happiness; for after all 'twas you who said, so long ago at that wonderful last Christmas Hunt luncheon at Château Quatreaux, that I should try the married state. Remember? But you were not correct when you claimed the love born of free choosing did not contain the stamina to last the distance; for I *did* choose mine own husband and I be disbelieving, *ma chérie*, of the love existing between Raoul and I ever dissolving. Ever! Ever! Ever!

I sometimes wonder how many women have been offered a proposal of marriage whilst upon the back of a horse, albeit a magnificent animal of course. One of Raoul's own, a great roan that carried us both, during the last tension fraught miles of our escape to the pirates' vessel, anchored in the hidden reaches of a little known river mouth. I shall forever honour the worlds' population of pirates: without them, and their swashbuckling total disregard for danger, especially in approaching an enemy's vessel in time of war, we should never have escaped to England. Raoul laughs at me and maintains that they remain scoundrels, as likely to slice off one's head as look at one—without the amazing amount of gold coinage he paid them and wonders the vessel did not sink beneath the weight! However that may be, I am extremely stubborn regarding this issue!

On your visit for our wedding you did note that my dearest Raoul remained restless and taut. He went on in such manner for many months, ever looking over his shoulder. I can only assume that his work, ever intricately interwoven with that of our *père*, and Emile of course, was hazardous in the extreme! But he is now much relaxed following the death of Robespierre, Saint-Just and the rest of that scurrilous collection of heinous individuals! And to go beneath Madame Guillotine: oh what poetic justice! In particular Robespierre, following his failed suicide attempt— apparently they dragged him, face half blown away but still alive, to the guillotine. I am afraid that I cannot muster one grain of compassion for him.

366

I am brought to fearfully wonder though, whether yet another leader of diligence and virtue; one also unable to master his over-powering zeal; shall rise up out of the ashes of poor beloved France's demise. This appears to be the way of things when nothing but flotsam remains; and all history does bear me out. I pray with love for her recovery, our beautiful France, but Raoul says that we are settled now in England, which he is beginning to like and is held in enormous respect by our friends and compatriots.

He is ever busy with our estates, always the journal for the improvement of farming methods in his hand. In this he and Emile are alike: the soil, the drainage, the weather, is their new elements to battle! Is man *born* to fight I wonder? Socially we are blessed in our acceptance amongst our immediate circle and have met the reigning Monarch, George III, whom I liked very much. Much of this is of course Rochelle's doing, along with Lady Lambeth and Louisa Frane, though the Earl of Cleaver did warn me regarding the royal court. I shall not go into that just now but imagine all courts are alike!

Madame Bayette remains with us, her love for Monseigneur Vermont apparently unassailable. I bow to her; her love of extreme depth apparently, for she grieves silently and deeply still; I am honoured to give her a home. This is no hardship for either of us, for she does occupy the east wing of our lovely old 12th century house. In point of fact I work hard to wean her out, from time to time: her attitude now one of complete recluse. This house, which you much admired but I did not have the time then to explain it to you, once belonged to a family who may trace their roots back to, yes you have guessed it, France; following William into England after 1066. It was consequently built after the French fashion and of course appealed to Raoul when he was searching for English property as far back as 1790! I can only thank Our Lord for his far sightedness. He bought it from a renowned and irretrievable young gambler of the House of Rambulét, the loss to the family felt keenly apparently. Raoul says that the young idiot would have felt the taste of his ire, should he have been a son of his! Now why do I feel that he shall be a severe disciplinarian toward our offspring? I tease him often about it and he says that, tempered with deep love, strong discipline is of a necessity. That I shall leave to him!

And now, dear Clarisse, I come to the point of discovering for myself soon whether he speaks sense or not! I am with child *ma chérie* and am revelling in all the apparently usual, but new to me, sensations of accomplishment. This accompanied by the not so wonderful early morning physical sensations but that is past now and I am well. If it be a boy-child, I feel that I must of course unite with Raoul but also watch carefully, for the times are changing, with the young demanding greater independence than we ever could even imagine. This, I see, could spark struggles between father and son, as Raoul becomes more serious minded with approaching fatherhood! I smile, in memory of the behaviour and antics of our brothers and no doubt that of Trifane also, but this is apparently to be relegated to the archives!

I continue to write and wonder how *mon père* would feel about that now; for I am told that my work is good and even that once finished, shall stand some chance of being published. Can you imagine that: a published work of a female? Such freedom as does exist within England must surely be an example to the world. I do miss dearest *père* severely; he was so much alive, was he not? One can only pray that his death was not in vain. Mayhap some other poor prisoner survived in his place and that one day the Guillotine be destroyed and the Place de la Revolution redesigned and renamed.

My love, I must away now, tonight we have the Cowpers coming, along with several others of their circle, for an evening of music and play, in the French style. The English love it but Raoul insists the gambling remains at low rate—in memory of Louis? Mayhap he feels that the old house has witnessed enough of the deep play that ruins many men—and women, apparently. I myself stay with loo and occasionally faro if pressed or supplying numbers but the senseless gamble on the throw of a card or dice does nothing for me. I am happy drifting around the rooms, simply observing the relaxed, tension-free, untroubled faces at play—this is utter joy to me.

My love, please do put quill to parchment and let us know what goes forth, for you are close to the borders and snippets must reach you. Do you grow closer to your return to Château La Costa? And Quatreaux... dare I ask how *that* stands now? How great is the threat now I wonder. Once divorced from it all it is difficult to imagine that the civil unrest and riots still go on! It all seems a bad dream now. Please do have a care *ma chérie* and my great love to y'self, Stanilaus and the children; they must be fluent in the Italian tongue now, I am jealous!

Your ever loving,

Angelique.

P.S.

Some day we shall meet again on French soil—never feel defeated, my dear sister: as yr missive does appear to indicate—for our family name shall rise from those ashes and once more small offspring shall gambol over the hills and eventually tend the estates. I hold this in great heart and hope and dream of our descendants vibrantly alive: and living in peace in our beloved old Châteaux Quatreaux, immersed in the real work of future French men and women—that of reversing ignorance to knowledge, anger to harmony, and dispute to peace; and the building of a better France for all. We shall prevail! Au'voir, *ma soeur*. Au'voir.

# APPENDIX A

*Ancien Régime*: Rule by Absolute Monarchy: king ruled by divine right, answerable to none but God. Assisted by:

> Law courts/'*Parlements*' = 13 through out France—run by local judicial courts headed by *Seigneurs*, acting in the name of the king. Affairs of Province administered by *Intendants* acting by his commission.

> *Ministers*: answerable only to Monarch;
> > Finance.
> > Foreign.
> > Interior.
> > War.
> > Navy and Colonies.

*Ancien Régime*, **administration of:** Ecclesiastic: consisted of 156 *diocèses*. Military: consisted of 33 governments. Administration and gathering of taxes: consisted of 20-35 *Intendances*, (see Intendant). Judicial system, based on feudal land tenure: consisted, roughly, of 500 *baillages* (feudal jurisdiction) and *senéchaussées*: these boundaries uncertain: more than 1800 parishes were uncertain as to where they really belonged. One map contradicted another and the word Province provided a blanket cover for these ambiguities.

This system: run by the 1) *intendances* (royal bureaucracy), 2) the *bailliages*, (feudal jurisdiction), 3) the dioceses, (ecclesiastical conclave) and 4) the governments, (a military system), served to keep the people down. Therefore were high on the list of radical changes by the new Revolutionary Regime after 1789.

**Aristocracy:** 1st born: often very severe upbringing but could look forward to a life of privilege and ease; inherited all. Younger son/'s; could not expect substantial inheritance but his/their family could pull strings, have him/them introduced to court and presented to king, who, if he took a liking, offered chance to rise to high rank in the military or church (sold or offered in thanks for services rendered by said family to the king).

*Armée Révolutionnaire*: emergency army. At this time France had 13 armies. The 14th, of the above named, consisted of hurriedly 'recruited' untrained peasants/*sans-culottes*: disbanded October 6th 1793.

**Assembly of Notables**: (Extraordinary Council) called by Calonne: Controller-general of Finance, Feb.1787 to lay before them his propositions to pull an utterly weak and helpless France out of financial disaster, by means of reforms of the entire system of administration and taxation.  This Assembly of Notables, nominated by the King was thus: 7 Princes of the Blood Royale, 41 Nobles, 12 members of the King's Council, 12 Ecclesiastics, 34 Representatives of the *Parlements* of France, 2 representatives of the *Chambre des Comptes*, 2 of the *Cour des Aides*, 16 deputies of the *pays d'ètat*, 1 lieutenant general and 25 *chefs municipaux* of the principal towns. To these the king added his ministers—the four Secretaries of State and his Controller-General of Finance. This Assembly however, comprising almost entirely of privileged persons, proved recalcitrant.  But the winds of change had begun to blow and those few who approved these changes, were now determined that they should be made by an Assembly representative of the Nation.

*Assignats*: paper currency printed during the Revolution; eventually cancelled.

*Auberge*:  Inn.

*Baignoire*: Bathtub.

*Baillage*: Administrative and judicial district of the ancien régime: rendered, during the revolutionary period, 'constituency'.

*Baille*: Magistrate.

*Barriéres*: Barriers at city entrances for tax purposes; later used to seal exits.

**Bastille, fall of: 14th July 1789: Immediate causes:** Louis' dismissal (11th July) of Necker, the finance minister, (distrusted by the privileged classes but popular and trusted by the people), added to the simultaneous increase of Royal Troops within Paris at this time, escalated the rioting already in existence.  In search for arms to defend themselves against a perceived royal suppression of the people, the mob attacked the prison fortress, the Bastille: symbol of royal tyranny but also believed to be a storehouse of arms and ammunition. They killed, (among others), Launay, the Governor, and took the fortress.

*Bourgeois*: not the 'rude' meaning sometimes attached to the 'middle classes' but 'one who enjoys the rights of citizenship' or the whole body of those who do so: businessmen, lawyers, doctors and entrepreneurs of the towns and cities and wealthy farmers of the country.  These made up the people of the **Third Estate** of the *Ancien régime*. (The lower classes: serfs, peasants and *sans-culottes*—urban workers, were not included in the Third Estate.)

**Bread:** from the summer of '87 to February '89 the cost had doubled. Av. daily wage of manual labourer was about 20 sous, a mason, at best, 40 sous.

**Bread Riots, causes of:** suggestion by two Parisian manufacturers in late '89, Réveillon and Henriot, that the distribution of bread be deregulated, thus reducing prices and reducing cost of production, caused the first bread riots of the Revolution. Labourers took violent action against them, reading the cut prices as an effort to cut wages. For Bread March on Versailles: see 'Versailles'.

**Brunswick Manifesto:** document signed by Prussian general. Issued at Metz; fathered by French *émigrés* de Lemon and Mirabeau's old secretary Pellenc declaring to put an end to 'anarchy in France and stop attacks against the Throne and Alter: to re-establish rule of law'.

*Cabinet Noir*: part of spy system within secret policing prior to 1789: censorship of the post.

*Cahiers*: address/letter. At the calling of the States-general, as was customary for the occasion, *cahiers de doléances* (memos of grievances) were drawn from the people regarding their grievances, hopes, ideas and complaints. Close examination of these appears to reveal that the people of France did not attack the monarchy and were not republican in thought. What was found was: **a)** of the privileged classes: resentment of 'ministerial despotism', **b)** of the provincial citizens: resentment of 'centralization', **c)** of the 'thinkers', philosophers - and admirers of the English style of constitutional monarchy: a dislike of the Absolute Monarchy – of Divine Right of a king. Other issues were the wealth of the clergy, inequality, the burdens of the serfs/*sans-culottes* and feudalism.

*Caisse d'escomte*: discount bank.

**Caput (Louis):** derogative nickname given Louis by the Revolutionaries, particularly during his trial. Even he never knew just why they picked out that name. The last Caput king of France died childless in 1328. (Perhaps, some surmised, because they now planned to rid France of the last king: their plan/desire, to exterminate the entire *Famille Roi*.)

*Casaque*: Priest's cassock.

*C-devant privilege*: a law ordering recompense by the Privileged Orders; of taxes that they had evaded in the past under Direct Tax Exemptions.

**Church Establishment Bill of July 12<sup>th</sup> 1790; (to bring the Church under state control);** as decreed by the Ecclesiastic Committee, comprising four parts:
  1. *Titrel, des offices eccliasticques*: reorganization of the old diocese and parishes.

2.  *Nomination aux bénéfites*: the appointment of bishops and *curés* by local election, as were the departmental officials: required to swear the oath of loyalty to Nation, Law and King. Refusal stripped these of stipend and rights and to organize resistance gained arrest.
3.  *Du Parlement des Ministers et de la Religion*: fixed stipend.
4.  *De la Loi de la Resistance*: fixed the residence of all Clergy and placed the whole beneath the disciplinary control of the State.

**Church Property**: Nationalization proposed, (end of 1789) by Tallyrand: Bishop of Autun, and supported by Mirabeau. The Assembly, as a way of mobilizing these new resources, issued *Assignats*, or bonds (at this time) against this landed property.

**Citizen, 'active'**: see; voting rights of the new order.

**Citizen, 'passive'**: see; voting rights of the new order.

*Claqueurs*: Hired hand clappers. (In parliament)

**Clubs of Paris**: evolved due to the austere attitude of the first deputies of the National Assembly of 1789.  No deputy owned any experience, had any template to follow, within this new Assembly.  They sat waiting words of inspiration from the speaker of the moment, said little and thought of themselves in general as representative of the nation and attempted vague improvements for the local interests.  These deputies belonged to no political party as viewed by modern politics.  Therefore: here, at the newly evolving clubs of Paris, (situated mainly in the grounds and arcades of the *Palais-Royale*), political discussion and debates of opposing ideologies raged, eventually influencing National Assembly decisions. Various clubs drew like minds. Thus: the development of the first political parties, eventually, within this new method of governance.

*Colporteurs*: street sellers.

*Commissaires du Châtelet*: Police *Registrates* of Châtelet Prison.

*Comité*: Generally, a 'standing committee'.
   **Special committee:** set up to deal with a particular question/problem.

*Comité* **of Public Safety:** immediate object/initial aim: to have an executive sufficiently strong to bring large armies rapidly into the field. This became very powerful and was soon directed by Maximilien Robespierre, supported by Couthon and St Just.

*Comité* **General Security:**  Body to superintend measures taken for detection of political crimes.

*Comité des Recherches*: committee of investigation set up by the *Commune* (municipal). Replaced police inquisition of the old regime and exhorted members of the public to denounce one another, to the *Comité des Recherches*, as display of patriotism.

*Comité de Surveillance*: police supervision or 'Vigilance,' set up all over the country by the law of March 21 '93. These bodies ensured the enforcement of the decrees against 'suspected persons'. Further purging of local authorities was carried out by the Popular Societies. See: *Societés Populaires*.

*Comités* vs National Assembly:   Though the Assembly met twice in the morning and twice again in the evening, this was only part of the day's work for the Deputies. The most important—constitutional, feudal, military, diplomatic, ecclesiastic and financial—of the 31 standing committees of the House, met singly or jointly almost every day and here their powers progressively encroached upon those of the Executive.

    Here, their *rapports* initiated legislation and their instructions guided local administration: the *comité des recherches* issued warrants of arrest, the *comité ecclésiastique* imposed the clerical oath, the *comité diplomatique* read the ambassadors' despatches, to mention just a few.

*Commune*: Inhabitants of any place bound together in a common interest and administration, especially a town with a municipality.

*Commune of Paris*: September 1790: recognized, in accordance with a special law, being divided into 48 sections, each of which had its primary assembly, composed of active (entitled to vote) citizens. Had permanent committee: business: to carry out orders of the municipality and police regulations within the sections—and occupied an independent position alongside the Committee of Public Safety. Administered the affairs of the capital but in reality took the lead in directing general affairs of France. Became the strongest power in France and had armed bands of ruffians in its pay. The National Guard was under its orders, ministers and generals were appointed by its selection and laws were made in accordance with its wishes. No one risked collision with it. **Origins**: in night of Aug 10th 1792 when the Insurrectionary Commune established itself at the Hôtel de Ville (Town Hall) and began to give orders to the National Guard: in effect challenging the Legislative Assembly and creating a *Revolutionary Government*: its members were elected by 'active' citizens.

*Compagnie des Indes:*   big overseas trading corp. founded by the Bourbon finance minister; Calonne and protected by the Girondin Minister Claviere. This soon attracted envious attention of a group of unscrupulous Jacobins.

**Constitutional Church:** state controlled church: under the new, Revolutionary Civil Constitution of the Clergy: denying the Pope authority.

**Constitutional Revolution; 1<sup>st</sup> Principle of:** to replace arbitrary rule with code of law, the National Assembly its guarantee, allowing the nation to speak as one man but freely appointed and empowered to represent the people.

**Cordeliers Club:** *Société des amis droits de l'homme et du citoyen*; met in the Franciscan monastery on the south bank of the Seine and acquired special notoriety: of later foundation than the Jacobin and of lower social status. Subscription: *gros sou* a month (equivalent = 1penny). Here presided the orator Danton, distinguished among his fellows by his ability, zeal and energy. Here the shopkeepers, students and artisans of the Latin Quarter could learn the ramifications of the Declaration of Rights and current case of the day against the Assembly. Pushed for a Republic in '91

*Corvee:* unpaid labour (by law) of one day per week, by vassal to seigneur.

*Coucher:* **King's:** Morning and evening dressing ritual, traditionally attended by the Princes of the Blood (any legitimate male-line descendant of the king) and those chosen by the king. Here, a word or glance from the king could make or break a career.

**Court Nobility:** known as 'absentee landlords' living at (drafted to) Versailles: a tradition instigated by Louis X1V. Though the Versailles chateau was built as a representation of glory and prestige, it also served as a gilded cage, especially in its isolation, to control those parochial nobility building seats of power too distant to be controlled by the throne, in spite of the Royal Intendants: the king's overseers of nobility.

**Court: invited to by king**: also could mean a possible offer of concessions/finance/lands, arranged marriage for one's offspring or high military rank for younger sons, in return for services rendered.

**Courtyards of Versailles, right of entry by carriage**: privilege extended to the Nobility of the Sword only.

*Deputies en Mission*: deputies sent into every department with authority to take all measures necessary to hasten the levy of army recruits and for providing supplies for the army. These men established special committees to act as their agents, compelled the sale of corn and arms and dismissed suspected administrative officers whose affection and loyalty for their country was held in question. These Deputies were always present within the armies (spies against the generals) and were responsible only to the Convention and *Committee of Public Safety*.

**Departments (83), of the new order:** replaced the Provinces of the old order, each with an administrative body for management of affairs.

**Districts (374):** subdivisions of the *Departments*. The Districts devised elective administrative bodies, styled the *Directories* and were subordinate to the *Departments*.

**Directories:** elective administrative bodies of the *Districts*.

***Donjon:*** A keep: of a castle.

**Ecu:** 3 livres; value of 'half crown' in English currency.

**Egout:** sewers, drains.

***Elle:*** measure of material = 1 1/4 yards/ 1.25 metres.

***Emigrés par execellence:*** French aristocrats of the Revolution—political refugees: criticized for deserting king and country.
     1$^{st}$ wave of *émigrés* 1789: led by the Comte d'Artois, d'Polignacs—had led decadent way of life and now feared vengeance. 2$^{nd}$ wave 1791 *émigrés*—could not face life, stripped of their properties and luxuries. 3$^{rd}$ wave 1792 *émigrés*—had contributed to change but could not stay longer under the increasing severity of The Terror that attempted to take all lives of nobles regardless of innocence or guilt of any crime.

**Empire, the:** Austria.

**Estates, The three:** Social divisions of France within the *ancien régime*.
     1$^{st}$: The Clergy.
     2$^{nd}$: The Nobility—together with the Clergy, 2% of the population.
     3$^{rd}$: The Bourgeoisie: of the towns and cities and wealthy farmers.
     An eventually recognized 4$^{th}$ estate, the peasants/serfs/*sans-culottes* (urban workers); the bulk of the population, (98% together with the *bourgeoisie*), came into being very briefly, during the Revolution, prior to the abolition of all class divisions.

***Estates-general:*** (from 1789 called States-general): A body, drawn from the three estates (see above) of France, represented by deputies, for consultation during times of extreme emergency. Origins in the middle-ages, whereby the king took into account their opinions but retained power (Absolute Monarchy) to make the decisions. Crisis over, it was dissolved. Called into being very rarely: sometimes centuries apart; last called, prior to 1789—1614.

**Fashions:** only Nobles could wear fine clothing. Silks, satins, furs and jewellery were illegal possessions to the lower classes: the lowest class wore, by written and unwritten law—course linen, wooden clogs and leather boots.

***Female Triumvirate:*** Paris gossip 1792: reference to Louis' 'weakness and inability to make decisions', declaring that a 'female triumvirate', that of the queen at the

Foreign Office (contacts with Austria), Madame de Lamballe at the Home Office and Madame de Stael at the Ministry of War, now managed the affairs of the nation.

**Feuillants:**  Result of a schism within the Jacobin party, following the massacre at the Champs de Mars. This caused a complete severance between those bent on maintaining the constitution and those extreme 'left' of the Jacobins: the ultra-democrats or republicans.  The Constitutionalists founded a new club: the Feuillants, named after its (new) meeting place: a convent formerly belonging to the monks of that order.  Amongst these were the '*Truimvirate*'of 1791: Lameth, Barnave and Duport – the most prominent men of the centre-left.

**Forced Levy:**  a levy on all wealthy citizens: of 1 ml. livre. Definitively voted; on Sept 3$^{rd}$ '93.

**Four Aristocratic Grandparent Regime of the Old Order**: ensured that eligibility for commission within the military was drawn only from nobility of this ancestry.

**Gabelle: salt tax:** a poll tax within Nth France.

**Gallerie des Glaces**: famous hall of mirrors (17) at Versailles.  These, on the eastern wall, reflected 400,000 candles at night; and by day, reflected summer sunshine and what daylight could be captured in the winter months: through the tall western windows opposite the mirrors.  These windows also gave perfect view of enchanted blue distance.  Could hold 6000 guests and here gold, diamonds and finest crystal glittered seemingly forever: a place where courtiers often assembled to meet Marie Antoinette.

**Gendarme**: at this time: a body of armed police, a military body. Not organized as the English police.

**Générale:** call to arms.

**Gentlemen of the Wardrobe**: those chosen to attend the king's am and pm ritual of dressing for the day and undressing for bed; an ancient ritual. At 1130 am a page shouted 'Gentlemen of the Wardrobe' and the Princes of the Blood and chosen ones entered the bedchamber and the toilet began. When the king eventually donned his coat a page shouted 'The Bed Chamber!' and the pages, chaplains and courtiers could enter.

Being invited, during this ceremony, to cross the barriers that separated the royal bed from the rest of the room was a sign of favour much sort after; as was being invited to talk to the king and or having a positive comment made by the king relayed to oneself.  None refused the invitation to act as a Gentleman of the Wardrobe: the following exclusion and ongoing repercussions would be extreme.

**Girondins:** moderate political party that led the French at the beginning of the Revolution. By 1792, though they agreed with the 'leftist' Jacobins: in the war, the

Republic and the Convention, they continued to believe in templates cut from the old regime.

*Grande Peur*: 1789, following the convocation of the States-general, evolved into a year of the Grand Fear: the king of the Assembly, the privileged classes for their privileges and the Third estate of the nobility and a royal counter-attack.  Paris was over crowded with refugees and the unemployed and the mob believed that the nobility were plotting against them.  This infectious fear caused the eruption of riots all across the country.  From this, rumours commenced of brigands and looters burning chateaux and whole villages even: exacerbating the *Grande Peur*.

**Great Book of Public Debt:** the compilation of which, was decreed by the Convention, Aug. 24 1793 in which all debts of the 'old regime' and the new, were 'Republicanised'. *Guarde du corps*: household troops.

**Guillotine**: ancient (centuries old at this time) beheading machine still in occasional use (in 1789) in Italy, Spain and England.  Revised and improved by Dr Guillotin, for the execution of large numbers of persons at a time, at the height of the revolution.  Contrary to common belief the aristocracy did not supply most of the victims. Close study of registered figures of the times suggest that the aristocracy were far outstripped by members of the middle class and lower orders. Towards the end of the revolution, any word, thought (exposed by facial expression) or deed by any person, seen to be *un-revolutionary*, was decreed treasonable: the perpetrator ending beneath the guillotine.

**Guillotine-Travelling:** a dismountable guillotine for the purpose of reaching any and every town and village for the execution of political 'suspects' and ordinary criminals

**Holy Roman Empire:** Complex of European territories under rule of German king (origin, the Franks), bearing the title of Roman Emperor. 1st: Charlemagne—800 AD, last Francis 11.  Dissolved 1806: following Francis' defeat by Napoleon at Austerlitz.

**Hôtel:**

1.  In 18c France, a nobleman's large Paris town house/residence/mansion belonging to only the most wealthy of Nobles.
2.  Public building ie, Hôtel de Ville - the Town Hall.

*Hussiers*: ushers.

**Imprisonment**: included capital sequestered and revenue confiscated.
    *Condemned to death*: revenue *and* capital confiscated: leaving family destitute. This also encouraged the family to keep their own in line.

***Intendants*, royal (of the old regime)**: provincial officials of France: Supervisors/ managers, courier/messenger for king, *collecteur* of taxes.

***Intendants d`armies***: old form of *Deputies en Mission*. Civil control over armies, or royal precaution against over-powerful generals, maintained throughout 18c.

**Jacobin:** originally the nickname of the Dominicans of the Church of S. Jacques on Rue Saint-Honoré. The church had been assigned to them in the 13th c when they first arrived in Paris. These premises were, (throughout the Revolution) occupied by the *Amis de la Constitution* (friends of the Constitution): the Jacobin Club. Meetings were first held in the Dominican refectory, then, needing more space, the library, then the chapel, of which it was remarked, did not appear to increase any spirituality of outlook. Throughout '90/91, it spread through France, in a time when all other bonds of cohesion had been destroyed or fallen away; and perpetually interfered with administrative bodies. From Oct. '91, they debated in public, drawing large audiences by their passion and zeal to indiscriminately tear down the old and build the new, by any means that worked, including wholesale slaughter. From August 1792, these became acknowledged as the political 'Jacobin Party' of the extreme radical left, a much feared dictatorship; intimidation their methods of persuasion. Became republicans; following the overthrow of the throne.

***Jureurs***: Constitutionalist priest. Priests that took the Revolutionary 'oath of allegiance' to the country excluding the church and the Pope: following the Revolutionary Civil Constitution of the Clergy, denying the Pope authority.

***Jurés*: Jury:** jurymen: specially appointed officials: not any casually elected twelve citizens.

***Lanterne***: street lamp of duel purpose: hung from a strong bracket or cord across street: convenient gallows.

**Law of Suspected Persons:** defined who could be arrested for treasonable activities. Enforced by the Revolutionary Tribunal: created by President Armand Martial Herman: who, with Fouquier-Tinville (Public Prosecutor), interviewed Marie Antoinette at her Preliminary Examination preceding her official trial.

***Lettres de Cachet***: of the *ancien regime*: a sealed letter, (indefensible royal warrant) for a persons' immediate arrest without explanation. Perceived enemies of the crown could be detained indefinitely without judicial process, usually within the impenetrable Bastille. Victims were mostly intelligentsia and aristocracy.

***Levée*: (morning rising/ evening retiring dressing ritual):** attended by the Princes of the Blood and others. To be summoned to the king's levée was both an honour and an opportunity to be noticed.

***Louis***: gold coin.

***Louis d`or***: 24 *livre*. Rough value: English sovereign.

**Madame:** Used as form of respectful address, crossing all social ranks, from the queen down. Also title for married woman and for older unmarried woman: as mark of respect. Also could be used as mark of respect: for young unmarried lady of nobility. Some documentations state that this evolved from '*ma dame*': My Lady.

***Marc d`argent***: money to value of about 54 English shillings or 50 day's labour.

***Marchaussie***: mounted police.

***Manège***: riding school.

**Marriage:** could only be contracted between those within the same class/estate, by law.

**Maximum Laws:** prevented prices from rising in the open market due to scarcity. The farmer soon found many ways to conceal his corn or shift it outside the country sooner than send it to Paris or larger towns where the Maximum Law was rigidly enforced. This circumvention brought about the Law of Suspected Persons. His reluctance to part with his corn under the maximum laws now could be viewed as 'originating in an ill will towards the Republic', leading to the guillotine without trial.

**Monseigneur:** my Lord, as highest form of address: His Highness, His Eminence, His Grace, His Lordship. Also used as demonstration of extreme respect by son to father; and/or in satire/humour/sarcasm.

***Monsieur***: title of address for those with no rank: (English Mr) but also polite form of address: used within, and crossing, all estates and ranks, as mark of respect: equivalent to the English 'Sir'.

***Montagnards*** **(the mountain):** the political faction sitting in the highest seats at parliament (to the left of the presidents chair): became the extreme radical 'left' of the leftist Jacobin Party, dominated by Robespierre, supported, among others, by Danton, Couthon, Saint Just and Marat.

***Mouchards***: agents.

**Mount/Mt (as prefix to names):** contrary to expectation of geographical mountains, this prefix to many village and town names was in honour of the extremist Jacobin political party: (the ***Montagnards***: who commandeered the highest seats in the new assembly.)

**Municipality, of Paris:** consisted of a general council of 96 and executive of 44 members. In difficult position at its birth: work scarce, crime rife and prisons crowded. No laws now existed to suppress political agitation, even though it took the form of treason to the constitution. With large numbers of men of moderation withdrawing from politics into private life, these ultra-democrats were able to gain the upper hand. In the poorer sections agitators undermined the popularity of the Assembly.

**Municipalities of the countryside:** owned direct control over the *Communes*. This became increasingly ignored, as the *Communes* grew more and more powerful. Members were elected by men with voting rights: of 25 yrs of age, inhabiting the *Commune* and paying direct taxes to the value of three days labour.

**Necklace, That**: plot, involving Cardinal Rohan, to sell an exquisite diamond necklace of priceless value to Marie Antoinette; falsely claiming that she had ordered it be made. She admired it when offered; but rejected it. The lies and heinous gossip stuck to the Queen, thus branding her further as frivolous and wasteful when the country was in famine.

**Nobility**: Figures on this issue appear to remain stubbornly differing: some historians claim the number to be approx. 150,000 (at 1789) and suggest roughly 6% of these claimed feudal nobility descent (Noblesse de l'épée)—from before the 15th c. Others claim the figure to be closer to 340,000—approx. 80,000 from the traditional Noblesse de l'épée.

Nobility was generally hereditary but many were previously awarded by a king for loyal service, or sold to carefully vetted families—after three generations of land and château ownership or possessing certain important official or military charges - these generally of two generations duration. Yet other non-nobles usurped titles by living nobly and devising some way of avoiding the official *taille* lists: the benchmark of the Second Estate. Several hundred years of this saw these accepted as 'Noble'. This practice of usurpation however, was brought under control by Louis X1V, who commenced authentication of all nobles: by means of written proof that their nobility extended from before 1560: by production of birth certificates, marriage certificates and land documents.

**Nobility—classes of:**

Noblesse de l'épée **(Nobility of the Sword or *Noblesse Ancienne*):** hereditary nobility going back centuries: only nobility with the right to wear a sword and use a coat of arms. Became a closed society; closing ranks ever more protectively against the *Noblesse de la Robe*. (See below)

*Noblesse de Chancellerie*: (nobility of the chancery): title of nobility given for holding high offices for the king.

*Noblesse de Lettres*: (nobility acquired by *Lettres Patentes* from the king.) Began in reign of Francis 1st, as method of raising revenue: non-

nobles possessing noble fiefs, payed a year's worth of revenue from these fiefs: to gain nobility.
*Noblesse de la Robe*: nobility; bought, acquired, earned (from king). To replenish state coffers the monarchy habitually sold noble ranks.
*Noblesse Militaire*: (military nobility). Nobility granted by king after two to three generations of a family holding military office.
**Distinctions between the nobility, based on age of titles:**
*Noblesse Chevaleresque*: (of knighthood)—from before the 14thc.
*Noblesse d'extraction*: nobility of four to five generations.

**Non-Jurors**: Refractory priests. Priests refusing to take the 'oath of allegiance to the country', which excluded the Church and the Pope, following the Revolutionary Civil Constitution of the Clergy.

**Oath, of Allegiance: to the nation, law and king by the clergy (personally and individually):** proposed by Voidel, on the grounds of clerical opposition to the Church Establishment Bill: declaring that too many clergy were unpatriotic toward the new regime. The point within the debate regarding the Constitutional Church, article XXI, over which the bitterest controversy arose. The opposition to the oath regarded it as the first step towards the separation of church and state. The first principle of the Revolution, however, sovereignty of the people, was at stake if it could not claim rights over the church. The Assembly therefore declared the law must be enforced. A decree, November 27th 1790, declared all clergy, officiating at public function must take the oath on Sunday morning after High Mass, in the presence of their congregation, which must contain, as witness, a representative of the General Council of the *Commune*.

**Obligations of the Noblesse:** Certain military, ecclesiastic and civic positions were reserved for the nobility. In return the noblesse owed certain activities to the crown: a) honour and faithfulness—i.e. military service (the 'blood tax') and b) council and assistance to the king. Strictly prohibited were manual and commercial activities; though they could profit from their lands through their vassals' land taxes, portions of his harvest and taxes on his usage of the granaries, mills, mines, forges, ovens and wins presses.

*Oeil de Boeuf*: a vast salon; into which the king emerged from his bedchamber following his morning *coucher*. Gentlemen granted an audience waited him here.

**Openness, of Royal Court to the public at Versailles**: an ancient tradition of the French court, allowing the public to observe the *Famille Roi* throughout their daily rituals of the bedchamber, dinning hall etc. To do so, members of the public gallery had to be clean and appropriately dressed. Origins: some thought prevailed that this custom of openness had commenced many centuries earlier, to allay fear of royal subterfuge against the people. Nothing for the royal family was private, every move of daily living freely observed.

*Parlements of France*: speaking assemblies, ancient bodies of magistrates.  *13c* through to *1789*, these were law courts with power to act on political events as well as the lawful and had the right to veto king's decrees.  Disappeared after the States-general, the only 'real' parliament, was recalled after 175 years of absence; and recovered its rights permanently, in 1789.

*Par order*: vote by order (1$^{st}$ 2$^{nd}$ 3$^{rd}$ Estates.)

*Par tete*: by person (vote)

*Petit Bourgeoisie*: section of Bourgeoisie with lowest social status at that time; shop-keepers/clerical.

*Peur le Grande*:  the 'grand fear' or great panic, which overran France during the 2$^{nd}$ half of 1789: beginning in 5 different places (Paris not one).  Fed rumours of pending orchestrated starvation of the people, by the nobility to bring them to submission: it spread by word of mouth from house-to-house, market-to-market.  Burning of châteaux, sackings and killings followed: ensuring, eventually, the routing of aristocratic feudalism and attacking the throne from behind.

*Phrygian*:  red cap of soft material worn by revolutionaries; adopted from ancient times (symbol of slavery)

**Pike:** rude, unwieldy weapon: a long (8-10 feet) pole with metal spearhead.  Cheap weapon used by the peasants and issued by the government during every riot/uprising.

**Policy of intimidation:** declared by Robespierre, 1794, an essential companion for virtue, in times of revolution. Without intimidation, said Robespierre, at such time virtue was powerless.

*Porte*: court or government of the Ottoman Empire.

*Possédant fief*: feudal tenure.

*Pots de Chambre*: a tiny, pod-like, open carriage: (taxi of 18$^{th}$c Paris): with room only for one passenger. The derogative nick-name stuck.

**Princes of the Blood:** relatives of the king: legitimate male-line descendant of the king.

**Provinces of France (of the old order):**  These, under sweeping changes as the Assembly attempted to complete the Constitution (1790/91), were swept away and replaced by 83 *Departments*, with an elected administrative body for management of affairs. These departments, in turn, were divided into 374 *Districts* with an administrative body; styled the *Directory*, subordinate to the Department.

*Regime Sensitaire*: qualifying to vote.

*Représentants en mission aux armies*: the means by which the *Committee of Public Safety* kept itself informed about the state of the armies and behaviour of the generals. Also was a channel through which it sent its orders.

**Revolutionary Tribunal:** tribunal to be faced by all perpetrators of crimes against the Revolution and France.  Enforcer of Law of Suspect, the brainchild of Danton, who organized its creation: giving it special powers, 10$^{th}$ March 1793, to try political prisoners: ie royalist sympathizers. This became the key instrument of The Terror. The 'widow Caput'; Marie Antoinette, was tried by the Revolutionary Tribunal.

**Riposte**: counter attack made immediately after a parried attack, (sword fighting/ fencing).

*Riposte-en-Quinte*: 5$^{th}$ of eight basic positions from which a parry or attack may be made in sword fighting/fencing.

**Robe, The**: See *Noblesse de la Robe*.

*Sans-culottes*: technically means 'without trousers' but evolved during the Revolution as an urban worker, from the slums of Paris; so called because he preferred proletariat trousers to the aristocratic breeches. These people were so low in the French social strata that originally no word existed to describe them. Eventually accepted as a Fourth Estate: briefly, during the Revolution.

**Scheldt:** closed to trade at the beginning of the Revolution, by European arrangement, agreeable to England, Holland and France but ruinous to the trade of Antwerp. After the French armies were in occupation of Belgium, the French National Convention proclaimed free navigation of the *Scheldt*, giving offence to England by breaking this agreement.

**Secret Allocution of March 10$^{th}$—of Pope Pius:** Condemned all the works of the French National Assembly—from the *Declaration of Rights* to the new *Civil Constitution of the Clergy*, rendering the new Constitutional Church illegal.

**Service of State:** a means of avoiding the proscription, the surest means of avoiding imprisonment and the surest means of acquiring wealth.  Government offices were flooded with incapable clerks and graft seekers particularly throughout 1793. Municipal officers and administrators had abundant opportunity to benefit themselves and their relatives at the expense of the state. The multitude of agents employed by the army also could; in making their military requisitions, enrich themselves by extortion and breach of the maximum laws.

**Seven Years War:** of France against Britain 1756-63.

**Single *chambre***: A clamour (in the very first sittings of the States-general turned National Assembly) for the three estates to sit as one meeting: instead of three separate entities: 1$^{st}$ estate: the Clergy, 2$^{nd}$: the Nobility, 3$^{rd}$: the People. King disagreed: *single chambre* implied abolition of class distinction; producing a threat of a swamping of the nobles by the Third Estate.   Also: to make one *chambre* would tear away the nobility from the crown…putting all people on one footing.  He saw this as the illiterate and uneducated masses taking control with disastrous result.

***Sociétés Populaires***: a Jacobin weapon. These '*Société Patriotique*' '*Société Republicaine*' '*Amis de la Liberté et de l'égalité*' and many more were in effect groups of enthusiastic men who ran the Revolution within their towns, villages. Became the spies and censors for the Jacobin regime; keeping the fires of hatred and fury burning.  All the real power lay in the hands of these men, before whom wise men trembled.

***Sou***: = 5 *centimes*. *Gros sou*: equivalent; one English penny.

**States-General:** (emergency council of the *ancien régime*.) Convoked by LouisXV1, took place on 5$^{th}$ May 1789 at Versailles to deal with famine effects and financial crisis. It had last met in 1614 - 175 yrs earlier, its deputies then being elected by the three Orders: 1$^{st}$ estate: the Clergy 2$^{nd}$ estate: the Nobles, and the 3$^{rd}$ Estate: the Bourgeoisie.  This precedent was followed on May 5$^{th}$ 1789.  The serfs/peasants (98% of the population) were not included, had no rights and were viewed at this time as simply a work force.

Prior to 1789, it was called **Estates-general:** an emergency council, consulted during crisis.  **Formation** 1328: at death of past Caput King (childless.) Crisis over, it returned to the archives and the King's Council took control again.  In 1789 however, this, the only proper parliament of France, remained entrenched and caused the old law court/'*Parlements*' to disappear. (See *Parlements*.)

**Storming of the Bastille 14 July 1789**: Did not 'begin' the Revolution, a common belief, but was only the first physically active demonstration of it; over and above the common (escalating at this time) street rioting.  Cause: the dismissal of the popular finance minister Necker, by the king; and import of extra troops into Paris, for the unrest caused by that dismissal. The people, foreseeing martial law, began to arm themselves: the Bastille one of the armouries pillaged.

**Sword, of the**: See *Noblesse de l'éppée*.

***Taille***: Property tax.

**Taper:** pine or birch single candlestick: cheap and did not smoke but was not very bright.

**Tax Collection by the Sword:** did not mean taxes were extracted at the point of a sword but collected by the local *Seigneur* (*Noblesse de l'épée* – nobility of the sword).

**Temple:** medieval fortress, owned by the king's brother, Comte d'Artois, in which the king and his family were held prisoners before his (the king's) execution, January 1793.

*Terreur*: Policy of intimidation: brought into being by a decree September 5th 1793 and became the order of the day. A period when the government used force instead of persuasion—then formed into a fine-tuned *system*, by Robespierre, to ensure greater efficiency. Its first move was to imprison 'suspects': on the denunciation of local, patriotic revolutionaries. A special 'Revolutionary Army' of 6000 'good revolutionaries', assisted in its enforcement outside Paris.

**Three Estates of France, the**:
   **1st Estate: The Clergy**—together with the Nobility = 2% of the population; owned large areas of land but was not required to pay taxes and answered only to the Pope in Rome.
   **2nd Estate: The Nobility**—owned all the rest of the land, paid few taxes and enjoyed many privileges.
   **3rd Estate: The Bourgeoisie**—lawyers, doctors, businessmen and entrepreneurs: paid the bulk of the nation's taxes but had few rights. These supposedly represented the serfs/peasants and urban workers. Eventually these, serfs/peasants, were accepted as a *fourth estate*, briefly, during the period of the revolution prior to the abolition of the classes.

*Tierce*: third of eight basic positions from which a parry or attack can be made: within sword fighting/fencing.

**Titles (in address)**: titled people were usually addressed by title. Jean-Pierre Vermont, *Comte de Quatreaux* therefore, would be addressed as *Monsieur le Comte de Quatreaux*, or simply 'de Quatreaux' by those who knew him by sight or association. Close intimates only; as a mark of affection and claim of close tie, used family name; Vermont.
   This advertised much more than simple hierarchical order: a person using another's family name was establishing to those around him that he stood on intimate terms with said person. If the king used one's family name in lieu of title, then one could be flattered and rest assured that the king held him in favour and trust.
   The reverse of this: to address an intimate friend by title, sometimes indicated anger, sometimes expressed comfortable affection/satire/formal occasions etc.; to decipher this depended on tone and current situational event/dialogue.
   The social divisions were strict at this time, many aspects enforced by laws. A noble might dine with member of the Bourgeoisie of the countryside whilst residing in his château but that man could expect to dine in the servants' hall if he called on the noble in the city. This did not arise out of snobbery, though this did evolve

among many, but simply acknowledgement of the division of classes by law. Both understood this and the many deeper subtleties. The result was one of high degree of vocalized respect. A Comte would, *or should*, use the same degree of respect in addressing all persons across the entire social scale: respect for all was mandatory to the point of fanaticism in polite circles. This respectful politeness reflected amongst all societies within France and has survived, in many ways, to this day within France.

**Traces:** leather straps either side of carriage horse—connected to whiffle tree: a crossbar in carriage harness.

*Tricoteuse*: knitters.

*Tric-trac*: mild gaming card-game indulged in by Louis. He refused to play higher-stakes games and encouraged his intimates likewise. He did not often lose more than 2 gold *louis* (half the salary of a mason).

*Tumbril*: crude cart for rubbish/manure etc: used to transport prisoners to the guillotine.

**Versailles, the gilded cage: invited to:** to refuse, or leave once established there, spelled disaster for a noble. All official positions, charges and appointments were made at Versailles. Many provincial nobles, unable to attend, were locked out of important positions within the military or state office.

**Versailles, attack on, Oct.5<sup>th</sup> 1789:** The fall of the Bastille, total collapse of authority and the effects of the *Grande Peur*, caused resistance by the privileged classes within the Assembly, to weaken. Rallying from this however, a 'right-wing', royalist party, wishing to restore the king's executive powers in the face of total anarchy, had begun to appear in the Assembly. The extreme revolutionaries, using forceful tactics to maintain the upper hand against this 'party', then manipulated the mob to march on Versailles. Six thousand: mainly women marched on and then attacked Versailles and the royal family, taking them by surprise. In triumph they forced the *Familie Roi* to Paris and to live thereafter at the Tuileries Palace. This, in some way, appeared to act as a guarantee against famine. The Assembly followed soon after.

**Voting rights of the new order:** a voter (male only) must be: living within the *commune* in which he votes, of 25 yrs of age and paying direct taxes to the value of three days labour. These, amounting to 1-500, were then required to serve in the National Guard but owned the title; '*active*' citizen with their indirect voting rights: as opposed to the '*passive*' citizen—one who payed less than three days labour in tax or no tax and owned natural and civil rights only.

A rise in the qualifying value for a direct elector (representative of 100 indirect electors) increased to a tax equivalent of ten days labour. Qualification to sit in the Legislature: demanded that of direct tax to the value of fifty days labour, or the *marc d'argent*. This very few could afford.

**Wheat**: typical family of five required sixty bushels of wheat per year or: with triennial rotation of crops, about 15 acres of land for food.  However the majority, about 70% after they were able to buy land, owned less than 2 ½ acres.  This fact, drought and harsh winters of the '80's, and medieval farming tools and techniques, helped to create the famed bread shortage.  However even under these conditions it was better to own a tiny piece of land than exist as an urban dweller.  The farming peasants could at least hope to grow enough for his Seigneur, the government and himself.  His burdens however were heavier, owing taxes to his feudal lord, the crown and the government.  Added to this, he lived under the law of the Seigneur; who had sole hunting rights across all lands and levied dues on fairs and markets and owned power to enforce his peasant farmers to bring the wheat to his mill; and his grapes to his press.

**Wheel, breaking on:** Form of punishment of the ancient regime whereby a person was tied spread eagle to a cartwheel and beaten with iron bar: to break all limb bones.

*Whisht*: intimation to be quiet.

*Whist*: card game for four in which the two sides try to win the balance of the 13 tricks: fore runner to bridge. (a 17c game; referring to the sweeping/whisking up of the tricks.)

**Women's rights at time of revolution:** enjoyed no civil or economic rights, totally subservient to fathers and husbands and in all areas of marriage contracts. Marriages were indissoluble. Noble women had no power even on properties that they held/inherited and these automatically went to her husband on marriage. Working women lacked economic rights and protection of any kind.

**Women of the Third Estate at the period beginning just prior the Revolution,** desired all the political, economic and social rights that they had heard now existed in England and America. To those two nations the most important rights of the people were political and civil – the right to participate in government, freedom of expression and equality before the law. Change approached, albeit at a snails pace.

# APPENDIX B

## Historical Figures

**Barnave, Antoine-Josephe-Marie-Pierre:** Son of protestant solicitor and penniless aristocrat, he resented exclusion, both as bourgeois and Catholic, from the society of his mother's noble birth. His personality, described by some, was overt: a hot temper leading to an attack on Mirabeau and Brissot and a duel with Cazalès but then an over-generous streak led to his champion of those of the aristocracy who appealed to his heart. Barrister of and from Grenobles and a Deputy of the National Assembly, he was a born orator. Was one of the three National Assembly representatives, along with Latour-Mauberg and Pétion, sent to meet the recaptured royal party between Epernay and Dormans. Instantly liked, and liked by, the queen and Madame Elizabeth; thereafter called the 'new friend of the queen'. At Assembly, he now argued that to depose the king would destroy the new constitution and that it was time to end the social Revolution: before it further degenerated into total mayhem and caused the destruction of France. The queen hoped that he might influence a full restoration of the king. To the public eye, he had been a 'man of the people' in'89: due on the one hand, to his hostility toward his family's exclusion from polite society but then a 'man of the court', in '91. Cartoons and caricatures depicted him as Monsieur 'Facing-both-ways'. This however was not born of a prudently 'swinging personality' but of the ability to see accurately from opposing aspects at the same time.

**Bishop of Aix:** debated hotly against the Assembly's *Church Establishment Bill* of July 12th 1790 (to bring the church under the state.) Maintained that the bishops descended through the Apostles from Jesus Christ himself and could not be touched by the State.

**Bouillé, de, Marquis:** Royalist: General of French army. Wrote to the king at beginning of the Revolution that, of his 125 battalions of infantry and eighty squadrons of cavalry, he could only rely on five battalions of foreign troops, should they be needed to put down an uprising. Conspired with Mirabeau and Lamark: for the removal of the King, under armed escort, to Campiènge or Fontaineblau.

**Brewer, Jacques-Rene:** Journalist/editor of Hébert's *'Père Duchesne'*. Along with Chaumette, became director of all action taken by the (newly developed and eventually very powerful) *Commune*. These two became a threat to Robespierre, leader of the Jacobins, provoking his hostility.

**Chaumette, Anaxagora, previously Pierre Gaspard:** Seaman, surgeon, schoolteacher, political journalist, member of Cordeliers Club; became leader of the *Commune*.

**Desmoulins, Camille:** Orator and journalist- leftist; and friend of Danton and Robespierre. Eventually destroyed by Robespierre and guillotined, along with Danton and others wishing to relax the Terror, April 6th 1794.

**Francis II—1768-1835:** Last Holy Roman Emperor; also (1792-1806) as 1st Emperor of Austria: hostile towards France; regarding treatment, by revolutionaries, of his aunt, Marie Antoinette.

**Géurin:** commissioned, May 5th '94, by *Committee of Public Safety*, to ensure the *surveillance intérieure* of Paris and paid equivalent of £200 sterling. Given four assistants (later increased to 10) to frequent public places in Paris, note names, occupations and addresses (gathered personally or from their informants) of those guilty of any crime: actual or rumoured. Passed daily reports to the Committee on intriguers and or conspirators thus discovered. The list of offences against the Revolutionary Government to be searched out was long: secret correspondence, gambling, profiteering, speculation on *assignats*, casually dropped words considered to be seditious, apparent royalist 'thought'- bound in dialogue; denigration of the Glorious Revolution by word, action or facial expression, the word *Austria* in any context and expressed sympathy for the interned *Famlie Roi*, but a few. Paris streets at this time were almost empty of carriages, dress simple and conversation stilted and wary. Salon gatherings of philosophers and serious minded beings, so constricted their dialogue, that jests were made regarding the new English influence: that of long discussion of nothing more important than the weather.

**Guillotin, Dr:** Modifier of the guillotine. **Also:** *Commissaire* of Assembly; resolved the issue of lack of room for reporters of Paris papers, within the new establishment at the *Manège* behind Tuileries. The *Journal Nationale* was given the *chassis grille* in a corner of the hall and others were found places to the left and right of the raised platform that held the President's seat. Thereafter the speakers spoke the more to the invisible audience than to their fellow Deputies. Ordered a twice/daily sprinkling: of vinegar and herbal solution to the Assembly, to combat the 'bad air'. Resolved the issue of slow executions: by the rapid blunting of the swords – comprising soft steel at this time - by improving on the beheading machine: found still in use within Spain, Italy and England.

**La Fayette, Marquis de:** With enough wealth and background to enter the best company of Europe, Lafayette turned his back on it all for adventure and a life abroad: exhibiting an enthusiasm for liberty. Financing his own army to take to America, he fought there in the American War of Independence, becoming a close friend of Washington. On return to France, he saw a new world developing within the rumblings of a rebellion and expected a gradual and peaceful change from feudalism to social equality. Organizer of the National Guard, night of the July 13th 1789, from the milling masses of the escalating rebellion: that took the Bastille July 14th 1789. Also tireless organizer of the construction of a business government which would secure property and profits and at the same time funded foreign emissaries financing agents of public disorder. Executed by the Revolutionaries.

**Marat:** anti royalist; called the 'Friend of the People' after the title of his journal. Gave patronage to the Popular and Fraternal Societies springing up during the winter of '90-'91, their aim: to popularise, among the illiterate, Rousseau and Republicanism. Became one of the eleven men elected to the *Comité de Surveillance*, jointly, with others, involved in/guilty of but difficult to prove, the September Massacres. His goal: a Democratic State and a government that provided bread and labour for the masses. His means: the re-establishment of absolute power (dictatorship) and use of force to crush under foot the possessors of wealth and talent. Encouraged murder and insurrection, advising, within his journal, writings and ravings, the people to 'secure their happiness': by rising and killing their enemies in a body. He openly accused the *Girondins* and constitutionalists of being sold to the court. Assassinated by Charlotte Corday, one of many who could no longer, by 1793, watch the establishment of a body of ruthless tyranny in their midst without attempting resistance - the moderate *Girondins* had weakened to the point of silence. The few who dared, by word or deed, to venture opposition to the *Mountain* or the *Commune of Paris* (powered by Robespierre,) paid the penalty by loss of liberty if not life. Seeing Marat as one of the major leaders of mayhem and slaughter, Charlotte, to gain audience with him, offered intelligence of the *Girondins* operating still in Normandy. He invited her in: (he was in his bathrobe, soaking within his bathtub). On request, she gave the names of these deputies. Marat, writing them down, said, 'In a few days, I will have them guillotined in Paris.' Any hesitation now in Charlotte dissipated. She killed him by knife on the spot, (in his bathtub) July 13th 1793.

**Mirabeau: Comte de—the Honoré-Gabriel Riqueti 1749-91**: Deputy working for the commons within the new Revolutionary National Assembly but pursuing a moderate policy – believing in abolition of absolute monarchy but to be replaced by a Monarchical Constitution: giving some stability to the new regime, as a template on which to develop the new. Whilst supporting the left, and denigrating the old order, spent the last two months of his life, prior to a sudden and inexplicable death, conspiring with Lamarck and General de Bouillé for a withdrawal of the king, under armed escort to Compiègne or Fontainebleau.

**Narbonne Comte de:** Natural son of Louis XV: made, by Louis XV1, Dec.06th 1791, Minister of War, replacing the inactive Duportail. Narbonne; an able soldier, with knowledge of foreign languages and affairs, hastily carried out inspection of the frontier fortresses then settled on a plan of campaign, with the newly appointed marshals: Luckner and Rochambeau. The Assembly was assured (Jan.11th) that some 120,000 men were ready to defend the frontier. He also conveyed the king's aunts, Victoire and Adelaide to Rome during their flight from France prior to the royal flight to Varennes.

**Orleans, Duc d':** of the Orleans family: Grande Master of the French Freemasonry and traditional pretenders to the throne and the recognized opposition at court. At its head, he sat as one of the richest men of France, with uneasy—some said evil—reputation, owning enormous estates, at the time of preparing for the States-general recall. Issued 100,000 copies of Instructions to his agents: to be delivered to, and hopefully direct the ideas and policies of, his tenants all over the country. He attempted at every turn, during every uprising, to usurp the throne and applied every strategy possible to gain popularity with the people. Received loud applause when he appeared dressed as a Deputy, not as a Prince, for the opening ceremony of the States-general at the Notre Dame. Attack on Versailles, Oct.5$^{th}$ and 6$^{th}$ 1789, was believed to be incited by the Duc d' Orleans but never proven. On news, Jun 21$^{st}$ $^{1791,}$ of the royal flight to Varennes, the Duc drove his cabriolet up and down the Carousel continuously; reminding Paris that it had a third alternative to a restoration or a republic. To augment this he disassociated himself from the royal family and changed his name to Egalité. None showed inclination to adopt this discredited Prince as king or regent. Cousin to Louis, he voted for Louis' death penalty at his trial then followed the Girondists to the guillotine Nov. 6$^{th}$ 1793.

**Robespierre, Maximilien de:** barrister of small municipality of Arras, leader of the Jacobin club, sat on the extreme left of the Constituent Assembly, elected to the Commune 1792, became a leading member of the Committee for Public Safety, established the Reign of Terror; then fine-tuned it into a 'system', inaugurated the worship of The Supreme Being (man: in opposition to a God of any kind) and reorganized the Revolutionary Court. Puritanical and incorruptible; he became a guillotine enthusiast as a swift, clean, painless means of execution of the impure. He owned a power that 'caused strong men to tremble'. Himself guillotined, July 1794, during the coup d'état of thermidor.

**Roland:** Sober, censorious, author: of *Dictionaires des Manufactures*. He was pushed by his young and politically ambitious wife to accept position of Minister for the Interior 1792. He insisted upon the literal meaning of the oath to the nation, law and king, within the Church Establishment Bill. Author of inquiry into state of prisons, May '92, showed dangerous over-crowding, insanitary and unsafe conditions. Attempted to claim no knowledge of the September Massacres (of prisons) until September 3$^{rd}$, after which he wrote a long letter to the Assembly, claiming the people were a little *effervescent* and describing the massacre as *une sorte de justice*. By September 4$^{th}$, massacre still raging, he ordered Santerre, in the name of the government, to employ legal means to bring the attacks on property and persons to a halt and thereafter worked, unsuccessfully, to bring the murdering to a halt. Said to have suicided by knife wounds, following the death of his wife, Madame Roland who followed the Girondins to the guillotine.

**Servan:** Minister of War: Aug 92-Feb.'93.

# APPENDIX C

## MINISTERS DURING REVOLUTION

| Finance | Foreign | Interior | War | Navy & Colonies | Justice |
|---|---|---|---|---|---|
| | Feb, '87<br>Montmorin | '87<br>Villédeuil | | Dec. '87<br>Luzerne | |
| Aug.25,'88<br>Necker | | | Aug.'88<br>Puységur | | Aug '88<br>Barentin. |
| | | July 12 '89<br>Breteuil | | | |
| | | Aug.3 '89<br>St Priest | Aug 7 '89<br>Tour de Pin | | Aug3 '89<br>de Cicé |
| Sept 4 '90<br>Lambert | | | | Oct 24, '90<br>Fleurieu | |
| | | | Nov.16, '90<br>Duportail | | Nov 21,'90<br>Duport-<br>Dutertré |
| Dec.4 '90<br>Delessart | | Jan25,'91<br>Delessart | | | |
| May 18 '91<br>Tarbé | | | | May 16,'91<br>Thévenard<br>Sept 18'91<br>Delessart<br>Oct 4'91<br>de Moleville | |
| | Nov 28 '91<br>Delessart | Nov29 '91<br>Cahier de<br>Gerville | Dec 6 '91<br>Narbonne | | |
| Mar 23 '92<br>Clavière | Mar 17 '92<br>Dumouriez | Mar 23 '92<br>Roland | Mar 9 '92<br>de Grave | Mar 15 '92<br>Lacoste | Mar 23 '92<br>Roland<br>Apr 13'92<br>Duranthon |
| | | | May 9 '92<br>Servan | | |
| June18 '92<br>Beaulieu | June14 '92<br>Naillac<br>June17 '92<br>Chambonas | June13 '92<br>Mourgues<br>June18 '92<br>Tirrier de<br>Monciel | June13 '92<br>Dumouriez<br>June 17 '92<br>Lajard | | |

| Finance | Foreign | Interior | War | Navy & Colonies | Justice |
|---------|---------|----------|-----|-----------------|---------|
| | | June 21'92 Champion de Villeneuve | July 23 '92 d'Abancourt | July21'92 Dubouchage | July3 '92 Dejoly |
| Aug 1'92 Leroux de Laville | Aug 1 '92 Bigot de St Croix | | | | |
| Aug 10 '92 Clavièrre | Aug12 '92 Lebrun | Aug 10 '92 Roland | Aug10 '92 Servan | Aug11'92 Monge | Aug 12 '92 Danton Oct19 '92 Garat |
| | | | Feb 4 '93 Bournonville | | |
| | | Mar14 '93 Garat | | | Mar20 '93 Gohier |
| | | | Apr4 '93 Bouchotte | Apr10 '93 Dalbarade | |
| June15 '93 Destournelles | June14 '93 Deforgues | Aug 15 '93 Paré | | | |

www.ingramcontent.com/pod-product-compliance
Lightning Source LLC
Chambersburg PA
CBHW020832030726
47496CB00001B/204